TO VALOR'S BID

Monster Girls in Space Book 1

M. Tress

M. Tress LLC

Copyright © 2024 M. Tress

All rights reserved

The characters and events portrayed in this book are fictitious. Any similarity to real persons, living or dead, is coincidental and not intended by the author.

No part of this book may be reproduced, or stored in a retrieval system, or transmitted in any form or by any means, electronic, mechanical, photocopying, recording, or otherwise, without express written permission of the publisher.

ISBN-13: 9798329278880
ISBN-10: 1477123456

Cover Art by: Kiera
Edited by: ApocMora
Library of Congress Control Number: 2018675309
Printed in the United States of America

CONTENTS

Title Page
Copyright
Chapter 1	1
Chapter 2	14
Chapter 3	22
Chapter 4	39
Chapter 5	55
Chapter 6	69
Chapter 7	74
Chapter 8	83
Chapter 9	90
Chapter 10	95
Chapter 11	107
Chapter 12	125
Chapter 13	139
Chapter 14	152
Chapter 15	164
Chapter 16	175
Chapter 17	182
Chapter 18	188
Chapter 19	198

Chapter 20	207
Chapter 21	220
Chapter 22	235
Chapter 23	244
Chapter 24	254
Chapter 25	266
Chapter 26	271
Chapter 27	283
Chapter 28	295
Chapter 29	302
Chapter 30	314
Chapter 31	332
Chapter 32	351
Chapter 33	363
Chapter 34	374
Chapter 35	387
Chapter 36	397
Chapter 37	415
Chapter 38 <3<3<3	438
Chapter 39	459
Chapter 40	467
Chapter 41	478
Chapter 42	488
Chapter 43	497
Chapter 44	509
Chapter 45	517
Chapter 46	532
Chapter 47	540

Chapter 48	549
Chapter 49	565
Chapter 50	573
Species Glossary	586
Character Glossary	590
Author's Note	593
About The Author	595

CHAPTER 1

Terran's have a strange dichotomy in their souls. Both a boundless capacity for kindness and a level of brutality that demands respect. Which face of the Terran psyche you encounter on a given day is far too often up to chance.
~Lila Tre'jira, Adept-Guard and Historian.

There was something sublime in the feeling of a perfect throw. Desmond had read stories about a marksman calling the target to him, then simply dropping a shot into a channel that guided it to strike where he wanted.

Desmond had never felt that, but he still knew a perfect throw when it left his hand.

The smooth feeling of the wooden grip as it slid out of his hand and the subtle way his torso tweaked to the side to give the throw more 'oomph' was all in perfect form, and he didn't have to look at the large wooden target on the far end of his lane to know the hit landed exactly where he wanted.

There was a loud 'thunk' as the axe bit into the center of the silver-dollar sized circle at the far end of the twelve foot lane that marked the bullseye. The spectators cheered, and Desmond felt a thrill run down his spine. Sure, there were only a dozen folks watching the competition at Al Axe-Hander's, but it was still satisfying to score a bullseye. Regardless of the dumb pun that the owner had made with his name and the bar.

"The hell? How did you manage that, McLaughlin?" howled his competition, and Desmond just shrugged with a small smile, double checking the lane before heading down to collect his axe. The polished mahogany handle felt good in his hand as he pulled the axe free of the target. His grip under the axe-head kept the tool balanced as he headed back to the prep table.

"Don't be too bitter, Kincaid. You bet me the bar tab on the game, so pay it up," Desmond chuckled. He caught the sour scowl on his opponent's face and rolled his eyes.

Nicholas Kincaid was almost an exact opposite to Desmond. While Desmond was short and broad shouldered with big hands and clean shaved, Kincaid towered over almost everyone with a meticulously sculpted bodybuilder's inverted triangle form and a carefully sculpted Van-Dyke beard.

"It's bullshit is what it is. No way you can aim that good without cheating somehow," Kincaid continued to gripe.

"You just refuse to believe that anything besides power determines accuracy, Kincaid. I'm out for the night." Desmond drained his pint before strapping the polished throwing axe next to its partner in his bag and shouldering the whole thing.

He had gotten the set as a graduation gift to himself, and he wanted to get his money's worth out of it. Some folks bought their own pool cues, Desmond bought throwing axes.

Too bad it's basically impossible to make money doing WATL events. Desmond mused, thinking of the World Axe Throwing League events, which were as close to professional as it got in this hobby. He pushed past the spectators and headed out to the front of the bar. As he went by, he grabbed the half finished bag of Wendy's that was his dinner.

"Kincaid lost again?" Grunted the lantern-jawed man behind the bar while he cracked open another can of PBR. The barkeeper slid the can of beer across the bar to another man there who was wearing designer ripped jeans and an immaculate band shirt, but a beanie that looked like he had stolen it from a construction site.

"Yeah, you'd think he'd learn, but hey, it's nice to drink for free occasionally, right Al?" Desmond chuckled as he slid a ten into the tip jar on his way past the bar. The bar owner rolled his eyes and nodded his thanks for the tip.

"Sure. Are you ever gonna try to compete in the WATL, bud? I bet you could make some money doing it." The way Al said it made the acronym sound like *waddle*, and it made Desmond roll his eyes. Al fished through the box he kept under the bar for credit cards, before handing Desmond back his and combining the slip with his tab onto Kincaid's.

"Yeah, not enough to live on. The pros for WATL are a small group, Al. I prefer to just have fun with it. Have a good night." Desmond threw a wave at the man before sliding his credit card into his pocket and pushing out the front door. *Glad I could roll Kincaid like that, can afford a pizza tomorrow or something.*

The walk back to his house wasn't a terribly long one, but Desmond made it a point to keep to the well-lit streets.

North Denver wasn't particularly rough, but the area around Al Axe-Hander's bar was an industrial zone by nature. It had to be for Al to have enough space for the dozen throwing lanes he had installed to draw folks to his out-of-the-way bar. This meant that it was often a place where the local homeless folks slept. Most were of them were harmless, but Desmond had been robbed before. So he kept the leather pack with his axes close at hand and walked with a purpose.

Desmond's steps slowed as a canine whine from a nearby alley caught his attention. Turning to look, he caught a bit of movement from behind a couple of dumpsters down the alley before a fuzzy head poked out from behind one of them.

"Hey there," Desmond muttered under his breath. He glanced around to make sure there weren't any folks loitering nearby that might take advantage of his distraction before crouching down, his chest angled away from the apparent stray in the alley to be less threatening.

He hadn't needed to bother, as the fluffy form of a ragged yellow lab emerged from behind the dumpster and padded over with its ears flopping and tail swaying slightly. The dog was clearly a stray, no collar on its skinny neck and the fur matted from time spent out in the weather.

"Hey boy, how are you doing tonight?" Desmond said in a low voice as the dog stopped an arm's length away from him and tilted its head in that way dogs do, ears flopping to one side and one had turned itself inside out. Desmond grimaced. He could see ribs through the animal's fur and bit back a sigh. He'd always had a soft spot for animals, but there wasn't much he could do to help this stray.

"Sorry buddy, you can't come home with me. The apartment manager is too much of a hard-ass. I can give you this, though." Desmond carefully opened the bag of cold fast-food and unwrapped the half-eaten burger, laying it and the rest of his fries out on the waxed paper wrapper.

The dog watched him hesitantly for a moment before padding the last few steps towards him, tail wiggling again as it edged towards the food.

Not wanting to crowd the stray, or risk getting bit if it decided he was trying to take the food away, Desmond slowly stood up and took a few steps away. As soon as he was moving away, the dog darted forward and snatched up the hamburger, wolfing it down in two large bites.

"Go easy, buddy. Not gonna take it from you. Enjoy. Hope you have many more good meals like it in the future," Desmond said quietly. He adjusted the bag with his axes on his shoulder. Crumpling up the paper bag from his dinner and stuffing it into a pocket, he hurried down the street towards where his apartment was.

Would have really liked to take it home, at least give it a few more good meals. Couldn't just take it to the shelter either, doubt they'd do more than keep it for a few days before putting it down... He knew that the animal shelters did what they could, but the number of abandoned house pets and strays was always increasing and there just weren't enough homes for them. It tugged at his heartstrings, but there wasn't much he could do. A welder's income was decent, but it wasn't good enough to overcome his situation. The college degree that his teachers had promised would open doors had only dumped a boatload of debt for him.

"My own damn fault. An English degree with a focus on history and mythology wasn't likely to get me much unless I got a job working for, say, the museum," Desmond muttered to himself. He glanced back over his shoulder one more time. The dog had vanished back into the alley, the crumpled wrapper from the food licked clean entirely. "Hope that helped make the night a little nicer, buddy."

The rest of the walk to his apartment building was quiet, with only the distant thumping of music being played in someone's backyard and the hum of cars on the overpass to really break the silence.

Desmond walked around the small house that fronted the tiny apartment complex he rented out of. The run-down house that his landlord inhabited had its red paint peeling in a dozen spots and the siding was warping on the left side of the house. All of which didn't bode well for the condition of the narrow row of apartments on the back side of the building.

The actual apartment building was behind the landlord's property, taking up most of the backyard like the leg to an uppercase T, with the top being the landlord's house. In the complex there were six tiny apartments, four one bedrooms and two studios in the building. Desmond heaved a depressed sigh as he walked around to the rickety wooden stairs that lead up to the second floor. The cars of the usual occupants were parked in the tiny alley parking lot, though one resident must have had a guest over, since there was a shiny black SUV parked in the empty spot that would have been his if he had a car.

Shaking off the melancholy, Desmond stomped up the stairs to his front door and unlocked it. Pushing the door open into his living-room-slash-bedroom-slash-everything-else, he let out yet another long sigh and reached to flick the lights on. He nearly shit his pants when a voice echoed from the darkness.

"Good evening, Mr. McLaughlin."

<><><>

The surprise quickly turned to anger as Desmond's hand shot up to the bag on his shoulder, fingers tugging down the zipper and diving in to grab the handle of one of his competition axes as he slid to one side of the doorway to get some cover. Someone had broken into his apartment and was sitting there in the dark waiting for him. He had no idea what they could want, but it couldn't be good.

"Easy there, Mr. McLaughlin." The deep bass voice of a man came from directly in front of the door, roughly where the couch that contained his fold out bed should be.

"I don't know who the fuck you are, but you have three seconds to get the fuck out of my apartment before I call the police. This is your only goddamn warning," Desmond snarled as he tugged the weapon out of its carrying case. His body was humming with the adrenaline dump that came with the scare. *Wish I had a gun, but this will have to do.*

"You will put the weapon down, Desmond McLaughlin, or I will put a bullet in you through the wall." Replied the bass voice as well, all traces of professionalism vanishing to be replaced by restrained anger. Desmond heard a hammer draw back with a quiet click from inside his apartment.

"Sure, sounds like a brilliant move. Some fucking stranger in my apartment, sitting with the lights off like a serial killer waiting for his victim, tells me to drop my weapon. Sounds like a bloody brilliant idea," Desmond retorted. His fingers tightened on the mahogany handle, thumb caressing the slightly rough bit of grain on the back of it as he got ready to do something that would probably be considered stupid by the vast majority of people.

Moving slowly to not give it away, he pulled his cell phone

out of his pants pocket, preparing to alert the police.

"If I wanted you dead, I'd have put a bullet in you as soon as you opened the door." There was a quiet creak from within the house and a click as the side table lamp turned on. "My name is Agent Carter, with the CIA. Get your ass in here before I shoot you for threatening a federal officer." Desmond blinked in surprise before shaking his head.

"You know what, Agent Carter? Go fuck yourself. Breaking and entering is still a felony unless you have a warrant, regardless of whatever alphabet-soup agency you work for." Desmond didn't believe for one second that the man inside the apartment was actually a federal agent. It was likely just a stalling attempt.

Which is working, you damn idiot, Desmond chastised himself before shifting his weight to finish working his phone out of the too-tight pocket of his pants.

"Subject is non-compliant. Please advise." Desmond heard the man mutter quietly, as if speaking into a radio. A brief thrill of worry raced down his spine.

What if he really was with the CIA? If so, why the hell was he here bothering me? Desmond wondered.

A moment later, Desmond's phone rang just as he finally wiggled it out of his pocket. The crescendo from *To Glory* by Thomas Bergersen made him jump in surprise and nearly drop the thing.

"Answer your phone, Mr. McLaughlin. Since you don't seem willing to take my word for it." The man's deep bass voice continued at a more normal volume.

Blinking, Desmond drew his phone out of his pocket and glanced at the cracked screen. An unlisted number was calling him. *This night can't get any weirder, can it?* Mutely, he hit the answer button and lifted the phone to his ear.

"Desmond McLaughlin?" A feminine voice from the other side of the phone asked politely.

"Speaking."

"Mr. McLaughlin, this is Agent Tessa Stuart. As I

understand it, Agent Carter has caused you a bit of a scare and you are unwilling to speak to him?"

"If, by a scare, you mean surprising me by hiding in the darkness in my living-room and then threatening to shoot me if I don't walk blindly into said darkness on his command before tossing his agent title at me, then yes. That is correct," Desmond said gruffly. He fought to keep his temper under control. This Tessa had yet to do anything and was at least being polite. She didn't deserve his anger.

It didn't slip Desmond's attention that, with him being on a call, he wouldn't be able to call 9-1-1. Instinctively, his hand tightened further on the axe handle and he lifted it to rest over his shoulder, shifting slightly to change his position to make it harder to guess where he was through the wall for the other man.

There was a moment of silence that stretched out before a long sigh came through the phone line.

"I apologize for my partner's crass approach, Mr. McLaughlin. He is correct in that we need to speak with you, though, on a matter of relative urgency."

"And can you offer anything convincing that this isn't some kind of prank or fucked up robbery attempt?" Desmond asked curtly. There was the sound of movement from inside his apartment and he took two quick steps away from the doorway and ducked low so he wasn't in front of the large window that broke up the wall there, scooting further while crouched down to ensure he had some cover.

"Agent Carter has official paperwork and his badge that you can inspect. Otherwise, the only way I can prove we are legitimate is for you to extend some trust and to come with him. There should be a black SUV parked near your apartment. Agent Carter is to give you the paperwork, then bring you to Buckley Air-Force Base for a briefing on the situation. That is all I can tell you over the phone," Agent Stuart said in a precise and professional tone.

Desmond remained silent for the moment. The odds of

this sort of situation were all sorts of messed up in his head. He'd expected to come home from the bar and read a bit before passing out on his couch/bed. Not coming back to find some stranger in his apartment that claimed to be a CIA agent and to get a random phone call from another stranger also claiming to be a CIA agent on his phone.

There was a distinct chance this could be a prank or some kind of stunt. But who would do something like that to him? It wasn't as if he had any close friends who had the connections or money to do this.

What if this is real, though? But what would the CIA want with someone like me? What if they are both serial killers and this is some kind of hoax?

"Mr. McLaughlin?" Agent Stuart's voice brought him back from his moment of distraction.

"Okay, if you guys are legit, then your partner shouldn't have any problems with getting the hell out of my apartment."

"Hey, shit-stain, I'm right here." The voice from inside his apartment rumbled, and Desmond took a deep breath and shifted the grip on his axe slightly, indexing with one finger along the shaft.

"I'm quite aware of that, supposed Agent Asshole. You've threatened me and entered my home without probable cause. I currently fear for my life, so *if* I decide to crease your skull here, 'Make My Day' has me covered as self defense," Desmond snapped back. He shifted again so that he was far enough away from the doorway that he could make a throw if needed, and so that if the idiot tried to shoot through the wall, he'd miss him.

"A reasonable request, Mr. McLaughlin. Please wait a moment," Agent Stuart said. A moment later, his phone gave a quiet hum as he was put on hold.

"Are you fucking serious, Tessa? We were told to bring him in, not baby him." Desmond could hear Agent Carter snarl from inside his home. "So what if I was waiting inside? It's not like he's going to...fuck, okay fine. Whatever." A moment of silence passed before a shadow cast itself through the doorway and the phone in his free hand gave a pop as the line picked up again.

"Mr. McLaughlin. Agent Carter will be exiting your domicile shortly and heading down the stairs to wait by the SUV. He will leave the documents in question on your couch. Once you have had a chance to examine them, please proceed down to the SUV to speak with him." With that, Agent Stuart hung up, and the line disconnected with a click.

"Sure, whatever. Just get him out of my house and I'll consider not pressing charges," Desmond muttered to himself, since Tessa was no longer listening. Agent Asshole definitely was.

"You are welcome to try that shit, kid," growled the man from inside his apartment. "I'm going to walk down to the SUV and wait for you for exactly five minutes. Once that's up, I'm going to come back up here and drag your skinny ass out by your nut-sack."

"You may test that assumption at your convenience. Now get off my property!" Barked Desmond in return.

There were a few seconds of silence before a brick wall of a man in a black suit stepped out of the front door and spun to his right, stomping pointedly across the wooden porch and down the stairs towards the ground floor. Distinctly ignoring him with each stiff step.

"Jesus dude, the little blue alien was in Hawaii, not friggin Colorado!" Desmond muttered, staring at the back of the massive black man's shaved head. Agent Carter snapped his head to one side, glaring at Desmond over his shoulder for a moment before he continued down the stairs, holding his hand up to tap his wristwatch over his head, as if to state *the clock was ticking.*

Desmond waited until the man was well away from the front of the building before he ducked into his apartment. Slamming and locking his front door, he set to surveying his studio apartment.

There wasn't much to examine. The front room held all of three pieces of furniture. His combination couch and fold away bed, the computer desk with his crappy PC, and the tiny entertainment center that held his old gaming consoles and the small TV he played them on.

Nothing was obviously out of place or like the agent had disturbed it. The only thing that was different was a large manila envelope sitting on the center cushion of the couch and a black leather wallet that was flipped open to show a card-ID stating it was for one 'Art Carter' of the CIA, complete with a photo that could have matched the ape that had just walked down his front steps.

"Sweet baby Buddha in a birch-bark canoe...Well I can rule out Al having slipped me something. If this was a hallucination, he'd be named Bubbles," Desmond muttered under his breath. He examined the card for a moment before tossing it aside to open the manila envelope and pull out several sheets of paper. Skimming over them, there were three things that immediately stood out to him.

First, they were matching what Agent Stuart had said; It amounted to a draft notice ordering him to present himself immediately at Buckley Air-Force Base for assignment.

Second, there were half a dozen official seals and stamps on them. Additionally, the orders were signed by a 'General Whitton', so it looked legitimate as far as he could tell with his limited knowledge.

Third, there was a very concrete statement on the last page that if he failed to comply with the draft notice, he would be charged with treason against his country and could serve time, if not receive the death penalty.

"Son of a..." Desmond shook his head as he paled. This was the sort of thing he expected to see in a movie or a video game, not show up in his living-room. What the hell could the military possibly want with a journeyman welder that was still struggling to pay off student loans in one of the most expensive cities in the country?

There wasn't any further time to consider the situation as a pounding of a fist against the door broke him from his fugue. Still holding his axe, Desmond shifted his grip to a throwing one again and glared at the front door.

"Fuck off, Carter. I swear to all that is holy," Desmond called. "Now listen up, I don't care how many ribbons and seals you put on shit. I don't trust your ass."

"Your choice, fucknut," boomed the man from outside his door.

Desmond waited to see what the big man would do, his arm cocked back with the sleek handle of his throwing axe resting in his palm and ready. He still wasn't sure if this was for real, but he refused to take a chance right now. There was nothing in the envelope that stated he needed to go with Agent Carter, only that he was to report immediately.

He'd expected the big man to go away or to knock again. Maybe, on the outside, to kick the door down. What he didn't expect was for Agent Carter to punch a hole in the large window that sat over his computer monitor and shoot him in the chest.

The 'pop-pop' of the gun firing was almost entirely lost amongst the sound of the plate window shattering, but Desmond felt the 'thump' of something hitting him in the chest and, on instinct, whipped his arm down and launched his throwing-axe at the window.

The cross-body throw was awkward. Most of his practice was on the lane, and it required specific posture and pose for each throw. The axe slammed through the already damaged glass of the window, sending the blinds clattering out to hit the big agent. Unfortunately, what hit him was the back of the handle. The window itself had fouled the throw.

Desmond had no more time to react. As the taser darts that hit him, since that was what the agent had fired into him, lit up and a surge of fifty thousand volts caused his whole body to seize. Despite his wishes, Desmond collapsed to the ground in a twitching heap.

"Son of a whore, you little shit-stain," barked the big agent from outside Desmond's apartment. There was a loud crunch and splintering of wood from somewhere above him as the agent slammed through his front door. "Going to make you regret pulling that kind of shit." The agent stomped across the floor towards Desmond, but the young man could do nothing at the moment as he fought to get control of his body once more.

Dimly, through the floor, he could hear a concerned voice rising from the downstairs neighbor. Unfortunately, that neighbor was an older Mormon woman that he'd met a few times. She liked to bring cookies around to the other residents and would try to strike up a conversation that she'd always turn towards religion.

There wasn't a chance for Desmond to chase that thought train any further as Agent Carter's shoe connected with the back of his head and the world abruptly went dark.

CHAPTER 2

Initial reports show humanity to be a fragmented species. It is, therefore, the recommendation of the Intelligence Bureau to approach each of the 'nations' to find their stance on things and take the integration into the Hegemony slowly to allow these disparate factions to come to terms with reality. We recommend additional ships to be stationed within the Sol orbitals to watch for pirates seeking to victimize the humans until they can step fully onto the stage. A final recommendation is that immediate integration begin, so that we can draft new Adepts from the populace to allow for closer study and help pave the way forward for their species.
~Inquisitor Yolanda Hammerfist, Intelligence Agent attached to the diplomatic ship *Empress' Benediction*.

The first thing that Desmond noticed as consciousness swirled around him was that his entire body ached like he'd been going at it with some MMA heavyweight. Groaning quietly, he shifted on the lumpy surface that he was lying on.

Squinting against the bright fluorescent white of the overhead lights, he looked around the room.

"Don't move too much. I don't need you throwing up in my office." A familiar feminine voice said from the other side of the room.

Still squinting, Desmond turned towards the voice and saw a dark blur that slowly resolved itself into a wooden desk of old oak that had several stacks of manila folders on it. Seated behind the desk was a no-nonsense looking woman with her blonde hair pinned up in a bun behind her head. Perched on her nose was a delicate pair of reading glasses, adding an almost secretarial look to her that was immediately dismissed by the sharp black suit she wore.

"Agent Stuart I presume? Why the fuck did Carter shoot me?" Desmond croaked, working hard to get enough saliva in his mouth to make his throat work properly. The woman behind the desk arched an eyebrow and flipped closed the folder that was in front of her.

"According to Agent Carter, you attacked him as he came to pick you up," the woman said in a neutral tone. Desmond rolled his eyes before carefully working himself into a sitting position on the lumpy couch that he discovered was as ugly to look at as it was to lie on. The blue-gray tartan weave of the couch was faded and frayed in several spots and his back popped several times, just sitting upright.

"Well, I do not think that you believe that. Given that I'm sitting in what I guess is your office, and not a cell. Speaking of cells, I hope Carter is sitting in one for assaulting me. If he isn't, I will be pressing charges." Desmond spoke with a forced calm. He still didn't know exactly what was going on here, but snapping at the woman wouldn't solve his issues right now, and he had worked hard to master his temper.

"You are correct in that I do not believe Agent Carter's story," Tessa Stuart said, her voice still neutral. "Though it was more because of the goose egg on the back of your head, combined with his actions earlier in the night than anything else. Care to fill me in on your side?" The woman did not move from behind the desk and continued to stare at him over the reading glasses with eyes that betrayed no emotions.

It took only a few minutes to walk Agent Stuart through what had happened that night. From when he came home to the surprise of Agent Carter in the dark, to reading the paperwork, and then to being ambushed as he was making his decision. Throughout the entire story, Agent Stuart didn't move more than an inch, only nodding slightly or blinking every so often as she listened without interrupting.

"So, yeah. He broke into my house not just once, but twice. I will be pressing charges for both assault and breaking and-entering, unless you have some compelling evidence, such as a warrant, that would provide an excuse for his actions." Desmond did his best to meet her stare evenly. While he had never really tangled with the law in his life, he'd had to stand up to enough asshole supervisors at work that he knew how to stand his ground and what sort of demands he could make without sounding like a complete fool.

"There will be no charges pressed at this time," Agent Stuart said after a moment of silent digestion of his words. Desmond opened his mouth to protest, but stopped when she held up a hand. "Agent Carter is being treated for a mild concussion and is receiving stitches for a blow to the head. A blow that came from you, if your story checks out." She continued, her hard stare drilling into Desmond.

Frustration was welling up in Desmond's chest as he glared back at the woman. Earlier, Agent Stuart had been the one to be a voice of reason while trying to work out the situation. Now, though, it seemed like she was preparing to spin this against him.

"As I stated on the phone, Agent Stuart," Desmond growled out. "I was well within my rights. I was under attack, threatened both outside and inside my home, and feared for my life. Under Colorado's Make My Day law, I was well within my right to use up to and including deadly force to remove what I believed was a threat to my life. He's lucky he didn't catch the blade on that throw. It's not often I miss what I'm aiming at."

The temperature in the room dropped several degrees as the two of them continued to stare at each other. Long moments passed before Agent Stuart spoke again, though she never broke eye contact with him.

"Be that as it may, Mr. McLaughlin, Agent Carter was there under direct orders to bring you in to report, as your orders stated."

"Bullshit, lady. The orders told me to report for drafted duty. Nothing stated about going with a suited gorilla in the middle of the night. This is the end of the conversation now. I'll be going, and you can speak to my lawyer." Desmond began to rise from his seat on the couch, turning towards the plain door that sat to one side of him.

"Mr. McLaughlin, sit down before you get yourself shot." The icy tone that agent Stuart used made Desmond's back straighten like he'd just been shocked again.

"Congratulations, Agent Tessa Stuart. I'll be adding your name to the lawsuit now for threatening me," Desmond said. His voice shook with rage. "I may just be a welder by trade, but I know that members of law enforcement and government agencies aren't just allowed to threaten the life of citizens. I know that all evidence right now is hearsay, but I guarantee you I will make this a *very* public trial."

"And I can guarantee you, Mr. McLaughlin, that you will not be seeing anyone from the press or any legal team anytime soon," Agent Stuart said, her tone still cold and neutral as she continued to stare at him. "As a member of the armed forces, you are outside the range of normal legal proceedings for a citizen."

"And you also know that without a national emergency and an act of Congress, the draft laws don't mean shit. You've burned any goodwill that you had earlier for dealing with your partner, Agent Stuart." Being bored one day, Desmond had found the information while researching something unrelated. He'd never expected to use that bit of fact, though.

The question had come up during his ethics class and he'd done some digging on what could actually reinstate the draft. His anger cracked a moment later when Agent Stuart held up one folder from her desk.

"Well, it's fortunate for us then. That is exactly what has happened. If you will sit down and stop throwing a tantrum, I will explain why you are here."

"Don't talk down to me, Agent Stuart," Desmond snapped.

He turned to stride back over to stand in front of her desk. The woman didn't flinch. Her unblinking gaze remained locked on Desmond. While he was furious at his treatment and the situation, Desmond wasn't the kind of person to just lash out at anyone, let alone a woman. "My attitude is a direct result of the situation. Start talking or I start walking."

The CIA agent in front of him continued to stare up at Desmond for several seconds before she took a deep breath and, for the first time in the entire conversation, broke eye contact with him.

"I apologize for my tone, Mr. McLaughlin," she said a moment later before looking at him again, her eyes still hard despite her apology. "The situation that is occurring is both unique and strange, and it has caused stress for everyone," she said a moment later before looking at him again, her eyes still hard despite her apology. She held up the folder again in her left hand. "What I have here is the officially signed paperwork from Congress reinstating the draft because of a national emergency. While I would have preferred to give you more time to prepare, situations prevent us."

"Okay, enough with the secret-squirrel shit. Just tell me straight up. I'm a freaking welder, not some special agent," Desmond said crossly. The anger still boiling in his gut finally slowing now that it looked like he was going to get some actual answers.

Rather than answer his question, Agent Stuart reached over to the sleek black phone that was on her desk and pushed a button on it. After a moment, the speaker-phone clicked and a younger man's voice picked up.

"Yes, Agent Stuart?"

"Mr. McLaughlin is awake. Will you notify the Academy representative? She was the one who requested him specifically, and he has questions," Agent Stuart said into the phone.

"Yes, Ma'am. She should still be with the General and the Ambassador still. I'll get her right away." The man's voice said with a hint of excitement in it before the line clicked again.

"Academy?" Desmond asked with a quirked eyebrow. "I already did college, and it's done nothing for me. How is that a national emergency?" The CIA agent in front of him just stared at him for several more moments before shaking her head.

"There are more things in motion than you are aware of, Mr. McLaughlin. The sheer amount of information that you do not know makes the starting point of an explanation difficult."

"So pick a spot and start, because stalling is just making it harder to give anything you say credence." Desmond stood in front of her desk with his arms crossed and waited. Agent Stuart looked down at her desk for a handful of seconds before shrugging.

"As of around 2000 eastern standard yesterday, humanity had the answer to one of the significant questions that has plagued modern times." Agent Stuart shifted in her chair to grab one folder out of the stack and sort through it before turning it to set the open folder in front of Desmond. "The question of whether or not we are alone in the universe was answered with a rather resounding 'No'. These photos are from the Hubble telescope of the area near one of Saturn's moons. Saturn LV, official designation as 'Angrboda'," she said dryly and pointed to the photos in the folder.

The agent had flipped the folder open to show a photograph of a golf-ball sized sphere of white that was partially occluding the multicolored pattern of Saturn in the background.

What stood out more, however, was the rough, arrowhead-shaped object that was drifting on the space side of the blob that was the moon. The bronze-colored wedge had a corona flare of blue light coming from the back half of it that Desmond guessed was the engines. The wedge-shaped object was just as long as the moon it was moving past, but only about half as wide. Along with it were a half dozen tube-shaped objects of the same material that were roughly a tenth the size, and another oval ship roughly half its size but of a polished silver color.

"Roughly an hour after the ship was spotted, the ship sent a smaller craft out that arrived in Earth's orbit less than ten minutes later. The ship engaged some form of anti-detection technology as it approached the outer orbit of the Earth's Moon and vanished from sensors. Roughly twenty minutes after that, at around 2140 eastern standard, the smaller ship contacted multiple nations via some type of long-range transmission that we have yet to discern. The United States was one of those nations."

The agent paused for a moment and Desmond was glad for a chance to process the information presented to him before looking up from the photos. His pulse was thundering in his ears as his mind raced over what she had said. There was no way that this was a hoax or some prank, there was just too much to it. That, and what kind of monster tased someone as part of an elaborate lie?

But aliens? Really? Why?

"Okay, so aliens are real and they came by to say 'hi'. What the heck did they want with me? You said that someone had asked for me, right?" Desmond blinked rapidly as the rushing sound of his heartbeat got a little louder.

"You'll have to ask them specifically. What they want with you is not something I have clearance to know, just that part of the demand of the Academy representative was to speak with…" The CIA agent paused and flipped another of the folders open before reading directly from the paperwork. "A twenty-six-year-old human male of the nation of the United States of America, by the name of Desmond McLaughlin, who resided at your address. They even provided your social security number." The agent looked up from the paperwork blandly. "How they have the information, I am unsure. But it doesn't bode well for the informational security of the nation. Regardless, they want you for something. Their 'ambassador' is currently speaking with the President and his chiefs of staff at the Cheyenne Mountain NORAD base."

Desmond stared down at the photos again and let his mind wander. The idea that aliens existed and had some reason for wanting to speak to him was bizarre in the extreme.

"I...don't know what to say. I feel like I should be worried or even irritated. But I don't really feel anything right now," Desmond muttered. He continued staring at the photograph of the ships hanging in space by one of Saturn's moons.

Agent Stuart's eyes softened slightly, and she removed her reading glasses before dropping them on her desk.

"I understand the idea. If I hadn't received orders from who I did, I'd not really be believing it either," she sighed. "And it's got every single person on edge right now.

"Have you seen one of them?" Desmond was rather proud of the fact his voice didn't waver with the question, but he could only chalk that up to the numb feeling that was replacing the anger that had filled his chest earlier.

"No, though from the verbal reports I have, the Ambassador and her staff are from several species that are foreign to us, and a few that seem familiar."

"Okay, where are we, anyway? How long is it going to take this person to get here?" Desmond glanced around, looking for a clock to try to ascertain the time. Since his unwilling trip into unconsciousness, he had no clue what time it was.

"Oh, I've been here for a while. I just didn't want to interrupt you," A light but professional voice said from behind Desmond, startling him for the second time that night.

CHAPTER 3

The galaxy is a tiny space amongst the absolutely massive stage of the universe itself. Just as we have no idea what lies outside the galaxy beyond supposition; many species are unaware of what lies outside their home systems. May the discovery be as benevolent to us as we are to those young races taken into the fold of the Hegemony. The last thing we need is to get punched in the clam by karma.
~ Monika Irongrip, Head of the Irongrip Consortium.

Desmond was gratified to see Agent Stuart also jump in surprise at the words that came from near the door to the office. Though that didn't stop him from turning to face the speaker.

There were some expectations that he had for what an alien race looked like. Considering how much science-fiction media there was in the world at this point, he had a decent number of guesses as to what one should look like.

She looked nothing like what he'd expected.

The woman, because he had no doubts that the person was female from her figure alone, was a few inches taller than his five foot six inches of height. Slender of build with wide hips and a modest bust, she stood with her shoulders back and her left hand on her hip. The woman's clothes were simple enough, resembling a pantsuit in the same shade of green as verdigris covered copper, with polished highlights of actual copper on the creases and joints of the suit. The suit made her look somewhat like a copper statue that someone had just begun to polish up with the contrast in colors. Differing from the normal look, a thick belt hung around her hips to hold the jacket of the suit down. What appeared to be a holstered sidearm sat on her right hip, and a leather pouch large enough to fit a hardback book sat on her left. A thin scar bisected her left eyebrow, and a thick rope of scar tissue marked the right side of her throat just below her jaw.

Despite the relatively familiar clothing, Desmond was more fixated on the fact that her skin was a dark blue-purple that glittered slightly in the bright fluorescents of the office, like she had mica powder scattered over the top of her skin. Her eyes glinted a bright cyan that almost glowed against the whites of her eyes. Dark-auburn hair was pulled into a chunky braid at the back of her head, revealing ears that came to an angled point several inches long.

The alien woman stood there for several seconds, her posture not changing as she waited for the two of them to take her in before she finally shifted and took several steps to cross the room to stand in front of Desmond.

"You are Desmond McLaughlin." Her words were not a question, just a statement as she stared down at him from less than a foot away. Desmond blinked a few times before nodding. Her eyes were easier to see now that she was closer. The woman's iris was a slightly darker blue than her cornea, making it seem oddly like she didn't have them. There was a faint scent in the air, one that reminded him of ozone and the scent of rain.

"You must be the representative from the Academy?" Agent Stuart said after clearing her throat. The elf-eared woman glanced at the agent for a moment before looking back at Desmond, her eyes focused.

"Yes, I am Instructor Camilla Tre'shovak from the Academy Ship, *Valor's Bid*," she said simply. The woman's neutral expression dropped off as she continued to stare into Desmond's eyes. "I apologize for dragging you out of bed as we have, Desmond McLaughlin. The Academy does not wait for anyone though, and our transport to it will only remain in your system for another six hours and we need to be aboard before it leaves."

"Wait...what? Why?" Desmond gaped at the stunning woman. Tre'shovak's split left eyebrow raised slightly and a small smile crossed her lips.

"I'm not surprised that you are confused, Desmond. We do not have time to answer all of your questions. The simplest, but not quite complete answer, is that you were identified as a potential adept by the Academy's scanners. There are a number of other potential adepts on Earth, but you were selected to be the first to enter training as you are at the ideal physical age to begin training. All adepts are required to be trained aboard the Academy ships, and *Valor's Bid* is one of the best. I don't expect you to understand the honor of it, or what is expected of you just yet, but first I have to complete testing."

Desmond just blinked at her, his ears hearing what she said, but his brain still wrestling with the idea that an alien was standing in front of him and that she wanted him to go with her. The tinny ringing that had started up again didn't help either, as he felt the world slip sideways a bit while he tried to cope with what was happening.

"Well then, go right ahead and complete your testing, Instructor Tre'shovak. I have already prepared the paperwork necessary to release him into your custody," Agent Stuart interjected. Tre'shovak broke from her staring contest with Desmond for a moment to glance at Agent Stuart, an expression of irritation crossing her features for a moment before fading again.

"The young man must give his consent for the testing. While all adepts are required to be trained in the Academies, it is still a question of his willingness to receive training. There are measures that we will have to take if he declines."

"Like what? Imprisonment? Execution?" Anger was what managed to finally unstick Desmond's tongue. It gave him a handle to get a grip on mentally, and the warmth of it in his chest was enough to get him past the shock that had filled his veins.

"No, of course not." A startled look crossed Instructor Tre'shovak's face as she turned back to him and, surprisingly, her ears flared out laterally from her head to accent her surprised look.. "What made you think that?"

"I was forced to come here against my will, with barely any notice or explanation," Desmond said, doing his best to remain neutral. "Part of the discussion we were having when you arrived was revolving around the situation of my... abduction from my home."

A look of horror crossed the instructor's slim features before she shook her head sharply, sending her braid bouncing and her ears swaying slightly.

"That is...no...no! What we requested was to speak with you expediently and nothing more, Desmond McLaughlin. If you decline further testing, I am to administer a treatment that will neutralize the gene expression that would make you into an adept for your own safety and the safety of others. Once that is done, I would proceed to the next candidate from your nation. *Valor's Bid* only has room for one Terran student at this time and, as I stated, time is short," she explained in clipped and precise tones.

Desmond thought that he saw a hint of anger behind her cyan eyes as she locked her gaze with his, but he didn't feel like she was directing the anger at him.

"You've said it a few times. What do you mean by 'Adept'?" Desmond desperately needed more context as to what was going on. She mentioned something about a treatment and gene manipulation. That concept made the hair on the back of his neck stand on end.

"There is a lot of context that I do not have time to explain to you, Desmond McLaughlin, but to answer your question..." Tre'shovak hummed for a moment, one long finger tapping at her pursed lips.

Desmond couldn't help but note that there were a number of small scars on her hands, on her lips, and cheeks as well.

Fine lines and blemishes that highlighted the fact that she was not one to shy away from trouble, it seemed. "An adept is one who has the ability to intake and manipulate mana in order to produce a number of unique phenomena. Not the least of which is in taming and subduing Rifts which, by coincidence, is what led us to discovering your species."

"Huh?"

Tre'shovak just smiled and shook her head, the fingers that had been tapping her lips shifting so that her hand was held out between them, palm up with her fingers splayed out evenly.

"I believe your people call it 'magic', Desmond McLaughlin," the elven woman said with a hint of laughter in her voice.

She muttered something under her breath and a wisp of green light formed in the palm of her right hand, spiraling upwards and shifting like a miniature Aurora Borealis above her palm. "Mana is a natural substance in most known space. Your system, the Sol system, has been outside the fields of mana for thousands of years. A natural disaster in nearby space drew the mana away from this sector of space, and that fact is what led to your people spending so long outside the fold of the Hegemony. That and the motion of this solar system has continued to drag it away from that section of space and into a 'dark zone' where mana was far thinner. No one thought to look here, as species developing without the influence of mana is extremely difficult and dangerous. Tell me, were there any cataclysmic events that occurred in your planet's history that accounted for a mass extinction?"

Staring at the moving wisp of light in her palm, Desmond took his time before responding.

"There have been five mass extinctions that science knows of, at least that's what I remember from high-school history...major events like climate change, a super-volcano, and a meteorite strike?" It took an effort of will to tear his eyes away from the shifting bit of light and look up to meet

Tre'shovak's eyes.

"Likely the last two, one of them at least. I would bet that this 'asteroid strike' was not actually an asteroid, but the effects of a Rift collapse," Tre'shovak replied. She gestured with one hand, causing the wisp of light to sway like a candle flame. "Rift's that are untended do one of two things. They explode or they implode. It is quite lucky that the Rift exploded in the fashion it did. It sounds like it spent most of its fury in the ethereal. The ripple effect would have driven mana away like a stone dropped into a pond. If it had gone the other direction...well it's possible the planet would have imploded with it. Rift's tend to be even more explosive in their reactions than anything science has designed, some of them causing destruction on a scale measured in light-years. Though, I doubt the impact site was where the Rift itself was. Even small collapses tend to shatter the planet they occur on."

Desmond choked slightly at that, his head whirling at the thought. The idea that magic was real was hard enough to swallow on its own but the fact that a beautiful, purple woman with ears like an elf was standing in front of him, her palm full of what she claimed was magic as well, was enough to tip him into wondering if he was hallucinating.

As he watched the glittering veil above the instructor's hand, its swaying shifted slightly and started to stretch in his direction slightly.

"Oh, now that is interesting..." Tre'shovak murmured and Desmond glanced up at the purple-skinned woman to find her gaze had also dropped to the veil of light in her hand. "Desmond McLaughlin, do you consent to testing?" Desmond nodded slightly, his eyes dropping back to the drifting shroud of glimmering light above her hand as he wondered what this testing might be. "I need you to say it, Desmond McLaughlin," she said again, a slight smile tingeing her voice.

"I consent to testing, Instructor." Desmond replied, the

shifting colors of the mantle of energy almost hypnotizing as he watched it.

"Okay, take a deep breath. As you inhale, focus on drawing in everything around you. The most important factor of an adept is the ability to draw in mana from the environment. Without mana, they cannot do anything special. Your planet is extremely barren of mana, but my presence here will have drawn a small concentration to this place. Like calls to like, after all. The presence of mana draws more of it together. The drift is slow but, like an avalanche, it can build up momentum and become quite disastrous."

Nodding once, Desmond moved automatically to follow her directions. Slowly, he drew a breath like he did when he was standing at the line for the targets, in through his nose and deep into the pit of his stomach in one long flow. The veil of light above the instructor's hand continued to flicker back and forth like a sheet in the wind. As he watched, the light danced from green to blue to a deep purple that almost matched the woman's skin.

"That is good. Draw deep in through your lungs. If you cannot draw mana in, that is fine. It is possible that there just isn't enough mana here to start the reaction," Tre'shovak said kindly. She watched him intently, her cyan eyes flicking from Desmond towards the agent who sat behind her desk, watching the whole thing intently. "In fact, it's likely that nothing will happen. If that occurs, we simply need to head back to my shuttle and we can attempt it there again. Perhaps that would...be...better?" Her voice trailed off as Desmond drew another long breath in and the shroud of light in the woman's hand flickered sharply, like a candle flame caught in the wind.

Desmond focused intently on the act of breathing, his eyes lit with the dancing of the veil of light above the instructor's hand. The third breath he drew in, Desmond felt something catch in his sinuses, a feeling of congestion not unlike the beginning of a head-cold. Moving without thinking, he sniffed sharply to clear his sinuses and continued the deep inhalation.

To his astonishment, threads spun off that glimmering mantle of light on which he had fixated his attention for the last several minutes. They spiraled up into the air and crossed the foot and a half of space between them in less than a second, before they siphoned through his nose and into his body.

A cooling wash of energy soaked into his head and throat before sinking slowly into his lungs. The persistent ache from the taser immediately faded from his body and he felt energized. It all happened before he could stop himself from the motion and he let out a rush of air from his mouth in surprise. His chest began to ache sharply, like he couldn't get enough air despite having just finished breathing a second ago.

"No, don't stop Desmond. Continue to draw in." Tre'shovak's sharp voice drew his attention to her eyes, which watched him intently. "Again, breathe deep again." She gestured with her left hand while her right, the one that had held the aurora above it, glowed slightly and a twisting shroud of light began to rise from her fingers. "Focus on that sensation you just had and breathe deep."

Doing as she asked, Desmond focused on that cool sensation that was, even now, fading from his body. Focusing, he drew a deep breath again. This time, the entire ribbon of light leaped from Tre'shovak's hand and flowed through the air directly to his face, rather than slowly fraying into threads. A chill feeling that reminded him of strong mint gum washed through his sinuses and down his throat. The feeling soaked into his core and began to spread through his body, both chilling and invigorating him, causing the ache to fade again. The ribbon didn't fade either, connecting the two of them with a band of twisting light.

While he breathed out, the ribbon floated away from Desmond's face and began to draw back towards Tre'shovak, but Desmond drew another long breath in and the energy snapped back to him and swirled down his throat.

The energy gathered in the pit of his stomach, and a burning sensation not unlike heartburn began just below his breastbone where the ache had been. A grimace crossed his expression, but he continued the cycle of breathing. There was something happening, but Tre'shovak hadn't said a thing to him about stopping.

Ten deep breaths later, Tre'shovak closed her hand, extinguishing the ribbon of light. A slight flush crossed her cheeks, only discernible by a darkening of the purple on her speckled skin that shifted the tone of the glimmering points of light that sparkled there.

The burning sensation in his chest continued, but the cooling feeling helped soothe it somewhat. Desmond coughed and patted his chest where the ache was located, pulling out his shirt slightly to look down at the skin with its dark patch of hair that sat above his breastbone.

"What you are feeling is the beginning of the dynamo that will fuel your mana cache," Tre'shovak said gently. Her left hand came up to rub at her right palm with her thumb like it was sore. "I had not expected such a vehement reaction." She gave him a searching look before continuing. "Regardless, you definitely have the aptitude to be an adept, like your genes stated." She straightened and assumed a position that was reminiscent of a military parade-rest, and her expression became stern. Out of reflex, Desmond mirrored her.

"Desmond McLaughlin, you are hereby drafted from the Terran military to attend training on Academy ship *Valor's Bid*. Your term of training will be no less than two years and no more than five. Once you complete your training, you will be assigned — with a team of guards — to serve the Hegemony. Either aboard a ship or on another station. You will utilize the skills you acquire during your time aboard *Valor's Bid* to serve the Hegemony for a minimum term of ten years. Once that time is up, you will be released from mandatory service to the Hegemony, if you wish. You will receive a stipend while attending the Academy and the military will pay you a salary during your time there as well." Her expression softened slightly before she continued. "This is compulsory, as you have tested and begun the process of spinning up your dynamo. Now that you have begun this, you cannot remain on Terra."

"Why is that?" Agent Stuart butted in for the first time in a while and Tre'shovak glanced at the agent for a long moment, as if weighing whether she should answer, before she spoke.

"Because, if he remains on this planet, in its mana-starved state, his dynamo will sputter and die. Which will cripple, if not outright kill him. Once his dynamo spins up and his cache is steady, then and only then will he be able to venture into mana-starved regions such as the Sol system without support." Tre'shovak's expression was neutral as she answered the agent's question before she turned back to Desmond and her eyes softened. "Sol is now under the authority of the Hegemony and its councils. Terra will receive support in elevating the people, as is right. However, Terra will also be expected to provide a tithe of soldiers to the military of the Hegemony. The most important of those being the ones seeking to achieve an adept's mantle. I'm sorry I didn't explain this to you earlier, Desmond McLaughlin. We skipped a few steps, but this is not something that you can take back." There was a hint of sorrow in her cyan eyes as she spoke.

"May I speak with Mr. McLaughlin for a moment, in private?" Agent Stuart asked primly, shifting several of the folders around on her desk. Desmond glanced over at her and it occurred to him that the woman hadn't stood once from behind her desk. He couldn't tell if this was an attempt at a power play or just her being uptight. *Either way, it feels rude that she didn't even offer to shake hands with Instructor*

Tre'shovak...

"Of course. I can give you a few minutes while I prepare the shuttle I brought." Tre'shovak turned back to lock eyes with Desmond for a long moment, searching him for something. Whatever she found, it seemed to satisfy her. "Desmond McLaughlin, I will come back here in a few minutes to retrieve you. If you have any personal effects you want to bring with you, then please have them ready."

"I wasn't really allowed to bring anything with me when they dragged out of my apartment..." Tre'shovak's eyes hardened at Desmond's words before she let out a long breath through her arched nose.

"Don't worry, the Academy will provide necessities to you and the stipend that is paid out each week is moderate enough that you should be able to acquire anything else you need. I will tell you more once we are underway. You will also have the opportunity to meet my team as well." Tre'shovak glanced between Desmond and Agent Stuart once more before she turned and walked back to the door of the office and vanished through it.

"Half expected her to dissolve in some kind of transporter beam," Desmond muttered under his breath. The sound of Agent Stuart clearing her throat drew his attention back to her.

"Mr. McLaughlin, I want to wish you well on your training with the Academy and assure you that your effects will be gathered and stored at no expense for yourself while you are away." Agent Stuart began, selecting one of the manila folders she had been sorting through and flipping it open, nodding once before closing it and holding it out to him.

"This details an offer from the United States government for employment after your mandatory term of service is up. What the instructor did not mention is that there are going to be adepts selected and recruited from most of the world's nations. The UN had tried to vote on who would get the nominations, but the Ambassador had a specific list of picks.

You were at the top of the list for the United States and, while we are unsure of the criteria that they used, we want to support you."

The abrupt shift in her tone and approach threw Desmond off balance as he carefully accepted the folder from her and flipped it open. Inside was a contract that looked very official and dense with legalese.

"Examine it at your leisure. When you decide to accept our offer, just sign it and have it forwarded back to Earth. The Ambassador has assured us that one of the first things they will get set up is a means of communication to help in bringing tech up to parity, though it may take a few decades for everything to disseminate effectively," Agent Stuart continued.

Meaning that the rich and the politicians are going to be controlling how and when the tech gets shared, and with who. Standard bullshit...wonder how many lobbyists are going to lose their collective minds over this situation once it's more widely known. Desmond thought to himself as he skimmed the packet.

He could glean a few highlights from the front page. They basically wanted him to return to Earth as a specialist, having lived amongst the aliens for a while, and bring back any information that would assist the country. The section on 'expected duties' was summed up as 'advisory and training as needs dictate'. What caught his eye more than anything was the eye-watering salary dictated at a little over a half million dollars a year.

"This...this is accurate?" Desmond choked out, glancing up from the paperwork. Alarm bells were ringing in his head at this. There was no way this was legitimate. Not with how they had treated him earlier and with Agent Stuart's insistence on not pressing charges against Agent Carter. *Makes sense what she was saying though, no way I'd be able to press legal charges if I'm off-planet and I doubt I'll be back before the statute of limitations expires, not sure how long it is but yea...*

"Yes, if you want to sign it now, I can get the paperwork processed immediately. There is a great deal of reassurance in the security of knowing your future is waiting for you," Agent Stuart said coolly. Her bland tone did more to alert Desmond than reassure him, and he snapped the folder shut.

"I'll let you know, Agent. I appreciate that my things will be stored. I trust that the agency will handle the repairs needed for the damage that Agent Carter did to my apartment? And, as I am returning to school, will my student loans and other debts go back into deferment?" *Because, of course, they wouldn't just forgive them. No way any lender is going to let you just walk on a debt. Even one as useless as student loans...*

"I can have that arranged. Are you sure that you want to wait, though?" It was as if she could read his mind as she added another enticement onto the pile. "I'm sure that if you were to sign now, we could work out something to have your loans forgiven as well, given that you will be training to work for a government position?"

"No. I appreciate the offer, but I need to read the contract first. My father taught me to always read something before I sign it and I don't have the time right now to do that. I appreciate that you had this ready." Desmond patted the folder before tucking it under his arm and turning to head out of the office.

"Well, best of luck, Mr. McLaughlin," Agent Stuart replied, and he could hear just a hint of irritation in her clipped tone. He still wasn't sure about the whole situation, from the random 'draft' notice he got to the military of the United States, to the abrupt realization that aliens were real and apparently looked a lot like an elf dipped in sparkles and rolled in berry syrup. And he was going to be training with them to learn magic, of all things.

The fact his government had drafted him, then basically handed him over to a space-elf without really any warning or paperwork was concerning in its own right.

Desmond took a deep breath and felt the pressure under his breastbone pulse slightly, the faintest wisp of the wintergreen feeling entering his lungs before fading once more. *She said 'like calls to like'...was that the last of the mana in the room from her being here? I wonder what it will feel like when there is more of it...wonder how this is going to change everything with science and how folks understand stuff?*

Opening the office door, Desmond was surprised to find Instructor Tre'shovak less than ten feet down the hallway. She was standing with one hand on her hip, right above where her sidearm sat holstered, and was watching the door.

"Good, glad you did not tarry. The sooner we can get back to the shuttle, the better. While you have enough mana to last you for a few hours, I would rather get you somewhere where you can safely get your dynamo started properly and begin to fully cultivate your mana cache." The instructor's eyes dropped to the folder in Desmond's hand and the raised eyebrow shifted sides before she shrugged slightly and gestured for him to follow.

"I would rather not end up crippled, so I agree," Desmond said, falling into step slightly behind the instructor.

"A smart move. You will learn quite a few things that are unexpected in the next few days." Tre'shovak gestured towards the sky with one hand, the other tucked behind her back. "How you react to them and how fast you adapt will be a key factor in how well you do in the future."

"I can adapt. I don't doubt that I will be surprised often, but I plan to do everything I can to adapt and grow as quickly as possible." Tre'shovak shot him a half smile that showed stark white teeth behind her dark plum lips.

"Good, that sort of adaptability will serve you well, but wait to make assurances until you are completely positive that you won't freeze. The trip back to *Valor's Bid* should help you acclimatize a bit." Desmond could see a metal double door ahead of them that looked like it led outside, based on the faint yellow light from floodlights that he could see coming through the window.

"There is something that I'm wondering about," Desmond asked as they approached the doors.

"Ask. I may have an answer, I may not."

"This all seems very fast." Desmond tried to piece together the misgivings that were hovering in his chest. "The government is infamous for taking its sweet time doing anything really, the fact that they are just...rolling over and accepting the fact that our entire planet is now under someone else's jurisdiction and handing over citizens like this...it feels wrong."

They approached the doors in silence, Desmond waiting to see how Tre'shovak responded.

"It's not too terribly surprising, really. What other choice did they have?" Tre'shovak said at last. "The Ambassador contacted every nation that we felt would be amenable to peaceful contact. The ones that we were unsure of, like the one known as 'North Korea', will remain in the dark until you Terran's can work as a cohesive whole. Your species is not the first one to be discovered and inducted into the Hegemony." Desmond pondered what she had said for a moment before skipping ahead to push the door open and hold it for her, which earned him a slight smile from Tre'shovak.

"That will be one thing of many that is going to be different for you." Tre'shovak stepped through the doorway and out into the evening air. Desmond ducked through after her and glanced around. There was no sign of a saucer or any other sort of space-ship parked in the open parking lot, just a collection of what he guessed were employee cars. Tre'shovak gestured for him to follow her and headed towards the back corner of the lot.

"Your action of opening the door," Tre'shovak continued as they walked, "as I understand it, that is considered chivalrous and a male's duty to do for a female by your species?"

"Yeah...let me guess, it's not in the wider Hegemony? Did the feminists get to you all already?" Tre'shovak chuckled at his response before shaking her head in the negative.

"No. It most definitely is not. Though not for the reasons you may be thinking. Equality is a matter of capability, not gender, but there is some dissent between the genders. The vast majority of life so far in the galaxy follows similar gender lines to Terran life. Male and female split, though there are a few with tertiary genders." As they talked, Tre'shovak fished a piece of metal roughly the size of a pack of cigarettes out of her hip pouch. "What differs is the gender ratios. They vary a great deal depending on species. For example, in my species, there are at least six females for every male born."

"Wha? Six to one? Why?" Desmond shook his head as he tried to wrap his thoughts around the concept.

"Simple mathematics of evolution, Desmond McLaughlin. One male can breed with several females. Most species experienced either some sort of evolutionary pressure that caused the females to compete over the males. Either from some sort of mass die-off of the males, or environmental pressures of that nature. Some of the more warlike species, the males ended up culling out enough of the other males that a similar setup occurred. Add in the fact that survival is not nearly as difficult on many of the worlds in the Hegemony as it is here on Earth because of the mana densities, and you end up with more females. It's a running theory that the overall pressure of breeding partners in the galaxy will cause even the equally spaced species, such as your own, to adopt a similar ratio as interbreeding between species is fairly normal. Almost all known species are compatible genetically, which is still a mystery that our scientists are stumped on."

Desmond's brain fought to shut off at that point, but he shook away the feeling. *Six to one? Just for her species? How do they survi—wait a second...*

"So…what is the most skewed ratio? And what is the least?" Desmond asked as they came to a stop near the back of the lot where there was a large open spot.

"The largest ratio? I'd say probably twenty or thirty to one, usually amongst smaller species. They usually breed rapidly, so that has further exacerbated the ratios. Least skewed is three to two, though that species is insular, so we don't know too much." Tre'shovak did something with the device in her hand before tucking it back into her pouch. "They should be here to pick us up in a minute or two. Questions?"

Taking a moment to think, Desmond tried to quiet the whirl of thoughts that occupied his mind. There were hundreds of questions rattling around in his head, but it was hard to select one over the others. Settling on one finally because they didn't have long, Desmond shook off his confusion for a moment.

"What's your race? If it's not rude to ask…" Tre'shovak smirked at his question before nodding once.

"A fair question, and no, it's not rude to ask, especially given that you have no way of actually knowing. Our species is known as 'Aelfa', my sub-race is 'Va'Aelfa' as I was born in zero-gee aboard the Academy ship. I've lived aboard *Valor's Bid* for most of my life." The smirk remained as she waited for Desmond to process that thought before turning back to the empty space in front of them. "And here is our ride."

CHAPTER 4

Mana is a strange and wondrous thing. It breaks so many known laws of science and existence that they end up being more of 'suggestions' than anything else. The only law that mana obeys is that it takes joy in being unpredictable.
~Karla Tre'killandra, Advisor to the Empress.

A moment after Tre'shovak finished speaking, a small, van-sized vehicle that was roughly shaped like a fat hammerhead shark dropped out of the sky without warning. Flares of blue light occurred from several points underneath the vehicle as it came to a stop and hovered in front of them silently. The entire ship was made with a brushed metal that reminded him of antique bronze and decorated with strips of a darker metal accented by a few angular symbols in bright blue.

"Here we go." Tre'shovak stepped slightly to one side as a hatch swung out and forward on the side portion of the vehicle where 'gills' would be on the shark. "After you, Desmond McLaughlin." The instructor stood to one side and gestured for him to climb in, which he did after a moment of staring at the strange vehicle.

The interior was straightforward in its construction and it reminded him vaguely of some of the military documentaries that he'd seen that included interiors of helicopters. To his left, a row of seats sat on each side, facing towards the midline of the ship, each with a complicated-looking harness strapped to them. Large lockers sat above each of the seats, securely latched closed, though they looked large enough that he figured he could have fitted several pieces of luggage into them. None of the seats were occupied. To his right was another door like the one outside, but it split in the middle on an angle, sliding into the walls on either side, exposing the view into the cockpit of the vehicle. Directly across from him, on the other side of the ship, was a door identical to the one he had just entered through.

"Hey Camilla, is this the new recruit?" A melodic female voice came from the front of the ship and Desmond caught sight of a slender woman of average height, which meant she stood roughly as tall as he did, sitting in the cockpit. She, like Tre'shovak, had pointed ears, though her skin was a dusky brown that reminded him of coffee with plenty of creamer added. Her hair was a shimmering black like spilled ink and hung loose around her jaw.

"This is him. Desmond McLaughlin, this is one of my team, Ryaan Summers. She is an instructor at the Academy as well. But not one you will personally be working with," Tre'shovak said as she stepped aboard the shuttle right behind him. Her sensible boots made a quiet *clunk* on the metal grating that made up the floor.

"Yup! Gotta keep the mundies trained up. But, you will have your own training. We might cross paths once you begin selecting your own team," Ryaan chirruped from where she sat. She turned slightly in her seat to wave at him. Desmond nodded to her and dropped into the first seat to the left of the door. It took him a minute to figure out how to belt himself in, but once he figured out how the harness attached to itself, the rest worked itself out.

"Mundies?" Desmond asked quietly as Tre'shovak settled into the seat across from him and flipped the straps into place with the ease of long practice.

"Mundanes. People who cannot harbor mana. Adepts are rare, even with the population density of the galaxy. Maybe one in ten thousand or more, depending on the species. The vast majority of citizens of the Hegemony are such. 'Mundies' is a playful term for them," Tre'shovak answered before she turned to face the cockpit. "Strapped in and ready, Ryaan. Get us back to the others. The Ambassador messaged me a minute ago that her meeting was wrapping up. Once we are all together, we can head back to the transport and split off back towards the *Valor's Bid*. I want to get our new recruit stabilized as soon as possible."

"Roger that, Camilla," chirped the grinning elf in the driver's seat, before she began working with the controls in front of her. A minute hum rippled through the ship and then a tiny lurch, like a car hitting a small ripple in the road.

Glancing forward into the cockpit, he could see the lights of Denver rippling away from them as the ship slipped up at an angle and wove through the night.

"I'm surprised," Tre'shovak said after a minute of silence.

"Oh? About what?" Desmond blinked back to reality. He had been staring at the back of the pilot's chair but not really seeing anything.

"You must have hundreds of questions. Newcomers always do." Tre'shovak crossed her arms under her modest bust and watched him with a curious gaze.

"He's just in shock right now, Camilla," Ryaan called from the front of the ship. "Give the boy some time and he'll start swimming right along. Or he'll drown." The laughter in her tone blunted the sting of her words.

"Well, until about an hour ago, I didn't know elves existed. Magic was a fairy-tale, and I had no idea that there was intelligent life out there. I mean, I figured it was, but we didn't *know* that it was," Desmond replied defensively.

"Aelfa. Not elves. Though we resemble legends from your world, there are differences," Tre'shovak interjected before Ryaan interrupted.

"Don't worry, bucko. Things'll work out," Ryann replied cheerily. "Though, the biggest thing is going to be figuring out what questions are the most important and asking those, since you won't have a ton of time until term starts."

"Okay? So, what would you say is the most important

question to ask right now?" Desmond prodded, and Ryaan laughed gaily while she manipulated the controls to send the ship into a dive towards the ground once more. He watched as her ears twitched rapidly, flicking like those of an excited cat's as they rotated and moved. *Or like tiny radar dishes, tracking where we are going.* He thought to himself.

"Smart choice there," Ryaan cooed. Her eyes never left the view-screen in front of her that displayed an asphalt paved lot tucked into a fold in the Rocky Mountains. Desmond could see several shapes of people standing by a metal door as they approached, but he couldn't get specifics. "So, in an emergency situation where you are thrust into the unknown with a culture that is not your own, what is the most important thing?"

"Knowing where the bathroom is?" Desmond replied wryly as the ship came to a stop with another tiny shudder. Ryaan glanced over her shoulder and grinned at him. The fact she hadn't finished landing yet made his stomach lurch, but they settled down without a problem.

"Close, but in the same vein. Language. If you know enough of the local language that you can ask for the bathroom, then you are set, right? You haven't asked why we are all speaking a Terran native language, let alone the language of your nation." Ryaan continued to grin at him for several seconds as Desmond pondered that thought before he shrugged.

"Translator or something like that? I mean, you have a technological edge and a magical one over my species, so it could be anything."

"Close," Tre'shovak interjected with a wry smile of her own. "There is a translation spell that allows your brain to interact with the language of other sentient species and gives feedback that you are familiar with. One thing that we had to do before approaching your species was expand it to include your native languages. It was one of the first things I cast when I arrived in the room with you and the agent."

Huh. Translation magic. That is pretty cool. Makes me wonder if 'magic' is the answer to all their problems or not. Desmond thought wryly as the door to his right slid aside once more and admitted the rest of the group.

In trooped an odd collection of creatures. At the front was a short, broad-shouldered woman with a mane of blonde ringlets that fell to the back of her thighs. It was hard to tell just how short she was since he was sitting, but by comparing her to the others that followed after her, Desmond had a hunch that she was around four feet in height. Along with her was another pale skinned Aelfa woman much like Ryaan, another female Va'Aelfa like Tre'shovak, and a trio of taller, moss-green beings that were heavily muscled and had pronounced lower jaws. Of the green-skinned folk, one was male and the other two were female, given their large breasts and wider hips. Everyone but the short blonde woman were wearing variations of some kind of armor and carrying obvious weapons, so by a process of elimination, Desmond assumed she was the Ambassador while the others were Tre'shovak's 'crew' as she called them.

"Is this your new recruit, Instructor?" The short woman asked in a lilting tone as she strode onto the ship and past Desmond.

"Yes, this is Desmond McLaughlin, Ambassador. He's already showing promise, so I think he will do well at the Academy. Sorry we had to drag you away from your meeting, but we need to get you back to your ship and on our way to the Academy," Tre'shovak responded. She nodded to the short ambassador respectfully, but did not rise from her seat.

"Not to worry, we have covered the majority of issues already. The people of this nation will need time to digest and discuss what their situation means and how they will adapt to the situation. I doubt they will decide to fight it." The ambassador sighed before turning her intent gaze to Desmond. Her eyes were slightly larger than normal and a brilliant blue that stood out against her pale skin. She regarded Desmond for several long seconds before nodding once. "Best of luck to you, Desmond McLaughlin. Your people will need a good first impression to set the tone for future interactions with the larger Hegemony. You represent your nation, at least for the time being. To many, you will represent your entire species, though."

Desmond just nodded his understanding to the short woman as the rest of the boarding group settled into their seats. The majority of Tre'shovak's crew were quiet other than a few words of greeting to the instructor before settling into their seats and strapping in. The trio of green-skinned beings eyed him up for a moment before proceeding past him. Desmond noted the fact that, despite most of the crew carrying some kind of firearm, these three had an assortment of melee weapons on their belts. The male had a long sword at his side while both of the females had sharp faced hammers on their hips that they had to rearrange to sit. *As if they needed help to be more intimidating.* Desmond thought wryly.

"Everyone settled? Okay, back to the Ambassador's ship to drop her off and then to the *Nebula Ghost* for the trip back to the Academy!" Trilled Ryaan.

<><><>

Without a point of reference, or a window of some kind, Desmond could not tell how fast they were going once Ryaan had the little transport shuttle aimed towards the star-speckled expanse of sky. It was maybe a handful of seconds before the moon came into sight and he was treated to a more personal view of Earth's closest celestial companion than any others, save the select few that had visited its surface.

But despite the up-close encounter with the pale white expanse of the lunar surface, it didn't get more than a quick glance before Desmond turned his gaze to the larger ship that hung in the shadow of the moon.

The 'shuttle' that Agent Stuart had shown him pictures of was easily ten times larger than the smaller ship they were currently in and he guessed it had to be somewhere between two hundred and three hundred meters in length.

What the images he'd seen with Agent Stuart had failed to illuminate was the stout shapes of what could only be weapons that sat close to the ship's sides. The angular barrels stuck out of turret mounts that blistered the smooth hull every so often, and it was clear that the 'shuttle' was a full warship in its own right and armed to the proverbial teeth. A trio of oval engines stuck out from the back of the ship to give it thrust, though all three were currently dark.

"Transmitting docking clearances," sang Ryaan from her pilot chair. A happy beep sounded from the console and an airlock irised open on the top of the ship, just ahead of the engines. A faint green glow extended over the opening like a soap bubble, but it didn't impede their ship as it eased through the opening. "Heading in to drop off the Ambassador then we will be off back to that cute ringed planet to meet up with the *Nebula Ghost*."

The Ambassador had already started undoing her harness and was standing by the exit door waiting patiently as the ship came to rest in a metallic corridor. Desmond leaned forward enough to see through the pilot's view-screen better and he could see a trio of other ships like this one sitting against the far wall of the immaculate bay, as well as a half dozen other beings, all the same race as the Ambassador, waiting ahead of the ship.

"Thank you for the escort, Instructor. The show of force for the Terran's went a long way to helping them to understand that violence was not the answer here," the short woman said as the door popped open with a hiss and slid to the side.

"Anytime, Ambassador. We are glad to assist the integration." Tre'shovak turned to look at Desmond with a raised eyebrow. "Desmond McLaughlin, any advice on Terran's that you can give the Ambassador before she leaves?"

Desmond shook his head for a moment before shrugging and turning to look at the Ambassador, who was peering at him with one hand on the door frame, an eyebrow lifted in question.

"Uhh...Dunno how true it is in the wider galaxy, but human politicians tend to be very money motivated? If there is a profit to be made, they tend to work more towards that?" He shrugged slightly before another thought crossed his mind and he sighed. "And things that damage profits for existing major companies tend to get stonewalled... Especially if that company can't get a slice of profit off what might be replacing them. At least that's true in America, but I bet it happens all across the world. That and a lot of folks are focused on the 'where's my share' rather than working as a community..."

"Sounds standard for most primitive worlds, to be honest. 'Haves' and 'have-nots' and all that. I'll keep it in mind though. Thank you for the advice, Desmond McLaughlin." The Ambassador bobbed a nod to him before disembarking and the door swung shut. There were several seconds of pause before she appeared with the group standing in front of the ship, after which Ryaan lifted them off and they re-entered the void of space.

A thought occurred to Desmond, and he turned to Tre'shovak. "Question on something that had been bothering me but I hadn't noticed till now...Why does everyone keep using my full name when talking to me? Is it normal? Also, how should I address you?" One of the green-skinned females chuckled, but when he looked at her, she gestured to direct his attention back to Tre'shovak.

"A fair question. I'll answer the simplest one first. For now, it would be best to address me as Instructor, or Instructor Tre'shovak. Despite appearances otherwise, we are heading to what would qualify as a military academy." Tre'shovak gestured to her outfit. "This isn't exactly a standard uniform. What the others are wearing is more appropriate and you will learn to read the ranks in your first week of classes. Given that you are from a new world, you will have some catching up to do in what is considered general knowledge of the Hegemony."

Desmond shrugged at that, glancing over at the others of Tre'shovak's team and noting what he guessed was the rank insignia that each of them had. "I figured I'd be behind the ball. It just comes with the territory. Any advice on getting caught up?"

"You'll get issued a data-tablet and a comm-cuff when you get to the *Valor's Bid*, until then though…"

"I've got a spare tablet he can use," the other Va'Aelfa spoke up for the first time, and her gravely voice startled Desmond.

Turning to look at the speaker, he spotted the edge of a knotted scar across the base of her jaw, which he guessed had been from an injury that damaged her vocal cords, explaining her gravelly voice. Like Tre'shovak, she had auburn hair in a braid, but her eyes were a delicate shade of pink.

"Appreciate it."

"Sure, just make sure I get it back so I don't have to 'lose' another one to get a spare," the Va'Aelfa woman said with a raspy chuckle. "I'll get it for you once we are back aboard the *Nebula Ghost*, since my kit is there."

"Anyway, back to your original question, though, Desmond McLaughlin. You asked why I use your full name when I address you. It is considered polite when meeting someone new to use their full name as such, if it is given to you. A cultural affectation, you could say." Tre'shovak said after rolling her eyes at the other woman of her species. "As for your early studies, I will send you some files to read over that will help you acclimate to the academy. There will be things that you will have to get used to that will surprise and likely may make you uncomfortable. Ultimately, that is just the way things are."

"Coming up on the *Nebula Ghost*," Ryaan commented from the front of the little ship. Desmond blinked in surprise and turned to look out at the view-screen. Ahead of him, he could see the ringed bulk of Saturn looming in the distance as well as a collection of ships in orbit around a misshapen lump of rock that he assumed was the moon he'd been told about.

"All right, team. You know the drill. Disembark and get your gear stowed. I'll get our recruit squared away and we will be riding a Wake to meet with the *Valor's Bid* inside the hour since we are ahead of schedule," Tre'shovak called. She shifted in her seat as they neared the largest ship in the group.

The big ship reminded Desmond a lot of a Star Destroyer, but far more sleek in design and built in three dimensions. Its angular surface was built like a broad-head arrow where the three blades stick out at different angles. At the moment, they were approaching the ship to land on the larger central body between two of the raised 'blade' fins, with the third one falling below the side of the ship opposite them. The entire thing shone like polished bronze, and he could see interlocking panels that made up the hull of the ship that he guessed were the armored exterior. Similar to the Ambassador's ship, turreted weapons stuck out at regular intervals along the hull, though he could see several hatches that looked like they concealed other weapons, but what sort? He couldn't guess. The entire ship came down to a bluntly pointed nose that had an odd pattern to the hatches on it.

Ahead of them, another hatch irised open with the same green glow emanating from the mouth of it as had from the Ambassador's ship. The rest of the group shuffled slightly in their seats and, as soon as Ryaan set the ship down with a near silent 'thump', immediately began stripping off their restraint harnesses.

Following their lead, Desmond quickly removed his own restraints before stepping to one side to let the others pass. Tre'shovak waited, remaining seated as the others moved past her and out of the ship, only unhooking herself from the restraints once the last of the group offloaded and one of the green-skinned women turned to give her a nod.

At Desmond's questioning look, Tre'shovak chuckled before gesturing for him to lead the way out.

"This team has worked with me for decades. It's become a habit for them to clear and secure routes ahead of me, even on friendly vessels. The only time this protocol doesn't happen is when we are aboard the *Valor's Bid*. The team is some of my closest friends, my coworkers, and my personal guards," Tre'shovak explained as they disembarked.

"Wait, if they are your personal guards, why did you come to get me alone?" Desmond stopped halfway down the aisle, the incongruity bothering him.

"Oh, that was partially due to them being needed to escort the Ambassador, and the other half that there wasn't anything that actually *could* threaten me in that base. We decided it would be easier for you to just meet one person at first to let the whole 'other life in the galaxy and they are recruiting me' thing sink in. And Ryaan was standing watch just above the base just in case," Tre'shovak explained. She gestured for him to follow again. Once they exited the ship, she paused for a moment to let Desmond get a look at the hangar they were in.

The entire room was a dull gray in color, with lines and diagrams marked on the floor to show different 'landing' areas that could be used as well as safe walkways to guide people to and from the different landing zones.

Six other ships, much the same shape as the one they had just exited, sat along the walls, an odd four-pronged 'hand' adhered to the top of each of them around the middle of the ship, keeping them suspended above the deck. As he watched, a seventh arm extended from the wall and settled over the ship he'd just exited. There was a quiet hissing noise and a 'clunk' of metal meeting metal before the ship powered down entirely and the arm took its weight. Ryaan skipped out of the cockpit with a smile, hopping down to the deck beside them. A moment later, the arm whisked the little shuttle away to join the others, settling it into a cradle at the end of the line.

"Well, let's get you settled into a berth. The *Nebula Ghost* will be heading out shortly. Its Wake drive will get us back to the *Valor's Bid* in a day or two, but it has to navigate out of the system first. Firing a Wake drive in-system is a good way to cause a lot of damage," Tre'shovak said at last. She led the way across the docking bay. The group of other instructors/guards were waiting by the thick hatch-like door that led into the rest of the ship. The trio of green-skinned beings led the way down the hall, with the other Va'Aelfa falling in at the back and both Desmond and Tre'shovak sandwiched between the others on either side.

"So. Have they ever had to protect you while on a friendly ship like this?" Desmond asked as they walked down the hallway, their steps echoing down its length.

"Several times. Just because a ship is friendly doesn't mean that there aren't dangers. Adepts are one of the most powerful tools in the Hegemony's arsenal, and bring a great deal of honor to a family that includes them. So political assassination can still happen, as well as accidents. I doubt anything will happen aboard the *Nebula Ghost*, but it is better to be wary. The only reason it is relaxed aboard *Valor's Bid* is because there are so many adepts around, it would be foolish for someone to try something. Not to mention, the security to get aboard the ship itself is extremely tight."

"Not to mention that we are expected to train as well," Ryaan butted in from his left. "Still, there's usually at least one of us with Camilla whenever she's out of our suites, even on board the Academy. Anywhere else, we tend to move in no less than groups of four. You get used to always being in close groups. Especially once you start selecting your team. Those girls will be lucky!"

"Lucky? How so?" Desmond glanced over at the grinning Aelfa who's ears flicked nearly vertical with excitement.

"Camilla already gave you some details, right?" Ryaan looked up at the Va'Aelfa adept as she spoke. "You give him the details on the ratios?"

"We covered a bit of it. He held the door for me on the way out so I brought it up," Tre'shovak replied with a roll of her eyes. Ryaan smothered a laugh. Though her eyes danced with amusement, she tried to be serious.

"You'll see the other side of that now. I don't know the exact ratio of the genders aboard the *Valor's Bid,* but male adepts are even more rare than adepts in general. It's possible you might be the only male in this year's class, though there will probably be at least one or two males and maybe someone from the handful of races that have a third gender." Ryaan shrugged, her expression going thoughtful for a moment before her eyes returned to Desmond with a wicked grin spreading over her face. "What Camilla probably didn't go into specifics about is that out here in the wider galaxy? Women chase the men, since there is a lot more competition for partners going in that direction." Clearly, the mischievous woman had been waiting to drop this revelation on him as she watched expectantly to see how he reacted.

Desmond's head jerked back in surprise at the idea of being pursued by a woman rather than the other way around. The feeling was such an alien idea that he honestly wasn't sure how to react. And, of course, Ryaan proceeded to blow his mind even further.

"Not just one to one either in relationships. Polyamory is common enough, even cross species." The wickedness in Ryaan's tone made Desmond flush red.

"It's not the rule though," rumbled the green-skinned male who walked ahead of them, his eyes remaining forward.

"True. But it is *generally* correct, with some exceptions. Like you." Ryaan blew a raspberry at the muscled man's back, drawing deep laughter from the two green-skinned women who bracketed him, before turning back to grin at Desmond, bent over slightly so she could look up at him through her eyelashes despite being taller than him normally. "But you don't really have the option to stick to your own species, since you are all alone up here. Besides, there are going to be a lot of hot girls looking to get your attention for all sorts of reasons! And some might chase you based on how sweet the other girls are, too. Girls can't be too picky when guys are harder to get hold of out here."

"Ease up on the poor boy, Ryaan," grunted the green-skinned male again. "Remember, he's just a prim, fresh from his world, and still doesn't know how everything works. You saw the reports. They are nearly one-to-one back there."

"Yeah! But that's why it's so much fun to see him react!" Ryaan whined at the large male, her ears wilting slightly, before turning back to Desmond and her grin slipping back across her face. "So! You are in for an interesting time, for sure. Between being prim, being a male, and being an adept. You are going to get a lot of interest from different angles. And not all of it is going to be good." Her grin flickered a bit at that, but she resolutely maintained it.

"Prim?" Desmond asked, latching onto the odd word as a means to distract from the confusion that was swelling in his mind.

"Primitive. Basically means that your people are fresh inductees into the Hegemony. It refers to species that are still bound to their home-world and that the Hegemony is actively working to bring up to speed. It's...not the most polite way of phrasing it. Something else you are likely going to have to get used to. A lot of folks look down on prims," answered the other Va'Aelfa in her raspy voice. Her pink eyes continued to scan their surroundings.

"More importantly," interrupted Tre'shovak, "you are going to need to give a lot of thought to what you pick when you select your team. It's not something you have to decide right away. The first selection doesn't occur until partway through the first term. But your team will be your closest friends and allies, so you need to understand them and have a plan in mind. The Academy will have you training with a variety of different setups at first, to let you get a feel for how you want to operate. Once you figure it out, you start building your permanent team. These people will be with you during your time in the academy and during your posting afterwards, barring deaths, of course."

The hall was silent except for the quiet 'clonk' of their boots as they wove through the ship. Desmond was caught up thinking about the whole situation and considered carefully what Tre'shovak was saying. There was just too much information going through his head right now. All the new things that he had discovered today, lumped in with his change in environment, it was just entirely overwhelming.

The grand procession of the group finally came to a stop after several minutes of walking and Tre'shovak guided him to a door set in the wall. A gesture with one hand in front of a sensor and the plain gray door slid into the wall, revealing a spartan room with a double-sized bed against one wall and a small desk with a chair in front of it. A small door attached to the left wall led into what he guessed was a bathroom, based on oddly shaped fixtures, and what looked like a shower stall that he could see. There were no decorations in the room and it was the same dull gray color as the hallway, though the bedding was a deep midnight blue. The dark color was stark against the bland walls and it pushed Desmond out of his fugue.

"This will be your room for the next few days while we catch back up with the *Valor's Bid*. Your rooms aboard the Academy will be much nicer, but this is the best option for now. You have privacy and our suite is right next door."

Tre'shovak gestured to a larger door about twenty feet down the hallway. "For now, you should get some sleep. I expect you are feeling overwhelmed currently, considering most recruits are, and they know about the Academy's existence for most of their lives."

"Yeah, my head is still spinning on all this…" Desmond's neutral expression dipped into a frown and Tre'shovak made a questioning noise, which drew his attention back to her. "Oh, I was just thinking that the taser shot probably didn't help my mental capacity much either."

"Taser? What?" Muttered Ryaan from the back of the group, but Tre'shovak made a patting gesture in her direction before turning back to Desmond.

"That is probably correct. Get some sleep, Desmond McLaughlin. When you wake, come to my suite and we can get you that tablet and see about answering any other questions you have for now."

"Okay. Sure thing, Instructor," Desmond sighed before stepping into the room. The door slid shut behind him and Desmond slumped onto the bed with a second gusty sigh. Part of him wanted to go test out the shower or give everything a good think, but right now, his brain felt like overcooked pasta.

Falling back across the bed, Desmond let out a low groan. The cushions were so much softer than that awkward couch in the agent's office that he'd woken up on.

The thought crossed his mind that he should get his work-boots off and get under the covers, but sleep swallowed him whole before he could really make good on the idea. Only one thing crossed his mind before the darkness took him to dreamland was to wonder about the names of the people he'd met so far.

For aliens from another culture, they have remarkably human-sounding names.

CHAPTER 5

Mana starvation is a terrifying thing. Mundies don't really understand it, I can't fault them for that as it's impossible to understand without context, but it's bad. Imagine starving, drowning, and suffocating all in one go and you might get close to it. Mana is a drug, a state sanctioned one, but still a drug and the drop is terrifying.
~Camilla Tre'shovak, Adept and
Instructor to the *Valor's Bid*.

The pressure on his chest was what eventually drug Desmond from his dreams. It felt like there was a weight resting on top of him. It wasn't the crushing sort of feeling that you got when you are sick and struggling to breathe. It just felt like an object was resting on his breastbone, like a weighted blanket all folded up.

Peeling his eyes open, Desmond winced and shut his eyes again as he ended up looking directly into the recessed light that was above his bed. He'd fallen asleep the night before, still wearing his street clothes, and apparently without shutting off any of the lights, so he felt rather groggy.

A quiet groan pushed out of his mouth before Desmond shifted slightly and the weight on his chest rolled off to one side. Blinking several times to clear the blur from his vision, he sat upright. A pile of…stuff had been sitting on his chest. Chief among the pile was a slim metallic screen that was roughly the size of a page of notebook paper and about as thick as his finger. Beside the tablet was a set of dark-gray clothing threaded through with black in an irregular pattern to break up the outline in a style that reminded him somewhat of digital camo. A pair of sleek looking, calf high black boots were next to it, though they looked like they were constructed of some kind of flexible metal fabric rather than leather.

"The heck?" Desmond muttered, yawning once as he shifted the pile to one side and sat up fully to stretch. Without a clock on any of the walls, he wasn't sure what time it was, but it had been a while. Fishing around in his pocket, Desmond extracted his cell phone and glanced at the screen to check the time.

So it's 11am back on Earth, but no idea what time it is onship. Do they even operate on a 24 hour day? Hell, for all I know they work in a different 'time zone' and it's like 4 in the afternoon. Desmond thought idly as he swung around to plant his feet on the floor. The hollow feeling in his gut told him that he'd been asleep for some time. It'd been a long time since that half-finished takeout burger back home and hunger was gnawing its way through his stomach, headed for his spine.

"Suppose I better clean up...guess this is my uniform, or a loaner or something." Desmond glanced over his shoulder at the pile of metallic cloth.

With nothing better to do, Desmond got to his feet and went to inspect the other room connected to his.

The bathroom was easily the same size as his sleeping quarters, with half of that space taken up by a massive shower alcove. The entrances were easily large enough to accommodate someone half again as tall as him and twice as wide.

Stripping out of his clothes, Desmond dropped them on top of the counter that ran under the mirror. The counter contained a sink almost big enough to be a small bathtub. Shaking his head, he headed into the shower.

It took a bit of experimentation to figure out the controls, but there were only a handful of buttons on the wall and after poking three of them, he found out how to turn it on.

Apparently, a cleansing agent was added to the water because he felt his skin tingle as it washed over him. The water was pleasantly warm by default, and Desmond let his mind wander as he enjoyed the soothing sensation.

There was still that dull pressure in his chest, just under his breastbone, but it didn't ache as much as it had back in Agent Stuart's office. His empty stomach actually ached more than his chest did in the moment, but there wasn't much he could do about either.

It's still so jarring...I'm on a space-ship right now. Desmond glanced around at the brushed metal walls of the shower. It was the same design as the walls in his room. The only bit of color was the buttons on the wall and the drain in the floor, which was a much brighter polished shade of gray.

Can't even pretend it's not real. Last night definitely happened. There was no denying that fact no matter how hard I try. Turning his face up into the water, Desmond intentionally pushed his thoughts away from the question of why the CIA and, by extension, the government, had been so quick to hand him over to the Hegemony for training. Had the Ambassador threatened them? Was there something else going on? *Need to read that contract closer...*

The water shut off after a few minutes and Desmond was left dripping in the large shower stall. Poking the buttons earlier had revealed that one of them opened a hatch that contained a number of extremely soft towels, the same dark blue color as his bedding had been. Retrieving one, he quickly dried off and strode into the other room with the towel around his waist to change into the new clothes that had been so graciously dumped on his chest while he slept.

A throat clearing from the doorway made Desmond jump back on reflex, backpedaling into the bathroom as he turned towards the door to find Tre'shovak standing there in the open doorway with both eyebrows raised.

The instructor had changed out of her verdigris green pantsuit and into a uniform much like his. The fundamental differences were bands of a dark, metallic green piping that ran up the outside of her legs. Embroidered above her breast was a bright silver emblem, as well as several other symbols that he guessed were rank on her shoulder. Her auburn braid had been drawn over her right shoulder to hang over the edge of her modest bust and dangle slightly in the air. A thick cuff of polished silver wrapped her left forearm for about half its length, exposed by the short sleeves of her top. The only thing that remained from the outfit of the night before was the holster and pouch hanging from her belt at either hip.

"Ah, sorry Instructor. Didn't know you were there," Desmond coughed. He could not suppress the blush that crossed his face and quickly checked to make sure his towel was secure.

Tre'shovak blinked at him, her bemused expression turning to one of amusement before she made a quick gesture with her left hand and tapped on her bracer, causing a symbol to light up with dark blue light before it faded.

A tugging sensation in Desmond's chest, right below his breastbone, made him wince slightly. Tre'shovak raised an eyebrow at that for a moment before speaking.

"I had forgotten about the translation spell, Desmond McLaughlin. What was that again?"

"I was apologizing for walking out half dressed, Instructor," Desmond repeated. The flush still burned high on his cheeks. Tre'shovak chuckled slightly at that and shook her head.

"Don't be, you will have to get used to communal bathing, eventually. Many of the smaller ships do not have private or even segregated bathing. The reason you have a private shower right now is that this is a spare officers' room. Considering you will fight, bleed, and some will die with each other on assignment, it is imperative that such things like modesty take a back seat when necessary," Tre'shovak said bluntly. She leaned her shoulder against the open doorway. "Again, one of those things I mentioned you will be needing to get used to as you acclimatize to the Academy. Though you are free to bathe in your suites if it makes you uncomfortable during training, as the cadet-adept suites do have a private bath. Some males and the more shy females do so, though unless there is a religious or serious cultural reason to prevent you from baring yourself to others in the line of duty, there is no exception to be made if such things make you late to classes."

"I...see," Desmond said slowly before nodding once and straightening his back. He strode across the room to collect his clothes before returning to the bathroom, using the edge of the wall to get a modicum of privacy while he dropped his towel and changed into the clothing provided as the instructor did not appear to be leaving anytime soon.

He found a set of underwear inside the folded pants as well. The underwear was like cyclist shorts, skin tight and stretchy. His pants were long and had several pockets on the outside and, unlike the instructor, his outfit did not have a pinstripe of any sort. The top was more like a tunic in its build, hanging to mid-thigh with short sleeves that left his forearms bare.

Once he was fully dressed, Desmond headed back into his sleeping room to find Tre'shovak was still waiting for him without having moved from her spot. Her cyan eyes scanned over his body as he collected his boots, fishing out a pair of thick socks from inside them and putting them on. Desmond pointedly ignored her watchful eye as he worked to get the boots on. There were no laces, and it took him a minute to find a line of concealed magnetic studs that held the heavy metallic cloth shut around his ankle. Once they were secured on his feet and he was relatively sure he had it right, Desmond stood up and turned to the instructor.

"How can I help you, Instructor?" Desmond asked, doing his best to assume an 'at attention' posture. Tre'shovak smirked at him for a moment before gesturing towards the data-tablet where it sat on the bed.

"It is more about how I can assist you at this time, Cadet-Adept McLaughlin. And this will be how you are referred to by the instructors now that you wear the uniform. Your title will change as you gain experience and prove competence. Collect your borrowed data-tablet and follow me. First thing is some food. I imagine your mana cache is aching and your dynamo needs fuel to get it up to speed. The ambient mana you absorbed aboard the ship and from me yesterday kept it going long enough, but putting it off further will cause problems."

"Of course, Instructor." Desmond collected the brushed metal data-tablet and tucked it under his arm. He wasn't sure how to turn it on, but he had a feeling Tre'shovak would teach him how when she was ready. "You made it sound like it was rather urgent back on Earth, after all."

"And it was," Tre'shovak replied as she led him out into the hall and down the opposite direction from the way they had approached before. The trio of green-skinned beings from the night before were waiting for them and fell in around the two in a triangle formation, with the two females leading and the male in the back.

"If you'd remained on Terra, which you should get used to referring to your home-world as since that was what your administrators decided to call it while I was in the meeting. Either Terra or Sol-3, they at least narrowed it down to that..." Tre'shovak made a dismissive gesture with one hand before continuing.

"Anyway. As I was saying, if you had remained on Terra for more than a few hours, your cache would have collapsed and it is likely you wouldn't have been able to jump-start your dynamo again. There are dangers to allowing your cache to fall empty and remain there for long. If you are in an area that is mana dense, like a Rift or aboard the Academy, it is far less dangerous as the ambient levels will be enough to keep your dynamo flowing until you recover, but it's not recommended."

"Okay...how can you tell when your...cache is running low?" Desmond asked, one hand going up to rub at his breastbone where the ache remained.

"You will develop an innate understanding of your relative reserves. But you will also have a bit of mechanical assistance." Tre'shovak tapped the brushed silver cuff on her forearm. "You will be issued one of these once we get to the *Valor's Bid*. They don't function unless the wearer has a dynamo up and running."

"How do I get it up and running?" Desmond asked as they strode up to a door that slid open, allowing a rush of noise to envelop them, though he couldn't see past the pair of tall women in front of them.

"That is precisely what we are doing right now, Cadet-Adept McLaughlin," Tre'shovak said with a small smile as she led him into what could only be the ship's mess-hall.

The large, arched room was filled with a number of tables that appeared to be topped with polished dark wood with benches attached to them. Everything was bolted to the deck in orderly rows and half the room was full, with a number of life-forms in varying modes of dress. Tre'shovak's team was easy to pick out because of their matching uniforms off to one side.

Doing his best to not stare, Desmond followed after Tre'shovak. There were easily a dozen different species on the ship, some obviously Aelfa like Tre'shovak and Ryaan, others something far different. He saw one massive person that took up an entire bench by herself. He wasn't sure, but he bet they would stand around seven feet in height when she stood up and was as broad as the tables were.

"Really need to research the species more," Desmond muttered to himself. He followed Tre'shovak around to the far end of the room and collected a tray.

"You should. In fact, it is one of the assigned reading pieces I'm going to give you. While many of the species that you will see in the coming weeks will be familiar to you, since your fantasy stories contain similar creatures, there are key differences in some of them," Tre'shovak replied blithely as she led him through the line. "Take as much as you think you can eat. Don't skimp. But eat nothing until I tell you." The last part was delivered in a sharp tone that sent steel down Desmond's spine.

"Understood, Instructor," he said automatically. Desmond caught a bit of laughter from a nearby table, which he chose to ignore. His casual glance around the room had proven the instructor's words to be true about the gender disparity. The vast majority of the crew members that he saw were female, if the cloth covered bulges of breasts on display were to be indicators. He followed their lead as they moved to a line of servers that were like miniature versions of the trio of unnamed green-skinned beings that surrounded them.

In short order, Desmond's platter was loaded with steak, eggs, hash-browns and thick cut bacon.

"Surprised?" the green-skinned male behind him rumbled as they moved towards the table where the rest of Tre'shovak's team was waiting.

"Somewhat? It looks so familiar to me."

"You get used to it. Evolutionary pressures tend to push species along similar tracks. Each species has some unique food types that are only found in their natural habitats, but somewhere like this, with the broad range of species, they tend to focus on foods that are common to everyone. All that changes is the ratios," the large male replied. He gestured to his own platter, which was mostly meat with only a small serving of the shredded and fried potatoes.

"Fair, I suppose. Is that why so many species share characteristics?"

"You mean bipedal and mammalian?" Tre'shovak shot over her shoulder, to which Desmond nodded. "It is the running theory. No one knows exactly why and it has infuriated the eggheads for the lifetime of the Hegemony. You'll get the occasional lunatic that preaches about

'Precursor' species that seeded the known universe with life or the presence of seventh-dimensional beings that would be referred to as deities, but no one can show it as fact."

"So gods don't exist, then?" Desmond couldn't help the question as it spilled out of his train of thought before he could stop it.

"Oh, no. Creatures from alternate dimensions do crop up occasionally and they can gain a cult following. There are a few benevolent ones that lead smaller theocracies, but the more dominating ones tend to get stomped out rather rapidly. The only ones that are allowed to persist are those that attach themselves to a culture peacefully in the time before integration with the Hegemony," the green-skinned male added. Desmond had to fight surprise again at his eloquence. Given his larger stature and rough voice, it felt strange that he was so well spoken.

"Ko'an is correct. But we have more pressing things to discuss. Sit." Tre'shovak gestured to the table where the other members of her team had shifted to open up two spaces in the center of the bench. Desmond ended up sandwiched between Tre'shovak and the other Va'Aelfa that he had yet to be introduced to. His back was to one of the bulkhead walls of the room, and he had a good view of the rest of the mess hall. He noted idly that they had an open space roughly the size of a single table around them in all directions as well, as if the regular crew apparently did not want to crowd them. That didn't keep the curious looks and stares of the crew from following them.

Once they were settled and the others had their places around or across from them, Desmond turned to Tre'shovak with a curious look on his face, waiting for the next instruction. His stomach was not as patient and let out a low groaning noise at the smell of the bacon and potatoes in front of him.

"You remember the breathing exercise I had you do back on Terra?" Desmond nodded his understanding of her question. Tre'shovak quirked an eyebrow at him and her expression became stern.

"Sorry. Yes, I understand, Instructor." Desmond winced as he realized his training was already starting. Tre'shovak nodded, a small smile on her lips.

"Remember, being respectful is never the wrong choice when dealing with another adept or an instructor. Especially when you are learning something from them."

"Oh, don't bust his balls too much, Camilla," groaned Ryaan from around a mouthful of breakfast roll. While he was not allowed to eat yet, that hadn't stopped the rest of the group from digging in. "He's going to get enough of that at the Academy."

"Precisely why we have to get him ready now. I don't show favorites. Since I'm the one who picked him up; McLaughlin's actions will reflect on me and, to an extent, the rest of you," Tre'shovak replied primly before turning back to Desmond. "Resume the breathing exercise, and focus on drawing in energy. Remember the sensation from the office. You'll feel your dynamo start pulling in the ambient mana. Once it starts drawing, you'll feel a tugging here." She tapped his chest right below his breastbone. "The ambient mana here aboard the ship isn't enough to keep it flowing properly with your cache so low, so as soon as you feel it drawing in strongly, like it's trying to suck your ribcage into itself, start eating."

"Understood, Instructor," Desmond replied, drawing a snicker from the two green-skinned females on the other side of the table as they dug into their food with gusto. "I assume there is something in the food that will fuel the reaction?" Desmond asked as he looked between the food on his plate and the plates of the others.

"Yes. All food in the wider galaxy has trace amounts of mana in it. Even the mundanes can process it and it helps their bodies grow, but for an adept, it is fuel for the engine inside you. Though, before you start..." Tre'shovak gave him a long look before she continued. "Yours is going to get a boost. I am...curious what will happen. On the *Valor's Bid,* they will customize your meals to your power level and the state of your cache to help you recover. But here we will need to do something different, given the situation of your homeworld."

"Don't blow up the Cadet, Camilla," warned the Va'Aelfa on his other side around a mouthful of fruit. Tre'shovak did not respond, instead just raising her nose dismissively and reaching into her jacket to extract a vial of clear material with a metal stopper. Inside it lay a glowing, opalescent powder that took up half the vial.

"Refined mana can take many forms. Crystallized shards being one of the more common ones. You will learn how to harvest and purify such things from Rifts during your first few weeks at the academy. You are not to use them like this without an instructor supervising," Tre'shovak warned before unstopping the vial and reaching out to shake it over his food lightly, like she was salting it.

The sharp, cool feeling of mint stung Desmond's nostrils again as soon as the vial got near him, and he inhaled sharply in surprise.

The powder that had been falling down over his food flared a bright wash of color before burning off into an iridescent smoke that flowed towards him. Tre'shovak cursed under her breath and yanked the vial back away from him. Before she could stop it, the reaction flowed back up the powder and into the vial, burning off half the contents into the expanding colored smoke before she stoppered it. The rest of the team leaned back from the billowing cloud of multicolor smoke that began to expand on the table, several of them cursing.

"Cadet, draw now. Quickly! Get that dynamo going," Tre'shovak barked.

Desmond fought the urge to choke as the cloyingly thick feeling of mint filled his lungs like he was trying to breathe a peppermint patty. The ache in his chest sharpened with a cracking sensation that felt like when he popped his spine after sitting wrong. Letting his breath out in a long flow, he took another deep breath and the cloud of multicolor smoke changed directions and raced toward him.

The first breath felt like breathing mint jelly with hints of the burn of cinnamon. The main mass felt like someone had jammed two tubes of wintergreen toothpaste into his nostrils and clamped down hard. To make the sensation even worse, the tugging feeling in his chest latched onto that thick flow of energy and began yanking it down his throat like it was forcing him to swallow through his sinuses.

Fighting the choking sensation in his throat, Desmond fought to continue the steady inhale despite the cloying feeling of the gaseous mana rushing into him.

"Camilla," one of the others said warningly, but Desmond couldn't spare the attention to figure out which one had said it.

"Hush. He's handling it," Tre'shovak whispered urgently. And indeed, Desmond could handle it. The bulk of the iridescent cloud vanished into his body and he felt a lurching sensation as his ribs compressed slightly before the pressure increased under his breastbone and the tingling sensation raced throughout his entire body.

"Shatter and void it!" swore one observer and Desmond noticed the rest of the room had gotten quiet as all eyes were turned towards him as the last of the cloud vanished into him. Blinking slowly, he continued the steady breathing as the tingle reached his fingertips and bounced back like a ripple in a pond reaching the shore.

As the ripple of energy returned to his center, he felt his muscles swell sharply. The swelling was noticeable enough that he saw the eyes of those directly across from him widen. He felt a seam in his shirt tear where his shoulders met the sleeves. After several more deep breaths, and the swelling began to subside. Desmond shrank back to his normal size while letting out a relieved breath. Just behind his breastbone, he felt a slight humming sensation as the tugging slowly continued. Like someone had put a wind-up toy on his chest and let it clatter away.

"Did not need to Hulk out of my clothes in the middle of the mess hall," Desmond muttered to himself before he continued the steady breathing.

The tugging sensation in his chest happened again, like something was being drawn into it through his ribs, but slowly. Desmond also felt the weight against his chest again as he tried to draw breath in through his lungs, as whatever was being drawn inwards piled up there. It felt as if his entire rib-cage was sucking inward. Remembering Tre'shovak's advice, he snatched up his fork and began shoveling the mound of scrambled eggs into his mouth.

"Thatta boy!" cheered Ko'an from across the table. A broad grin spread over his face, revealing that all of his front teeth were sharp points. Relieved laughter broke out amongst the group seated there.

Tre'shovak watched him intently as he ate, not touching her own meal for the moment as she watched.

"Cammy, what the hell was that?" asked one of the green-skinned females.

Orcs...I bet they are orcs, since Instructor Tre'shovak is like an elf, or Aelfa as she called herself... Desmond thought as he continued to shovel food in his face. The pressure in his chest was easing up as he ate, but it felt as if he transitioned from being very hungry to absolutely starving in the time it had taken to do the breathing exercise with the multicolored smoke.

"Mana-starved. It's the only explanation I can come up with," Tre'shovak said, pity dancing in her cyan eyes while she watched Desmond eat like a starving hound. "His home-world was so barren of mana, it felt like breathing the air inside of a blast-furnace. Like it was actively drawing the mana from my body. As soon as his body got a whiff of pure mana, it latched on and drank deep."

"Dangerous...you should warn the Ambassador," Rumbled Ko'an as he dug back into his food.

"I'll pass the word back as soon as I get back to the quarters. McLaughlin, how are you feeling?" Tre'shovak had not looked away from Desmond yet, nor had she blinked. It honestly was creeping Desmond out a bit to have her intense cyan eyes staring through the side of his head.

"Like my leg is hollow and I'm trying to fill it, Instructor."

"No pressure? Can you tell if your cache is filling or not? Answer between bites, but don't stop eating," Tre'shovak insisted as she fingered the stopper on the half full vial in her hand.

"No pressure. Though I can feel that sucking sensation you mentioned." Desmond started cutting up the steaks as he answered, chewing the meat while he thought and cut more. "Feels like...when you try to drink a milkshake through too small a straw? Does that make sense?"

"Yes, that sounds about right, but you don't feel any pressure at all?"

"No, none. At least none going out. Like, I don't feel 'full' in any fashion, not even my stomach..." Desmond said carefully around a mouthful of the steak.

"Ryaan. Go get him another plate of the same," Tre'shovak ordered. The bouncy Aelfa hopped to her feet and scampered off to comply. Desmond noted that, while none of the others rose to follow her, at least two of them kept watch over Ryaan with their eyes the entire time she was away from the table.

CHAPTER 6

What did I think of the Terran the first time I saw him? Feisty and resilient. He didn't have that 'lost puppy' look that you would expect from an out of depth male in the greater galaxy. He jumped in with both feet and ran with predators. Probably seduced a few of them by accident too, now that I think about it.
~Ryaan Summers, Adept-Guard, on meeting Desmond McLaughlin.

The hunger pangs didn't fade away until Desmond finished the second plate of food. Even then, he felt a persisting ache in his system. The sensation of pressure in and around his ribcage had shifted to a dull ache as well. The only time that it had faded completely was just after he had finished inhaling the iridescent smoke from the powdered mana.

"All right, now that you aren't going to keel over and your dynamo is running properly," Tre'shovak drawled. The others had finished eating while he had downed his second serving, and Ko'an had won a bet between his fellow guards that he would finish everything. "Let's walk through what happened there, and why you had such a powerful reaction to the presence of the purified mana."

"You said something about being mana-starved?" Desmond asked as he pushed the plate away and took a deep breath. He should feel like an overfull balloon, stuffed beyond the point of no return, but he just felt...full. Not even full, actually, just not hungry anymore.

"You understand what dehydration is? Imagine something similar, but with mana instead," Tre'shovak explained slowly. Her eyes turned to one side as she considered. "Your body has acted for so long without mana to the point that your species adapted to survive without it entirely. Or maybe they evolved specifically because of the absence. Either way, your body realized that you could give it something that it desperately needed and started drawing it in as quickly as possible."

"So I unconsciously caused the powder to react like that?" Desmond squinted at the table as he thought it over. The mechanics of it didn't make sense to him.

"Somewhat like that." Tre'shovak waved a hand back and forth as she spoke. "More that…you sparked a chain reaction and your dynamo did the rest, doing what it needed to in order to get started. It just happened a lot faster than expected. You did exactly as you were told, and it was a good thing you followed instructions after it happened."

"What would have happened if I hadn't?" Desmond asked before wincing slightly. "Instructor?" He tacked on quickly, but Tre'shovak didn't seem to notice or care.

"Mana is inherently unstable. Crystallized mana is its most stable form, and the reaction caused the contents of the vial to burn up rapidly. You or I would be fine, but if the others had breathed in the smoke, it could have caused injury in the most conservative of cases, or mutations in the most extreme ones."

Eyebrows shooting up, Desmond gave her a look of horrified surprise. Tre'shovak just nodded, her face serious as she let the moment sink in before continuing.

"You aren't expected to know this yet. But, when teams are deployed into areas that have high concentrations of raw mana, they wear special protective gear." Tre'shovak tapped one long finger against the table for a moment before she continued. "Think of it like…oxygen. You need to breathe it to survive, but excessive exposure in high concentrations is very dangerous."

"Okay. So is that going to happen every time I'm around

something with high concentrations of mana? That sounds pretty dangerous, Instructor."

"Doubtful. You should adapt just fine. This was likely just an extreme reaction to your first exposure to concentrated mana. But we will be keeping a close eye on the situation." Tre'shovak finally slid the little vial of crystalline mana powder back into her jacket. "All right, let us have a look at this data-tablet and get your reading assignments loaded up for you."

"Is there going to be any training before we get there, or just reading?" Desmond asked as Tre'shovak pressed the upper left and lower right corners of the data-tablet screen at the same time, which caused it to light up and begin displaying text in a menu.

"No, training begins at the Academy. Triggering the dynamo is the only thing that we do in advance, so that your body has time to adapt to the feeling before classes begin. When I spoke with the Captain, they expected us to arrive in roughly thirty hours at the rendezvous point with the *Valor's Bid*. Until then, you are to work through as much of these as you can." Tre'shovak tapped through a series of menus and pushed a few things around before turning the data-tablet back over to him. On the screen were nearly a dozen titles in a language he didn't recognize.

"I can't read this, Instructor." Desmond looked up at Tre'shovak with a worried expression. Tre'shovak rolled her eyes and gestured at the data-tablet again.

"Tap the corners like I did. That way, it keys to your biometrics."

Doing as instructed, Desmond watched the strange, angular characters shift and flow until they slipped into a standard English text.

"How does it do that? I get that your spell is translating the words for us in my head, but..." Desmond continued to stare at the data-tablet in confusion.

"Technology. Our systems were able to build a lexicon

of the various Terran languages as we approached your home planet. It's been loaded into the universal database to ease transition. You will be expected to learn Hegemony Standard, or Standard, during your time at the Academy." Tre'shovak tapped her cuff again with one finger. "The translator spell that will be imbued in your cuff will only work for the first year of studies. You don't want to end up held back a year, so make sure you study. Starting the second year, your reading assignments will be in Hegemony Standard."

"Short amount of time to work with, but I get it. Can't have folks relying on the crutch of the translation spell. Anything like that can end up backfiring on you at the worst possible time." Desmond nodded as he started tapping through the menu.

"Yes. And not everyone is an adept or has access to one that can cast the translation spells. So the universal trade language of Hegemony Standard is necessary. The handful of species that cannot vocalize the full range of sounds have ways around it." Tre'shovak sighed before standing and collecting her tray. "Let's get you back to your room. Focus on reading while you can. I'll have an assigned study list sent to your personal data-tablet when you have one assigned that will include these titles as well, so make sure you return that to Jenneth when we disembark."

Juggling the data-tablet and the two trays took a bit of doing, but he managed to get them to the window that held the staff working to clean the trays and the entire group trouped back to their rooms.

"Doesn't it ever get...stifling being surrounded like this?" Desmond asked Tre'shovak, which drew a number of looks from the others. "Not that there is a problem with it. It's just not something I'm used to. Being surrounded everywhere I go, always moving as a group. I'm used to being alone most of the time."

"You'll get used to it," grunted Ko'an. The big male walked

behind them, again taking up the rear like a mobile green wall.

"As Ko'an said, you will grow accustomed to it during your time in service and at the Academy." Tre'shovak stopped at the door that led to their suite and gestured for Desmond to head down the hall to his room. "Go, rest and read up. We will come and retrieve you for the next meal. If you feel anything odd, come and get me. And I mean anything, Cadet McLaughlin." Tre'shovak locked eyes with him, a stern expression creasing her features until he voiced his agreement. "Best of luck, and congratulations. You have taken your first and, arguably, hardest step onto the road of the adept."

"Thank you, Instructor. I look forward to being able to do something with this. It still feels a little far from genuine right now," Desmond replied. The data-tablet was tucked under one arm securely.

"You are dismissed, Cadet. You'll learn about proper protocol at the Academy as well. Do not leave your room without an escort, for your safety. You can come and get one of my guards if you need to, but do not wander on your own." The stern expression faded from Tre'shovak's features once more and she turned to lead her collection of guards into their rooms. Desmond caught a glimpse inside and the room was far more lavishly furnished than his simple accommodations, with what appeared to be paintings hanging on the walls and velvet chairs scattered about the room, but that was all he could see before the door slid shut.

Fancy. Wonder if I'll get the royal treatment one day. Desmond pondered as he headed back to his room to read up on the various bits of subject matter that he was expected to memorize.

CHAPTER 7

What did I think of meeting all the non-human folks? I'll be honest, I was overwhelmed enough with the whole 'space-wizard' thing that I spent a fair bit of time looking for laser swords. Once that wore off, I was used to the people. And that's what they were, just people. Sure, some of them were really different looking, but have you ever been to Comic-Con?
~Desmond McLaughlin, on his first experiences in the Hegemony.

Desmond spent most of the next full day reading. He had debated going out to explore the halls of the *Nebula Ghost* but decided against it given the warning from Tre'shovak the day before. He was still wondering about just how serious the dangers of being an adept might be, but since the instructor was wary, he figured it was best to do the same.

After the stunt in the dining hall, the rest of the crew had kept a watchful eye on him. Not enough to make him feel singled out, but enough that he didn't feel comfortable being alone with the strangers either. So instead, he set to the reading with a vengeance, only pausing for meals and to do some light calisthenics every so often when he felt stiff. The chair in his room and his bed were remarkably comfortable, but there was only so long one could sit still before needing to move.

His tablet provided a wealth of new information. The material contained both hard facts and random trivia that he was unsure would prove to be useful, but was interesting nonetheless.

The knowledge that the Hegemony was actually known

as the Hegemony of Velvet Stars by its full designation felt extraneous, but Desmond filed that bit of information away in his mind.

More importantly, the knowledge that, at the time of the document being written, the Hegemony held claim over more than a third of the Milky Way as its base of holdings made his brain seize up slightly. He spent half an hour just staring at the wall, trying to comprehend the sheer number of stars that included. The document had stated that there were over forty billion individual star systems, and inside that number were over four dozen different 'home-planet' systems that were the dominion of the various member races of the Hegemony.

Another bit of information that was surprising to uncover was the number of Academy ships that were in service to the Hegemony. Fourteen. Fourteen ships that provided the training to the adepts of the Hegemony and provided training to their bodyguard teams and elite military. It didn't feel like nearly enough, given the sheer number of stars that they patrolled, but apparently it was.

The reading also gave him the answer to another question about adepts and that was related to their duties.

An adept's primary role was as a force multiplier. Either with their personal guard teams, or when dispatched with a patrol ship or regiment. From there, their principal duty was helping to eliminate Rift incursions, which tended to occur when enough mana congregated in one location. Untended Rifts could be catastrophic to nearby settlements, and only by closing the incursions and disbursing the collected mana was it possible to avert some rather nasty consequences. It didn't, however, go into the details of *how* the adepts went about the process of it. Only that mana tended to have a snowball effect on the environment, larger concentrations drawing in exponentially more mana from the region until they were dealt with or the Rift went critical.

Desmond was also suspicious since the book he was

reviewing didn't specify exactly what happened when a Rift went critical, just that it was 'Very Bad News'.

Tre'shovak and the others collected him for several meals over the following days and Tre'shovak stopped by to examine him again to make sure that his dynamo was still doing its job properly.

"It's important to monitor it closely until you are safely on Academy grounds. The ambient mana on site will allow you to grow just fine, but I don't want to risk you having a reaction and something going wrong just because I didn't look," she explained during the second check up. Desmond just put up with it and did his best to not complain.

He had learned several things about his traveling companions. First was that the name of the species for the green-skinned beings had turned out to not be anywhere near the 'orc' he had suspected. According to his readings, they were called Hyreh.

Also, while Tre'shovak's flavor of Aelfa was known as the 'Va'Aelfa', what intrigued him was that both the home-world and native language for Tre'shovak's sub-species and Ryaan's were the same. Apparently, both had evolved on the same world or that their 'root species' had developed there.

Ryaan's sub-species name came up as 'Tu'Aelfa' and shared a suffix to denote the 'elf' connection. Desmond spent quite a bit of time wondering what might have caused their species to diverge enough that they needed specific subcategories for each variant, as there were over a dozen listed in the species compendium, all uniting under the single heading of 'Aelfa' in their native language. The fact that it reminded him of the word 'elf' in Terran didn't escape him, but he didn't have access to the Internet to confirm his suspicions.

<><><>

They arrived at their destination a few hours after

breakfast and Ryaan had come to pick Desmond up to take him to one of the forward viewing decks.

"You've never seen one of the Academy ships before, so you gotta get a good view of our baby before you board it. Would be a waste not to," Ryaan chirped as she led the way down the hall. It was just him, Ryaan, Ko'an, and the stoic Jenneth right now. Camilla was already waiting for them on the deck.

"I dunno, Instructor Summers," Desmond replied. He'd learned that, while her name came across in his language as something familiar, it was apparently an entirely different word when translated from English, to Standard, to her native tongue. It had summed up to something along the lines of 'Dancing-sun-on-broad-water' the one time he'd had her explain it during a meal. "It isn't like I have anything to compare it to. The *Nebula Ghost* is already the biggest single construction I've ever seen."

"Trust me, you need to see it," Ryaan asserted before dragging him through the sliding door and into the large viewing space with one arm, while the other gestured wildly over her head.

There was a scattering of regular crew at various tables around the large open space. To his left was a viewing port that was easily as long as a football field and half as tall, built into one wall. The rest of Tre'shovak's team were standing near one corner waiting for them, as the ship slid through the expanse of darkness between stars. A faint ripple of light flared away from the ship, like the wake being shed by a speedboat, and it distorted the view through the window slightly.

"Uhh..." Desmond stopped for a moment before Ko'an chuckled and gave him a push from behind to get him moving again.

"Go on, boy. It's safe enough. That view port is several feet thick and made of a crystalline alloy that can take hits from a ship of similar displacement to the *Nebula Ghost*,"

Ko'an urged. They crossed the distance just as the ripple-like distortion began to fade away from in front of the viewing port.

"Looks like you arrived just in time. The *Nebula Ghost* just arrived in the system and it looks like the *Valor's Bid* is waiting for us near the outer orbitals of the star," Tre'shovak called. The Va'Aelfa instructor gestured for Desmond to join her by the glass. Hurrying over, he met the instructor there and peered through the crystalline view port into the vacuum of space.

Thousands of distant stars twinkled against the inky backdrop and Desmond blinked as a bright purple planet slid past, distant enough that it was about the size of a watermelon, but still close enough he could see the varying bands that made up its surface.

"The local star is a type-O. So it is going to wash out the colors somewhat, but the filters in the view-screen should keep it from blinding you via reflection. Just don't stare into it if the star itself comes into view," Tre'shovak warned. She then reached into her hip pouch and produced the small device from before when she called for the shuttle. She manipulated it for a moment before raising it to her mouth and speaking into it. "Captain? Can you swing a little wide? I want the Cadet to get a good view of the Academy as we approach without having to deal with the local star blinding him." There was a quiet noise of affirmation from the unit before she tucked it away again. Moments later, the ship shifted slightly on its trajectory and a shape slid into sight.

"Well, Cadet Desmond McLaughlin. That," she gestured broadly through the window ", is your new home for the next several years. Meet the *Valor's Bid*." The smile on Tre'shovak's face was obvious in her tone, despite Desmond not being able to look towards her. Instead, he was fixated on the sight in front of him.

They were approaching the academy ship from the side and the first mental image that Desmond had was of an ocean sunfish that he had seen once on a Discovery show. The ship was flat from this angle, shaped roughly like a broad lizard scale. It had two stubby 'fins' that rose from the top and bottom of the structure, each 'fin' being nearly as long as the main 'body'. It was impossible to tell the correct size of it as there was nothing of a scale he knew nearby, but given that it dwarfed the moon that it hung next to, the *Valor's Bid* was absolutely massive.

As they grew closer, Desmond could make out more details. On either flank of the ship, along what would be the 'sides' of the fish, were a series of ridges that extended out like ripples or the whorls of a fingerprint. There was a brief flare of light from a spot on one whorl and Desmond saw something move inside the whorl. Squinting as they approached, he could make out several small ships launching from inside the ridges and details on the side of the ship. It looked like there were hundreds of small launch bays on either side of the massive ship and as they drew closer, Desmond began to truly understand the sheer size of the behemoth that he'd be living on in the future.

"The *Valor's Bid* is classed as a 'super-dreadnought' by the Hegemony's ship classifications. It's eight kilometers long and nearly eleven tall at the engines," Jenneth murmured from behind him. "While it isn't the largest in its classification, only another Academy ship would be larger than it."

"Are all the Academy ships that big?" Desmond asked as the *Nebula Ghost* drew closer. A trio of other ships slid into view as they patrolled in an arc around the Academy ship. Each was easily the size of the *Nebula Ghost* and they slid protectively in between them and the Academy ship for several long moments before their engines fired again and they swung out of the way.

"Some are, some aren't. They all class in the super-dreadnought category, but the *Valor's Bid* is one of the longest serving Academy ships in the Hegemony's navy," answered the Va'Aelfa. Desmond glanced at her to see a proud smirk cross her lips before he looked back at the ship they were approaching.

"Look closer towards the aft of the ship," Tre'shovak broke the silence suddenly. Desmond's gaze snapped to the back half as directed.

"What am I looking for, Instructor?"

"You'll understand it when you see it," was the only response he got.

Desmond squinted and looked closer around the engines and the back half of the broad ship. A handful of seconds later, he noticed the odd ripple that surrounded the engines. The void of space danced slightly, causing the light of the stars there to waver as if seen through a heat mirage.

"What is that?" He gestured towards the ship, tracing the distortion that extended behind the massive ship.

"That, Cadet McLaughlin, is the entire reason the Academy ships exist." Tre'shovak gestured at the distortion as well before continuing. "You've read about how the Rifts form, correct?" Desmond nodded along, and she continued. "The Academies are built into the super-dreadnoughts, like the *Valor's Bid*, in order to patrol and hunt them down in cooperation with freelance teams on independent ships. That is their first duty after training the new generation of adepts. But the other half of it is that the sheer amount of mana manipulated within their walls leaves a wake behind the ship. The Academies literally draw a wake of mana behind them. If they stay in one position too long, Rifts can begin to form both around the ship and inside of its halls. There are shields and dispersion devices aboard to prevent such things from happening, but one thing that we have learned is that mana will find a way around the most stubborn of technology."

"So that distortion, that's what? Raw mana?" Desmond turned his incredulous gaze on Tre'shovak to find her somber expression and a nod waiting for him.

"Yes. You notice how the *Nebula Ghost* is coming around from the side and not approaching from the rear? The distortion of the mana wake could rupture the ship's systems as surely as a cannon shot. And that mana wake isn't just because of the engines running either, it's also because of the sheer number of adepts aboard the *Valor's Bid* and the amount of mana being utilized every day."

"The engines don't help none, but she's right. The vast majority of the wake comes from adepts and the instructors teaching them," Ko'an added as well.

"That's...slightly terrifying. What happens if one of them breaks down?" Desmond's gaze was drawn back to the ship as he thought.

"We pray such things happen in the void between stars, or in uninhabited systems." Tre'shovak's tone was solemn as she spoke. "Such things don't happen often though. The Academy ships are heavily staffed and under constant maintenance to prevent something like that happening. Generally, if something major like that is about to happen or major repairs and refits need to occur, there are a handful of outposts that can do such repairs but most times they are taken care of by on site staff and occur in the void between stars."

"What happens when an Academy ship needs to be decommissioned, or is scuttled? What about during war?" Desmond asked, tracing the obvious armaments the massive ship carried. The dimensions on such weapons were hard to grasp but there were a trio of cannons mounted ahead of each of the massive 'fins' above and below and the barrels looked large enough that Desmond imagined he could have crammed a Challenger space shuttle into them.

"Again, something done in the void between stars," Tre'shovak said sharply. Desmond glanced over at her to find the Va'Aelfa was watching him with a severe expression. *Probably not a subject that a cadet is supposed to ask about...*

"So are we taking a shuttle over there? Is something

coming to get us? Does the *Nebula Ghost* dock with it?" Desmond asked several questions to get away from the more tense topic. Tre'shovak seemed happy to turn the conversation away to a more safe subject and nodded.

"The Academy is sending over a shuttle now." She glanced down at her cuff and, with a press on one of the embossed symbols, a small green screen slid open on the back of the cuff. "It looks like it is on its way now, so we should go and collect our things."

The group pushed away from the window as one and began to walk back down the halls. Again, Desmond was shifted to the center of the group with Tre'shovak while they walked.

I don't know if I will get used to this ever...hope whoever I get paired up with isn't quite as...stifling.

CHAPTER 8

The Adept-Guard is one of the most elite organizations amongst the Hegemony's military. They are the sword and shield of the adepts, the most treasured resources of the Empress, and as such are expected to rise to peak standards and be able to adapt on a moment's notice. Adept-Guards will see sights and experience things others can only dream of and will clash with the foes of the Hegemony as the tip of the spear! Can you measure up to this demanding standard?
If so, do your part and apply today at
your local recruitment office!
~Recruitment poster on the factory world of Lind-4.

The shuttle ride over to the *Valor's Bid* was uneventful, though Desmond ended up sitting next to Ryaan, who grumbled the entire way. The smaller Tu'Aelfa apparently did not like to be relegated to a passenger role, but the shuttle-pilot that had picked them up had outright refused to let her take over or even to open the door to the cockpit. It had taken Tre'shovak ordering Ryaan to sit before the smaller woman had plopped down into her chair with a huff of irritation.

Desmond had tried to distract her by asking questions about what to expect when they got there, but Ryaan refused to be distracted from her irritation. While she answered questions in general, she managed to find a way to wedge in comments about the slow progress of the pilot and how she could have gotten there so much faster if they'd just let her fly the shuttle.

The awkwardness of the situation was only exacerbated because Ryaan was wearing her full combat kit and had been brandishing what looked suspiciously like a heavy bore, sawed-off shotgun the entire time.

By the time that they had landed, Desmond was ready to disembark, and it was only partially because of his excitement to see the inside of the Academy.

When the light above the exit hatch flipped over to a cool blue color and it slid open, the group let out a collective sigh and, as one, popped their restraints off with a practiced coordination.

"Well, let's get back home then. Glad we weren't gone long, but I still hate these babysitting trips…" Grumbled Jenneth the Va'Aelfa. "No offense intended, Cadet McLaughlin."

"None taken, Instructor. I'm sure that you all had things you would have preferred to do than escort me from a backwater world."

"That's part of it, yeah. But it's customary for a team from an Academy to accompany an ambassador on first contact. The fact that the system scans picked you out of the database as a match was a bonus. It saved us a side trip to pick up another potential on the way back." Jenneth sighed as they all filed out of the ship in a column.

"I had meant to ask about that, by the way, here's your data-tablet back, thank you." Desmond handed her the device back, which she accepted and slipped inside the carry bag that hung under one shoulder with practiced ease. "How did I get picked again? I know that your tech is wickedly advanced, but there are billions of people on Earth."

"You were part of one of the DNA databases your people had. The standard for the Hegemony is that each citizen is registered in the system databases at birth. It's how a number of things are tracked after all, everything from bank accounts to arrest records. The potential to manipulate mana is dictated by your genetics, so it's important that they are kept track of," Tre'shovak answered for her, tossing the comment over her shoulder as she led the way out the door.

"I think the one they accessed was one of those 'ancestry tracing' services. They had enough data that the necessary sequences to wake your dynamo were easy to spot when we ran it through the computers. They spat out a short list of potentials that will be contacted in the next few years as Terra comes up to speed and more Academy ships rotate through nearby space."

"That's right, they all patrol to keep that 'mana wake' that you mentioned from building up and pick up new cadets along their paths, right?"

"That's correct. When we found the proverbial harvest ready in Terra's databases, we sent word back to the Academy and you were selected from the short list as the best potential for this year's class. Came in just under the wire too since there were only two other slots open, and others filled them by the time we made it back to the *Nebula Ghost*."

Desmond opened his mouth to ask another question, but the words died in his throat when he finally emerged from the shuttle and saw the massive hanger in which they stood.

The hanger for the *Nebula Ghost* had felt large, with enough space to launch all seven of the shuttles at once if necessary, but the hangar that they stood in held two dozen of the shuttles in ready racks against just one wall and there were other racks of two different models of ship. The open space was easily three or more football fields in size and dozens of techs jogged back and forth. He saw the flash of a welder off on the other side of the open space as a ship was being worked on by a ground crew. *And this was only one of hundreds of bays I saw from space*, he thought in wonder.

The trip from the hangar to the dorm space aboard the massive ship happened in a daze for Desmond. His group led him through a series of causeways, the halls easily large enough that he could have driven a semi-truck down them with space to spare. The occasional decorations of potted plants and various bits of art that were clearly from unique cultures broke up the vastness. Elaborate paintings of galaxies hung beside hand-carved statues of wood, depicting what Desmond guessed were tribal heroes or deities. They passed several open-air atriums, larger than the hangar had been and full of different types of life, from sentient to arboreal. The floor was carpeted in a stiff material with a slight cushion to it and was colored a dark yellow that bordered on gold that accented the brushed gray walls well.

Throughout the entire trip, Desmond listened in silence as the group of instructors that surrounded him chatted back and forth, far more relaxed in the familiar surroundings. He had questions that he had wanted to ask them, but his focus was drawn inward instead.

The steady thrum he had felt behind his breastbone for the last day and a half had picked up tempo. There was a flood of different 'flavors' entering his nostrils every time he breathed in. The tang of cinnamon here, a blast of wintergreen there, the faint scent of rosemary wafting through them all. *Is this the ambient mana that Instructor Tre'shovak mentioned?* Desmond wondered as he continued to breathe in slowly while they walked. Every time the 'flavor' of mana changed, he felt that the hum in his chest changed pitch slightly.

It wasn't until they arrived at the cadet wing that Desmond realized he was being watched. Both Tre'shovak and Jenneth were watching him closely as the group came to a stop in front of a pair of doors that were colored a deep bronze with a symbol he didn't recognize pressed into the door.

"This is your dorm wing, Cadet McLaughlin," Tre'shovak said. She shifted slightly and adjusted the strap of her carry bag on one shoulder. "Select a suite from the unoccupied ones and settle in. For now, you will have the suite to yourself. You read up on the document outlining the first year that I assigned you, correct?"

"For the first year, adepts will work with the various members that have been selected for advanced training.

Some of which have mana sensitivity but cannot actually start their dynamo. During this time, it is the cadet-adept's responsibility to begin forming their guard-team who will work with them for their term of service. The first three members will be selected during the first year, as the minimum team size is four. Additional opportunities to build the team out from there occur in year two as well, but are optional depending on the cadet-adept's abilities and planned approach," Desmond quoted verbatim. He'd studied the pamphlet about what to expect extensively and, while it hadn't had as much as he hoped, it had given him at least a basic understanding of what to expect in the coming years.

"Good. But remember one thing." Tre'shovak crossed her arms as she took up a stance directly in front of Desmond with her feet shoulder width apart and expression stern. "Once you select someone for your team, there is no 'trade in' if things do not go to plan. Working with what you have is also an expectation in the field. You will eventually be assigned to a combat role and have to work with the crew under you as well as your guard, and you need to adapt to the situation as needed. This is also important for male adepts to remember that they cannot just swap around female members of their team at a whim. Exceptions are made in extreme situations, but it requires a severe conflict of personality and review by a board of instructors. It is an exception, not the rule."

Desmond was rather proud of the fact he did not blush at the underlying implication to Instructor Tre'shovak's words. Your guide book mentioned that the Academy did not care what 'consenting adults' did in their off hours and relationships were encouraged as long as they were positive because it helped build 'team dynamic'. The outline of consequences for rape was severe regardless of which gender instigated the situation and apparently 'diviners' were called in to suss out the truth of accusations as well to prevent false allegations. The guidebook hadn't gone into details about what a 'diviner' was, but Desmond had an inkling that they'd learn more in the coming classes.

"The areas you are cleared to have access to will be marked with a bronze trim and the symbol for the cadet-adepts, like the door behind you. Once you get settled in and get your comm-cuff, it'll also only open doors you are cleared for. For now, all the cadet-adepts are confined to the dorm space, classrooms, and training areas. Once you have selected your first guard, you will have expanded access on the *Valor's Bid*. This is for your own safety." Tre'shovak explained carefully, indicating the rune on the door as she explained it. Desmond nodded his understanding.

"Do you have any last questions, Cadet McLaughlin?" Tre'shovak's words rang with a finality as she stared at him with her large, cyan eyes.

Desmond took in her team as they arrayed themselves behind the instructor as he thought. Ryaan stood directly to Tre'shovak's left, with the other Tu'Aelfa that had remained silent the entire time beside her. The front wedge was completed by Jenneth on Tre'shovak's right. The three Hyreh stood in a V formation behind them, with Ko'an in the middle and slightly back. With their armor on and weapons shouldered, the group made an intimidating spectacle. Rather than feeling oppressed by the team in front of him, Desmond felt encouraged slightly. He could vaguely imagine himself heading up a team in the future, several large shapes bracketing him with others arrayed like points on a star.

Shaking off the daydream, Desmond snapped to attention. The guidebook had given him the proper steps for a member of the Hegemony military to salute a ranking officer. His heels came together with toes apart in an 'at-attention' much like from the Terran military, but rather than a flat hand to his eyebrow, Desmond made a fist with his left hand and tapped it to the base of his breastbone, right above where the hum of his dynamo emanated. As an adept, it was a sign of respect and an indication of the status as an adept of any rank. A normal member would salute with their fist at the top of their breastbone, to symbolize shielding the body of the Empire.

Instructor Tre'shovak returned the salute a moment later before gesturing for him to proceed through the door. As neatly as he could, Desmond stepped back into an 'at ease' position and turned to march towards the door that led to the dorms. The door slid open with a quiet hiss and he passed through it a moment later without stopping. Once the door slid shut, Tre'shovak let out an inaudible sigh and relaxed.

"Think he'll survive?" Ryaan's normally bouncy voice was subdued slightly.

"Boy has grit and wants to learn. I think he'll do fine," Grunted Ko'an. The group devolved into muttered conversation as they turned as one and headed towards the staff dorms, but Tre'shovak was lost in silent thought as she followed her team.

CHAPTER 9

Cadet-Adepts are assigned personal suites of rooms. This is not to prevent them from interacting with other cadets-adepts, but to foster close bonds with their eventual guard teams. The rooms, like most things that are provided for the cadet-adepts, are only basically outfitted as each cadet-adept is provided a weekly stipend for their necessities. This is to allow them to furnish and equip themselves and their rooms as they see fit. An approach that is followed in all their gear, to allow each cadet-adept room for their talents to grow.
Cadet Handbook version 7.23, regarding Housing.

Telling if a suite was occupied took a bit of experimentation, but Desmond figured it out rather quickly. If the suite had been claimed, the doors refused to open to him when he walked past them. He only figured this out after walking past several obstinately closed doors until he caught sight of someone ducking into one that refused to open when he went past. The fact the halls were empty right now made him wonder what time it was aboard the ship. Was the lack of other people because of the late hour?

There were two doors on each side of the hall before it split off at a four-way junction. Each direction had two doors in each wall, staggered slightly, and the grid continued. The hallway itself was quite similar to the ones outside, except for two things. The carpet was the same shade as the main entrance had been, and there were no bits of art on display. Just the brushed metal walls and the bronze carpet.

Desmond found an empty suite at the end of one of the side paths a fair way from the dorm entrance and when he poked his head through the door, he was stunned at the size of the suite.

"Dayum," he murmured and began inspecting the large room. There were nine doors heading off the circular main room. To one side of the door was a massive conversation pit sunk into the ground with soft sofas that ran around it. In the middle of the pit was a round table that put some banquet tables to shame. Opposite the conversation pit, but still closer to the door, was what he guessed was a kitchenette, as there was something that resembled a griddle top cooking surface with a large oven like construction underneath it. A fridge sat next to those with a sink on the opposite side of the refrigerator and a high topped table taking up the rest of the floor space. Besides these necessary pieces, the room was entirely unfurnished.

"So, this space is all mine for now?" Desmond couldn't help but wonder aloud as he paced around the room. It felt strange to be alone in such a vast room, but Instructor Tre'shovak had told him to pick a suite after all. Did he want to take this one or keep looking? *No, she said that there were only a few slots left, and they'd been filled as well. For all I know, this is the last suite in the dorm, so might as well stay here.*

A cursory inspection of the other doors leading off the room revealed that eight of the nine lead to empty and unfurnished rooms without a single object in them. The ninth room held a luxurious bathroom with a shower three times the size of the one he'd had on the *Nebula Ghost* and a quintet of sinks sharing one wall with a large mirror above it. Besides the fixtures in the bathroom, it was entirely bare without even a towel rack. In fact, the only two things that he found loose in the entire suite were sitting in the middle of the kitchen table. One was a cuff like the instructor had worn. The only difference was that this cuff was a polished bronze in color, similar to the decorations in the hall. Sitting next to it was a data-tablet similar to the one he had borrowed, which lit up when he picked it up. Desmond read the notice that popped up immediately on the screen.

Greetings Cadet-Adept. These rooms will be yours for the remainder of the year. Please note that defacing or damaging them will incur charges to your stipend. Please keep the rooms tidy. If you choose to remain in this suite, please equip the cuff that is included. Be sure to wear it only over bare skin, as direct contact is needed to sync with your genetic signature.

Glancing between the screen and the cuff, Desmond shrugged and fiddled with it for a moment before latching the cuff onto his left forearm like he had seen Tre'shovak wearing. *Huh...were the others wearing a cuff like this?* Desmond thought as the cuff vibrated slightly, almost like an engine starting up, before constricting on his arm to fit snugly against his skin. There was a sharp pain as something pierced the back of his wrist and Desmond let out a yelp of surprise. A moment later, he made a second startled noise when he felt the spin of his dynamo pick up for a moment before a cool sensation entered his wrist and soothed the pain.

"Bloody hell, did this thing bite me?" Desmond tried to remove the cuff, but the latch that he had flicked closed earlier had merged seamlessly with the rest of the cuff and he could no longer find it. No blood oozed from under the cuff, so he had to hope it wasn't serious. *Maybe it just pinched something when it was fitting...rather wish I had someone I could ask questions of to figure out what the hell is going on.* He was grouchy that the others had just dropped him off at the dorm door and left, but he swallowed that irritation. *Can't expect a hand-holding the entire way.*

"Greetings, Cadet Desmond McLaughlin," a neutral, mechanical voice spoke, making Desmond jump in surprise.

"What? Who is that?" He spat in surprise, whirling to look about the room rapidly as his heart raced.

"I am the Singular Artificial Universal Liaison assigned to monitor your suite and assist you with orientation, Cadet-Adept Desmond McLaughlin." The neutral voice replied, the acoustics of the room making it impossible for him to spot where the sound was coming from.

"Oh good, I have a computer minder. Does every cadet have one looking after them?" Desmond asked gruffly, doing his best to calm his racing heart.

"Yes, Cadet-Adept Desmond McLaughlin. My specific designation is SAUL-474, and it is my responsibility to watch over your suite and help you to coordinate your schedule," the neutral voice stated, enunciating each letter in the designation. Desmond quirked an eyebrow at that before glancing at the data-tablet, which had gone dark when he set it down again.

"Anything specific I should call you so that you know I'm talking to you?"

"I may assume any designation that you wish to give me, Cadet-Adept Desmond McLaughlin," the robotic voice replied. "Your data-tablet has a full listing of unique tones and voices that can be used to make you more comfortable. The English Language lexicon has already been uploaded to my database, as you can tell, but if you prefer, the language I use to address you can be altered."

"Are you an artificial intelligence or just a program? I'd hate to change you around if you don't want to."

"I am not a fully artificial intelligence, Cadet-Adept Desmond McLaughlin. The simulation of a fully sentient mind is something that is possible, but I am not one of them."

"Hmm." Desmond thought for a minute before he chuckled and nodded. "I'll call you SAUL then, unless that designation is being used by someone else?"

"At this time, no one has decided to just use the initials. Accessing..." there was a brief pause. "Confirmed. There exists a name that is spelled as such in your language. I will respond to SAUL if you speak to me in this suite. Let me know if you want me to use a different name."

"Got it, SAUL. So what time is it? What kind of clock does the *Valor's Bid* operate on?"

"At this time, it is two hours past midnight shipboard time. The *Valor's Bid* operates on a twenty-six hour clock," SAUL answered in the same genderless neutral tone. *Going to have to pick out something to make him sound less like a murderous Synth or something...* Desmond thought before glancing around the common room once more.

"Gotta say I'm already looking forward to picking out a team...if only to make this feel less cavernous. So SAUL, is there a way to get a bed or something?"

"A basic bed can be deployed from the wall via a command on your data-tablet. Further furnishings can be purchased with your stipend or any hard currency you wish to deposit to your student account for now." Desmond winced slightly at the answer.

"Well, damn. Didn't think to bring any cash with me. When is the stipend deposited?"

"Each student's stipend is deposited to them at the beginning of term. Which is in three days."

"Okay. So basic furniture only for the next three days. I can work with that. Can you wake me up when breakfast is served and can you give me directions to the mess hall?" When SAUL gave him an affirmative, Desmond scooped up his data-tablet and paused to look across the room once more to pick one room as his. "Not like it matters, they are all the exact same..." Desmond muttered before heading into the room next to the bathroom at the back of the suite with a shrug.

A bit of fiddling with his data-tablet got the basic bed that SAUL had described to deploy. A twin sized bed popped out with a pneumatic hiss and despite not feeling all that tired, Desmond was unconscious within minutes of laying down.

SAUL dimmed the lights in the suite as the sole occupant's biometrics slipped to a baseline indicating sleep. There was a quiet 'clunk' from the front door as the locks engaged and the digital guardian of the human cadet-adept settled in for the night watch.

CHAPTER 10

I met a lot of people during my years on the Valor's Bid. Made friends as well as enemies too. It was a social space, and I was visibly different, so it was expected. Thankfully, the friends outweighed the enemies, though some of them did their best to kill me regardless of what side of that fence they were on.
~Desmond McLaughlin, regarding life on the *Valor's Bid*.

Desmond woke to the sound of a gentle beeping from just above his head and the lights steadily growing brighter.

"It is time to wake up, Cadet-Adept Desmond McLaughlin," SAUL's neutral voice piped in from somewhere above his head.

"Right, getting up. SAUL, can you just...randomize a voice each time we talk so I can get a few samples?" Desmond grumbled. The addition of the neutral voice to his wake up had shaken off his sleep as rapidly as a cup of ice water poured on his face. "The neutral tone just sounds so soulless."

"I can do that, Cadet-Adept Desmond McLaughlin." The neutral tone had been replaced with a throaty female voice that made Desmond wince.

"Ack, no. Okay, randomize through *male* voice tones please. Keep the English language for now as well. Also, just call me Desmond or Des."

"That is acceptable, Desmond or Des," answered the gruff voice that reminded Desmond of a New-York cab driver from a movie.

Desmond fought the urge to facepalm. *Okay, so definitely not a true AI. Or SAUL is just messing with me...*

"Either call me Desmond, or call me Des. One or the other, not both, please."

"Understood Desmond." The voice had switched to having a distinctly British twang to it this time. "You wanted to be woken in time for the morning meal. It is being served in the first-year mess hall presently. Directions are available on your cuff interface and on your tablet."

"Appreciated, SAUL. Is there somewhere that I can get additional uniforms? And what about laundry?"

"Place laundry through the chute in the corner and it will be washed and returned to you. A week's worth of uniforms are in the drawers underneath your bed near the foot of it. The drawer closer to the head contains basic supplies for your classes, though more will be issued as classes are attended." This time, the voice that SAUL used reminded Desmond of an older movie about a boring bank clerk that found a wooden mask that changed his personality and voice and colored his skin green. Desmond couldn't help but chuckle at the mental image.

"Appreciate it, SAUL." Desmond fiddled with the cuff for several minutes, pressing different symbols on it and figuring out what each did as much as he could by the process of elimination. He had memorized the one that set off the translation spell and made sure it was engaged before he changed into a fresh uniform and headed out towards the mess hall, following the directions that the cuff gave him.

<><><>

The route to the mess hall was a short one that led through his dorm section. In contrast to the silence of the previous night, the halls were positively busy with people moving back and forth. The words Instructor Tre'shovak had said about the gender ratios echoed in his head again as passed through the halls, noting that every person he passed was female.

He did his best to not be awkward or stare at the different species that he saw, instead just nodding to them in acknowledgment if they met his eyes and keeping moving. He did note that, for whatever reason, the higher majority of people he saw were of a sub-species of Aelfa.

"It's like fucking high-school all over again," Desmond muttered to himself as he heard whispers start up behind him, but no one approached him. "Whatever, just gonna focus on studies and classes. I need to get caught up first before I can worry about anything else." Though he did chuckle slightly at the sharp about-face his mind had taken.

Aboard the *Nebula Ghost*, he'd wondered how he would put up with being surrounded by people. Now, though, Desmond was missing having that insulating layer of other people with him. *Definitely made it easier to ignore the stares.*

The mess hall was at least familiar to what he'd seen on the *Nebula Ghost*, so he could get a hearty breakfast and get settled with his back to a wall to eat and watch the people in the room. He made sure to load the plate with a bit of everything he was already familiar with and included a few new things to try. *It looks like an orange but it's electric blue. I have to try this and see what it tastes like...*

All different races came and went. Aelfa in a dozen different colors and styles, the short folk like the Ambassador that he later learned were a species were known as Dwerg, a name that triggered familiarity but he couldn't latch onto it either. There were at least three different breeds of Hyreh as well, based on the different shades their skin took. It was always a variant of green, though. Two of the other girls he'd seen had delicate wings that were soft pastel colors, like fresh bloomed flowers, with enormous eyes that dominated their skulls, though they were not the strangest ones that he saw moving through the mess hall. That seat was taken by what he could only describe as a lizard-centaur girl who stood almost seven feet tall but had a squat lizard body that extended almost a dozen feet behind her, like someone had grafted her at the waist to an over-sized Komodo dragon. That was the only time he got caught staring as he'd been surprised enough he dropped his fork, and the noise drew her attention.

Rather than continuing to stare, Desmond nodded a greeting to her and forced his eyes back to his food as the mess hall continued to fill up. So when another tray landed on the table in front of him, the sharp 'clack' caught him by surprise.

"So what the hell are you, anyway?" an airy female voice asked. Desmond looked up in time to catch the speaker as she slid into the seat across from him.

"Uh...hume...er Terran?" Desmond replied, fork poised halfway to his mouth. The woman sitting across from him was an Aelfa, though she was one breed that he hadn't met explicitly yet.

Se'Aelfa, I think. Yeah, she has fin-like ears and her skin is so pale. Can't see gills to confirm, though. He thought for a moment before shaking it off.

"Is that a statement or a question?" the Se'Aelfa asked with a quirked eyebrow. Her left ear flicked out and down before tucking back against her pale blonde hair, which fell loose down her back. Dark red eyes the color of tart cherries watched him intently as she forked up some sliced fruit from her tray and took a delicate bite.

"Statement, sorry. Wasn't expecting company. My name is Desmond McLaughlin."

"Olianna Yu'tona. I've never heard of a Terran before. First time I've seen you around," she replied after finishing the bite of fruit she'd started eating. She managed to maintain a haughty glance throughout the entire process too, looking down her nose at him while chewing.

"I'd be surprised if you did. Apparently, they just recently inducted us to the Hegemony. I'm...uh...the first one here as far as I know." Olianna's eyes widened in surprise and she nearly dropped her fork as well.

"So you are that fresh off the shuttle, then? Oh wow, you are doing surprisingly well for a prim thrown to the predators like this." A wicked smile crossed her lips and Desmond was startled to realize that every one of Olianna's teeth looked to be serrated like a shark. "Most prims hide out in their rooms until someone comes to drag them along. At least that is what my sister told me of the one she saw in her time at the Academy. Poor thing was little better than a wild animal."

The Se'Aelfa's snide tone grated on Desmond's nerves, but he pushed the irritation away and forced a smile onto his face.

"Well, I'm happy to break the mold on that. I have too much shit to do and there are never enough hours in the day to get things done." He punctuated his statement by stabbing his fork into a cube-cut fry and stuffing it in his mouth.

"Fair enough. What class set are you in?" The Se'Aelfa looked down at her meal before slicing and downing a large mouthful of steak. Her mobile ears shifted slightly, the tips angling towards him as if to put to lie her nonchalant attitude.

"Dunno yet. Got in late last night, only had the time to figure out how to get a bed deployed and then sacked out. First thing I did was change and come here." Desmond did his best not to stare as Olianna's razor-sharp teeth shredded her meat rapidly.

"Well, at least you got your comm-cuff on right. Though you eat like a barbarian…" Olianna said again in the same snide tone as she reached out with her fork to rap the edge of Desmond's bronze cuff. All the while, her eyes traced over the pile of food on his tray with a hint of disgust.

What's wrong with her? Is she a 'food separatist' or something? Desmond wondered and glanced down at her far more sparse servings, which were neatly organized and not touching. *Called it…*

Fighting the urge to jerk his arm back when she tapped

his cuff, Desmond glanced down at the cuff as if he had only just realized he was wearing it in order to check and see if she'd left anything sticky on the polished metal. It was clean, thankfully. A casual glance noted the one on Olianna's wrist, and he nodded.

"Looks like you got yours figured out as well, too. That's good. Instructor Tre'shovak implied that we are expected to produce results quickly." While he hadn't quite intended to return the dig to her, the way that Olianna's ears tucked back tight to her skull and the scowl that bounced across her face for a moment told him she thought he had. *Well fuck it, she's the one who was digging at me anyway earlier.*

"Of course, the competition for class placement is high and fierce, after all. How much practice have you had? Have you even sparked your dynamo yet?" Olianna didn't wait for his response and continued talking. "Of course you have. The comm-cuff wouldn't work for you otherwise, but I doubt you've had it going for long. You said you just arrived after all."

"Yes, I arrived last night. I 'sparked' the dynamo about two days ago under Instructor Tre'shovak's guidance during the trip here. Why?" Desmond didn't like the cruel grin that crossed Olianna's lips before she opened her mouth to say something scathing. He was beginning to like this woman less and less by the second.

"Oh shove off, Olianna. Let the poor man be. The last thing any of us need to listen to right now is you harping on the only male in our dorm block." Another voice cut into the conversation and Desmond turned just as another tray hit the table with a quiet 'clack'. The tray was stacked with a pile of different breakfast foods that nearly blocked the owner from sight.

The speaker was one of the Dwerg and she would have not even stood as high as his ribcage if he was on his feet. As it was, only her neck and shoulder showing above the table they sat at and her eyes barely peeked over the pile of food.

Bright and lively red hair was cut in a bob at a sharp angle along her jawline and sparkling sapphire blue eyes sat in a round face the color of toasted almonds. Those bright blue eyes were twinkling with mischief.

When the speaker hopped up onto the bench, Desmond noted that the Dwerg was stacked, built broad and deep, with an abundant bust, wide hips, and thick forearms. She had the scars on her forearms of someone who worked with her hands for a living, and Desmond immediately felt a kinship for the short woman.

"Ugh, I didn't invite you to sit at my table, Irongrip," sneered Olianna, turning a glare at the short woman.

"Didn't ask. 'Sides, it isn't your table, is it Olianna? It's been his since he was here first. Mind if I sit here, buddy?" The Dwerg rolled her eyes at Olianna before turning a broad grin towards Desmond that revealed a bright white smile and a rather cute gap between her two front teeth on top.

"Be my guest, always happy to have pleasant company at a meal. My name is Desmond McLaughlin," Desmond said with a smile. He was already liking the Dwerg's brusque attitude a great deal more than Olianna's high minded one.

"Monika Irongrip. Call me Monika for now, though if you are always this nice, you'll get to call me anytime you want." Monika held out her right hand to shake, which Desmond did automatically. "Ooh, you got the hands of a laborer! Good to know you weren't raised soft like so many of the boys out here," she said with a grin as they shook hands. "Now, I heard from Olianna's crowing that you were a new arrival in the Hegemony. What did you do for a living before getting scooped up here?"

Monika's grip was firm, but not crushing, and Desmond could immediately tell that she, at least, took her family name seriously. Her hand had no give to it. The handshake felt like he was gripping a steel gauntlet rather than bare flesh.

"Welder. I was certified in all the styles of welding. Before

Instructor Tre'shovak scooped me up, I was working welding for a construction company that built skyscrapers and the like." Desmond set back to eating as he turned to the more comfortable conversation with Monika. However, Olianna wouldn't be so easily ignored.

"Sounds like plebeian work, and simple at that, you just worked in atmosphere? No exo-atmospheric work?" Olianna dug as she delicately sliced a selection of fruits on her plate that looked like oranges but had solid flesh more like a peach inside of a thick rind. Those finned ears were tucked back against her skull still, and Desmond was beginning to interpret that as irritation.

"It was simple work, but I was also just fresh out of college. Loans needed paying back, and it got the bills paid and let me start paying off the money I owed," Desmond said with a shrug. He'd had to get used to folk looking down on his chosen profession awhile back, a lot of people looked down on construction and trade jobs, but it paid well enough even at entry level. And he was more concerned with not carrying that student debt for the rest of his life.

"Nothing wrong with simple and solid work," Monika cut in, waving her fork again between two thick fingers.

It looks kinda like a messed up wand with half a potato stuck on the end of it. Desmond mused with a smile as he cut into some meat on his tray.

"Besides, it isn't as if McLaughlin knew he was going to be an adept. Not everyone gets to test when they are a sprout, or even bother until they get the notice of the draft. Hell, I almost didn't get tested myself. I was too busy working in the family shop." Monika's gaze cut back to Desmond and her expressive eyebrows bounced like a pair of foxes discovering a trampoline for the first time. "My family builds starship hulls. You rode one of the standard shuttles to get here, right?"

"The one that looked like a fat shark?" Desmond's response amused Monika and angered Olianna, it seemed.

The former burst into loud laughter, having to shift sharply to not spray him with crumbs. The latter's eyes narrowed, and she glared at him more.

"Aye, that's it. My great-great-great grandmother pioneered the design and we've been making them ever since. The damn things are sturdy as hell and can pack a wallop in a fight, but the Hegemony still goes through them like condoms in a brothel." The mirth left Monika's expression for a moment and she turned stern. "Not because they are flimsy, mind you! The Hegemony just uses so many and for a number of different things that it's like trying to shovel rainwater to keep them all repaired!"

"Never even crossed my mind, Monika. And in case I didn't tell you earlier, call me Desmond. It's only been a few days and I'm already tired of hearing my last name all the time. My culture preferred using first names unless you were in trouble or in the military."

"You are in the military," snapped Olianna. The scowl still sat firm on her face.

"Yeah? No one has gone over regulations that require I be addressed by my full name. Instructor Tre'shovak told me that it was my discretion in who used my first name only anyway," Desmond said dismissively. His patience was already wearing thin with the Se'Aelfa.

"As much as I hate," Monika coughed. She slammed one large hand against her chest to clear her throat, not having bothered to stop chewing while she talked and ended up choking a bit. "Ahem. As I was saying. As much as I hate to agree with Olianna here, she's right. You should get used to being addressed by your last name. During classes, the instructors will be calling you by your last name. When we go on active duty, you'll be 'Adept McLaughlin.'"

"And you'll be, Adept Irongrip. Doesn't mean I have to make my friends use the whole mouthful right now," Desmond said with a shrug before digging into the pile of biscuits and gravy he'd dished up.

His dynamo hummed behind his breastbone and he felt it taking in the mana that was imbued in the food, adding an odd hint of rosemary to the rich gravy. *That is going to take getting used to.* The food distracted him just enough that Monika's next words caught him by surprise.

"What if I enjoy a full mouth?" The redheaded Dwerg gave him an entirely too innocent smile as Desmond proceeded to choke on the bite of biscuit. "Aye, kind of like that. The gagging and panting is part of the appeal after all." Her continued comment only made the coughing worse, which caused Monika to break out into deep belly laughs.

It took a full minute of coughing before Desmond remembered his drink and managed to free the blockage in his throat. The entire time, Monika laughed at him like it was the funniest thing in the world.

"You'd fit right in with the guys back on Earth," Desmond said at last, once he could breathe again. "I mean Terra. My home-world," he amended. Meanwhile, Monika wiped tears of amusement from her eyes.

"Sounds like a good place if they can appreciate a proper laugh."

"Especially one at another's suffering," Olianna said bitingly.

"Laugh or cry, pick one or the other. I'd rather folks laugh at me, and I get the feeling that if I was actually in distress, Monika would have done something besides laugh."

"Maybe," the Dwerg woman shot back. This time she was brandishing a roll of something that looked like ham between her thick fingers.

"Maybe." Desmond agreed with a chuckle of his own.

"Fine. I suppose I will leave you two simpletons to your crude amusements," sniped Olianna. She tossed her flatware back onto the tray of half finished food.

"Awww, there goes your chance at a threesome then, Desmond," laughed Monika while Olianna got up from the table. The Se'Aelfa's nose was raised in the air like an image of an offended cat as she got ready to storm off. An image that was immediately ruined as she sputtered and turned a fierce glare at Monika.

The Dwerg affected an unconcerned look as she, quite indelicately, slid a breakfast sausage into her mouth and held it there for a long moment between her lips, before sucking it into her mouth with a pop and a grin.

The Se'Aelfa looked like she wanted to say something scathing but held herself back with a sniff and stormed off with her tray, leaving the two of them alone at the table again. Desmond could hear murmuring from other nearby tables and knew that they were being watched, but couldn't find it in himself to care at the moment, instead turning back to Monika.

"Yeah, well if you keep chasing off girls like that Monika, you'll get stuck on your own handling the problem."

"Trust me, Desmond, you don't want any of that." Monika's jovial appearance faded for a moment as she watched to ensure that Olianna had gotten far enough away. "Some girls will lay into you for being a new-blood. Others will do it just because you are the lone male in the group. Some will want a toss in the bed first just as a status symbol. But you are the only guy in our dorm section and there are only ten or twenty other male cadets on the *Valor's Bid* in our year. There are three thousand female cadets among the twelve dorms and another fifty thousand mundies."

"You gotta be jerking my chain." Desmond nearly dropped his fork as he turned to stare at Monika.

"Nope. I don't jerk at the breakfast table. Makes a mess." Monika's lewd rejoinder, combined with her bouncing eyebrows and her bobbing left fist, made sure the point came across.

"You are such a pervert." Desmond turned back to his food with a chuckle.

"You say that like it's a bad thing."

"Naw, actually reminds me of home and the guys on the

job site. But seriously, are the numbers skewed?" Desmond needed the confirmation then, if only to get his brain to stop whirling. The instructor had told him that the gender ratios tended to be pretty harsh, but not that they were *that* bad.

"Had a look at the registry when I got up this morning since I got an alert that our dorm was full up. Wanted to know what kind of folks were living near me? Dunno the exact ratio for the mundie cadets, but as far as our dorm and classes? You got the only swinging sausage in the mix for our dorm." Monika had another breakfast sausage between her fingers, which she was gesturing with like a baton this time.

"That...could be good or bad, really."

"Hey, it is what you make of it." Monika shrugged, popping the meat into her mouth and chewing rapidly. "Regardless, I couldn't just stand there and let O400ianna bully you like that. Didn't feel right."

"Well, I appreciate you coming to my rescue, regardless of your motivations. She was just being snide for the most part."

"Ya, they do that. The Aelfa-breeds vary a lot. Some think they are better than others. You'll get a feel for them as time goes by." Monika had another link of sausage in hand, but she was holding this one like a cigarette between her fingers. "Now, I'm not encouraging you to profile folks by race, but there are some things that are just more common."

"Like all Dwerg being dirty minded?" Desmond poked back with a smirk.

"Naw. I'm special like that," Monika shot back primly, raising her nose in the air like Oliana had earlier.

The two of them continued to fire back and forth for the rest of the meal and Desmond began to relax more and more as he felt at home with the saucy redhead the longer they worked their way through the stacks of breakfast food they'd both taken.

CHAPTER 11

Biology is a fascinating and frustrating thing. Vestigial traits remain behind long after their purpose is lost to time and new mutations show up every day! There has to be a method to the madness out there and one day I will find whoever planned it and slap the silly out of them.
Rebecca Heartsblood, Lead Research
Scientist aboard *Valor's Bid*.

Monika taught him a few of the functions on his comm-cuff that he hadn't been able to figure out by just poking the engravings at random. The cuff operated as a basic interface for secured doors that he had access to, like his rooms or the dorm. It also tracked him through the ship and monitored his life signs, ensuring that if anything went wrong, it could summon a medical team to him.

Besides just keeping track of him and opening doors, the cuff had a very simple interface that allowed him to send text-based messages via a holographic keyboard that would pop out when he pressed on other glyphs.

"The most important thing the comm-cuff does is track your growth." Monika had led him to one of the open park type areas to laze in the simulated sun while they finished digesting breakfast. Desmond pointedly ignored the stares he was getting from several small groups of females nearby, instead focusing on learning what he could from his friend. Monika was sprawled on her back in the short grass with her arms spread, while Desmond sat up with his legs crossed, inspecting his comm-cuff.

"How does it track your growth?"

"You remember the pain when you put it on? That was the comm-cuff bonding with your body. We'll go through calibration and assessment in the next month. They'll do some testing so the comm-cuff has a baseline of your abilities and cache size. From there, the comm-cuff monitors it and you can check it at any time." Monika tapped through a few options on her comm-cuff before holding her arm out to show Desmond.

"I...can't read that." Desmond stared at the angular glyphs displayed in dark orange holograms above the cuff, noting the different color from his own green screens.

"Ah bugger, forgot to reset the language from Dwerg. Can you read Standard yet?"

"Nope. Still figuring out what buttons do what. Wish the translation spell worked on writing too. I'm just lucky that they can turn the study material over to my native language. Learning Standard is going to be a pain in the butt."

"You say that now, but it shouldn't be too bad. If it worries you that much, you can use some of your stipend to pay for a subliminal training in the language nuances," Monika said dismissively. She let her arm fall back to her side. "Like most problems: if you can't solve it with a good pounding, you can pay for it to go away."

"Yeah, but it's not like I have a ton of funds. The stipend will be the only cash I have on hand, though it is good to see that the almighty dollar still solves most problems eventually," Desmond said with a sigh, triggering the glyphs that Monika had shown him to open his account balance. It still read out as a collection of zeros, just like it had the last three times he'd checked it.

"There are other ways to earn funds besides the stipend. That's just what we are paid up front for supplies and the like while we train." Monika rolled over to lay on her side, propping her head up with one hand. "There are part-time jobs you can do, like working in the kitchens or on board the ship. Hell, you might put your welding skills to use working in the repair bays. Dunno how they translate from your Terran equipment to what we use, but if you are in a pinch, gotta do what you gotta do, right?"

"Yeah, I suppose so. There is just so much reading I have to do to catch up on shit too…" Letting out an explosive breath, Desmond dropped his arm to his side again.

"Going to have to pick what you are willing to give up and what you can't, then. You are behind on a lot of things, Des." It had only taken an hour before Monika had decided to shorten his name even further. "You aren't gonna have the time to learn it all. Something has to give, and the only way to keep up is to abuse some stuff." Monika's normally joking tone had turned more serious now as she watched him with her bright sapphire eyes.

"Fair. I suppose I'll have to look into those subliminal language training things. Instructor Tre'shovak said we only have a year before they turn off the translation spells and expect us all to know and use Standard. Though you have an advantage there, right?"

"Yup, I already know Standard from working with my family. All the blueprints for the ships we made were in Standard and the merchants that shipped them to the various fleet depots only spoke it, so my Ma taught me when I was a sprout. Never thought I'd be an adept, though." Monika's eyes crinkled up with a smile before she flopped back down on her back, an action that sent her anatomy swaying in a distracting fashion. "Never thought I'd be meeting a whole new species either at the academy. They don't find new worlds often and it's been more than a decade since the last one was folded into the Hegemony."

"Well, I'm happy to pop that proverbial cherry for you," Desmond snarked back, drawing a laugh from Monika in response.

"Glad to see you can fire back, was worried that you forgot to pack your wit when you shipped off that backwater world." The Dwerg shot back at him, her expressive eyebrows cavorting back and forth for a moment before they broke into laughter again.

<><><>

The next several days, Desmond spent getting used to navigating through the section of the *Valor's Bid* that he had access to, as well as reading up on what he could on his data-tablet. He'd exchanged contact information with Monika and they'd met up to hang out for a while each day.

Desmond had come to learn that the Dwerg was as blunt with everyone as she had been with him and Olianna, given that she'd greeted more than a few of their classmates with rather flirty comments on each of the outings, as well as giving two women a piece of her mind when they started loudly denouncing the Academy for accepting a 'filthy prim' within earshot.

Honestly feels like, rather than not having a filter, she physically uninstalled hers. Desmond thought with a grin as he navigated the broad corridors to the first class that he'd been assigned.

The message had come through his comm-cuff midway through the previous day, a broad range message that everyone had gotten at the same time. It had interrupted a conversation he'd been having with Monika, describing what he could remember about the basic space shuttles that humanity had developed, much to the amusement of the Dwerg.

It had been a simple notice, like a calendar update with time and room location for him to report to. Unfortunately, Monika had been assigned to a different block, so they wouldn't have the class together. She had been quick to remind him to be on his best behavior since the individual classes did cross paths for the larger combat exercises and she'd be happy to stomp him if he got too big for his britches.

"Crazy midget that she is," Desmond chuckled, before

turning his focus back to the present. It hadn't taken him long to find the room that he needed, his previous scouting having given him an idea of the layout of the area surrounding the dorm floor.

Examining some of the limited maps he'd been given access to from his cuff showed that the different first-year classes basically each had a floor to themselves in a block in roughly the middle of the ship towards the rear. The second years were in the block above them. All the rooms that he would be going to classes in were on the same relative floor as his and forward of the dorms, with the large ranges and physical training gyms, were towards the rear of the ship, some of which spanned between floors.

The classroom that he was in reminded him of a combination between a lecture hall and a science lab. Large tables were spaced out in ascending ranks from a lower central pit that was placed like the stage of an auditorium. Each table had seats for three people, and Desmond snagged a seat in the back on the upper tier so he could overlook the entire room.

The room rapidly filled over the course of about ten minutes. Several of the cadets eyed him up suspiciously before giving him a wide berth, though many just pointedly ignored him. Thankfully, his table wasn't the last one filled, as a pair of Taari with matching fur colors, but with a slightly different swirling highlight to the fur, were seated there.

The Taari were a race that he had read about but had yet to speak to. While they varied a great deal in their coloration and subspecies, they apparently all tied back to a single home-world that had actually produced six different stable subspecies along with fairly similar genetic coding. The two that sat with him had a mix of sandy brown fur with white highlights that covered their forearms that he could see exposed from their uniforms. Hand-sized fox-type ears emerged from the tops of their heads, which reminded him of a fennec fox from their size and mobility, each one rotating rapidly as the two chatted with each other. If he remembered correctly, their subtype was just grouped together under the phenotype of 'vulpine Taari'.

The two Taari also had more slender figures than many of the women he'd seen. Monika had pointed out several appreciable specimens of the female form to him the other day, though usually at far too loud a volume for him to be comfortable. These two had more of a runner's build, with compact breasts and narrow hips that tied into muscled legs, which pulled the uniform pants tight on them as they sat. Their faces were only vaguely human, with a lightly furred muzzle extending from their face and bright gold eyes set above it. A fluffy tail also extended from a special slit in the back of their pants, dancing back and forth as the two held an animated conversation.

He had nodded a hello to them when they glanced at him, getting a nod in return before the two returned to their conversation. It was also the first time that bits of the native language began to leak through the translation spell. While he could understand what the two were saying, he could also catch the underlying high-pitch chatter of the native tongue that the two were using. It only served to reinforce the fox-like appearance to him since it reminded Desmond of several YouTube videos he'd seen of someone playing with a group of red foxes.

Silence began to spread throughout the room and it drew Desmond out of some last-minute reading that he had been doing on his data-tablet. Looking up, he caught sight of what could only be their instructor striding down the broad and shallow steps on the far side of the room.

The instructor was a female, that was obvious from her tight fitting uniform that clung to a generous chest and muscled hips. It was hard to get an exact read on her height given the distance and the stairs messing with his perception, but Desmond had a feeling that she had two feet on him at least based on the others she passed on her approach. Her stone gray skin matched her uniform in a way that made it hard to distinguish where one ended and the other began. Dark blue hair cascaded in a thick mane down the back of her head and brilliant orange eyes that were actually luminescent glowed under deep brows in a handsome face that was marked with a number of small scars across her cheeks and forehead. The specific name for her species evaded him at the moment and it bugged at the back of his mind.

"Cadets. At Attention!" the instructor barked as she stepped up onto the podium, her husky and deep voice echoing around the room. Desmond immediately got to his feet and assumed the position as Instructor Tre'Shovak had shown him. Surprisingly, he was one of the first to get into position, and the neutral expression on the instructor's face turned into a scowl as she looked across the room. "I said, ATTENTION!" She roared a second time and there was a great clattering of chairs as those that hadn't moved the first time leaped to their feet and assumed the pose.

"That is better. In each class, you will greet your instructors properly when they call you to attention. As of today, you are no longer citizens of the Hegemony. You are cadets! Gods and my patience willing, you will be adepts one day. Now, salute!" The instructor's scowl remained, but at least didn't deepen, as she observed the salutes that the class threw her.

Desmond fought the urge to look around and see if anyone else was doing it right, instead keeping his attention fixed on the instructor. Several long seconds passed as the big woman radiated displeasure before she nodded once before snapping to attention herself and saluting with a fist over her breastbone as an adept would.

"At ease. Take your seats. This is your orientation class, so you understand what to expect in the coming weeks. Take notes, as I will not be repeating myself." The instructor waited for several seconds as the cadets got their data-tablets ready. Desmond already had the note taking function ready. It was one thing that Monika had shown him how to call up during the previous day, and he wanted to be sure he was ready.

"Now! My name is Instructor Maya Throneblood. But you will address me as Instructor, or Instructor Throneblood. You will respect me or I will see you loaded into one of the gravity catapults and launched into the nearest black hole." The instructor smiled wickedly, putting a mass of sharp teeth on display that would have made a guard dog proud. "As you can tell, I'm an Uth'ra and I can personally guarantee you, you do not want to make me angry."

Desmond made a note on his data-tablet to research more about 'Uth'ra' to get an idea of what to expect from the big woman.

"Your first week will be training the basics on how to manipulate and conjure mana and its various applications. After that, you will begin combat training and begin learning how to actually use your mana as a weapon. You are expected to monitor your cache's status and any deviance in your dynamo and its action of drawing mana will be reported immediately. Likely, your comm-cuff will notify Medical before you notice, but if you sense any variance, do not hesitate to notify a staff member."

Instructor Throneblood strode across the stage with her arms tucked behind her back, taking a moment to look over every cadet in the class. Desmond felt it when her eyes landed on him and noted that one of her thick eyebrows popped up questioningly, but the instructor did not say anything, only continuing to scan the class.

"I also expect decorum from every one of you. The adepts are some of the most highly regarded members of the Hegemony's military. Your actions could save or damn an entire planet if you are assigned a Rift in populated space. Your actions reflect directly upon the academy and the Hegemony as a whole. Now, Cadet McLaughlin. Stand up."

Desmond was in the middle of noting down her statement when his brain caught up and he jerked his head upright to meet her gaze once more. Finding the instructor staring directly at him and that almost every head in the room was turned towards him, Desmond scrambled to his feet and stood at attention on one side of the desk.

"Yes, Instructor Throneblood?" he said once he was at attention, keeping his eyes on the instructor for any clue as to what might happen next.

"Cadets, this is Cadet Desmond McLaughlin. He is a Terran from the Sol system and one of the handful of males in this year's program. The Terran are being integrated at this moment. I am telling you this not to single him out, but to make you aware of the fact that some information you may take for granted will be new to him, so do not judge him harshly if he asks questions that seem inane. This is the only allowance I am giving you, Cadet. Do you understand me?" the instructor barked, her deep voice echoing the silent room.

"Yes, Instructor Throneblood." Desmond replied, his back stiffening. He did his best to suppress the blush that was threatening to take over his face at being stood up in front of the group like this.

"Good. You can take your seat, Cadet." Instructor Throneblood turned her sharp gaze back to the rest of the students as they murmured quietly to each other before her gaze snapped to one in particular. "Do you think something is amusing, Cadet Yu'tona?" The snarl that emerged from her lips put her fangs back on display and Desmond craned his neck to spot Olianna halfway down the other side. He hadn't noticed her in the class before, but he hadn't exactly been looking for familiar faces. The spiteful Se'Aelfa had sniped at him a few times in passing, but he had avoided her for the most part when out of his room.

Olianna had a startled look on her face for a moment before she shook her head and answered the instructor.

"No, Instructor."

"Then keep your comments to yourself." There was a long moment of silence as the gray-skinned instructor continued to glare at Olianna before she turned sharply and stomped back across the stage in the middle of the room.

"Now, all of you should have sparked your dynamos. But I will ask once to ensure that you are all on the same shuttle here. Has anyone here not triggered the dynamo reaction to allow yourself to draw in ambient mana?" There was silence from the group for several long moments before the instructor nodded. "Good, no need for remedial training, then. There is nothing that I hate more than wasting my time. What do you need, Cadet?"

The cadet in question, a Va'Aelfa girl who had raised her hand, jumped slightly to be immediately under the instructor's molten gaze, but cleared her throat and spoke.

"When do we begin Rift suppression, Instructor?" The girl's voice was shaky compared to the instructor's far deeper tone, but she still asked the question.

"You will begin Rift suppression in a month of time and you will begin team selection roughly around the same time. It varies from class to class, as your instructor has to approve you before you are allowed to enter the first Rift. Before then, you need to focus on stabilizing your mana and learning what applications fit your skill set the best. Remember this!" The last two words were barked at a roar, making a number of people jump. "Sole-specialization is for insects! I expect each of you to be competent in an expanding pool of skills in each of the disciplines. While I don't expect anyone other than a Transport specialist to trigger and guide a Wake-Ripple, I expect each of you to master the basics of astral navigation and be able to support a specialist as needed. Speak, Cadet."

This time, Instructor Throneblood addressed a cadet that was entirely behind her as she paced, somehow knowing that they had raised their hand before turning that direction.

Desmond also made another note to look up what the hell a Wake-Ripple drive was.

"How do we learn what our specialties are, Instructor? Every book I've read states that it is just 'part of the training' at the Academy."

"First, not everyone has a specialty. One in three adepts will have a school that they specialize in," Throneblood replied as she turned, her eyes scanning over the group as she talked. "For those that do have one, the methods for discerning your specialties are different for each Academy. As far as how we handle it aboard the *Valor's Bid,* though? You will be exposed to every class of mana use that we are aware of. Some of you will have an affinity and find it easier than others. Once your affinities are known, you can begin developing your personal style in your own time. The Academy will ensure that you can meet the baseline of skills required, but your choices in your team building and style will decide if you are just passable or a front-runner when it comes to salvaging the Rifts."

<><><>

The instructor answered a handful of standard questions about the housing, mess hall arrangements and special needs regarding religious or cultural observances for a few of the other cadets, but Desmond wasn't really paying attention. He was spending most of the time imagining what sort of specialty he might end up with and how it could be applied in different situations. He was broken from his daydream by the instructor's sharp increase in volume.

"All right cadets, you are dismissed for lunch. Return to this room in two hours for your first class on mana manipulation. Do not be late. Attention!"

After the entire class scrambled to attention and exchanged salutes with the instructor, Throneblood strode out of the room and the entire class let out a sigh of relief and started to talk amongst themselves.

"Why'd she single out the prim? Does he think he gets special treatment?"

"Ugh, I hope it didn't bring anything on board with it."

"I forgot Uth'ra were that big. I thought she was gonna take a bite out of that one girl."

"He's cute. I like the color-pattern of his head-fur."

"Why did they even bring a prim on board? It's not like he's going to be able to do anything."

The muttering of both quiet and not so quiet conversations surrounded Desmond, and he sighed. *Instructor Tre'shovak warned me about this. Just going to have to prove them wrong. I know I can do this and the Instructor seemed surprised at how fast my dynamo got going.* Desmond thought to himself as he tucked the stylus he'd been using to take notes away and stood up.

The two Taari that he'd shared a table with had scurried off as soon as the instructor had left the room, so he quickly threaded through the ambling herds of other cadets and headed to the dining hall to get his food.

Doing his best to shut out the comments of others, Desmond almost missed the quiet voice that called his name as he neared the doorway.

"Cadet McLaughlin?" Turning, he looked for the speaker, but didn't see anyone right away. Most of the other cadets were pointedly ignoring him at the moment, actually.

"Cadet McLaughlin, over here." A flutter of movement caught Desmond's eye, and he turned to find a slight woman around his height that was on the other side of a mass of students that flowed between them. He'd only caught sight of her because one of her long-fingered hands was waving over the crowd and the emerald green mass of her hair bounced slightly when she jumped to get his attention.

"Coming. Excuse me, pardon me." Desmond worked to thread through the mass of other cadets to where the green-haired woman was standing by one wall. Once he got past most of the other cadets, he could get a better view of the person who called him out.

She was around his height but far more slender of build than he was. A narrow waist met slim legs while supporting an average sized torso. What stood out the most about her was the bouncing mass of her green hair that fluffed out from her head like a halo of curly green, with what looked like leaf ornaments braided into the hair all over. The color of her hair contrasted sharply with the mocha color of her skin. She wore a standard uniform like his, but had a different symbol on the shoulder. Desmond kludged at his memory to track down what the symbol meant, but it was the comments of a passerby that triggered it.

"What does a med-tech want with the prim?"

Ah, she's from Medical. That's right, that is the symbol for one of the cadet-medics. He made the connection at last as he came to a stop in front of her, but she didn't say anything at first, just staring at him with dark brown eyes that were full of curiosity.

"Yes, Miss? I'm McLaughlin," he prompted, and the woman started in surprise.

"Ah, yes! Come with me, Cadet McLaughlin. Doctor Astrid needed to speak with you in Medical after your class was finished."

"Of course, lead the way Cadet...?" Desmond let the question hang for a moment to prompt her and the woman blushed sharply before leading the way off down the hall.

"Sorry about that, I'm Connie Leafsong. Assistant to Doctor Astrid for the term."

"Pleasure is mine, Cadet Leafsong."

"Oh my sweet stars, he did have something. Ugh, I hope he didn't infect anyone in class." The sharp comment from behind them made Desmond scowl, but he shook it off.

"Did Doctor Astrid mention what she needed to speak to me about?"

"No, just that I was to retrieve you from class as quickly

as possible. Something about a variance in your biorhythms that she wanted to confirm that wasn't important enough to pull you directly out of class," Leafsong said, shaking her head and sending the mass of hair flipping back and forth. Desmond watched as two of the little leaf-charms shifted in her hair, adjusting slightly as they passed under a light source in the ceiling to present the maximum surface to the overhead light.

Is she...one of the plant-folk? Desmond wondered. He'd read about a few of the different species that were plant based rather than fully animal-mammalian, but the specific name escaped him.

"I am sorry about that. I didn't think it would cause a problem to call out to you in the hall," she said after a moment or two of silence as they walked.

"Huh?" Desmond responded cleverly.

"The comments of the other girls. I don't know why they would assume something like that. I mean, if you were infectious, we would have quarantined you as soon as it was detected. Not that any normal pathogens can get past the filters of the ship," Leafsong rambled along as they walked. She was clearly getting more nervous the longer he listened to her. "That and the sensors or the room Liaisons would have alerted us of anything worrisome. I'm sure it is just something routine, but the Doctor wanted to be sure since you are the first Terran stationed here."

"It's fine, Cadet Leafsong. They were sniping at me in the classroom too. I'm a little surprised since Instructor Throneblood warned them to be polite earlier, but she'd already left the room at that point." Desmond shrugged with a 'what can you do' expression on his face.

"Throneblood?" Leafsong's nervous expression morphed to one of vindictive glee. "Oh, they will regret that. Throneblood has a reputation for laying out spying spells in her classrooms to catch people misbehaving or cheating. Not to mention she's one of the strongest Divination specialists on board. Keep an eye on the folks who badmouthed you over the next few days."

"Really? Divination? She didn't seem the type..." Desmond was thoughtful as they walked. The massive Uth'ra woman had not struck him as someone who did subtlety, *but that would be the perfect sort of cover for that kind of thing,* he thought before shrugging. "I appreciate the heads up on it. I'll be sure to not step out of line in the classroom."

"Oh, Instructor Throneblood can scry anywhere in the ship if she wants to. She's that good," Leafsong added airily. She led him through a large doorway that was painted a dark ruby red with the symbol for 'medical' engraved on the front. "Last I'd heard, the rumor mill put her range out to encompass an entire solar system at a casual distance. Further if she has a focus to aim with. But at that point, it's like looking for a needle in a forest and the area to search can be an effective deterrent unless she has a means to lock on to someone. So it's not like she knows everyone's intimate secrets."

Desmond's brain refused to comprehend the idea of someone who could spy on an entire solar system as they entered the Medical wing and he pushed the thought off to the side. *Just need to make sure to never give her a reason to suspect or spy on me.* He swore, following close behind Cadet Leafsong.

The Medical wing was far more simple than he'd expected. There were no regeneration tanks or complex operating suites with dozens of little assistant arms hanging from the ceiling. Instead, it was a stark white room with over a dozen doors leading off in all directions and a desk that a stern looking Hyreh woman sat behind, tapping away at an interface in front of her with a scowl twisting her lips.

"Cadet Leafsong, what do we have here?" The Hyreh woman's sharp gaze pinned Desmond in place.

"Cadet-Adept McLaughlin reporting as requested by Doctor Astrid for a check-up," Leafsong chirped. She was apparently immune to the stern Hyreh's glare.

"She's seeing a Taari right now, came in after getting into a fist-fight with another mundane student over something. Take him over to exam three. I'll buzz the Doctor to let her know."

"Thank you!" Leafsong gestured for him to follow her as the Hyreh at the desk tapped a few more things before rapidly typing a message into her interface behind the desk.

Following the other cadet closely, Desmond went through the door into an adjoining hallway. He heard a bit of muffled yelling from one doorway that they passed, but it sounded more like an argument than a fight and Leafsong didn't react at all, so he just continued.

A short way further down the hallway, she stopped and opened a door, gesturing him through. Inside was something both similar and entirely different from a traditional exam room that Desmond had been expecting.

A counter lined two walls with a number of dispensers for everything from syringes to gloves alongside an enormous set of sinks. A rolling oval chair was tucked under the counter as well, but what was more odd was the exam table that was more like a queen-sized bed in the corner and the multitude of mechanical devices hanging over it.

Ah, there's the mechanical murder-bot worth of surgical appliances...

"Just have a seat on the examination bed. Doctor Astrid will be with you shortly," Leafsong advised. She shot him a smile before disappearing back through the doorway.

"Sure. Just sit on the bed with the giant murder-bot hanging from it. Totally not a dissection table, you swear, right?" Desmond muttered as he eyed the mass of mechanical limbs above the bed.

To be fair, most of those look like sensors or scopes of some kind. Only a few look like surgery tools and only one has a saw on it. Deciding that trying to comfort himself through sarcasm wasn't going to work properly, Desmond edged over and sat on the edge of the high exam bed. When none of the metallic limbs lashed out to snatch him up, he relaxed a bit.

Any relaxation was immediately tossed out the window when the door slammed open and another massive gray woman stormed through the door and into the room. She was built much like Instructor Throneblood, but rather than a bush of dark blue hair, her hair was a dark brown mane and her brilliant, orange eyes twinkled behind a pair of clear crystal goggles. The doctor also lacked the many obvious scars that the instructor had sported as well. She was dressed in an open lab coat in a sky blue color over her uniform, but the soothing doctor vibe it would have given her was ruined by the stain of blood marking the bottom edge of her coat.

"Ah, there's the Terran!" boomed the woman. A broad smile showing off a rather ferocious mouthful of teeth rode on her lips.

"Yep, I'm the Terran. I assume then you are Doctor Astrid?" The Uth'ra woman nodded, bustling across the open space to loom over him, brandishing her data-tablet like she was a priest giving a benediction to him.

"Yes, I am indeed Doctor Astrid. Your comm-cuff has been reporting some odd numbers for your dynamo activity and I wanted to have you checked out."

"Odd numbers like bad?" Desmond asked worriedly. The last thing he needed right now was something wrong with that reaction.

"High numbers, to be honest. Your dynamo is spinning at a consistently high speed that is abnormal. No elevation in your biometrics though, so no injuries or anything driving it..." The nearly eight foot tall and rather intimidating doctor hummed to herself for a moment as she examined something on her data-tablet.

"Doctor, I've been meaning to ask, what the hell is a dynamo, anyway? Is it an organ or something? I feel a pressure in my chest and I can feel it humming, but as far as I know, huma...er Terran's don't have an organ there."

Desmond had been trying to find an answer to that question in his books, but none of them had mentioned anything specific on it. Asking the doctor was probably the best choice here.

The Uth'ra woman looked up from her data-tablet and blinked owlishly at him for a moment before she laughed and nodded.

"That is right, you wouldn't know about it! So the latent potential of mana adepts is stored in what your species calls 'junk DNA'. The dynamo is actually a metaphysical organ that exists within your astral self. It refines mana, then feeds it back into your body and also acts as a valve to keep mana from draining back out without direction. The idea of the 'cache' of mana, as if you had it all stored in one spot, is actually flawed. The mana refined in your dynamo spreads throughout your entire body. So when you use some of it from your cache, you are actually sapping it from where it's stored in your cells."

"Ah...okay?" Desmond just nodded along. The idea that it was a ghost organ of some kind in his body just didn't make sense, but fact mana was stored in his cells like some kind of spare battery felt even stranger than the idea of it being stored in one spot like a fat deposit. "Feels odd, but I trust you, Doc."

"A good outlook to have. Trusting your doctor. Actually... that might be it." The Uth'ra woman's mind appeared to jump tracks in an instant. "Your dynamo is likely overworking because it hasn't had a chance to spin down yet. It's churning away despite not having much mana to process. We just need to give it a bit of a jolt..."

"Jolt? What do you mea..." Desmond started to ask, but he learned what sort of jolt the Doctor had been implying when she punched him in the chest.

CHAPTER 12

I didn't believe in fate. The idea that there is some master manipulator out there pulling the strings in our actions and the universe was dancing to their tune was disturbing. All the woes of existence could be laid at their feet and they would have to account for them. Then I met Chloe, and I realized that fate might not be all that bad.

Desmond McLaughlin, regarding life on the *Valor's Bid*.

There were many things that Desmond had expected when sitting in a doctor's exam room. Being poked and prodded was one of them. But being punched in the chest by a fist roughly the size of a gallon of milk was not on that list.

The blow threw Desmond back onto the bed with a gasp as pain radiated through his chest. His breathing hitched and locked up for several seconds before he could get his lungs back in action and suck in a deep breath.

Internally, he knew that Doctor Astrid could have hit him hard enough to cave in his ribcage, but that didn't stop the litany of curses running through his head as he fought to breathe.

"Rest for a bit, then you can head back to class. I will continue to monitor your dynamo remotely and ensure that it remains at a steady pace, though this adjustment appears to have gotten it back to normal." He heard Doctor Astrid say distantly, but Desmond couldn't get his muscles to function enough to sit upright or even look at the Uth'ra doctor as she left with a click of the doorway, already tapping away on her data-tablet.

Desmond wasn't sure how long he laid there and fought to master his breathing. His entire chest ached sharply, and he was sure a bruise was forming under his uniform, but nothing felt broken. The humming sensation that he'd felt from his dynamo had faded to a distant whir that reminded him of hearing a bee on the other side of a window.

When he felt like he could do so without falling over, Desmond groaned as he slowly sat upright, a dull throb in his breastbone.

"Doc didn't break anything. But sure as hell feels like she cracked something." Desmond touched the spot at the base of his sternum gingerly. Finding no blood, he shakily got to his feet. The desire to be anywhere but the exam room right now kept him moving.

Walking was a bit of a challenge, his head swimming slightly as he crossed the room, but he made it out the door and paused in the hallway for a moment, leaning against the wall.

The hell? She hit me in the chest, not the head. Why does my head feel all jacked up?

Gingerly, Desmond unbuttoned his uniform top and looked down at his chest. The skin was already turning red and darkening further to form a bruise.

"That is going to suck in a few days," Desmond muttered, closing his eyes and taking a deep breath to steady his irritation. *Seriously, what kind of doctor just punches a patient in the chest?*

His internal grumbling distracted him from the sound of the door just ahead of him sliding open with a quiet hiss.

"Oh, hey. You okay?" A deep female voice broke him out of his introspective grousing and he looked up at the speaker.

Directly in front of him, leaning heavily against the doorjam, was an absolutely beautiful giant of a woman. While both Instructor Throneblood and Doctor Astrid were large and well muscled women and he had yet to find someone he would consider ugly here, the one ahead of him was a different class. She stood roughly as tall as the two Uth'ra had been, topping his height by at least two feet, if not more. Broad shoulders supported a thick neck and flaring lats, as well as an enormous bust that was straining the already tight uniform top in monotone gray and black. The closely tailored uniform came in to hug a trim waist before flaring into wide hips and tree-trunk legs that lead down into broad feet in sturdy boots. Perched on top of that thick neck so far above him was a face that was beautiful, even under several bruises and a stitched cut above her left eyebrow. Both her upper and lower lips were split in different spots as well, though it didn't look like she was missing any teeth. The bruises stood out starkly against her pale skin. Her right eye was puffy, partially blocking his view of her bright green eyes. Her nose was swollen and angry looking, like it had been broken and set recently. Surrounding the whole mess of her bruised face was a shaggy mane of dishwater blonde hair that was all snarled up around a pair of black horns that emerged from her skull slightly back from her temples and curved forward over a foot from her head, much like those of a bull.

It made Desmond's chest ache in an entirely different fashion to see the bruises and other injuries across her face and how she was favoring her right side.

"You there? Hey, you okay?" she said again. Her voice was low and melodic as she leaned towards him, still supported by the doorway to her room.

Unfortunately, the change in posture must have thrown off her balance as she stumbled forward. Desmond reacted on instinct, lurching forward to catch her. The fact that her horns could have easily impaled his face didn't faze him as he ducked slightly and caught her around the chest with his arms, though he groaned as her weight landed on him.

The ache in his chest grew sharp for a moment before it faded from his mind as concern took over.

"Easy there, you look like hell, lady." Desmond chided. He had to set his feet wide to support the much larger woman's weight as she regained her balance. He did his best to ignore the plush flesh that pressed against his face and shoulders.

"Like you can talk," she rumbled in a pained voice. Thankfully, the big woman did not struggle to get away from him, taking his assistance and getting her feet back under her. "Who hit you?"

"What? Why does that matter? Who beat you up, anyway? Tell me it wasn't the doctor..." Desmond brushed her question aside as he helped her get stabilized. Once the woman was standing on her own, he stepped back slightly, but still kept one hand on her to keep her upright, just in case.

"No. Why would a doctor hit me? It hurt like a bitch when she set my nose, but that was it." The horned woman wrinkled her nose in confusion before wincing again at the pain that had caused. Desmond's heart ached seeing that look of pain on her face, and he wished there was something he could do to help her. Instead, he remained silent, making a 'go ahead' gesture with the hand that wasn't helping support her left side at the moment.

"Got in a fight with one of the other cadets. Was winning until the coward's group of suck-ups decided to all jump on me at once," she replied sullenly, staring at the deck in front of them.

"How many?" Desmond's voice shook with anger.

"What?" She looked confused at his question, blinking her unswollen eye as she looked at him.

"How many folks jumped you?" Desmond spoke with barely restrained fury, fighting the urge to grit his teeth. The horned woman stared at him, a look of surprise writ large across her broad features before she spoke.

"Six the first time, but four more joined in once they started losing." There was just a touch of pride in her voice and Desmond swallowed his anger to nod.

"And did they end up worse than you?"

"Yeah, I...I think I broke one's arm and got a few good hits in on pretty much every one of them before they piled on me as a group," she said shyly. She turned away from him again, though her good eye remained locked on him. "What about you? Where'd you get that enormous bruise? I mean, who'd hit a guy?"

A crackpot doctor with a fetish for corporeal treatment.

"Doesn't matter. You good? They all done with you?" Desmond brushed it off, flipping his shirt closed for the moment to hide the growing bruise over his chest.

"I was just going to head back to my bunk and rest until conditioning. I don't want to give them the satisfaction of making me miss a class."

"Cool. You guide the way and I'll walk with you." *And if anyone tries to jump her on the way, I'll kill 'em.* Desmond shifted his data-tablet into one of the large pockets in the side of his uniform pants while he did his best to keep the murderous thoughts off his face. With it secured out of the way, he shifted slightly so that she could push off the wall and stand upright again. As he repositioned, he considered the difficulties of supporting someone so much larger than him and what he'd have to do differently.

"I can get back on my own…I appreciate the offer, though," she said gruffly, adopting a stoic expression and reaching up to flick her hair back over her shoulder. The stoic pose was ruined by the wince that ran through her entire body when her arm got halfway there and Desmond shifted to be ready to catch her as she swayed.

"Don't argue with me. Come on, put your arm over my shoulders and I'll walk you back. Sooner you listen, the sooner you can lay down." Desmond switched sides so that her good arm would drape over his shoulders and pushed up against her side, wrapping one arm around her waist. Given their difference in heights, he had to reach high so his arm wasn't cupping her ass, but he made it work.

"Fine…" The mumble of assent was quiet, and he caught a dark flush marring her milky complexion, but Desmond didn't comment on it. A large arm draped over his shoulders and Desmond fought down a smirk at the idea that he must look like her kid brother trying to help her based on size alone.

They were silent as he helped her down the hall and past the Hyreh, who was on desk duty. All they got was a raised eyebrow from the green-skinned woman as they passed.

Once they were in the hallway, Desmond flicked his head to one side.

"Which way is your suite? I've got another hour or so till I have to get back for class. So, as long as you aren't on the other side of the ship, I should be good." The big woman glanced down at him again and Desmond fought the urge to flinch back as the smooth black length of her horn swept in front of his face. She was clearly aware of them, though, and they never touched him.

"My bunk is that way." A gesture with the arm over Desmond's shoulder directed him to the hallway opposite of the one that he had taken to get here. She glanced back down over his uniform and her eyes went wide. "What..." he felt her shift against him for a moment before she gasped slightly and he felt her shift again, this time away from him and they almost fell over.

Taking a quick step to the side, Desmond slid out from under her shoulder and got his back against her broad chest to catch her from falling, acting as a sort of improvised kickstand to catch her rather than trying to haul her upright. *Good thing I thought about this in the hall earlier, otherwise I'd have tried to just hang on to her and she'd have drug both of us down.* Desmond thought, again forcing his mind away from the two soft weights that sat on his shoulders now, pressing against either side of his head.

"Adept! I apologize for inconveniencing you. I did not mean-" She started, starting to push away from him before letting out a grunt of pain.

"Knock it off, you over-sized walking bruise," Desmond snapped, and she froze. He could hear her panting for breath just above him. "I told you I was going to help you back to your room. Are you trying to fall over and injure yourself worse? Now, knock it off and let me help you."

"I couldn't, Adept. It's shameful enough to have a male help me, but..."

"I'm not an adept. I'm just a cadet right now. Now, are you going to listen to me or do I have to knock you out and go borrow some kind of alien wheelchair from the scary Hyreh nurse in there?" Desmond snapped back, leaning his head back so he could glare up from between her breasts at her.

The horned woman was silent for several long seconds, staring back down at him in turn. The heavy blush on her cheeks making the bruises stand out even more. Desmond noted idly that she had a light sprinkling of freckles on her cheeks and wondered if more were hiding under the bruises.

"Don't argue with me. You won't win," Desmond said as she started to speak. Instead, she let out a huff before a small smile crossed her lips that led to a wince as her split lower lip began to bleed again.

"As you say, Adept."

"Not an adept yet, just a cadet," Desmond grumbled again. "You going to let me help you now? I can still go and get that wheelchair. It's not like you can run away right now."

"I will comply, Adept."

"You are trouble, you know that?" A small bit of laughter caused her to shake against his back before Desmond sighed and resumed his spot under her arm and they began the slow walk down the corridor.

"How did you know I was a cadet-adept?" Desmond asked while they walked.

"The patch on your shoulder indicates you are one of the adepts. Someone at your station should not be helping a regular recruit like myself. You have more important things to do." Came the murmured reply.

"I swear to all the stars we flew past on the way here, if you keep doing that I'll knock your ass out and drag you back to your room by your hair. I'm just another recruit and you deserve help," Desmond grumped at her. Keeping his eyes focused forward, he ignored the surprised look she shot him.

"So. What started the fight?" Desmond asked after they walked for a short distance in silence, as much to learn more about her as to break the awkward silence.

"Unkind words about my stature." Came the pained reply and Desmond glanced up to check on her. She winced with each step they took, but soldiered on without a complaint. When he didn't respond, she continued to elaborate. "She complained that I took up too much space in the mess hall. There were other tables she could have chosen, but she chose mine. When I refused to respond, she threw her tray at me."

"That seems a bit extreme," Desmond added as they turned a corner and passed a pair of Tu'Aelfa that stopped to stare as they went by.

"I think she was trying to show off for some males among the regular recruits."

"Well. Sounds like she roundly messed that up, didn't she? Got her ass handed to her as well as most of her posse, too," Desmond said with a chuckle. He squeezed her waist lightly with his arm around her hips. The big woman laughed as well, a low and husky noise that made a thrill run down Desmond's spine.

"That she did. I doubt she will try such again, though both of us will get punishment detail for brawling…Doing that with several cracked ribs will not be fun."

"That does sound like it is going to be rough." Desmond couldn't help the question that came next. "Why the hell didn't Medical patch you up better? Looks like they just stitched up what was bleeding and made sure you weren't going to die or something."

"That is…accurate. Brawling like that is frowned on and the instructor who broke up the fight said that we would receive only basic treatment in Medical as part of the punishment. Pain makes lessons stick."

"That's bullshit!" Desmond exploded, a burning indignation in his chest. "You were attacked and defending yourself! What the hell!?" He trailed off into incoherent grumbling and missed the surprised smile that crossed the larger woman's face as she watched him out of the corner of her eye. And the surprised glances of a Hyreh and a Dwerg cadet shot their way at his exclamation.

"Regardless of who started the fight, I escalated it. She threw first, but I also threw her across the room," the horned-woman replied stoically and Desmond glanced up at her to find that she was looking ahead, her eyes hard as she watched another group of recruits emerge from another hallway and start in their direction. "That will be trouble..."

"What? Those folks?" Desmond glanced in their direction to see at least a dozen of the green-skinned beings marching down the hall towards them, stern expressions on every one of their faces. At the head of their group was a well muscled Hyreh woman with matching scars running parallel on both her cheeks, the stern expression on her face fading slightly as she saw Desmond glaring in their direction.

"Yes. They are companions to the one who jumped me," the horned woman mumbled quietly. She shifted away from Desmond to take more of her weight off him and give herself room. She swayed slightly but remained upright this time and rolled her shoulders back with a quiet popping noise.

"Then they are gonna learn to leave well enough alone." Desmond's response made her glance down at him sharply in surprise.

"Male! Step aside. We need to have words with the Taari behind you," growled the scar-faced leader of the group. They came to a stop in front of Desmond and she crossed her arms over her broad chest. The group of Hyreh grouped up behind her, all of them muttering to each other and most of them ignoring him to glare at the horned woman behind him.

"How about you take a long walk off a short cliff? And when you hit the bottom, find something sharp to go fuck yourself with," Desmond snapped at her. He shifted to stand directly in front of the horned woman in open defiance.

Absolute silence descended on the hallway as all eyes turned to him. Desmond crossed his arms over his chest, which sent his partially unbuttoned uniform gaping open slightly. He locked eyes with the scarred Hyreh woman and met her glare for glare.

"I can teach you manners as easily as I can teach the cow-titted bitch manners, male. What sort of fucked up Aelfa are you? Someone already clip your ears to put you in your place?" the Hyreh snarled, her skin darkening in rage as she took a step closer.

"Terran."

"What?" His response startled her, and she balked a moment.

"I'm not an Aelfa, I'm a Terran," Desmond replied coolly while glaring up at her.

"The fuck is a Terran?" asked one of the women.

"It's a species devoted to 'fuck around and find out' is what it is," Desmond shot back. He turned slightly to glare over the leader's shoulder at the woman who had just spoke for a moment.

Surprisingly, the Hyreh he locked eyes with flinched and took a step back, so Desmond turned his eyes back to the scarred Hyreh that loomed over him. A staring contest ensued for several long moments before the green-skinned woman snorted and twisted her head to one side.

"Fine. We will find her another time to finish this." The green-skinned woman shifted to turn to one side, but the smirk that crossed her features set Desmond's blood on fire and he acted on instinct.

The Hyreh wasn't expecting his actions and a moment later Desmond had the big green woman by the throat and backed against the nearest wall. Their difference in heights made it awkward, but Desmond had gotten used to it over the years because of his shorter than average height. Getting her by surprise allowed him to put her off balance and get the hold in place rapidly.

The sudden shift in their positions put her eye to eye with him rather than looming over him. Leaning in close and putting a bit of pressure on her neck with his hand, Desmond snarled directly in her face.

"Lay a damn finger on her and you will definitely find out what it means to 'fuck around' with a Terran. I don't hit women unless they start shit. So if you start shit with her, I'll figure out what Throneblood meant about loading your ass into a gravity catapult and punt you against the side of the nearest moon."

"Throneblood? What does…shit, he's an adept!" one of the other Hyreh snarled. The rest of the group dissolved into swearing and backed away. The Hyreh under his hand, who had been winding up to take a swing at him, glanced down at his uniform again and her eyes went wide, the color draining from her face abruptly.

"Yes, Adept!" she grunted quickly, going limp under his grip. "As you say, Adept. We will leave this Taari alone."

"Friendly talk." Desmond let her go and stepped back rapidly in case she decided to take a swing at him. The Hyreh immediately scrambled away from him and the group beat a rapid retreat up the hall.

"That was…" the horned woman said as Desmond continued to glare after the retreating Hyreh.

"That was necessary. Not only is this supposed to be a place of learning, we should be learning to work together, not fight with each other," Desmond spat before turning to look back up at the big woman.

"The competition to perform the best amongst the mundane recruits is high, as we each wish to be selected to work with an adept later in the year." Her words were quiet and eyes downcast as she refused to meet Desmond's eyes.

"Doesn't matter. Good competition can push folks to perform better. What that was isn't good competition. That was an attempted beat-down." Desmond hooked a thumb over his shoulder. "I know you can defend yourself, but you're injured. I don't know what the expectations are out here. I'm fresh off the turnip truck as it is, but you damn well better expect me to step in when it's needed."

"Turnip truck? What does a root-vegetable transport have to do with this?" Her confusion took the wind out of Desmond's sails and he blinked up at her for a moment before laughing.

"Means that I'm new here. Just arrived a few days ago. Last week I didn't even know the Hegemony existed." The horned woman shook her head, her eyes wide in surprise. She started to say something, but stopped before it got out of her mouth. "Anyway, let's get you back to your bunk. I need to get my ass in gear if I'm not gonna miss Instructor Throneblood's first class. I don't wanna learn what the hell a gravity catapult is from inside one, after all."

Without waiting for her agreement, Desmond resumed his spot under her arm and began guiding her down the hallway.

"I appreciate it...I do not want you to anger Throneblood, either. She is...notorious for harsh punishments and well known."

"Good woman to stay on the right side of."

They were silent for the rest of the walk down the hall, both lost in thought for the moment.

Desmond grumbled internally still that Medical let her go back without doing anything to actually help her. *This is a damn alien space ship with magic in it. They gotta have healing potions or some kind of spell to fix the damage. Sure, pain is a wonderful teacher, but it could take her weeks to heal from cracked ribs and those bruises.* Glancing up, Desmond bit back a growl. The swelling around her eye had only gotten worse, and it looked like it would eventually block her vision entirely.

An ache built in his chest as Desmond worried about the

big woman. She acted stoic, but he could tell she was having trouble walking and navigating with the injuries. Training with them was going to be next to impossible. As the worry built up, the ache turned into a sluggish pressure in his chest that moved to a burning feeling in the back of his throat.

A lurch from his dynamo made Desmond stumble, and a brief wash of weakness slipped through his limbs. The only thing that kept him from falling was the arm wrapped around his shoulders, which gave him just enough stability to catch himself, then catch her before she followed him over. A tingle of that wintergreen sensation from before soaked out through his limbs and Desmond felt the dull ache in his chest from when Doctor Astrid had applied her 'treatment' to him fade abruptly before the wash of tingling energy slid out of him.

The horned woman who was pressed to his side twitched slightly and looked down at him sharply for a moment. She'd felt a brief tingle through their contact, but she wasn't entirely sure what it was. Shaking off the confusion, she spotted the heavy bronze door that led to her bunk-room and pulled him to a stop. Thankfully, her injuries ached less than they had when she left Medical, though she wasn't sure why.

"My bunk is through there. I can make it the rest of the way." Desmond shot her a dubious look that made her roll her eyes. "Seriously, Adept. You can't just escort me all the way to my bunk. I have a bit of pride left."

"Fair. But if you fall in the twenty feet to the door, I'm going to throw you over my shoulder and carry you the rest of the way like a sack of potatoes," Desmond shot back. Taking a moment, he got her balanced on her feet before slipping out from under her arm again.

As before, she caught herself and straightened slightly, a series of quiet pops emanating from her chest and shoulders.

"Ooh...that felt odd, but good. I think something might have been dislocated, but it's back in now," she muttered, rubbing her ribs on the left side, just under one large breast.

"Well! Glad I could help. If they give you any problems, let me know and I'll make sure to deliver on that promise I made to her. The name is Desmond McLaughlin." Desmond offered her his hand, and she took it with a firm grip. Her large hands dwarfed his, but her grip was gentle, despite the heavy calluses on her palms. *Clearly used to mitigating her strength, which I appreciate*, Desmond thought to himself, as she didn't crush his hand.

"Chloe Vandenberg. I doubt she will cause any problems. While brawling amongst the regular enlisted is frowned upon, one of us getting into a fight with an adept, even a cadet, is grounds for immediate dismissal and incarceration. The Hegemony doesn't risk its adepts lightly."

"That's good. If she does, contact me. I made her a promise and I do not want the reputation of someone who breaks promises." Desmond tapped the activation runes on his cuff to bring up the comm system. It turned out that regular military recruits didn't get a fancy comm-cuff like the adepts did, but Chloe gave him her contact codes and he sent a message to her data-tablet.

Once that was finished, the two separated ways. Desmond waited in the hallway long enough to ensure that Chloe got to the door on her own before he turned to head back the way he had come. Thoughts of Chloe and the situation she had been in swirled in his mind.

She's different from the other Taari that I've met. She's got a normal face rather than an animal one, but the horns...huh, wonder why? He thought to himself as he walked. One thing in particular kept coming back up in his mind that he hadn't noticed until she was walking away from him in the hallway. *She had a cow tail coming out of the back of her uniform pants... it was kinda cute swaying like that...*

CHAPTER 13

All adepts can manipulate mana, but around forty percent of all adepts have a specialization. What that means is that they are more predisposed towards a particular 'school' or process of mana manipulation. Either their spells are more efficient or their personal twists that develop bend in that direction. It is because of these two factors—the specialization and the twists—that adepts get so much freedom in designing their teams and their approaches to situations. The Hegemony learned to embrace this difference rather than try to stomp it out long ago. Do not abuse this freedom, or I'll be doing some stomping of my own.
~Instructor Maya Throneblood,
lecturing a new class of cadets.

The distraction of introspection lasted for most of the walk back, but Desmond's cuff gave him an alert that he was going to be late getting back to class, so he picked up a jog that got him into the classroom just as Instructor Throneblood came in through another door.

"Take your seat, Cadet," the Uth'ra woman called as she started down the stairs on the other side of the room. Her sharp orange eyes flicked over his mussed and partially unbuttoned uniform with a disdainful air.

A quick glance around at the available tables showed Desmond that the only place left was in the very front row next to a Dwerg and a Hyreh woman who were pointedly ignoring him. *Oh well, I didn't expect everyone to be my friend.* Desmond thought, hurrying down the stairs to take the seat and doing his best to get his uniform back in order.

"All right, Cadets. This is your first class on mana manipulation. Today, you will be receiving a comprehensive review of the different flavors of mana manipulation that exist, examples of how they function, as well as a collection of exercises to practice in order to refine your own mana manipulation. Can anyone tell me what is regarded as the most critical specialization that exists in the Hegemony?"

Several hands went up. Desmond's was not among them. He had been doing all he could to get caught up on general information, but it would take more than a few days of occasional reading to do so. Instead, he listened while he got his data-tablet back out of his pocket and got it set up for notes as the instructor pointed to someone in the back of the room.

"Transportation is the most critical specialization in the Hegemony, though some would argue that Evocation, or combat magic as it is sometimes called, is the most important."

"That is correct on both accounts. While Evocation is a required skill set for all adepts to be able to survive in the field, given the dangerous nature of Rifts; Transportation is the most critical of specializations." Instructor Throneblood graced them with another tooth-filled smile before continuing. "Without a Transportation adept on hand, Wake-Ripple drives larger than a cruiser would be impossible to direct or sustain as the reactions used within them are too energetic. They would either fire off in random directions or burn out the cycle too rapidly and consume all the fuel in one go."

Wake-Ripple? That's right, I wanted to look into that more. Desmond thought to himself. His confusion must have been obvious on his face as Instructor Throneblood caught it and nodded to him.

"To further elaborate for those who may not be aware of it." Several of the class groaned but shut up when Instructor Throneblood glared at them. "The Wake-Ripple drive is how star-ships of the Hegemony travel. The specifics of the reaction are a closely guarded secret known only to the teams that assemble the engines, but an adept is needed to carefully guide the reaction. An adept specializing in Transportation is preferred as their mana is far more efficient in the process and they can guide exponentially larger engines. For example, the *Valor's Bid* has a standing team of five specialists, so that there is one on hand at all times as well as two spares should something occur to the drives. The drives create what amounts to an explosion in the fabric of space-time, the ethereal foam of existence if that example fits better in your head, and the drive array allows the ship to 'hook on' to the ripple and ride behind it. By remaining close to the distortion created by the ripple, star-ships can circumvent certain natural phenomena and exceed speeds that would normally be the limiting factors of travel. Please note, the Transport specialist is not the ship's pilot! Their one and only job is monitoring the reaction in the Wake-Ripple engine and steering the ripple itself. Not the ship."

They what? Desmond nearly dropped his data-tablet in surprise. *They...literally set off explosions in space and ride the* explosion *through space?* He felt a brief surge of panic before he forced it down. Clearly, this was something that they understood and had been doing for some time. *Just... don't think about it, like with flying on an airplane. Sure, there are ways for it to go wrong, but clearly people who know it are handling it. Don't think about it and hope you don't have the transport specialty.*

"Now, for a demonstration of the transport specialty." Instructor Throneblood's words were punctuated by a whip-crack noise of air being displaced. The section of the podium behind the instructor was now occupied by eight different cadets standing at attention. Squinting, Desmond could tell that they were second years from the rank marking on their chests, and only one of them was male, but that was all he could tell at this distance.

One of the group of eight stood slightly ahead of the others, a thick-waisted Aelfa woman with a scar on one cheek that was eclipsed by elaborate tattoos in blue and green that swirled over her face and down her neck into her uniform top. He couldn't spot any defining marks to tell which subspecies of Aelfa she might be.

"Thank you, Adept Ko'toran." Instructor Throneblood saluted the tattooed Aelfa, who returned it before stepping back into line with the others. "These are your upperclassmen. You will not assume the title of adept until your second year here. At that point, you will be considered a full adept in rank. Though you will continue to be addressed as 'cadet' or 'cadet-adept' until you fully graduate. Your second year will be devoted to refining your specialties. Those you see before you are some of the second years that have distinguished themselves above all others. As such, I will address them today as adepts." The line of second years on the stage puffed up slightly at the complement. "Ko'toran is the current leader amongst those with Transportation as her specialty. She transported the group from the second-year dorms two decks away. Without line of sight."

Throneblood's comment drew several gasps of surprise, and a ripple of whispers flowed through the room.

"I see that many of you understand the challenges that poses. It is considered a general rule of thumb that, for mana manipulation to work properly, one must have eyes on the target. Transportation is one of the few situations where that does not hold true." Instructor Throneblood's words cut through the conversations like a gunshot, and the entire room went quiet. "Understand this! It is only with the consent of the staff and long hours of practice that Adept Ko'toran attempted this. I will be very displeased if any of you attempt this, specialty or not."

The entire class shrunk under the instructor's glare for several moments before turning back to the group of second years behind her.

"Now, as it has already been brought up, Evocation is arguably the second most important skill set in the Hegemony. Adept, you may begin."

A Dwerg woman with skin the color of dark chocolate and shockingly bright blonde hair cropped close to her head stepped up next and saluted the instructor before turning her attention to the rest of the class.

"Evocation, or combat magic, is one of the most destructive specialties and necessary for large conflicts. To those of you who are hoping to have it as your specialty, you may come to regret that decision. Evocation specialists are always in the thick of things and you will see destruction up close. May you all have stomachs made of iron if it is your fate." A few gestures of her arms and a swirling globe of blue flames formed over the Dwerg's left shoulder, hovering there waiting. "Evocation specialty will force changes to your lifestyle as well. I don't risk long hair anymore, given what my personal twists have done to my spells. Got tired of setting it on fire. And for those of you who aren't aware, 'twist' is the colloquial term that we all use to describe how our personalities affect our spells. You'll learn more about those as they start popping up, I'm sure, but if you end up practicing a spell and it suddenly changes how it acts out of the blue? That's your personal twists starting to show up, and one of the many reasons that the Hegemony lets us run a bit more 'loose' than normal military units." The Dwerg muttered something and the sphere of flame shifted shapes into a broad crescent that hung in front of her head like half of a halo and flared brighter.

"Adept. Strike here," Instructor Throneblood spoke from the far side of the stage where she had moved while everyone was focused on the Dwerg. Before calling out, the instructor had gestured a few times, murmuring under her breath, and a broad wall of what looked like metal blocks formed in front of her with edges that glowed a dull orange.

The Dwerg turned and, with a flick of her chin in a

nod, sent the crescent of flame screaming across the stage to impact the wall. The boom of the impact pushed against Desmond's chest like a physical blow, and the accompanying flash had him blinking spots out of his eyes.

When he could see again, Desmond could see a scar across the conjured barrier that was easily three feet long and several inches deep into the conjured metal blocks.

"Adroitly done, Adept. Take your place," Instructor Throneblood said from behind her wall and sent it dissolving into the air once more.

Desmond felt a small tug at his dynamo, and the tang of metal filled his mouth for a moment. *Huh? Is it drawing in leftover mana from the spells they used*? The thought distracted him enough that he missed the introduction of the next adept. Her actions drew his attention like a magnet.

The next adept was another Dwerg and spent several moments singing quietly to herself in a rhythmic rate, gesturing with her hands as blocks similar to the ones that Instructor Throneblood had conjured began to form in the air and after less than a minute, a similar bulwark of stones existed in front of the adept. But her singing didn't stop as the blocks solidified more and began to shift and glow brighter, waves of heat emanating from the stones.

"Construction specialization is a mixture of Evocation and Conjuration that is distinct enough that it has received its own classification. Many look down on it because of the stationary nature of what we do. But, in a prolonged battle or during repair work, everyone wants a construction specialist as we are fortresses on legs." The Dwerg said proudly as the walls continued to shift and adapt, spikes growing in some spots while shifting notches appeared along its length for firing points.

"Well done, Adept. Dismiss your construct and resume your place," Instructor Throneblood called. The Dwerg snapped her fingers, and the emplacement vanished back into her hand. Desmond felt a bit of a tug from his dynamo again, but ignored it for now.

"Next we have Medical. As I do not expect anyone to injure themselves for the adept to practice on, he will instead explain the benefits that come from it." The sole male of the group stepped up at the instructor's gesture. He was a wiry Va'Aelfa with long limbs that gave him a somewhat hunched appearance as he stood there.

"Medical is one of the most stable specialties. With it, your guard team will probably never lose a member unless something goes *horribly* wrong. It does put heavier weight on your guard team though, as they have to do more of the work in a Rift." The man went on to explain the various spells that could be used to stabilize injured and certain non-combat procedures that required such a high mana investment that only a specialist could handle them.

It really seemed like, of the specialists that had spoken so far, the biggest draw of the Medical one was safety during deployment and prospects after finishing the military term. Excellent physicians were always in high demand and the special types of procedures they could perform would no doubt command them a splendid position in any hospital. Desmond made a note to make sure he learned all he could. That sort of skill would be great to bring back to Earth.

"Enhancement is often looked down on as an inferior specialty, as it isn't as flashy as the others." The speaker was a Taari woman who was built more along the lines of what Desmond would imagine a traditional werewolf would look like, with dark gray fur and piercing blue eyes. "Enhancement is something overlooked by some as well, as it does require constant attention to keep the various parts in place. But with it, even the most mild-mannered can become a juggernaut in combat. Standard Enhancement can allow for damaged equipment to fulfill its purpose far past the point that it should give out, or allow equipment to survive blows that it should not."

Reinforcing equipment? That could be pretty handy...and

flexible too. Desmond made a note to research more about what kind of things Enhancement could do. If it was just strengthening things, it would be disappointing, but he could accept it. If he was able to do other things like increase agility or sharpen vision, then that would be a tool in his toolbox he would want to cultivate.

Instructor Throneblood introduced three other second-years to talk about Navigation as well as Divination. Desmond took notes on autopilot as he pondered what he could potentially do with Enhancement depending on its limitation. It was only the warnings earlier about Instructor Throneblood being a specialist in Divination that kept him from researching it right then and there.

"And lastly, we have the Conjuration specialization. Adept." Throneblood gestured to the last of the group, another Taari, but this time a feline one with tawny fur and a long, slender tail that twitched actively behind her. The Taari woman pranced forward with a broad grin on her lips.

Unlike the canine Taari's he'd seen so far, this one had a more humanoid face, though her nose was still upturned like a cat. Desmond briefly wondered about the variance he'd seen so far as well. All the other Taari he'd seen had a muzzle of some sort, but Chloe had a very human face with her features just being a bit more blunt than normal.

That and she wasn't sporting bovine ears or anything, but she did have that cute tail...

Desmond was pulled out of his introspection when the feline Taari began to speak.

"Conjuration is one of the broadest of specialties. It relies heavily on the creativity and knowledge of the caster. Many use it in conjunction with other classifications of mana manipulation to create shields, emplacements, and even to conjure physical weapons in the event of one being damaged or destroyed. The more complicated a construct is, the more mana it takes to maintain, so don't think about conjuring a starship or rail-cannon." The feline Taari winked broadly at the group, her nose twitching as she glanced back and forth through the room. "A lot of folks use it to conjure disposable fodder as well to distract creatures inside the Rifts."

The adept muttered to herself a moment and with a flick of her hand, a squat lizard that looked like a Komodo dragon had decided to walk on its hind legs materialized in front of her and flicked its tongue at the nearest cadet, who shrunk back in surprise.

"Those with the specialty are only constrained by their creativity, though. Most adepts can maintain a handful of conjurations at once around the size of this one. But..." she began to mutter again, her tone taking on a singsong quality that her tail matched as it flicked back and forth. After a moment, additional instances of the squat lizard formed with each flick of her tail until more than two dozen crowded the front half of the platform, tongues flicking in all directions.

"The options increase as your skill increases too, as well as reserves. The more complex or large the conjuration, the more mana it costs to sustain. It is slightly more efficient to make multiple copies of the same smaller creature than it would be to make one massive one. But experimentation is key and the twists you develop with conjuration will dictate what angle you lean towards best. Of all the disciplines, Conjuration benefits the most from chants. So! Don't be like me and try to phase them out too soon." The Taari woman said the last part with a sardonic grin twisting her lips. Another gesture dismissed the collection of creatures, and she stepped back in line.

"Thank you all for your presentation. You are dismissed, Adepts." Instructor Throneblood came to attention and saluted the second years, who did the same before the transportation adept made a couple of gestures at the group and they vanished with another whip-crack of air moving.

Instructor Throneblood strode to the center of the stage and turned to look out at them with a stern expression on her face that softened only slightly as she beheld the eagerness of the cadets watching her. Even Desmond felt a surge of excitement at seeing an actual demonstration of magic like this had been.

"Now, I'm sure all of you are itching to begin practicing, but first we must begin the exercises to control your mana."

<><><>

The rest of the class period was Instructor Throneblood walking them through a series of meditation exercises that would allow them to sense their mana and begin to collect it in one place, and utilize a basic spell to make their palm emit light. She echoed the previous information that Desmond had learned about how mana was imbued throughout their body and lectured on several rules about magic use that the academy had. Things like 'practice in your suites is allowed for any non-combat mana use.' Combat mana use was required to be in one of the various ranges that existed and they were forbidden from using them until their first full Evocation class was over and they were certified to practice on the range without supervision.

Amusingly, Desmond noted that Throneblood kept calling up different cadets to use as 'examples' and they always ended up being one of the girls that he'd heard making snide comments about him being called to Medical. *I guess Cadet Leafsong was right. Throneblood is always watching. That's both reassuring and a little terrifying too.*

"The most important thing to remember is not to overdraw your cache. Remember, one of the biggest rules that exists around mana is that 'like calls to like', the more mana you have in your system already, the faster you will recover what you have spent. Overdraw and your mana will be slow to recover. Draw it too far and you can die. None of you are to draw your cache lower than half at this time." The instructor's words rang out as a declaration as the group practiced the basic spell.

Unfortunately, Desmond was having trouble already. He could feel the thrum of his dynamo whirling away in its little metaphysical pocket in his chest. He could also feel that tingling sensation that he had come to recognize as his mana cache as it settled through his body like water in a basin. But while he could draw it to the surface of his hand, the light his palm emitted was a weak and flickering blue-white glow. All around him, the other adepts were conjuring a wreath of light around their hand like they held different colored fluorescent bulbs in their palms.

"Cadet, you seem to be struggling." Instructor Throneblood had snuck up on him while Desmond glared down at his flickering palm. Desmond jumped and his concentration slipped, causing the light to go out entirely.

"Ah! Yes, Instructor," Desmond replied, sitting up straighter in his seat. He vaguely heard someone behind him tittering and pointedly ignored it.

"Do the exercise again and I will observe," Throneblood ordered. She stepped down off the stage to stand directly in front of Desmond's desk and waited.

Taking a deep breath, Desmond worked to steady his nerves before trying again. The breathing exercise that Instructor Tre'shovak had used to get his dynamo going helped to get his mind focused. Desmond was able to urge that tingly, wintergreen feeling up through his arm to his hand, and his hand began to glow brightly for a moment before flickering and going out.

"Hmm, nothing wrong with your process. Cadet McLaughlin, let me see your com-cuff." Desmond let the focus drop away and held out his left arm to the instructor, who tapped her bright silver cuff against his bronze one before clicking through several interface screens with a scowl on her face.

The scowl only deepened when she found what she was looking for, and the instructor turned her sharp gaze back to

Desmond.

"Cadet, your cache is already down to thirty percent. Were you using mana between classes?" Desmond felt like the instructor's glowing orange gaze was boring a hole straight through him.

"No, Instructor. I went to speak to Doctor Astrid in Medical at her request. She wanted to check something since I am the first Terran on board. Other than that, I spoke with a few other cadets, then came back to class, as I didn't want to miss it."

"You didn't eat lunch?" The Uth'ra's piercing gaze did not look away from Desmond, and he felt like she was somehow divining if he was lying to her. *Wouldn't be surprised if she could, actually.*

"No, I didn't have time, Instructor. Between Medical and the others, I didn't get a chance to."

"Hmm, that might be the source. And you swear you did not use any magic between classes? It's not against the rules, but you should maintain your cache better, especially as someone who was only recently exposed to mana."

"As far as I am aware, I did not use any magic. Doctor Astrid did say something about my dynamo running fast and needing to be...adjusted so it might be related to the treatment." *Or it could be from her punching me and somehow knocking mana out of my body. Friggin psycho doctor...*

"All right then. Do not continue to practice, Cadet. I don't want you to draw your reserve down any further. For now, I'll send you some reading material. Study that for now and make sure you get a large dinner. Practice tonight only if your cache rises above fifty percent and do not draw it lower than that. Do you understand?"

"Yes, Instructor." Throneblood nodded once before turning back to the rest of the class and striding over to check on another of the cadets. A moment later, his datatablet flashed as it received an upload from the instructor. Desmond took a moment to check the readout on his comm-cuff, and he struggled to remember which of the combinations that Monika had shown him was for his vital numbers.

- Physical Condition -
Condition - Healthy
Cache Status - 32/100
- Stats -
Strength - Pending Assessment
Endurance - Pending Assessment
Dexterity - Pending Assessment
Accuracy - Pending Assessment
Mental Flexibility - Pending Assessment

Wonder when we are going to do the assessments for the other stuff... Desmond pondered for a moment before shrugging it off. He watched as the '32' ticked up to '33' a moment later before closing the interface and picking up his data-tablet. It was irritating that he couldn't continue to practice, but if there was one thing that high-school weight training had taught him, it was that sometimes you needed to rest so you didn't hurt yourself.

Don't even want to think about overdrawing too far...I didn't get this far to blow out my ability to do all this stuff.

CHAPTER 14

Terran's had so many funny ideas about space. Des told me about the little green men and their fixation with probing people. I'm pretty sure that was just some bizarre fixation of people way too into butt-stuff. Not saying that is a bad thing, but for it to be a fixation on the species...? Maybe it's something to do with their messed up gender ratios. Then again, I've heard that some species that get off on smell. Glad I'm not one of them. I'd never have survived in my parents' workshop.
~Monika Irongrip, Head of the Irongrip Consortium.

Desmond was so caught up in reading the descriptions of the various specialties and unique examples of their powers that when Throneblood dismissed the class, it came as an abrupt surprise to him. As a result, he was a beat behind the others in getting to their feet to salute the instructor before she left.

Allowing the class to get moving first, Desmond took a moment to finish the paragraph he had been reading and carefully secured his data-tablet into a pocket.

"That was rather pitiful, you know that?" The accusatory tone pulled Desmond's attention to one side to see Olianna had snuck up on him while he was distracted. Apparently, he had looked confused because she began to elaborate. "Blowing your load so fast that the instructor had to intervene and tell you to stop. A male should have more control than that."

"Wow, where do you come off saying shit like that to me?" Desmond just stared at her, irritation warring with embarrassment in his chest as he glared at the Se'Aelfa.

Olianna flipped her blonde hair over her shoulder and smirked at him.

"Just wanted to point it out to you, prim. You need to have better self-control than that. No girl likes a man that can't keep himself under control." Her barbs delivered, Olianna walked off with a sway to her hips that might have been sultry if it wasn't for the venom she'd used on him.

"She's right..."

"He's cute when he's flustered!"

"Why would she say something like that to his face?"

"Eww...gross!"

The muttering of people around him only made it worse, and Desmond flushed red at being put on the spot. He wanted to say something, to defend himself, but there wasn't much he could say that wouldn't make it sound worse in the moment. So he said nothing and just walked out of the classroom, intent on separating himself from the situation.

<><><>

Desmond made it halfway back to his rooms, still burning with shame, when something short and heavy plowed into his back and nearly carried him to the ground. The redheaded attack-dog in question laughed gaily as she clung to him like a backpack.

"Nearly got you, you giant git. Were you daydreaming about Instructor Throneblood's tits or something?" Cackled Monika, the stout Dwerg wiggled in her position, clinging to his lower back and hips in an attempt to twist and throw him to the ground. Desmond stumbled finally and had to catch himself on the wall, but managed to avoid going down.

"Get off me! Are you a Dwerg or some kind of crazed squirrel on a sugar high?" Desmond demanded, his grumpy mood and embarrassment over Olianna's comments washed away by the enthusiasm of his redheaded friend.

"What in all the swirling nebulas is a squirrel?" Monika

paused her attempts to wrestle him to the ground and peered up at him from the space between his arm and his side, still attached to his lower back like a tick.

"A tree-dwelling rodent with way too much energy that likes to cause trouble and steal nuts." Desmond glared back at her before reaching back to try to grab hold of the back of her uniform and drag her off.

"I am not a tree-dweller!" Monika let go of his back, dropping to the deck with a solid 'thunk' of her boots.

"But you don't deny being a rodent?" Desmond turned to mock-glare at her with his fists on his hips. Monika paused for a moment, rubbing her chin as she considered it. The fact that she didn't have a counter to that ready took the wind out of Desmond's sails.

This, apparently, was exactly what Monika was waiting for. She immediately lashed out with a punch to the outside of Desmond's left thigh that made pain shoot through his hip and the entire leg folded up under him.

"That was for calling me a rodent!" Monika laughed, lunging forward to catch Desmond before he landed on the deck.

"Why? Why would you do that?" Desmond gasped, his entire leg pins and needles. Thankfully, the sensation faded quickly, and he was able to stand up after a few seconds.

"What, I thought you boys preferred not to take a shot to the ole 'floppy disk', was I wrong?" Monika sassed, cocking one eyebrow at him and winding up with her fist again.

Instinctively, Desmond flinched away, twisting to shield himself.

"No! I appreciate you not tagging me in the Three Amigos. If you did, that would be a declaration of war…"

"'Three Amigos'?" Monika gave him a confused look.

"It's a loan word from another ethnic language. English as a language likes to steal shit from other languages…It means 'buddy'." Desmond shook his head, taking a careful step to make sure he didn't lose his balance. When his leg supported him, he relaxed and sighed in relief.

"Ah, that is going to get confusing quickly. Unless you swap over to Standard. Did you take a look at the cost of going through subliminal training on that?" Monika fell into step beside him as they continued down the hallway.

"Haven't had a chance to. Was going to take a look and skip dinner but I guess I shouldn't do that." Desmond scowled slightly. "Instructor Throneblood ordered me to eat since I missed lunch."

"Throneblood? Gods and stars, you ended up with a hard-ass as your instructor. My condolences!" Monika threw her head back and laughed. "Why did you miss lunch?"

"Got called to Medical. Apparently, something was fucked up with my dynamo and they needed to check me over."

"Makes sense. The Hegemony doesn't take chances with their adepts. Well…that's not true. They kinda throw us to the wolves during training, or Uth'ra in your case." Monika shot him a wicked smile as she bounced along at his side.

"Yes. I missed lunch and apparently overdrew myself in class." Desmond tapped into his comm-cuff to check his current cache levels. "Only back up to 38% total."

"Ah yeah, that's not good. Let's get you fed and you can furnish that barren hole you call a suite." Monika broke into a trot to lead the way to the dining room and Desmond had to speed up to keep pace.

<><><>

It wasn't until he sat down in the mess hall with his food that Desmond realized just how hungry he was. He suffered through Monika's teasing in silence, just focusing on getting his stomach filled. Thankfully, he didn't gorge as much as he had back when he had first gotten his dynamo spinning.

Once they had finished dinner, the two of them headed back to Desmond's suite of rooms.

"Okay, so how the hell do I go about getting some

furnishings so this isn't so bleak?" Desmond asked, as the two of them flopped onto the low couch in the conversation pit. "What do I furnish it with, anyway?"

"Depends." Monika had sprawled out on the couch opposite him, laying on her side rather than actually sitting.

"There really isn't a ladylike bone in your body, is there?"

"Nope! Haven't met a lady that could bone me yet either. Though I hear they have pills for that," Monika shot back with one of her regular eyebrow waggles. Desmond had to smother a chuckle lest he encourage her. "How you furnish it is simple. SAUL, Desmond wants to furnish the rooms finally."

"Understood, Cadet Irongrip. Sending relevant catalogs to your data-tablet, Desmond." SAUL's voice this time sounded like an old time radio personality.

"You still haven't picked a voice module yet?" Monika winced at this voice mode and turned a pointed look at Desmond. "It took me all of five minutes of browsing to settle on one for my Liaison."

"Well, aren't you special then, hmm?" Desmond shot back before glancing up at the ceiling, a habit that had formed when addressing the digital helper-slash-housekeeper. "SAUL, keep that voice module."

"Understood, Desmond," replied SAUL with a flourish. Desmond didn't bother to hide the smirk.

"That is going to get annoying fast."

"Totally not the reason that I selected it, I swear."

"Suuure. Anyway, get to furnishing. Your stipend isn't going to be enough to fully furnish the place, but you can at least spruce it up."

Desmond dug his data-tablet out of the cargo pocket of his uniform pants and began to poke through it. He spent almost ten minutes paging through different options, staring at the various things listed.

The stipend he'd been given for the first week wasn't much, only a hundred and twenty Hegemony Interstellar

Credits, or HICs, or credits depending on who you asked. He could get very simple furnishings for now or try to save the funds for something better as time went by.

"What else can we spend the HICs on?" Desmond asked at last, glancing up from the tablet to find Monika sprawled on her back now with her feet up and over the back of the low couch. It presented him with a view down her uniform top, but he studiously avoided looking.

"Oh, a lot of things. You can get supplemental reading, rent specialist range time, games and other media as well as subliminal training on various subjects. The Academy covers the basics, but the stipend and credit system is part of how folks can specialize early on."

"Oh? They haven't gone over it in class yet." Desmond poked through more of the menus until he found the section on subliminal training and started going through it.

"That's because they don't want folks to prejudice things just yet. My cousin is an adept, and she told me about it. They'll let folks know about it once we start forming our teams. Up till then, it's better not to do any of the heavy training and the like, or only do the language and knowledge classes."

"Kind of annoying that they don't allot stuff like that for 'filthy prims' like me. Would make catching up that much easier." Desmond scowled when he saw the price tag for the language training that Monika had mentioned. Training in Standard would cost him two hundred credits, while a comfortable chair would cost him almost a hundred credits. *Cheap for language training that might take months naturally, but is still annoying.*

"The academy is big on equal footing."

"Sure, totally equal footing. I've seen what your suite looks like. You are totally on equal footing with me," Desmond shot back at the Dwerg in mock irritation. She just winked at him from her position upside down.

"It's not my fault that my family decided to send me off

with a gift of credits."

"Not everyone is born to a family that builds shuttles for the Hegemony."

"Make sure you add the complaint when you send a report back to your home-world. You mentioned that they tried to get you to sign some kind of employment contract for after your service term?" Monika's words reminded Desmond of the contract that the agent had foisted off on him and he sighed.

"Yeah. Still glad I didn't sign that. No idea what the conversion rate for dollars to credits is, but I really don't wanna sell my soul to the government for a couple of bucks... I'd rather have to work a bit harder now to not be in debt to them. Student loans already got me that way once."

"Just gotta make good on the bounties once they have us doing Rifts in training and you'll get ahead of the curve, no problem. Just gotta manage your equipment costs well."

"Equipping costs?"

"Yup! The Academy issues basic gear themselves but you can buy better or more specialized gear depending on the style your team goes for. Specialized or enhanced ammo, enchanted gear, stuff like that. That sort of shit can make the difference between having to abort a run and not. While the Academy always has backup teams ready to bail us out if we really fuck up a run, if you have to get pulled out, it cuts into your earnings."

"Okay. You gotta elaborate on this shit, Monika..." Desmond set the data-tablet aside and stared at the shorter woman.

"Only if you elaborate on what happened in Medical. I know there's more to that story just based on how you tried to gloss over it earlier." She'd been badgering him about it the entire time they'd eaten dinner, but Desmond had resolutely denied it, still feeling somewhat guilty for basically bullying that Hyreh, despite her plans to attack Chloe.

Speaking of, I should check in with Chloe and make sure she's doing okay. He snatched up his data-tablet and typed up a quick message to the taurine Taari to check on her.

"Who are you messaging?" Monika was on him in a flash, launching herself off the other couch and scrambling to check his data-tablet, but Desmond had already locked the screen. Something he'd had to learn quickly because of Monika's nosy nature.

"Nope, you gotta go first. Fill me in on this earnings thing, Monika. I know that the instructors will cover it eventually, but I hate feeling like I'm behind in everything." Desmond sighed, stashing the data-tablet under his butt and pushing the redheaded Dwerg back onto the couch.

"It's simple enough," Monika said with a huff, crossing her arms and looking put out at his insistence. "Rift runs are a duty that the Academy takes up." Desmond nodded. He'd read about that while studying up on everything. "The Academy ships patrol the Hegemony's space and close Rifts where they find them. The rating on the Rift decides which year gets first crack at it, for us at least. They also work to contract out with freelance teams lead by retired adepts for Rifts that are out of range or off patrol routes. Also, there are teams assigned to active duty ships for the actual military term who range out and around the Academy ships to act as longer range runners. So that might end up being your posting when you finish your training, depending on the whims of the officers."

"Yeah, I understand all that. What I'm not getting is the whole 'being paid for it' thing?"

"I'm getting there, Des. Just let me finish!" Monika fired back at him before she began ticking off points on her fingers. "As my cousin told me, each Rift is usually breached by a collection of teams for Academy work, or a solo team for the freelancers depending on crewing. From there, it's a race to clear and stabilize the Rift. Your comm-cuff keeps track of what your team does to contribute to clearing the Rift and you get a percentage of credit at the end for how much you did. That calculates your share of the value of mana distilled from the Rift to safely collapse it. You also receive a bounty for materials recovered inside the Rifts."

"Things like crystallized mana?" Desmond asked, remembering the powder that Instructor Tre'shovak had shown him.

"That or infused metals. Some alloys only form inside Rift's due to how mana likes to play weird with the natural scientific laws. If you get bailed out, the team pulling you is awarded no less than half your total earnings as decided by the Instructors overseeing the Rift. As for what everything is worth and what is worth bringing out or not? My cousin told me that it's a shot in the dark." Monika shrugged before flopping back against the couch again. "Some things are guaranteed payouts, crystallized mana being one of those things, but the quality can vary drastically depending if its pure or needs refinement, or if it is elementally aligned. Finding pure crystals is like…finding a sapphire in your sock drawer. Sure, it's possible, but the odds are super long."

"Huh…okay. Any idea what the average payouts are? Just trying to get an idea of what sort of budget I might see in the future." Desmond tapped his chin in thought, staring into the distance as he tried to imagine what sort of loot they might find in these Rifts and what the best way of securing and returning with it was.

"My cousin said she averaged a few grand for completing the Rifts. But the bonus for recovering supplies varied so much it was hard to say what to expect. Team size matters too, since you are required to split it with your team. The mundies still have expenses too and they expect a fair cut. The Academy pays them a stipend as a guard team, but it is expected to share the payouts from Rifts. Not required to be an even share, but a share nonetheless."

"Naturally. Everyone should be paid for their work," Desmond agreed. He continued staring into the middle distance as he considered. *It would be better to invest the short-*

term earnings into preparing for the Rift's coming up, right? Rather than hoarding credits for something like paying off my loans when I get out or for a fancy bit of gear, I should try to prep as extensively as possible for Rift runs since one of those could pay out better than potentially years worth of the stipend.

"Okay, I showed you mine. Now spill about what happened in Medical!" Monika scooted around the couch so that she could poke him in the side.

"Ack, okay fine. Doctor Astrid decided I needed to have my dynamo 'adjusted' as it was running too quick for no reason. She did this by punching me in the chest, which apparently caused it to jump and stall or something because it stopped humming so damn much."

"You got punched by an Uth'ra?" Monika gave him an impressed look that turned suspicious. "There's more. You wouldn't be so cagey unless there was. Spill!" Desmond rolled his eyes and continued.

"Once I could breathe again, I limped my ass out of there. Apparently, another cadet was getting treatment for having a fight and she stopped me to ask if I was okay since I'd unbuttoned my top to look at the bruise the Doctor left on me out in the hall."

"Ooh, flashed your pecs and got some girl's attention. How risque!" Monika bobbed her eyebrows at him before she got a devious look in her eyes. "Where were you bruised? Was it here?" She lashed out, smacking him in the chest right over his breastbone before he could stop her.

"Ow! Damn it, yes!" Desmond protested, though it didn't hurt nearly as much as he'd expected. After fending off several more attempts from Monika to smack his bruise, Desmond undid the top two buttons of his shirt to check on it and was startled to find an expanse of unbruised skin that was only red where the Dwerg had smacked him. "The hell?"

"What? You grow a third nipple or something?" Monika pestered him, shifting to peek over his shoulder. "Wait, I thought you said she left a bruise?"

"It was starting to turn purple already in the hall. That was why Chloe stopped me to check on me. Though she definitely looked worse than I did," Desmond said thoughtlessly.

"Ooh? Chloe? Got her name and everything. Spill!" Monika prodded, plopping down next to him, her attention redirected again with the speed of an over-sugared toddler.

"Ugh, fine. Okay..." Desmond proceeded to describe Chloe's injuries and Monika hissed in sympathy.

"Now that was quite a thorough beating she went through...She sounds cute, though. You take a shot at her?" Monika's sympathy immediately turned to teasing. "Is that why you missed lunch?"

"No. I escorted her back to her room because the girl could barely stand upright. That was it. I did put the fear into a group of Hyreh who wanted to take another shot at her, but that was it," Desmond countered with a sigh. Monika was fun to be around, but her boundless energy felt exhausting.

"Ooh, how scandalous! So, are you going to take a crack at her?"

"What? No! Chloe is just someone I talked to for a bit and helped out."

"Ya, but that whole 'defending her honor' thing can really get a girl's panties wet. Flipping the script can go one of two ways, and since she didn't get pissed at you, I bet she was soaked!" Monika barked, laughter tingeing her voice. "Besides, if you aren't going to take a crack at her, I might have to give it a shot. I like 'mountain climbing' if you know what I mean, and she sounds like she's got some good 'handles'. You said she was a mundie?"

"Lay off, Monika," Desmond growled. Irritation was welling up in his chest. Monika shot him a sly wink and held her hands up.

"No worries, Des. I see you are staking a claim there. Just do me a favor and ask her if she has a brother next time you see her."

"Monika, I said lay off," Desmond rumbled, but Monika just kept her hands in the air and hummed innocently. Desmond knew better than to believe that lie.

CHAPTER 15

Logic doesn't play into it. It took a very long time to not cringe while using chants for the magic. Phenomenal cosmic power and all that and I had to yell incantations like I was doing a LARP pretending I was a teenage wizard...
~Desmond McLaughlin, on life aboard the *Valor's Bid*.

The following week sped by with little time to think about his plans for the future. Chloe had sent Desmond a simple response: that she was recovering just fine, and that the other cadets that had bothered her before were leaving her alone now. They'd exchanged a few messages back and forth, Desmond inquiring what sort of training the regular cadets were going through and learning that most of their time was being taken up with what sounded like regular army style training.

Olianna continued to make snide comments about his longevity and the like, and there were always whispers from many other girls in his class, but Desmond ignored them as best he could, focusing on his studies. Whenever it started to get to him, he just reminded himself that he needed to perform well to dispel the idea that he was a 'useless prim'.

The few messages he continued to send to Chloe were lighthearted, just chatting in general as he wanted to keep in touch with the large woman and it was easy to commiserate about the abuse from the trainers. There wasn't much time to chat, because after the first day 'introduction', their instructors had picked up speed to a run. Desmond spent most of his free time working to manipulate his mana throughout his body.

During class, Throneblood pressed all the cadets to the point they could tap into and shift their mana throughout their bodies at a moment's notice. Even their day off had seen Desmond and Monika practicing in earnest in Desmond's suite, taking turns calling out different amounts of mana and locations for the other to shift, learning how to measure and separate off a portion of mana and move it to different spots. An exercise that would come in handy the next week when Throneblood finally took them to the practice range for their first lessons on combat casting.

<><><>

"All right, I want each of you to take a lane and begin cycling the mana in your body to your dominant hand." Instructor Throneblood's thunderous orders echoed throughout the massive chamber that was within the combat range. The section that the class took up was only one of six that stretched across the large room. Each of the other sections were occupied by other classes of cadet-adepts, but shimmering green fields prevented noise from the others intruding on their space.

Each of the lanes was roughly sixty yards long and divided by low walls that stood roughly waist high. A console to one side of the belly-button high counter could summon targets up at varying ranges and amounts of cover as well as adjust the height of the counter at need. Everything past the starting line was heavily armored by an alloy that Desmond didn't recognize, but he could see a number of shallow scars from where spells had damaged, but not pierced, the decking.

Desmond moved quickly to grab a lane, already sinking into the breathing pattern that he'd learned to help reach his mana. He'd made it a habit to continually collect and release his mana throughout his body. The idea had come after walking Monika back to her suite the previous week, as the silent halls had led him into a naturally meditative mindset and he'd unconsciously taken to pushing the mana into his feet with each step but not releasing it. The washing tingle of mana moving through his body had helped keep him awake despite being exhausted.

"Now, you are each going to practice the most basic of Evocation spells, Bolt." Instructor Throneblood paced down the line, glaring at each cadet that wasn't already in a lane and ready. "The standard incantation or chant for Bolt is customizable for each person. Remember, incantations are not required but they can help focus a casting. Which is why, right now, you are all going to utilize Bolt with an incantation."

The idea that most incantations were just a mnemonic effect for the body to condense a pattern for the spell had thrown Desmond at first, but the more he'd thought about it, the more sense it made. It helped that the more familiar someone became with a spell, the less necessary the mnemonic was. He didn't want to spend all of his time muttering cringe-inducing spells after all.

"All right, once you have the mana gathered in your dominant hand as we have practiced, repeat your mnemonic and project the Bolt spell towards the target in your lane. A throwing gesture is acceptable at this time, but I expect you to project the *Bolt* spell without it by the end of the week. Make sure you keep an eye on your cache levels and break to rest if you begin to get down to half." Throneblood had reached the far end of the line at this point and was doubling back, marching with her hands behind her back and her wild mane of blue hair bobbing slowly with each step.

Okay Desmond, you got this. Just start with around one percent of your mana for now and see where that goes. He thought to himself, focusing on gathering up that small section of mana and portioning it out to his fingertips on his right hand.

Since this was their first time actually practicing the

expression of their magic, he wasn't sure what his latent regeneration rate was yet and wanted to keep things slow and steady. More shots to practice his aim were better than overdoing it.

As if to mirror his thoughts, the *crack-boom* of a lightning strike echoed through the firing range and made everyone wince and caused Desmond to lose his hold on the fragment of mana he'd sectioned off.

"Too much! Way too much mana for a simple Bolt! Dial it back, cadet!" Throneblood roared, wheeling to shout at the now woozy cadet who had incinerated her target with a brilliant green bolt of energy. The bolt only left a dark smudge on the alloy of the decking, though.

Pointedly shutting out the ass-chewing that was going on four lanes over from him, Desmond took a deep breath through his nose and tugged free a small bit of the mana he had cycling through his body again.

"Bolt..." Desmond muttered under his breath, deciding to keep his first attempt at the mnemonic simple and pushed the mana out of his fingertips, focusing on the target twenty yards ahead of him.

At first, the mana resisted his push, pooling against his fingertips like he was pouring water into a glove but after a moment of resistance the power flowed out and a sky blue blob flicked out from his hand to land less than half-way to the target.

"Okay, that...was lackluster. Was it the amount of mana or the force?" Desmond muttered to himself, ignoring the snickers of one of the other cadets nearby.

Focusing again, Desmond repeated the same movement and made a throwing gesture with his right hand and this time the blob flew the full distance, though it splashed against the target awkwardly, not doing any actual damage and smoking off into the air.

"Good, Cadet. You can push a bit more energy into it. What are you envisioning as you throw?" Despite

Throneblood's size, she had managed to sneak up on Desmond while he was focused on the target. Strangling the urge to jump and cuss, Desmond turned to his instructor to reply.

"A sphere, just like with the light exercises for now. It's the most familiar at the moment." Throneblood nodded once at his explanation, her piercing orange eyes studying him intently for a moment before she turned her stern expression to the woman to his left.

"Cadet, what are you using as a visual?" The instructor barked. Being put on the spot made the vulpine Taari jump as well and bobble the spell that she had been readying, causing it to splash against the armored deck ahead of them. Once she had recovered, she turned to the instructor with wide eyes and stammered out a response.

"Ah, I...uh...a spear head, Instructor!"

"Good idea. Images as such will help you focus your will so that you can continue to build mnemonic pathways. Continue." Instructor Throneblood turned back to Desmond with a nod and a gesture for him to attempt again. "Before you try again, Cadet McLaughlin, watch the others. Note the shapes their *Bolt* takes and consider that."

Taking another breath in through his nose, Desmond did that. Turning back to the lane he was in, he looked back and forth at the others nearby. Several were conjuring spheres, others were using flat planes, though the ones having the most success were launching wedges or points. So he focused on the target and began to gather the mana together in his hand again as Throneblood spoke behind him in a lower tone.

"Find an image in your mind that feels comfortable. Bolt is the bread and butter of an adept's arsenal. It is one of the first spells to begin developing twists to match an individual's personality. You remember what 'twists' are, right Cadet?"

"Unique changes to a spell that reflects the adept using

them." Desmond remembered the lecture from the previous week. Twists could be the shape of the spell, secondary effects, or any number of changes that opened the pattern beyond its standard.

"Good. Remember not to push *too* much energy into it, but it is okay if your image calls for more."

The rumble of the instructor's voice helped guide Desmond's mind as he thought before a smile twisted his lips. *A comfortable shape? I sure as hell have one of those.*

Without conscious effort, the mana slipped from his fingertips down into the palm of his hand and his hand moved from a cupping shape to gripping a handle. His empty left arm came up in front of his chest, parallel with the ground as his right pulled back behind his shoulder further. The haze of mana flowed out of his palm and into a familiar shape that settled into his grip like the touch of an old friend. Moving on autopilot, Desmond twisted his hips and let out a sharp breath through his lips.

An axe that appeared to be made of mint-green glass whirled down the lane and slammed into the humanoid shaped target's mid chest, sinking partway into the polycarbonate form and lingering for several seconds before dissolving into nothing.

"Very good, Cadet McLaughlin! You didn't use the incantation, though. How much did that take from your cache? No, don't check your comm-cuff yet. Tell me what you *feel*," Instructor Throneblood boomed as Desmond smirked at the target. The motion had felt so natural, just like throwing one of his axes at the competition range. He took a moment to assess his cache before he answered.

"It felt like roughly three percent?"

"Check your comm-cuff and keep track of it. You have the visualization down and your accuracy seems quite solid. How familiar are you with that weapon?" Throneblood eyed him intently and Desmond quickly accessed the comm-cuff to find that between the three attempts he'd made at the Bolt spell, he'd only used around six percent of his cache, and as he watched the number on his comm-cuff ticked up from 94% to 95%.

"I used to throw as a hobby. That weapon is one I am very familiar with, at least on a practice range like this, Instructor," Desmond replied after looking up from his comm-cuff. "I believe the comm-cuff confirmed it at three percent usage."

"Good, I want you to practice refining it. Use the incantation next time and see if that mitigates the amount of energy necessary. Your accuracy is already good, so work on reducing the amount of mana it takes and focus on practicing. If you are lucky, you'll start developing twists to the spell during the next week. Remember, repetition of the pattern is key."

"Understood, Instructor." Desmond saluted her before turning back to the range and taking a deep breath, his arms moving into his ready pose. The mana flowed up and into his palm, pooling there instinctively and the glassy shape of the throwing axe formed almost without conscious thought. This time, Desmond did as the instructor had ordered and worked to restrain the amount of energy that flowed into it to the barest minimum.

<><><>

Time got away from him as he moved steadily, launching an axe through the air and watching it strike his target. Using an incantation made it feel stiff and awkward, but it did reduce the cost of mana once he came up with something that fit for him.

"Kill shot," Desmond muttered again as he made the gripping motion before launching the axe down the lane one last time. Using a term from his WATL league made it feel more natural, since a 'kill shot' was the kind of throw that had to be called out before it was thrown to count. He didn't bother to watch, knowing the blade would strike in the same dense cluster of cuts that he'd left in the center of the body-outline where the breastbone would be. Instead, he checked his comm-cuff and grinned. "Outstanding! Got it down to a single percent…"

Glancing to his left, Desmond noticed that he was one of the last ones still standing in the lanes. Most of the rest of the class was clustered at tables back along the wall, resting and watching those still remaining. Olianna was glaring at him from amongst a group of other Aelfa subspecies, but after noting her, Desmond just ignored her.

Checking the readout on his comm-cuff, Desmond noted that he had kept his mana cache at roughly 75% of full. He'd found the rhythm that let him form and throw a single one of the Bolt axes and how long to wait till it regenerated and kept around there.

"All right! Pack it in, Cadets," Instructor Throneblood called, her voice booming throughout the room and drawing everyone's attention to her. "Good work today. Each of you was able to properly form and launch the Bolt spell. You have the afternoon off to rest and recover. Since this is the first time you've expressed mana in large volumes, you are going to be tired."

"Instructor?" A female Dwerg asked, raising her hand to get the Uth'ra's attention. She had been one of the other cadets that was still launching the spell when Desmond had come out of his practice trance. "My cache is already back to ninety percent. I don't feel tired right now. Can I keep practicing?"

"For today, I want all of you to rest. Even as your cache recovers, you are going to be tired. Expending mana always has a cost, remember that!" Throneblood swept her gaze over the collection of students firmly before she continued. "Managing your reserves and keeping them high will prevent you from injuring yourself, but you are still exerting your body. Just like with working your muscles, you have to rest to let them recover. Read, relax, or take a nap. No more casting until class tomorrow. You will regret it if you don't listen. Tomorrow morning we are going to be doing physical assessments. Now that you are working your first spells, we can also begin to work your bodies. You want to be rested for it! Dismissed!"

After saluting, the class began to break apart and head back to their suites. Desmond remained on the range and, with a few pushes of the buttons, called his target forward to inspect it.

The polycarbonate figure was roughly his size and shape, and the cluster of cuts had been worked deep into its chest. Prodding at the material showed that it was firm under his touch and it definitely took a powerful hit to deform it.

Wonder what sort of twist is going to develop first? Desmond bent close to inspect one cut that was deeper than the others, eying the edge of the cut. It looked smooth, which would indicate the blade had been sharp, but how sharp he wasn't sure. *Not like I bothered to test the edges, I just formed and threw them...felt good to throw an axe again.*

Sighing, Desmond turned to leave and nearly tripped on one of his classmates, who was standing close behind him. It was one of the vulpine Taari he'd sat beside on the first day.

"Oh hey, can I help you?" The Taari woman blinked at him a few times before her gaze dropped to the ground and she blushed slightly.

"Just wanted to say you did good today. Most of the others didn't think you'd do this well. They were betting you'd not be able to figure it out, even with the instructor helping you." Her voice was higher pitched than he had expected, and he could still faintly hear the sort of chitter/squeak of her natural tongue through the translation spell, but he shook it off.

"And what did you bet on?" Desmond asked, keeping his expression neutral. The vulpine Taari blushed slightly and glanced up to meet his eyes before looking away again.

"I bet that you'd figure it out. Honestly, they were being petty. Just because you are from a primitive world doesn't make you an idiot. It'd be like saying that you couldn't work mana just because you were male." Desmond made a noise of surprise at that. He'd remembered her and the other one he had assumed was her sister making snide comments the first day.

"Well, thank you. I appreciate your support for that. Means a lot to me." Desmond couldn't help the small smile that grew on his face and when she glanced up at him, he winked subtly.

"Sure! Anytime! I gotta go!" The vulpine Taari squeaked, her flush growing even darker under the light fur of her face and she scurried off, her tail flipping back and forth rapidly in what he guessed was embarrassment.

"Huh...that was odd, but nice," he murmured, watching her go before heading back to his suite as well.

A subtle tone and a vibration at his wrist notified him of a message, as he was partway down the hall. Checking the interface on his comm-cuff, he smiled when he saw it was from Chloe.

Hey, I heard through the grape-vine that the first years were getting their first chance to try combat spells today. Is that true, and how did it go if so?

It went well. We learned a basic combat spell called 'Bolt'. Was fun to practice like this. I'd been hoping that I'd show a specialization in Evocation, but it doesn't seem like it. We had a few that showed one and let me tell you, it SHOWED. Desmond sent back after a moment to consider what to say. He'd stepped out of the general flow of traffic to type one handed on the cuff's interface and he wasn't sure he could keep from bumping into someone if he tried to do it while walking.

Desmond made it most of the way back to his room before his cuff chimed quietly and vibrated again.

That's cool that you got to do that. I can still only imagine what being able to work with mana must feel like. It's unfortunate that you don't have a specialization for Evocation, but also nice since that would put you in the middle of combat. I mean, more than an adept normally does, right?

Desmond smirked at her questions. He and Chloe had talked off and on and most of it had been about what her classes were going through, but he'd shared a couple of tidbits, especially after the demonstration from the second year cadet-adepts. She'd been just as curious about what might occur as he was. Deciding to wait till he got back to his room to reply, Desmond hurried down the hall. It was good to have friends. Between Monika and Chloe, this place wasn't feeling quite as lonely anymore.

CHAPTER 16

Uth'ra as a species are terrifying to encounter for most species. Imagine a creature that stands between six and seven feet tall and has a mouth like a steel trap. Their eyes glow, literally glow, and standing in front of one is like standing in front of an apex predator. They are a warrior race that didn't leave that ethos behind when they left their homeworld.
~Species of the Hegemony, a report sent
back to the nations of Terra-Sol-3.

"Come on, Cadet! Is that the best you can do?" Spittle flew as Throneblood closed in behind him.

Desmond's breath was coming in fits and starts, his lungs clawing for more air as he raced through the maze. Reaching out, he grabbed a slot on one wall to take the corner at speed and hopefully get some distance on the Uth'ra instructor that was hot on his heels. He didn't have the breath to say anything in response and just focused on getting the hell out of her way.

"Clever! But if you can't keep pace, it won't save you." The crackle of electrical discharge gave Desmond just enough warning for him to dive forward into a roll as the stun-bolt arced through the space his torso had been in moments before, instead it just discolored the clay-colored wall in front of him.

Allowing his momentum to carry him forward in a roll, Desmond came to his hands and knees and scrambled through a low hole in the maze wall that he hoped the instructor couldn't follow him through. As soon as he was clear of the opening, he got back to his feet and bolted forward. Thankfully, the hole had led into another 'hall' rather than one of the access shafts.

This is such bullshit! They said they would be doing physical assessments today. How is being chased through a maze by our instructor an assessment?! The thought had crossed his mind several times as Desmond made several turns on the route to try to distance himself from Throneblood before slowing down and trying to catch his breath. It was harder than he had expected to slow his gasping down, but he did it while he went back over what the instructor had told them all in the waiting room.

"Each of you will take a turn being assessed. Your name will be called and you will proceed through the doors on the far wall. You are to do your utmost to complete the objective given to you when you go through the doors. You are not allowed to use any mana manipulation during the exercise. If you do not follow the rules, you will be disciplined and forced to run the assessment again tonight rather than having free time," Throneblood had said before stomping through the indicated doorway.

A few minutes later, the first name had been called over the intercom. Time had passed slowly, and they'd spent nearly an hour waiting before Desmond's turn came up. His directions had been printed on the digital board in front of the maze. It had just said 'reach the end, don't get shot'.

"I can hear you, Cadet." Throneblood's voice echoed through the maze and Desmond whirled, looking every way possible to try to figure out which direction the Uth'ra was approaching from. "You are going to have to try harder than this."

The entire maze was built more like a honeycomb than a traditional labyrinth, with tunnels branching off at odd angles and at different heights, and he'd done his best to make the most of this while escaping the instructor. Thankfully, his smaller size was an asset here, as he could wriggle through the smaller passages that the much larger

Throneblood wasn't able to squeeze into. This had let him keep ahead of her for the most part. He'd gotten less than half a minute of a head start before the Uth'ra had begun her noisy chase.

Desmond wanted to shout something in response to her taunts, but he restrained himself. *What if she doesn't actually know where I am? What if she's trying to bait me into giving it away?* Biting his lip, he edged down the route he had been going and checked the three-way junction he'd been heading for. A flash of movement on the left-hand side got him to draw back and wait for a handful of breaths before checking again. Seeing nothing on the left-hand side, he hurried around the corner and down the right-hand path.

"Don't assume that you've evaded me, Cadet. You forget one important thing!" Throneblood's voice was slightly more distant now, and he gave a quiet sigh of relief as he scooted around another corner and ducked low, tucking back into a recessed tunnel in the wall and checking all the directions before letting out a long breath. "You don't know if I'm the only one hunting you in here."

A chill went through Desmond and he had to fight the urge to bolt right then and there.

It was a good thing he didn't, because a moment later, Instructor Tre'shovak turned the corner to his right, her auburn mane bouncing as she scanned the tunnels. Only the fact she was facing away kept him from being spotted immediately.

Desmond began to duck walk backwards, further into the alcove and down the low tunnel so that he was out of sight. He could hear the click of Tre'shovak's boot-heels as she stalked down the tunnel and had to fight the urge to leap up and sprint. Rabbiting like that earlier was what had nearly gotten him caught by Throneblood.

The sound of Tre'shovak's steps slowed as they came to the junction that he'd ducked down. Desmond glanced around frantically for an escape in the low tunnel he was duck walking backwards through. A sudden opening above him provided the avenue he needed and Desmond could lever himself up into a small bubble of empty space that grew over the top of his tunnel. There wasn't anywhere he could go, but he was out of direct line of sight.

A moment later, he heard the scrape of Tre'shovak's boots in the tunnel he was just in. Holding his breath, Desmond waited, his heart thundering in his ears. Each second felt like it lasted for an eternity, but eventually, he heard the quiet scrape of Tre'shovak's boots head away down the tunnel.

Should I try to take the instructor from behind? Desmond wondered. *No way I could do it to Throneblood. She'd crush me like a bug, but I might surprise Tre'shovak and overpower her...* Desmond turned the idea over in his head before deciding against it. His directions had just said 'reach the end' not 'defeat your attackers' after all.

After the sound of Tre'shovak's boots had faded away, Desmond lowered himself back down into the tunnel and emerged from the tunnel back into the main corridor. Another handful of twists and turns and he saw the exit goal in sight. It was marked by a cool, green field of light and a rune that he had come to recognize as saying 'escape'. The problem was that the goal was also on the other side of a large, open room that was easily twenty meters across and had multiple tunnels opening onto it.

Prime spot for a last-minute ambush...

Desmond had been paint balling all of once in his life, but he'd played enough 'capture the flag' type games in first-person shooters that his instincts were warning him from just charging across the open area. The prickle that danced up and down his spine warned him that someone *had* to be watching the exit. Especially since he'd already seen two different instructors.

Crouching low against one wall, Desmond edged closer to the mouth of the tunnel, carefully peeking around the corners, looking for something that might indicate where the ambush was coming from.

It was because of his low profile that he noticed the strange protuberance near the mouth of his tunnel, a rounded hump shape that was a slightly different shade than the wall and about hip height.

Is that some kind of sensor or trip mine? That...would be just like them. Moving carefully, Desmond examined the exits from other tunnels that he could see. All the larger, hallway style tunnels had small bumps that he could see at the edges, all around hip height. None of the smaller crawlspace-like tunnels that honeycombed the walls showed them.

Okay, don't take a chance. Double back and take one of the small ones. He decided and crept backwards. He'd passed the access point to one of them earlier, and had decided against it since the tunnel had been so small that he would have had to do a pull up to get into the hatch in the ceiling, and then army crawl down the small tunnel. Now, though, it felt safer than taking a chance.

And everyone always said 'games don't teach you anything'. Desmond thought with a snicker as he wiggled his way up into the crawlspace. *All I need now is a zippo lighter and I could call myself McClane instead of McLaughlin.*

Moving as quietly as possible, Desmond wiggled through the crawlspace, his breath coming faster as he grew closer and closer to the exit space until finally he came to the rounded opening of the exit for the vent. Unfortunately, he was going to have to emerge headfirst as it came to a dead end at the exit, which was in the ceiling of the large room, and the space was too small to turn around in.

"Fuck...okay, this is going to suck," Desmond muttered and wiggled forward to peek over the edge of the drop. He tried to gauge the distance to the floor before swearing quietly to himself again. *That drop is at least ten feet. How the fuck do I get down without breaking something?*

Searching the room with his eyes, Desmond found nothing and was about to start edging backwards to try another exit when he caught sight of the struts in the roof of the main room. He hadn't noticed from the floor, but the ceiling of the room he was peering into now was criss-crossed with struts that had just the barest of lip, like a miniature I-beam.

It's not much, but I think I can get hold of that... With no better ideas, Desmond edged forward and stuck his head out of the hole, doing a quick check of all the different halls that he could see to make sure no one was lying in wait for him. After confirming the coast was clear, he wiggled forward, turning slowly as he did so, so that he was emerging from the ceiling hatch on his back with his arms out. As soon as he got a good grip on the ceiling strut, he pulled and levered his body out of the ceiling hatch at an angle. The strain on his fingers was immense, but Desmond held on, holding himself nearly parallel with the ceiling for half a second before his grip began to fail. However, it was long enough to pull his lower legs all the way through the hole and he tumbled free to land with a loud *thump* on his feet.

"He's at the exit!" Throneblood's roar echoed from the leftmost tunnel and Desmond turned, launching into a sprint for the escape hatch as he heard boots coming from several directions. Throwing himself forward, Desmond slapped the plate that would open the 'escape' hatch and ducked through just as one of the stun-bolts crackled through the air behind him. Desmond landed face first on a padded mat on the other side of the opening.

"Cadet clear," crackled a robotic voice much like the one SAUL had used when Desmond first spoke with him.

"Congratulations, Cadet McLaughlin. You are one of the very small handful who has made it through," Throneblood called with a laugh. "Go get cleaned up and get some lunch. Report to the Gold combat range at fifteen hundred for afternoon classes."

"Yes, Instructor!" Desmond wheezed from where he lay on the mat. His head was spinning from the adrenaline dump that had occurred during the last ten seconds of the training exercise and all he wanted to do was just lay there for a while.

"Good man. Your assessment results will be posted to your comm-cuff in the next few hours. Don't be late to the range, the upperclassmen are going to be giving you lot a demonstration on team dynamics."

"Yes, Instructor!" His lackluster response must have amused the Uth'ra woman, since she let out a cackle of laughter before he heard her stomping away.

"All right, ladies. You have two minutes to get back into position before I pull the next cadet in."

"You have way too much fun hunting your students like this, Maya." Desmond heard Camilla Tre'shovak's voice echo from the other side of the open hatch.

"Oh, like you don't enjoy it, Camilla. This is much better than the boring monitoring that the other side is doing. I'm sure that the cadets would prefer it to static measuring, anyway. Besides, most of them need to be reminded that they aren't the biggest predator around just because they are adepts!" The rest was lost to Desmond as the hatch spiraled closed and the instructors got further away.

"Sure. It is more exciting. But I think I'd rather just do push-ups," Desmond muttered before levering himself to his feet. He needed a shower and food. The idea of seeing different team dynamics as well as what sort of demonstration the upperclassmen might be putting on gave him the burst of energy he needed to pry himself away from the cool embrace of the padded flooring.

CHAPTER 17

Did I enjoy teaching? Of course I did! Instructing and preparing the next wave of adepts was a worthy job for someone who's seen what the wars are like out there. I did my absolute best to prepare those young minds for their future service to the Empress. Accusations that I would occasionally hunt my students for sport are nothing more than the lies of my detractors. All the instructors did it, not just me.
~Maya Throneblood, Memoirs of The Unblinking Eye.

The afternoon demonstration of the upperclassmen was apparently a multi-group affair. Desmond discovered this when he was ambushed by Monika while minding his own business.

The irrepressibly spunky Dwerg had brought a friend along, a female Uth'ra cadet that had been introduced to him as Dianne Sagejumper. Dianne was slightly smaller than Instructor Throneblood and built more along the lines of a sprinter, if that sprinter snacked on professional bodybuilders while modeling for Playboy in her free time. *Seriously, how does someone look that fit with that large of a bust?* Rather than the common loose mane of hair, she kept her hair braided back into a tumble of smaller black braids that she secured out of her face.

After Desmond managed to peel Monika off of his back, he could get an introduction. Despite being so much larger than both of them, Dianne was rather shy. The three of them secured a suitable spot to watch the proceedings.

Unlike the firing range that they'd all been shuttled to

the previous day, the Gold combat range wasn't sectioned off into individual lanes. Instead, the direction of the range had been changed to run the full length of the room and obstacles had been added to the combat floor. The first years had a raised section to stand on to observe as well as several hanging screens to watch the proceedings from safety in the area that had been behind the firing line normally.

"Wonder what sort of demonstration we are going to get?" Dianne had remained mostly silent until this point, only speaking a few times and content to let Monika do most of the talking.

"Throneblood said something about 'team dynamics' when she told me about it." Desmond shifted slightly, nearly dislodging Monika from her position on his shoulders. The shorter Dwerg had demanded to sit on someone's shoulders to see over the crowd. Apparently, this was a normal thing for her because Dianne had immediately responded with a 'not it' and shot Desmond a smirk. He'd tried to protest, but Monika had climbed up his back like a chimp before he could say anything.

"Guessing that they are going to run a gauntlet for us. Maybe simulating a Rift assault?" Monika shifted slightly, keeping her thighs spread wide to help with the balance, which Desmond was thankful for. If she'd been clinging tight to his head, it would have been impossible to focus.

"That would be pretty wicked. I'm guessing since she said it was team dynamics, it's supposed to get us thinking about what sort of team we want to assemble." Fighting the urge to pinch the wiggly Dwerg on his shoulders, Desmond checked the screens again.

The various screens showed different 'engagement areas' throughout the obstacle course, each of which had varying levels of cover or debris scattered over them. All the engagement areas were empty at the moment, but given that they were on one of the firing ranges, Desmond expected that to change soon.

"Attention, Cadets!" An unfamiliar female voice echoed throughout the space.

"Admiral on deck!" Throneblood's voice thundered through the space like an angry god a moment later. Both Monika and Dianne stiffened and immediately went to attention, which was an odd sensation with Monika on his shoulders. Doing his best to do the same, Desmond glanced around furtively to find the speaker without turning his head.

Movement on the screens caught his attention and Desmond looked up to see an avian Taari woman stride into frame, with the instructors following right after her. The avian Taari stood roughly between the heights of Instructor's Throneblood and Tre'shovak, so Desmond guessed her around seven feet in height though more than half of that was leg. Her head and upper body were covered in long, delicate looking white feathers that tucked back into a bobbing crest behind her head that reminded Desmond of a secretary bird. An image that was further reinforced by the curved yellow and orange beak that dominated part of her face below shimmering gold eyes. She was dressed in an immaculate uniform with the sigils for adept with three glittering stars embroidered under it marking her as a Vice-Admiral. What was even stranger to Desmond was the fact that the hands that emerged from the ends of her cuffs were covered in a gold-and-black spotted pelt, with heavy claws tipping her fingers.

Is she some kind of hybrid? She reminds me of some kind of griffin? Desmond wanted to ask the girls, but didn't want to risk breaking the absolute silence that had descended. His mental image of a griffin was further reinforced as the woman turned slightly and he caught sight of a pair of white wings with black tips folded neatly against her back. Each step the griffin-woman took was a long and measured pace.

"Good afternoon, Cadets," the officer said. Her voice was very deep for her slight build, and it rumbled nearly as much as Throneblood's booming tones did. "For those of you who do not know me, I am Vice Admiral Roaring-Feather. I am the head of the academy aboard the *Valor's Bid*. Today you will be observing a selection of your upperclassmen in a simulated environment that will echo a Rift incursion, as I am sure some of you have guessed." The Vice-Admiral paused at that point, slowly turning her head as she regarded the herd of cadets for several long seconds before she continued.

"Additionally, those of you who were able to successfully complete the entire challenge put forth to you for your assessments will have an additional benefit bestowed upon you. We are currently en route to support the freelance cruiser *On Wings of Fire* in suppressing a Rift that is destabilizing. We received the request to reinforce them less than an hour ago and will be on site in the next three hours."

The silence was broken by a rumble of murmurs, some happy at the chance and others irritated that they would be missing out. The Vice-Admiral let it go on for a few moments before flaring her wings out to either side. Her gesture was the only warning before the entire combat range echoed with a *crack-boom* like a close proximity lighting strike. The Vice-Admiral tucked her wings back behind her back and gave the group a stern glare.

"This is a unique opportunity for those of you who have already excelled and will serve as encouragement to those of you who are still lacking. You will be accompanying the second year teams during their excursions to help suppress the Rift. If you have the energy to grumble about not getting to go, you have the energy to improve. Selection to build out your teams is coming up fast, and those of you with higher scores will get first crack at the lists for who you want on your teams." The Vice-Admiral paused again, her sharp golden eyes seeming to pierce every one of the cadets standing at attention, even through the view-screen. "So for those of you who will not be observing a second year team directly, pay attention to this demonstration! And those of you who will be, this is the opportunity to see what a variety of people do to overcome similar challenges. Do not miss this chance, as it will risk your lives and those of your future team!"

With this final declaration, the Vice-Admiral turned abruptly and paced back across the open space at the entrance to the obstacle course before hopping lightly onto a squat podium in the corner and turning to assume an 'at-ease' pose where she could watch the second year teams.

One instructor, a thick-waisted Dwerg that he didn't recognize, stepped out of the line of instructors to address everyone next.

"The second-year students will be entering here in full combat regalia. They will proceed through the gauntlet in turns to face matching challenges and varying scores will be displayed on the viewing monitors to reflect their performances as if this was a real Rift assault. Remember, not every team will be ideally suited to address a challenge. What you are here to ascertain is what style you think will fit your mindset and goals. In order to replicate this as close as possible to a Rift assault, we will not be using the firing range's dummies."

"Oh shit," Monika murmured, her voice tight with excitement. Desmond could feel the short woman vibrating with anticipation.

"What?" Desmond asked, but the instructor answered his question before Monika could.

"The Vice-Admiral herself will be using her Conjuration specialty to manifest creatures like would be found in a standard Rift. Vice-Admiral, at your signal." The instructor turned to salute the Vice-Admiral, who nodded once before turning her attention to the simulated combat zone in front of her.

Without moving or speaking, light began to flicker along each of the long, delicate feathers that emerged from the back of the Vice-Admiral's head. That light collected into beaded drops before flicking through the air to land in the various 'engagement' zones before swelling to take the form of true monsters.

CHAPTER 18

The variety of approaches that each adept can take to any given situation is curtailed by three things. Their personal twists, their creativity, and their wallets. The last two are ones we can help them with, either with training or their paychecks. The first one, though, that's the tough one. No one can tell at a glance what way an adept's magic will twist when put to the test.
~Gemtooth, Weapons Instructor on the *Valor's Bid*.

"By the fangs of the queens..." Dianne's oath broke Desmond out of his surprised stupor. In less than ten seconds, the Vice-Admiral had manifested well over fifty creatures of some four different breeds. Two of which were absolutely massive things, one that looked like some sort of armored lizard the size of a city bus. The other reminded Desmond of an ape the size of a Volkswagen Beetle, but with six arms rather than two.

"That...is amazing," Monika breathed. The joy was obvious in her voice. "That is what a master in their specialty can do! I can't wait to see her controlling them all at once. I heard that the Vice-Admiral has closed a Rift on her own once, when her guard team were all injured during an initial assault."

"That sounds like suicide," Dianne shot back in disbelief.

"The Rift was about to go critical and take out a nearby colony world. She didn't have time to call for back-up and to retreat would have cost millions of lives. It's what got her the rank of Vice-Admiral."

"I'm more astonished by the fact that you know all of this, Monika. I don't think I've ever caught you reading even once,"

Desmond prodded, craning his neck to look up at her with one eye. This turned out to be a mistake as Monika took the opportunity to clamp her muscular legs around his head and choke Desmond for a moment before releasing him.

"They made a vid-drama of it, you ass. I've got a copy in my personal things. I was going to let you borrow it, but if you are going to sass me, you can find your own copy," the Dwerg replied primly.

"Stop fighting, you two. The first team is coming in." Dianne reached out to smack Monika on the back of the head.

"Ow, why did you hit just me?" Monika whined, mock-pouting at the Uth'ra.

"Because. You are an instigator," Dianne shot back before pointing to the main viewscreen.

The line of instructors had retreated to stand by the door that led to the staging area. Six cadets were now forming up in the open space. Only one of them, an Aelfa with pure white hair, wore the mark of an adept, and she stood at the back of the group. Arrayed in front of her in a wedge were her guard team. All five were heavily armored and bearing stubby rifles in one hand, with heavy shields in the other. Short swords hung from their belts on the left hip in a fashion that reminded him of a Roman Legionnaire. The five guards were all Hyreh and easily twice as broad as the Aelfa that they guarded and three times as heavily armored.

"Looks like she went for a phalanx style. Solid and aggressive. Five HICs say she's an Evoker," Monika murmured, using the common nickname for those with the Evocation focus.

"Just because the phalanx is the most common build for Evokers doesn't mean she is one," Desmond countered. But he didn't put much effort into it, given the haughty look that was crossing the Aelfa's face.

Monika didn't get a chance to respond before the group began to move at an unseen signal.

The quintet of Hyreh crossed the decking in lockstep,

bringing their shields to bear and locking their rifles into a cutout slot on the right side of the shield. The Aelfa followed behind them, just barely tucked into the broad wedge that they formed. As soon as they emerged into the first challenge room, the conjured enemies let out roars of challenge and charged the quintet's shield line.

The first group of monsters looked like someone had taken a pangolin and up-sized it to be the size of a mastiff. Not being satisfied with this, they'd also given it razor-edged armor and a mouthful of teeth to use on its enemies. To finish it off, they then painted the whole thing a mottled purple-gray color.

Moving with easy familiarity, the Hyreh guards opened fire on the approaching wave of armored creatures, their rifles coughing up a fusillade of projectiles that shredded the wave of creatures in moments. The wedge continued to move across the room as a score ticked up in the corner of the view-screen and the guards picked off any stragglers. The adept followed in the safety of the wedge without having to contribute anything. This pattern continued for the next two challenge rooms until they reached the first 'boss' creature, as Desmond had been thinking of it.

The armored lizard surged forward, charging the shield line like its smaller brethren had. The guard's rifles left glowing welts on the armored lizard's hide but were unable to penetrate.

"Dangerous and wild, raise the flames and build them high, sings this sparkling child," called the Aelfa from the back of the group. Her hands moved through a series of gestures before her right rose above her head, her arm moving in a circle like she was spinning a lasso.

The Hyreh guards reacted with well drilled instinct, dropping to one knee to brace behind their shields as the massive lizard closed even faster. A spinning wheel of flame coalesced above her fist, following the lasso motion of her arm until she launched it forward with an audible *thump*. As soon as the spell began to move, the Aelfa stepped forward and took cover behind the three forward-most shields of her guards.

The spinning blade of flame rocketed across the remaining twenty feet between the quintet of guards and the fast approaching lizard before it blossomed in a shock-wave of flame. When the wash of heat and fire cleared, the massive lizard lay sprawled across the deck, its head a scorched crater on its shoulders.

The Hyreh guards checked the body rapidly to ensure it was dead before leading the charge into the next room. No problems presented themselves as the phalanx cleared the rest of the area, with a repeat performance of the massive fire spell when they reached the second 'boss' creature. The only spot that they struggled in was when a second wave of enemies attacked the group from behind in one of the rooms leading up to it, but the back two guards had heard them coming and turned to form up while the adept had eliminated the threat with a series of wheel-shaped *Bolt* spells that were like miniature versions of the massive one she'd used on the boss.

"Told you she was an Evoker," Monika needled as the first team cleared the obstacle course to the applause of the first years.

"Little disappointed that she didn't show more spells... I guess it makes sense though, since this was supposed to simulate a real Rift and they wouldn't want to waste mana," Dianne replied. She ignored Monika's needling with an ease that told Desmond the big Uth'ra was used to it.

"What do you think, Des?" Monika patted Desmond on the top of the head. "Think the phalanx build is right for you?"

"I dunno, it definitely seems effective, but...also feels cheap to me?"

"Cheap, how so?"

"Like...the adept barely did anything besides handle the

boss-monsters. She could have reinforced her team or taken potshots as well. She wasn't even carrying a weapon." Dianne nodded in agreement with Desmond but didn't interrupt him. "Sure, she may have wanted to conserve mana, but it wouldn't take that much to add into the fight. Ultimately, the faster you take down the enemies, the better for everyone, right?"

"Yeah. But, to add into the firing line, it would have exposed her to return fire. Not every beast in the Rifts will focus on melee, just the lower end ones like what we will face later this year," Monika reminded him. Though a smirk tugged at her lips while she rested her chin on her hand and dug her elbow into the top of his head. "I can't imagine you hiding behind a group of women though, even big brawny girls like those were."

"Damn straight," Desmond muttered as the next group entered the staging area.

This second group differed vastly from the first group. Instead of a cohesive gun-line, this honestly reminded Desmond more of something he'd expect to see in a sci-fi crossover table top adventuring party.

The adept was a male canine Taari that carried a stubby-looking rifle that reminded Desmond of a trench-shotgun. To either side of him were Dwerg women bearing large shields and their own shotgun looking weapons with broad-bladed swords on their backs. Behind the trio stood a Tu'Aelfa with a long-barreled rifle that was covered in electronic gadgets and whatsits that sparkled and blinked lights. Beside her was a vulpine Taari wearing a heavy harness that had all sorts of medical tools on it and held a chunky-looking pistol with a collapsible stock in her right hand.

The second group mirrored the first in their approach, with the smaller wedge leading the way at a charge. Their approach changed as soon as they staged in a room, with the trio forming a bulwark with their backs to a wall. The Tu'Aelfa proved to be a skilled markswoman and devastating to anything that failed to close. Any enemies that managed to reach mid to close range were torn to shreds by the forward trio.

The adept appeared to be focused on enhancement, as his shotgun took on a glowing silhouette and rather than shot, it fired a whirling storm of miniature blades. At the back of the group, the medic added in potshots and kept an eye on their back. The group handled the massive lizard boss without a problem; the Tu'Aelfa bringing it down with a shot through the eye before it closed. The gorilla proved to be slightly more challenging, as it could close to melee by sacrificing two of its six arms as shields. The adept was ready though, dropping his rifle on a sling and, with a howling roar, summoning a massive two headed battle axe and meeting the ape in a melee clash. Meanwhile, his two shield-women moved to flank the much larger creature and hamstring it with a careful application of their own shotguns. From there, it only took a handful of strikes from the adept and the sniper to take it to pieces.

"A good flexible build that one. Enhancers tend to go for that kind of thing. Surprised he didn't enhance any of his team." Monika's commentary drew a nod from Dianne as well.

"He was using them as anchors, known quantities. I bet that if his charge had failed, or the creature had countered him, they would have covered his retreat behind a shield wall or moved to flank it to distract the creature. Pack-tactics like that work well for big creatures. Good of him to have a medic with them, though, shows he values the team individually." Dianne cut in before gesturing to the next team that was taking its place in the staging area.

<><><>

There were another six teams that ran the gauntlet, all of them with different makeups. Desmond saw larger bodied species carrying heavy weapons, teams that were organized around melee, and several variations on the 'phalanx' build with an Evoker leading them.

The one that was the most surprising was the four-person team led by a hard-eyed adept that had to be a transportation specialist. The adept was by far the strangest being he'd seen yet, a woman's body leading down into the body of a large hunting cat, with her waist attaching to where the cat's neck would be. She'd been heavily armored and carried an assault rifle. Her team had been two 'riflemen' armed with standard rifles and an Uth'ra with a rotary-barreled Gatling style gun.

The group had marched through the walkways to each room, but as soon as they entered the room, they opened fire on the enemies, drawing them close. As soon as the monsters had closed to mid to close range, the group had vanished with a *pop* to appear in another corner of the engagement space. Every time the enemy closed, the adept shifted them to another location. Each time they shifted, they remained aiming towards the enemy group, despite being transferred to the other side of the arena.

Their fight with the two bosses had taken longer than any other engagement, but they were never once in any danger as the adept nimbly moved them across the arena and actually caused the large lizard to plow into the debris and injure itself more than once.

Once the last group had cleared the gauntlet, the Vice-Admiral had descended from her podium to stand facing the cadets. Monika climbed down off of Desmond's shoulders at Dianne's urging, given that they had more notice this time that the officer was about to address the cadets.

"All right, Cadets. I hope this has been informative for all of you. Begin planning how you think your team will work best. As most of you do not know your specializations yet, now is the time to experiment and think. You will be running practice sessions soon with experienced teams from the standard army to expose you to firsthand experience. To those of you who will be going on the Rift observation with the second years, return to your rooms. A standard armor kit has been provided and is waiting for you there. You will receive your orders of whom to report to shortly. Get geared up and head to the port shuttle bays. You have twenty minutes, so don't dawdle. The rest of you are dismissed!" The Vice-Admiral snapped off a salute before stalking away. Moments later, the instructors descended on the cadets to begin chasing them out of the practice range.

"Well, this is going to be interesting."

"What is?" Monika prodded Desmond as the trio of them joined the flow of cadets heading back to their various dorms. "Don't tell me you actually cleared that damn obstacle course?"

"Okay, I won't tell you. But I will tell you all about the observation when I get back. Ow!" Desmond tried to dodge the punch, but Monika tagged him on the thigh with her fist and he feigned a limp for several feet before walking normally again.

"How, by all the glory of my petite buttocks, did you get past Throneblood?" Monika's oath made Desmond grin. "What? Something wrong?" Monika glared at him for a moment, but Desmond brushed it off. *She does have a nice butt, but I can't say that. Don't wanna make things weird.*

"Got lucky, was able to hide in one of the crawlspaces in the walls. What about you two?"

"I got herded into a dead end by two of the instructors. I couldn't find any of the crawlspaces that I'd fit in," Dianne sighed. Desmond was distracted from the conversation for a moment when his comm-cuff chimed and vibrated. Thankfully, Monika was too distracted discussing the exam to notice.

"Tre'shovak got me. That Aelfa is way too quiet!" groused Monika as well. "Fine, you better tell us all about the Rift then, Des! We won't get to see the inside of a Rift until after first selection, so it could be a month or more before we get a crack at it."

"I'll make sure to tell you both about it when I get back. I gotta run to get kitted up. I hope the armor is relatively intuitive or that SAUL can talk me through getting it on," Desmond said. He glanced at his cuff and noted that he had a message pending from Chloe, which made him smile.

"Oh, I'm sure if you have trouble suiting up, one of the girls would be happy to help you figure it out," Teased Monika with a saucy wink. Desmond rolled his eyes, catching the blush on Dianne's cheeks but not commenting on it.

She's gonna have to get used to Monika being salacious like that if she hangs around with us for long, Desmond thought before jogging away down the hall, hurrying to get his gear in order.

As he jogged down the hall, he opened the waiting message.

Hey! I heard from one of the girls that they are letting some of your first-years go on an observation? I told her she was full of it, but she insisted that her sister, who is a guard for a second-year, told her about it to rub it in her face. Is she serious?

Glancing around, Desmond ducked into an alcove in the hall to type out a quick response to Chloe.

Yep, I got tapped to go, actually. Apparently, the testing we did a bit ago was a ranking set and they are having the top group go on the observation. Should be safe enough though, since we'll be with full teams of the second-years and their guards.

Chloe's response popped through only seconds later. She'd clearly been waiting for him to respond.

Be safe, Des. The second years should have at least four guards to the adept, since that's minimal team size, I think. Have they been drilling you with weapons yet?

Nope, but I have 'Bolt', so I won't be helpless. I'll let you know how it goes. I promise I'll play it safe though. Gotta go get suited up, though. Talk to you later!

Desmond watched for a moment as the '...' showing him that Chloe was typing a reply popped up, then vanished.

Then popped up again, only to vanish again. This occurred three more times over the course of a minute before a simple message came through.

Okay, stay safe. Was all it read.

"Darn, half hoped she'd offer to come help me get geared up," Desmond chuckled to himself. The bawdy joke that Monika had made was still lurking in his mind.

Would that be so bad, though? He thought while he finished the jog to his rooms, remembering the curve of Chloe's bust when he'd seen her last and the look of genuine concern on her face for him. They had talked off and on, and he'd flirted with her a bit, but the impression he got from her messages was that she didn't know how to handle it.

I'll try again later. She seems like a sweet gal, regardless, he resolved.

CHAPTER 19

Rifts are weird things. Mana seems to take it as a challenge to confuse the observer, but Rifts make it personal. They are basically pockets of folded reality caused by the accumulation of large amounts of mana. That mana then causes a bulge in reality like a cyst in a healthy body. We have to drain those cysts before they kill the host. The downside is that the host in question is reality itself.
~Astrid Wristbreaker, Adept and
Doctor aboard Valor's Bid.

The standard issue armor was, thankfully, easy to put on. It consisted of an armored jacket with a double breast that had reinforcements built throughout the jacket much like a motocross jacket had, but with more hard plates attached throughout and a high, rigid collar. The leg armor strapped into place over top of his uniform pants, attaching to and hanging from a harness that was built into the bottom edges of the jacket much like chausses for plate armor.

Once he had it on, Desmond followed the directions that had been sent to his comm-cuff and jogged down to meet the second year team that was escorting him in the hangar. Desmond saw a handful of other cadets moving through the hallway, some of them just carrying bits of the armor kit and others fully geared like him.

Arriving in the cavernous hangar, Desmond split off and headed for Pad 11. The shuttle was already parked there and the second years were standing around it, checking over each other's gear while they waited.

"Cadet McLaughlin, reporting as ordered." Desmond

saluted the entire group after coming to a stop outside the 'stand clear' line painted on the decking around the shuttle. The group was a larger one, consisting of the adept and six guards. The adept of the group was a vulpine Taari with delicate red-gold fur that shimmered in the bright lights of the landing bay.

"Well met, Cadet McLaughlin. You are in excellent hands for this trip. My girls will make sure you stay nice and safe while you get a taste of the Rifts. Right, girls?" The regulars all nodded as one, broad smiles on their faces. Two were kitted out with standard rifles, two with heavy weapons, and the last two were clearly kitted as skirmishers.

"Like hell we'd let a guy get hurt on our watch. Much less an underclassman," grunted a stout canine Taari as she swung what looked like a chunky machine gun up onto her shoulder.

"Right? He's far too cute to let him get his first scars because one of us fucked up," snickered a slender Se'Aelfa. She was checking and rechecking the pistol on her hip before clearing the saber on the other side.

"Have you ever been in a firefight? Any combat at all?" The adept that led the group stepped closer to him, her bright red-gold tail flicking back and forth slowly as she crowded Desmond just a bit, hooking her arm through his elbow and drawing him into the group. "Need to know if you might freeze up on me out there, Cadet."

The second year was gentle in her inquiry, but firm and Desmond relaxed slightly. He'd been worried that they would pick at him like Olianna had, but that fear was laid to rest as the others settled into a perimeter around them as naturally as one could hope. Though several of the girls seemed to be standing a bit close to him for being in the spacious hanger, several bumped their buttocks against him 'innocently' and it was distracting as hell.

"Never an actual firefight. Did some war-games a few times with friends, but nothing more than high-speed paintball or digital games. I'm familiar enough with most firearms that I won't be a liability."

"Ooh, we got ourselves a warrior-prince, girls!" The other heavy weapon bearer, he guessed her to be an ursine Taari, crowed loudly, her sharp teeth sparkling in her short muzzle. "No lily-handed, mincing fop this time!" Desmond couldn't help matching her smile before turning back to the adept.

"Dunno if they would issue me a weapon or not, but I'd rather carry if given a choice, Adept…?"

"Sorry about that. You can call me Adept Marsden or just Marsden. Your class hasn't gone over weapons training yet, am I right?"

"No. Instructor Throneblood had us on the range yesterday to practice *Bolt* for the first time."

"Then you haven't been issued your sidearm yet. Until you get it issued, it's against regulations to lend you something. Sorry Cadet McLaughlin." Adept Marsden had an expression of genuine regret on her lupine features, but Desmond waved it off.

"That's fine. It's more of a matter of comfort for me, anyway. I'll focus on staying out of the way. Even if you could lend me something, I'd be worried about throwing off a dynamic since I'm not part of your regular group."

"Smart lad, he is," grunted one of the two Hyreh to the other. They were both armed with the standard rifle kits and looked like they could be sisters, especially standing next to each other. "Don't worry, we'll make sure you get back to the ship in one piece. Just listen closely."

"They are right. Trust in us. We've done this before. The big thing is to keep moving and stick close to me. I'll be running in the middle of the formation." Adept Marsden, who still had her arm through his, gave his biceps a squeeze. "Let's get loaded up. Come on girls, if you haven't got it secured now, it isn't important enough that we can't live without it." The group all gave a cheer of assent before they piled into the shuttle and shuffled into position.

Desmond ended up sandwiched between Adept Marsden and the other one of the skirmishers, a heavily muscled Dwerg woman whose weapon of choice was a pair of long-barreled pistols that connected via an ammo belt to a rounded pack she wore on her back like a tortoise shell. Desmond wanted to ask more questions, but he didn't want to interrupt the patter as the group began tossing information back and forth once they were secured, so he just listened in.

"Okay girls, the veterans out of *On Wings of Fire* stated that the Rift had swollen to where the clock was ticking, but not that an evac order was necessary," Marsden explained. She had yet to relinquish her hold on his arm, and Desmond wasn't really fighting to get it back. "Report I got was that the Rift is primarily filled with earth mana and creatures, so make sure you are loading AP or aiming for joints to cut past the armor. Watch for traps as well. The environment on the far side of the Rift is in the pattern of a hollowed out asteroid. Think 'empty mining colony'."

"So, no explosives then?" grunted the Se'Aelfa with a disappointed look on her sharp face.

"No. Negative on the explosives. Our team is on a sweep and clear while escorting Cadet McLaughlin. I don't need to state this, but his safety is priority one. We do not want to be the girls that got a fresh recruit hurt or killed, so no racing off to scoop something up. We move as a group, loot as a group, and leave as a group. Last report I have is from half an hour ago and it stated that the veterans off the freelance ship had cleared what they suspected to be the first half of the complex but it was taking long enough that they wanted back up to sweep through while they focused on pushing to the Core and pacifying it."

"Ugh. Of course they did. Means they get to tag or harvest the Core, while we get left with whatever bits and pieces are in the wings," sighed one girl out of Desmond's line of sight. "Still. It's good for the first year, right?"

"Right. So standard formation and don't deviate. Got any questions for me, Cadet?" Marsden turned her attention back to Desmond, her eyes piercing him abruptly and he stared for a moment before he shook it off and was able to come up with a question. Two of them, actually, as a second jumped to mind as well.

"Two questions, really. What did you mean by 'Core'?" he asked first, wanting to pin down the newest question before he forgot it.

"All Rifts form around a 'Core' of super dense mana. It tends to crystallize towards the center of the Rift and acts as an 'anchor' to the rest of the Rift. High-value stuff: pure, crystallized mana. It's what they use to create the emergency mana-gas inhalers that you can buy from the Armory in case you need a pick-me-up mid run. Though using a Core for that is a waste, as they also can be processed into the focusing lenses of the more powerful ship-grade weapons too. It's one of the few times you'll find non-aspected, solid state mana. And the monsters inside the Rift fight hard to protect it, since they are drawn to sources of strong mana. It's the adept's job to find, pacify, and secure the Core, since we are the only ones that are safe to approach it. The *Valor's Bid* has a trained team of harvesters who come in to collect them, but you'll learn later in years how to do it safely. Do not let your guards near it. They will die from the sheer amount of mana it puts out," Marsden explained quickly. "Next question?"

"What sort of specialty do you have?"

"Ooh going right for the juicy bits, aren't ya? Normally I'd wanna show off for a guy first, but I'll spill for you." Marsden shot him a coy look that was interrupted by the sniggers from several of the other girls. She turned to glare at them for a moment before looking back at Desmond. "To be honest, I don't have a specialty, though my style relies on enhancing the girls while saving my big damage for larger enemies. So, if you wanna see me in action, watch my girls for most of the run unless we run into something that is resistant to conventional weaponry. Now, none of you wenches can say I never did anything for you." The last part she shot at the rest of her team, which elicited a laugh from them all this time.

<><><>

The group continued to banter for a bit, with familiar jabs being passed back and forth between the girls. Desmond was so caught up in it all that he didn't even notice the telltale rumble of the shuttle taking off. What did catch his attention was the sharp tingle that suddenly raced over his skin before being sucked down into his dynamo, which began to whirl a little faster.

"Ugh, that still makes my butt pucker even now," growled the Se'Aelfa. Desmond had to fight to keep the smile off his face. He'd had the idea that Aelfa were 'delicate' creatures forcibly ejected from his mind after watching some of the different varieties of them in the mess hall, but she'd been even more blunt than others.

"All right, girls. You know what that means," Marsden called. She released his arm from hers and unhooked her helmet from where it clipped to her belt before tugging it over her head. A clear faceplate allowed Desmond to still see her through it, though her ears were pressed flat to the top of her skull. All around him, the regulars were securing helmets as well and doing a last weapons check.

"Do I get a helmet?" Desmond prodded as they got ready. Marsden chuckled and reached up to squeeze a toggle on his collar. A brief flash of energy surrounded Desmond's head before the barrier faded from sight.

"That's all you get today, Cadet. You are in light armor, after all. Don't want you getting any ideas. The force-field will keep you safe without blocking vision as well."

"Touching down in three, two, one." The voice of their nameless pilot came through the intercom and this time, Desmond felt a solid bump as they settled and the door beside Marsden slammed down. The two skirmishers were the first ones out, followed by the rifle team, then Marsden tugged him out while the heavy weapons girls came out last.

"I take it we are already inside the Rift?" Desmond asked, staying close to Marsden as the group fanned out slightly around them.

"Yup, that tingle you felt coming in was us breaching the barrier to the Rift. We are officially in a folded pocket of space," Marsden replied. Her hands flicked back and forth as she wove spells. The weapons of the surrounding mundanes took on a glow as the enhancements settled into place.

Leaving her to her work, Desmond took a slow, deep breath to center himself and surveyed the landing zone.

A half dozen other shuttles had settled in around them and groups were forming up as well. The space they were in was an irregular, oblong cavern hewn out of a sandy gray rock and illuminated by the spotlights of the shuttle and a dull glow that emanated from all around them. The ground underfoot was more of the same rough stone and irregular in texture. A trio of large tunnels pierced the far wall of the cavern and led off in different directions. Back the way they came yawned an iridescent, wavering veil of light that was one and a half times the size of a football field.

The entrance to the Rift..., Desmond thought in awe. That shimmering bubble was the only thing between them and the vacuum. He'd heard from the second-years that the Rift had formed on the side of an asteroid, so there was no atmosphere for them outside of this environment. *Good thing I have the atmosphere from the helmet...* he did not want to think what might happen if the Rift collapsed. A bit of experimenting confirmed that he didn't have anything to worry about from suffocation, at least at the moment, as the force-field projected a basic Heads-up Display with half an hour of oxygen listed for emergency and a tiny blinking reminder that a safe atmosphere was detected so it was held in reserve. *Wish I knew where the tank was stored, or maybe it's just 'magic'.*

Once the group was clear of the hatch, the shuttle's door folded closed and the ship lifted up vertically before scooting in reverse to exit back through the shimmering veil. The wash of pressure from the thrusters stirred Desmond's clothes, and he was momentarily distracted by it.

"Come on, Cadet," Marsden's voice called him back to reality, and a gentle hand on his back got him moving. "We gotta clear the landing zone. There's another wave of teams coming in."

"Is it normal to have this many teams heading into a Rift like this?" Desmond asked as the entire group trotted clear of the landing zone, just as another shuttle came zipping in behind them to thump down in the spot they had just cleared.

"No. Usually Rifts are maybe one to six teams, but the reports stated it was unusually large. I guess that is part of why the teams from *On Wings of Fire* called for backup. Now, once we go into the tunnels, don't argue. Me and the girls will keep you as safe as possible, but if you don't listen, you can still get hurt or killed. Keep right on my ass and let my girls do their jobs."

"Got it, Adept," Desmond shot back as the group came to a halt outside of the far left tunnel. One team had already disappeared into it and another team queued up behind them.

"Good. The first team will follow the tunnel till it branches, then mark which branch they took. We follow after and do the same as soon as it branches. From there we leap-frog. Once we play out a branch, we double back and take the next unmarked branch. Your comm-cuff can send a distress call. You know the code for it?" Desmond nodded, sparing a glance down at the unit on his arm before looking up again. "Good, don't touch it unless one of the girls goes down and needs evac, or you get separated. You wanna be useful?" Desmond nodded again, keeping his eyes moving as he listened to the adept. "Millie, pack!"

The ursine Taari behind him dug into her armor before extracting a folded up duffel style pack that she tossed to Marsden, who tossed it to Desmond.

"You are in charge of carrying any loot we find. Firsties don't normally get a cut from this, but I'll give you ten percent of my share if you hump the bag so the girls can stay focused on guarding us. They'll collect shit and pass it to you. One of the first things I got the girls was shielded gloves so they can handle the mana infused shit they find for short times. Anything else, you or I have to go 'hands on'. Make sure to keep your senses open. One of the other reasons they send us adepts into the Rifts is our 'mana sense'. While the girls have to rely on mechanical means, we can feel the pressure of mana a lot finer. You and I might sense something that they miss." The flirty tone she used made Desmond's ears burn, but it turned back to serious just as fast.

"Glad to help. I remember what you said earlier: stay as a group, no separating to loot. I'm just going to carry the bag and stick tight to your ass."

"Good man. All right girls, let's find us some trouble." The regulars all let out low cheers and, as one, the group charged into the open mouth of the tunnel, clicking on shoulder mounted lights as they went.

CHAPTER 20

Proper preparation prevents getting stabbed in the ass by a pissed off Rift monster.
~Millie Sanders, Adept-Guard to Iris Marsden.

The ambient light died rapidly and Desmond was grateful for the broad beam lights that the guards all had on their gear. *Gotta remember that, just in case it's not part of the standard kit. Wouldn't be surprised if it's one of those things that doesn't come standard just to test folks.* The tunnel that they followed wound back and forth several times before splitting in three directions, one heading down and to the right, one going left, and the other continuing straight ahead. The first team had marked the left-hand tunnel with a long streak of reflective silver paint.

"Take the right," called Marsden. The group pivoted and angled down and to the right, smoothly. As they entered the offshoot tunnel, Marsden pulled a stout cylinder from her belt and marked the wall with a streak of paint as well, hers being a brilliant yellow. "When we come back and have cleared the offshoot, we strike through the mark. That way, the survey knows that side is cleared," she explained before tucking the cylinder back into its slot on her belt. "Each team is issued a different color at the start as well."

"Got it. Anything I should keep my eyes open for?" Desmond kept to an easy trot with the group. He was wearing lighter armor and the shorter stride of the Dwerg in the lead ensured that the pace was something he could keep.

Going to need to do more cardio training...as if the assessment earlier today wasn't proof enough of that. Desmond thought as they turned a corner and the tunnel branched out again to the left and right. *Still need to check the results, forgot to do that earlier.*

"Keep right," Marsden called directions and drew another stripe of paint as they passed that wall. "Eyes on everything, you're here to learn. Leave looting to the girls. You feel threatened by something, you confirm you have a clear line of fire before you unload *Bolt* into it. Got it?"

"Throneblood hasn't cleared anyone for independent practice on that yet." Desmond hated to admit it, but he didn't want Marsden to get in trouble over it either, given that she'd refused to lend him a gun earlier.

"Didn't ask that, Cadet. Down here in the tunnels, my word goes. You get a clear lane of fire and feel threatened? Drop the hammer and send it," Marsden replied with a wink.

"Trust the Adept. We got you covered. We know better than to step into the line of fire, and that's not exactly a sneaky spell for any adept," added the canine Taari from behind him. He was about to respond when the distant rumble of weapons' fire echoed through the tunnels from behind them.

"Stay sharp, girls. Some others already found playmates. Remember, no markings from the teams out of *Wings of Fire*, so this area is considered hostile until we secure it."

Marsden's words proved to be a herald of warning as only a handful of seconds later, the two in the lead opened fire with pistols as the tunnel opened into a larger room and they fanned out to either side. Moving with a practiced precision, the two Hyreh followed up, sliding into position at the center of the formation with the two skirmishers spread out to either side of them. Marsden slid to a stop in the very middle with Desmond right behind her and the heavys taking position right behind them.

The natural cave that they had stopped in was filled with thick stalactites and stalagmites that threw dancing shadows on the walls from the rapidly moving spotlights each of the girls carried. The rock was powdery and dry, showing that they were formed long ago, though several had a translucent hue to them. Desmond was more concerned with the leaping forms that bounced between the rock outcroppings.

The creatures looked like a nightmare fusion between a goblin and some sort of spider. A stumpy pair of legs sat at the bottom of the body while between four and nine chitinous legs sprouted from the torso to propel them forward. The head bore a razor-edged maw filled with teeth under a trio of dull red eyes. Their resemblance to goblins was only vague at best, but it still gave Desmond chills and he immediately began to cycle his mana to be ready to throw a *Bolt* out if the need presented itself.

The fight was over in only moments, with the precise shots of the front four of the team putting down the scuttling horrors without issue.

"Room appears clear. Secure it," ordered Marsden and the two skirmishers peeled off, darting forward and scouting ahead. There was only a single burst of gunfire from out of sight before they returned a moment later.

"Confirmed clear, the tunnel continues on the other side," the Dwerg said before tossing a lump of what looked like quartz at Desmond. He caught it more out of instinct and nearly dropped the cluster of smoke-white crystals. No sooner had his hand touched them, than the whole cluster vibrated slightly against his skin, even through the thin, armored gloves he was wearing.

"Good find. Tuck that away, Cadet," Marsden urged before sending her team forward with a gesture. Desmond did as ordered after staring at the humming crystal for a second more. *So this is what crystallized mana looks like...I can feel the pressure and buzzing of the mana from it. Guess what Marsden said earlier makes sense now.*

<><><>

They cleared four more rooms after that before doubling back to the second branch, the girls taking it in turns to clear and secure each of the rooms of the squat spider-creatures. They'd only found the initial cluster of crystals and a lumpy stone that hummed with a quiet resonance that continued long after it was touched. Marsden advised him that it was likely a geode of some kind, given the high concentration of earth aligned mana in the Rift right now.

"We can crack it open once we are back on the ship and see what is inside. Better to do that in a contained environment anyway. Sometimes they have less than fun surprises tucked away inside them."

"Like what?" Desmond inquired as they backtracked to the branch. He could still feel the geode vibrating through the pack against his back.

"Poison gas, sometimes dangerous insects or caustic liquids. It acts odd, so it comes back to the academy. If it's something that can be refined for something useful, we get paid for it."

"And there's nothing on the creatures that is useful?" Desmond cringed internally at the idea of having to root through the corpses, but he wanted to make sure that he had all the information he could.

"Naw, not on chaff like these. Something bigger maybe. You can usually tell if a critter has something useful on it since either they'll throw magic around too, glow in strange ways, or you can feel the emanations." Marsden paused to strike through their initial mark on the right-hand tunnel before they routed down the left. "Or you can sense it. You'll be able to feel the vibrations of the mana. It's how I track important stuff. The girls have learned to spot most things out of habit nowadays, though, so I let them collect it."

The left-hand branch took them for another hundred yards before opening up into a much larger cavern space that yawned away in all directions. Exiting the tunnel mouth, the guard team promptly took up an oval formation around the two adepts. The skirmishers up front, the assault on either side and the heavies anchoring the back of the formation.

"Opens up quite a bit. Looks like it has a drop off ahead as well. Gonna put a flare out in the middle of the room to see if we can't scare up whatever the hell is in here. Be ready," Marsden called before she began to murmur an incantation under her breath.

A pinpoint of light formed in her right hand that Marsden then lobbed forward. Desmond had the intelligence to not look directly at the dot, looking off to his left as the light bloomed into a hovering globe that filled the room with a bright red-orange light.

What the flare revealed was something Desmond would have been happier not seeing.

The cavern they were in went even further back than the light revealed clearly in many directions, the flare's light only barely showing the shape of the ceiling directly above them. The entire space was shaped vaguely like an egg laid on its side and they had entered around the midpoint. Gently, the floor sloped away before vanishing into a cliff some two hundred yards ahead of them.

It was hundreds of reflective red eyes that suddenly lit up in the dark around the far side of the chasm that had sent chills down Desmond's spine and he heard several of the mundanes curse around him.

"Spawning room. Looks like we have a horde on our hands. Even money on their being something big and nasty down that cleft. Funnel them into our heavy weapons girls. I'll lock down our backs first, then add in. No explosives for now. We are still in a cave system," Marsden growled. The playfulness that had haunted her voice for most of the trip so far vanished.

"Additional ingress above, keep a wary eye up in case some of them flank in," called the Se'Aelfa, drawing Desmond's eyes away from the shifting mass of reflective dots and up. Several other tunnel mouths gaped open at irregular intervals along the rough wall and Desmond noted them. He could keep an eye on those while the girls laid down the heavy fire.

The mundanes worked like a well-oiled machine, shifting spots around so that he and Marsden dropped to the back of the pack and they swept off to either side. Rather than clumping up shoulder to shoulder, the girls spread out, ensuring they each had a bubble of space around them and limbered their melee weapons and checked ammo counts on their primary weapons.

"Skirmishers, hang back for now. Let the girls with range bring them in. You all know the drill," Marsden ordered before she began to chant again.

The scrabbling of claws on stone was loud enough that Desmond couldn't hear what she was saying, but what it was doing was rather obvious as the walls on either side slowly extended to cover the outer flanks in a low wall. A shifting under his feet as well drew his attention behind them to where the tunnel narrowed such that it was only one person wide.

"Give the signal, Marsden. We are in position," called the canine Taari. She'd deployed a long-legged bipod for her machine gun to steady it and stood ready behind the weapon. A thumb-thick blue cable ran from one side of the stubby weapon to a pack held low on her back that he could feel the humming from there.

"All right, girls. Send the hate!" Marsden called a moment later as she finished securing their rear, and her team was happy to oblige.

Desmond had seen the other four of Marsden's girls lay into the enemy before. Until that point, the two heavy weapons troopers hadn't actually fired their weapons yet. He learned why at that moment.

The canine Taari let out a howl that was matched by her weapon a moment later. While the other four all had weapons that fired some manner of solid projectile, the canine Taari's weapon launched what Desmond could only describe as a pulsing stream of lasers. The blue beams seared brilliantly across the room, carrying a corona of purple light from where they clashed with the light of the flare around them and overpowered it. The beams both illuminated and decimated the skittering swarm of spider-legged horrors that was approaching them. Enemies fell in squealing waves that only grew more numerous as the other girls added in with their weapons.

Beside Desmond, the ursine Taari's weapon coughed twice, sending oblong shapes arcing up and over the wave of enemies to crash to the ground in the ranks further back. A moment later, a wave of violet flames washed out, outlining the creatures like gruesome torches as they began to flail about while the flames ate away at them. The flames gave another point of illumination in the room and Desmond swallowed, his heart pounding in his chest. More of the spider creatures were boiling up out of the crevice ahead of them and swelling in their direction like a wave.

"If you have a clear lane of fire, add in, Cadet. There are plenty of targets for everyone," Marsden grunted from one side. She made a sharp gesture with both hands, like she was kneading dough. A moment later, the ground in front of their formation boiled sharply and spines of stone shifted and rose up from the ground for a dozen yards or more, creating a deadly bulwark between them and the charging mass.

"Got it, Adept," Desmond called over the chaos. He took a moment to check on each of the regulars, none of which looked concerned as they methodically tracked and fired on their targets. A check above confirmed that the walls were clear and there was no sign of the enemy moving to change that. "Okay Desmond. You got this. More than you expected today, but this is literally what you are training for."

Taking the stance that was as familiar to him as breathing, Desmond sucked a breath in through his nose as he sighted down on a clump of approaching enemies. *Don't know what kind of range Bolt has. It acted just like my axes normally on the range. There isn't any weight to it, so the strength behind the throw isn't what propels it...standard throw to start.*

"Kill shot," Desmond murmured. The cycling mana flowing out of his fingertips to form the silhouette of an axe in his hand that he lobbed forward. The spell arched up slightly before slamming low into the legs of the front runner of the group he had been aiming at. Unfortunately, the blow didn't do more than shear off the tip of one of its leading legs and make the creature stumble.

"Good shot, Cadet. Again! But more *oomph* this time," Marsden urged from nearby. A moment later, a wedge-shaped javelin that crackled with lightning arced away to crash and explode amongst the same group, the crawling forks of lightning cooking half a dozen of them in one go. "Remember, these have thicker armor than standard because it was earth oriented mana that gave rise to them."

"Got it." Desmond doubled the infusion, still taking the time to properly direct his mana before launching the *Bolt*. This time, it plowed a straight line from his hand to the enemy with a whistling hiss, shattering the armored chestplate of the creature and blowing it backwards into its allies.

"That's it, Cadet! Keep it up! If you need to rest, step back behind one of the girls," Marsden encouraged, forming another crackling javelin of energy before launching it forward.

"I'm happy to provide cover for ya, boy. Just don't distract me by getting grabby," chuckled Millie, the ursine Taari, shooting Desmond a wink that looked both macabre as well as flirty in the flashing light of the battlefield. She underscored the macabre by launching another series of canisters into the swelling wave of chittering horrors, creating a bulwark of chemical flames and forcing them to flow around it.

Desmond winked back before focusing on what he was doing. They had a relatively ideal killing field, with a mostly open space between them and the chasm that these creatures were originating from. For the moment, the massed fire of the girls was keeping them from pushing closer than about fifty yards. The mass of enemies would swell and push forward before a well placed spell from Marsden would break the charge and combined fire would drive them back. He had no idea how long they'd been fighting. It was likely only minutes, but it felt like an eternity had passed. He kept count of the only thing that he could focus on at the moment.

Twenty-one. Desmond thought as the *Bolt* left his hand, whirling across the empty space in a wheel of flashing blue light before it split the head of one of the creatures. *Twenty-two.* The next *Bolt* missed the creature he had aimed for but sunk into the side of the neck of one directly behind it. His mana was draining fast, but he could feel his dynamo spinning away, pulling and refining fresh mana from the rich environment they occupied.

A brief movement on the edge of his vision drew Desmond's gaze upwards to the ceiling. The scuttling creatures had finally changed tactics.

"Up high," Desmond shouted. He angled his torso back and launched the *Bolt* spell upwards at the group, pushing another double of the power into it so it would make the distance. Marsden tracked the whirling spell upwards to spot the ripple of enemies moving across the ceiling.

"I got them. Ches, Miri, you two are on ceiling duty," Marsden replied, sending her next lightning javelin into the ceiling.

This time, the spell detonated short of the actual ceiling, but the dancing corona of bolts expanded even further than before. Dozens of the crawling beasties seized up and dropped from the ceiling to land with sickening squishing and popping noises. The two Hyreh shifted their fire to picking off the crawlers on the ceiling and the surging horde ahead of them pushed even closer to the group.

"Power cells are getting low," called the canine Taari. "Need a minute to swap it out."

"Empty the cell and swap it out. Cover her," Marsden called from her position in the back of the group. Sweat matted the vulpine Taari's facial fur as she continued to conjure her lightning javelins with both hands.

The steady 'pop-pop-pop' from the pistols of the two skirmishers doubled up. A moment later there was an even brighter flash of the heavy repeating laser as the canine Taari drained the last of the power out of her unit before reaching back to shift the cable around on her pack to another on the same side. The barrel of her weapon was glowing a dull red that made Desmond worried.

That kind of heat on a regular machine gun would give them a warped barrel. I can only imagine it's worse on something like a laser where all the power comes from heat.

The concerns were resolved a moment later when the weapon picked up firing again, allowing Marsden a moment of breathing room. Rather than launching another of her lightning-infused javelins, a cool blue glow surrounded the weapon and a ghostly cable arced back to the ammo pack on the small of the canine Taari's back. The formerly black energy cell began to glow again, the small charging meter beginning to fill.

"How the hell?" Desmond mumbled as he drew the mana together for another *Bolt*.

"Heat is just energy, redirecting it back to the battery. Can't do it too often or risk the battery. But this is necessary," Marsden panted next to him. The adept pulled a vial full of glittering dust from the inside of her armor and dumped it into her hand. Desmond felt the tug from his dynamo increase and immediately recognized it as powdered mana crystal. Marsden caught his look and shook her head as she popped open her faceplate before tossing the small mound in her hand into her mouth and swallowing. "Sorry, Cadet.

Can't risk giving any to you. Too easy for you to overdraw. Would be different if I had an inhaler, but didn't bring one. How are your reserves?"

"Sixty-ish percent? Haven't had a chance to check the comm-cuff, but I know it's closer to three quarters than half."

"All right, don't draw below fifty. You are contributing, but it's not so dire you should risk it. If we have to, we can fall back to the tunnel and use that as a funnel." Marsden perked up almost immediately and launched another of her crackling bolts of lightning.

The horde was pushed back again, the falling enemies from above helping to thin the ranks some when they landed on their compatriots. Their numbers were inexhaustible, though, and the creatures seemed more than happy to build bulwarks out of the bodies of their fallen. The only thing that kept them from piling too high was the chemical fires that Millie kept setting with her launcher, turning the piles of bodies into smoldering wrecks that were eventually toppled as another wave pushed on them.

"We need to push forward. There has to be a nest or something in the chasm," called one of the girls, Desmond was too distracted to tell which, as he lobbed his *Bolt* up into another of the creatures on the ceiling.

"I can get an angle on it to drop some party favors into the chasm," shouted Millie as she laid out another barrier of chemical flames.

"Didn't want to risk damaging any loot down there, but we gotta do something. Do it," Marsden responded. "Low yield only, go for maximum spread. See if we can't pen them in."

Millie grunted and fumbled with her pack for several moments before she loaded the first one into her weapon.

"Ranging with air-burst," she called and popped off her first shot. Desmond watched as the round arched upwards and was lost in the darkness for a moment before it shattered with a bright pop and cut down a swath of the scrabbling horde just shy of the chasm. "Got the range. Sending the heat."

The light in the cavern tripled after only a handful of seconds as the area around the chasm was saturated with violet flames that stuck to the stone and flesh alike. The ground underfoot rumbled as something let out a piercing shriek inside the chasm that was picked up by the smaller creatures.

"Sounds like we woke up the momma. Clean up the field, girls." The regulars shouted wordless agreement to Marsden and kept at their grim work, their rate of fire increasing as the skirmishers deployed grenades as well now that low-yield explosives had been approved. "Hold up, Cadet. Save your juice for the big one. The girls rely on me to crack shells for things like this."

"I don't think we are going to be able to clear all the little ones." Desmond kept his voice steady as he leaned back against the wall, mopping the sweat from his face. He hadn't realized how hot it was getting until he stopped to take a breather.

"Don't have to. The girls will keep clearing them out whenever the big ugly shows its face. Once we get eyes on, we can figure out what to do next. We got this, Cadet. The girls and I have been in tighter spots. Remember, we can drop back into the tunnel and turn that into a killing floor as well."

"Got it." Another flash of movement above caught Desmond's eye, and he flinched, twisting to look up while summoning another *Bolt* to his hand on instinct.

Several bright beams of light emerged from one of the tunnel mouths in the wall above them before weapons fire began raking the critters off the ceiling even faster.

"Sounds like one of the other teams finally caught up through a different tunnel," Marsden laughed. "Was too much to hope that we'd get to hog the whole thing. Still, we've got a hell of a score so far on the ground and first claim to anything loose. Eyes forward, big momma is showing."

Snapping his eyes back to where the chasm was, Desmond saw that the violet chemical fires were burning low, and the ridged back of something massive was pushing up and over the chasm edge.

CHAPTER 21

I'd say that I've been sold a false bill of goods about being an adept-guard. The recruiter said that I'd see sights that others can only dream of. I bought into the lie; bolt, washer, and screw. The bitch never mentioned that those 'dreams' she mentioned were nightmares.
~Overheard in a bar frequented by off-duty adept-guards.

The multiple sources of light bounced off the iridescent carapace of the larger creature, giving it a mottled appearance. They also made it harder to see the creature's outline until another of the napalm rounds landed on it and the fire outlined its shape.

Rather than just a larger version of the creatures they had been slaughtering wholesale, the bigger creature leaned more towards the insect aspect. Its body was as long as a city bus, with at least a dozen tree-trunk legs emerging from each side, each ending in deadly spikes that dug deep into the stone as it shifted and turned. The front end split open like the mouth of a flower but lined with teeth in a fashion that reminded Desmond of an old horror movie about tunneling worm monsters. Rather than a rubbery hide, the entire thing was sheathed in articulating chitin that struck sparks as it deflected rounds from both teams.

The massive creature let out a low bellow that made the floor vibrate before it began to shamble towards Desmond and the group along the floor. A fresh wave of the smaller creatures flowed around the larger one, parting like a wave around a rock and giving it plenty of space. The reason was quickly illustrated, as it did not step lightly, stomping one of the smaller creatures to pieces that didn't get out of its way fast enough.

"Whenever you are ready, Adept," called the Dwerg as the horde of smaller creatures closed the distance. They were moving even faster than before, as if bolstered by the presence of the larger creature. The Dwerg and Se'Aelfa were firing into the horde as fast as they could while the canine Taari was sweeping her fire back and forth in a steady stream over the group, trying to get ahead of the larger creature.

"Mars, the sooner the better," added the Se'Aelfa, yanking her scimitar out and readying herself as they grew closer.

Desmond steadied himself and launched his *Bolt* spell into the head of the gigantic creature. The glittering mana axe sparked off its hard shell as well, vanishing in a puff of mana a moment later.

Gotta put more oomph into it again. Desmond thought, pushing mana into his hand faster and fighting to focus as the ground shifted under his feet, nearly losing it as Marsden finally let fly with her spell, having been focusing the entire time.

While before, the bolts she had been throwing were more akin to a javelin in size, what rocketed forward from the slight vulpine Taari was more akin to a missile of pure electric fury. It crossed the sixty meters left between the adept and the creature in a flash and impacted with a boom, sending the beast stumbling to one side and tearing off a section of its armored carapace the size of a sedan along one side and entirely severing one of its legs.

Taking aim at the opening, Desmond sent the overcharged axe he'd held ready into the opening. The blade sunk deep into the wound, but the massive creature barely reacted to the blow. Even with the armor stripped off, its sheer mass likely made it feel like nothing more than a pinprick.

"Come on, Marsden. You can do better than that," a haughty voice called from above them. A moment later, a swirling ball of fire impacted further back along the creature's spine, blowing off two of its legs and sending it to the ground while creating a shock-wave throughout the room. The adept for the other team had decided to finally join the fight.

"Watch the explosives!" snarled Marsden as bits of the shell rained down on them.

"Watch yourselves, our job is to bring these things down," called back the other adept as another sphere of flames crashed into the creature. The blow removed another section of carapace and kept it from getting back to its feet.

Desmond winced as several hunks of its carapace bounced off his armored chest, one causing his head to rock to one side but the energy field around his head robbing it of dangerous momentum.

"Shit, we need to bring it down fast before someone gets hurt from collateral," bit out Marsden, her hands making clawing motions as she gathered another larger spell together. Desmond silently agreed and focused, pushing more energy into his hands.

The mental image of his throwing axes had worked for shaping the *Bolt* before, but he needed something bigger. Just like Marsden's javelin became a missile, he needed to pack more energy into it. Even pushing the maximum he could into the construct earlier, it had only accepted roughly five percent of his cache before it stopped.

A memory of a different competition flipped through his head, and he shifted his stance with a grin. Rather than one hand over his shoulder, both hands met, one atop the other, and reared back behind his head. A large, double-bladed, felling axe formed out of mana, still green but growing darker by the second as Desmond poured more energy into it. Growling his incantation, Desmond took a half step to the side to get a clear shot and wrenched his whole body forward, levering the spell over his head and towards the enemy.

The axe actually swelled in size as it crossed the distance

rapidly before slamming into the opening that Marsden had made, nearly shearing through another 'petal' of its razor edged mouth now that the shell was broken. The creature shrieked in pain before the whole body lurched a third time in response to another searing ball of fire landing in the area clear of armor on its back. It let out a coughing, retching noise that made Desmond's heart race with hope that it was starting to die, but that was washed away a moment later as the creature spat something at the other group.

There was a crash of something impacting the stone above them, followed by a yelp of surprise. Desmond felt something bite into his shoulder a moment later and his whole left arm erupted in pain.

"Fuck! Cadet is hit with shrapnel," shouted Millie, turning towards Desmond with worry obvious in her eyes. "Do we fall back, Mars?" Marsden shook her head, in the middle of a chant at the moment. She made a gesture with her left hand that Desmond couldn't interpret. He was gritting his teeth against the pain at the moment.

Something was lodged in the meat of his left shoulder, coming in from the front and going through his upper trapezius, emerging just above his shoulder-blade. Turning his head slightly, Desmond caught sight of a wicked-looking shard of white ivory sticking up out of his shoulder and bit back the urge to scream.

It spat out a bunch of its damn teeth. The thought sent a shiver down Desmond's spine that was further reinforced by the spreading, sticky feeling down his back. A sick feeling in his gut made it hard to focus, and his vision went blurry.

A moment later, there was a series of muffled 'booms' that preceded another arc of yellow lightning. Distantly, he heard something collapse, which caused the ground to pitch beneath his feet, and Desmond swayed hard to stay upright.

"Shit, he got hit good. Looks like it ricocheted from above. Lucky that." He heard Marsden's voice from his right and turned slightly to try to focus on the other adept. "Easy now, the ricochet robbed it of a good amount of force, and your armor did what it could to blunt the hit, but it got you on a seam. Gonna need to extract it to get a look at the injury."

"Big momma?" Desmond croaked, his vision swimming as his gut churned. The air felt thick to him and he struggled to breathe. His dynamo rocked in his chest as it fought to draw in mana as well.

"Dead. Crammed a spell down its throat. I had meant to do it sooner, but the other dumb bints kept distracting it and I couldn't get a clear shot lined up," Marsden growled. She carefully began working the catches on Desmond's armor. "Hey, eyes on my tits. I know they aren't much to look at in this armor, but focus on me." She gripped his chin as his gaze tried to wander and forced Desmond to look down at her chest.

The rest of the regulars were mopping up the smaller creatures that had scattered now that the bigger one was dead. Desmond could hear cursing distantly. He guessed the other team was dealing with its own injuries, too.

"Gonna take off your jacket, focus on breathing, Cadet. This isn't gonna kill you, but it is gonna leave a scar," Marsden muttered as she finally got the catches on his armored jacket open and carefully began peeling it open where she could without jostling the injury. A quick swipe with her knife cut away his uniform shirt to lay the injury bare. "We are gonna have to pull that out to get you exposed. I have enough mana on hand to keep you from leaking out, but we are gonna have to backtrack to the shuttle to get you patched up."

"Loot..." Desmond shook his head. They'd worked for it. There had to be something valuable in this room to make it worth the effort. *Not going to cost them their bonus just because my dumb ass got hurt.*

"Nope. You need to be seen to, not gonna risk a cadet for a few extra credits," Marsden shot back. "Now focus, eyes on tits and breathe deep." Desmond did his best to focus on her compact breasts through the armor plates and sank automatically into the familiar breathing pattern of drawing in mana. He felt his dynamo lurch again as Marsden gripped the bone spike in his shoulder. "Sorry about this..." Marsden whispered before yanking the spike out.

Desmond screamed. There wasn't really any way around it. Even the semi-meditative state he'd assumed didn't do anything to blunt the pain as the serrated ivory spike emerged from his shoulder in a gout of blood. He felt something pinch in the pit of his stomach before a tingling sensation of mana washed out of his core and up to his arm. The second it hit the injury, he felt the pain fade and begin to cease.

"Oh, thank perky tits and all the good things in life," Desmond groaned. His head cleared abruptly as the minty sensation washed through his sinuses and he could see straight again. The other girls had formed a protective half circle around him but were casting worried glances over their shoulders while he was being seen to. "Thanks, Adept. That feels...great. I think I can keep going."

"What are you talking about? I haven't done...anything," Marsden trailed off. The spiky tooth still held in one hand. Her eyes darted from his face to his injury before going wide. "What the?"

"What? What's wrong?" The canine Taari turned to check on them, her nose wiggling as she sniffed the air. "Is he okay? There's so much blood I can't tell."

"He's...well look." A moment later, all six of the regulars were crowded around him. Desmond jumped when Marsden prodded his shoulder, a spike of pain washing through him but only a pale shadow of what had gone through him when she'd pulled the spike out. Craning his head, Desmond looked down to see the hole in his shoulder closing like a bulkhead irising shut. Blood had stopped flowing already and he could see muscle tissue pulling together as fresh skin slid over the injury.

"What the fuck?"

<><><>

In less than a minute, the wound was fully closed. Desmond stripped off his armored jacket and undershirt, to be sure, but none of the others could see any sign of the injury that had previously pierced his shoulder. Marsden swore up and down that she hadn't done anything to heal him yet, having literally just yanked the offending item out of his body. She'd insisted on cleaning the injury site to confirm he had no other injuries and that it was healing properly.

"Shatter me, how did you do that, Cadet?" Marsden pressed. Her eyes were hard as she stared at him.

"I don't know, Adept. First time that it has happened that I remember. All I can remember from that was the feeling of pain in my shoulder, my dynamo humming away to try to replace what I'd used during the fight, and then I felt a cool sensation wash through my body and the pain stopped. I thought that was you doing something."

"Again, I hadn't had the time to yet." Marsden stared down at Desmond's bloodied clothing for another long moment.

"What about his species? He does kinda look like an Aelfa. And you know how they are with weird mana reactions," prodded the Dwerg from the other side of him.

"He's most definitely not an Aelfa. He's not nearly skinny enough," huffed one of the other girls. Desmond couldn't tell which.

"Well, Cadet? Anything special about your species that we should know about?" Marsden asked quietly.

"Nothing special. I mean..." Desmond thought for a long moment before shrugging helplessly and spitting out the first thing that came to mind. "I mean, human's biological adaptations basically begin and end with simple things; we developed tools, we can eat pretty much anything, we were persistence predators relatively recently in the timescale of our species, and we heal quickly in comparison to other species on our homeworld."

"Healing quickly would count for this, you think?" Marsden came back from her thoughts with a glare.

"By quickly, I mean at all. It can take weeks for a small puncture to heal without assistance. A lot of other mammals on my homeworld wouldn't survive long enough to heal properly. A majority of our medical practices revolve around taking pills or cutting off whatever part is causing the problem, then focusing on letting the body heal it naturally," Desmond protested. "By all rights, that injury should have taken months to a year or more to heal back on Terra."

"Still. You are going to report this all to Medical. I'm sure they have a file going on humans already and they will need to document this. Especially if you are having some kind of reaction to the Rift. The last thing we need is for you to start mutating wildly," Marsden snapped before turning to scan the area.

Nearby, a thick metal cable had snaked down the wall and the other team was in the process of lowering themselves to the cavern floor. Marsden growled quietly, the fur on her tail bristling as she glared at them.

"Okay girls, split teams. Half with me, the other half stay with the cadet till he is presentable. Once he is, start casing the room. I want anything of value packed up before those greedy bitches get a chance at it." The vulpine Taari didn't wait for their response and began to march away from the group. Her team was clearly well trained as they split in half, the Dwerg, one of the Hyreh, and the ursine Taari going with her in a protective triangle formation while the others gathered around Desmond.

"You heard the boss. Get yourself sorted and we'll cover ya," the canine Taari said with a broad grin on her muzzle. The larger woman planted herself directly between Desmond and the other team, both blocking his view of them and their view of him while he struggled with the bloody and tattered armored jacket.

"How's the shoulder? Still tender?" The Hyreh, who had largely remained silent up till that point, asked, her voice surprisingly musical for someone so rough looking. She took up a position opposite the Se'Aelfa, the three of them forming a pretty solid bulwark with their backs to give him some privacy.

Only a little since all three are staring at me...eh fuck it, if they wanna stare, whatever. My pants aren't what was damaged.

Testing the shoulder gingerly, Desmond winced at a small twinge but could rotate it without problem and ended up stripping off what was left of his uniform top, it was soaked with blood anyway from the injury and shredded from where the adept had to cut it away, anyway.

"Woo, free show. Wish I had some credits on me," teased the Se'Aelfa with a wink at Desmond that nearly broke his resolve, but he shook it off, glancing down at his somewhat toned torso. He'd been doing his best to keep in shape and thankfully his old job had kept him from going too soft before coming here, but he wasn't a chiseled Adonis by any measure.

"Glad you like the show, but I'm not exactly impressive." Desmond shrugged, using the tattered remains of his shirt to mop as much of his blood off as possible before using a handful of what he could only describe as alcohol wipes that one guard had produced for Marsden while they were checking the injury earlier.

When he was as clean as he could get, Desmond piled the used wipes on top of his damaged uniform top and tossed them to one side of the doorway. The entire time he'd been cleaning up, he could hear Marsden arguing with the other team in a low snarl that echoed dully in the cavernous room. The magical flare she had lit still hung in the middle of the room, throwing macabre shadows.

"Here, let me get those. Get buttoned up." The canine

Taari gestured with her weapon and Desmond raised an eyebrow. "You shouldn't leave anything with clean genetic material behind in a Rift if you can help it. Blood being one of those things, especially not adept blood. Something about the mana causing issues, Marsden can tell you more. I just know she always has us incinerate any medical supplies from treating ourselves or her."

"Noted, go ahead." Desmond gestured for her to do it and the small pile of cloth was soon just glowing embers from the laser impacts. "I gotta see about getting training on one of those. Big guns have always interested me." Desmond said with a half smile, deciding to tease back a bit.

The results were immediate as the canine Taari's bushy tail began to wave back and forth from where it emerged under her armored pants as she opened her mouth to say something before slumping slightly as she changed her mind.

"I'd let you take a shot, but if Marsden didn't wanna lend you a pistol earlier, I'd better not. What?" Desmond's attempt at flirting had flown right over the big canine Taari's head, but the Hyreh was snickering and the Taari turned to glare at her green companion.

"No worries, I don't wanna get any of you in any more trouble. Besides, I can just appreciate the gun show for now," Desmond tried again. He gestured to where the canine Taari had the machine gun resting on one muscled shoulder. She turned back to him with a confused look for a moment before seeing his gesture and her eyes bugged out as her mind finally caught up.

The canine Taari sputtered in surprise while the others burst into full bellied laughter. Desmond just let it go for a moment, a light blush dusting his cheeks, but he did his best to remain entirely stone-faced while buttoning up the front of his jacket over his bare torso. The material itched slightly against his bare skin, but it wasn't as uncomfortable as he had expected it to be. Eventually, the big canine Taari began to laugh with her companions as well, though he could detect a blush through the thin fur on her face.

After letting them laugh for several more moments, Desmond hefted what he had been coming to think of as his 'loot sack' onto his shoulder and gestured towards the still steaming dead 'big momma' that had been killed earlier.

"Let's get this taken care of. Adept Marsden can only stall the others for so long, I think."

A glance over his shoulder showed Desmond that the vulpine Taari adept was now in a heated argument with what looked like a heavily sunburned Aelfa woman with bright orange hair. The two were standing nearly chest to chest and snarling at each other. Admittedly, Marsden looked more intimidating with her fangs, but the Aelfa didn't seem inclined to back down. None of the guards had their weapons aimed at each other and were just watching with bored expressions.

The three guards with him nodded, and they ducked into the piles of dead critters carefully, moving slowly from pile to pile and being cautious to keep the dead or the base of a massive stalagmite between them and the other group by silent consensus before ducking back behind the massive arthropod.

It was even more disgusting close up, with a thick slime covering its carapace and legs, while blood and other stinking fluids drooled out of its massive mouth.

Desmond glared at the oozing maw, eying the serrated teeth that were still in its wide mouth.

"I should take a trophy with me," he muttered quietly before jumping slightly when he felt something hard bump into his side. Glancing over, he found the canine Taari with something in her broad hand that she had thumped into his side. Sticking out of her fist was the same serrated tooth that Marsden had pried out of his shoulder.

"Here, I bet that'll look right wicked mounted on your armor once you get your kit issued. Or you can put it on a display or something," she said before dropping the big tooth into his hand. It was over a foot long and as thick around as three fingers at the base, tapering down rapidly to a wicked point.

"Feels...appropriate to take the tooth it got me with. Hadn't even thought of grabbing it until now." He smiled up at the much larger woman, who blushed a bit darker before winking at him.

"Figured. If you hadn't asked about it, I was going to give it to you on the shuttle back anyway," she mumbled. Turning back to the big monster and clearing her throat, the canine Taari wound up to kick the thing in its belly. "Better make sure this bastard is dead, though."

Smiling to himself as she worked to hide her embarrassment, Desmond tucked the big fang into his belt like a knife before joining her and the other two, who were staring at the abdomen of the creature.

"So, how do we know if this thing has anything worthwhile on it? The shell looked pretty sturdy, but I can't exactly take it with me." Desmond gestured to the shimmering black armor that still covered most of the beast. "Besides that, it doesn't look especially shiny to me."

"Most monster bits aren't worth as much to the Quartermaster. They claim anything they want from the dead once a Rift is pacified, anyway. If you see a small hunk of the armor, grab it and bring it with. Especially if it's a bit from where Marsden blasted the bitch open. Proof of kill and all that to help confirm contribution, though the cuffs will document it still, never hurts to have extra. One this size likely has a core, though."

"That I can do." Desmond carefully pried up a cracked bit of the shell from the injury on the front of the creature and stuffed it in the bag. The sheer size of the creature went a long way to keeping his stomach stable with the idea that he was ripping bits of its body off. "What's next?"

"Next, we go check the chasm. Make sure there aren't any

others of these beasties around. We can come back for the core," the Se'Aelfa jumped in. She'd drawn her saber as soon as they got within arm's reach of the creatures and she'd been using it as a prod to ensure that the different creatures were actually dead. Only one had shifted slightly when she'd stabbed it, and she'd been quick to drive her sword into its skull.

They trooped deeper into the cavern with the Se'Aelfa leading and Desmond bracketed between the other two. His dynamo was still spinning away, but he could feel the bone-deep ache in the pit of his stomach that was his cache telling him he'd drawn heavily on it. While they walked, he flicked open his comm-cuff to check the readout.

Condition - Healthy, tired.
Cache status - 21/100

Flicking the display closed, Desmond rubbed at his eyes. *Tired is right, been a long ass day already. Gotta keep moving until the job is done though. That last Bolt I threw took a lot more power than I had expected...I need to work on refining it.*

From a distance, the chasm that the larger monster had crawled out of looked like it had split the room in half. Up close, though, it really just dove into the base of one wall with only a clear strip of about twenty feet on the other side of it. Other than the entrance they had come through and the other entrances that honeycombed the walls above, no exits existed on the far side of the cavern.

The mundane guards refused to let Desmond get close to the edge first, instead having the Se'Aelfa go first as she was the lightest. Once she'd checked to make sure it would support them, she gestured the others forward.

"Gonna need a line to get down there, but I think it's gonna be worth it," she said as they approached gingerly. The pitted stone underfoot was solid despite their combined weight, its durability shown from the many shallow gouges from the monster's clawed feet from earlier. "Take a peek, Cadet." She gestured to the end before reaching out and grabbing the back of Desmond's belt to keep him from slipping over the edge.

While Desmond wanted to protest, he held it back, reminding himself that they were supposed to be keeping him safe and he'd already been injured once. Admittedly, it was a freak accident, but he was sure these girls were jumpy enough that he didn't need to make it worse. *Be a man and all that, gotta put forward a strong face for them as well. I'm sure they are feeling guilty that I got hurt already. So I don't need to rub salt on the wound by doubting them without reason.*

Once she had a secure hold on him, Desmond leaned over and peered down.

The chasm itself wasn't a sheer drop off, instead it angled down at around a sixty to seventy degree slope for a good twenty yards before leveling off into a pile of loose stones and scree. Right in the middle of the chasm, along its widest point, was what could have only been the creature's nest, an organized bowl of material that was big enough you could park a school bus in it. Desmond could feel the raw mana emanating from the bottom of the chasm like heat rising off a stove. His dynamo lurched as the wave hit him in the chest like a punch and he felt a rush of energy surge through him. *This has got to be what Marsden meant by 'mana sense'. Oof, definitely feel it now.*

"Ugh, that...yeah I'm going to have to go down there." Desmond winced and pulled back, his eyes watering.

"Like hell you are," growled the canine Taari. She'd begun unwinding a thin metal cable from a spool at her waist while he'd checked over the edge.

"Look. That nest is literally radiating mana like a stove. I remember Instructor Tre'shovak telling me that high concentrations of mana can be dangerous to normal folk. And trust me, it's high coming up out of there. Is your gear shielded? I know you girls were handling the loot earlier, so it's at least partially shielded, but that would be like walking into a nuclear reactor. I'm surprised it isn't affecting you already. The stone of the floor must be deflecting it," Desmond asked pointedly. He rolled his formerly injured shoulder to make sure it would do its job before shifting the 'loot sack' on his back to make sure it would stay in place.

The canine Taari looked like she wanted to argue more, but bit it back with a sigh.

"No...you are right. I've had mana poisoning before and it is not fun. I've seen it kill girls before, too. The bag you have is shielded, but that's the only bit we've been able to get so far. Mana shielding is pricey. The one time we let Marsden go ahead of us is when it's too thick to be safe. If we can't guarantee it, we walk away, though." Desmond's eyebrow quirked up at that.

That's right, we all have to buy our advanced gear ourselves unless we wanna make do with the standard kits...suppose that makes sense, so folks think harder on what kind of kit they bring. Odd that they protect adept's so heavily, but make us buy our own gear like this.

"Then you know it's best for me to be the one down there. It's gonna be hard enough for you three to be exposed to the fumes, let alone below."

"He's right. Just checking it earlier made my head swim, and that was through my helmet," chipped in the Se'Aelfa. "Lets get him harnessed up so we can get this over with."

CHAPTER 22

I've often thought about the fact that the Hegemony talks about how they care so much about the adepts and their teams. How they care so much about our disposition and protection. And then on the flip-side, they expect us to literally dig our paychecks out of the gross insidy-bits of the Rift monsters we kill. Bureaucracy at its finest, I'm sure.
~Desmond McLaughlin, on life as an adept.

The armored jacket he was wearing had several attachment points along the shoulders that they threaded the cable through before looping it around his waist and securing it to itself. While Desmond was pretty sure that this was not how someone rappelled, he also had no idea how to properly rappel either, so he just went with what the girls told him to do for now.

Sliding down the steep slope on his butt, Desmond felt quite a bit like the worm on the end of a hook.

At least this worm has three chicks with guns watching his back if something comes crawling out to eat me, he thought wryly as he reached the bottom of the chasm and began searching around. The mana was so dense down here that it felt like he was standing in a sauna. His dynamo was humming away happily and the ache in his chest from having a low cache was fading rapidly.

"Wonder if one could bottle the air like this and turn it into a booster. Marsden mentioned not having bought something like that before, so they must have something like it. Would be a heck of a way to top up in a fight. Just take a puff off an inhaler," Desmond muttered to himself as he picked his way across the uneven ground. He could feel a vibration through his boots, but it was very slight and emanating from the nest ahead of him. The security line that they'd wrapped around him had enough range that he could get to the nest and back but not wander too far as they kept the tension on it tight to ensure they could recover him if something went wrong.

Glancing over his shoulder, Desmond confirmed that the canine Taari had the line well in hand, ready to reel him in while the other two kneeled with weapons ready to cover him. All three were just barely over the lip of the chasm, the limit of what was safe for them with the lighter shielding on their armor against the radiant mana that welled up here. He gave them a quick wave with one hand and got one in return from the Se'Aelfa.

Another quick look around the chasm confirmed that there wasn't any sign of the spidery monsters they'd slaughtered wholesale in the cave, and Desmond edged up and over the lip of the nest.

The density of mana in the air abruptly tripled as he crested the edge of the nest and slid down inside of the shallow bowl. He could feel the texture of the air as it was forced into and out of his lungs, and the fact that it felt different going out than coming in made him shiver. *Feels rougher going out, like it's leaving behind moisture or something in my lungs...really hope that is just the mana being stripped out of the air and that I'm not gonna end up with some kind of magical pneumonia or some shit...*

What he had come for lay at the very bottom of the nest. Desmond could feel the vibration picking up through where his feet and his hands connected with the ground as he approached. A pile of rough, oblong dull gray stones striated through with bands of shimmering black so dense that it looked more like the stone itself was the banding, while the black ore made up more of it.

Moving quickly, Desmond unslung the duffel pack and

began loading the stones into it as quickly as he could. Each stone he touched buzzed against his fingers and he felt his dynamo surge slightly with each touch of the ore on his bare skin.

"No idea what you are. But you gotta be valuable," Desmond whispered. He carefully stacked the ore-laden stones into his bag. He made a mental note to study more about the different exotic materials that they might recover from Rifts as well. The fact that Marsden was giving him a cut of their proceeds definitely motivated him to find everything he could.

Once the ore was secured, Desmond cast around and flipped a few stones over, recovering almost a dozen of the muddy crystal clusters as well that had fallen into the cracks in the rocks. Several looked distinctly odd, like they'd been chewed on and he pondered that while he crawled back out of the pit with the help of the security line.

"Oof, it definitely feels like you got a haul there," grunted the canine Taari as she levered him up and over the edge of the chasm.

"Yeah, most of the bag is full now. Got some ore-bearing rocks that I can still feel humming in my teeth right now." The pack felt solid on his back, but oddly Desmond didn't find it heavy, though the Taari woman panted from the exertion of dragging him out.

"Blasted adepts and the freaky stuff mana does," she muttered with a good-natured grin. "I won't piss and moan too much. If you stuffed the sack full, then that means we are getting a hell of a payday for this run. Well, more than we already get as a stipend."

"There's more too, but I dunno if you wanna dig for it." Desmond pulled one of the crystal clusters out of his pants pocket. He'd kept that one as it was the most 'chewed on' of the ones he'd found. "I think they were eating these..."

The mundane guard's eyes had narrowed when he'd produced the crystal from his pocket, but their faces relaxed as he explained and the Se'Aelfa made a disgusted gagging noise.

"Ugh. You want to cut the big one open and check its stomach, don't you?"

"I don't want to. But I need to. Gotta make sure you girls have the best payday you can, both as thanks for taking care of my ass and because Marsden said she'd cut me in as well. Bigger payday for you all, bigger payday for me." Desmond shrugged, swinging the pack around to tuck the crystal into it before securing it closed again.

"Well, far be it from me to stop a man from anything. Let's see if he changes his mind when he cracks it open," laughed the Hyreh. As a group, they trotted back to where the big arthropod lay.

The smell had only gotten worse as time had passed and more fluids leaked out of the dead creature. Desmond had to fight back a gag as he examined the length of the corpse. While the heavy shell armored its top, a comparatively thinner shell covered its belly, but he still was unsure of where its stomach would be.

On a hunch, he placed one hand on the still warm carapace of its belly and carefully walked its length, hoping to feel that telltale vibration that told him something charged with mana was nearby, as Marsden had told him before. Just touching the creature made him nearly vomit from the gross feeling of its carapace, even through his gloves. *How can something be hard, soft, and sticky all at the same time?*

The first pass was unsuccessful, mostly because of the constant buzzing of the backpack full of ore-bearing rocks he carried. Setting it down, he made another pass. This time, Desmond could pick up a faint, resonant humming through the carapace two-thirds of the way down from the mouth. Borrowing the Aelfa's scimitar, Desmond carefully cut the creature open, dodging out of the way in case he'd cut into one of the organs. The smell that came out of its open body actually made him heave, but at this point, there wasn't anything in his stomach.

The regulars that were watching over him muttered bets back and forth while they stood guard, letting him work.

Desmond was so distracted by trying to discern which of the gross sacks inside the body was the stomach that he didn't hear Marsden and the others approaching until the vulpine Taari called out to them.

"The hell are you three making my cadet do?"

"We didn't make him do anything. He volunteered to go digging for extra credits," chuckled the Hyreh. She gestured to the duffel that sat between her feet. "That's after he crawled down into the critters' nest and dragged off anything that had a trace of mana in it as well. I think the poor guy has earned his cut."

"Agreed. Cadet McLaughlin, are you having fun in there?"

"Oh tons," Desmond gagged and continued sawing with the knife. "If you want to climb in and help me, go right ahead." He was currently headfirst in the large cut he'd made and doing his best to not get any of the creatures' innards on him. When he'd cut the creature open here, he'd expected to find the stomach with maybe fragments of mana crystals in it. Instead, he found something far different. He carefully worked it free of the surrounding tissue while Marsden laughed behind him.

"Oh no, I wouldn't wanna take away from your first experience of the joys of looting a good kill."

"If," Desmond grunted with effort as his find finally came loose and dropped into his arms, "you are sure." Turning away from the cut, Desmond presented his find to the onlookers, who all gave varying expressions of surprise.

In Desmond's arms was a hexagonal spire of crystal that came to a pointed termination on both ends. The crystal was as thick around as his thigh and around two feet in length. The crystal was a mottled brown and green color, like moss growing out over rich earth.

"Damn," someone muttered in surprise. Desmond had to restrain the grin that threatened to cross his face. Marsden didn't bother to fight the urge at all.

"Very nice, Cadet. Looks like you found its core. Let's get that packed up with the rest and keep moving. We need to finish clearing zones, and the other team can have whatever is left in this room. I think we got our share."

"Whatever is left is likely only small stuff, anyway. The creatures seemed to be eating the crystals and, while I checked for its stomach, I couldn't find any remains there," Desmond said with a shrug. He used a swatch of cloth that one of the girls handed him to wipe down the crystal before tucking it into the bag and getting the whole thing secured on his back again.

"Damn, boy is like an ox."

"You sure you got it, Cadet?"

"Yeah, I'm fine. Let's get moving." Desmond nodded back the way they had come. The guards fell in around him and Marsden, who studied him intently, was still clearly wary about his previous injury. Desmond kept up without a problem, his formerly injured shoulder not even twinging.

<><><>

They spent two more hours clearing another half dozen tunnels before the signal came to fall back to the staging area. Desmond added another two dozen small crystals and nuggets of ore to the pack and pockets of his uniform pants and jacket. The girls hadn't even hesitated when he declared the bag full and began filling his pockets instead. Several of them had loaded bits and pieces into their spare carry space as well, but most of their space was taken up with their kit.

During that time, they encountered only the smaller variants of the spider-goblin creatures and wiped them out without a problem. Desmond was kept firmly back between the two heavy-weapons geared girls, though. It was clear they were taking no risks with him after his earlier injury. Marsden made sure to remind him not to exert his mana any more either since he would be recovering for a while, though Desmond noted that his cache was back up to the seventy percent range by the time they all got back to the staging area. Apparently, the time in the chasm's mana rich atmosphere had helped.

Being one of the last groups to get back to the staging area, a level of exhaustion had settled over all of them as they loaded into the shuttle and it scooted off to return them to the *Valor's Bid*.

"Did good, Cadet." Marsden sighed, prying her helmet off and rubbing at the base of her ears, groaning quietly as she ruffled the fur that had been smashed flat by her helmet. All the others were busy unbuckling their helmets as well, but several nodded in agreement. "You still gotta report to Medical to get checked out, since your comm-cuff will have reported the injury. I'll include in my report that your injury was not life threatening either, but you still gotta report in. They'll wanna give you a clear marker for the injury, and I'm sure they will need to run some tests to figure out how the hell you did that."

"Ugh, fine, but can I take a shower first?" Desmond shifted the 'loot-bag' where it was wedged between his knees, the contents of the lumpy bag digging into his thigh oddly.

"Nope, report to Medical as soon as we are dismissed from the flight deck." Marsden gave him a tired smile. "Sooner you get that done, the sooner you can get a shower, Cadet. Seriously though, you did good. Here, flip me your contact details and I'll get your share wired over when the Quartermaster is done logging it and pays me."

Tapping their comm-cuff together lightly, Desmond transferred his contact information to the vulpine Taari before letting out a gusty sigh.

"Fine, just hope it's a more...gentle encounter than my last one."

"Oh? Sounds like you have a story there."

"Kinda. So I had just gotten out of class," Desmond related the first encounter with Dr. Astrid while the shuttle carried them back, much to the amusement of the girls.

"Yeah. That sounds like Astrid. She's rough around the edges, but very focused on her work. She and her team saved my left leg, actually. It nearly got taken off during a Rift suppression a year ago, back when I was still a fresh recruit on my first run with Mars. She had me up and running in time to make our next Rift," the canine Taari added from the other end of the cramped shuttle.

"Ya, I wanna hear more about this Taari gal you ran into," prodded the Dwerg with a wicked smile as they bumped down into the flight bay.

"Not much to say. I helped Chloe back to her bunk space and had to scare off some folks trying to single her out." Desmond brushed it off, but he couldn't hide the slight blush. The girls all chuckled at him but didn't prod further as they filed out of the shuttle.

"She sounds like a half-breed. You mentioned she didn't have a muzzle like I do?" Marsden murmured to him as they began to disembark and Desmond nodded. "She's gonna have a rough time of it. Half-breeds get a lot of shit from pure-bloods on top of any problems she might have had in the wake of that fight, too." Desmond turned that over in his head, but nodded his thanks to Marsden.

"Appreciate the head's up. I'll keep an eye out for her. She deserves better," he replied as they filed out of the shuttle. Marsden nodded, shooting him an encouraging wink before they emerged.

Instructor Throneblood was waiting nearby with her data-tablet out, checking teams in as they disembarked.

"Cadet McLaughlin, report to Medical," the tall Uth'ra called to them. She made a mark on her tablet before flicking her heavy mane of blue hair back out of her eyes. "Adept Marsden, report to the Quartermaster with your take. You know the drill. I expect a report on McLaughlin's performance tomorrow by noon." Throneblood gave his damaged and bloody jacket a suspicious look before shrugging it off and gesturing for them to get moving, apparently content with the fact he hadn't fallen over on the flight deck.

"Yes, Instructor," chorused the group, Desmond right in time with them, before they split off with a few last goodbyes.

Marsden re-iterated her promise to send him his cut once the Quartermaster got it tabulated and paid out, as well as made him double check his pockets to ensure nothing got left behind that might set off the sensors in Medical. Desmond also got several flirty winks from the mundane guards before they headed off to the lifts that lead down to the second year dorms.

"Well. Off to face the music," Desmond muttered. He adjusted his armored jacket to cover his bare and bloody chest before starting off towards Medical.

CHAPTER 23

How long does it take to develop a twist? If you could put a number to that, then I think the Empress would give you a noble title outright. Honestly, the reason it's so hard to nail down is the free-form way that most adepts shape their mana. If everyone operated off of more fixed spells besides the core handful like the 'Bolt' or 'Shield' spell, then that would probably help. But ultimately, that stifles growth amongst the adepts. So we have to adapt on the fly.
~Camilla Tre'shovak, lecturing her
current class of cadet-adepts.

The trip to Medical was anti-climatic, thankfully. Desmond reported in as requested and was handed off to Cadet Leafsong, who put him through a series of scans on one of the treatment beds before sending him back to his room with a clean bill of health and orders to sleep as much as he could. She also said she would pass the information on to the doctor when all the scans were done being processed and reviewed.

Thankfully, Dr. Astrid was busy elsewhere, and he didn't encounter the punch-happy Uth'ra before he made his escape from Medical. He was able to get back to his suite without encountering anyone else, as it was already nearing midnight by the ship's clocks.

A quick shower was the only thing that slowed Desmond down before crashing hard on the bed and passing out.

SAUL's brazen radio-announcer voice woke him the next morning and, despite the brief night's sleep, Desmond actually felt like he was in good shape as he got changed into a fresh uniform. His ribcage ached from the strain on his dynamo. It felt like his solar-plexus had a pulled muscle, but that was the worst of it.

"SAUL, what do I do with the gear from the Rift? The jacket was damaged." Desmond had just dropped the bloodied and damaged gear on his table when he'd gotten home the night before, and now he had to figure out what to do with it.

"I can send a request to the Armory to have someone come and pick it up for repairs if you would like, Desmond. That armor kit has been issued to you as part of your standard kit," SAUL replied cheerily.

"No, I can take it down to them. Would be good for me to go swing by, so I know where the hell they are."

Desmond was gathering the leg armor into the damaged jacket when a pounding echoed from the door to his suite.

"Desmond, it appears that Cadet Irongrip is at the door," SAUL volunteered.

"Really? I never would have guessed that was her pounding the door down. Let her in before she kicks the door in." Desmond sighed and tossed the last plate on top of the pile and set the tooth he'd taken to one side.

The door to his suite slid open right as Monika wound up to pound on it again and the redheaded Dwerg stumbled through, catching herself on the edge of the entrance so she didn't land on her face.

"Des! Why didn't you respond to any of my messages?" demanded Monika. She crossed her arms over her abundant chest and planted her feet shoulder width apart to glare up at him.

Still getting used to someone having to look up to me like this, almost the same difference in height between me and Chloe. He thought with a smile.

"Messages?" Desmond prodded his comm-cuff and sighed when he got to the message section, noting that he had twenty-six unread messages from Monika that were time stamped as having been sent while he was in the Rift. "Because none of them were delivered until I got back aboard, Monika."

"Then why didn't you respond when you got in?" She stamped one foot to punctuate her irritation.

"Because I got back and passed out. Come on, I need to take this to the Armory and you can show me the way." Desmond brandished the armored jacket at her and the Dwerg's ire broke as she noted the bloodstains on it.

"Wha? How the hell did you get injured!?"

"Walk and talk, I'll tell you while we walk. Still need to get food and I don't wanna have to skip it to make class."

It took a bit of urging, but Desmond managed to corral his excitable friend out of the room and into the hall. Answering all of her questions and giving Monika the full rundown of the Rift suppression took the entire trip down to the Armory and most of the meal.

Turning over the armor to the Armory's staff drew a few curious looks, but they logged the armor in under his name and advised him that it would be washed, repaired, and returned to him in the next three days. They did advise that it would take slightly longer as they were prioritizing the gear from the upperclassmen at the moment. Desmond reassured them that he understood and would be patient.

<><><>

"That is so crazy." Desmond had been forced to retell the story when they got to the mess hall and met up with Dianne. Monika had continued to badger him with questions the entire time. The Uth'ra had at least listened without butting in like Monika had, content to just take it all in while she ate.

"Yeah, it was definitely an experience. Still need to sit down and thrash it all out in my head. I wanna find out what our standard gear is going to be so I can figure out what sort of important gear to pick up and in what order." Desmond went to work on the, now-cold, omelet that he'd gotten for breakfast. His bottomless hunger had thankfully abated finally and he could eat normal portions again, now that his dynamo wasn't straining.

"But the academy issues gear, doesn't it?" Monika prodded. The excitable Dwerg was on her third mug of what Desmond had taken to referring to as 'space-coffee' in his head.

The idea that coffee out here comes from bacteria like beer, rather than hot bean juice, is weird. Okay, it's just as strange when I think of it that way.

"Ya, we got a basic kit from them. But like you told me before, you flesh out the kit more from your bounty payouts. Given that my wallet is going to be thin until we get our first Rift runs done? I gotta be smart about it," Desmond said around a mouthful of eggs and sausage.

"It makes sense. I'm still surprised that they only issued you armor and no weapon." Dianne stared into her own mug of the 'coffee' like it held the answers to all her questions.

"Adept Marsden said it was because we hadn't had weapons training yet."

"Honestly? What throws me is that we were practicing combat magic before we even went over sidearms or weapons. I hadn't thought about it till you mentioned it, but it feels weird." The Uth'ra continued to press.

"Maybe we'll be going to weapons training soon. I mean, the Vice-Admiral did make it sound like that bit of an excursion was an unexpected diversion and the like," Monika suggested. Desmond didn't add to it, focusing on getting through his food in time for class.

<><><>

It turned out that Monika was partially correct in her guess. Once they got settled into class, Throneblood declared that they would be going over the ratings for their assessments, then heading to the firing range to begin a review on the standard weapons of the Hegemony in preparation for the selection process of their first permanent teammate.

It did strike Desmond as odd that they hadn't even been taking classes for two weeks yet and they were already getting a chance to pick a member of their guard.

"Remember, you need to plan and build out your team from the beginning. For the first few runs, you will have assigned guards from the veteran crew of the *Valor's Bid* to fill your teams out. Once you have the minimum team size of four, you can elect to go without the veterans there to assist you. While the veterans are part of your team, they are to be paid a fair cut of whatever bounty you recover," Throneblood boomed from her place on the podium.

The Uth'ra instructor had been waiting in the classroom when Desmond arrived, going over something on her datatablet, but she hadn't said a word until class started. Desmond fought the urge to take a peek at his assessment numbers. His restraint proved to be a good idea as Throneblood had torn into several of the class, who had immediately opened up the readouts on their comm-cuff to check.

"The assessment information is purely to give you a baseline for comparison. The rating is on a scale of one to twenty," Throneblood said after finishing her chewing out of the students. "Your comm-cuff will continue to measure your abilities as time goes by and will update to reflect the changes you make as conditioning starts next week."

The statement jogged Desmond's memory, and he raised his hand. Instructor Throneblood nodded to him a moment later.

"Instructor? It occurred to me the other day, but I wanted to ask now. Why was it that we began training with mana first and progressed into the first combat spell before any type of conditioning or mundane weaponry was discussed?"

Dozens of eyes turned to stare at him and he did his best to not curl up and hide at the sudden massed regard of all of them. Normally, the weight of regard from everyone wouldn't bother him so much, but he could feel the heat of irritation from several people, like the sun on his skin.

"That is a legitimate question. Especially for someone who so recently joined the Hegemony. You wouldn't quite understand the scope of things and it is easy to miss it in the general reading," Instructor Throneblood said first. She took a moment to glare at the other students, who looked away from Desmond sheepishly. "Simply put, you can be disarmed of a weapon and even injured to where bodily conditioning isn't functional. But, at your core, you will always be able to manipulate mana unless you catastrophically overdraw your cache."

Desmond considered her words for several moments. *It does make sense, training the skill that is hardest to take away...*

"But Instructor, if the only actual way to damage one's cache is by using it too much, why start us on that first? I would think training accuracy or trying to determine specialties to isolate and improve learning speed would be first on the list. Not that I'm challenging your methods. I just want to understand the purpose of our training style better," Desmond hastily tacked the ending on when he realized how it must have sounded.

"Not to worry. While I don't get this question often, it is one that comes up on occasion." Throneblood waved off his concerns. "The other factor that plays in is that, at the core of each of you, is a mana adept. That is why you are here. That is why you are being trained, and why you are allowed to select your own teams to specifically act as bodyguards and aids. While you will be receiving weapons training, it is not to be the first tool you reach for. That is your mana manipulation. So we start with that. As to why we don't try to isolate specialties early on, it is because we don't want you to limit growth in any areas. While a specialist may be superior to a generalist in their chosen field, that doesn't make the generalist useless or unable to keep up."

"Thank you, Instructor." Desmond made careful note of what Throneblood had said, and the subtext underneath it. He wasn't sure if there was something darker about why the Hegemony was focused on them learning magic first over weapons. Perhaps to keep them more dependent on their 'mundie' guards for protection when not engaged, thus tying them more firmly to the military?

Or maybe it really is just a matter of priority. I've been here less than a month and that isn't enough time to really go over everything.

"Now, back to the assessment readouts. As I was saying, they are measured on a scale of one to twenty, and across five different definitions. Most species have a broad enough range of potential to begin with, though some standards can be applied for baselines. However, that doesn't mean that you should not strive to improve."

A couple of gestures from Instructor Throneblood brought up a holographic screen behind her with the standard readout on it.

- Physical Condition -
Condition - Healthy
Cache Status - 100/100
- Stats -
Strength - 10
Endurance - 10
Dexterity - 10
Accuracy - 10
Mental Flexibility - 10

"Now! Condition measures your current physical condition when compared to the baseline you normally inhabit. It won't tell you if you are just sleepy, but if you start to suffer from malnutrition or receive an injury, it will show up here. This changing is what gets Medical on your back. It does record physical exhaustion levels as well, but that is more of a measurement from standard so you don't over-train and that doesn't alert Medical unless you remain in that zone for several days, showing you aren't taking care of yourself. Your cache status, as you should already know, is the relative energy levels stored in your cache. Note that your cache will increase in size, but this ratio will remain out of a hundred. A skilled adept has a far higher density of mana in their bodies compared to a recruit. Even amongst the Aelfa, who naturally have a higher density because of their species adaptation." Throneblood highlighted the first two lines before moving further down.

"The status, or 'stats', is where things get a bit more nebulous, but should still be easy enough to comprehend. Strength is a measurement of the potential energy of your muscle cells. How heavy an object can you lift? How far can you throw something? While Endurance is more of a measurement of how long, you can keep doing something like that. Having a low number in Endurance can and will correspond with a lower mana density in your cache as well. It doesn't measure just purely your physical exertion." The first two words flashed with a white outline before settling.

"A ten in strength would put you roughly on par with someone who works with their hands and can lift roughly fifty kilograms over their head. By comparison, my strength is eighteen. Each species has a 'cut off' point where they reach their peak, and the results after are logarithmic in expansion. For Uth'ra, such as myself, the cutoff was at seventeen and it took me a decade to get to fourteen with regular training."

The midnight-blue maned instructor leaned forward, flexing her arms and upper body to make her physique tighten and the muscles cord under her skin.

"While it is impractical for everyone to push themselves

high in every stat measurement, it does give you an idea of where you stand and where you can go when you compare yourself with top performers in your species. For example, an endurance of ten is common amongst the blue-collar workers who lift or move heavy objects for extended periods."

So far, it sounds like the 'tomato analogy' applies to the stats. Desmond thought to himself as he took notes on what Throneblood spoke on. Dexterity was fine manipulation and reaction speed. Accuracy was just that, the ability to hit a target and hand to eye coordination. Mental flexibility was a more nebulous concept than the others, a combination of intelligence, neuro-plasticity, and adaptability. Each of them had a 'standard measurement' point, and she gave examples at different points to prove that ten was not the 'standard'.

When she finished explaining them, Throneblood gave the class permission to examine their scores with the reminder that these were only initial assessments and would change during physical training in the coming months. She stated very specifically that she would make sure of it.

Desmond accessed the proper menus on his comm-cuff and scanned the readout.

- Physical Condition -
Condition - Healthy
Cache Status - 100/100
- Stats -
Strength - 9
Endurance - 10
Dexterity - 7
Accuracy - 12
Mental Flexibility - 8

"Huh," Desmond muttered to himself. The scores made sense for the most part. As a welder, he wasn't moving lots of heavy materials around. Anything heavy that he had to weld was usually held in place with rigging or fastened via clamps or something else. His kit was heavy, but it wasn't like he had the welding rig strapped to his back. Endurance made sense since he had worked long hours often and kept that up with studying. Dexterity disappointed him slightly, just as Strength had, but he wasn't sure what the human baseline was after all. The Accuracy score made him smile though, it made sense since he spent so much time at the range with his axes.

Gotta ask Throneblood about qualifying to practice on my own. That time on the range practicing Bolt really helped me focus and relax. The Mental Flexibility made him shrug. It was hard to really give perspective on that, since he was surrounded by aliens that strongly resemble fantasy creatures from fiction daily. The fact he was coping with that made him think that he should have high flexibility, but again, no point of contrast really to compare them with.

"All right, class. Now that you are finished with that, we will be heading to the drilling range. The rest of the morning class will be put to practice with *Bolt*. Afternoon class, you are to meet back up at the range and we will begin going over firearms, armor, and standard kits. After observing the upperclassmen the other day, you should have an idea of what different team layouts can do. Those of you who accompanied the upperclassmen on a Rift suppression should have an even better idea." Desmond shrunk slightly as he felt eyes on him again, but after a moment, threw it off. He had no reason to be self-conscious right now. Just because he'd gotten that bit of extra didn't mean he should feel bad about it.

Straightening, Desmond focused his attention on Throneblood as she finished giving directions for which range they would meet in, pointedly ignoring the stares of his classmates. *Besides, it's not like I was the only one who got to ride along...*

CHAPTER 24

I remember the lectures about specialization and how they talked it up. It reminded me of classes back in tabletop games I'd play back on Terra. Finding my specialization was somewhat anticlimactic. No glow, no angels singing. Nothing fancy like that. It just worked, and it worked way more effectively than I'd expected.
~Desmond McLaughlin, on life aboard the *Valor's Bid*.

Drilling with the *Bolt* spell was soothing and, by the end of class, Desmond had joined the score of others that were cleared to practice on their own. This was both a bonus and a punishment, it seemed. Throneblood had informed them that they were cleared to drill without supervision and then promptly ordered them to log a minimum of an hour on the range every night after classes, as they would be drilled on different spells to continue expanding their repertoire, while the others would instead keep drilling *Bolt*.

The afternoon at the weapons range had been more of a lecture than Desmond had hoped for, unfortunately. Rather than having racks of different weapons for them to examine and try out, there were individual kits laid out with an armor set and a selection of weapons in front of each.

"The pool of regulars that you will be selecting from for your guard are being trained in a number of different disciplines. Much like each of you will have preferences and some of you will have distinct specialties. Today, I will be introducing you to the specific load-out given to each specialty. While these load-outs are not the only gear they are allowed to carry, it is all that the Academy will issue them. This is part of why your team will all receive a cut from your bounty payouts for Rift suppression. They can drill with samples in the ranges, but only the gear issued or items purchased from the Quartermaster will actually go out with you for Rifts. When you are deployed for military term, your gear goes with you. Remember, as adepts, you are the pinpoint strike, the tip of the spear, the elite. Be flexible! We will provide you with the basic equipment, but do not be afraid to customize and improve upon it. You and your teams are one of the few groups allowed to customize, so embrace it." Throneblood lectured from behind the sets of gear.

There were six different 'kits' laid out on several tables in a half circle at the back of the range and at Throneblood's urging, the class filed past them to examine them. Each kit had a different style of armor on a stand behind it, with a selection of different weapons.

Two were 'light armor' variants that shared a table that contained a large pistol on one rack, a pair of smaller pistols on another, and a compact rifle that reminded Desmond of a P90 on the last, but with a glowing power-supply cable that trailed off the side of the gun. The armors were similar in layout, varying in whether it was smaller armored plates scattered around, or larger segments that left the joints exposed.

Three of the options were what Desmond would consider 'medium armor' and they all varied, like the lighter versions in where the armor was concentrated. One had thicker plates on the upper body with lighter on the legs and seemed to focus on maintaining mobility. The second was smaller individual plates that focused on flexibility and actually had a medium-sized rectangular shield with a rifle slot cut out of it leaning against the rack. Lastly, the third kit had more heavy plates across the body that reminded him of a medieval knight's armor with the large single plates. The racks in front of them held a pair of rifles, cutting down the options from the previous set. At a glance, the difference between the rifles seemed to be whether they operated on a battery or through solid projectiles given the power cells on one and the magazine well on the other.

In the last rack was the 'heavy' variant armor, which Desmond noted that he hadn't actually seen anyone using in the previous demonstrations, even the members of the teams with 'heavy weapons' like what was on the table. That armor honestly reminded him more of something like a powered suit than actual armor, the large plates being over an inch thick in critical places. The table in front of it had a shield similar to the medium set, but the cutout being sized to match a heavy weapon instead. For weapon option, it had the solid projectile and energy variants of the chunky machine gun that the canine Taari had used the previous night. The same multi-munition launcher that the ursine Taari had used. Finally, the last option was a broad barreled shotgun with a drum magazine on it that Desmond was sure had a large enough barrel he could stick two fingers into it and not touch the sides.

"Instructor, the upperclassmen all had close combat weapons as well. Why aren't those here as well?" One of the other cadets asked the question that had been teasing at the edges of Desmond's mind.

"Melee weapons are part of a different kit for them. You can rest assured that each will have one that is best suited for them. As you are not expected, or supposed, to be too close to melee range, you won't receive training on them until your second year. Though that does segue nicely into next week's lessons, Enhancement will be the next class of mana manipulation you learn."

The rest of the class was taken up with each of them getting to test-fire the weapons that intrigued them. Instructor Throneblood advised that, while they would each be issued a sidearm and a standard rifle in the design of their choice, it would still be good to experience what each weapon could do, as the regulars would have their kits already decided when the first round of bidding for teams came around.

<><><>

The rest of the week flowed by like honey. In the Evocation classes, Desmond learned how to infuse proportionally larger amounts of mana into the *Bolt* spell and how that would affect its outcome. After discussing it with the instructor, his larger 'double-bit' axe didn't actually qualify as a twist yet. Instead, it was more of a feature of pressing more mana into the spell, and his mind restructuring what it was using as a visualization.

Nearly a dozen of his classmates showed specialization in the Evocation class of magic, having already started to develop their twists to the *Bolt* spell, like one cadet who manifested multiple copies without effort and another that was able to infuse a corrosive effect into the spell on their third day practicing. Desmond kept up with his dogged focus, launching copy after copy of the standard spell into his target as his efficiency continued to rise but it appeared that his own twist on the spell would take far longer to manifest and it became obvious he did not have a specialization in the Evocation class of magic.

Firearms drills became just as monotonous as well. The first few days were interesting as they got familiar with the different weapons and Desmond got to be very familiar with the slug-thrower that he had selected as his sidearm. The chunky pistol reminded him of an M1911 pistol from back home, but it fired a much larger projectile via a caseless system. Despite the larger projectile, the fact it was caseless allowed him to load more rounds in the magazine, which held twenty-one rounds.

It took a day or two to get used to carrying the pistol on his hip, as all cadets were ordered to always have their weapon with them, as it would help familiarize them with it.

Throneblood did warn them that unholstering it outside of the range or their private suites would send an alert to the ship's security and that they had better have a damn good reason if they did.

He did get a chance to talk to Chloe for a bit during training, having decided to hit her up for recommendations on different weapons. It was actually her suggestion to go for the slug thrower over a smaller laser pistol, as the stopping power was just as high, but the intimidation factor of the larger pistol would come in handy. Plus, since he would be issued a rifle as well in the Rifts, it was a solid back-up weapon if something closed to closer distances.

With the issuing of the sidearm, Desmond's evenings became even more crowded. Once the afternoon classes were finished, he put in his hour on the magical range before heading over to the firearm range as well, to put in a half hour with the pistol and the power-cell rifle that he had been issued as well. The rifle stayed locked up in the Armory when it wasn't in use, but he was determined to be used to the equipment he was issued. He was one of the few cadet-adepts that actually practiced beyond the mandatory two hours a week with their mundane weapons.

When Monika had asked him about it, Desmond had pointed out that the practice helped build fast-twitch reflexes which would come in handy with time as their combat magic increased in speed as well. After that, Monika joined him on the range and occasionally dragged one of her friends with her as well.

While Desmond checked his account regularly, he had yet to receive the cut that Marsden had promised him, but on the fourth day he did get a message from the vulpine Taari stating that the Quartermaster was dragging their heels on it, having to process the materials first before a payout came and theirs was not the only big score brought in from that Rift.

The third week of classes started normally, though the

morning lessons switched focus as the last of the class had finally qualified to practice their *Bolt* spell unsupervised. They learned several variants of the spell and how to conjure different effects. They had been working on adding piercing to explosive effects first, and then on how to force a specific elemental alignment into the spell. These were beyond the automatic alterations that some of the cadet's twists had begun to show as. Towards the middle of the week, they shifted gears and began to expand beyond basic Evocation. As Throneblood had promised, they started learning more about the Enhancement classification of mana manipulation and Desmond found it fascinating.

<><><>

"Now, Enhancement is a section of mana manipulation that crosses borders with several other disciplines. It could be argued that Enhancement can be blended with all the different disciplines. This is because the focus of the spells is to further enhance the abilities that are already present in different targets. It can target equipment as well as people, so having a flexible mind is very important as you have to be ready to shift purpose rapidly." Throneblood had them all gathered up on the mana range again for this lecture. At the far end of the range, a heavily damaged personal shield was propped up in front of one of the polycarbonate dummies.

"It is often a secondary focus due to what it can do to enhance a primary. Evokers, this means you. Enhancements can further boost your spells if you can get your mind around the idea. An already twisted *Bolt* can be further enhanced if you take the time to layer in an extra bit. Those of you without an Evocation focus, this is what allows you to keep up with those that have the specialty. Though, more importantly, the defensive benefits cannot be ignored."

Instructor Throneblood gestured towards the distant shield and the entire class watched as it shimmered with a faint golden hue before fading back to its pitted and scarred gray color. The instructor then launched her own *Bolt* spell at it. Her spell manifested as a spinning saw-blade of deep purple energy roughly as big as a dinner plate and crossed the space to the target in the time it took to blink once.

The energy blade shattered on the shield, dispersing into a cloud of purple fragments. All that it left behind was a dull flare of gold light on the surface of the shield and no damage beyond what had been done to it originally.

"That was with a basic protection enhancement. Without it..." Throneblood dismissed the enhancement, and her second *Bolt* tore a finger wide slot in the shield and shredded the dummy behind it. "While I don't expect you to fully negate a blow from another adept right away, time and practice will allow you to improve, and it may mean the difference between life and death for your team. Enhancement specialists occasionally go down a different path though and can permanently imbue equipment with enhancements. This is even more rare than triple specialties, so don't get your hopes up!" The instructor admonished before continuing to lecture and give examples on different things that could be targeted by enhancements.

It turned out that individual limbs could be reinforced, or specific traits could be improved as well, such as strength or dexterity. Instructor Throneblood gave the example of an enhancement to the eyes of someone with strong low-light vision, making it possible to see without light, though it did run the risk of blinding them if a sudden light source was applied. Enhancements to strength would allow for momentary super-powered exertions, though most enhancement boosts did not last long enough to do more than give someone a brief advantage or a temporary shield.

The applications had Desmond's mind whirling through dozens of different potential uses at a time, from enhancing a single bullet to boosting someone's grip strength to prevent recoil from causing muzzle climb, to enhancing the cutting edge that formed from his *Bolt* spell. Despite his distraction, he focused on what Throneblood was saying intently.

The instructor stressed several times that the intent had to be very strict on how much and what was being enhanced.

"You don't have to focus on all the minutiae of it. You won't cause someone to spontaneously shatter a bone by enhancing their muscles unless you *specifically* focus on that. Enhancing maliciously can be quite difficult, as well as dangerous, too. You can never be sure what your opponent is doing and most Rift creatures resist it naturally because of their own native mana fields," Throneblood warned before turning the class loose to practice the basic enhancement, which was focused on increasing the durability of a target.

They were ordered to group up at random and each cadet got several sticks issued to them made of synthetic wood that were two inches wide, a quarter inch thick, and two feet long. They were told to push mana into the wood with the intent to enhance the durability. Once that was done, they were to pass it to the left, and that cadet was to attempt to snap the wood in half.

Desmond was grouped with a pair of Dwerg women who just nodded to him before focusing on their work, which he was glad for. Over the last week, the muttering and grumbling of his classmates had waned somewhat, but that also meant that the flirting and suggestive murmurs were easier to make out and it had gotten to be somewhat uncomfortable.

It wasn't that he was unhappy with the attention, more that the *tone* was the problem. Too many of those he caught talking when they thought he wasn't listening were being rather crude about it. More than a few had suggested 'taking him for a ride', whether he wanted it or not. He wasn't afraid of them, but the fact it was being discussed in a classroom setting so bluntly was concerning. It made for a poor impression for sure, not to mention explained why there were so few men in this sphere of the Hegemony.

Pushing his concerns aside, Desmond inspected the first of his pieces of wood. The grain of the wood was even and clear throughout the length and it was a pale blonde color. Testing it with his hands, he found the stick to be surprisingly flexible. Taking a moment, Desmond thought back to the metalworking classes that he'd gone through while getting his welding certificate. It was the microstructures in steel that made it durable and flexible. He wanted the wood to be strong but not brittle.

Unbidden, a poem floated to the top of his memory, one that he'd seen framed on the wall at a friend's house once, and Desmond smirked.

"Good timber does not grow with ease, strong winds make stronger trees..." The chant shifted over his lips and a trickle of mana flowed out of his fingertips before sinking into the wood. The wood only took the barest drop of his mana before it ceased to draw on his energy and vibrated slightly in his grip.

A poke in his side broke him out of his concentration and he looked over to the brunette Dwerg that was scowling at him, her stick held out after having jabbed him in the side.

"You done daydreaming, Terran?"

"Name is Desmond, but yes," Desmond shot back, rolling his eyes at her. While most of the women had stopped calling him a prim, except for the dedicated few that seemed to just hate his guts for no reason he could come up with, most of those that had stopped still refused to use his name.

"Whatever. Pass it over so we can get this useless practice out of the way," the Dwerg snapped. She spoke while jabbing at him again with her stick. Desmond snatched it away before she could drive it into his side, passing his stick over to the other Dwerg as he studied the stick he'd been handed. He could feel bits of mana running through it, like rebar through concrete, but it felt no more solid.

"All right, Cadets. Now that you have passed to the left, attempt to flex your classmates' sample and break it,"

Instructor Throneblood called out over the class.

A moment later, there was a cacophony of cracks and snaps as the cadets began snapping the bits of wood. A few strained for a moment but snapped the length of wood after more force was applied.

Desmond gripped either end of the stick and snapped it without issue. Inspecting the broken ends, he found that they had shorn through cleanly without splintering.

"Huh. Almost like it snapped on a fault line." Desmond mused as he examined them. His focus was broken by the two Dwerg arguing nearby.

"Oh, give it here. You clearly aren't trying hard enough," snapped the brunette Dwerg who had poked him earlier.

Desmond looked up to find the blonde that he had given his enhanced stick to turning red with exertion as she fought to flex the wood. It bent slightly but didn't break or crack. Blowing out her held breath, the blonde passed the stick over to the brunette.

"Give it your best shot," growled the blonde. The brunette took the stick and, using her knee as a leverage point, tried to break the stick over her knee. Desmond watched as it bent slightly but still refused to break, a small smile creasing his lips.

"Bloody...hell..." grunted the brunette. She stopped pulling on the stick for a moment, taking a deep breath before yanking the stick back against her knee, trying to crack it by impact. "Ow! Shatter and space it!" She yelped, dropping the stick of wood with a clatter and clutching at her knee.

"Hey are you okay?" Desmond stepped closer to check on her but backed away at the glare she shot him.

"What is the problem?" Instructor Throneblood had come up while they were distracted and was staring between them with her piercing orange eyes.

"I believe she may have injured her knee attempting to break my stick, Instructor," Desmond answered smartly, coming to attention on reflex. The two Dwerg stiffened and did the same, though the brunette hissed as she put pressure on her leg.

Throneblood's eyebrow went up, and she looked between the three of them for a moment before stooping to pick up the bit of wood. Desmond could still feel the faint hum of mana through it as Throneblood examined the stick for a moment before she glanced at the brunette Dwerg and sniffed.

"How badly have you injured yourself, Cadet?" Throneblood sniffed again before shaking her head. "Nevermind, I can smell blood. Go to Medical and get that checked." Desmond glanced down and winced. He could see the knee of the cadet's pants starting to darken with blood.

"Yes, Instructor," the brunette hissed, shooting Desmond a glare as if it was his fault she was injured.

"Don't glare at McLaughlin. You injured yourself, now go!" Snapped Throneblood, causing the Dwerg to stiffen and start limping away. "Help her get to Medical." Throneblood ordered the other Dwerg, who saluted before hurrying after her classmate.

"Sorry, Instructor."

"You don't have anything to apologize for, McLaughlin." Instructor Throneblood had gone back to inspecting the stick, but her bright orange eyes flicked up to meet Desmond's green ones. "She tried to bring it down over her knee to break it after failing to snap it normally, right? Her mistake, given what has been done to it."

Gripping the stick on either end, Throneblood flexed hard with a grunt. Desmond watched in surprise as the stick bent at a nearly thirty-degree angle while the Uth'ra strained for a moment before it sprang back straight once more when she relaxed.

"Looks like you found a specialty, Cadet." Throneblood chuckled and tossed him the stick, which bounced off Desmond's chest. He was too surprised at her failing to break it to catch the thrown stick. "Keep practicing. You are going to have a hard choice coming up when team selection comes around."

CHAPTER 25

Allowing adepts to choose their own team compositions has been a controversial topic amongst those that believe themselves to be the 'military elite' for a long time. They'd prefer if everyone fell into a neat mold so they can plan for them. The problem is that mana laughs at plans and organization. It's something that only those who've done time inside of Rifts will really understand. It's not just nice, it's necessary.
~Admiral Lo'Unath, discussing what to expect on one of the academy ships with her niece.

Desmond was deep in thought during his evening practice at the range. He'd already finished his mana-manipulation practice, his Bolt still refusing to show any personal twists yet, and was working his way through his second box of ammunition for his sidearm. He'd been cleared by Instructor Throneblood to practice Enhancement, as well as Evocation, without supervision, but the instructor had been very pointed on the fact that he was to not injure himself doing it.

Desmond briefly experimented with enhancing his hand-to-eye coordination, which brought his accuracy to more pinpointed levels. The drain of the enhancement was minor as well, proving the instructor's previous statement about a specialty showing for him. Now, though, Desmond had released the enhancement and was back to honing in his focus.

After all, if the base is even stronger, the enhancement has more to work with.

A flick of a gesture and Desmond focused additional

dexterity into his hands, reloading the blocky magazine with the stubby caseless rounds in under three seconds. He was just seating the magazine back into the pistol when his comm-cuff vibrated slightly against his arm.

Checking the interface, he found a message from Chloe waiting for him.

While the two of them had exchanged a few messages back and forth, it had been a few days since Desmond had heard back from the big woman. Most of the messages were him checking up on her and her reassuring him that everything was fine and no one had been causing her problems. While no one seemed to be bothering her, she hadn't mentioned making friends with anyone, only referenced what they were being drilled on when he asked how she was doing.

The message itself was simple and short.

Our instructors said that selection is coming up for our teams next week. Have yours said anything? Trying to find out if they are just pulling our tails or not.

Desmond fired one back at her quickly. It had taken him some getting used to, typing with one hand, but he'd gotten the hang of it thanks to Monika bombarding him with messages between classes.

Throneblood mentioned that it was coming up, but nothing concrete yet. We did go over kits this week, so we know what the basic load-outs are. I know a lot of the girls already have plans for their teams. It's the most common conversation to hear in the halls. Monika won't stop talking about it at meals.

Chloe must have been waiting for his response, as he had a reply back by the time he finished emptying the magazine into the target.

Good, that it's coming up. Really tired of physical conditioning. There are only so many times we can run around a track in increased gravity or do firing drills before you start to lose touch with reality. Her message read.

Fair point, I can only imagine. The two hours I spend at the range every night are really getting to me. I'm just glad that they don't make us buy practice ammunition out of our stipend. Desmond shot a glance at the four empty boxes on the table beside his lane and smirked. He still had two more to go before he finished for the night, but the messages with Chloe were refreshing, actually.

Two hours on the range a night? I thought you were a cadet-adept, not a grunt like the rest of us :)

Only one is on the firearm range. Gotta practice, so it's instinctive after all.

Still, an hour a day? You know that's what us 'mundie' are for, right?

Yeah. But it doesn't hurt to have the skills in case I need them. Plus, you never know how something might factor in later.

Sounds like you have a solid plan already. Desmond read back over the message again. He wasn't sure what it was, but he felt like there was something extra to the message from Chloe.

I'd like to think that, but plans never survive first contact. At least, that's what the military folks back home used to say.

Well, hope your plans go well. I'll stop distracting you from your range time.

All right, have a good night Chloe.

The rest of the evening passed with Desmond spending more time thinking than practicing with his sidearm, considering options. If the first selection for teams was coming up soon, then he needed to figure out what he wanted to do. However, his mind kept drifting back to Chloe.

<><><>

Three more days passed without any actual changes. Desmond had moved from enhancing the durability of objects and his own stats to focusing on maintaining multiple instances of different enhancements. Instructor Throneblood had him in the range, enhancing a collection of wooden boards at once, while taking shots with his sidearm at random. He had to keep as many enhanced as possible while still firing, but he wasn't allowed to only enhance the one board he was aiming at. He wasn't sure how she noticed, but she was on him every time he lost focus, like a glowing eyed bulldog on a meaty bone.

The rest of the class continued with the basic enhancements, and a few others showed signs of specializing in Enhancement as well. None had caught on as quickly as Desmond did, though. He practiced enhancing at the magic range as well, enhancing the durability of the target dummy, the edge on his axe-formed Bolt spell, and different muscle systems to spread the focus out more, even if he wasn't using that muscle group yet.

Even Olianna had been leaving him alone, aside from the occasional snide comment. At least as far as he could tell. Desmond continued to focus heavily on his own work and ignored most of the rest of his class. He had not subscribed to the bullshit when he was in school the first time and refused to do it now.

They had just finished up the fourth day of working with Enhancement spells in the mana manipulation class when Throneblood announced that got the entire class excited.

"Tomorrow morning, you will be meeting in the Gold combat range, the same space you observed your upperclassmen before. I hope that you all have been thinking hard about your plans for your teams, as the first round selection will occur tomorrow." Throneblood gave the class a minute to quiet down before she continued.

"Selection will occur by contribution. Your performance in class will be weighed against your contribution in various different ways. As only a small handful of you have been to a Rift, they will obviously lead the class. First to bid does not guarantee you that the person you are bidding on will join your team. We do not force assignments here." Throneblood stopped for a moment to level a piercing glare that covered the entire class and made each of them feel like she was staring directly at them the entire time. "You will place your top five bids in ranked order and they will be accepted or denied in that order. All of you have the afternoon off to make final decisions. You will receive a roster link to this year's prospectives so that you can review them. Tomorrow, you will set your bids digitally. Your interface will let you know how many others have placed their bids ahead of you for a prospective guard member, so you will know what odds you have of them accepting yours. Those of you who participated in the Rift suppression after assessment, you will put in your bids tonight ahead of the rest of the class."

Desmond felt the eyes of many of his classmates on him. Of the hundred-odd cadets in the room, only two of them had actually gone on the suppression. He and Olianna. He kept his eyes focused on Throneblood as he considered again what he should work towards and how his specialty with Enhancement might work best with a team. *Stronger base means it has more to work with.* He thought to himself again, something he'd proved empirically with his time on the range as he considered.

Enhancement means I'll need to rely on my team a lot, too. Not going to lie to myself, I'm leaning towards Chloe just because I know her and she seems like a great person. He pointedly did not think about the attraction he'd felt to the large Taari woman, though, so he did lie to himself a little.

"Remember! This is the first of the team of people that will be responsible for keeping you alive and protecting you while you go into some of the most dangerous environments imaginable. Don't rush this and *chose wisely!*" Throneblood growled at the class again before dismissing the class.

CHAPTER 26

We were told to choose wisely. I chose the only way I could and still be able to look myself in the eye every morning. I've never regretted that choice.
~Desmond McLaughlin, regarding his team composition.

With the afternoon classes canceled, Desmond met up with Monika and Dianne at the lunchroom, as they usually did when the opportunity arose. The two women had gotten the same news that he did and were quite excited over it all.

"The way Tre'shovak said it, it's like we are picking the captain of our guards tomorrow." Dianne's surprisingly delicate voice was muffled by the mouthful of sandwich, but her enthusiasm remained undiminished despite the mouthful of vegetables and meat.

"Ya, but we can always change that later," Monika dismissed, levering a large spoonful of purple mashed potatoes into her mouth before continuing. "I think I'm going to go with a standard build. The teams that were heavy on the medium kit with the standard rifles did the best in the demonstration."

"That's because they were backed up with an Evocation specialist, Monika."

"Ya, but even without being one myself, you can still fill the gap with equipment. I've got the funds to bump my standard kit up to something with a bit more 'pow' to it. That'll cover more bases. Right, Desmond?" The Dwerg took the opportunity to elbow Desmond in the side as she asked her question.

The elbow to the gut broke Desmond's distraction, and

he wheezed, spitting out the half masticated mouthful of vegetables onto his plate so he could breathe again.

"Wha? Why did you hit me?" he groaned, turning his glare on the redheaded terror in the seat next to him.

"A heavier weapon can make up the difference in a tough encounter, right? You saw more first hand stuff on that suppression run you tagged along with," Monika said shamelessly, not at all contrite about hitting him.

"I did see a fair bit. But the heavy weapons that the group had were one of the laser repeaters and the multi-munition launchers. One of the first things the adept said when we stepped off the ship was 'no explosives' because of the tight cave system. I would imagine that would be true for most settings we encounter that attach to something in space rather than form in the void. Though that doesn't guarantee it, right?" Monika's face fell at his reply and she went thoughtful again.

"Yeah, I remember one of our classes talking about how the location of the Rift doesn't always play into what's on the other side of it. But it does influence it somewhat. Anything else?" the Dwerg asked after silently considering his words for a minute.

"I did remember that pretty much every girl I saw there had no more than the medium kit armor. So it's likely they started with the standard load and swapped in equipment from there," Desmond added after a bit.

"See! Makes the most sense, especially with the very first one to find someone whose focus is the basic gear. Most adaptable and all that," Monika crowed at her friend, her enthusiasm quickly returning.

"But that still doesn't narrow it down any. Standard kit is standard for a reason. I'm still kinda surprised we didn't see as much dedicated melee in the demonstration from the upperclassmen," sighed Dianne. "They all carried a melee weapon, but not many seemed focused on it."

"Well, of course. There was no reason to. Not like they had

to worry about running out of ammunition, and I doubt the Vice-Admiral would have actually hurt anyone if there was a weapon malfunction," Monika shot back. The put-upon expression on the Dwerg telling Desmond that this was not the first time they'd had this back and forth.

"There is another reason," Desmond cut in and both women turned to stare at him. "Think about it! If only one of the team was melee focused, then they'd have to wait for something to get through the support fire for one, and then once that enemy closed the rest couldn't easily fire on it for fear of hitting an ally."

"But what about the entire team going for melee?" Desmond nodded at Dianne's question. But he had considered this as well.

"Ultimately, they are with us to keep us safe, not to be an idealized combat unit. If their entire focus was letting enemies get into melee range, then that puts the adept at the maximum risk without outright having them on the front lines. The exception being melee focused adepts like that one Taari we saw at the demonstration."

"I guess that makes sense...but still! It was supposed to be a demonstration of what the different builds could do!"

"Clearly 'all melee' wasn't a viable build. I mean, when we got a chance to examine the kits, we were told that melee weapons were issued separately..."

A buzz on his wrist cut Desmond off, and the others at his table also looked down at their comm-cuff before opening the notification.

"The roster!" squealed Monika. The excited Dwerg immediately began scrolling through the list of names on her comm-cuff.

"Oh sweet, I thought it would take longer to get the final build." Dianne's grin was filled with excitement that tempered the ferocity of her fang-filled mouth.

Desmond didn't speak though. He immediately shunted the list to his data-tablet and began sorting through the prospective teammates.

"Ooh, he's cute!" Monika yelped only a moment later.

"Damn it, Monika. Stop thinking with your snatch and be serious," Dianne growled back at her while rolling her glowing eyes.

"Dianne, I never stop thinking with my snatch. It's how I got this far."

Desmond shut out their bickering while scrolling.

The prospectives list was organized by build first and then could be customized from there to include load-out, accuracy rate, physical scores and more. Out of curiosity, he sorted by gender and saw that the hundred or so male recruits all had flags on them, showing that bids had been registered for them to join a team already.

Damn, there were only twenty-four of us that had a slot for the early bidding. So that means the girls mostly bid on one of the guys since they are in short supply…and each of the girls bid on multiple guys. I suppose a shotgun approach is needed when the numbers are this low, but seriously?

"Short sighted," Desmond muttered before he began to reorganize the list. A boot to the side of his leg made him wince again, and he turned to glare at Monika. "It wasn't a height joke, Monika!"

"Oh? What were you muttering about, then?" The redheaded menace shot back, the anger draining from her eyes to be replaced with mischief.

"Apparently, all the male mundane recruits have bids on them. Dianne's comment about 'thinking with your snatch' got me curious, and it looks like the girls who got in early are doing the same."

"Awww really? Damn! Well, it doesn't hurt to put a few bids in on them too! Never know, some might have a thing for us 'fun-sized' lovers." Monika's mood swapped back and forth fast, and Dianne just sighed before nodding at Desmond's data-tablet.

"That's a good idea, Desmond. Bigger screen makes it

easier to parse." Desmond just nodded and kept paging through the recruits. While he could organize the sort in a number of ways; the accuracy scores and load-out had most of his attention.

"Oh, she's really cute! Love the horns!" Monika's excited outburst drew Desmond out of his thoughts as she started making a motion with her hands that looked like steering a motorcycle while her hips bounced on the bench seat. "Oh hey, Des. It's your mysterious friend you met in Medical."

Turning to see what Monika was talking about, Desmond had to dodge back slightly to avoid being punched as the Dwerg thrust her comm-cuff clad arm into his face.

Chloe's readout was there on the screen and he grabbed Monika's wrist and noted down a few things before using the search and sort functions to find her on his tablet after releasing Monika.

"Ooh. Looks like Des has his eye on someone and didn't tell us," teased Monika. She gasped when Chloe's picture popped up in better resolution on Desmond's tablet. "Oh, she's not cute. She's downright gorgeous. I couldn't tell as well with this smaller screen."

The mugshot style image of Chloe was only from the shoulders up, and she had a stern expression on her face as she stared into the camera. That style didn't hide her large, leaf green eyes or the way her full lips looked soft even in the military picture. The wickedly curved and pointed lengths of her horns glinted in the image as they emerged from the mess of dirty blonde curls cut close to her head. The lower edge of the picture dipped enough to show off both her heavily muscled shoulders and the upper swell of her large breasts, too.

"Huh...she apparently chose a 'heavy' kit as her load-out...ooh that's why." Dianne had done the same as Desmond and looked her up on her tablet as well. "Makes sense. Bet she needed the extra volume of fire to make up for that low accuracy." The accuracy range that Chloe was sporting was in the low sixties. Desmond was running in the high eighties himself, with both his sidearm and rifle, but could push that up to the high nineties with the enhancements he laid out.

"Still. She looks big enough to rock that heavy kit load-out and make it look *gooooood!*" crooned Monika. "Too bad they don't have any full body pics of her, or some shots from behind! I'd love to climb that mountain!"

The growl that emerged from Desmond's chest surprised all three of them, though Monika recovered the quickest, which was unsurprising given the sheer amount of energy she always had. The hyper Dwerg shot him a grin and held her hands up in surrender.

"Right, right...She's yours Des. If you don't snap her up, though, I'm totally going to take a shot at her."

"Chloe is a friend, Monika." Desmond restrained the growling and pushed the glare away to focus on looking over the readout for Chloe. *Where did that come from? Monika is a friend too, but her talking about taking Chloe really...well it infuriated me.*

"Doesn't mean I can't shoot my shot, Des. If she's half as built as she looks in the photo, then she's gotta be a brick house. And clearly a crossbreed." The questioning look he shot at her got the Dwerg to explain further. "Taurine Taari are like all of their kind: the animal head remains as well as dense fur across most of the body. One of her parents has to be another species. My money is Uth'ra based on the height and weight numbers."

"Huh...never bothered to ask." He remembered Marsden mentioning the same after his story about helping Chloe, but he'd been too tired to follow up on it and had forgotten until now.

"You should be careful if you do." Dianne cut in, shooting a firm look at Monika. "Most half-breed Taari are a little touchy on the subject for good reason. Taari are the only species in the known verse that doesn't breed true. Usually, the offspring of mixed parents follow the mother or the father, depending on gender. With Taari crossbreeds, the features get mixed and muddied and some breeds of Taari can be as haughty about 'pure blood' as the Aelfa get."

"Noted. Don't ask her where she got the pretty face." Monika made a show of scribbling something into her palm before miming crumpling it up and throwing it over her shoulder. "Still, Des, you should totally put a bid in on her. I'm sure she'll take your bid."

"Maybe. That accuracy rate is going to really eat through ammunition quickly. Plus, it looks like she has some outstanding medical debts that come with her. She's gonna be a drain on resources at first since they are going to garnish her pay. Means she'd be unable to flesh out her gear or buy upgrades till it's paid off," murmured Dianne.

"Medical debts? From what?" Desmond prodded at the entry, but all it listed was that she had 'Elective service to annul debts: Medical. Pay to be garnished until settled or minimum service term completed' in her entry. "Now that is just bullshit. Why would they make her pay for injuries taken during training? I thought the Medical bay was free for the cadets."

"To the cadets, yes. But sometimes folk enlist to pay off debts. It's possible she was dealing with the medical debts and signed up to defray them. Poor girl. The private sector medical costs can get exorbitant. The kind of fee that would drive one to active service to annul the debt could have been limb regeneration or something even more ridiculous, depending on how long she's been paying it. Military service is still better than slaving away to pay it off. At least it has an end date," Dianne said with a shrug.

Desmond felt his heart clench at the thought of Chloe laboring under debts. He'd known more than enough people back on Earth that had spent their lives paying down medical debts, let alone home or school debts. Hell, his student loans from his failed attempt at college had throttled his attempts to get a decent place to live for years. He'd been barely able to keep afloat because of the overtime he put in.

Without thinking any more on it, Desmond thumbed the 'bid' option on the tablet and the 'priority one' bid was entered into the system. He then thumbed the entry four more times, placing his other four bids on Chloe, and closed the interface.

"You sure about that, Des?" Monika's eyes were wide as she looked at him. She'd seen all five bids pop up on Chloe's listing.

"Yup." Desmond stood from his spot at the table. "Gonna go hit the range. Got nothing else to do tonight, anyway."

"Yeah. Because you flushed all five of your bids out. What if Chloe gets a different one she wants to go with instead?"

"Then I guess I get dropped to the back of the list and have to bid again. That's a problem for 'Future Me' though, and that guy has it coming. Not sure why yet, but I know he does."

"But why?!" The redheaded Dwerg followed him to the dish return, her tray remaining behind with Dianne, who just watched them with wide eyes.

"Because I can."

"But her debts…"

"So what about her debt? Debt doesn't define someone." Desmond's response was sharp as he cleared his tray and set it in the cradle for the automated cleaners to sanitize.

"You know what? Whatever, Des." Monika's worry melted away, and she just shot him a warm smile. "You know what you are doing. I'm sure you've got it planned out. I'll have faith in that. If she turns you down, then I'm sure I can talk Dianne into consoling you."

"What? You aren't gonna offer to do that?" Desmond shot back, his irritation relaxing slightly as Monika let up on her inquiry. The fact she trusted him went a long way to allaying that irritation.

"Nope, you aren't tall enough for me, anyway. Like I said earlier, I wanna climb a mountain!"

"I'm nearly two feet taller than you!" Desmond protested.

"Two feet does not make a mountain, more like a short hill. Go hit the range and blow off some steam." The wicked eyebrow wiggle that Monika sent his way made Desmond roll his eyes at the innuendo. "Try not to get caught with your pants down, though."

"Whatever. Tell Dianne that I'm sorry for bouncing early. I just wanna get the practice done so I can relax."

"Will do, Des." Monika shot him one last wink before bouncing back to the table, the motion sending little ripples through her body that her tight fitting uniform did nothing to hide. Desmond stepped on his libido, using the irritation at the idea of Chloe buried under medical debts to get hold of himself again.

*Monika flirts a lot, but she isn't serious...*He reminded himself. He had watched the Dwerg woman flirt with SAUL for over an hour while they had been relaxing after classes the other week.

<><><>

The Bronze combat range that Desmond used to practice his casting and shooting was nearly empty when he arrived. Most of the other cadets were likely still eating or reviewing the prospective guard lists. He spared a moment of thought that he might have been hasty throwing all five of his bids onto Chloe but he shrugged it off and got his mana cycling for practice.

Desmond had been drilling his Bolt spell for a good twenty minutes when his comm-cuff chimed to alert him of a new priority message.

Desmond, what the hell?! Apparently Chloe had been notified of his bids.

Sup, Chloe? Looks like your instructor was right. Throneblood told us selection was tomorrow, but the handful of us that were part of that suppression exercise a while back got the first shot at picking teammates.

But why me? Why all five bids?! Desmond chuckled. He could just imagine the frustrated look on Chloe's face as he reread her response.

Because, I want a heavy on my team and I trust you.

You barely know me, Desmond. And you didn't answer why all five bids, McLaughlin... Desmond thought for a second before letting out a sigh through his nose and deciding to be blunt.

I wanted you specifically, Chloe. Easiest way I could see to make that obvious.

Desmond, you are one of the handful of male adepts. You could pick anyone to be on your team and be guaranteed to get priority over almost anyone else.

Yeah, but I'm also a 'prim', and the other cadet-adepts have shown that most aren't willing to look past that. You don't have to take my bid if you'd rather go with someone else, Chloe.

Not what I am asking, McLaughlin. You read my whole entry, right? The reply from Chloe was quick to come in.

Yup, that's how I know you roll the heavy kit after all.

Then why? I'm not the only taurine Taari in the line-up. There are at least a dozen other 'heavy' kit users.

But you are the only Chloe Vandenberg on the line-up. Look, I think you are a solid pick for a teammate and want you on my team. That and I know you already. That's what matters. Don't let my reasons cloud your judgment, Chloe. Do what you feel is best for you.

Desmond turned back to the target in front of him when Chloe didn't send an immediate response. Instead, he focused on honing his spell. As astral axe after axe thudded home into the same three square inch space on the target, Desmond let himself sink into the meditative mindset that his practice always brought him to.

It was some time later when he got another chime on his comm-cuff, but this was a different tone. Pausing with the bolt manifested in his hand still, Desmond checked the readout.

Chloe Vandenberg has accepted your priority one bid for Adept-Guard team posting. Reassignment of housing processed.

"Oh...shit that's right. She'll be moving into my suite..." Desmond felt the bottom drop out of his stomach at that thought.

Letting the Bolt that he was holding dissolve into the air, Desmond rushed out the door and headed back to his suites, frantically trying to remember if he'd left a mess behind.

As he was heading out the door of the range, Desmond got another alert on his cuff in the messaging tone this time. Glancing down as he hurried through the halls, he noticed it was from Adept Marsden. As he opened the message, he got a third alert with an entirely different tone from the others, but focused on reading Marsden's message.

Hey McLaughlin! So the Quartermaster finally got the payout for the loot from the Rift suppression, despite it taking waaay longer than it should have. And since I got paid, you get your ten percent of it as well. You sure as hell earned it. Should hit your account soon-ish. Heard your class is going for initial selection this week, so best of luck on that. Hope the seed funds help you get your team squared away. ~Iris Marsden

A grin spread across Desmond's face that morphed to astonished excitement when he checked his account. The cause of that third alert. He'd been saving his weekly stipend almost exclusively, only spending a handful of credits for extra reading material over the four weeks he'd been at the academy. That morning, his account had read: *452.7 Hegemony Interstellar Credits available...*

Checking it now revealed that the number had changed and changed drastically. The readout for his account now showed: *11,616.9 Hegemony Interstellar Credits available.*

"And that was only a ten percent cut of Marsden's share...I bet the bulk of that was from the 'big momma' bug but still... we can make this work, should let me kit us out as well as furnish the suite finally!"

CHAPTER 27

When I heard Desmond spent all five of his early bids to get Chloe's attention, I laughed my pert little ass off. It was totally like him to pull that shit. The man pretends to be mysterious, but he's not. If anything, her problems made him want to help Chloe out more. I honestly think the physical attraction between them wasn't even a second consideration, maybe a third. He's a better person than I am in that way. Noble idiot that he is.
~Monika Irongrip, Head of the Irongrip Consortium.

Desmond made it back to his suite in less than ten minutes and had what little mess he had produced cleaned up within another five. It wasn't as if he even had that much to make a mess with, but he got it tidied up regardless. With nothing else to do and unable to make himself go back to the range, Desmond decided to finally start browsing through the shop to get the place furnished better and see what all was within his budget.

He had just settled into the conversation pit with his tablet when his comm-cuff chimed on his wrist.

So...accepted your idiot bids. You cool with me moving my stuff over tonight? I want out of the barracks. Chloe's message was brief and to the point.

Come on over. You can help me figure out how the hell to furnish the place. Desmond was quick to respond and sent permissions to the system to give her directions to his suites.

Chloe's response came in the form of the door sliding open less than ten minutes later to allow the broad woman into the suite with a loaded duffel over her shoulder.

The large woman was just as attractive as Desmond

remembered, even more so actually, since she wasn't covered in bruises and limping this time. She ducked slightly as she entered the room, in what seemed to be an ingrained habit to ensure her horns didn't catch on the doorway, though they didn't even come close. Her uniform was neat and creased on her enormous frame, though it pulled tight across the chest, shoulders, and hips.

"Cadet-Guard Chloe Vandenberg, reporting for team reassignment." She came to a stop two steps inside the doorway and snapped off a salute with her free hand. Desmond raised an eyebrow at the official tone she was using now, given the tone she'd used in their messages earlier.

"Hey Chloe, feel free to pick any room you want. Mine's the one to the right of the bathroom. Go ahead and get settled in and then come help me get stuff figured out for furnishings. I've got a budget for your room set aside already. Figured it would be best to hold off organizing the main room till I had someone else here and didn't wanna furnish the rooms without the occupants' input." Desmond decided the best way to make her feel welcome was to treat her as if she'd always been there.

Chloe blinked at him owlishly for a moment before nodding and letting the salute drop.

"Sure thing, Adept…"

"Desmond, or Des," Desmond cut her off abruptly. "I'm not an adept yet, just a cadet. We are roommates and teammates now. Better to be familiar."

"It is inappropriate for me to be that familiar with the adept I am assigned to, regardless of cadet status or not," Chloe argued quietly. Her gaze dropped to the floor. It surprised Desmond how someone so large could look so much like a scolded puppy, and the change in personality from her messages bugged him.

Dropping his data-tablet on the couch next to him, Desmond hopped to his feet and out of the conversation pit. Chloe glanced up at him before dropping her gaze back to the floor as he approached.

Coming to a stop in front of the much larger woman, Desmond caught her down-turned eyes with his and stared up at her for several seconds in silence.

"Chloe, I don't care what is inappropriate or not. You are part of my team now, yes?" The big woman nodded. "Then call me Des or Desmond. Cadet-Adept McLaughlin may be what my uniform reads, but we are going to basically be living in each other's pockets here. I'll make it an order if I have to, but you are my friend first, Chloe."

The muscular wall of a woman considered his words for several moments before cautiously nodding.

"Okay, Des...if that is what you want. I will warn you that such familiarity is...discouraged."

"What are they gonna do? Talk behind my back? Not like the other cadet-adepts don't already do that. Either calling me a prim and deriding me or just talking about my ass like I'm a piece of meat," Desmond said with a shrug. He almost missed the flash of anger that crossed Chloe's features before her normally placid expression covered it up once more.

"Understood, Des. Let me drop off my things." Chloe stepped past him carefully, as if she was afraid of running into him, and hurried over to the door just to the right of his, putting her room between his and the entrance to the suite. Desmond watched her disappear into the room and sighed before going back to sit in the conversation pit.

"SAUL. Make sure she has anything she needs and has access to all the rooms in the suite," Desmond spoke aloud to the digital liaison, who replied a moment later in his overly enthusiastic radio-announcer voice.

"Including your personal rooms, Desmond?"

"Yeah. She'd be a shite guard if she's unable to get to me at any point she needed to after all," Desmond replied before looking back at his data-tablet. He missed the surprised look that Chloe shot at him through the open door to her room, since he was already reading through different furnishing options and considering how much of the windfall he had would be reserved for gear or not.

<><><>

It took Chloe less than ten minutes to settle her things into her room and emerge once more. Desmond had given up on the room furnishings for the moment and was staring up at the ceiling as he pondered what the best way to divide the funds was.

The light was blocked abruptly as Chloe loomed over him with a concerned look on her face. "Des? You in there?" The way the overhead lights glinted on her horns made them glow slightly around the edges, like they were translucent.

"Ya, just thinking a lot. Are you ready to get your room furnished and whatnot?" A smile zipped across his face at her concern for him before vanishing once more.

"I don't need anything extra, Des," Chloe murmured, holding a hand out to stop him. "Just being out of the barracks is enough. Having my own room is a huge upgrade from what I had before." Desmond made a questioning noise, so she continued. "The barracks are communal. Ten girls to a room as big as the one I have to myself now. The bunks were built into the walls. It's part of why I don't have much with me."

"That's gonna get bleak fast. Trust me, I've spent the last month in a basically empty room with just the tiny standard bed. Come on, have a seat. You got your data-tablet?" When Chloe shook her head, Desmond shoved his tablet over to her. "Have a poke through that, you've got a budget of…" Desmond paused for a moment to think. "Five hundred? Yeah, that should be enough to furnish the room."

Chloe shook her head again with a frown.

"Five hundred? That is way too much, Desmond. I'd rather spend that on gear than furnishings for my bedroom."

"Oh, there's another budget for gear. I figure five hundred

each for our rooms, a grand to get some stuff done out here, then the rest on gear and supplies. Wanted to pick your brain on that and see what you thought. Maybe run some drills or spend some time on the range first, so we get a feel for each other's skills. Your kit in the Armory?"

The blonde-haired, taurine Taari just stared at him with wide eyes.

"What? Something on my face?" Desmond patted his cheek for a moment.

"Desmond...that...how do you have that much money? I know cadet-adepts get a larger stipend than us 'mundie' recruits, but how?" she asked finally, shaking her head side to side slowly.

"Oh, that is easy. I told you I went on a Rift suppression already as an observer, right?" Chloe nodded slowly, still staring at him with wide eyes. "The second year who was leading the team said she'd pay me a cut if I carried the loot. I think she just wanted to make sure I didn't cause any trouble or get hurt. Not like that worked, but we did fill up a duffel with bits and pieces, so I have some funds to make sure we are properly geared up with something besides just the basics."

"Des, you realize my salary is only like...thirty credits a week before they pull the garnishment, right? And that is with me volunteering for adept-guard training? It'll double now that I'm on a team, but still..." Chloe's voice was small as she stared down at the tablet in her hand, refusing to meet his eyes now.

"So? You are part of the team. You'll get an equal cut of the loot in our next run, and I plan on making it a good haul. If the bit I got cut in on from Adept Marsden stays true, then this is just peanuts. Trust me." Chloe still kept her eyes on the tablet and shook her head.

"You went along on a second year suppression run. The mana density is higher on those. They are more dangerous and there is more to collect. Anything they have the first years running on is going to be just a fraction of that."

"Still, we can make it up in volume. Don't sweat it, think of this as an investment. Pick out your room stuff. If you don't spend the budget, I'll just transfer the credits over to your account. In fact..." Desmond trailed off and began accessing his comm-cuff with a few rapid presses.

"Des, what are you...Don't you dare!" Chloe looked up, her face twisting in an expression of worry that made Desmond's heart clench.

"Too late, Chloe. Transfer is processing. You can spend the credits to dress up your room, or hang on to them. Your call. I recommend at least getting a better bed. The basic fold out one they have for each room is shite." Desmond waved it off again. It felt good to toss money around like this. He wasn't rich by any extent. He'd done the pricing to realize that just getting a few alternate guns and upgrading his personal armor would eat up most of the rest of his budget, but it still felt good. And that was picking bottom end gear to get more than one item.

Chloe glared at him now, her brow furrowed and nostrils flared in irritation. Desmond refused to look up or acknowledge the look of irritation on her face and, in the process, missed when her expression softened to a smile before she schooled herself to a neutral expression.

"Okay, fine Des. But no more. I want to earn my share."

"Trust me, you will earn it by keeping my skinny ass alive. But I'm going to make sure our entire team is properly kitted out," Desmond replied without looking up from his comm-cuff. "Equal shares and we work together. I expect you to call me out if I do something stupid that puts us at risk. Just like I'm going to do my best to make sure my guards have everything they need to do their job."

Silence descended on the two of them as they made the selections they wanted for their rooms. It wasn't an awkward silence, despite the newness of their situation. Instead, it was a peaceful one. Another hour passed as they got several extra furnishings for the main room, mostly individual comfortable chairs, so they had somewhere besides the table or conversation pit to sit. With the orders logged in and distraction removed, the silence finally turned a bit awkward as they stared at each other.

"So…want to go get some dinner? I kinda skipped most of lunch. It'll give you a chance to meet the others that I hang out with," Desmond offered after the silence got too thick to tolerate.

"Sure, that sounds good. Since I'm officially assigned to your team, I'm supposed to stick with you any time you leave the room," Chloe said. She hopped to her feet with a surprising amount of dexterity. Desmond frowned as he also got to his feet.

"Sounds stifling. If you need some time alone, just tell me. I don't expect you to hang on me at all times while we are here in the rooms."

"It's my job, Des," Chloe said with a soft smile. "I'll let you know if I need a break or something, but this is what I signed on for. It's not a burden." Desmond caught the hint of a blush crossing her broad cheeks before the big woman turned away from him and led the way to the door.

"Oh, that reminds me, do you have a sidearm?" Desmond checked and settled the chunky pistol on his hip out of habit. He was still getting used to having it, but the belt and drop-leg holster were slowly becoming natural.

"Mundie guards don't carry sidearms onboard the *Valor's Bid*," Chloe answered. She paused to check both directions at the door before leading the way out. "As our instructors told us, the only reason the adept-cadet's get to carry them all the time is more self-defense than anything else. And to get them used to having them for the future."

"Suppose so. Seems odd, though. That the 'guards' that are required to be with us at all times aren't allowed to be armed."

"It's an academy ship. If something that could threaten

the cadets got on board, a sidearm isn't going to make a difference."

"At least for outside threats," Desmond muttered. Chloe could only shrug, glancing back to check on her charge and make sure Desmond stayed close. As they walked, the long, tufted, cow-tail that emerged from the back of her uniform pants switched back and forth happily.

<><><>

The mess hall was, unsurprisingly, still messy with people. While the massive space wasn't anywhere near filled to capacity as it was sized to accommodate the cadet-adepts and their entire teams, after all, it was still busy.

A quick glance around spotted Monika and Dianne with their heads down over their tablets at the usual table. *Honestly, it looks like they haven't moved since lunch.* Desmond thought wryly before following Chloe through the food line.

The two of them got more than a few odd looks, and murmurs chased after them as the nearby cadet-adepts noticed Chloe. Given the taurine Taari's size, she was hard to miss. It only took a glance at the rank insignia on her shoulder to know she wasn't a cadet-adept. The murmuring didn't faze the bull-horned woman as she gathered her tray of food and stood watch over Desmond while he got his.

While Chloe had led the way to the mess hall, once they had food, she fell in a step behind him and to the left, letting him guide the way to their table. *I wonder...* Desmond thought over Chloe's practical personality and smiled slightly. *Is it because the pistol is on my right hip and she wants to ensure I have a clear draw? Would fit for what I know of her.*

"You two still drooling over your bid picks?" Desmond said as he sat down at Monika and Dianne's table, gesturing for Chloe to take the seat next to him, which she did.

"Yeah, you hear back...whoa!" Monika finally looked up

from her tablet and did a double take at seeing Chloe's broad form next to Desmond. This drew Dianne's attention, and the Uth'ra blinked in surprise, too.

"Monika, Dianne, this is Chloe. She agreed to join my team, so you two will be seeing a lot of her. Chloe, these two are the only other cadet-adepts that bothered to get to know me. Well, Monika kinda dragged Dianne in and forced her, but she hasn't complained much." Desmond shot the Uth'ra a wink, and she just rolled her eyes.

"Like the pint-sized terror could actually drag me anywhere."

"Oh, I'll drag you somewhere. Don't discount me on my size alone. I'll just hack you off at the knees to bring you down to size. That or just get you by the panties!" Monika said with a grin.

"Still wouldn't be enough to put me at your size," snarked Dianne before turning back to Chloe. "It's good to meet you, Chloe. You have my permission to smack either of them if they get too lippy. Especially Monika."

"You can smack me anytime you want, cutie." Monika apparently had already decided to switch gears and flirt with Chloe rather than argue with her Uth'ra friend.

"It's good to meet you two," Chloe said carefully, clearly lost in how to respond to the two cadet-adepts. Desmond flicked Monika with his spoon, making the Dwerg jump and yelp.

"What was that for?" Monika demanded with a glare, rubbing her forehead while staring at him.

"Stop flirting with my guard and get your own," Desmond mock-demanded.

"Fiiiine. If you get bored with dealing with the sour-puss here, let me know Chloe. I'll make a spot for ya." Monika's whine morphed into her familiar flirting before she turned back to her tablet. Dianne chuckled and did the same.

"You guys narrow your selection down?" Desmond asked as the table returned to its previous quiet. Chloe ate in silence, her eyes flicking back and forth warily as people passed near their table, clearly taking her role of guard seriously already.

"Somewhat. Neither of us are Evocation or Enhancement specialists, so I'm leaning more towards staying balanced. The challenge comes in picking someone that can keep up with me," Groused Dianne as she prodded the screen in front of her. "Got any suggestions, Chloe? You were in class with most of these girls already."

"Who are you considering? I can give you some info, but I didn't spend a lot of time observing the others. I was more focused on my own thing." Chloe glanced over at the Uth'ra and accepted the data-tablet when it was offered to her. She flipped through the list for several seconds before tapping and marking several of the women listed and passing it back. "Those six are the ones I'd avoid. They had attitude problems that had to be 'adjusted' multiple times. Two of them by me personally."

"Were they the ones that sent you to Medical?" Desmond's voice was icy, which drew a surprised look from all three women at the table.

"Uhh...yeah actually. Those two were part of the group that piled on after I dropped the first one who started in on me. Broke one's arm and the other's face before they got me on the ground."

"Oh, I hadn't heard this part. All Des would tell us was that you got into a fight! Spill!" Monika bounced into the conversation as well and pushed her tablet across the table towards Chloe. "Can you look at mine too?"

Chloe set her fork back down and poked through Monika's tablet as well, flagging several that were on Monika's shortlist as well. She briefly went over the fight that led to her meeting Desmond in the Medical wing, even including the brief verbal altercation with the other group in the hall on their way back that Desmond had described previously.

"They didn't bother me after that, at least not physically,"

Chloe said with a shrug, digging back into her food. "And I'm not telling you to avoid them just to be petty! They legitimately had poor attitudes. A few even got time in the stockade for shit they got caught for."

"We know, Chloe. They asked you for your opinion," Desmond reassured her. He'd finished eating while she'd explained the encounter to Monika and Dianne. "Right?" The other two nodded, already diving back into their updated lists with fervor.

"Thanks," Chloe murmured quietly and Desmond just smiled at the big woman. The dichotomy that was already showing between her assertive self on duty and the quieter face she showed in social situations amused him. Desmond looked forward to her relaxing more.

Desmond made small talk for another hour with Dianne and Monika, while the two continued to debate what the pros and cons of different team layouts might be. Chloe chimed in occasionally with suggestions from the other side of the fence, alternately approving or shutting down different ideas that they had.

After they had finalized, for now at least, who they'd be bidding on in the morning, the group broke up. Desmond and Chloe headed back to their suite of rooms. The furniture that they had ordered had been fabricated and delivered by that point and they got it unpacked and arranged how they wanted before heading to bed for the night.

Desmond lay awake for more than an hour, his ability to sleep at the moment stymied by the knowledge that Chloe was just on the other side of the wall. He'd helped the bull-horned woman get stuff in her room and, as he'd expected, she'd gone for a spartan layout. Just the bed, a weapons rack, and an armor rack, along with a small cabinet for storing media. Not that Desmond could comment much. The largest expenditure he'd made was getting a much larger bed with more comfortable sheets, as well as expanding his media library. It still hadn't taken that much, and he ended up saving most of his funds for 'future use' as planned.

Eventually, Desmond gave up and used his tablet to queue up the subliminal language training that would help imprint at least the spoken language for Hegemony Standard into his subconscious. It wouldn't eliminate the need to practice on his own, but given how much of his free time had already vanished into extra-curricular training, this was necessary.

He was asleep within minutes.

CHAPTER 28

It was dorm life. I didn't mind it as much, being from the family that I am. It was actually nice to have someone around once we got to the first guard selection. Tense until we got to know each other, but nice.
~Dianne Sagejumper, on life aboard the *Valor's Bid*.

Waking with a start, Desmond was extremely disoriented at first. Waking up on the much larger bed with the new bedding was strange enough for him, but his dreams had made it even stranger.

"Gotta be the subliminal training," Desmond croaked, shaking his head to try to clear the disorientation from his system. "Man, I hope that doesn't continue...the program is supposed to take weeks to fully master."

Shaking off the last of his lethargy, Desmond got out of bed and stumbled out into the main room, heading for the bathroom. The fog still lingering in his mind cleared up enough to notice that the door to the bathroom was cracked slightly and the light inside was on. Pausing to stare at the light streaming through the crack, Desmond flogged his brain to figure out why in the world he'd left the lights on.

It was fortunate that he paused as he did, because that gave his brain the time needed to process the fact that he could hear water running. Which led him down the path of 'who could be in the shower'.

"Oh...that's right. Chloe moved in yesterday," Desmond murmured, rubbing at his face again. The lethargy was fighting him hard today, and he turned to stumble back to his room when the water shut off and he heard someone humming distantly. A glance down at himself reminded Desmond that he was only wearing his boxers and he hurried through the door to his room just as the bathroom door swung open behind him.

"Morning Des," an overly-cheerful Chloe called as she crossed directly in front of his room, heading for her door. Desmond threw a glance over his shoulder as he heard her pass and nearly swallowed his tongue.

Chloe had a towel wrapped around her waist just below her belly-button and nothing else. Her skin shone brilliantly with the leftover moisture from the shower and drops of water pearled on her pale skin, tracing adventurous paths down across her muscled back or down along her side to race along the defined channels of her abdominals. His mouth went dry as he could only imagine the view from the front, since he could see the generous curve of her breasts swelling to either side of her back. Fortunately, or unfortunately, he wasn't entirely sure. She'd already made it past his room before he turned, so he could only imagine. *Not sure I'd even be able to think straight if I saw her head on like this.*

"Ah, uh. Morning Chloe, are you all done in the shower?" he called back, voice strained.

"Yup, all yours, Des. Breakfast when you are done?" Chloe's voice echoed through the common area as she vanished into her room. Desmond distantly heard the 'thump' that had to be the towel around her waist hitting the ground, and he groaned low in his throat.

"Sure...yeah...let me get a shower real quick," Desmond choked out before snatching up a clean uniform and sprinting to the bathroom, latching the door shut behind him as soon as he was inside. He'd managed to resist the urge to glance toward Chloe's room, since he'd not heard her shut the door either.

A rapid adjustment of the heat slider in the shower had a cascade of cold water pouring down over him. The chilly water washed away the last bits of his disorientation. While

Desmond shivered and scrubbed at himself, he thought back to earlier and played it back in his mind. He hadn't heard her close the door...before she'd dropped her towel.

<><><>

The cold shower had helped Desmond get his libido under control. He'd known that Chloe was attractive, but the sheer amount of femininity in her nearly eight foot tall frame had hit Desmond like a truck all in a single moment. Once he was showered and dressed, the two of them headed to the mess hall.

"Looks like I'm not the only one who's already shifted dorms." Chloe nodded to a mass of women that were crowded around several tables in the corner. Among the women, Desmond could make out the large frames of several men of differing races.

"Guessing those are probably the other front-runners that did well in the assessment. It certainly looked like they'd all had bids put in for the males last night." Desmond rolled his eyes. He'd seen Olianna in the middle of the group, sitting directly on the lap of a large male Hyreh, who looked a little uncomfortable with all the attention he was receiving from the cadet-adept females. Though the thunderous look the female Hyreh cadet-adept behind him was directing at Olianna hinted that she was likely taking liberties with someone else's guard at the moment.

Probably tried and failed to bid for a male guard herself. Desmond thought with a grin, noting another Aelfa watching Olianna carefully in case the Hyreh cadet-adept got violent.

"Not surprised in the least. At least here with the adepts, they'll have fewer females all over them. The men are in short supply in general amongst the regular army. At least with the adept-guard, even the cadet-adepts, they'll be left alone. No one wants to piss off an adept, except maybe another cadet-adept." Chloe explained as they got their food and headed back to their usual table, which they had to themselves for once.

"Good to know. So they only have to fend off the attention of the cadet-adepts rather than the entire ship's complement of marines...Glad those girls left you alone before. Are they going to give you any trouble when you go back to regular classes?" Desmond dug into his stack of biscuits and gravy with gusto.

"I don't have regular classes anymore, Des," Chloe said with a shrug. She began digging into her own breakfast, a pile of scrambled 'eggs' as big around as his head. "The regular army folks only spend six to twelve months on the academy ship before shipping out to a duty post. Only the first three months of that is mandatory training and I'm at the four-month mark, anyway. Anything after the third month is specialist training."

"So what, you just follow me around to class now?" Desmond mumbled through a mouthful of biscuits. Since Chloe wasn't bothering to not talk with her mouth full, he figured he might as well too.

"Sorta. The way it was explained when I signed up for selection was that, if we were chosen, we'd accompany our adept constantly. Any practical classes you go through will give us time on the range to practice as well. The classroom ones are free periods for us to do as we see fit. They did mention that there is group training as well and that second years could largely train as they saw fit to further hone team dynamics. Once you get more folks on your team later on, we'll likely drill situations where you are incapacitated or separated from us while you attend a lecture."

"Huh...okay I'll ask Throneblood today. I know she said to meet in the Gold combat range for the first half of the day. I assumed it was going to be for the bidding, but everything is supposed to be done electronically."

"Ya, likely going to fill everyone in. If we are lucky, she'll give you part or most of the period off since you already got your selection done." Chloe shot him a sidelong glance with one large green eye as she chewed. "I haven't even seen you on the range yet, and you haven't seen me either, so that will be important to do."

"Agreed. I have some ideas that I wanna test out as well." Desmond paused to chew for a moment before rolling his eyes as a thought occurred to him. Chloe caught the mild expression of irritation that slid across his features and made a 'continue' gesture with her hand. "Just realized I hadn't filled you in yet on it. Training had me so distracted, combined with getting you settled yesterday. I tested with an Enhancement specialization, so you got that to look forward to."

Chloe's eyebrows shot up at that and she turned to face him directly, her jaw moving rapidly to finish chewing her mouthful and swallowing before speaking.

"Enhancement specialization? That's good, right? They didn't fill us in on all the bits and pieces of mana manipulation, since we weren't ever going to be adepts ourselves."

"It means, sweet cheeks, that Des is going to be relying on you most of all." Monika interrupted their conversation in her usual enthusiastic and brash fashion as she tossed her tray up onto the table and hopped onto a stool to join them.

"How so?" Chloe flushed slightly but turned her focused attention to the Dwerg instead.

"Enhancement adepts specialize in making things stronger, faster, durable, and accurate. Regular ole adepts like myself can usually enhance one factor and only by a modest amount. Des here is going to pump you up like an Uth'ra berserker on a blood rage *and* make sure you are lucid enough to thread the needle at a hundred yards."

"I'm not that good, Monika," Desmond sighed. He had to snatch his mug of space coffee off his tray when he caught the Dwerg eying it, getting the mug just before she did.

"Not yet, you aren't. I give it six months and you'll have Chloe here doing trick shots that a skilled markswoman would struggle with."

"Don't set expectations too high, Monika. I haven't even tried to enhance another person yet."

"Well, who knows? The rest of us will have our first guards today. Maybe you'll get to practice this afternoon. I bet Chloe is looking forward to it." Monika glanced between the two of them with a wicked smirk on her face. Chloe just shrugged, continuing to eat at a steady rate and giving nothing away at the moment.

<><><>

As it turned out, Monika was right. When they arrived at the Gold combat range, Throneblood had immediately called Desmond over so she could meet Chloe. The interaction had been interesting since even the Uth'ra instructor had to look up to meet Chloe's eyes. Despite the size difference, Instructor Throneblood hadn't had any problems staring down the bull-horned woman before turning her glare on Desmond.

"McLaughlin, you and Vandenberg are to report to the Bronze combat range and begin familiarizing yourself with each other. There's no reason for you two to hang around right now, since this period is going to be given over to introductions between the cadet-adepts and their guards. I know Vandenberg already moved into your suite last night, anyway." Desmond fought to keep the blush off his face at what Instructor Throneblood said, despite the fact they hadn't actually *done* anything other than get their rooms furnished.

It's not what it sounds like. Stop being an idiot. He reminded himself.

"So, instead. You two get to have a jump on the rest of the class. Drill for the period, break for lunch, then report back to the Bronze range for afternoon class. The rest of these yokels will be doing then what you two are now, but more time to drill will always be useful." Throneblood glanced to one side when a gaggle of cadet-adepts entered the room, giggling at each other. "The entire class is going to have the next day off. Unfortunately, the first years don't qualify for shore-leave so you won't be allowed off the ship, but it gives you time to get to know each other as well. No enhancements for Vandenberg until the afternoon class. I don't want you trying that shit without supervision. Dismissed."

Desmond and Chloe snapped out salutes before ducking out the door.

"Gotta swing by the Armory to pick up my kit first," Chloe muttered. She glanced back over her shoulder at Throneblood, who was tearing into one girl for her uniform being mussed.

"No worries. Are you going to store it in your room on the stands?"

"That was the plan. I can do maintenance and cleaning on all my gear myself. Armorers prefer it if we actually take the time to maintain our gear. We weren't allowed to store our gear outside the Armory when I was in the barracks. Not enough room, but now that I'm on assignment, that restriction is lifted since my entire focus is keeping you safe. It's getting in the habit for now, even though I'm not allowed to carry it outside going to the range and back."

"Don't sweat it too much. I have money set aside for gear, so we can check that out this weekend. Let's get your current gear though and get to the range. Throneblood is a Divination specialist, so I wouldn't put it past her to have a mana construct tracking us to make sure we actually go to the range."

CHAPTER 29

The Hegemony of Velvet Stars is a tolerant nation. They do not overly interfere with their vassal states' lives and laws, allowing many of the species to dictate much of their own internal structures. Though several laws are required to be observed throughout the Hegemony. You do not meddle with Rifts, and all adepts are required to be trained aboard the academy ships of the Hegemony. The restrictions on organized religion are meant to protect rather than oppress. Because of several encounters with seventh-dimensional creatures posing as deities in the early years of the Hegemony, such things are heavily vetted when a new culture is encountered. As such, the vast majority of citizens distrust and avoid them.
~Lila Tre'jira, Adept-Guard and Historian.

Desmond learned several things during firearms practice with Chloe before lunch.

The first being that, while Chloe had been issued gear, it wasn't new gear, like his sidearm and rifle had been. Her armor kit, which had been wheeled out on a stand for her to show him, was serviceable, but obviously worn. The laser-repeater, which she carried to the range under one arm like it was a loaf of bread, was in the same condition, though clearly both were well maintained.

The second thing was that Chloe had something akin to performance anxiety. If he was watching her directly, or after several of the other cadet-adepts and their teams showed up, her accuracy tended to go downhill. Desmond fixed this by shifting their firing lanes away from the others, putting Chloe against one wall, and he took the lane next to hers to act as a bulwark between them. As long as he didn't stare at her while she shot, her accuracy numbers climbed steadily and settled in the mid-seventies rather than low sixties.

Lunch was a lesson in madness, as all the cadet-adepts had their teammates with them. Despite there being plenty of room in the mess for them all, folk still argued and clumped up. What they argued about varied from whether they all needed to queue up, or if they would queue as groups, or if the cadet-guards should 'fetch a meal' for their cadet-adepts.

Desmond dealt with it using the bluntness that had served him well on dozens of construction sites. He just plowed through the groups with Chloe at his back. Between the fact he was a male and her size, no one really voiced a complaint when he pushed past groups that had devolved into arguments over the lines and the like.

They did get to meet Monika and Dianne's teammates. Monika had ended up going with a broad Hyreh woman named Oril'la with severe features and a strong resting bitch face that hid good humor when she decided to join the conversations, though she observed silently most of the meal. Dianne had settled on a willowy Yu'Aelfa named Mona Lu'toru who was an opposite to Oril'la. While the Hyreh looked severe but had a good humor, Mona looked like she was daydreaming but had a very serious attitude, which she displayed by getting up in the face of another cadet that had 'accidentally' bumped into them while they were getting their food. She was around Desmond's size, at least in height, but far more slender.

While the cadet-adepts were friends, Desmond did notice that the cadet-guards were more wary of each other. *Like cats meeting each other for the first time.* Desmond thought as he watched the cadet-guard's eye each other warily. *Wonder if they will relax more once they have extras on their team. I know Chloe is serious about keeping me safe. She just about chewed my head off when I tried to wander off at the range.*

The afternoon classes went very similar to the morning ones, but with far larger numbers of people in the range. Desmond had left the mess hall early with Chloe to get back to the Bronze combat range in order to secure their lanes along the wall. He hadn't told Chloe yet that he had noticed her issues when being watched before, and simply mentioned that he needed to get more ammunition set up and wanted to get there early, before the rush.

"All right, Cadets!" thundered Instructor Throneblood when the afternoon classes began. "As some of you have already heard through the rumor mill, you are all getting leave tomorrow to help your new cadet-guards settle in with you. As I've already had to field this question two more times today than I should have had to." Throneblood shot a withering glare around the group of cadets that made several of the cadet-adepts cringe. "Yes. The teammate you selected is going to be sharing your suites with you. You are expected to cooperate and cohabitate with them. They are your guards, not your servants or slaves. If I hear reports of you mistreating your team, I can guarantee there will be consequences that you won't like. This goes double for any of you who selected a male guard-cadet. They are not your personal gigolo, they are your bodyguards. You will respect them."

There was a chorus of assent from the cadet-adepts, punctuated by a handful of 'yes, Instructor!'s from the more aware cadet-adepts. The cadet-guards remained silent, one and all doing their best impressions of potted plants as the instructor bawled out her class.

"I'm sorry. I think I heard a bunch of children muttering! What was that again?" Throneblood roared. Apparently, her temper was up at the moment as a crackle of purple lightning arced between the curls of her dark-blue mane while her orange eyes quite literally flared brighter.

"Yes, Instructor Throneblood!" Roared back the cadet-adepts. Those that weren't at attention immediately snapped to it.

Instructor Throneblood continued to glare at the cadet-adepts for several long moments before she snorted like an angry bull. Running one large hand through her still crackling hair, she gathered the purple lighting into her fist and squashed it with a loud *pop*.

"Do not make me repeat this lecture or every one of you is going to be running an additional assessment," snapped Throneblood before she gestured for them to move to 'at ease' stances. "Now, this afternoon is for you and your new cadet-guard to get to know each other's abilities. As I stated before, tomorrow will be for you to get them settled into your suite. Your entire guard team will eventually be sharing the space with you, so get used to it. If you think sharing those suites is cramped, just ask your cadet-guards about the ship barracks they were in, because that's where you are going to end up when on assignment later." Throneblood paused to throw yet another glare around the room, and Desmond had to wonder at just what had set the instructor off so badly. "First years do not get shore leave, so don't expect to get off ship unless you earn special exception. However, there are retail and relaxation zones that you can visit now that you have at least one of your guards with you. Cadet-adepts are required to be escorted by their guards whenever they leave their rooms. This is to get you used to it. You are the future of the Hegemony and the bulwark against Rifts. Your guards will be your bulwark against other threats. Do not cause problems."

After her lecture, Throneblood directed them to begin practicing so that they could familiarize themselves with each other's level of skill, working her way down the line from one end of the building to the other, giving direction and pointers while observing. Desmond noted that there was a trio of other instructors that he didn't recognize observing and assisting Throneblood.

Nudging Chloe, he pointed to the unfamiliar faces with a

questioning expression.

"Some of our old weapons instructors. They likely got reassigned to help Instructor Throneblood ride herd on this group," Chloe muttered. She only glanced up at the trio before going back to setting up her laser repeater with familiar motions.

Desmond watched as she attached two of the three power sources she'd brought with her to the charging ports on the top of the shooting bench before slipping the third into a belt rig that hung on the back of her belt. The portable power sources were baton shaped rods roughly two inches across and a foot long that had a glowing meter on one side to show their current charge.

"Makes sense. So, are you ready to see what the enhancements can do for you?" Desmond had laid his sidearm on the bench in front of him, as well as the four magazines he carried for it. The six boxes of spare rounds landed beside them. He'd loaded the magazines up before heading to lunch, but it didn't hurt to have things arranged neatly when Throneblood came by.

"What...what does it feel like?" Chloe asked, her hands slowing on her weapon but her eyes not looking up at all.

Desmond was about to shrug off her question but stopped to think on it, staring up at the ceiling for a moment to consider.

"It kinda feels like...you ever pop your neck and feel you can think better afterward?" Chloe nodded, twisting her head to face him. Desmond fought the urge to duck as her dark horns swung towards him, despite the fact they were several feet above his head. Chloe didn't seem to notice his twitch.

"It's kinda like that. You'll feel a *pop* or a *click* kind of sensation and then it all sharpens. At least when I'm boosting my awareness or hand-to-eye coordination. Strength enhancement feels...more like the burn after a good stretch." Chloe seemed mollified after the explanation and nodded slowly.

"Okay, that doesn't sound too bad…"

"I should hope not!" Desmond laughed, smiling up at the much larger woman. "Don't want to hurt you or anyone just to give them a boost. I mean, if push came to shove, and it was necessary to survive? Yeah, totally. But not on the regular. Though…that does make me wonder if I can enhance my mental-flexibility while studying and retain more information." Desmond tapped his bottom lip thoughtfully as he turned it over in his head.

Chloe, however, was much more blunt and to the point. Rather than just ponder it, she glanced over at the group of instructors who were maybe a dozen lanes away from them at this point and waved her arm to get the attention of one of them.

The instructor, a sturdy-looking woman of average height with slate-gray skin, bright-yellow eyes and a smooth, hairless head, trotted over to them after excusing herself from the group. A pair of membranous gray bat-wings were tucked neatly against her back.

"Yes, Cadet?" Her voice was deep, even deeper than Throneblood's was, and sounded like two rocks being rubbed together.

"Instructor. My cadet-adept was pondering something about the application of his Enhancement magic off the range that we wanted to ask about." The gray-skinned instructor nodded slowly, her head tilted to the side in an oddly bird-like gesture. "Can enhancements be applied to cognitive functions while studying to improve retention? And if so, is it something only the adept can benefit from?"

A broad smirk spread across the instructor's face, revealing dense, square teeth in her mouth that were as dark as obsidian.

"Yes, actually. That is one of the many benefits of working with an adept." She glanced to one side at Desmond, quirking an eyebrow at him. "Cadet-Adept McLaughlin, right?

Enhancement specialist?" Desmond nodded. "As I suspected, you lucked out on this one, Vandenberg. Take good care of him and you will see the benefits. Now, I have to get back to Throneblood. She will want to talk to McLaughlin before he actually enhances you, so hold off on that till she gets to you."

The two cadets saluted the instructor, who trotted back to where Throneblood was working her way down the line. A brief conversation was had between them before Throneblood nodded and continued on her way. Desmond and Chloe only had to wait a handful of minutes until they got there, and the two of them used it to ensure their lanes were set up and ready.

"McLaughlin. Starting next week, I want you bringing your rifle to class. Your skill with the sidearm is acceptable at this point. Vandenberg can help train you with it in your spare time. I don't have to tell you to practice both diligently, do I?"

"No, Instructor." Desmond replied with a nod.

"Good. Now, I'm sure you are itching to share an enhancement with Vandenberg so she can get used to the sensation. Start slowly. It is going to be stranger for her than when you were enhancing yourself. Especially since you are developing a specialization in it.

"While you aren't going to require chants for long, it might be good to retain some basic ones to warn your team of what is incoming, so they know. Start with something simple and go from there." Throneblood glanced between him and Chloe a few times before gesturing over her shoulder at the gray-skinned instructor.

"Instructor Gemtooth tells me that it finally occurred to you to try enhancing your mental faculties for studying?"

"Yes, Instructor. I'm unfortunately behind on a lot of things, and I know the language deadline is coming faster than I want it to. I bought the subliminal training course on it, but it really messed with my sleep schedule. It occurred to me while I was explaining what the feeling of the enhancements would be to Cadet Vandenberg that I might use it to...ease the transition?" Desmond finished lamely.

"It is an idea, but don't leave an enhancement in place overnight. It is a good way to drain your mana cache. Given time, you will begin to develop the ability to put a limiter on them, to say shut off after consuming a set amount of mana or a set amount of time has passed. At this time, it's not safe. However, you can put them into place to study." Throneblood reached out to tap the center of his chest with one thick finger. "Though only do so in short bursts to start with. You've already got approval to practice Enhancement and Evocation without supervision. Don't make me regret it."

"I will ensure that he does not, Instructor," Chloe spoke before Desmond could, her fist meeting her chest in a salute.

"Good woman. That is your duty to your adept. Ensure they are safe as can be in all things. Now, back to the lesson. McLaughlin, one aspect at a time. Start small and ramp up as Vandenberg gets used to it. Vandenberg, you need to learn to perform with and without the enhancements, so I expect you to drill both ways as there will be times that McLaughlin will not have them in place for you or you have to react before he does."

<><><>

Starting small helped a lot for Chloe. Desmond decided to begin with a dexterity boost when he noticed her hands shaking slightly as she readied her weapon. Clearly, having all the instructors watching them was kicking her nerves up.

"You got this," Desmond murmured before winking at her. Turning slightly, he took up the 'at-ease' position half a step behind her right shoulder. A position that put her 'at guard' as it was how they normally walked through the halls when she led the way.

The move worked, because Chloe's shoulders firmed up and she brought her weapon to bear on the target. Desmond spun up the first enhancement, a light increase to hand-to-eye coordination as the instructors watched on.

"Shooter ready?" Desmond infused the words with the enhancement, pushing it into Chloe by using them as the chant. Chloe grunted her assent. "Begin."

Chloe snapped off a volley of shots at the target in a storm of blue beams. While her shots earlier had been accurate enough that they all connected with the polycarbonate dummy, the muzzle climb of her weapon being negligible because of the lack of recoil, they tended to spread out in a clump roughly the size of his head at this range. This volley, however, was tightly focused. A cluster of scorch marks settled over the chest of the dummy, smaller than Desmond's closed fist. Chloe blinked in surprise and lowered her weapon, punching the buttons to bring the target forward to observe it.

"Very good. What did you enhance there, McLaughlin?" Throneblood said curtly.

"Hand to eye coordination, Instructor. About a third of what I have practiced on myself. I wanted to ensure that my partner felt the increase but wasn't startled by it."

"A third?!" Chloe choked, turning her wide-eyed gaze onto Desmond.

"Yup. You wanna go whole-hog?" Desmond shot her another wink, but a confused look crossed Chloe's face.

"Whole-hog?"

"I mean, 'do you want the full increase'?" Desmond clarified.

"Give her the full increase, McLaughlin," Throneblood cut in. The Uth'ra instructor stepped around them and adjusted the controls, sending the dummy sliding back on its rail until it was the maximum distance away at around a hundred and fifty meters. "Cadet Vandenberg, I expect you to aim for the head on the target."

"But Instructor, the scatter pattern on a repeater..." Chloe protested weakly, only to be cut off by Throneblood.

"I didn't stutter, Vandenberg. Trust in your adept," Throneblood said with a flat stare before stepping back from the controls.

Chloe took a deep breath and let it out through her nose before she squared her shoulders and faced the target.

Desmond took up his position behind her and to her right, hands behind his back as he thought furiously. *This is as much a test for me as it is for Chloe…the accuracy of the repeaters goes to shit beyond a hundred yards. They can scatter up to a foot and the head of the dummy is just over half that wide.* Thinking for a moment, Desmond frantically cudgeled his brain for inspiration until it landed on a chant that might work. Just the regular hand-to-eye coordination increase wouldn't be enough like this. *The chant guides the magic when you are unsure of where to place it after all.*

"Let her aim be true and her hand faster than those that seek to destroy me, grant her victory over my foes and those that wish to do harm to me and mine…" Desmond chanted, modifying the Gunfighter's Prayer to something that would fit Chloe's mindset. He remembered his uncle having it tattooed on his biceps. The man was ex-special forces and Desmond remembered him using it as a mantra while doing competition shooting later in life before lung-cancer had claimed him, and it felt perfect for the moment.

Desmond felt the mana spin out of his body like a handful of gossamer threads, settling into Chloe's body and her weapon. He felt a noticeable drop in his cache, more than he was used to for enhancements, but Desmond did not react.

A brief shiver ran through Chloe before she went still as stone. The firing stud depressed on her weapon and a volley of bright, violet-colored lasers arced into the target.

"The hell?" muttered one instructor behind Desmond, but Throneblood just chuckled.

"McLaughlin, I told you just to boost her accuracy, not give her 'the works'," the Uth'ra instructor chided him. "That, Vandenberg, is what an Enhancement specialist adept can do. I, personally, would use a similar chant to achieve the boost you got on the first try. Now, though, you have the unenviable task of getting used to operating under both the variety and depth of enhancements he can spin out. And when your team expands, it's going to be your responsibility to teach the others."

Chloe didn't respond. She was staring down at her weapon in confusion still.

"How...what?" she muttered. Her surprise drew laughter from all four instructors, which finally broke Chloe out of her fugue. She blinked owlishly at them, her confusion still obvious.

"You are wondering about the color shift, aren't you?" Instructor Gemtooth asked, her yellow eyes dancing with mirth.

"Yes! I've used this weapon for months. It's never done that."

"That's because McLaughlin enhanced your weapon and you at the same time. It's why I chided him about giving you 'the works'. Though that is inaccurate, since you aren't wearing your armor yet. McLaughlin, how are your mana levels doing?" Throneblood cut in to explain.

Desmond checked his comm-cuff with a glance, noting that he was down to around ninety-five percent and, as he watched, it ticked down another percentage point. *Oh, that's right, the buffs are still running,* he thought. And, with an effort of will, recalled the threads of mana. Chloe shivered slightly as the spell faded and she returned to normal.

"Down about five percent, Instructor." Desmond closed the comm-cuff and looked up at the group of Instructors with a smile.

"Good, I want you to continue your enhancement practice. No boards this time, just focus on enhancing the durability of the dummies, yours and Vandenberg's, as well as the accuracy for you both. No more than accuracy for each of you and nothing on the weapons themselves. We do not need an 'ultimate spear vs ultimate shield' type of clash in the range considering what you did to Vandenberg's dummy already," Throneblood finished before leading her group of instructors away.

"What did she mean?" Chloe asked, still turned towards the range with her repeater in her hands. Desmond shrugged and keyed the commands to bring the target back to them to check it out.

The head of the dummy had a silver dollar sized hole melted nearly all the way through it, without a single scar on either side of the head.

CHAPTER 30

The Boghet are industrious people. Small of stature and lightly muscled, they often find positions in technical work where their size is an advantage. There is something of a friendly rivalry between most Boghet and Dwerg, as both species adore technology and share a similar ecological niche with that and their size. Boghet families are large, with one of the most skewed gender ratios of the known species of the Hegemony. This is because of a disease that ravaged their homeworld and actually drove them into colonizing space to escape it.
~Species of the Hegemony, a report sent
back to the nations of Terra-Sol-3.

They spent the rest of the afternoon practicing with Chloe, moving from different levels of enhancement. While the instructors hadn't told them to, Chloe had asked for him to begin randomly shifting the amount of increase she was allotted so she could start feeling for the changes.

"We can work out verbal and nonverbal cues later. Right now, I need to get used to it as much as possible. We can try some more physical boosts later on," she had urged him. Desmond was happy to comply. After their performance with the instructors, Chloe had been more confident and a great deal more focused.

Desmond did notice that she still became even more focused when he took up what was rapidly becoming his position to her right. Before lunch, her nerves had made her less accurate when he was observing her, but for whatever reason, she focused down tightly when he stood there. *Must put her in 'guard mode' there. Will have to remember that for deployment.*

After they were done at the range, the two of them got Chloe's gear moved back to the rooms and laid out on the racks that the bull-horned woman had purchased in her room. Desmond left his armor and rifle in the Armory for now, as he needed to get racks still. He had decided he would wait until they had a chance to 'shop' on their days off. *Still got over eight thousand credits to spend. I know I could just shop using the data-tablet, but I want to actually handle the weapons and touch the armor. Maybe I'm old-fashioned.*

Both Desmond and Chloe were too exhausted after training all day to do much more than get dinner and crash out in their rooms.

<><><>

Desmond was woken early by the distant thunder of a fist on the door to his suite. The groggy sensation left by the subliminal language training faded rapidly as he applied an enhancement to his mind. While he got out of bed, SAUL's voice rang out, punctuated by the clatter of Chloe tumbling out of bed and the metallic rattle of her snatching her repeater off the rack.

"Cadet-Adept Irongrip is at the door, Desmond," SAUL sang out once the AI had detected he was awake, and Desmond sighed.

"Thanks SAUL." He rolled out of bed as a fresh bout of knocking echoed dully through the room. "Irongrip is right... to put that much noise through the solid door." Desmond muttered as he tugged on his uniform pants. "It's okay Chloe, just Monika being her obnoxious self."

He had to call the last bit out because Chloe was already halfway across the common room, repeater in hand and wearing nothing but a pair of utilitarian gray panties. The bull-horned woman turned an acidic glare on him that softened almost immediately. Unfortunately, a portion of

Desmond hardened at the sight of Chloe's ridiculous chest bouncing as she turned. Each of the soft teardrops stood proudly on her well-muscled chest, only sagging slightly from the effects of gravity on their sheer size. A pair of silver rings pierced the nipples, glimmering against the horned woman's pale skin.

Huh...didn't realize she had pierced nipples before... The thought chased itself across Desmond's mind before he drug his focus back up from her chest to her face by sheer effort of will.

"It's a day off, Des. You gotta be just as tired, if not more so than I am. Go back to sleep," Chloe insisted, her hands moving over her repeater automatically as she took another step towards the door. He noticed that the energy cell attached to the power cable from the weapon was actually tucked into the waistband of her panties and smirked.

"Naw, it's fine Chloe. You can get some more sleep, if you want. I'll just find out what Monika wants now. If she doesn't get an answer soon, she's just gonna keep pounding away." Desmond gestured for the big woman to head back to her room, but Chloe shook her head.

"Nope. Even on days off, I'm your guard, Des."

"Fine, let me at least answer the door. I've got more clothes on than you do." Desmond gestured to his uniform pants before nodding to her panties. "Not that I'm complaining about the view." He'd decided to tease her a bit, to see if she was giving him a show, intentionally or not.

Chloe blinked at him, her eyes going wide and a blush gracing her cheeks before she squared her shoulders and nodded. This had the added effect of presenting her breasts to him again, which did not help Desmond focus any better. But he resolutely turned his back and strode over to the door, taking the chance to 'adjust' himself so he wasn't tenting his uniform pants so much. *No way Monika wouldn't catch on and give me shit if she saw, just have to hope Chloe didn't notice.*

"SAUL, is Monika alone in the hall?" he asked as he came to

a stop by the doorway.

"No, Desmond. She has another cadet with her, her teammate, Cadet-Guard Oril'la."

"She can also hear you through the damn door, Des. Open up!" Monika's voice was muffled and tinny, coming through the plates of metal on the door.

"Not surprised I can hear *you* through the bulkhead," Desmond muttered quietly before keying the unlock commands into the door pad that sat to the left of the entrance. He could feel Chloe take up position behind him and to his left as the door cycled.

"You should have your sidearm on you next time you open the door. Build good habits now," Chloe muttered and there was a clatter of her cycling the firing system on her heavy repeater.

The door slid to one side, revealing Monika and Oril'la standing in the hallway. Oril'la had a put-upon expression on her green face that cycled to one of startled surprise for half a second before she reached forward to pull Monika back and put herself in front of the much shorter woman. Monika only made it half a step forward before Oril'la got hold of her and yanked her back again. She started to protest but her eyes bugged out when she caught sight of the two mostly naked cadets glaring at her from the entrance to their room.

"Holy shit! You two were banging?!" Monika screeched in surprise and Desmond let out a long, drawn-out sigh. Oril'la's eyes were fixed on the laser repeater held at ease in Chloe's arms, while Monika was staring avidly between the two current occupants of the room, no doubt more focused on the amount of bare skin on display rather than the weapon as her gaze bounced between Desmond and Chloe's bare chests.

"Monika, shut the hell up and get in here before I tell Chloe to shoot you..." Desmond stepped back from the doorway, his bare back briefly brushing against Chloe's pale skin before the horned Taari shifted to match his pace. She did not fully step away from him and Desmond felt a heavy, but wonderfully soft, weight settle against his head.

Is that...? It is. It's her tits...don't look, McLaughlin. There's no way you are going to live it down and Monika is right there. She sure as hell wouldn't let you live it down. Desmond's brain immediately went into overdrive, aided by the mild enhancement he'd laid on it to clear his head earlier, over-thinking everything and worrying about potential outcomes.

Monika gaped at them for several seconds before pushing on Oril'la, who had remained protectively in front of her cadet-adept, to urge the large green woman into the room ahead of her. Desmond could distantly hear other doorways opening in the hall and gestured for them to hurry up.

"Clearly, I'm not the only one who can hear you through the damn door. Get in here before we have to deal with others," Desmond hissed. This broke through the fugue that Oril'la was locked in, and the Hyreh woman allowed herself to be urged into the room.

"SAUL, close the door please," Desmond muttered, finally remembering that he could have just had the artificial liaison answer it for him earlier while he dressed. "Gods all damn it..."

"So, spill the deets, man! Did you two bang?" Monika bounced in place behind Oril'la, who was still remaining between her and Chloe. Admittedly, it was probably a wise choice given that Chloe still had her repeater in hand, though the weapon was pointed at the deck underfoot rather than either of them.

"Seriously? For the love of tits, Monika! Let the two of them get dressed!" hissed the Hyreh woman, shooting a half glare over her shoulder that did absolutely nothing to dim Monika's enthusiasm.

"Fiiiine. Dress if you gotta, but I want details!"

"Chloe, go ahead and go get dressed," Desmond said, rubbing his face with one hand to try to banish the tension headache that he felt coming on. "You two can have a seat over on the couch while we finish getting dressed. Monika, I'm still tempted to have Chloe shoot you for waking me up early on what amounts to our very first weekend ever, so don't push it."

"You mean like how Chloe pushed 'it' for you?" Monika's heavy accent on the word 'it' left nothing to the imagination for her bouncing eyebrows to dispel, but she still did it.

Chloe made a choking noise that drew Desmond's gaze immediately. This had the unfortunate side effect of causing him to twist his head to the left. Something he had been earlier resisting the urge to do as it planted his face directly into the side of her right breast. Thankfully, his eyes weren't entirely blocked with supple flesh. He could see Chloe was bright red, and the blush extended all the way down her throat to the top of her ample chest.

Is that her piercing pressing into my cheek? Desmond thought for a moment before forcibly taking his mind by the throat and putting it back on track. *Don't react. If you freak out, it's just going to make her more self-conscious.*

"Chloe." Desmond had the wherewithal to pull his head back, so he wasn't talking directly into her tit, but it took more self-control than he was willing to admit.

The bull-horned woman dipped her gaze to meet his over the curve of her right breast, her cheeks still on fire. Her eyes lingered on his only a moment before darting back upwards to lock onto the grinning Monika and her worried looking cadet-guard. It looked like the big woman couldn't figure out what to do at the moment.

"Chloe. Go get dressed and put your weapon away. Monika and Oril'la aren't going to hurt me. I'm going to go get dressed as well. I appreciate you being protective. But, for now, we need to get clothes on," Desmond said gently. *If I can tap into her role as a guard and reinforce that rather than the embarrassment Monika is drumming up, that should help, right?*

"I need you dressed so that we can head out to get breakfast, okay? If I have to deal with Monika this early, I need caffeine."

That seemed to give Chloe something to hang on to mentally in order to shift gears. She nodded, which nearly caused Desmond to duck on instinct again when her horns swung down towards him, but he mastered the urge. Chloe stepped back and turned on her heel to head back into her room. Desmond was glad that she had stepped back first, rather than just clubbing him upside the head with her tits as she rotated.

Watching after his guard, Desmond couldn't help but notice how her tail switched back and forth several times before settling to hang without moving over her toned and muscular ass. *I need to do research. I know for dogs wagging tails mean they are happy, but I should see if I can find out if such things carry over to Chloe's species or if they mean something entirely different.*

"Des...if you don't give me details, I'm going to explode here," pried Monika from only a few feet away.

"Nope," Desmond shot back with a glare over his shoulder.

"Desssss!" whined the redheaded Dwerg woman.

"There are no details to give, Monika. Regardless of what you *think* happened, you literally just woke both of us up. That's it," he stonewalled, turning away to head back to his room.

"So you did it last night, then?"

"If by 'it' you mean slept, then yes. Because that is all that we did. We slept. In our own rooms. You pounding on my door at..." Desmond paused to check the time on his comm-cuff, "five in the morning on a day off woke us both up. Which is one reason why Chloe answered the door in panties and her repeater."

"Just one reason?" Monika's whine transformed into a teasing tone and Desmond just sighed again.

"Nope, not gonna explain. You are just being intentionally annoying now. I'm going to finish getting dressed and then you are going to explain why the hell you are waking us up this early, Monika. And it had better be a good reason."

"Or what?"

"Or..." Desmond thought for a minute before a wicked grin crossed his face. "I'm not going to get you copies of that comic series I told you about from Earth. You'll have to wait until my people start exporting media to the Hegemony with the rest of folks."

"No! Not that one about the whole-steel chemist! You wouldn't dare clam-jam me like that, would you?" Monika whined. Desmond just shook his head and went back to his room to change. "Fiiiiine!" Monika called after him frantically.

<><><>

"I still can't believe that you tried to break down my door just to ask us if we wanted to go shopping, Monika." Desmond sighed for what felt like the hundredth time. He and Chloe had both gotten dressed and Monika had spilled her plans for the day while the four of them had walked to the mess hall.

"It's important! Besides, you got that fat stack from your Rift suppression run that you got for being epic and top of your class." Monika elbowed in the hip, making him wince on instinct. Thankfully, the half-sized terror only smacked him lightly this time rather than trying to give him a dead-leg.

"And how do you know that I haven't already spent that 'fat stack'?"

"Because your suite still looks like you just moved in, with a few extra bits. And you haven't bought anything cute for Chloe to wear yet."

Desmond started to protest but bit it off. *There is no safe way to counter that, the 'yet' is a trap.* He reminded himself and just focused forward.

The section of the massive, city-sized ship that they were heading to was affectionately called the 'retail zone' of the ship. Built amidships, ahead of the academy 'campus' area, the entire space took up nearly a kilometer of length of the ship and expanded to several decks. Which, given the size of the *Valor's Bid*, was only a fraction of space. There were open nature spaces with a variety of greenery and different places to sit, as well as the occasional massive screen that projected an image of space around the *Valor's Bid*. Scattered among the natural beauty were a variety of billboards filled with neon advertising, art installations, and food courts.

"This ship really is a mobile space station, isn't it?" Desmond muttered as they finally emerged from the walkways into the open atrium at the center of the ship that housed most of the retail zone.

The ceiling soared up and away, revealing all four levels of the expansive sprawl. Walkways spider-webbed their way between floors with mobile cart-style vendors scooting along the walkways and between floors to hawk their wares to different beings as they moved about the retail zone even this early in the morning.

"Eleven million souls call this ship home at any given time. The *Valor's Bid* only comes in to dock once a year to submit tribute to the Hegemony as it passes through the Core Worlds. Other than that, everything it needs is either made on board or shipped out to it on its patrol," Oril'la replied. Once the Hyreh woman had relaxed that morning, she'd been a font of information. Desmond had learned that she had originally hoped to be a combat-pilot for one of the fighter wings, but had opted to become an adept-guard instead as the pay was better with a lower fatality rate.

"Eleven million. That's more than the largest city in my home country..." Desmond shook his head slowly as he scanned the crowds.

Chloe urged him to one side to draw Desmond out of the flow of traffic, taking up position at his back and to his left while he tried to wrap his head around the number while still taking in the myriad of sights and sounds. Monika just smirked at the sight of the massive woman looming over

Desmond, entirely ignoring the fact that Oril'la was doing the same to her, though on a smaller scale.

"That's nothing. The hive cities on some of the Core Worlds have populations in the billions. And they aren't the only city on their planet, either," Oril'la continued. Her resting-bitch-face fell away for a moment as a smirk twisted across her lips.

"I can't even imagine."

"Most people can't. I mean, if I told you to image what a thousand of something looked like, most folks can't even do that. Take it up higher? It gets to the 'grains of sand on a beach' type of analogy. I remember my mom explained it like this…a million seconds is around roughly eleven days, while a billion seconds is equal to thirty-one years. Even in that context, the number makes my brain recoil…" Oril'la shrugged before shifting behind her partner. "So, what are we here for? If it's just browsing, we could spend a week of leave doing it and still not see half of what is on offer."

"Guns," Monika said immediately. Desmond opened his mouth to protest automatically before his brain caught up and he laughed.

Why in the world did I expect Monika, of all people, to insist on clothes?

"You know what? I'll agree with your first suggestion this time, Monika. Guns sound good. They sell that kind of stuff on board without issues?"

"Ya, the Armory just stores and issues the basic kits. The only thing they sell is repair equipment. Since the adept teams are supposed to furnish their own gear if they wanna go beyond basic kit, the revolving market is there. Some of the most high end shops on board actually cater to the adept-cadet's that come through, since they have the most free credits to spend. You can sometimes find more unique stuff when you get actual time off on one of the normal space-stations when the *Valor's Bid* does a close pass in a system for that opportunity, but still." She shrugged slightly and gestured around her.

"Huh...makes sense, I suppose." Desmond thought back to the 'cut' that he'd been given from Adept Marsden that came from her share of the one run. "Guess the only thing to see now is whether or not that actually is a little or a lot of money," Desmond muttered to himself.

"How much did you get anyway?" Monika prodded. Chloe made a curious noise as well from behind Desmond and he just shrugged. It wasn't like he was trying to hide the funds.

Besides, it might give them perspective on what to expect later.

"I've got about eight thousand left of the ten-ish that Adept Marsden sent me as my 'cut' from the run. She never told me if it was a lucrative or average run, though."

A low whistle came from Oril'la and drew the attention of the other three to her.

"What? That's a solid chunk of change. Maybe not top of the line gear, but you and Chloe can get some solid upgrades with it. Or you can get one high-end piece," the Hyreh woman said defensively.

Desmond turned to glance over his shoulder at Chloe thoughtfully. The bull-horned woman caught his gaze and scowled at him.

"Don't you dare."

"Don't he dare what?" Monika had a massive grin on her face.

"He's thinking of spending it on gear for me." Chloe sighed, rolling her eyes.

"What's wrong with him spoiling you?" Monika protested while Desmond just smirked.

"Because it makes my job harder!" Chloe growled, rubbing her face with one hand. "You need better armor than the basic cadet-adept kit. That should be your first step. My armor and repeater will work just fine for the time being, Des. It'd take an AP shell to get through the heavy armor, and even more to cut through my shield. Your armor only stops small arms fire and even then, that's iffy."

"She's got a point, Des." Monika immediately switched from stirring the pot to serious mode, startling Desmond.

"What? Why?" Desmond protested, turning a confused look on Monika. At receiving support from the half-sized terror for once, Chloe grinned.

"If you have better armor, that means Chloe can focus more on offense and her own defense rather than just guarding you. You wanna stand beside her, right? Not behind her?"

While Desmond had only known Monika for barely a month now, the Dwerg woman had figured out exactly how to push him when she wanted to. As much as he wanted to protest and insist on replacing the secondhand gear that Chloe had been issued, Monika had a point.

"Okay fine. Armor for me, then. But I'm not blowing the entire amount on just me," Desmond conceded with a put-upon expression.

"I can accept that, as long as you get something more than that armored jacket. I'd prefer you in at least the medium-grade armor kit, but *anything* is better than that jacket." Chloe's tone was relieved and happy at the same time.

"Does make me wonder why that is the basic kit issued to cadet-adepts. They give us regulars the option for up to nearly powered-armor, but only issue you guys something that they give corporate security in low-crime areas," Oril'la added as the group rejoined the flow of traffic.

"I don't really know. My guess is that they don't want us leading from the front. That and giving us the lighter armor forces us to focus on dodging and staying out of the line of fire. It still doesn't add up with how protective of us they are and how they make us buy our own gear. Unless..." Monika hummed thoughtfully as she led the way. As one, the group exchanged a look and sighed together.

"Bureaucracy..."

The group traded other theories back and forth as they

walked through the mass of beings. Desmond and Monika walked side by side, with Chloe a step behind Desmond on his left, and Oril'la in a similar position on Monika's right. The two adept-guards scanned the crowd as they walked, keeping aware of their surroundings but still adding to the conversation while Desmond and Monika led slightly. Both of them stayed close enough that they could quickly move to cover their charges from either direction if needed. The pairing worked out rather well as Monika was left-handed, so they both had a relatively clear draw for their sidearms in the event something happened.

Feels like they are always on watch...I thought it was just Chloe, but it's not...what kind of drilling do they do to instill this level of wariness in them? Desmond wondered as they threaded through the retail zone.

Large avenues and open spaces allowed for plenty of space for groups to stop and chat. The mobile vendors zipped by, jockeying for different spots that opened up along the various walkways, always chasing crowds of people on different levels. Stores both large and small bracketed the walkways and occasionally popped up in the open spaces. The scents of a hundred different types of food filled the air and Desmond was constantly distracted by different species he saw moving around. The majority wore some version of the Hegemony military uniform in its gray and black irregular pattern. However, hairstyle, skin tone, and accessories abounded. Armed guards patrolled in suits of combat armor with rifles at the ready, and about a third of the folk that Desmond saw carried some sort of sidearm on their hip and not all of them had an adept patch on their uniforms.

The variety of species still threw him the most often. For the first time since coming aboard, he saw another of the taurine Taari besides Chloe. The woman was only around seven feet tall and built a lot softer than his guard, but her bovine head reminded Desmond far more of a full minotaur than Chloe's human-ish features. The Taari in question had a number of metal bands on her horns with chains strung between them. Her horns were also much shorter than Chloe's and angled slightly higher, just little nubs that curved forward less than half what Chloe did. *That's right...Chloe's a half-breed right? I remember Monika or Dianne saying she was likely half Uth'ra? Wonder if she'd get that curly mane like Throneblood if she let her hair grow out...* Desmond thought, his mind drifting to Chloe's more closely cropped blonde curls and how they wreathed her black horns for a moment.

Desmond's thoughts were interrupted when Monika pointed and began to urge them to one side of the open lane.

"There! Second floor, I've heard good things about Shatterstar Armory!" It took a bit of maneuvering to find the lift that got them to the second level, as the crowds had only gotten thicker in the time they had wandered. Doubling back to the well lit shop, Monika led the charge through the broad doors.

Shatterstar Armory was well lit, with dozens of different display racks showing different armor configurations spread across the floor. Weapons hung on racks on three walls, while the fourth was heavy plate glass that looked out over the retail zone. An almost deafening quiet settled over them as soon as they crossed the threshold, and Desmond glanced around in surprise.

"Sound dampening field," a cheery voice explained from above him. Looking up, Desmond spotted a short, green woman standing proudly on a catwalk that hung above their heads. The system of catwalks crossed the entire shop like a massive spider-web and, now that he was looking, he spotted another half dozen of the short, green-skinned beings walking back and forth. They were all dressed stylishly but in matching outfits that had to denote them as staff.

"Makes sense, otherwise it'd be impossible to hold a conversation in here with how loud it is out there," Desmond replied. The woman snapped her fingers and pointed at him with a wink.

"This guy gets it. Haven't met one of your kind before, stud. I see you are with the Academy, cadet-adept on leave, I take it? I hardly need to ask given the two mountains of muscle you got following you two. Are you looking for armor or a portable hole-puncher?" The grinning woman spoke in a rapid fire pattern that had Desmond blinking and was very glad that he still had the assistance of the translation spell.

"Portable hole-puncher...I'm so stealing that," Monika sniggered, which got a laugh from the sales-clerk.

"Armor, for him," Chloe cut in. One of her large hands came down to land on Desmond's shoulder.

"Roger that! Let's take a walk!" the woman chirped happily and dove over the edge of the catwalk. Desmond lunged to catch her but stopped short when a flare of blue light fired from the broad belt around her waist and her fall abruptly decelerated before she landed in front of them with a soft 'pat' and Desmond got a more up-close look at her.

The shop-assistant had lighter green skin than Oril'la did and her short stature marked her as one of the 'goblin' race. Desmond had not had a chance to talk with any of them yet.

I think their official name was Boghet? Desmond thought to himself. The small number that were in his classes tended to stay grouped together and didn't interact much outside of their group.

This woman, though, was all smiles and friendliness. Her robin-egg blue hair was cut close to her head and inlaid with a zig-zag pattern that was shaved to the skin. Bright red eyes flashed with excitement as she gestured for them to follow her into the racks. Her close fitting clothes accented her streamlined shape and modest bust while remaining professional but without a skirt, for obvious reasons. She looked something like a mix between a secretary and a mechanic in that outfit. The large ears that hung low on each side of her head gave her a distinctly cute look on top of it all. He couldn't help but think that she was far cuter than the spider-goblin monsters he'd fought in the Rift with Marsden.

"So! Armor for the stud. Any particular style you are going for? What's your kit look like? I'm betting you are a first year since it's the first time I've seen you here, and you only got the one guard with you...I'm Shelly by the way!" she chattered while bouncing from foot to foot, making her small bust jiggle under the tight fitting button-down she wore.

"Thank you, Shelly. And yes, he's a first-year," Chloe again spoke before Desmond did. Her hand was still on his left shoulder as she remained in step with him. The Boghet just winked up at her, the smile on her lips growing broader.

"Already close, aren't ya? Don't you worry! We'll find something to keep your boy safe. Come on!" Shelly scampered off into the racks before Desmond could protest.

"She's got you pegged," Monika snarked at them both with a smirk, before following after the blue-haired Boghet with Oril'la in tow. Chloe coughed once before Desmond followed, still keeping her hand on Desmond's shoulder.

Does she do that so we won't be separated in the close space? Why didn't she do that outside? Chloe only did it when the shop assistant showed up... Desmond wondered as they wandered after the excitable short-stack woman who chattered on about different materials and weights. He didn't mind Chloe being so close to him, a thought that surprised him when it wandered through his mind.

"Chloe, do you understand what she's talking about?" Desmond muttered out of the corner of his mouth as they were led to a fourth different display stand.

"Some of it. We had more classes on materials and gear, I think. So I'm getting most of it," Chloe replied in a low tone. Her breath brushed the back of his ear and made Desmond shiver slightly. Swallowing hard, he crammed the rising arousal down as tightly as he could and focused instead on what the Boghet shop-assistant was saying.

"So! It really depends if you have a specialty and range-band that you like to work in. Since you don't have an entire crew with you, and you already admitted to being first-years, I doubt you have it figured out yet. This is the set that I think would best fit your needs for the time being while you figure out what works best for you." Shelly had come to a stop next to a rack that displayed a set of medium armor.

The armor on the rack consisted of interlocking plates that reminded Desmond a lot of Roman style armor, with each plate tucked under the next and arranged in such a way to give maximum flexibility to the limbs. It had a quartet of thick plates combined into the chest guard that also had a flexible material between them to strike a balance between protection and movement. A sturdy helmet with a wedge-shaped brow hung from the belt of the mannequin and the Boghet rapped her knuckles on it. She continued her pitch, "bonus is that this set has high end mapping functions and environmental seals."

"Huh, looks solid to me." Monika leaned forward to rap her knuckles against the thigh guard, getting a dull ringing noise from the metal in return. "What's the material?"

"Composite titanium for this model. There's a tungsten alloy version as well, but it's a bit..." Shelly rubbed her thumb and first two fingers together in the universal sign for 'expensive'.

"That's fair. What's the run-time like for the power supply?" The Dwerg was intently focused on the armor and quickly started delving into the specifics that had Desmond lost.

"What do you think, Chloe? You were the one who insisted I get better armor." Desmond glanced up at the horned woman, meeting her eyes when she looked down at him.

"I think it's an excellent set, would keep you mobile and safe. The tracking and mapping will be useful too. I've got a good directional sense, but my gear doesn't do mapping at all and it could come in handy. I'm worried about the cost though," the horned woman said while squeezing his shoulder gently with one hand.

"Cost is negotiable," chirped Shelly, having caught their conversation despite going into specs with Monika. "We have layaway programs and financing if you need it. The suit itself is twenty-two grand, with taxes and fees. I can get you a stripped-down model for around fourteen, but it won't have the advanced software or high-grade vacuum seals."

Desmond winced at the words 'financing' and shook his head sadly.

"Sorry. That's outside the price range. I could do about half of the base model you mentioned right now. Though I do like this one and I might upgrade to it in the future," Desmond said at last, and Shelly nodded. A disappointed expression crossed her cute features for a moment.

"Ah, yes. The constraints of a budget. I get it though. No interest in the financing?" Shelly made one last attempt, her expression inquisitive and innocent, though Desmond swore he could see the hint of a predator behind her eyes.

"No. I...dislike owing money in general. I appreciate the offer, though." Desmond did his best to decline gracefully, and Shelly nodded once.

"Okay! So used and refurbished models will be your best bet. Let's see what I can dig up for you in that price range!" The Boghet bounced back from her disappointment quickly and led them deeper into the shop.

CHAPTER 31

Was it weird getting to know so many species? I suppose you could say that. No more weird than dealing with people from a lot of different backgrounds. Rather than someone who grew up in the far north and had months of time without light; I ended up meeting people who literally had wings, claws, horns, or glowed. People are people. Rather than a fixation on calling a sport 'footie' or 'soccer', different species would just have their tics. Like the fact Monika was always tinkering with something, at least if she wasn't flirting with whoever was in arm's reach.
~Desmond McLaughlin, on life aboard the *Valor's Bid*.

It took another hour to narrow down a set of armor that would both fit the budget Desmond had, as well as satisfy the guidelines that both Chloe and Monika insisted on. Oril'la just watched, bemused, as the Boghet trotted them past dozens of different used models until they settled on an older generation set of medium armor that was similar in design to the set from earlier. Rather than more rigid plates for the torso, it was made up of smaller, interlocking 'scales' of straight titanium rather than the composite plates. The sensors were several generations older but would still retain the mapping functions though at a reduced resolution. Unlike the first set she'd shown them, the leg armor for this set was a series of narrow plates that flexed and articulated much like the arms, allowing for rapid repair and replacement in the field if extra parts were carried.

"It's a solid set. Was traded in about a year ago by a Va'Aelfa who was upgrading to more solid scouting gear. We cleaned it up, refurbished and repaired it. Total comes out to seven thousand eight hundred and change. It'd be seven if you could pop it on and walk it home now, but the extra eight and change is to get it refitted to match your build, stud," Shelly said as the group finally settled on the kit in question.

"Ugh. Easy come, easy go, I suppose?" Desmond muttered.

"I prefer 'gotta spend money to make money', cutie," Shelly quipped, throwing him a wink. "Besides, this model does have something the other didn't. Extra hard points on the back frame. Means you can throw on a hard-shelled cargo pod, which will let you carry more while you are doing your Rift suppressions. That's how you make the most money early on!"

"How do you know that?" Oril'la finally broke into the conversation, breaking her long silence as she stared intently at the Boghet.

"Cadet-Adepts talk a lot, and you gotta know the market if you are selling it, after all." Shelly shrugged before glancing over at the group with a calculating expression. "You know what? I'll throw in an extra for you guys. The gal who traded in this gear actually had an old cargo-pod that wasn't worth refurbishing. It's banged up but still seals. Was going to scrap it but just haven't gotten around to it."

"You are trying to throw in junk as an 'extra'?" Monika's tone was acidic as she stared at Shelly. The Boghet gave an innocent shrug and a smile to her before she responded.

"Only junk if you don't want it," Shelly said in a teasing tone.

"Why not take it?" Chloe cut in, having been silent for a while as she stayed close to Desmond and kept an eye on their surroundings. "Worst case, it's junk, but still spare materials. Only thing it's going to cost us is the effort to get it back to the suite, right? And I'd rather you have a carrier like that than the loose bag you described having used before, less likely to rip."

"That is fair. Okay, fine. Let's do this before I change my mind." Desmond sighed, which drew a little cheer out of the perky Boghet saleswoman.

"All right then, stud! Just need to get your measurements real quick and we'll have it refitted for you. Should only take an hour or two since you are being such a sweetie about it."

It only took a handful of moments for the cheerful green woman to get the measurements she needed. Chloe's looming presence was apparently enough to keep her flirtations to a minimum though, as the bull-horned woman remained extremely close to him with her hand on his shoulder the entire time. When she was done, Shelly took half the cost as a deposit to get the modifications started before reminding them to swing back by in an hour to pick it up, as delivery would cost extra.

"Well, what now?" Desmond asked as they strode out of the shop, his shoulders slumping slightly.

"What's wrong, Des?" Chloe asked gently, her hand falling off his shoulder as soon as they stepped out onto the walkway.

"Just irritated. I hadn't wanted to spend that much, even on used gear." Checking his balance and doing the mental math, Desmond had only a little under a thousand credits left in his account. *Given how expensive the armor was, I doubt I can buy anything useful for Chloe with just this much.*

The woman in question watched him intently, knowing that there was more to Desmond's depression than just what he was saying.

"I think we should go for a wander, see what else strikes our fancy. While I doubt any of us is going to top Des' spending today, since none of us have gone on a Rift suppression to earn the extra credits, we might find something interesting!" Monika interjected. "Could go for a snack or something right now as well."

"What are you? A stomach with legs? You are like...a third Chloe's size and you already eat more than she does." Oril'la smacked Monika on the top of the head lightly.

"I'm just not very fuel efficient, that's all!" Monika

countered with a mock scowl. The banter broke Desmond out of his depression, and he chuckled lightly.

"Yeah, sure, let's go walk around and see what we can find. Chloe, you had leave before, right? Any place you recommend?"

"Yup, I've had leave a few times since I came in a few months ago. I haven't wandered a whole lot, usually spent my days off at the range."

"Oh, you were with the previous wave of recruits then?" Oril'la asked as she worked to urge Monika along. The entire group slid into the crowd and began to wander the retail-district.

"Yeah. I came in with the last group. This is the first year of cadet-adepts that our class was viable for. Didn't realize we'd joined up during the 'bridge' period between years." Glancing down at Desmond and seeing the curious look on his face, Chloe continued. "The cadet-guards come in on six-month stints, like I told you before. They stagger it out during selection and those not tapped by a cadet-adept get folded into special forces. They stagger each 'wave' every three months in recruitment, so there are two 'classes' present for each of the selection cycles. So there are always going to be new people added in for each bid to add a teammate. Though if you don't qualify, you aren't part of the roster. Basically, fresh folk come in every three months or so, but cycle out after six."

"Interesting, and they are all roughly around the same skill levels when added, right?" Desmond had to wait as a trio of canine Taari females crossed in front of them without bothering to check. He slowed rather than run into them and the others matched him, though Monika grumbled about it.

"Yeah, I think it's better than having heavily trained people joining later on, because then our training would clash. Instead, we get someone with the baseline and can finish the training ourselves."

"There are benefits and risks to that," Oril'la countered,

stepping in between Monika and another passerby that was getting too close for her liking.

"I agree," Chloe commented. "It generally is better to get the medical slot taken care of early on if you are going to have a dedicated medic. While the adept can handle patchwork, having someone dedicated to it in the heat of a fight can save a lot of lives…"

"Sounds like a point of contention. I know when the second years were doing a demonstration there weren't many of them running with a dedicated medic, were there?" Desmond directed the last bit of the question towards Monika, who nodded in agreement.

"Yup. A lot of the cadet-adepts don't want to give up a guard 'slot' for a medic. I know a lot of girls in my classes were talking about minimum-size teams to maximize payouts from suppressions and minimize costs."

"Surprised that the academy lets it happen," Desmond countered. "Given how protective they seem of us, you'd think they'd aim for maximum guards for each of us."

"It's something to do with building styles and independence. Each adept will eventually have their own unique style of combat using their magic. No two adepts are exactly the same. While they teach us baseline spells to meet the minimum standard for the Hegemony, the way that twists develop on nearly every spell given time means that they have to let the adept grow on their own. Another reason adepts are generally assigned as sole units with their guard contingent, rather than forming their own battalions," Monika filled in. The Dwerg was acting surprisingly helpful at the moment and it made Desmond suspicious.

That suspicion was later confirmed when he caught sight of Monika sneaking her boot out to one side and tripping a Hyreh female that had been walking in front of her but moving way too slow as she was fixated on the data-tablet in her hand. The Hyreh stumbled off to one side and turned to snarl at her, only to nearly run right into Oril'la's chest when the cadet-guard moved to intercept her. Monika didn't slow down, and Oril'la just glared at her as they proceeded by.

"Little mean there, Monika," Desmond chastised.

"Shouldn't have her head up her ass while walking around. If you wanna read, do it sitting down. Not like there aren't places to do that. I'm not going to just huff and go around her. I got tired of being ignored because of my height, so I just take the corrections into my own hands now," Monika said airily. "Anyway, that's why they let us pick our own squads, as well as decide the size beyond the minimum of three guards to one adept."

"I guess that makes sense," Desmond murmured.

"Can always ask your instructor. I'm sure it'll come up in class the later in the year we get. I'm sure the next few weeks are going to be heavily focused on group combat training. Oh, those are pretty!" Monika came to an abrupt stop that nearly caused a pile up behind them. One of the mobile-vendors swooped down to claim a spot ahead of them, replacing a dumpling cart that had just zipped off. Monika immediately made a bee-line for the vendor.

The mobile-vendor was about the size of a Volkswagen bus with one side open to the air. Dozens of rings and necklaces sparkled on displays or hovered in the air on little leashes as the driver, a stick-thin avian Taari that reminded Desmond of a falcon with her hooked beak and sharp eyes, emerged from the cockpit of the vehicle into the workspace in the back with a happy twittering noise.

"Why thank you, young miss! I make all of these myself, actually! The materials are sourced from the local foundries. I even have a few pieces made with materials recovered from the most recent Rift!" The woman's voice was light and musical, despite the severe expression left by her beaked face.

Desmond stepped up as well when he realized that Monika wanted to look at the jewelry, regardless of if the rest of them wanted to or not.

"Really? Rift-metal is so expensive, I'm surprised you don't have your own shop to sell from." Monika carefully snatched one of the rotating rings out of the air to inspect it, the thin metal chain keeping it leashed to the cart.

"Oh yes, there would be no way for me to afford it if I was using the Rift-infused precious metals. Even Rift-silver is something outside of my means, though I do know how to work with it. No, I stick with the more common metals. Those that aren't snatched up by the smithies to use for armor, anyway." The last part was said in a conspiratorial whisper and a broad wink.

"Really? What sort do you have then?" Chloe asked with interest, standing right behind Desmond and leaning over him slightly to get a better look. Her increased height meant that he didn't end up crushed against the cart, but he still felt her press against his back slightly. Getting his libido by the throat, Desmond swallowed before tuning back into the conversation.

"Oh, I have a selection of the base Rift-metals. Iron, copper, steel, and nickel are most of what I have. Though I've got a handful of tungsten pieces too. Made them just the other day from some ore I bought that was sourced last week."

Tungsten? Was that the ore we dug out? The thought chased itself across Desmond's mind while the girls inspected the different bits of jewelry. The memory of the other taurine Taari and her jingling jewelry on her horns surfaced as well.

As slyly as he could, Desmond ran a few searches on his comm-cuff to confirm his suspicions before he asked a question while the girls were looking over some copper necklaces that looked like twisted strands of DNA, if DNA had three helixes that was.

"The tungsten you picked up, how much of it was there?" Desmond inquired idly, head tilted to one side to keep an eye on the girls.

"Oh, only about two dozen kilos came in, as I understand

it. The bits I got were only enough to make a small handful of ornaments, most of it got snapped up by the armorers. I think I got less than two pounds of it." The vendor darted a glance between Desmond and the horned woman basically pressed to his back and chirped in amusement, her feathers fluffing slightly before smoothing.

Desmond saw the smile in her eyes and tipped his head back slightly, indicating Chloe and tapping his temple slightly before flicking his index finger forward to indicate her horns. The vendor nodded once and set to work.

It did not surprise Desmond at all that the vendor was quick on the uptake. Anyone in sales had to be. She spread out a selection of rings in different types of metal on the counter, calling the girl's attention to them as she offered them different styles and colors to inspect, while nudging a small tray of them once with her elbow towards him.

Desmond glanced over at the items she indicated. Most were too small for what he wanted, but he saw one that looked to be the right size. A thick band that reminded him of blackened steel, polished to a high shine without ornamentation other than the variegation of the metal.

Reaching out to touch the band with one finger, Desmond felt a familiar vibration chase up his fingertips and smiled.

If I gambled, I'd put money that the ore I picked up with Marsden was tungsten ore from what the search showed... He thought to himself before he turned to look at a pendant that Oril'la had held up while tapping the one he wanted with his left index finger. The vendor nodded and held up four fingers, then two, then five. When Desmond nodded in agreement, she shifted the tray away and tucked it under the counter-top.

"Desmond, what do you think of these?" Monika dragged his attention to a collection of thin metal cuffs that reminded him of arm torcs with how the metal looked braided.

"Those are cool. I've seen that style before back home, actually. Whole culture used to use them as a way to honor a warrior as gifts from his liege-lord." Desmond did his best to act nonchalant about it as he inspected the rounded pieces of metal for a minute before finding one he liked. "How much are these?"

"Twenty credits for those, since they are just regular steel. Good and durable pieces for everyday wear." The vendor said, her eyes shining brightly. Desmond turned to the others and gestured to the tray.

"See any that you girls like?"

Monika and Oril'la shook their heads, going on to another set of necklaces that were three different types of metal braided together into intricate patterns.

"Too small for me," Chloe said with a small sigh, holding up her right arm to illustrate. The band would have had to be bent far larger open to fit on her arm and would barely have covered half her wrist.

"Maybe another time. I'll take this one though, for now," Desmond said, tapping the one that had a pattern that reminded him of intertwined vines.

"I do some custom work as well, I'll include my card in the bag so if the lady would like one I can do it up for you," the vendor said with a smile in her voice, sliding the torc that Desmond had selected under the counter. A moment later she produced a flat, opaque brown box of synthetic wood. She set a thin wafer of polished metal on top of it that had a communications code and her shop's logo imprinted on it. "Tap your cuff here and I'll send the bill to you." She indicated a section of countertop that was like polished black glass.

Desmond did as she directed, and his comm-cuff chimed with the message. Accessing the message, he found the invoice for his purchase there, the large tungsten ring at the bottom of it. He glanced up at her with an inquiring look and the vendor tapped the box with one finger and winked.

"*Thank you.*" Desmond mouthed before keying the interface to pay the invoice and picking up the box and tucking it into one of his pockets. The vendor just bobbed her birdlike head with a wink at him.

<><><>

They hung around the vendor for another ten minutes before Monika finally picked a necklace she liked the look of and haggled with the vendor for it. When they were done there, the group moved off, buying lunch from another of the mobile vendors before finding a spot to relax in one of the open areas.

Desmond had caught more than a few people staring and snickering at the group, most of them being one form of Taari or another. The girls had ignored them, so Desmond did as well. It bothered him to see intolerance even out here with this many species, but maybe it was a universal truth of some kind that eluded him.

"Maybe folks are just dick-bags though," Desmond muttered to himself.

"Hmm?" Chloe looked up from her meal, which was a collection of something that resembled a gyro, a bit of sauce on the tip of her nose.

"Nothing, you...uh, got some here." Desmond tapped his own nose and Chloe's eyes crossed for a moment before she rolled her eyes and wiped it off.

"Not quite as messy as barbecue, but still." The big woman said with a shrug before taking another bite of her food.

"Sometimes the best stuff is messy," Ribbed Monika. The comment earned her an elbow from Oril'la.

The Hyreh woman had become more relaxed as the day went on, clearly the exposure to the excitable and irreverent nature of her cadet-adept partner thawing her out some. Either that or the exhaustion of riding herd on Monika finally made her give up.

"Does she have any setting besides bawdy?" Chloe asked in a low voice that, unfortunately, did not go unnoticed by Monika.

"Only when I'm asleep or horny," Monika answered with a broad grin.

"All right, that's enough of flirting with Desmond's girl." Oril'la pushed herself to her feet.

"I'm not..." Chloe started to say, her eyes going wide.

"She's not..." Desmond began as well, but cut off as Chloe voiced her protest as well.

"Suuure. Chloe, you've been basically sitting on top of him this whole time. Look, I'm gonna drag the ankle-biting terror off so you two have some peace and quiet for a bit," the Hyreh woman continued. She got hold of the back of Monika's uniform shirt and tugged her upright.

"I am not an ankle-biter!" Monika protested, flailing her arms to try to fight the much larger woman off, but refusing to give up her grip on the massive burrito she'd been eating. So instead she sort of just flapped her arms like she was trying to do the chicken dance.

"But you admit you are a terror? Figures. See you two tomorrow." Oril'la gave Monika another tug to get her moving, and the two vanished into the crowd a moment later, Monika grumbling into her burrito like a petulant six-year-old.

"Uh," Desmond said.

"That was awkward," Whispered Chloe, her face bright red.

"So..." Desmond drug the word out for a moment, fighting the blush that was on his face as well. "What did she mean about you sitting on top of me? What's that supposed to mean?"

"Ugh...she didn't have to call me out on that so much," Chloe moaned, throwing her gyro down on the table and hiding her face in her hands.

"What?" Desmond asked cleverly, his embarrassment clearing as concern took its place. Chloe remained silent for several moments before peeking between her fingers at him. Seeing his concern, she sighed and dropped her hands.

"Look…how much do you know about the Taari subspecies?" she asked, picking up her food with one hand again and taking a bite, chewing slowly.

"That you all originated on the same planet, and evolutionary pressures caused a racial divide in a base species that eventually produced the different Taari breeds that exist now. Cross-breeding is possible between almost any of the Taari variants, but the subspecies breed true unless bloodlines other than a Taari is introduced?" Desmond recited from memory what he'd read weeks before while studying the different species in the Hegemony.

"Largely true," Chloe said before taking another bite to stall for time.

"And? How does that play into this?" Desmond's embarrassment was draining away now to make way for concern as Chloe struggled to explain what was bothering her.

"All the different sub-species of Taari have…holdovers from their more primal sides," Chloe explained slowly. "The canine Taari, for example, tend to move as packs and get very defensive of anyone outside of their 'established' pack structure. You can usually tell their mood by their ears and tails unless they've crossbred enough with a non-Taari to lose those traits, for example." She still refused to look up from her food.

"And?" Desmond thought for a moment, turning over what Oril'la said and comparing it with most of the earlier day. "I know you were standing very close to or touching me most of the day. Is that something like this? I mean, you are here as a guard but…"

Chloe winced and looked away, her shoulders coming up slightly in a defensive posture as she leaned away from him. It occurred to Desmond that, until that moment, she'd basically been pressed against his side the whole time. He'd just gotten used to it over the course of the day and, since she wasn't pressing her tits to him directly, he'd just ignored it.

"Yes..."

"Chloe, just explain it to me. I'm not upset." He spoke in a gentle tone, shifting slightly so he was leaning against her, taking a shot in the dark, guessing that it was probably something comforting or good as he waited.

"So, I'm not a pure-blood Taari, as you can obviously tell." Chloe sighed and dropped her food again, carefully wiping her hands before turning to look down at Desmond. He was gratified when she leaned into him as well.

"Yeah, I can tell," Desmond said with a snort and a smile. He reached up to tap her nose lightly with one fingertip, swiping away the sauce that had made it back there again from her gyro. Chloe's eyes crossed at the tap, and she followed his finger with her eyes as he pulled it away, her gaze intent before blinking herself back into focus and turning to stare at him.

"I'm guessing that it's something similar for you? This, I mean?" Desmond bumped his shoulder to one side against her arm, to indicate her leaning back into him now.

"Sort of. My mother's people have a lot of 'herd-tendencies' that can bother some folks." Chloe struggled for a moment to find the words before just letting them out in a rush. "The taurine Taari tend to lean into folks they trust. It's a herd thing. They stick close to and do their best to remain in contact with people that they like or are comfortable around. Touch is a big thing..."

"So...what you are saying is that you are a cuddler, and it's not your fault. It's just instinct?" teased Desmond, smiling as his thoughts were confirmed. He'd had an inkling that she liked him for a while, but he'd never been good at reading women's attentions in the past and Chloe was most definitely not human.

Oh jeez, what gave her not being human away, the eight feet of brick house muscle, the horns, or her tail? Stop trying to judge her based on human tendencies. Not to mention she's criminally shy, gonna have to just take a shot and hope I'm not misreading her, Desmond scolded himself internally as Chloe's flush just deepened.

"I...I'm sorry if it makes you uncomfortable, Desmond," Chloe stuttered, moving to lean away from him again and going formal with his name for once. She froze a moment later when Desmond wrapped his left arm around her waist to prevent her from getting away and pulled himself close to her again, trapping her arm between them.

"Okay. Just going to throw this out there so there are no misunderstandings, all right?" Desmond cleared his throat once before looking directly up at Chloe. The horned woman was frozen stock still and staring at him with wide eyes. "I think you are really attractive, Chloe. Given the chance, I'd like to get to know you better. But what I've known of you so far just makes me more attracted to you. I don't mind you leaning into me or touching me. Not just because you are my bodyguard, or just because I'm attracted to you. It's part of who you are, and I'm not just going to accept only a part of you."

"Uh...o...okay Des," Chloe stuttered, still staring at him wide eyed.

"Now. Any other behaviors I need to know about? I had figured that each of the species had non-verbal cues a while back, but haven't found the right reference material to figure them all out. I know that Aelfa's ears can tell a lot, since they move a hell of a lot more than I expected, but I've only pinned down 'angry' and 'embarrassed' really."

"Uh...grooming?" Chloe said quietly, blinking twice but still not breaking eye contact.

"Like how? Like me brushing your hair? Or are you talking more like...tongue bath grooming?" Desmond prodded, an eyebrow going up. "You okay, Chloe? You're...kinda staring at me. Did I break you?"

"Both?"

"Both what? Both types of grooming? Or you're okay, but also broken?" Desmond used the arm around her waist to squeeze her slightly, before releasing his grip on her and moving to lean away slightly, worrying that he might have crossed a line while teasing her.

Chloe abruptly dismissed his worries as she came back to herself and shifted to drop her right arm across his shoulders. She let out a huff that reminded Desmond of videos he'd seen of bulls about to charge a bull-fighter.

"Both sets of them. Des, you have no idea what you just did, do you?" Chloe sighed gustily and Desmond could feel her tail switch back and forth behind her for a moment before stilling.

"I cleared the air between us, told you that I think you are cute, and that I don't mind you cuddling me because you like me," Desmond summed up. His heartbeat was slowing back to normal now that Chloe was returning to her usual self. Leaving his arm around her waist, Desmond picked at the nachos he'd been working on as silence descended on them for several moments. "You do like me, right?"

"Oh, for the sake of the stars, Desmond! Yes, I like you!" Chloe swore, letting out another explosive breath. "You treat me like a person, which is not something I'm used to, especially as a half-breed Taari. You defended me even when it wasn't your place to do so. And you, an adept that I'm duty-bound to obey, *listen* to me when I give advice. Your first thought with the funds you had was to buy *me* gear and not yourself, when I'm currently better equipped than you."

"Yeah, but you can't throw mana around like I can," Desmond countered, brandishing a chip with his free hand.

"Not the point, Desmond. You are a selfless idiot, and I'd be a fool to not jump on the chance to get to know you better. The fact that you spent all five of your selection bids on me, in some kind of bizarre move to show your confidence in me, was like throwing accelerant on a bonfire."

"Well, a guy likes to buy things for a girl he likes."

"I forget that you are from a primitive world..." Chloe shook her head slowly before squaring her shoulders and pulling him against her side firmly. "That doesn't matter, though. You are different, that's all."

"Let the record show that I think you are beautiful the way you are as well," Desmond cut in. "Which reminds me, since we are both being awkward now, might as well get it all out of the way." Desmond fished the wooden box out of his pocket and popped it open.

"What? The bracelet you bought earlier?" Chloe looked on in confusion, twisting her head slightly as she watched him fiddle with it.

"Not the only thing I bought, actually. Here, bend that head down a bit more." Desmond removed the tungsten ring from the box. When Chloe did as asked, he reached up to slip the ring over the tip of her right horn and down its length until it caught two thirds of the way down with a quiet 'click' of metal against horn.

"What? You...what is this?" Chloe twisted her head away to peer up at an angle at the horn. It was close enough to the side of her head that she had a hard time focusing on it at first until the light caught on the metal band and she gasped, eyes going wide again. "Desmond, you didn't!"

"Yep, bought the pretty lady something pretty to wear. Figured it would fit on your horn and saw another taurine Taari wearing jewelry like this. Didn't have the budget to buy you gear, so figured this would work. So...hope you like it?" Desmond finished lamely.

"Des. Guys don't give women gifts like this out here," Chloe said slowly, reaching up to stroke the band with her fingertips.

"Well, this guy does." Desmond shrugged slightly before stuffing the box back into his pocket. "Hope you like it."

"I love it, Des..." Chloe murmured quietly, still stroking the metal band lightly. Desmond had a sudden thought and felt a chill run down his spine. He'd been so focused on trying to confirm if the ore he'd found was tungsten or not, to add another layer to the gift, that he'd forgotten to research any cultural connotations to the jewelry.

"Uhh, just gotta ask. Does the jewelry on horns for your kind have any special meaning?" Desmond tried to play the question off as nonchalant, but Chloe saw right through it and burst into loud laughter that got stares from several people around them.

"Just the thing a guy wants to hear when he asks a serious question..." Desmond grumbled to himself, prying another cheese-laden chip loose off the pile in front of him.

"Ahahaha, I'm...I'm sorry, Des. I shouldn't laugh at that question, but it does show your origins." Chloe wiped tears from her eyes as she chortled a few more times before she got control of herself. "Yes, and no. If you had horns and I gave you jewelry for them, it would have some meaning. It marks you as claimed, among my mother's people. Claimed and being courted."

"She's a full taurine Taari, right?" Desmond mumbled around the mouthful of hot cheese and chips.

"Yes, she's a full-blood. But yes, it would be like an engagement mark. Males of her species wear bands on their horns to denote each of their partners and proclaim their status. The closer to the skull, the longer the partner has been with them. When a courtship starts, the traditional jewelry would be a cap for the tip of the horn."

"And what about the females? Do they wear any ornamentation to mark relationship status?" Desmond asked, curious and wanting to learn more.

"No. The women can decorate their horns however they want except for one way. A band of precious metal with their husband's name or symbol engraved in it is placed flush with the skull on the left horn. That is only for when they enter an official relationship. Speaking of, what kind of metal is this, anyway?" Chloe tapped her fingers against the dark, glossy material of the ring.

"Something I thought was appropriate for you. Tungsten, one of the most durable metals in existence." Desmond shot her a wink and a smile, which caused Chloe to blush again. "I'm not one hundred percent sure, but I'm almost positive that it came from the Rift suppression I participated in. The vendor mentioned she got some of it that wasn't snapped up by the armorers, and the vibration of it feels the same as the ore I carried out."

Chloe dropped her gyro for the third time that day, her head coming around fast enough that her horns actually made a humming sound as they cut the air while she stared at him in surprise.

"It's *Rift-Tungsten*?!" she hissed, her eyes wide.

"Uh...yes? It has the same vibration I felt from the ore I collected and brought out. We found it in the nest of a big nasty beastie we killed. Dunno if any more was found and brought out, but I do recognize the feeling as like what we did recover."

"Shatter me..." Chloe cursed, shaking her head slightly, sending her horns swaying back and forth. "Desmond, that walks a fine line...I'm glad it doesn't fit to the base, otherwise this would qualify as a mating-band. If you'd gotten me a piercing, it would qualify on my father's side as well."

Desmond had been in the middle of taking another bite and promptly choked, a dangerous proposition given the sharp edges of the chip. Coughing to try to clear his throat, Desmond fought to breathe for several long moments before he finally got his throat clear.

"Really now? That's...great?" Desmond croaked, taking a long drink of his water. Chloe snickered at his predicament once she realized he wasn't in danger of actually dying.

"Yes. And I appreciate the gift. I look forward to getting to know you better, Desmond. But I will warn you now, I'm not going to make you into a loose man. While you continue to throw me off balance, I'll do my duty and keep you safe, while we get to know each other better," Chloe said and took a deep breath, squaring her shoulders as if firming her resolve.

What have I gotten myself into? Desmond thought to

himself as Chloe's arm settled across his shoulders like a comforting weight, and her right breast settled against his head. *Hopefully something wonderful…what did Monika say? 'I like mountain climbing.' Or something equally silly.*

CHAPTER 32

I wasn't sure if we were rescuing him from them, or if the guards were saving the three idiots from him.
~Sergeant Ral'toros, after-action report.

"So your father was an Uth'ra? How did your parents meet?" Desmond asked as they wound through the crowds back to Shatterstar Armory to collect the gear they'd ordered. They'd sat around the table talking for another half hour and Chloe had begun to open up more about her family.

It was clear to Desmond that Chloe cared about her family a great deal and missed them, based on the sad smile that crossed her features when she talked about them.

"Yeah. My dad is an Uth'ra. They met during a deployment. Dad was a ship's mechanic and mom was part of the complement of marines on the ship. She'd somehow gotten stuck in a vent on a dare and they'd had to call a mechanic to come and disassemble the vent entrance to get her out."

"I bet that was embarrassing for her." Desmond couldn't hide the laughter in his voice or the smile as he imagined Chloe stuck headfirst in a vent.

"Oh no! As she used to say, it was the best thing that could have happened to her. Since it made her stand out in his mind. Hard to forget her after seeing her like that," Chloe chuckled. She'd remained close to him as they walked, her right hand resting lightly on his left shoulder the whole time. Not quite pressed to his back like she had when they were seated, but close enough that if Desmond stopped rapidly, she'd bump against him lightly.

If she wasn't paying such close attention, I'd worry she'd run me over. Desmond thought with amusement. *Doubt it, though. She's far too aware of her surroundings.*

"What about the rest of your family? Got any siblings?" Desmond asked idly as they ducked around a pair of Dwerg women who had come to a stop when one of the mobile-vendors swooped down with racks of roasted meat on display.

"I've got a little brother actually..." Chloe's voice was affectionate as she said it, but the moment was interrupted before she could say more.

"What do we have here? The half-breed and some stunted Aelfa that she's paid for his time?" The loathing was thick in the deep voice as a trio of males in the standard uniform of the ship oozed out of the crowd. All three of them were taurine Taari's and stood more than a foot over Desmond in height.

Still shorter than Chloe, Desmond noted idly as he shifted his stance. *Wonder if that is because of her dad? The Uth'ra in her heritage gave her more height and build while retaining the horns and tail from her mother?*

"Beat it, Davis," Chloe growled. The hand that was sitting on Desmond's shoulder squeezed firmly before relaxing.

"No. We'd rather beat on you. What new hidey-hole did you find after you scampered out of the barracks? Or were you shacking up with your little Aelfa-toy? Going to dilute our blood even further?" The bull-man growled, blowing a snort out of his wide nostrils.

'Davis,' as Chloe had called him, was the shorter of the three males in front of them, but only by a few inches. Which meant he still had a foot or more on Desmond and at least a foot across as well. The other two were broader in build and just as sour looking. Though, Desmond noted idly, all three had shorter horns than Chloe did.

Gotta ask her about that...I got a feeling that it has meaning in their culture too. Desmond thought idly before interjecting himself into the conversation.

"Chloe, I thought you said people didn't bother you after I had words with the Hyreh and her pals?" Desmond drawled idly, slipping his right hand down to slowly unbutton the holster for his sidearm.

"*They* never bothered me again. Davis and his herd have hounded me since they arrived, though. I'm just glad I recovered faster than expected from that state you found me in, Des," Chloe growled while not taking her eyes off the trio in front of them.

The crowds that had been surging around them had parted. The other beings around them did not want anything to do with the argument amongst the much larger beings, though many watched with interest. Desmond did note the fact that several were pointing at him and whispering. He caught sight of one wide-eyed Yu'Aelfa murmuring urgently to her friend and pointing directly at him. Or more precisely, pointing at the markings on his sleeve that denoted him as a cadet-adept. That murmur spread like a ripple in a pond.

"Keep your mouth shut, shrimp. Our business is with the half-breed. I'll break you later," Snarled Davis, turning his glare to Desmond.

"You may test that assumption at your convenience," Desmond replied coolly, setting his hand on the butt of his pistol without bothering to hide it. The bull-man's eyes dipped to the sidearm and Desmond swore he could hear the grinding of gears in the big lunk's head before his eyes darted up to the rank marking on Desmond's chest as well.

"Adept..." the bull man snapped, his lip curling surprisingly higher. "He's just a cadet though...did you whore yourself out to the Aelfa for protection, Vandenberg?"

"Like I'd need protection from an ill-tempered calf like you, Davis," Chloe replied icily, her back straight as she met his hard glare. "Now. Piss off out of our way. Or I'll move you."

"You'd be welcome to try," Davis growled back, which was echoed by challenging snorts from the two males behind him.

Huh...just occurred to me, this is the largest number of men I've seen in one spot that aren't surrounded by a group of females...wonder what's wrong with them? Desmond could not smother the laugh that bubbled up a moment later, which drew all eyes to him.

"What? What's so funny, Aelfa?" Growled Thug 1 from Davis' left. Desmond could rein in his chuckles enough to answer after a few seconds.

"First of all, you guys suck at observing shit. Not an Aelfa." Desmond twisted his head to the side to show off his rounded ear before continuing. "Second, what crawled up your asses and died? What say do you have in who Chloe decides to spend her time with? Are you just jealous because she decided she doesn't wanna give you the time of day? Is it because you 'got no bitches' and are stuck in a sausage party?"

"What?" Davis' face had gone even more red through his brown fur and the big man was trembling with fury.

"I'm asking: what the fuck is wrong with you three? Every male I've seen so far has a whole bevy of women with him. But here are the three of you, all sad and lonely by yourselves with no women around." Desmond snapped his fingers and turned to look up at Chloe. "I know what might be the problem! Are they geldings? Is that a thing for them? I am still learning, after all."

There was a collective gasp from the onlookers and in the silence that followed, all eyes darted to the trio to see how they took it. Desmond heard a few mumbled bets from the onlookers and suppressed another snicker.

"No, sadly not," Chloe remarked a moment later, throttling a smirk of her own.

"He's the fucking prim!" snapped Thug 2 suddenly, breaking the silence and drawing eyes back to Desmond.

"I'm a Terran, yes. First of my kind out here and look at me, a lovely young thing already at my side," Desmond shot back at him, patting Chloe's hand on his shoulder with his right before returning it to the butt of his pistol. "Now. My guard asked you politely to move and stop causing a scene."

Davis was trembling with fury, eyes locked on Desmond the entire time. A loud *clack* drew Desmond's gaze down to the deck and confirmed one of his suspicions when he saw the broad hooves that the man's legs ended in stamping against the deck again.

"I will crush you," Davis gritted out between broad teeth, shoulders bunching as he lowered himself like he was ready to charge.

"I'd say that's enough of a threat on my life, right Chloe?" Desmond kept his eyes locked on the bull man and his two buddies, who looked like they were gearing up for a fight.

"Yes, sir," Chloe grunted. Her face was stony as she shifted to put herself ahead of Desmond on the left and dropped down into a loose stance with her feet spread wide.

The situation was diffused a moment later by a shout from one of the station security teams that had spotted the growing crowd and was forcing their way closer.

"Cease at once! Security!"

The crowd immediately split like a parting sea to allow the trio of armored and armed individuals access to the center of the ring. Coming to attention, Desmond immediately saluted the security, with Chloe only a half-beat behind him. The trio of idiots turned sullenly and assumed a loose 'at attention' stance.

"What, by all the stars, is going on here?" snapped the leader of the security team. Her clear faceplate allowed Desmond to note that all three were Hyreh women and clearly did not shy away from a fight given the multiple scars on their faces. "Why are four males arguing and gearing up like street thugs for a brawl?"

Quickly noting the woman's rank insignia on her left breast, Desmond stepped around Chloe to answer, still keeping to his at-attention pose. The movement brought all three's attention to him and their rifles twitched at his movement, but they remained pointed at the deck.

"Apologies for disturbing the peace, Sergeant. My guard and I were on our way to Shatterstar Armory to retrieve a custom order when these three waylaid us. They had unkind words for both of us and began to threaten our persons. I was preparing to defend myself when you and your team stepped in, which I thank you for," Desmond said in as polite a tone as he could manage.

While he hadn't had many encounters with any kind of law enforcement here on the *Valor's Bid*, he'd had run-ins with police back on Earth often enough that he knew being polite was the easiest way to get fair treatment, at least most of the time.

The sergeant gave him a once over, her eyes widening slightly when she noted the cadet-adept markings on his uniform and his unbuttoned holster, which he had not bothered to secure thinking that it would be good evidence that he had been under threat.

"What is your name, Cadet-Adept?" the sergeant asked gruffly.

"Cadet-Adept Desmond McLaughlin, first year," Desmond replied, repeating his salute at the end of it.

"You three are in a world of trouble, but not as much as it could be." The sergeant wheeled on the trio of taurine Taari males after another moment of examining Desmond. "Threatening an adept, even a cadet, is a serious infraction." The sergeant stomped over to glare up at the three of them as Davis began to protest. "Nope, don't want to hear it. There are at least two-score witnesses to this and my girls will be gathering statements as to what they saw. I can guaran-fuckin-tee that the observers would rather stay on the good side of a young adept over you lot, so don't expect them to lie for you."

The two other security guards split off and began taking statements from the observers while Chloe and Desmond watched.

Clearing his throat, Desmond waited for the sergeant to turn her sharp gaze back to him.

"Sergeant, I wanted to request your permission to secure my sidearm once more." The sergeant stared at him, a look of confusion crossing her face. "I didn't want to do anything to make you or your girls nervous, now that the situation is in your hands." Understanding dawned on the green woman's face, and she nodded.

"Go ahead, Cadet-Adept McLaughlin. I appreciate you taking the time to appraise me of it." Desmond buttoned the holster shut immediately before returning to 'attention'. "You can relax, Cadet. My girls are gathering statements, as you can see. You'll be on your way in a minute or two more."

True to her word, the sergeant had them on their way in only a handful of minutes more while she detained the three trouble-makers. Davis and his cronies glared at them both as they strode away, with Chloe taking up her position at Desmond's back and slightly to the left, as usual, one hand on his shoulder.

Desmond waited until they were a good hundred yards away from the group before letting out a breath.

"Well then, that was interesting."

"Interesting and entirely unnecessary, Des. I could have handled them myself," Chloe murmured quietly, sticking close to him as her eyes darted back and forth still.

"Maybe, but I'm your Adept as much as you are my Guard." Desmond emphasized the words 'Adept' and 'Guard' as he spoke. "It's as much my job to back you up as it is yours to guard me."

"Yes, but they only stopped us because of me." The self-recrimination was heavy in Chloe's voice and Desmond felt his heart twist to hear it.

"Which made them my problem. You are part of my team, after all. Besides..." Desmond didn't restrain the laughter. "I got to use one of my favorite lines there as well. Same thing that got the girls to back down off you last time, just rephrased."

"What do you mean?"

"'You may test that assumption at your convenience' is just a classy way of saying 'fuck around and find out' back where I am from." The explanation got a bark of laughter from Chloe before she sobered up.

"You don't fully understand the scope of the insult you dealt them, do you?"

"What, the gelding thing?"

"Yes. Among the Hegemony, gelding and castration is a punishment dealt to sexual criminals, as such deviancy is not something that the powers that be want passed along to the younger generation. Such crimes are seen as a reason for someone to be removed from the gene pool, even with the lower ratio of males to females."

"So I basically called them kiddie-fiddlers in a crowded place and they never got a chance to rebut it?" Desmond snickered again, but cut off when Chloe squeezed his shoulder sharply.

"Yes, Desmond. You leveled one of the worst insults to a man that can be had, while calling their status as unattached males forward as well as evidence. I dare say that Davis hates you as much, if not more, than he hates me now."

"Good, fuck 'em," Desmond snapped before taking a deep breath to control himself. "I have no patience for bigots. He came up to give you trouble because of your mixed heritage, after all, so he's scum in my book. At least that's what I took away from this."

"As I told you earlier, Taari view breeding with species outside of other Taari as an act of genocide. Taari are the only ones that clearly crossbreed with other major species like the Aelfa. Any other time that two different species cross, the children breed true to match the parent of the same gender. Though cross-species struggle with producing children at all, they breed true. That only happens when sub-breeds cross in the Taari species, like taurine or canine. Otherwise, the blood dilutes when Taari cross with any species outside their own."

"So? It's not like your species is teetering on the brink of extinction."

"You'd think that they were, if you listen to the bigots talk," Chloe muttered in a defeated tone.

Desmond abruptly turned and towed Chloe out of the flow of traffic before spinning about and grabbing the hand that had been on his shoulder. Looking up into her bright green eyes, Desmond stared at her intensely. Slowly, the look of depression faded and a light blush graced her pale cheeks as he continued to stare at her.

"What? Why...why are you staring at me, Des?" Chloe murmured, her wide eyes fixed on his unblinkingly.

"Because you are beautiful, Chloe. Now, let's not allow the bigots to ruin the day. We have armor to collect, and you were telling me about your little brother. I never had any siblings myself. Parents got more than they bargained for with just me." Desmond squeezed her hand in both of his before turning to tug her back into the crowd. He set her hand back on his shoulder and felt Chloe squeeze him back gently.

"Thank you, Des..." The words were quiet, almost too quiet for Desmond to hear.

"Any time, Chloe. Hey! I had another question too. It might be a bit insensitive, but I think you'll forgive me. Or if not, you'll only beat me lightly right now." He shot her a wink, and she just rolled her eyes before gesturing for him to continue. "Your horns. I saw a taurine Taari gal earlier, and hers were far shorter than yours. Davis and his crew even had shorter horns. Does it mean anything? Or is it just a side effect from your dad's blood, making you so big and strong?"

Chloe blushed at first, but burst into laughter at his question.

"What? Tell me it wasn't something insensitive to ask? I've been meaning to for a while, but Davis and his handful of idiots got me thinking and I wanted to say something before I forgot," Desmond pressed while bumping his hip into hers playfully.

"Yes and no, Des." Chloe laughed, shaking her head from side to side. "Horn length in my mother's people is seen as linking to virility in males. The more virile and vital you are, the larger your horns. For the females, it's a sign of strength. It's not uncommon for females to have longer horns than males, given that we tend to actively pursue our mates, having long and undamaged horns shows you know how to fight."

"Nice, so your horns show off that you are sexy, as well as strong. Love it." Chloe blushed at the compliment and Desmond decided to give her a break, so he deflected the conversation to safer territory. "Now, you were telling me about your little brother?"

<><><>

The stop into Shatterstar took only five minutes, as they had the armor waiting for him. Desmond transferred the other half of the payment for it and Chloe took possession of the large crate that it had been packed in, easily hefting it onto her left shoulder like the crate weighed nothing. Desmond was left with the battered cargo-pod that, thankfully, had some shoulder hooks that would interface with his armor, so he could get it on his shoulders like that and it would mostly stay in place.

The cargo-pod was a wide, curved shape with the bottom resting against the top of his hips like a good backpack should, while the top came up behind his head like an open cowl. The whole thing was segmented like a roly-poly shell and it flexed with him, though it squeaked and squealed from where the dents in it prevented effortless movement. Next to his right cheek was a broad stud that he could press to open the mouth of the pack behind his head to deposit items, as well as two smaller studs that opened hatches on either side for someone else to retrieve items or deposit them without having to throw it past his head.

"Feel like a frigging turtle with this," Desmond grumbled, not for the first time, while they walked down the far less crowded hallways towards the dorm blocks.

"You'll get used to it. The power pack for my armor felt awkward for about a week for me too, but once we started doing weapons drills with it, it became natural."

"Gonna see if I can't hammer some of these dents out." Desmond sighed as the pack gave another squeal as he rolled his shoulders.

"Probably a good idea. Armory might have the tools for it, or you can ask if they'll do the maintenance for you. Since it's not standard issue gear, they'd charge us some, but I doubt it'd cost as much as taking it to a commercial armorer." Chloe shrugged, bouncing the crate on her shoulder as she did.

"You are just too strong, damn it."

"No such thing." She replied airily.

"Sure there is, making me feel all weak with how you are toting my gear like that."

"You feel that way now. But if we have to evac, I can just toss you over my shoulder and run," Chloe shot back, sending him a wink.

She'd relaxed some as they had talked and retrieved the armor, telling him a few stories of her younger years and the mischief that her brother had gotten up to. There was a wistfulness to her tone when talking about him that made Desmond wonder. He'd noted that she only spoke of her parents a little and in the past tense as well, but he didn't want to pry.

I only really met her the other day, and it's not like we've been working together for very long after all. Desmond reminded himself. *Besides, it's gonna be odd enough with...whatever the hell we are doing right now. Dating? Maybe? Bugger, I don't know...*

Darting a furtive glance up at Chloe, Desmond saw her smiling quietly as they walked, her eyes scanning the hall ahead of them actively.

Does it matter? She's happy and I think she's hot. Plus, her personality is just too cute. The mental image of someone built like a brick-house like her being a snuggler is just too sweet too.

Firmly deciding that his worries could be put off for 'Future-Desmond' to deal with, he hitched the cargo pod higher on his shoulders and continued down the hall to their rooms.

CHAPTER 33

Group composition is key. You have to think about your specialization during all of it. Honestly? There were times I envied the other cadets that weren't specialized. They had the freedom to work with more options. The instructors made sure that we had basic competency with a wide range of spells as they walked us through each 'branch' of mana manipulation, but those of us with specialties always would fall back on them. We built our teams to maximize efficiency for those situations we could shine in while the true generalists could handle anything, given time.
~Desmond McLaughlin, on life aboard the Valor's Bid.

The rest of their day off was taken up with getting a stand for Desmond to store his armor on and taking the cargo-pod to the Armory for maintenance. The armorers were able to lend Desmond the tools needed to hammer out the worst of the dents and dings himself after he decided the fifty credits they'd asked to fully repair and restore the thing was too much, given his much diminished budget.

The following weeks oozed by, with most of it being on the range in at least half the day's worth of classes. Chloe and Desmond drilled, with him adding enhancements to her in the middle of her running shooting simulations where targets would emerge at random. The second week, Throneblood had them drop the divider between lanes and begin doing drills cooperatively.

The cadet-adept class was slowly becoming more cohesive while working with their cadet-guard. Desmond and Chloe had good times but weren't the fastest at clearing the different shooting courses, as they focused on a more conservative approach.

Twice during the two weeks, Throneblood lectured on different team compositions. Any day that she didn't lecture on team composition, she discussed Rifts and what sort of creatures had been spotted inside of them, reminding the class repeatedly that each Rift would likely be unique, but certain factors stayed common between types depending on the density of elemental energy inside.

One of the more interesting lectures that Throneblood held was concerning how the Rifts varied in type and what they could expect. Desmond's previous assumptions that the surroundings dictated the Rift nature were wildly off base, apparently. Most of the examples that Throneblood brought up revolved around the idea that they had no idea what to expect until the Rift was breached and they could inspect it. Though each Rift had a Rift Core that could be harvested by the team who found it, their main focus was in removing as many of the potential threats as possible for now, as the *Valor's Bid* had specialist teams for extracting the core for first years.

In private, Desmond and Chloe got to know each other better during the bits and pieces that they could. They'd taken to drilling in armor to get used to it, rationalizing that they'd most often be using their weapons in armor, rather than without. This had initially been to the amusement of the instructors and the other cadets. When several of the cadets had made snide comments, Throneblood had rounded on them, reminding the cadets that physical conditioning would begin in their seventh week and coincide with them learning another classification of magic. After that warning, a good portion of the class showed up in their armor as well.

In mana manipulation, they learned several new spells. For Evocation, the instructors drilled them on creating reactions and delaying them until they met a target, allowing them to build out what amounted to a magical grenade they could toss out. Desmond didn't like it as much since it cost so much mana to prepare. Enhancement was far more free-form, and he progressed into pushing individual enhancements into the shells in his handgun, and Chloe continued to practice with varying degrees of accuracy and reflex enhancement. None of his spells developed a twist yet, which was beginning to worry Desmond, since most of the class had gotten some sort of twist to occur with their *Bolt* spell at the very least. When he expressed the concern to Throneblood, she'd reassured him that it would happen in time when his mind was ready, since each twist depended on the adept using the spell to be ready.

Evenings ended early, with each of them exhausted both physically and mentally from the day. Though they would spend some time sitting next to each other, with Chloe draped over Desmond or him, leaning into her side and talking about training and bits of their history. Desmond ended up sharing more than Chloe did, but he didn't mind. Chloe seemed fascinated by the stories of Terra and how humanity had adapted to exist without the use of mana to help them.

Monika was her normal self, teasing Desmond mercilessly and prying for details whenever she could, but Desmond just shrugged her off, knowing that the mystery would drive the Dwerg woman crazy. He also figured that Chloe would tell him when she was ready to try anything besides cuddling. She'd been affectionate with him when they sat together, but it didn't move beyond the touches and glances, despite the fact she still paraded around after a shower with just the towel around her waist. Desmond did the same and was gratified to see her blushing when she caught sight of his bare chest. Desmond was gratified to note that he never saw Chloe without the ring on her horn, either.

While doing shooting exercises in his armor wasn't overly stressing on his body, it was adding more muscle definition to his build as he'd transitioned to using his rifle more.

Holding the stance and keeping his weapon up for hours on the range did help. Which made him feel less like a malnourished child when standing beside Chloe, who was still a mountain of muscle without any visible fat on her other than a faint bit of padding around her hips and chest to fill out the curves.

The announcement that they would be doing their first official Rift suppression in two weeks came out of nowhere at the end of a day on the range just after their second week completed.

<><><>

"All right, that's a wrap for today. Get your gear cleaned up and prepped tonight and tomorrow. You have tomorrow off from regular classes, but I expect the lot of you to continue training and getting ready. We are going to be doing simulated team drills with some of our veteran troops to prepare you for going into your first official Rift suppression once you come back from time off." Throneblood's thunderous voice cut through the crackle of weapons' fire as easily as it usually did, bringing everyone to a stop and drawing attention to her.

Once the Uth'ra instructor knew she had the attention of all the cadets in the room, she continued.

"Reports have come in that there is a cluster of mana Rifts forming in a nearby system. The *Valor's Bid* is diverting in that direction to take care of them. You'll each be assigned two more guards from among the veteran companies aboard the ship to fill out your teams when we arrive. There will not be bidding for the temporary teammates, but you can put in a request for someone with a specific load-out if you have a plan in mind. You will deploy in teams of four and no more. This is mandatory, as it is part of your training. Your veterans will be there to advise you, but if you get in over your heads, they are under orders to pull you out. They will only countermand you when they believe it is necessary to preserve your lives. So listen to them and take the opportunity to learn. While they aren't adept-guard trained, they are trained military members and you can learn a lot from them. Make sure you do so, as this will be the only Rift suppression you will all get before the mid-term testing and your next team-selection bid."

"What do you think? Any ideas of a team build you wanna go for?" Chloe murmured, keeping her eyes on Throneblood.

"Dunno. What do you think of three heavies with overlapping fields of fire?" Desmond stood in front of her and replied quietly as well.

"Aggressive wedge? Not a bad idea, but harder to move in closed spaces, plus, as you know, we tend to have shorter range bands for open spaces."

"Did you have a question for me, Cadets?" Throneblood had apparently heard their whispering and glared at the two of them.

"Just wondering if we have any idea of what the layout we are going into might be, Instructor," Desmond said quickly, coming sharply to attention. Throneblood stared at him for a long moment before nodding and turning back to the class.

"Cadet-Adept McLaughlin has a good question there. The answer to it is simple: it varies. The cluster of Rifts you will be deployed to haven't actually formed yet. Sensors are putting them at coming into being next week, which is why we are taking the time to bump your team training up to get you a feel for working beyond your pairing. Due to the number of Rifts and their proximity to each other, we have plenty of warning. As some are attached to nearby asteroids and others are free-floating, it will vary. It will be rare in the future that you know the layout of a Rift before entering it, as any team qualified to survey a Rift is also qualified to suppress it. You are the tip of that spear, so prepare for anything," thundered the big Uth'ra woman.

"Yes, Instructor," the class replied as one. They had

gotten used to what to do when Throneblood was using her 'command voice' to lecture.

"Now! If you have a request for team assignments, you have until 1800 the night before deployment to submit them. I'll remind you as we get closer to that time. And remember, just because you make a request does not guarantee you will be assigned that support! Also, your assigned veterans will be receiving a cut of anything you pull out as extras. They are to be treated as full team members for the duration. Dismissed!" The class saluted as one and began to gather their equipment and unload their weapons, packing ammo away into the carriers that each of them had taken to using.

"Think we should take someone from each load-out? Spread out the exposure so we can get a feel for it?" Desmond asked as he rapidly emptied his spare pistol magazines onto the shooting bench before arranging the rounds in their boxes.

Chloe was silent as she disconnected her power-cells from the charging ports, tucking them into their ports in the small of her back where the storage pack was for them. Once she'd policed her cells, something that took only a handful of seconds, she disconnected Desmond's spare cells for him and tucked them into the hip pouch for them on his belt right behind his left kidney.

"Chloe?"

"Hmm? Just thinking, Des." Chloe's voice was subdued and Desmond stopped what he was doing, rolling his head on his neck to look up at Chloe through the clear faceplate of her helmet.

"About?" Desmond prompted. Chloe glanced around them before keying her helmet to internal comms with a flick of a button. Desmond did the same before nodding for her to continue.

"Just worried. Up till now, this has all been drilling and range time. But you or I could get seriously hurt on this Rift run," Chloe whispered. Her voice was slightly distorted when coming through the speaker behind his left ear inside the helmet.

"Doubt it. We are two of the better armored folk here. And we know how to work in tandem," Desmond reassured her. "I mean, Throneblood has only a dozen of the pairs working on the combined lanes right now."

He resumed tucking the caseless rounds for his pistol back into their tray before stuffing that into the carry pouch on his belt and turning to face Chloe. Meeting her green eyes with his, Desmond paused to make sure he had her full attention before he spoke again. "What would make you most comfortable?" Chloe shook her head, refusing to speak. "Chloe, tell me."

"Two medics," the big woman said quietly before heaving a gusty sigh that made their comms crackle. "It's not practical, I know."

"We can request a medic for one slot then. Do you think another heavy weapon or long range would be better? Spread out or consolidate range bands? I can instigate at quite a distance with *Bolt* and my rifle. Anything that steps into your range is going to feel the hate, you know that."

"Better to consolidate range bands rather than spread them out," Chloe murmured, not looking away from him.

"You realize that the medic would be more for you, right?" Desmond reminded her gently.

He'd told her about the injury he'd suffered from the last Rift suppression and how it had rapidly healed. Desmond had heard back from Medical a few days after their time off and been informed that it was a result of his mana adapting to the naturally rapid process of human healing. More study would be necessary to quantify it, but he'd been advised that he should rapidly recover from most injuries as long as he had mana available.

"I'd...forgotten." Chloe took a deep and slow breath before letting it out again. "I'd still feel better if we had a medic, in case you get knocked out or down. Another heavy for the second slot to consolidate range bands. It'll give us a chance to experiment on that and see how they do or if we are stepping on each other's toes."

"Sounds like a plan. Let's get our gear stowed, I want a shower. Been sweating like a turkey the day before Thanksgiving."

"Fine...I suppose I could let you have the shower first," Chloe replied, though the mention of Thanksgiving had a confused look slip across her face, but she shook it off.

"You are welcome to join me." Desmond winked up at her, and a blush darkened the larger woman's face again before she cleared her throat and looked away.

"You are very forward, Des," Chloe murmured as he led the way out.

They fell into the familiar cadence with Chloe a half step behind him on his left. She had her laser repeater on her right shoulder and the massive slab of a shield in her left hand. Which was the only reason she didn't have her hand on his shoulder as they walked through the halls. Chloe had taken to doing that whenever they were moving between rooms or in public, explaining to Desmond that it allowed her to shift him behind her if needed, and keep track of him at the same time while she kept an eye on their surroundings. Kitted out like she was, the shield could be extended in front of him with only a flick of her wrist and she could drop the repeater into its slot on the shield in the same motion, basically trapping him between her body and the shield if necessary.

"Chloe, you prance around in just your panties or a towel after a shower. It's not like I haven't seen most of you, anyway. Besides, you're cute when you blush," Desmond teased with a light smile.

"This is what I mean, Des..." He could hear the blush in Chloe's voice as they joined the tail end of the cadets flowing down the hallway. "I know we've talked about it, you know that women are usually the pursuers out here..."

"So I'm supposed to be all demure and not myself, then? Come on, Chloe. I like you a lot and I want you to understand that. If it's bothering you, I can tone it back. The last thing I want is to make you uncomfortable." Desmond kept his eyes forward now as they navigated the halls.

"Maybe...maybe ease off in public some?" Chloe's voice was pleading as they turned down the hall to their shared accommodations.

"I can do that, but you know we aren't going to have the suite to ourselves forever. Throneblood said the next selection is after midterms after all and that is only three or four months away."

"That's different..."

"How so? They are going to be living with us, regardless."

"Yeah, but they'll be part of the team. For years, if not decades, depending on how things go after our service term. Not just classmates that we likely won't see after the academy is over," she whispered.

Desmond thought over her words. He'd not given it as much thought as she had, apparently. In his head, he'd likened their time in the academy to college, a phase of life that was only a small handful of years. Despite Throneblood's repeated reminders, the fact that he'd been with this team, and Chloe as a result, for the better part of a decade, if not longer, hadn't really clicked for him.

"Okay, I'll ease up some," Desmond agreed as he led them into their suite. "I had forgotten that we can take our time."

"Thank you, Des. I am interested in you, but I don't want to rush and have emotions get in the way of keeping you safe." Chloe's voice was near a whisper now as they came to a stop in the middle of the main room.

"Thanks, Chloe. I appreciate it. I'm...gonna get cleaned up, then send the team request to Throneblood. A medic and a heavy kit preferred, right? Sure you don't wanna wait till after the team drills?"

"Right. And yes, the drills will help us get more variance,

but I think that pairing will be best, regardless," Chloe said.

There was a moment of silence that stretched between the two of them before Chloe pulled him back against her in a hug, using the hand that was bearing her shield. It wasn't as enjoyable as a hug without the armor on, but Desmond could feel the emotion behind it and he snaked an arm behind him to hug her back as best he could before they separated again.

<><><>

Training with the veteran squads was an eye-opening experience for all the cadets. For the following two weeks, different groups of the veteran troops stationed on the *Valor's Bid* rotated through the different classrooms and worked with the instructors to ensure that the cadets had a good basis for comparison on what to expect. The entirety of the two weeks was spent on the firing range, with Throneblood occasionally lecturing on different spell combinations and applications while the cadet-guards drilled in the background.

Desmond learned several new applications of his enhancements, as well as how to apply them to people he wasn't looking at directly. He still used chants for most of them, and they were taught communication discipline as well in those weeks, while the different personnel rotated through the squads. One and all, the ones that worked with him and Chloe, commented on their surprise at the number of enhancements he could use at once. Throneblood forbade him from using the enhanced bullets on the range after he damaged the wall behind one of the target dummies. He'd only done it on a dare from the private that had been working with him on pistol drills, but he refused to throw the Hyreh woman under the bus and accepted the ass-chewing from Throneblood.

Chloe was put through her paces as well, spending a lot of time with the veterans drilling with different weapons. She worked through her anxiety about being watched with some gentle encouragement from Desmond, as well as a judicious application of accuracy increasing enhancements. Building up confidence and not wanting to make her partner look bad, Chloe rolled with any challenge the veterans gave her and did her best to deliver on the lessons.

The most enjoyable portions of the training was the various challenge scenarios they ran through. Throneblood advised them that, in the future, they'd have further classes where they'd run through physical obstacle courses and head-to-head fights with other cadet teams to further practice and drill in different tactics.

At the recommendation of the veteran teams that trained with them, Desmond had started putting aside a few credits for their next day of official leave, as there were several establishments that offered something similar to paintball on-board.

One of the most notable announcements that came from their instructor was that the ship had a simulation center as well, and they would be leaning on it in the second half of the year to give them further experience with what they might encounter in a Rift. When the Uth'ra was questioned by one particularly sassy cadet as to why they didn't do it now, Throneblood had just told them that without first experiencing a Rift themselves, the simulations wouldn't give them a proper feel of the danger and would lead to overconfidence. She then urged them to get back to training for the actual Rift suppression that was coming up.

The training continued until Throneblood announced that they were arriving in-system with the Rifts and that the teams would be deploying shortly, so they should make the final preparations and get their submissions in for their requested partners.

CHAPTER 34

Why don't we scout Rifts ahead of inserting a team to deal with it? They said it is because anyone who could safely scout a Rift should be able to close it up. I think it's because they are afraid of what happens when a Rift goes 'sploot' because someone was messing with it that shouldn't.
~Hailey Tre'novos, shuttle pilot for Valor's Bid, discussing Rifts with a cadet-adept in flight.

Preparations for the Rift run went without a hitch, as far as Desmond was concerned. He'd put in the request to Throneblood for their prospective teammates and got back a standard 'will attempt to accommodate' response. They spent the following day making sure their gear was ready and getting their kits settled. Desmond checked over the cargo-pod to ensure it was as serviceable as possible given time and equipment. Which was mostly pounding dents out of the material and applying lubricant, so it wouldn't squeal as much.

Both he and Chloe agreed that they should try to drag out as much loot as possible in order to further upgrade their kits for the future. Every credit counted right now. Though they disagreed on what should get upgraded first. Chloe had, of course, insisted on Desmond putting it towards another armor upgrade for himself, while Desmond had pointed out that improving her gear should be next on the list. Both of them secretly planned on using their share on the other.

Monika and Oril'la had come by for a planning session as well, and Monika revealed that she'd requested a pair of mid-range fighters to match Oril'la to maximize their adaptability in the moment. She'd spent a few minutes teasing the two of them, but thankfully had been dragged onto a different subject when Desmond had brought out the cargo-pod to work on while they talked.

Dianne and Mona were busy as well, spending more time on the range and missing several meals. Desmond worried about them getting too focused on the practice, but the Uth'ra woman had always been more practical than him or Monika, so he just had to hope she wouldn't push herself too hard.

<><><>

The morning of the Rift suppression saw the entire class staging in the Gold combat range in full kit. Orders had come down from Throneblood to assemble there and be ready to deploy so that they could meet up with their veteran escorts.

Desmond felt like something crossed between an armadillo and a roly-poly bug as he walked back and forth with the armored cargo-pod on his back. He'd done some stretching in their suite with it to get used to the pod, but every bit would help him move naturally with it. He pointedly ignored the giggling of some cadets around him as well as he paced carefully around Chloe.

For the moment, both he and Chloe had their helmets hooked on their belts. How Chloe's helmet worked had taken some time for Desmond to figure out, as it slotted onto her head around her horns before sealing tight. Armored plates would automatically extend forward to fully enclose her horns once the seals engaged, leading to an even more intimidating look for the bull-horned woman.

Chloe remained stoic as always, her repeater hanging on its sling in front of her with her shield leaning against her shoulder. She checked and rechecked the half-dozen power cells she had stowed in the compartment set in the small of her back, molded into her armor. The squat pod acted as a protected storage for the volatile energy cells. Desmond had learned that the model she had did not charge the cells like the canine Taari's had in his last Rift suppression. That had required an advanced module to draw in the ambient mana to recharge the cells, or something like the rapid charge trick Adept Marsden had done. While they would draw mana in naturally because of the pseudo-osmotic pressure that mana worked under, the trickle wouldn't be enough to fully recharge the cells in a reasonable amount of time. Completing Chloe's load-out was a thick telescoping baton that ended in a flanged mace-like head that was attached to the inside of her shield by a quick release clip.

Desmond had four more of the larger cells in the dump pouch on his left thigh, figuring that having extra for Chloe wouldn't hurt. He had half a dozen cells for his rifle as well, but those were tucked on the outside of his right thigh, strapped close behind the raised edge of his armor. A trio of spare magazines for his sidearm completed his load-out, leaving him with eighty-four shots spread between them. He had a spare box of ammunition in his dump pouch with Chloe's spares. It had been an easy trade-off to swap one of his boxes of sidearm ammunition for the larger power cells, as Chloe could put out far more shots than he could with the same amount of space.

"'Would be nice if we had some grenades,'" Desmond quipped to himself as he checked his ammunition one more time before checking the attachment point of the rifle sling to his armor to ensure it was secure, then letting the boxy rifle hang in front of him. He had ended up with a laser variant of the rifle that reminded him of the P90, so it was a chunky little thing shaped like a box of valentines chocolates with a holographic sight mounted on the top.

"What was that, Des?" Chloe inquired, her big head swinging to the side to regard him.

"Nothing, just quoting a movie. Gonna have to see if I can't get a line on Terran media here soon. There are a lot of cultural touchstones that you are missing out on."

"That might be fun. Would be a good way to unwind, and I bet you'd enjoy some media from the Hegemony too. Something besides reading, that is." Chloe shifted on her feet, her heavy boots clattering against the armored decking of the combat range before she settled once more.

Desmond took a moment to fully appreciate the striking figure that his girlfriend/bodyguard struck in her heavy armor. With the specialized helmet to protect her horns, the bulky outfit looked reminiscent of a powered armor suit. Heavy interlocking plates protected her arms and legs, while a segmented breastplate kept her chest protected as well without crushing her bust flat. He'd wondered about that and had asked, coming to find out that the armor was reinforced and designed to contour to the body to provide the best mix of protection and comfort to the largest variety of body types. Chloe's kit had to be modified for her size, specifically because of her height. Heavy shoulder-pads rose up on either side of her helmet with a raised neck-guard angled to deflect a blow up and over her head rather than into the side of her helmet, without being tall enough to block the line-of-sight. The whole thing was painted the same mottled gray-black as their uniforms, being a standard issue with the shipboard camouflage.

"I bow to your expertise then. Movie date when we get back?" Desmond replied as innocently as he could, walking slowly over to stand next to Chloe before leaning against her right side. The heavily armored woman reacted automatically, shifting her feet to stabilize them both and her gauntleted right hand coming up to rest on his shoulder lightly.

"Sounds...good," Chloe said after a bit of a pause.

"Looking forward to it. Oh hey, I think I see the vets coming in." Desmond didn't shift away from Chloe. He'd gotten into the habit over the last several weeks of leaning on her when not moving about. It had partially been because of her own penchant for doing the same and partially a conscious effort on his part to reassure her. Plus, it did feel nice.

Might as well give her what she wants. She's taking it real slow, but if this is what she needs to be comfortable, that is fine with me. Last thing I wanna do is make her uncomfortable and have things be stilted and awkward between us for our whole deployment. He thought to himself. It hadn't even crossed Desmond's mind to investigate if there was a way to remove the team members that disagreed. He just took it as a fact that Chloe would be beside him, regardless. Though, now that he thought about it, he remembered Tre'shovak talking about it back at the beginning of the term.

The motions that had caught Desmond's eye earlier were a flow of armored forms that surged through the wide gates at the far side of the room and hurried towards the cadet teams. They came through the same entrance that the veterans always did for the team lessons. This time, they were dressed in their combat gear rather than just regular fatigues.

Every one of the veterans wore well maintained armor in the variety of styles that were available to the regular enlisted. They moved with a sureness of stride that showed they had lived in that armor for a time as well and were familiar with their suits' individual characteristics.

The flow of veterans was mostly silent as they crossed the space, peeling off in ones and twos to meet up with their assigned teams. The groups that had trained with them had rotated, and while Desmond could spot a few that were familiar, most of the veterans crossing the range were unfamiliar.

"Cadet-Adept McLaughlin and Cadet-Guard Vandenberg?" A gruff voice called from nearby, and Desmond turned in tandem with Chloe to spot the speaker. It was a stout framed female of a species that Desmond had not encountered, beyond seeing one during the second year's demonstration. He blinked in surprise.

The veteran that approached them was similar in build to Chloe, heavily muscled and broad, but a good two or more feet shorter than the bull-horned woman. Her upper body was that of a muscled woman with blunt features and close cropped hair. What stood out the most about her was her lower half. Where her hips would normally meet thighs on every other species he'd encountered thus far, they instead met and meshed with the shoulders of a body that resembled a massive cat, though the details were hard to make out because of the heavy armor that she wore. She had the chunky shield of a heavy trooper in one muscled hand. An odd harness was attached around her shoulders that had a repeater attached to it, but the weapon was stowed along her flank at the moment with a complex frame supporting it in place along the feline body.

The woman eyed them up as she approached, her pale gray eyes took in the pair of them at a glance and snorted before rolling her eyes in amusement while a smirk twisted her lips, revealing hair thin scars that had been hidden before surrounding her mouth.

"Yeah, that has to be you two. No way there is another pair like this on the deck, considering you are the only Terran aboard currently, McLaughlin. Though I have to wonder if some still mistake you for an Aelfa."

"Ah...yes, that is us." Desmond quickly glanced over her rank markings and fought the look of surprise back, "Sergeant. We look forward to working with you." He considered for a moment before saluting her, but not stepping away from Chloe still.

She's my permanent teammate and bodyguard. I trust her more. Besides, not like I'm ashamed of this.

For her part, Chloe made her salute around Desmond, not pushing him away either as she watched the woman warily but respectfully, something the cougar-bodied woman noticed.

"Good, trust no one, Cadet. Especially in the field.

Especially if your adept starts making a name for himself. While it's not necessary here, building the habits is good," the half-cat woman said after a moment of inspecting them. "May I approach?"

"Yes, Sergeant?" Chloe said after another long moment of inspecting her and the other woman nodded again, a smile darting across Chloe's lips at the respect shown to her as a guardian.

"Sergeant Whist. My counterpart will be here shortly. She had decided to collect some extra ammunition from the Armory at the last minute." The half-cat woman sidestepped to stand on Desmond's right side and turned to look across the room at the other recruits as they met up with their veteran escorts.

"Looking forward to seeing how things go today, Sergeant Whist. Any idea of what we are heading into?" Desmond shifted slightly, still getting used to the cargo-pod on his back and missing the feeling of actually leaning against Chloe and feeling her skin against him. In this outfit, he might as well be leaning against the bulkhead.

"No more than you, Cadet. I know we have a low grade Rift to handle. The one tagged for us is one of the ones floating in the void. We've got three other teams with us for this run, but your cadet-adept class is one of three being deployed for this cluster. The remaining cadet-adept classes will be rotated through a series of low end Rifts like these over the next month."

"Sounds fair. What can you tell us about our missing teammate?" Chloe added, her head still moving on a slow scan of the room that had become a habit for her.

"Corporal Ry'taal is a solid mid-range assault. I was informed that you had requested a medic, but all the available medic class veterans that were part of this set had already been reserved at that point, so they pulled from the pool to ensure that everyone would rotate in."

"Did they ration out the lower count classes, like medic

or heavy, per class group?" Desmond asked, getting an approving nod from the sergeant.

"Yes, few people think about that. They usually are more interested in throwing a tantrum that they didn't get their picks, even though they are warned it's not guaranteed."

"Happens, best laid plans and all that." Desmond's response got a confused look from the sergeant and so he elaborated. "It's a saying from my world, 'best laid plans of mice and men oft go awry', meaning that you can plan all you want, but it still can go sideways."

"A fair summation, ah, there is the Corporal." The Sergeant looked up and nodded towards a slender female trooper bounding across the room towards them, her eyes fixed on the Sergeant. She was bearing the regular kit for one of the assault class, light armor meant to keep her mobile, but she clutched one of the broad barreled shotgun-style weapons to her chest. A bandoleer of magazines clacked against her chest plate and she sported absolutely stuffed dump pouches on both her hips that made her look comically wide as she came to a skidding halt five feet from them.

Up close, Desmond could tell that the woman in front of them was one of the Aelfa-breeds, a Tu'Aelfa from her slender build and fine-boned features combined with her shorter stature and the gossamer hair that was bunched in a messy ponytail behind her head. *I think they come from very low gravity worlds with high winds?* Desmond thought to himself as he tried to remember what he'd read about the 'wind elves', as he'd called them inside his own head.

"Corporal Ry'taal, reporting!" She snapped a quick salute to the sergeant before twisting in place to repeat the salute to Desmond. "Cadet-Adept McLaughlin, Cadet-Guard Vandenberg. Looking forward to putting holes in shit with you." She said with a broad smile before dropping into a relaxed 'at-ease' posture and bouncing from foot to foot gently as she did so, like she just wasn't able to sit still.

"Good to meet you, Corporal. I can see you are looking

forward to this as much as we are." Desmond couldn't help the smile that crossed his face at the excitable woman's bouncy presence, which wasn't at all suppressed by the weapon she clutched to her chest.

"Why wouldn't I be looking forward to this? Veteran duty for first years is easy-peasy, and we get paid well for it too! I see you are ready to bring home the credits as well," the corporal chattered while nodding towards the cargo-pod where it peeked over Desmond's shoulder.

"Yes. I need all the credits we can get to bring my partner's gear up to par. So the more we bring back, the more of a split we get to keep after all." Desmond reached up to pat Chloe's hand on his shoulder when she made a grumbling noise.

"Awww, it's so cute to see you getting along so well!" cooed the Tu'Aelfa corporal.

"Okay, can it you? I know things are more informal on the cadet escort runs, but be professional, Corporal." Sighed the Sergeant, getting a crisp salute from the Corporal before she went back to bouncing back and forth on her feet.

*This is going to get interesting...*Desmond thought as he swallowed his blush, chancing a glance up to see that a light dusting of red marked Chloe as well but she hadn't moved at all from her position at his back, not even a twitch.

< > < > < >

The groups trooped out to the shuttle bay shortly after that, splitting up to board the shuttles. Desmond's team shared their shuttle with another team that was heading for the same Rift and, while they were one of the polite ones, they didn't talk other than greetings.

Sitting in the flight chair was awkward with the cargo-pod on until the Sergeant showed him how to adjust the seat to conform for non-standard occupancy. The back pads shifted and molded to the pod, allowing him to sit more comfortably and less hunched forward.

"Entering Rift in thirty." The announcement came across the internal speakers from the cockpit. Desmond tugged his helmet off his belt and snapped it into place, followed only a half-second later by Chloe. The two veterans who were seated across from them nodded approvingly, securing their own helmets as well. The only person without a solid helmet was the other cadet-adept, a feline Taari woman that was from a different class. She watched them in confusion for a moment before one of her veterans showed her the force field helmet built into her collar like Marsden had for Desmond before.

"Sergeant, do we know if the landing pad is clear?" Desmond keyed his helmet to transmit to external speakers. The question brought a chuckle from all four veterans before his sergeant answered.

"No, it hasn't been cleared."

"Right. Chloe, you take point and sweep left. Sergeant, you sweep right. I'll stack left. Then Corporal, you go right. Announce contact before opening fire. Make sure we don't have friendlies in the line-of-fire. Once we have our exit secure, your team can exit." Desmond nodded to the other cadet-adept, who gave him an irritated look at being ordered around. Her veterans, though, nodded in agreement before speaking to her.

"He's voluntarily taking point. Would you like to breach an unsecured area instead? No? Then listen and watch. Eventually you'll be in his spot, so when he fucks up, you know what not to do."

"*If* we fuck up," Desmond shot back. His response got a nod and a wink from the other team's lead-veteran before turning back to his group. "Are you three ready for this?" There was a cluster of agreeing sounds from them and Chloe got to her feet, bracing against the wall in the entryway, shield at the ready and weapon in its notch.

"Why are you sending her out first?" Sergeant Whist asked on their squad-channel. Desmond switched his mic over to it and replied.

"I know Chloe has it covered. We've drilled similar before on the range. It's why I'm going left with her. She's the one I'm most familiar with, so I'll be most in sync with her."

"Good call. Most of the cadets are going to order their veterans to breach, if they think of it at all," the Sergeant said with an eye roll.

"Gotta learn someday, might as well be today." Desmond cycled his rifle, detaching and reattaching the power cell that lay on top of the stock before flipping the safety off and letting it drop to its sling and getting ready to move. The Sergeant was already prepared to dart out the exit hatch behind Chloe and the Corporal was already wiggling in her seat with excitement as she waited for him to go by.

"Rift breach occurring, standby." The pilot's words made them all brace, and Desmond felt the racing tingle rush up his body before it faded. He felt a brief surge of energy on his skin and his dynamo gave that energy a yank.

That's right, spin on up, we got shit to do. Desmond thought at the bizarre little metaphysical organ. He'd just decided to imagine it as a tiny, helpful gremlin that was working to keep his mana cache stocked, since he'd never been able to really understand the mechanics behind it before. Not to mention it amused him to imagine the little critter grabbing handfuls of mana out the air and cramming it into a pile like it was some sort of prize to present to him.

"Landing zone hot, repeat, landing zone hot. Hostiles present!" The pilot's voice was tight as the shuttle bumped hard as it came down for the landing and the door crashed out of the way.

Chloe slammed out the door, wheeling to the left as ordered. The Sergeant dove through and moved to the right, both calling out contacts as they went. The harness on the Sergeant's back unfolded with a mechanized hiss as she went through the door. A pivoting support arm came forward to present the Sergeant with a laser repeater that she snatched with her free hand to guide it into the socket on her shield before opening fire. The support arm remained in place, helping steady the weapon for her.

Desmond moved on auto pilot, charging through and slamming to a stop five feet from the exit, only three feet to Chloe's right. Energy was already pooling in his right hand and his left kept his rifle out of the way while he took stock of the landing zone.

The space they had landed in was a clearing that was surrounded by tree cover and thick vines and waist-high plants. Above them, a bright blue sky hung on a cloudless day. Desmond had a brief moment of déjà vu, thinking they'd somehow ended up in an Earth jungle like Vietnam. Yellow sunlight poured down over the riot of green and brown around him. The creatures charging out of the trees sharply dismissed that notion, though.

They reminded Desmond of gorillas that had gotten addicted to whey powder and arm day. Thick arms met solid, wall-like shoulders that rose up on either side of a coconut shaped head that was easily half mouth, which was filled with needle-like teeth. From there, they narrowed down to a tiny pair of stunted legs that dangled above the forest floor. Heavy, blunt fingers gripped the ground as they shambled towards the landing zone, screeching their fury. The creatures were covered in thick, coarse brown hair that was mottled with green in places to help them blend in with their surroundings.

Two lay dead at the tree-line in front of Chloe, and another was falling on the Sergeant's side. Desmond heard the sharp roar of thrusters behind him as the other shuttle in their group came in for their landing.

"Push! Hearts and minds!" Desmond called through the squad frequency, and flung his arm out, spinning the threads of his mana towards the two heavies in front of him as he bolstered their aim and reaction speed with the Enhancement spell he'd prepared.

Chloe was ready for the enhancements to settle over her and her sustained bursts dissolved into one shrieking spray as she capitalized on the brief surge of intense focus that came over her. The Sergeant was a moment behind her, laying down a withering storm of laser fire that was less effective on a per-target basis, but served to shred the foliage in front of her and send it collapsing on the creatures trying to push through the trees.

"Void it, they didn't tell me you were a goddamn Enhancer!" swore the sergeant and Desmond laughed in response.

"Sorry about that, Sergeant. I'll give more warning next time. If you hear me start rambling on about something nonsensical, brace yourself to get 'The Works'."

"Ooh ooh, I wanna get 'The Works' from you! Do me!" chirped the Corporal as she pushed up next to him. Desmond choked as he nearly tripped over the unintended innuendo from the bouncy woman.

"Another time, Corporal. Trust me, you are going to get it eventually, especially if this is going to roll how I expect it." Desmond snapped off one of his *Bolt* axes. The conjured bladed weapon arced across the clearing to cleave into the neck of one of the ape-monsters that the Sergeant's volley had injured, sending its head spinning up into the air.

"Can't wait! Let's clean up so we can get moving!" cheered the excitable corporal before opening up with her auto-shotgun, the steady 'chug chug chug' of the weapon providing a counterpoint to the shrieking bursts of the laser repeaters on either side.

CHAPTER 35

Was I impressed? Eh, the kid could have done better, but he could have done far worse in that first Rift. His girl? She had grit. Too bad that her mother's people look down on crossbreeds. That weighed on her heavily. Her father's people, though? I can only hope that she spends more time with other Uth'ra. If she gets the encouragement she needs, that woman is going to be an iron wall for her adept.
~Hailey Whist, Sergeant, 46th Battalion. After-action report regarding Rift activities of Cadet-Adept McLaughlin.

It took less than a minute to clear the landing zone to the point where the second team could safely unload.

"Send a flare through the Rift gate when you need pickup or evac, I'll remain on standby just outside," radioed the pilot before lifting off and backing out of the shimmering veil that hung above the tree-line behind them. Desmond signaled his assent before turning back to his team.

The second shuttle finished unloading its crew, as it had taken them too long to exit to contribute to the fight, but they worked to rapidly secure their half of the clearing.

"All right, McLaughlin. What's the play here?" Sergeant Whist called. She stood beside Chloe, facing outward, with Desmond and the Corporal inside their wedge. Corporal Ry'taal had her eyes on their rear, keeping watch in the clearing to make sure that nothing snuck past the other teams.

"All right...last time I was in a Rift, they had tunnels to scout but this one is relatively open..." Desmond scanned the tree-line. The undergrowth surrounding the clearing was thick enough that the only exits were a trio of paths, like game trails, that cut through the brush and trees to provide a path. The section of forest that the Sergeant had cut back with her laser didn't reveal anything of note other than that the undergrowth was deep on either side. "Sergeant, advise me?"

"It will cost you points in the final scoring, McLaughlin, but I can."

"Fuck the points, Sergeant. I'm here to train and I want us all to get out safely," Desmond shot back, drawing a bark of laughter from the quadrupedal sergeant.

"Okay, fine. I'll ask you this first, before I advise you: What is your first instinct right now?"

"Pick a path. Follow it and scout along. Mark any splits we take and treat it like the cave system. The undergrowth is thick enough that it makes it dangerous to deviate off the paths, but it is doable. Treat it just like the cave system, but be wary of shit coming out of the bushes."

"Not a poor plan. What kind of mapping software do you have in your helmet?"

"It's older gen, but I can keep track of the path and get us back here if we get lost."

"Can it do a radar ping?"

"No, that module cost extra and we didn't have the creds for it."

"Okay, keep your mana sense open then, Cadet. You are the next best thing we got to radar for mana surges. What's the order of marching?"

Desmond considered for a moment, glancing over his shoulder to see one of the other squads start hacking their way into the underbrush while the other two argued over which path they would each take.

"Chloe, me, the Corporal, then you Sergeant. Call out contact before firing if you can. We have Friend/Foe tags in all the armor, so we *shouldn't* need to worry about friendly fire. I'll drop pins in the mapping software as we move. Chloe, pick a path and get us moving. Pause if the path splits and I'll see if I can sense concentrations down either way."

"Stepping off," Chloe called and began moving forward, her repeater steady in the notch of her shield as she moved onto one path and started forward. Desmond heard shouts from behind them as the others noticed that he'd just grabbed a path, but ignored it.

They'll figure it out, eventually. He thought to himself, snatching the can of marker paint off his belt and tagging the trees on either side of the path they took with a brilliant bumble-bee yellow slash. *Huh. Okay, they issued me a yellow. Dang, I wanted a swanky metallic like Marsden had, but this works just fine. All that matters is that it's bright.*

<><><>

Ducking under the tree cover had an immediate effect. Desmond blinked several times to let his eyes adjust to the change in the light. The path they were on was packed dirt and just barely wide enough for Chloe to get through without a problem. On either side, trees and thick bushes blocked easy passage off the path and the winding nature of the trail itself prevented them from seeing more than a dozen meters ahead of them at any point. Above him, Desmond could hear the wind stirring the leaves in the trees, but other than the crunch of their boots on the path and the occasional distant shout from the clearing behind them, the forest was eerily silent.

"Too quiet," Desmond muttered into the team channel.

"Agreed, but this isn't a natural space. Remember that," Sergeant Whist replied. She watched the younger cadet-adept carefully with one eye as she scanned the trees on either side of them. The young man had promise, and if the enhancement she'd felt earlier was something he could casually toss out as early on a run as securing the landing site, then she wanted to see what the young man could do when pressed.

"Picking up movement around the bend. Clearing ahead with more of the natives it looks like." Chloe's statement drew them all back to attention and Desmond shifted to grip his rifle, again checking to ensure the power cell was firmly seated and that the safety was off.

Enhancements are cheaper, burn those first and focus on the rifle. Save two cells worth of ammo and switch to Bolt then. Chloe has more ammo than the other three of us combined, I think, unless the Sergeant has one of the charging modules. Desmond reminded himself before taking a deep breath.

"Lead the way, Chloe," he radioed to her as soon as he was ready and the big woman did not hesitate.

Chloe moved from the steady, slow tread that she had been using until that point, into a trot, then a charge as they came round the last gentle bend and saw the clearing fully ahead of them.

Chloe opened fire as soon as she had a clean shot out into the clearing, which was good as the creatures looked like they'd been getting ready to come charging down the path towards them.

A screech of laser fire heralded the end of two more of the ape-creatures before the rest of the team breached the clearing. The group opened out in a fan rather than crossing each other this time and Desmond opened fire with his boxy rifle, sending a cascade of shots into the torso and shoulders of one of the creatures as he mentally spun the mana out to each of his companions, growling the key phrase he'd chosen for the accuracy enhancement under his breath.

The fight was over in a matter of seconds. Between the combined weight of the two heavy weapons scything through the creatures before they could rally, while Desmond and the Corporal executed any who survived the cascade of shots in quick order.

"That was a rush!" exclaimed the Corporal. Her fingers moved rapidly through the motions of swapping magazines out on her auto-shotgun and topping up the partial magazine from her dump pouches.

"Get used to it, at least for today. Cadet-Adept McLaughlin is going to spoil us for regular duty doing that," Sergeant Whist chuckled, eyes darting around the clearing. "I see two paths branching off, one on each end of the clearing."

"Stick right. I'll tag as we go. Corporal Ry'taal, you have point this turn. Otherwise, same stack."

"Sweet!" chirped the excitable Tu'Aelfa. She bounced forward to lead the way down the path. Chloe queued up behind her with steady steps. Desmond swapped over to a private channel to the horned woman before speaking.

"You holding up okay, Chloe?"

"Doing good, Des. This feels sort of…odd. I expected to be more nervous going into a Rift like this."

"It's been something of a turkey shoot so far. I'm sure it'll get hairy later. I felt the same way when I went with Marsden's group. Even then it got tight with seven people at the end."

"Yeah, you mentioned."

Desmond was about to continue when he felt a sudden swell of pressure on their right from his dynamo that felt like walking next to a radiant heater. He swapped back to the team channel to radio the Corporal to stop.

"What's up?"

"Felt something off the path. Cover me." Desmond pushed at the greenery to his right, cursing for a moment before he had a thought. It took more effort than he had expected, but he could form and hold the axe that his *Bolt* spell took the form of and began chopping at the greenery. It took him a minute or two to clear away enough to spot what he had sensed, and a smile spread across his face.

A thick prism of green crystal stuck out from under a tree root on the backside of a tree that made up part of the barrier wall. A careful blow with the blunt back of his axe and Desmond leaned back onto the path to examine it.

The crystal was as thick as his wrist and almost a foot long, faceted like a piece of quartz and mostly translucent, with a heavy emerald tinge to it. It vibrated gently in his hand, the potential raw mana in it humming along with the tune of his dynamo.

"Very nice. Looks like we aren't going back empty-handed now," chuckled the Sergeant. Desmond nodded to her before slipping the crystal over his shoulder and into the cargo-pod on his back. It slid in to land with a quiet 'clunk' in the padded enclosure on his back.

"Got room for more in there, so let's keep moving!"

<><><>

The path that the Corporal led them down opened into another clearing that had more of the ape-monsters in it and three other trails leading off of it. They cleared it with no problem, and Desmond had them go right again. This led to a dead-end clearing that had a narrow river running through it and was suspiciously empty. Desmond had the others stand guard while he scanned the clearing with his senses. Nothing jumped out of the bushes, but he did collect a double handful of sky-blue crystals from inside the river that were hidden under several stones. Each of them felt cool in his hand, even through his gloves.

Doubling back to the triple split clearing, Desmond marked the branch they'd just finished with a second line to declare it cleared before they took the middle route.

Again, this route led them to a dead end clearing, but this time there was a large group of the ape-monsters waiting for them. He'd had the Corporal leading on this one again to give her another chance to get used to the sensation of the buffs. The sprightly Tu'Aelfa had proved adept with her weapon, downing four of the creatures before Desmond even made it into the clearing. Searching the clearing had yielded a trio of metallic yellow fruit shaped like pears that hung from a squat tree off to one side. The fruit themselves, despite having a metallic sheen to them, felt soft enough that Desmond was sure he could bite into one and wondered at what their purpose would be.

"Restoratives. You can eat them in a pinch, but they do better when turned over to the Armory. They can refine them down into an inhalant or injectable that is more potent. Medical has uses for them sometimes too," Sergeant Whist advised as Desmond inspected them. Tucking them away into a hip pouch rather than the cargo pod in order to keep them from being crushed, Desmond thought about what the Sergeant had said.

Wonder what kind of restoratives they have. Never even thought to look into those while browsing the Armory supplies. Was there even a listing in there for them?

The last path off the triple-split led them to a clearing that butted up against a low cliff. A short waterfall rushed off the cliff and into a pool on one side of it. Rather than a collection of the ape creatures in the clearing, there was only one. And it was easily three times the size of the others. The creature stood almost ten feet tall and nearly that wide, with arms as thick around as Desmond's waist.

The creature was drinking from the pool when they broke the tree line and Desmond urged them back to plan before it spotted them.

"Okay, has anyone spotted anything that stood out on the creature?" Desmond whispered, despite being on contained team comms in his helmet.

"Pile of round stones by the cliff. Don't look like they ended up there naturally. Could do some damage if it decides to chuck them at us," Chloe said after a moment of thought.

"Cliff looks like it's clear up above, but that might change as well," Corporal Ry'taal added after her.

"Pool looked deep enough that something might be hiding in it. Doubtful but possible." The Sergeant added at the end.

"Saw the stones and the cliff. Was surprised to not see trees up on the cliff. Gonna have to take a look up there once we clear this fucker out. I can sense mana coming from the pool and from that pile of stones you mentioned. Be careful if it starts throwing those. Chloe and Sergeant Whist, I want you two to enter the clearing first. Open fire as soon as you are ready. Corporal, flank wide left but keep a sharp eye on the cliff. If something is up there, I don't want it blindsiding you if it jumps down. I'll stick with the Sergeant and Chloe for the moment and push support."

The women made various noises of assent before shuffling past each other to change up positions in the tighter confines of the path.

"All right." Desmond took a deep breath before turning to the Corporal. "Gonna give you it all, so when you hear me start chanting, brace for it. Chloe, you and the Sergeant are going to get accuracy for now. If it starts chucking rocks, durability will hit your shields, so don't be afraid to block."

"Shit, kid. You can really do that much? I know you can do multi-targets, but really?" The Sergeant gave him an odd look and Desmond just shrugged.

"Enhancement specialist. Throneblood's had me targeting multiple things for the last half month or more."

"Sounds like her. That woman is a terror in a fight. She knows what she's doing. We'll wipe the floor with this bastard." Laughed the Sergeant before doing a weapons check. "On your mark."

"Mark," Desmond called, and the group started forward at a sprint.

Chloe and the Sergeant burst into the clearing, moving out into the open and splitting to either side, leaving a five-foot gap between them for Desmond. The Corporal darted left, circling widely away from the pool, while Desmond slid to a stop, shouldering his rifle as he spun up the mana for the enhancements.

He laid the accuracy into his heavies first before spinning

up the full strength of 'the works' for the corporal.

"Let her aim be true and her hand faster than those that seek to destroy me, grant her victory over my foes and those that wish to do harm to me and mine…" Desmond chanted out the modified oath, flicking the strands of magic out to the Corporal as the ape-monster spun in their direction, its maw snapping open with a roar that was met by a fusillade of laser fire from Chloe and the sergeant.

Immediately, the creature was driven back on its heels as the blasts seared into its flesh but, unlike its smaller counterparts, the lasers did not scythe through it. Instead, only blowing bloody chunks from the creature's forearms and shoulders. In response, it hunched forward, turning slightly to shelter its head behind one thick shoulder and side-shuffling towards the stack of boulders as they had expected.

The Corporal struck with a whooping cry as the creature snatched up one of the rounded rocks and turned to fling it at the group. Darting forward with unnatural speed, the Tu'Aelfa opened fire with her auto-shotgun. To Desmond, the 'chug-chug-chug' of the weapon sounded like a chainsaw starting to turn over, and the elbow of the arm holding the rock abruptly erupted in a cloud of blood and shredded flesh.

The creature bellowed in pain when its arm was blown off below the elbow. With the sudden change in its body-mass threw its balance off and it fell backwards onto its ass. The trio of women converged on the downed creature but the Corporal made it there first, landing lightly on its chest before pumping half a dozen rounds into its face and sending its bowling-ball head flying into chunks.

"Woo! That was a rush!" exclaimed the Corporal from her perch on top of the creature as it slumped over dead.

"Get back over here!" demanded the Sergeant as another series of howls echoed from the cliff above them. Thankfully, the Corporal didn't turn to look, instead lunging forward to sprint towards the three of them. A moment later, four more of the enormous creatures leaped down off the clifftop to land beside their fallen fellow.

CHAPTER 36

I was there, and I didn't believe it either.
~Gwen Ry'taal, Corporal, 46th Battalion. After-action report regarding Cadet-Adept McLaughlin.

No orders were required as Chloe and the Sergeant laid down covering fire for the Corporal while she sprinted back towards them. Not bothering to look back, Corporal Ry'taal emptied the remains of her magazine over her shoulder, blowing chunks off of one of the brutes as they all howled after her.

Two of the enormous creatures started forward, their massive paws slamming into the ground hard enough to make it shake. The other two whirled to snatch stones from the pile that their fellow had been standing beside.

"Incoming!" Called Desmond as he watched the stone throwers turn back to lob their projectiles at the group. "Good timber does not grow with ease!" He snapped, spinning out two more enhancements, latching on to the shields that the two heavies carried and reinforcing them as the melon-sized projectiles arced towards them.

The Corporal dove into a slide that sent her between the Sergeant's front legs with an ease that showed this wasn't the first time she'd done it. The moment the Corporal slid past her, the Sergeant planted the edge of her shield and hunkered down behind it. Chloe did the same with her shield, and Desmond stepped up to shelter behind her just as the stones crashed into them. One stone hit each of the heavy's shields, shattering with a detonation of thunder and a storm of stone shards that exploded in all directions.

"Shatter and Void it!" cursed the Sergeant, gritting her teeth as the blow against her reinforced shield rocked her back slightly and her arm went numb from the impact.

Chloe grunted in agreement. She'd been slightly better braced and took the hit at an angle rather than square. Both of them resumed pouring fire into the two beasts that were charging them. The bobbing movement of the creatures as they jogged back and forth on their hands made it difficult to stay on target, the enhancements from Desmond showing their worth as much as possible.

"Reeling it in, Corporal," Desmond growled as the Tu'Aelfa rolled onto her stomach and rapidly swapped magazines before adding her fire into the mix. He could feel his dynamo straining to maintain the flow of energy for everything he had running right now. Desmond reeled in the energy that he had dedicated to enhancing her, leaving just the accuracy enhancement behind. The five that he was managing, three accuracy and two durability, were still chipping away at his cache and while he wasn't drawing low, that could change quickly if the fight was prolonged. His cache would last longer now after consolidating.

The one charging the Sergeant went down first, the creature going down to the ground in a heap when a lucky shot from the Corporal took out one of its hands right as it planted its weight on the limb. This allowed the Sergeant to pour concentrated fire into its head, which finally burst.

The one charging Chloe ducked its shoulder as it neared and threw itself at her in a straight-up football tackle. Desmond saw it start to duck and slapped his left hand into the small of Chloe's back, shoving a stability enhancement into her legs and pushing more durability into her shield.

"The mountain does not bow to the wind!" he snapped out the first chant that sprung to his mind that sounded like it would fit and slammed his mana forward just as the creature connected with Chloe's planted shield.

The impact sent her sliding back several feet, the toes of

her boots leaving trenches in the earth as she went. Desmond had, thankfully, stepped to one side to fire, so he wasn't bowled over as she slid past him. Unfortunately, the shield Chloe held bounced back and slammed into her helmet. The impact caused a crack to spider-web through her faceplate and yanked a snarl of pain from her throat.

Even with the reinforcements on her shield, the metal cratered at the point of impact and dented heavily. As a result, her back-up mace snapped free of its restraints on the back of the shield and clattered across the clearing towards the trees.

"Shatter and burn it," growled Chloe while she fought to bring her weapon around on the creature in front of her. "I think my arm is broken."

Desmond brought his rifle up and let go a salvo into the creature's head while it fell backwards. The ape-monster hadn't survived the impact without injury, landing on its ass to wrench at a dislocated shoulder with its other hand. Chloe was able to join him, her face a mask of pain as she forced her arms to respond despite the shooting pain on her shield side.

Fury filled Desmond when the creature that had injured Chloe fell still, its face a smoking ruin. The barrel of his rifle glowed red hot and the indicator on the side of his power cell blinked that it was nearly drained.

"Incoming!" The words from the Sergeant barely made it through his funk as Desmond whirled towards the two remaining monsters. His right hand released the rifle to fall on its sling, before swinging back into the throwing posture and snapping forward, hurling the anger he felt along with his mana toward the enemy.

The axe that formed from his normal *Bolt* spell was normally the size of a tomahawk, just under two feet in length with an angular, wedge-shaped head. Even when he'd summoned the larger one, it was only the size of a double-bit axe.

Instead of that, what Desmond sent whirling through

the air like a rocket, energy snapping and crackling along its edges, looked like it would have been more at home in the hands of a fur-wearing barbarian king. The *Bolt*-axe slammed into the leftmost of the stone throwers with a crash like the aftermath of a lightning strike right as the creature pulled back to recover from its own throw. The impact blew the creature's right arm clear off, sending the limb flipping through the air to slam into the other thrower and knock it off balance.

Unfortunately, their stones were already in the air and Desmond was out of position, having moved forward to pursue the enemy that had injured Chloe. Both of the rocks were aimed for him and he tried to skip backwards to get away from them, but his own balance was shot from the *Bolt* throw.

Like a blast-door slamming down, Chloe surged in front of Desmond. She snatched him with her right arm, having dropped her repeater, and pulled him against her chest. Her left arm still hung limp, shield dragging it down and away from them. But, with a wrench of her upper body that sent a scream of pain between her teeth, she got it up and propped against her shoulder moments before the stones impacted, one on the ground in front of her shield and the other just above the other dent.

The world was consumed with a ringing explosion of noise and Desmond was jostled in Chloe's arms as the woman weathered the impact with only a jerk and a sway. The only thing that cut through the ringing in Desmond's head was Chloe's whimper of pain only inches from him.

"Stay down!" snapped the Sergeant, before the scream of her repeater filled the clearing, punctuated by the 'chug-chug-chug' of the Corporal's shotgun putting rounds into the downed and injured throwers.

"Chloe! Talk to me, are you okay?" Desmond's head was ringing from the close proximity impact of the strange, explosive stones. Chloe shook her broad head, her horns clacking against the back of her distorted shield.

"It hurts," she whined, her face rapidly going pale behind the cracked faceplate. Desmond pushed at her restraining right arm.

"Let me up, Chloe. I gotta take a look at you, hon," he urged, as the sounds of gunfire died down.

"Arm...fucked up bad," Chloe panted, releasing her death-grip around Desmond and allowing him to slip free of her arm and take stock of what had happened.

The first explosive stone had only scarred her shield, but the impact from the creature's tackle had dented and warped it, leaving a broad concave bend in the shield that had managed to strain Chloe's armor underneath it and snap her arm. The impact from the second explosive rock, as well as the strain of trying to maneuver the injured arm, had driven one of her arm bones through the skin and caused the fabric under her armor to distort.

"Sergeant! Need a hand here!" Desmond shouted over his shoulder, forgetting that he was on comms with the others. No one said a thing as the Sergeant raced over, her four legs pounding across the clearing from where she'd been checking the dead to ensure there weren't any faking it.

"Blast, it's broken. We need to get it set and sealed. I have medical supplies to get it secured," swore the quadrupedal woman when she saw the injury. "We will have to evac. I can't let you continue with her injured like this. Get her shield off, gently now." The Sergeant began rifling through her pouches while snapping orders to the Corporal to keep watch while they worked. Chloe took a knee when her balance went off from the pain.

Thankfully, Desmond had gotten used to helping Chloe put her gear on over the last few weeks, so he could follow the steps in reverse to release the clamps that secured it to her forearm and get the slab-shield off of her, tipping it over to land in the dirt. Her armor was more tricky, but thankfully it had only bent some plates slightly and he was able to get the catches to release and open the piece, letting it fall to dangle off her elbow.

One of the bones in her forearm was sticking up at an odd angle. I had punched through her arm and emerged into the open air, blood gushed from the wound. Chloe hissed in pain, gritting her teeth hard as she fought to keep from screaming.

"Easy, girl. I got you. You'll be in Medical for a while, but you should bounce back from this no problem," reassured the Sergeant as she produced a medical kit and started unpacking it rapidly.

Desmond froze as her words triggered a series of memories.

Chloe in the Medical wing. Chloe leaning on him and could not walk. A wash of the wintergreen sensation he'd come to feel as mana. Chloe walking down the hallway to her barracks, still in pain but not as bad. Finally, the wash of sensation and the vanishing of pain as his shoulder injury healed suddenly while in the Rift.

"Sergeant, set the bone."

"I have to give her painkillers, Cadet. Setting the bone is going to hurt even then!" protested the Sergeant.

"Set the bone. Now." Desmond's voice held an undercurrent of ice as he gripped Chloe's elbow in both of his. He met Chloe's pain-filled eyes for a breath of a moment. "I got you, hon. What does not kill us makes us stronger," he murmured, keeping his eyes on hers. When Chloe nodded in agreement, Desmond *shoved* almost a third of the mana he had left into her body, around twenty percent of his total, directing it into her forearm with a specific goal in mind.

The mana coiled around Desmond's hands before bursting into Chloe's body and racing down her arm. Chloe let out a startled scream and, acting on instinct, the Sergeant grabbed her hand and jerked forward. The exposed bone slid back under the skin and all three felt an eerie 'click' of the ends of the bone connecting automatically like they were guided by magnets, and then suddenly fusing. Seconds later, the bleeding from the injury stopped and the puncture wound sealed up before the swelling began to rapidly fade.

"What... the hell did you do, Cadet?" breathed the Sergeant, watching in awe as the wound healed before her eyes and the swelling across Chloe's arm that had been only growing until a moment ago began to fade, leaving only dried blood and unwounded flesh behind. "I know you haven't been trained in healing yet. They explicitly told us that during the briefing. Any injuries beyond minor scrapes were 'recover immediately' unless you had a trained medic pulled for you."

Desmond didn't respond. He was busy fighting vertigo from the sudden outpouring of mana. He'd never blown quite that much energy in one go other than his own injury, and it made his head swim. His dynamo hummed angrily at him from its place in his chest as it fought to draw mana back into his cache.

Chloe was there, using her newly healed arm to steady Desmond, color already returning to her face and a soft smile decorating her lips.

"Shared it with her," Desmond mumbled, blinking away the dizziness before patting Chloe's healed arm again to make sure it was fully repaired.

Breathing deeply, Desmond pulled on the threads of enhancement mana he had spun out, canceling the buffs and drawing them back into his body, reclaiming what mana he could from them. The cable that he had forged for Chloe had been the largest, and it brought his mana back up enough that his balance firmed up again.

"Shared what? Explain, Cadet!" snapped the Sergeant. She was trembling in a mixture of fury, fear, and relief at seeing an injury that might have ended up leaving Chloe a cripple healed so rapidly.

"Healing. Huma...er...Terran's heal fast. Medical told me even faster with mana involved. Used myself as a template and gave that to her," Desmond explained. "How are you doing, hon?" Desmond turned back to Chloe, bending down to peer through her cracked faceplate to make sure she was okay.

"I'm fine, Des. You made sure of that. Lemme up," Chloe laughed, a bit of a manic edge to her tone. She was a little lightheaded as well, but the supercharged healing that Desmond had given her had pushed her bone marrow as well, replacing the blood faster than she'd lost it. Most of her remaining disorientation was because of the sudden switch back in blood pressure and the gnawing hunger that was rising in her stomach.

Stepping back, Desmond let Chloe get to her feet, standing close by in case she stumbled, which she did not.

"Shatter me…that was a hell of a rush. Felt like you poured about a gallon of mint extract into me. Swear I could feel it in my lungs…" Chloe muttered, stretching her arm and back, making both click and pop as they settled back into place. "These flea-bitten monsters better have something worth this…going to be a pain in the ass to replace the shield." Chloe nudged her damaged and dented shield with the toe of her boot before flipping her armor back in place and working the damaged catches to secure it for now.

"Yeah, not something I want to do often…that costs me a lot of mana…" Desmond collected her laser repeater, having to use both hands to lift it, and handed the weapon off to the horned woman. "You sure you okay, hon?" Desmond didn't let go of the weapon right away when Chloe took it, holding it and looking up at her intently.

"Yes, I'm okay Des. Let's finish this up. Need to make sure we get paid for this." Chloe glanced back down at the damaged shield and sighed. "I won't fight you on getting me some better armor now. Anyone see where my mace landed?"

"Good girl," Desmond said with a wink before turning back to the Sergeant, who had watched the whole interaction with a bemused expression. "Sergeant, we got some looting to do. You have a knife I can borrow?"

<><><>

"I definitely need to get me one of these," Desmond muttered as he sawed the broad-bladed knife through the thick hide of the last of the larger ape-monsters. He'd already gone through the first four, extracting the mana crystal buried next to their hearts with the keen knife, and it wasn't showing any signs of dulling yet.

"Bought it off a blade-smith years back. I can send you his information. He's got a shop on the *Valor's Bid*," the Sergeant called. She and the Corporal were standing watch while Chloe loomed over him, observing while he did the gristly work. Desmond had decided to get the messy part out of the way before delving into the other sources of energy that he'd felt in the clearing, especially since one of them was in the pond that the creature had been drinking out of before they'd attacked.

"Appreciate it, Sergeant. Should be done here…presently." The hide popped free and Desmond could reach in and wrench out the crystal from beside the creature's heart, freeing it with a sickly *pop* that made him extremely glad he was wearing gauntlets. "All done. Okay, let me check out the pond next and get this cleaned up."

"Roger that!" chirped Corporal Ry'taal. The excitable corporal had gone back to her normal happy self once Chloe was on her feet. She had been set to patrolling the clearing by the Sergeant in an effort to 'put that energy to some use.' Thankfully, the Corporal had located where Chloe's mace had landed, and the taurine Taari now had it secured on her belt, since the clips on her shield had snapped right off during the fight.

The group shifted over to the pond and Desmond peered through the choppy water to try to discern the ripple of energy he was feeling from it.

"Hmm… let me see." Desmond squatted down, leaning

over the water before Chloe stopped him.

"Hold up, Des." She cautioned before getting a grip on his belt with her left hand, the right occupied with her repeater now that her shield was a pile of twisted scrap.

"Thanks, Chloe." Desmond nodded and waited for her to get a good grip before he stuck his helmeted face under the water. Once he was past the choppy surface, it was much easier to spot the source of the mana pulse that he felt trembling through the water.

A collection of shimmering silver nuggets sat just below where the waterfall hit the pond, and Desmond pulled back to relay the information to the others.

It took a handful of minutes to strip off the pieces of gear that he didn't want to get wet before Desmond engaged the environmental seals on his armor and waded into the pond. He then spent another few minutes collecting the sharply vibrating silver nuggets together and stowing them away into a sealable pouch that the Corporal had thrown to him from the shore when he'd asked them.

"Rift-silver, now that is going to bring in good credits," cheered the Corporal when she saw the clear plastic pouch of the metal.

"More than that, I bet there is some more above the waterfall, too. These bastards came from somewhere and I wanna go up there to check it out. But first, let's finish up down here," Desmond said with a grin, tucking the pouch inside his armor. The silver vibrated gently against his skin. He had no idea how much it might be worth, but he did remember the girls saying that precious metals that absorbed Rift energies were some of the most expensive items for the jewelers. Inside his armor was the most secure spot to stow it to ensure they got something out of this run.

Inspecting the pile of stones that had been thrown at them revealed that they were just polished river rocks. However, they had faint traces of mana in them at a higher concentration than the surrounding stones. Not wanting to weigh himself down, Desmond left them there for the time being while they debated what to do with the sheer stone cliff.

"You aren't going up there alone. That's final." Chloe was very insistent as she stood with one hand on her hip, the other resting her repeater on her shoulder.

"I didn't say I should. The cliff is like...ten or fifteen feet tall. If you lift me up, I can scramble the rest of the way up. Corporal Ry'taal can come up with me while you two keep things secure down here. If anything seems off, we drop back down and hightail it out of here," Desmond repeated for the third time.

"I think the Corporal should go up first to scout it," interjected the Sergeant finally, drawing the two out of their argument. "She's fast enough that I doubt anything up there could catch her, and we need to get moving. The longer we hang around, the more likely that something goes wrong, and we still have to finish securing the Rift so that the *Valor's Bid* can send a team in to drain and collapse it safely."

"That's right...these Rifts get more unstable the longer they sit," Desmond muttered to himself before glancing over at where the Corporal waited for them to decide.

"Yes. But this thing just formed. There are weeks to months before it actually destabilizes, though we are supposed to treat it as if we only have hours," reminded the Sergeant.

Desmond nodded in agreement to her before turning his attention back to the Corporal. "You up to scout a bit, Corporal? Just give it a quick once over and let us know. I'll join you to snatch anything worth bringing back. I don't sense enough emanations coming up there to be any risk for you."

"Sure thing!" the Corporal sang, throwing him a sloppy salute before darting over to the rough cliff wall. Before anyone could reach her to assist, she was already halfway up the cliff.

"Huh...nimble doesn't even begin to describe her," Chloe said, her tone impressed.

"Yup." Desmond chuckled, shifting so he could lean back into Chloe's hip. It was partially because he knew she liked it, and partially to reassure himself that she was okay. *Been getting more and more used to this...*he thought idly as he settled into his familiar spot.

They watched as the Corporal made it up and over the edge and vanished from sight. Less than a minute later, her head popped back over the edge and she waved down at them.

"All clear up here. Another clearing up here with a path leading away from it. Creek comes out from between some rocks and flows down to the waterfall. Looks like some kind of nest near where the creek comes out of the rocks."

"Gotcha, stay away from the nest. Last time there was one of those, the mana concentration was high enough to cause problems for normal folk," Desmond replied, before turning to look up at Chloe. "Give me a boost, hon?"

"Sure," Chloe said with an exaggerated sigh before squatting and putting her hands together to make a stirrup. Desmond stepped into it, and with a surge, Chloe tossed him upwards.

Desmond sailed a lot higher than he had thought he would and smacked stomach first into the edge of the cliff, scrabbling to get a grip before he slid back off of it. Thankfully, the Corporal was there to help pull him up and over the edge. Chloe watched him warily, flexing her formerly injured arm with a bit of surprise still.

The clearing was laid out just like the Corporal had described it and Desmond was quick to check the nest. Unlike the spider-goblin nest that he'd seen before, which was made of stones piled in a rough circle, this was made of the foliage torn out of the edges of the clearing.

As he'd suspected, he could feel a ripple of mana coming from the nest and, while it wasn't as dense as the spider-goblins nest had been, he felt it pressing in on his dynamo as his body scrabbled and scraped at the loose mana in the air, working to refill his cache.

"Okay, stay here and keep watch. Cover me and do not be afraid to radio if anything looks suspicious," Desmond ordered the Corporal, which got him a snappy salute and she began to fiddle with the auto-shotgun before turning to survey the clearing.

"Desmond, keep in contact on the comms, okay?" Chloe's voice echoed through his helmet and he nodded in agreement before remembering she couldn't see him right now.

"Sure thing, Chloe. You two keep watch down there. While nothin's come out of the trees since the landing zone, I don't want to take a chance." He got noises of assent from the Sergeant and Chloe before proceeding forward.

The rough nest was his first goal. The ripples of mana coming from the bundle of plant debris were enough to obscure his senses of anything else in the clearing. Up close, it was...disturbing, more disturbing than he'd expected.

Plants and mud made up a good portion of the nest, but there were also odd bones and a few skulls worked into the thing like it was completely natural. Thankfully, none of the bones looked like recent additions, and the three skulls he could see were obviously similar to the creatures they'd killed.

"Nest is clear, looks like they took trophies from others of their kind that they killed. Makes me wonder if they compete over this space or resources."

"Rift beasts do tend to compete over the concentrated mana sources. It's part of why the adept teams are sent in to sweep and clear them of hostiles before the harvesters are sent in to collect the ambient mana and collapse the Rift safely," Sergeant Whist replied back. "If they haven't covered it yet, I'm sure they will soon."

"I'm sure they will. Throneblood was just more focused

on making sure we had the skills to get by rather than including 'academic facts' in her lectures, I bet," Desmond sent back to her.

Sorting through the nest took a bit of effort as Desmond had to snap branches and crumble the loose packed mud to get down to where he could feel the humming vibration through his hands. But the digging was rapidly proved worth it when he unearthed more than a dozen of the humming green crystals, all the same size or larger than the one he'd recovered already, laid out like the floor of a log cabin and held together by the rough mud-pack.

"Jackpot! Crystals, and lots of them." Working the crystals loose carefully, Desmond got them brushed mostly clean and stowed in the cargo pod on his back, one at a time.

Surprisingly, the weight of the cargo pod hasn't changed all that much. The crystals aren't exactly light, but the pod doesn't feel that heavy.

Desmond paused to try to check the weight and was surprised to realize his heart was still thundering from earlier, not as fast as when Chloe had been injured, but still faster than normal. *Okay, maybe it is more to do with the adrenaline after Chloe got hurt...that sucked. I need to figure out a better way than just enhancing the durability of something. There's gotta be more to it.*

Stowing the last of the crystals, Desmond gave the nest one last check over before moving to his next step.

"Okay. Dropping the cargo pod next to the Corporal and going for a swim. Corporal, keep an eye on my gear."

"Desmond, I don't like you going into the water with only one covering you..." The concern in Chloe's voice was obvious.

"If it wasn't for the fact I found Rift-silver in the lower pool, I wouldn't chance it, Chloe. We need all the credits we can get to get our gear square and be ready for our new addition after the next selection," Desmond replied. He began rapidly stripping his gear off a second time and piling it next to the cargo-pod. The Corporal gave him a sharp nod before going back to scanning the clearing. "Anything of note, Corporal?"

"Nothing to report!" she chirped back happily, bouncing slightly from foot to foot with her auto-shotgun at the 'low ready' position. He spared a moment to wonder how the motion must distract others when she wasn't wearing her armor, but shoved it away with a snort.

Chloe is plenty distracting, even in armor. Focus on what you are doing right now.

"Good woman, thank you for keeping an eye out and ensuring I'm safe. I'm sure that Cadet-Guard Vandenberg is much happier having you here to cover me."

"Damn straight I am. Otherwise I'd be climbing up there myself," quipped the big woman from her place below.

"I rest my case," Desmond deadpanned and got a giggle out of the Corporal before he turned and headed into the river.

Checking between rocks and following the gentle vibrations in the river, Desmond worked quickly to recover several handfuls of silver nuggets and three large clusters of the sky-blue crystals that they'd found in the other creek. The biggest score so far occurred when Desmond tracked the water back to where it emerged from the rocks and found several large chunks of shimmering gold that sang as soon as his fingers touched the metal.

"Mother f..." Desmond strangled the urge to swear, reminding himself of the fact the Sergeant and Corporal were on the radio with him too. "We got something here."

"What? Desmond, are you okay?" Chloe's voice had a note of panic to it and he was quick to reassure her.

"I'm fine, but I think I found gold nuggets in the stream too. These definitely look like gold."

"Stars and suns, Cadet! What kind of brother-humping luck do you have?" The Sergeant apparently had no compunctions on swearing at all. "There should be no way

Rift-silver forms in a low end run like this, let alone Rift-gold."

"Get it all!" chimed in the Corporal.

"Keep your eyes peeled, Corporal!" snapped the Sergeant, her astonishment giving way to concern. "If the haul is that good, the Cadet-Adept is going to be a damn beacon to the Rift-beasts. I wouldn't be surprised if he starts drawing them out of hiding and into the paths, too."

"Hmm, that didn't happen last time I was carrying the loot, and it was worth a lot more since I was with the second year groups."

"You probably had a shielded bag. I don't know if your cargo-pod has shielding to contain the mana signature or not, so we shouldn't test it."

"Roger that, Sergeant." Desmond had gathered up the four thumb-sized lumps of gold from where they were wedged between rocks.

Muttering a quiet thanks to the fact that his armor was air and water tight because of the environmental seals, Desmond carefully checked the rest of the small, bowl-like basin that the water landed in, finding a half-dozen smaller nuggets that were still large enough to be recovered.

Standing up to stretch his back out, Desmond stared at the crack that the water gushed out of. It was maybe eight inches across and four feet tall, with the water gushing out of the bottom three feet of it to land in the pool before chuckling away in the stream. *Wonder if there is any more inside the crack...one way to find out.*

The spell to conjure light was something he was quite familiar with and it took only a moment to summon up the mana and then sink it into the palm of his glove. With that set, Desmond dove into the flow of water, bracing as it battered against his chest-plates, and ran his hand into the crack.

Light shimmered off of more than a dozen spots inside the rough split in the stone and Desmond began to scoop them out with his un-lit hand, dropping them into the pool at his feet after his hand was full.

"If this was somewhere stable, I'd say I found the end of a lode or vein of ore here."

"Seriously?"

"Yeah. The nuggets are small and rounded off, so I figure wherever the water is coming from is running over the lode, but I don't know how far back it goes, either. Going to grab what I can. Sergeant, do you know if they'll send a mining team in if we let them know there might be a vein here?"

"No, Rifts aren't stable enough to set up long-term mining, even with drones. They are strictly a 'grab what you can and walk' type of resource extraction among the Hegemony. The last group that tried to mine inside a Rift triggered an early collapse by destabilizing it. Damn thing ate up nearly a light-year of space and triggered a localized black hole that pulled planets off their orbit." Desmond's eyes widened at the thought, and he started shoveling faster.

"Don't worry. There are early warning signs that a Rift is destabilizing. The one the Sergeant is talking about is just a more infamous one in history used to illustrate greed," the Corporal added on, her voice finally robbed of cheeriness because of the somber topic.

"Noted. I think I got most of it out. Just need to bag and secure it. You got another of those pouches on you, Corporal?"

"Several! Never know what you are going to find on a mission, and these come in handy if I have to snatch something up that is mana-charged and don't wanna risk getting burned."

Desmond chuckled at the mental image of the bubbly corporal carefully inverting one of the bags over her hand to pick up a mana crystal like it was a steaming pile of dog-doo.

"Great, I'll have to pick up a bunch. I'm sure they will come in handy for isolating stuff in the future and I can guess that the Quartermaster will be happier if he doesn't have to sort through a pile of mixed metals." The Sergeant snickered at Desmond's words and answered his question before he could voice it.

"It normally takes years before adepts make that connection. Keep the Quartermaster happy and your life is that much easier."

"I mean, it makes sense. Look after your support crew, since they support you," Desmond replied idly, already collecting the nuggets out of the pool at his feet. He couldn't see the pointed look the Sergeant sent Chloe, and he was pointed in the wrong direction to see the wink and thumbs up that the Corporal threw the horned woman from her spot on the edge of the cliff. Chloe just blushed furiously at both of them.

CHAPTER 37

As a part of the greater Hegemony, the Aelfa species is one of the more numerous and ancient races. Their species has unique features that allow and encourage them to adapt to a number of different environments within only a handful of generations. As the founders of the Hegemony, theirs is the longest recorded history. The Empress' family traces its lineage back to the beginnings of the Hegemony and it is considered a mark of a family's nobility to have such records. As such, Aelfa of all of the sub-species tend to have a high opinion of themselves, something that is not always shared among the other species.
~Species of the Hegemony, a report sent back to the nations of Terra-Sol-3.

It only took a handful more minutes for Desmond to collect and stow the loot. He had to tuck the Rift-silver into the cargo pod as the Rift-gold took its place inside his armor. While he had a larger total quantity of silver, as that was most of what he'd raked out of the hole in the rock, the gold was still far more valuable. *That is, if the disparity in prices are similar to the ones back home...* Desmond thought idly as he made the swap.

Getting down from the cliff was a bit more difficult than getting up had been. The Corporal was able to shimmy down the rock face without a problem but none of them had thought to bring a line of any kind. Making a note to add a strong cable line to his kit in the future, Desmond had been forced to slide off the edge and dangle before dropping down into Chloe's arms.

While being caught by a woman was somewhat

emasculating for him, the fact that Chloe was entirely unperturbed by his weight and he'd heard the Corporal coo an 'awww' again when she saw it, Desmond resolved to not let it bother him. Things were different out here, after all.

Desmond had offered to head downstream next to see if he could catch any more of the nuggets that had been washed further down, but the Sergeant argued against it. The greenery was too thick, and they did need to get moving, so the group headed onward. Chloe dragged her busted shield with her, citing that even if the shield was warped and damaged, it might still be useful, despite the fact she couldn't get the clamps to line up right with her forearm armor after they'd gotten it off her.

The third branch that they hadn't checked yet turned out to wrap around and up to the upper nesting area, much to Chloe's quiet irritation. Desmond understood her frustration. If they'd taken this path originally, they could have ambushed the larger group while they didn't have access to the throwing stones, which were only piled on the bottom of the cliff.

Reminded of the stones, Desmond had them double back and load them up in his cargo-pod. While the mana signature on them was faint, they still would be worth something and they could always dump them to make room for other things if they found them.

Finishing off the trio of branching paths allowed them to double back to the point the path had first branched after leaving the landing pad clearing, and mark the completed direction with another slash of paint. Taking the left path wound through several clearings, each of which was occupied by the regular sized ape-monsters. Desmond found a trio of the green crystals while winding between the clearings and one of the clearings had been two smaller groups of the ape-monsters fighting over a fourth crystal that was growing out of a rock formation in the center.

Chloe's busted shield came in handy, but in an unexpected

way. She'd taken to jamming the bottom edge into the ground before using it as a rest for her laser repeater. When one of the smaller ape-monsters had managed to close the distance towards them at a charge, she'd kicked it hard from behind, sending the bent slab of metal careening forward to slam into the creature's face and split its head open.

"Chloe, smash!" Desmond hadn't been able to resist the line and chuckled for a good ten minutes until Chloe had made him promise that he'd show her what he was quoting at their next earliest convenience.

The linear chain of clearings terminated in one much like they had hit before, but with only a pair of the larger ape-creatures and no throwing stones. The two of them had been engaged in a fistfight just as the group was approaching, and they could pick the two alpha-predators off at range while they were distracted. Desmond harvested their core crystals, as he had been coming to think of them, using the sergeant's knife. With that taken care of, the group rapidly backtracked to the landing zone.

Arriving in the landing zone, Desmond was surprised to see that two of the other three teams were already there, waiting for them. The only team still missing was the one that he'd seen start hacking their way into the brush.

"Where are the others? Anyone find the Rift's core?" he asked, keying his suit to external communications.

"Dunno. They vanished off that way, and no one has their team frequency to call them back. And yes, we found the core. It's tagged and flagged for recovery. We didn't want to risk extracting it with our gear," replied the feline Taari that had ridden in on the same shuttle that he had, shooting a smirk over her shoulder at the other team's adept, who was pointedly ignoring her. "Now that you are back, I can call the shuttle for us."

"No, don't call the shuttle yet. I'm going after the other team," Desmond denied with a wave of his hand.

"What? Why?" The other cadet-adept gave him a startled

look, while Desmond spotted relieved looks on the veterans that were with her.

"They might have run into trouble. No one left behind." Desmond shouldered his rifle and turned to head into the cleared section of undergrowth. He couldn't hear it, but from how the other cadet-adept's head snapped towards her veterans, he guessed that they were reinforcing what he'd said. *Or warning them to not risk it.*

Desmond's team fell into their familiar positions as they entered the wide swathe that had been cleared. Chloe was to his immediate left and slightly ahead of him, the Corporal a few steps further to his right with the Sergeant anchoring the far right of the squat bowl shape they formed, mirroring Chloe.

"The other team is following us," Corporal Ry'taal's words were quiet over the team channel and Desmond nodded.

"Surprised the veterans didn't push her to go after them already."

"Their job is like ours. Your pair is our top priority. It's only if you risk yourselves unnecessarily that I'm to take command away from you," Sergeant Whist explained. The quadrupedal woman kept her eyes forward. "Even though I'm sure they were itching to go looking for the missing team. No emergency flare has gone up either, so they are either fine or entirely incapacitated."

"Let's hope they are fine then," Desmond shot back before going quiet.

The clear-cut section they were in continued for another hundred or so yards before taking a roughly thirty degree turn to the right and continuing. They found the first signs of fighting a few feet past the turn. A quintet of the smaller ape-monsters had been shot to pieces before the clear-cutting had continued.

"Sloppy...they got the drop on the other team it looks like," The Sergeant added as they pushed past the bodies. "You can tell from how the injuries are scattered on the bodies and how spread out they are. Let's hope they were more disciplined after they got further in."

The cut path they were on continued to turn and bend at odd angles, and it took two more of the sudden directional shifts before Desmond figured out why. He felt the barest trace of mana from under a fallen log and glanced under it to find the broken stump of one of the green crystals.

"That makes far more sense now…their cadet-adept is leading them from source to source. Either she knew what direction to go or got lucky and has been leapfrogging the crystals, tracking mana signatures," Desmond said, this time over the external comms.

"Smart idea. Wish I'd thought of it," called back the feline Taari from where her squad was spread out and behind them roughly twenty yards back.

"Not really. I found plenty of them just off the paths. And this group had a chance to pick one of the paths first while you and the other adept were arguing," reminded one of the other cadet-adept's team members.

Desmond craned his neck to look further back behind the other squad and noted that no one else was with them. "Looks like that other team is still holding the landing zone. Not a bad idea to make sure it stays secure."

"Doubt it, they likely view their part of it being done after clearing what they did," the other cadet-adept replied. "Lazy bints…"

Desmond didn't reply to that, instead focusing forward to continue tracking the path that had been cut.

The two groups followed the clear-cut path for another ten minutes before finding more signs of combat. Bodies of the smaller ape creatures started appearing regularly and Desmond spotted one of the larger 'alpha' creatures as well amongst the mess. Noting that its body hadn't been harvested for the core, he made a note to get it on the way back if they had time. *It's entirely possible the other team didn't realize it had one. I only knew because Marsden's girls taught* me about it. The creature's native mana signature can conceal it unless you know the crystal is there somewhere.

The distant screech of laser fire got them to pick up their pace to a trot, which turned into a full charge when they turned the last corner and spotted a fight going on ahead of them.

The group of four was in a staggered wedge formation, a shorter woman who he guessed to be the adept at the point with the others alternating on either side of her.

It was rapidly confirmed that the point member had to be the adept, as she was in the process of conjuring a wheel of fire to throw at one of the alpha creatures that was yanking at one tree, trying to rip it out of the ground to either throw or use as a club. A dozen or more of the smaller ape creatures were forging towards the group, either using their own dead or hunks of rock and trees as shields while they approached.

"Move up and support!" Desmond called, using the external speakers again so the other team could hear him, before cranking up his volume even further. "Friendlies, coming in from behind!"

Two of the four ahead of him snapped a glance back and nodded their helmeted heads. Desmond guessed those were the veterans attached to the other squad.

Turning his head, Desmond called to the other cadet-adept behind him, "we'll take left, you go right!" She nodded sharply. Desmond could already feel the mana spinning into shape around her left hand as she got ready.

Their team swung to the left, slotting in next to the wedge shape of the other team as best they could and adding in their own shots. The weapons fire had shredded the undergrowth ahead of them, opening up a pseudo-killing-field.

Realizing that they wouldn't all be able to get good vantage points, Desmond fell back slightly, calling into his team channel to let Chloe and Sergeant Whist take the lead as they could do the most to support the other team, who was entirely made up of the mid-range kit folks with their rifles and had no heavy support.

"Fall back, catch your breath!" Desmond called to the other team, which got a mixed response. The two veterans started to move backwards, but the cadet-adept glanced in his direction and shook her head sharply, planting her feet and refusing to move. Desmond caught a flash of blonde hair in the helmet, but she was turned back to the fight too quickly. As the cadet-adept was refusing to fall back, the others had to remain, and they firmed up, stepping back onto the fighting line.

"Idiot pride..." Gritted Chloe as she braced herself before scything her shots over the smaller enemies at an angle, forcing some to change what direction they were holding their improvised shields in.

"Get the best angle you can on them. Corporal, be ready to step in if one of them needs to reload," Desmond barked the orders to his team. He got a quick bob of the head from all three before he began to spin up his enhancements for them.

Three counts of accuracy. I'd toss some to the other team, but I have no idea if they know what to expect with it. Do not need to jar them right now. Nearly fucked that up when we landed with the Sergeant. Desmond thought to himself as he got the spells locked into place. *I'll put dexterity on the Corporal and whoever needs to reload too.*

It had taken some mental gymnastics, but Desmond had learned that thinking of the enhancements in general terms as 'strength' or 'accuracy' worked best for him, rather than enhancing specific factors of the feature. By focusing on just accuracy, he could enhance muscles, tendons, and everything else included to assist with preventing muzzle climb. This also had the side effect of improving fast twitch reflexes. While hand-to-eye coordination only did reflexes and mental acuity, and the dissonance between just the reflex and expected muzzle climb would cause issues.

The enfilade fire, while not quite true to the word, ended

up being the turning point once the third team got into position. Because incoming fire came from three directions, it was enough that the charging enemies could not protect themselves. Instead, they were all cut down by the combined fire, as they couldn't coordinate a defense. The big one had gone down to the focused spells of the first cadet-adept, as she'd ignored the smaller ones as they approached to focus on the larger threat.

"We didn't need your help!" snapped a familiar voice as the dust settled and Desmond quickly checked on his team. A glance over his shoulder at the fuming face of the cadet-adept they'd shown up to support revealed why she'd looked familiar in the quick glance he'd snagged earlier.

"Olianna, good to see you are okay," Desmond grumbled. It had been a week since he'd been anywhere near the snide Se'Aelfa. She always seemed ready to overtly poke and prod at him, being a prim ever since Monika had defeated her subtle attempts the first day. "How is your team doing? We've cleared the paths from the landing pad and your team was the only one who hadn't checked back in."

"Because we weren't finished harvesting this place!" snapped the Se'Aelfa, gesturing to the forest all around them. "There are concentrations of mana all around us!"

"That's not our job though, Olianna." Desmond rubbed at the brow of his helmet and fought back a sigh.

"What?"

"We are supposed to secure the Rift and suppress creatures in it. Not go off treasure hunting."

"What do you call what we were doing?" Olianna pointed at the dead ape-monsters ahead of them. "We have suppressed dozens of the creatures!"

"That you have been provoking into attacking you. Do you realize that you've likely been just skirting the edge of the enclosed space of the Rift this entire time? I bet if you went," Desmond paused to think for a minute and extended his senses, "that way for another two hundred meters, you'd find the edge of the Rift space."

"Cadet-Adept. He is correct, as I have tried to advise you before. While you have harvested a good amount of resources doing this, foraying into the trees like this has put your team at undue risk because of lack of clear sightlines," one of the veterans for Olianna's team piped up. The veteran didn't react when the Se'Aelfa whirled to glare at her. "We need to return to the landing zone, anyway. We are getting dangerously low on ammunition. And if the others have finished locating or suppressing the Rift Core, then the harvesters can get set up and collapse the Rift."

"The Core was located and flagged already," chipped in the other cadet-adept that had followed Desmond. "My team located and flagged it since we don't have the equipment to recover it." The feline Taari's tail whipped back and forth behind her with smug satisfaction.

Olianna made a noise of incoherent fury before turning sharply and beginning to march back towards the landing pad. Sighing, the trio with her fell into step behind Olianna.

Desmond glanced at the alpha monster, which hadn't been harvested yet. The feline Taari started off after Olianna as well, after letting the grumpy Se'Aelfa get far enough ahead of them to not cause problems.

A glance at the Sergeant had her producing the knife he'd borrowed before and a few moments of quick work had the crystal extracted from the alpha before they fell in as the rearguard of the group. Desmond stopped to harvest the other alpha ape along the way too, keeping the bloody crystals in hand after cleaning and returning the knife to the Sergeant.

<><><>

Arriving back in the clearing, Desmond found that the shuttle for the other team and Olianna's were already settling into place on the trampled grass of the clearing.

"Olianna!" Desmond called out, jogging ahead of his team and waving to her to get the woman to stop.

"What do you want, prim?" snapped the irate Se'Aelfa. Her eyes narrowed in obvious hatred at him as he came to a stop a few feet from her. Less than a second after he came to a stop, Desmond felt Chloe settle in behind him, barely an inch away from leaning into his back.

"Look, the big ones? They had crystals in them. Figured you didn't know since you didn't harvest them. Here's the two from the ones you killed." Desmond held out the bloody crystals to Olianna, who sneered at him.

"I don't need charity from a prim." She slapped the crystals out of his hand with a flick of her wrist before whirling to stomp through the entry hatch to her shuttle.

"What crawled inside her snatch and died?" Desmond heard someone murmur. It wasn't a voice he recognized, so he didn't respond. Desmond just sighed instead and bent to pick up the bloody crystals and turned to the cadet-guard that was about to follow Olianna onto the shuttle, a slightly built woman who was also a Se'Aelfa, and looked familiar.

"Miss, do you want them? I'd say she declined her right to a share of them?" Desmond offered the crystals to the guard, who flatly ignored him, following her mistress aboard the shuttle. "What about you two?" Desmond offered them to the veterans, who smirked with the toothy grins that he'd gotten used to from Hyreh.

"I ain't gonna turn away gifts from a cute male," the first one said and snagged one of the two from Desmond. The second of the veterans nodded in agreement and blew him a kiss when she took the other one before the two loaded up.

"Earning brownie points with the enlisted there, McLaughlin." Desmond shrugged at the Sergeant in response to her comment.

"Never hurts to be nice to folks, especially those that are here to watch my ass."

"Cute ass that it is." The comment was likely not meant

for the squad channel, as the Corporal immediately flushed bright red when the three of them turned to stare at her. "What? It is?" She shrugged helplessly, doubling down on it instead of apologizing.

"Asses aside. Send up the flare for retrieval when you are ready." The Sergeant turned her gaze back to Desmond, and he nodded.

The retrieval flare was a rounded tube as long as his forearm, and it only took breaking the seal and twisting the back end to send a bright blue sphere of light rocketing up and into the shimmering veil that separated the inside of the Rift from regular space. Four seconds after the flare vanished through the veil, their shuttle emerged, circling once and coming in for a landing.

"Load up!" Desmond called as the airlock door slid open. "After you." He gestured to the feline Taari adept and her team, who nodded and hopped aboard, filing back to the same seats that they had used to ride out in.

Chloe was the last aboard, standing guard with her back to the side of the shuttle until they were secured. Once she was sure they were in place, she dragged her damaged shield through the hatch and settled into her seat.

"Ooh, I can't wait!" Corporal Ry'taal had apparently overcome her embarrassment from the gaff on the radio earlier and was wiggling in her seat happily. "Gonna get me so many new models with this."

"Wait, you collect models? What kind?" Desmond stared at her in surprise, wondering if that particular bit of nerd fandom continued here in the galaxy at large.

"Assemble and paint them too! Sure, the fabricators can just print them up already assembled. But I like making custom ones, so I buy kits that are disassembled and have the fabricators print those up as loose parts so I can do custom poses and the like! I've got a whole storage unit full of finished models on the ship since the barracks doesn't have room to display them all," she said the last part with a level of disappointment that Desmond could nearly taste in the air. "I have models of the different major starships, as well as famous adepts, characters from vid-dramas and all sorts!"

"She's not kidding. She usually keeps a handful of her most recent ones on display in her bunk and rotates them out as she finishes new ones," Sergeant Whist said with the sort of exhausted resignation that could only come from having to share space with someone that had this kind of hobby. "I'm just glad she's gone back to using the dura-plastics rather than having them printed in metal..."

"I said I was sorry when you stepped on that sword! I hadn't even realized I'd dropped it on the decking..."

<><><>

"You two aren't coming with us to the Quartermaster?" Desmond was surprised when the two veterans went to split off from them in the hangar.

"Not necessary. We are logged as part of your team and they'll send us our share. Besides, we trust you!" Corporal Ry'taal said with a cheery smile on her face. "Unless we shouldn't trust you?"

"No, it's fine. I'm sure Chloe would smack me upside the head if I tried to cheat you two."

"I would never strike you, Des!" Chloe protested vehemently. Desmond rolled his eyes at her before turning back to the two veterans.

"If you two are sure." Desmond patted his chest plate over where he'd stashed the Rift-gold and both of the women nodded in understanding. "It wouldn't offend me if you two wanted to come along. See the run all the way through to the end."

The two veterans shared a glance and Sergeant Whist nodded once.

"Sure, might as well. I want to see how the officer on duty reacts when you dump your pod out. Save the best for last."

<><><>

The Quartermaster's was bustling with teams returning from different Rifts for the first year cadets. Desmond noted that his team was one of the few that had all four members there. Most of the folks in line were other cadet-adepts and their guards, only three other folks in the crowd had the entire team with them.

No one commented on it, so Desmond just joined the shortest line, with Chloe falling in at his side. The group of four chatted while the line moved forward slowly. Desmond caught sight of Olianna in one of the lines on the other side of the room. She was still in her armor and her posture showing the sulk she'd sported while loading up in the Rift. That triggered the realization for Desmond that a good number of the others he saw in the queues had apparently taken the time to remove their gear and get a shower, since most of the cadets he saw were in their uniforms and not the armor kits.

"Feel like we are standing out a bit in gear here," Desmond muttered to the others. His comment interrupted a conversation between the Sergeant and Chloe as they discussed the stabilizing arm that the Sergeant had been using.

"Yeah? Well, whatever. We aren't the only ones in kit. Besides, your cargo-pod is a pain in the butt to unlatch and reattach. Even while empty," Chloe fired back, and the Corporal nodded vigorously with her. After all, she'd had to help him reattach it when he'd finished looting the upper clearing and the much smaller woman had struggled with the bulky pod.

After about ten minutes of waiting, it was finally their turn. The turn-in counters were manned with a collection of second-year cadet-adepts that had various instruments to measure and catalog the materials that were brought in. Scales, microscopes, scanners and more were on either side of a large receptacle that acted as an enclosure to keep mana emanations from causing problems.

"Cadet-Adept McLaughlin." The second year behind the desk was an Uth'ra with bright white hair and a bored expression. "Go ahead and empty your acquisitions into the receptacle. We will get them cataloged, and you will receive a notification when the credits are applied to your accounts. Do you have any special directions for how you will be splitting the cut between you and your guard?"

"Equal shares for all four of us," Desmond answered, as Chloe helped him unhook the pod from its attachment points on his shoulders.

"The veterans are guaranteed an equal share. But I'm sure they appreciate you ordering it, anyway." The Uth'ra chuckled before nodding to the deep tray in front of her and keying the button to turn on the permeable barrier that was the 'lid' to the enclosure.

Desmond began unloading his pack, laying out the lightly imbued stones and the crystals in a growing pile, separating the 'core' crystals he'd taken from the alpha-apes into their own pile. He also set the trio of fruit on their own to one side. As the Sergeant had directed him earlier, he held back the bags of the precious metals for the moment.

The inspector snorted at the stones, but her eyebrows rose at the number of crystals that Desmond laid out, coughing out a laugh before schooling her face to a more neutral expression and scrutinizing the fruit before nodding.

"I think you might have the largest haul so far, McLaughlin. You didn't steal any of this from another team, did you?"

"No, ma'am. Just got some lucky encounters and kept my senses open."

"Not many first years know about the core crystals." The Uth'ra's statement was leading and Desmond didn't see any reason to conceal where the knowledge had come from.

"I was lucky enough to go on observation with a group of

the second years. They taught me about them and made me harvest the one that we got from the only larger creature."

"Ah, that would explain it. That's everything?" The Uth'ra gestured towards the pile that was just shy of overflowing the suppression field.

"I have a bit more, but wanted to let you clear some of this away first," Desmond said politely.

"Okay. Tap your comm-cuff to the plate there so this load is tagged as your team's." Desmond did as directed and the Uth'ra began with the stones, pulling them out of her side of the field and running them through a series of scans. "These are barely worth bringing back, only a handful of credits each. If you didn't have the pod, I'd have said you wasted your time on them." She said as she worked.

"They would have been the first things abandoned if something else needed space."

"Makes sense. Since you had the pod, it probably wasn't too laborious to carry them. Gal in my year brought back an entire load of them, thinking they were geodes." The Uth'ra said conversationally as she worked. "They just get broken down for fuel, though I did read about some of the independent teams using them as ammunition for the ship's gravity cannons when they ran out of shells instead. Unstable, but in a pinch you gotta use what you have."

"Huh...kinda makes sense. Some of the beasts threw them at us and they were definitely more energetic than expected when they hit shields."

"You were lucky your team had shields. And your girl is lucky she didn't get hurt worse when hers failed." The Uth'ra's eyes darted to Chloe's damaged shield, which was leaning against the horned woman's shoulder at the moment. "Armory is gonna be pissed that it broke. But it was on duty, rather than during practice, so they can't fine ya for damaged gear. Just might take a while to get a replacement."

"Gonna pick up something nicer than the base stuff anyway, or at least hope to. Depends on the pay," Desmond said conversationally.

"Dunno if you are gonna make enough off this load for that, but good on you for looking after your guard."

They continued to make small talk as the Uth'ra finished weighing them and dumped the stones into a large bin behind her that had the rune for 'fuel supplies' on it. The crystals got similar treatment but were placed in a carrying rack for refining instead of being shipped directly to the reactors. When she finished the last of the cores, the Uth'ra gave Desmond a questioning look while she slipped the fruit into a small plastic container and tucked it into a cart.

"Well? You said there was more? You find some ores? Bang em on here and let's take a look." She patted the now empty counter and Desmond smirked, checking over his shoulder to make sure no one was watching. Olianna had already dropped her load off and left, and most of the rest of the folk in line were finishing up too.

With that confirmed, he pulled out the bag filled with various sized silver nuggets and slid it into the suppression field. Out of the corner of his eye, Desmond noticed all three of the women with him wince slightly and lean back like they'd been hit by a wave of heat from an oven.

Huh, wonder if the mana aura is higher while they are all in one spot like that? Guess the pod did have a suppressor built in since they didn't care till I pulled it out. Will have to be careful when it's the gold's turn. Though I gotta wonder why it wasn't bothering them. Does my suit have a seal too?

The second year sat up straighter when she spotted the bag of silver nuggets and swore quietly to herself, shooting a glance to either side and slapping a button that raised an opaque divider on either side of her station.

"You gotta say something if it's a precious metal, boy!" she snapped, her tone low but urgent. "The dividers draw attention, but not as much as flashing precious Rift-metals around like this."

"Why? It's not like someone would try to steal it from you,

right?" Desmond was legitimately surprised by her reaction. The Uth'ra shook her head once, tugging the bag to her side of the field and opening it to begin weighing the nuggets.

"No. No one would steal it. But, these things are worth hard credits, especially for a first year. Guys have it hard enough without people digging for their creds. Guy in my year got taken for a ride by this bint that somehow talked him into loaning her a bunch of credits against his stipend and nearly broke him."

"Thanks for the warning. I wouldn't let that happen to him though," Chloe spoke for the first time, glancing down at Desmond before gently resting her hand on his shoulder.

"I know you wouldn't, Chloe," Desmond said to her with a quick smile before turning back to the Uth'ra, who had a smirk twisting her lips, showing the trademark mouthful of sharp teeth that her kind had.

"Cute. Still, watch yourself. This will get you all a hell of a cut, put you further ahead of your year." She nodded towards Desmond's armor to make the point.

"This isn't the best part, though." Desmond gestured to the silver on the table before patting his chest.

"No...you got more? Oh, I can't wait to see this...too bad the bookies are closed on the highest scoring first year, I'd make some credits on you." The Uth'ra chuckled as she finished weighing the nuggets of silver and tucking them into an opaque, locked case that she carefully noted down the number stamped on the side, before having him swipe his comm-cuff and then setting it on a mostly empty cart labeled for the smelters. "Okay, the anticipation is already making me wet. Whip it out already."

The Corporal sniggered behind him and Desmond felt Chloe's hand tighten on his shoulder lightly, but the horned woman didn't say anything. Shrugging, Desmond carefully popped the pressure seal that held the overlapping layers of his chest armor closed and fished out the bag with the small collection of gold nuggets, which he palmed and slid into the field.

"Bless my tits...I'd have made a *lot* of credits on you..." was all the Uth'ra said, her eyes wide and smile wider.

<><><>

After everything was cataloged and Desmond had linked it to his party's signature, they'd headed off. Bidding the Sergeant and Corporal goodbye, the two of them had headed back to their suite to get cleaned up and changed out of their armor. Monika had left an excited message for them both that she wanted to trade stories about their Rift suppressions over breakfast the next day. Desmond agreed, as it was already getting late, and sent her a response to that effect.

He and Chloe had swung by the Armory to drop off the remains of the shield for recycling or repair. The Armory staff were less than enthused by the mangled state of the heavy plate of composite steel, but they said they'd be in touch once it'd been gone over to let her know if they needed to issue a replacement.

While Desmond had gotten used to Chloe sticking close to him over the last couple of weeks that they had been together, the bull-horned woman was getting even closer to him now. He'd noticed while in the line at the Quartermaster's depot that she'd basically been pressed to him the whole time, only their armor preventing her from it, and she'd dropped her hand on his shoulder as soon as she could switch her repeater to her other hand for carrying. She was keeping close to him the entire walk back to their suite, and the cargo pod on his back kept bumping into her while they walked.

Once they were back in the suite of rooms, Chloe didn't peel off to her room to remove her gear. Instead, the big woman remained close to him like she was intent on following him into his room. Desmond decided to say something, as clearly there was something bothering her and he was concerned.

"Hey, Chloe...you wanna help me get my gear off?" Desmond offered after they had stood in the center of the common room for a handful of moments.

"Yeah. That would be good, Des," Chloe said quietly, drawing his gaze up to her.

She'd removed her damaged helmet, leaving it behind in the Armory as well for repairs, while Desmond's hung from his hip. A bit of dried blood still marked Chloe's forehead at the edge of her dirty-blonde hair, which was matted with sweat. She resolutely refused to look down at him. Instead, her eyes were fixed on the door to his room.

"Okay. Come on, let's get changed." Desmond led the way into his room and started peeling the armor off. He could have removed it himself without help, but having Chloe there to help unhook the cargo-pod, as well as take each piece as he removed it, made the process easier.

In a matter of minutes, Desmond was stripped down to the skin-tight bodysuit that he wore under the armor to prevent chafing. The normally elastic material of the suit was even more tightly drawn to his body from the sweat that soaked it.

"Okay, it's your turn now, Chloe," Desmond said as he pulled at the moist fabric on his chest. He wafted it, trying to get some air against his skin. Desmond hadn't realized how much he'd sweat under the armor until he'd taken it off and the fabric felt weird against him.

Turning to follow Chloe to her room, Desmond instead bumped right into the big woman who hadn't moved an inch from where she was standing, staring at him in surprise.

Stumbling and nearly landing on his ass, Desmond was saved from the fall by Chloe, who snapped out her hand to catch him.

"Oh shi...sorry Des." Chloe flushed hard as she helped right him. "You, you don't have to help me gear down. I can do it."

"I want to, Chloe. Besides, you got hurt and I wanna make sure you are okay," Desmond said insistently. She attempted to look away from him and Desmond reached up to catch her chin in his hand, tugging her face down to look at him. "Chloe, please? I want to. It doesn't have to be more than that, but I want to help look after you. Besides, it's only fair, right?"

"Oh...okay, Des," Chloe's voice was small and reserved as she nodded slowly, her big green eyes focused on him. Desmond decided the moment might be right to take a shot at something that she'd mentioned before, but hadn't brought up since their day off when she'd explained her species 'natural instinct' type drives.

"After we get you out of your armor and get it hung up, I'd like to take a shower with you. Clean up my protector." Desmond gave her a gentle smile, hoping it would reassure her. It felt odd saying it, but he pushed that feeling down to focus on what he thought Chloe needed to hear. "Make sure you aren't hurt anywhere and thank you for taking that hit for me. You did save my ass earlier today. No idea what would have happened if that rock had hit me instead of your shield."

Chloe's eyes had grown rounder and her mouth hung open slightly while she stared at him like he'd just clubbed her over the head. Desmond gave her a few seconds to come back to herself, and she didn't move.

"Chloe? You in there, hon?" Reaching up, he poked her between the eyes gently before grabbing the tip of one of her horns and using it to shake her head back and forth ever so slightly. Chloe blinked in surprise, reacting to the horn shake more than the poke and taking a shuddering breath.

"Ah...yes." She swallowed hard as a flush blazed across her cheeks and she smiled down at him. "Yes, I would like that too, Des. You really are forward..."

"Naw, this is me being nice and taking things slow," Desmond said with a laugh, gesturing for her to head to her room. "Though it will be odd that I'm going to be showering with you before we kiss for the first time."

Chloe had started to turn away from him and promptly tripped on her own feet. Thankfully, she was able to catch herself on the door before turning back to Desmond with a startled look on her face. It was an absolutely adorable look on her, eyes still as wide as before and face blank in surprise. He could imagine if she had ears like a bovine, they'd be locked forward on him.

"What? Did I not make it obvious that I liked your face and wanted to kiss it?" Desmond shared her look of confusion. Chloe slowly shook her head from side to side and Desmond heaved a sigh. "Friggin alien gender practices and different relationship signals...get down here Chloe. I'm going to kiss you unless you tell me not to."

Chloe didn't protest, but she did turn back towards him, her expression hopeful but shocked still.

Well, it worked the first time. Desmond thought and reached up with his right hand to grab her left horn halfway down its length. Using that grip as a handle, he pulled Chloe down to his height. *Man, this feels weird kissing someone so much taller than me.* The thought came unbidden to the surface of his mind.

Their lips met and the sensation apparently power-cycled the horned-woman's brain. Chloe immediately squatted down, so they were more equal in height and wrapped her arms around Desmond's waist, pressing her lips to his. The kiss remained chaste for the moment, since Desmond didn't want to blow a fuse in the shy woman's brain. They separated a moment later, with Chloe breathing fast, her pupils dilated to the maximum as she stared at Desmond.

"I told you before, Chloe. I like you. Hell, I thought you were hot when I first met you, bruises and all. You've only gotten cuter the longer I've known you. You've put up with me being an idiot and are getting along with my friends. Plus, I can tell you like me too," Desmond said quietly, taking the opportunity to bump his forehead against hers lightly before kissing the tip of her nose. This caused Chloe to cross her eyes again and stare at her nose for a second before she looked back at him.

"You...you are serious? I thought you'd just been flirting before, to make our relationship easier on assignment." The disbelief in her voice was thick.

"What? No! I wouldn't do that, Chloe. If I was just focused on us being adept and guard, then I would have said so outright. You can always trust me to be honest with you." Desmond was astonished that she would have thought that of him.

"You aren't disgusted by me?"

"Babe, you are beautiful. There's a whole subset of Terran men that are going to hate my guts when they find out I was the first Terran to score the sexy, muscled alien gal as my partner. They can kiss my lily-white ass though, you're mine," Desmond reassured her with a wink.

"You don't want someone softer? Smaller than you, like your species normally go for? Even among my dad's people, women like me have a harder time finding mates." Chloe's voice was quietly hopeful and Desmond just leaned in to kiss her on the lips again.

"Chloe, I like you just the way you are. Mountain of muscle and all. You aren't lacking in feminine charms. I know that from how often you press them against me while we are just standing around." Desmond patted the armored top of her breasts that were, even now, pressed to his chest. Chloe glanced down and giggled slightly.

"I am pretty proud of them. You can thank my mother's side that I was able to keep them and be this strong."

"I'll be sure to do that. Now, come on. Let's get you out of this armor and go get cleaned up." Desmond patted her chest light before using the hand that still gripped her left horn to urge her up again. She complied without comment or complaint, a smile creasing her lips and showing just the barest bit of her fine white teeth.

Desmond chuckled, and she made a questioning noise, to

which he answered. "Oh, I was just thinking, I'm glad you got your mother's teeth. Kissing you with a mouthful of fangs like most Uth'ra have would be...challenging." Chloe just blushed at that, her smile returning in full force.

CHAPTER 38 <3<3<3

One of the most common questions I'm asked by other Terrans now that we are finally becoming more common in the Hegemony is either 'how' or 'why' in relation to Chloe. To most of those, I tell them that it's none of their business. To those few that ask with the kind of intensity that tells me they are wrestling with similar choices; I remind them that if you want something bad enough, you find a way.
~Desmond McLaughlin, on life aboard the *Valor's Bid*.

It took substantially longer to remove Chloe's armor than it had Desmond's, between the larger number and heavier plates that it was made up of and the fact that several of them had been bent in the same blow that broke Chloe's arm. With some time and effort, though, Desmond was able to get the armor off her and onto the rack instead.

"Going to have to get those plates repaired," Desmond muttered as he dropped the last of Chloe's leg armor onto the rack.

"How long do you think it will take for the Quartermaster to pay out?" Chloe asked as she came to a stop behind Desmond. She'd stayed as still as she could while Desmond had worked, but now that the last of the armor was off, she took up her normal position against his left side and wrapped her right arm around his shoulders and chest, pulling him back against her.

Desmond did his best to avoid looking at the blood-stains on her left arm, and the hole where the bone had poked through the under suit.

"Could be...ahem, a few weeks. Hard to say. I know

Marsden took awhile to pay me, but she said that it was because the second-year's hauls take more time to process." Desmond coughed once. The mixed feeling of Chloe's soft breast pressing into the side of his head and the hard muscles of her abdomen and hips pressing into his back was quite distracting.

"Fine, getting it repaired shouldn't take more than a day or two. I might be able to get them back into shape myself too, but that's a worry for tomorrow. Right?" Chloe's voice was quietly hopeful, her arm tightening around his chest slightly before releasing him.

"Yup, time for a shower. Come on, hon." Desmond patted Chloe's wrist with one hand and moved to take a step. Reacting naturally as could be, Chloe kept pace with him, her body barely an inch away from his the entire time and the side of her breast brushing his cheek and head occasionally as they shifted and jostled inside her skintight bodysuit.

While Desmond had opted for a dark forest green bodysuit, Chloe had gone with a midnight black bodysuit that clung tight enough to her body right now that Desmond could make out the individual muscles of her six-pack abs out of his left eye, as well as the stiff peak that could only be her nipple as it swayed into view on occasion, held firm and prominent by the slightly less obvious ring he knew that pierced it.

Entering the bathroom, Desmond tugged at the magnetic closure that held the bodysuit in place and began to peel it off himself. His heart was beating faster as he considered what was about to happen.

Don't get cocky, McLaughlin. It's just a shower together. Naked. With one of the cutest women you've ever met. Whose tits are quite literally bigger than your head, and she could likely snap your neck like a toothpick. Don't blow it, McLaughlin, he chanted to himself inside his head.

Fortified as best he could, Desmond tossed the bodysuit into the laundry chute and hurried across the open space of the bathroom to the large shower area. It was the work of a few moments to get it going, setting all the shower heads to run simultaneously.

"Uh..." Chloe's voice caused him to turn around and look towards her with concern. Desmond had to bite back a laugh.

Chloe was, once again, frozen stock still and staring at him in surprise. The big woman only had her bodysuit halfway off. The fabric was bunched at her waist in her hands, like she was about to roll it down off her ample hips, leaving her looking like she was just wearing black leggings for the moment. Her tremendous breasts hung heavy and ripe in front of her, only drooping slightly to the pressure of gravity into the shape of a teardrop with her nipples leading the way, sharply erect and highlighted by the bright silver rings she wore through them.

"Come on, hon. My ass can't be that captivating, can it?" Desmond teased her as he strode back across the room, doing his best to keep his own blush under control while his body reacted in its normal fashion to seeing Chloe with her breasts on display. This time, though, he didn't have any fabric blocking his reaction.

Chloe blinked once, slowly, as he strode closer, her eyes dipping to lock onto the part of his anatomy that was leading the way and her blush deepened further, but she still did not move.

"Yes, I am attracted to you. That should be obvious now, hon. Come on, I can't wash you down if you don't finish undressing, hon," Desmond said as he came to a stop a few feet away from her. Since Chloe was bending forward to push her bodysuit off, she was already within range, but he still reached up to take hold of her horn, this time the right one just ahead of the ring he'd given her, before he planted a kiss on her lips.

Starting in surprise, Chloe gasped into the kiss before returning it. She abandoned her bodysuit entirely and wrapped her arms around Desmond again while the kiss deepened. It took Desmond tugging on her horn with the hand he had on it to get her to release him after several long seconds of kissing.

"Got a one track mind, don't ya?" Desmond teased, using his grip on her horn to shake her head slightly. Chloe bit her bottom lip and moaned slightly, the blush firmly painted on her cheeks and unlikely to fade for hours.

"Please, Des. My horns. When you do that…sensitive." Desmond immediately released his grip on her horn and Chloe moaned again, but this time in disappointment.

"Come on, woman. Get your clothes off already so we can shower." Desmond bopped her lightly on the nose with one finger before wiggling furiously to get free of the grip that was smashing her breasts against him. His erection was already hard enough to hammer nails with, and she'd stared at it as he walked over, so Desmond stopped caring as it bumped against her stomach and thighs while he struggled.

Chloe released him, stripping off the bodysuit the rest of the way and tossing it on top of his in the clothes chute before following Desmond into the steaming shower, her cow tail twitching slightly in anticipation.

"You know, it's gonna be impossible to get things done if you keep giving me the 'deer in the headlights' treatment every time I surprise you," Desmond said without looking back. Chloe tried to blush harder at his chastising, but the blush had already bonded firmly with her face and down her neck, so it only deepened the colors.

"Sorry, Des. Still getting used to it," she apologized shyly, looking away while Desmond busied himself in the streams of water coming down. A moment later, she gasped and jumped in surprise when Desmond touched the soapy cloth he had been preparing to her stomach.

"What? I said I was gonna wash you. Stop wiggling!" Desmond teased with a smile, carefully rubbing the rough cloth over her skin. Chloe curled into the scrubbing motion with a quiet moan, a happy smile gracing her lips as she let him tend to her.

Desmond seized the moment to fully take in her body as well. Chloe was heavily muscled, that much was extremely hard to miss. She had deep grooves in her abdomen that outlined her six-pack like they'd been carved into stone. The same heavy definition clung to her legs and arms, outlining them like they'd been carefully highlighted to show power and grace. The fact that she hadn't lost her womanly curves in the process just further shone a spotlight that it had to have been a higher power at work. Her hips were broad and womanly, with a rounded bottom and not a single wisp of hair anywhere but her head and the tip of her tail. Full breasts, larger than Desmond's head by at least a third again in size each, hung from her chest. Those curved treasures drooped just slightly under their own weight and were a perfect fit for her large stature. It was only really obvious just *how* big they were when Desmond stood close and could use his own body as a reference instead of hers. Dusky nipples stood erect from those mounds with their silver crowns, begging him for attention.

Working slowly, he tended to her body and often went back to the dispenser on the wall to re-apply the lather to his washcloth. Desmond started from the bottom and worked his way up her body, the hot water cascading around them. Chloe was content to stand there and let him work as he kneaded tense muscles in the wake of the soapy washcloth. He paid special attention to her left arm, carefully kneading it to ensure that there were no tender spots remaining before moving on.

Chloe was in heaven. This kind of attention from a male was something her mother had described to her in the past. A fantasy of the kind of gentle, loving interactions between long time partners. It soothed both of the itches in her subconscious: grooming and physical contact with someone she trusted.

It'll be even better when it's my turn. The thought drifted through Chloe's pleased subconscious like a wisp of cloud as she reveled in the moment.

Her blissful relaxation was broken by a sudden jolt of arousal when Desmond brushed the cloth across her breasts and grazed her nipples with it. The sensitive buds tightened further in response and Chloe gasped as arousal raced down her spine, sending her tail switching in surprise.

"Oh? Sensitive are they? I guess they would be with these." Desmond flicked the silver rings through them lightly with one fingertip, making Chloe moan again and shiver. "Tell me if I make you uncomfortable, hon," Desmond murmured, smiling up at Chloe from between her massive breasts while he carefully soaped them.

Chloe just shook her head in denial as he carefully worked, yipping in surprise as he planted a kiss on each of her nipples and tugged lightly on the piercings between his teeth just after he had rinsed them with the warm water falling from the rain head.

Glad she just has the two breasts…would be odd if she had the whole 'udder' thing going. Wouldn't think less of her, would just be…different? Though it would be kinda kinky to see all of them pierced. Man, I'm turning into some kind of deviant, Desmond thought as he worked, smirking to himself at the last thought. *I think 'deviant' is a forgone conclusion considering my girlfriend.*

Chloe was responsive to his touch, and she clearly was enjoying herself. He could tell from the little happy noises and wiggles that she made to stay in contact with him as he worked and played with her gently. Each time he tugged lightly on her piercings, a full body shiver would roll through her. Those parts of her that were soft jiggling enticingly while her defined abs would ripple and her muscles would clench as well.

While he'd gotten a good view of her in the past, given her habit of parading about with just the towel around her waist, Desmond had still managed to underestimate the definition of her lower body and her thick and tight bottom. A sight he made sure to enjoy as he worked his way around her while scrubbing with the cloth. The cute, blonde, cow tail that emerged from the base of her spine switched occasionally, and Chloe let out the sweetest of moans when he massaged the bundle of muscles at its base. It was surprisingly softer than Desmond had expected as well, not being as rigid as a true cow's tail.

Maybe some kind of adaptation for their species? Desmond thought as he carefully soaped the appendage and rinsed it in the shower water. *What did she do in her armor? I don't remember whether it was tucked away or if it was out...*

Putting his questions aside for later, Desmond focused back on his work and lathered up her back again, working carefully over the thick muscles that criss-crossed her broad back. He hummed to himself as Chloe made more joyful noises at the attention.

He'd made it over her body a full two times before Chloe finally broke herself out of the pleasured haze and snatched the cloth away from him. Desmond quirked an eyebrow at her as she turned, her eyes hot with desire as she eyed him up and down.

"My turn, Des," the big woman purred in a deep and throaty voice. Desmond just shrugged and spread his arms out, surrendering to the larger woman.

Thankfully, Chloe was gentle as she returned the favor. Kneading into the tense muscles of his thighs and shoulders as she worked, but otherwise keeping her caress featherlight. Even in the brief moment she carefully washed his manhood, she was gentle with it, for which Desmond was infinitely grateful for. He had only been *slightly* concerned that Chloe's strength would get away from her, but he'd quashed that worry with the knowledge that she had not once hurt him during their training.

What Chloe did do, was steal several shy kisses from him during the process. It felt as if she was reassuring herself that he didn't mind when she kissed him. A worry he was happy to assist in dispelling. He was gratified that she remained very aware of her horns and, while they bumped his shoulders or sides on occasion, as she had to bracket his body with the long things, the tips never came close to him.

The item that had been more concerning for Desmond was just the sheer difference in their size. While he was a little above average for a human, he didn't want to disappoint Chloe, either. Add in the fact that she out-massed him by at least a hundred pounds of pure muscle, and Desmond knew he needed to get creative. Thankfully, he had an idea of something that should let him ensure they both had fun with this encounter.

After Chloe had a chance to soap him up and explore his body, Desmond turned in her embrace and got hold of her horns again, this time with both hands. Chloe let out a low moan as he tugged on them lightly, but bucked her head back rather than giving in to his pressure at the moment. A motion that physically lifted Desmond off the ground for a few inches before setting him down.

"Damn, woman. You are ridiculously strong," Desmond breathed. He'd managed to keep his balance when he landed on the slick tile, so there was no harm in Chloe's movement. "I like it." He reassured her when a moment of concern flashed through her dark green eyes.

"I'm...glad, Desmond," Chloe sighed quietly, acquiescing to the pressure of his grip and kneeling on her folded legs in front of him. This put them roughly at the same height and ended up with Chloe's bountiful breasts pressed hard against Desmond's abs. She still loomed over him, but only by a few inches rather than several feet at the moment. Still keeping his grip on her horns, Desmond pulled her down into a long and slow kiss that Chloe moaned into. Slowly, their lips parted, and they began to explore each other's mouths.

The kiss continued for more than a minute as they both lost themselves in each other. Chloe wrapped her arms around Desmond and squeezed him tight, wedging him between her breasts. While she was careful with her strength, she did manage to elicit a handful of pops and crackles from his back because of the pressure, which made Desmond groan happily as his back realigned again.

"Oh damn, Chloe…" Desmond groaned into the kiss and Chloe relented to let him breathe but did not release him. "I bet you give great massages with that strength. Didn't realize my back was that out of joint from carrying the cargo-pod."

At the unexpected praise, Chloe blushed hard. She tried to turn away shyly, but Desmond still had her horns in his grip and he tugged her gently to look back at him, which drew another low moan out of her.

"These really are sensitive for you, aren't they?" Desmond reflected. Knowing that he wasn't going to be getting free of her most pleasant grip until Chloe *let* him free, he leaned into it instead. Stroking the length of her left horn with his fingertips, tracing the edge of the tungsten band lightly before continuing to the base of her horn where it met her skull and the dense skin there to protect her head.

"Oooh, yes Des. Shatter and Void, I didn't believe mum when she told me," the big woman crooned, leaning her head into the caress. "Right there, around the base…" Chloe made a sound deep in her throat that felt like it was halfway between a moan and a moo. A second after she did that, her eyes popped open, and she looked absolutely mortified as she tried valiantly to blush harder.

"Don't be embarrassed. That was hot, and you clearly enjoyed it," Desmond chided her gently. He continued to stroke the base of her horn lightly, working his fingers into and around the spot where they met her head. Chloe's embarrassment faded slowly and she let her eyes slip closed, trusting in Desmond's words.

"Yeah. The point where it joins my skull is…itchy? It feels good when you stroke it like that. When you tug on the horns, too. I don't really feel it like…" She nodded down to her breasts before glancing back up at him with lidded eyes. "Like other pleasant spots, but I can feel the pressure. And knowing it's you and you are using them to guide me? It does something for me."

"Oh? My big, mighty guardian likes being led?" Desmond teased lightly, but Chloe just smiled and nodded lightly, her horns bobbing down towards him but not getting close to his face.

"It feels...right," Chloe said in a tiny voice, still watching him through her lashes. Her arms were still wrapped around him, keeping him trapped in the valley of her bosom, but her hands had taken up kneading his back again and Desmond was fighting his own groans.

"Well then, mighty one, let me lead you some more then?" Desmond urged with a chuckle. Chloe blinked slowly before nodding again just once.

Pulling back slowly, Desmond kept his grip on her right horn, just behind the ring he'd given her, and pulled away from her. Chloe allowed him to pull away, though she let out a disappointed sigh as they separated. That sigh shifted to a moan of desire when Desmond, using the grip on her horn, tugged her to stand up.

"Come on, my dearest Chloe. I want to know you better. But, somewhere more comfortable than the showers," Desmond murmured to her as she stood. Chloe's mind took a moment to catch up with what he said through the lust-filled haze that had colored it. Once back on track, she nodded slightly, as much as his grip on her horn would allow, a smile ticking her lips upward.

Turning in place with his right hand still above his head, Desmond was barely tall enough to keep his grip on the horn while Chloe was standing, but it worked because she angled a bit to make it possible. Tugging gently, but firmly, he started them out of the showers and through the rest of the suite.

Ignoring the water dripping from their wet bodies all over the floor, Desmond led Chloe into his room and to his bed.

Only when they were there did he stop, release her horn, and turn to look up at her again. His hands moved to rest on her hips as he looked up the length of her to meet her shy gaze.

"Chloe, I'm a blunt man. You know that already, so I'll just be blunt so we can dispel any doubts now, okay?" Chloe nodded her agreement, her breathing starting to speed. "I want to have sex with you, to explore your body and please you. When you got hurt today, it scared and infuriated me. I'd been content to let you take things slowly. But, in the weeks I've known you, I've gotten very attached to you. I think I've fallen in love with you, and I want to show you that."

"I want you too, Des," Chloe breathed. She took a knee in front of him so that they were nearly eye to eye again. "I don't know if it's love, but I know I want to stay as close by your side as you'll allow me to. I don't expect to have you to myself, but I'll take all you can give me. You'll have a herd, I know it. You have too much potential that I've seen. I just want to lead it for you."

Desmond blinked. He hadn't expected that. *Well, yeah, I knew Chloe had a thing for me. We talked about that weeks ago and we've been pacing around the edges of it, but the herd thing?* Desmond thought to himself, staring directly into Chloe's much darker green eyes as she waited for his response. *I mean, that is normal, isn't it? Group arrangements? I've seen the gender ratio firsthand already. Why not?* Desmond shook off those thoughts and instead tightened his focus on the woman in front of him. *No, that's a problem for Future-Desmond to deal with. Don't hate me dude, I'm focusing on the now.*

"Chloe, I'm in no rush for a 'herd', as you said. I know there are going to be others living with us, but I have no idea if they are going to be worthy of joining a relationship with us. I'm not going to go race off and man-whore myself around," Desmond said gently, and Chloe rolled her eyes in amusement. A faint blush colored her cheeks while she waited patiently for him to continue. "But yes. If something more happens. If more people join us. You were here first, my Chloe. My strong shield arm. For now, though, I just want you."

For the second time that night, Chloe made the odd moan/moo noise deep in her throat and leaned forward, shifting her head carefully to keep her horns away from him before burying her face in his neck, her arms going around him in a tight hug. Desmond returned it, one arm going around her thick neck to pull her against him while he slid the other along her horn to its base, using it as a grip to pull her into him.

"Okay, Desmond. You have me," she mumbled into his neck before drawing away. Her blush remained, but her expression firmed with sudden confidence and lust. "How do you want me?"

<><><>

"How do I want you? However, I can get you," Desmond said with a throaty chuckle. "For now though, on the bed with you, on your back." Desmond gave her a gentle push using the hand on her left horn and Chloe moved automatically, rising up to her feet before falling sideways onto the bed into a sprawl that left her in a heap of muscled limbs and delicate female curves. The motion sent her breasts swaying in a hypnotizing way that Desmond happily stared at until they came to a stop.

"I trust you, Des," Chloe said quietly, her big green eyes watching him intently. The infusion of confidence from earlier continued to bolster the big woman.

"And I trust you, Chloe. If you want anything, speak up. If I do anything you don't like, speak up. When you disagree with me, even outside the bedroom, speak up. I'll do the same, but I expect you to return it to me, all right?" Desmond locked eyes with her from the edge of the bed and waited until she gave him a hesitant nod before he continued.

"Communication is key. Never feel you can't talk to me. About anything."

"Okay, Des," Chloe refused to break eye contact with him, watching him intently as Desmond got up on the edge of the gigantic bed and settled on his knees between her calves. She'd had the sex talk with her mother and such conversations came up regularly in the barracks, even if she wasn't directly involved in them. But, since she was a crossbreed, she'd had fewer opportunities than others to have her first experience of intimacy as other Taari's disdained her for the 'dilution' of her bloodline.

"I've never…" Chloe started to say, wanting to warn him so it didn't take him by surprise.

"All right, I'll be gentle. Just relax, Chloe," Desmond reassured her with a wink before leaning forward to press a kiss to her muscled thigh. Chloe moaned again, the touch of his lips on her skin stoking the fire inside her and making her whole body tremble.

"Okay, Des," she groaned, gripping the sheets to keep her hands at her sides.

Desmond gave a low, lusty laugh at how revved her engine already was before settling in between her muscled thighs fully. His hands ran up and down the well-defined muscles of her legs. He left a trail of kisses up her thigh to the moist center that sat between her legs. Chloe moaned and writhed slowly, her hips twisting back and forth in response to the gentle kisses and nips that led up to her sex. Desmond paused, blowing a warm breath slowly across her full lower lips before kissing back down the other thigh while Chloe groaned in disappointment.

Desmond made several passes up and down her thighs, each time kissing closer and closer to her sex but never actually touching it. He took the time to find the spots that were sensitive, as well as sliding his arms under her thick thighs to wrap up around the tops of them and hold her in place. He had a feeling that Chloe was going to be a wiggler once he got to the main event.

Again blowing his hot breath across her soaked sex, Desmond inspected her womanhood more intently. He'd watched her lips grow fuller and redder as Chloe gained arousal with each pass. Dew glimmered on her sex and her thighs while her hips rolled in a slow rhythm. The blunt nubbin of her clitoris was poking out from under its hood, begging for his attention ever since his third pass over her. He was gratified to see that, while Chloe's sex was sized to match her, her sex looked tight enough that their difference in sizes shouldn't prevent either of them from enjoying themselves.

Surprisingly small opening for someone her size, I'm not gonna complain though. Desmond thought to himself with a grin, taking in another breath and blowing a slow stream of warm air directly over Chloe's clitoris.

The big woman hissed out a keening moan, one big hand coming up as if to grab Desmond's head but stopping halfway there.

"Des! Stop teasing me," she moaned. Her hips rolled up to present herself like an incoming wave.

"As you wish, precious one," Desmond murmured back. His words touched off a shiver down the length of Chloe's body and her sex gushed sharply. "Oh? Like that name, my precious one?" Chloe whined again in response, her hand gripping the top of her thigh hard to keep herself under control. "I'll give you what you want then, Precious," Desmond rumbled, his voice having gone husky with arousal at seeing her excitement, before leaning forward and kissing her clitoris.

Chloe came immediately.

It was only Desmond's grip on her thighs that kept her legs from slamming shut on his head hard enough to stun him. He'd had an inkling that she would be sensitive and he'd been ready for a reaction, something he was glad for. Just how hard she bucked had still surprised him. Chloe's whole body shook with orgasm as Desmond pressed kisses over the hyper sensitive nub of flesh and dug his hands into her thighs. He was losing the contest of strength rapidly as her thighs continued to tense up while Chloe grunted sharply with the contractions of her climax. Desmond could feel her abs pulsing against his forehead as she curled up and over him.

Double down or get out. Desmond ordered himself and shifted down from her clit. Chloe gasped in relief as the pleasant suckling on her clitoris released and she began to relax, her orgasm slowly dying away like a receding tide.

The tide came crashing back in as Desmond's lips found her opening and he thrust his tongue into her rapidly, bumping her clit with his nose.

"Des!" Chloe yelped in surprise, her abdomen tensing so hard that she literally did a sit up as she came hard a second time. The change in her posture kept her thighs from slamming shut on his head and Desmond did not let up, urging her through the second climax and into the third rapidly. Her body reacted and her sex gushed with juices, encouraging her lover in its own way.

Chloe could barely think. She'd played with herself before. A girl had to get relief on occasion and they had just as many desires as a male, after all. But she'd never come this thunderously or back to back like this. The ripples of climax continued to make her whole body tense and Desmond seemed intent on keeping her on the peak as long as possible. Needing something to do with her hands she clawed at her breasts, finding and squeezing her nipples, tugging on the rings, as well as kneading the soft flesh to add to the rising tide of pleasure while her lover drove her higher and over each new wave.

Desmond did not let up his oral assault for several minutes, Chloe's whining moans growing hoarse as she continued to twitch and tremble, her hips rolling from side to side as she tried to guide his tongue to the ideal locations.

Desmond was grateful for this, since it allowed him to find all her most sensitive spots and memorize them. It didn't hurt that, while she was moving like this, she wasn't trying to crush his head with her thighs. With each orgasm, her pitch shifted and got higher as she continued to make inarticulate sounds of pleasure that became more frantic by the minute.

Finally, after he'd lost track of time, Chloe's hand came to the back of his head and tugged gently, pulling him away from her.

"Enough, Des! Enough," she panted, sucking air hard. "I can't breathe, please. Mercy, Des…" she drew out his name in a whine.

"As you request," Desmond replied with a grin, working his jaw as he came away from her sex. It had been some time since he'd had the opportunity to express his oral skills and his tongue was sore. Though that ache faded rapidly as he felt the wintergreen tingling sensation through his aching jaw when his body's rapid healing fixed the problem, now that he wasn't straining the muscles.

Huh. Oh, I can't wait to see if that works for refractory as well. Desmond thought with an evil smile. He bent to wipe Chloe's juices off his face with the comforter, but found that the big woman had left quite a wet spot between her legs.

"Juicy one, aren't you, my precious Chloe?" Desmond teased and Chloe's whole body tensed again, her sex gushing a small measure of her sexual fluids to add to the wet spot.

"Please, Des?" Chloe moaned, tugging him weakly up her body. Desmond complied, only pausing to find a dry spot to use to wipe his face before settling on top of her body and between her breasts. His erection bumped her hot sex on the way up, drawing a gasp from Chloe and a grunt from him, but Desmond shifted so it was trapped between his stomach and her cut abdominals. On either side of him, Chloe's massive breasts spread out as if to present him with a pillow that would guarantee erotic, as well as sweet, dreams.

Something for later. I have other priorities right now. He thought with a wicked grin, pressing a kiss to the underside of her right breast and suckling sharply, leaving a minor bruise there on the curve of her breast.

Chloe whined happily at the sensation before her arms wrapped around Desmond and pressed him to her.

"Thank you, Des. No one's done that for me before," she whispered, her head lolling to one side so she could look down at him with a smile on her lips.

"Oh, I plan to do that and more. Glad you enjoyed it though, precious Chloe," Desmond replied with a wicked grin. He felt Chloe's abs tense under him in response to the pet name, and his grin deepened. "You *really* like that nickname, don't you?"

"Never thought that I'd be precious to someone. Hearing you say it like that, in that tone of voice? I bet you could make me come just whispering that in my ear."

"Something to try in the future, then." Desmond turned his head to the other breast and gave it the same suckling kiss treatment to leave a hickey there as well.

"Hmm. I love feeling you marking me like that," Chloe cooed quietly, her hands running up and down Desmond's back lightly as the two caught their breath.

"Oh? You like being marked by me?" Desmond teased gently. Chloe's blush, which had faded to just a rosy tinge up to that point, returned in full force. "I'd say that is a resounding yes from the lovely lady. You want them where others can see, or just where you'll feel them throughout the day?" Desmond punctuated the question with several nipping kisses against the base of Chloe's throat.

"Where...where others can see? I want a badge to show I'm desired." Chloe's voice was a thready whine of desire as Desmond kissed up and over the pulse point in her throat, feeling it pounding against his lips, before he bit lightly into her neck and set about giving his lover what she wanted.

Desmond left a handful of small bruise marks on Chloe's throat, high enough that they would be seen if someone looked, but low enough on her neck that she could simply turn up her collar and hide them from view. *Monika is going to have a field day when she sees these. Better give Chloe the choice to hide them if she wants to when she's not running entirely on horny.*

"Desmond, I want you," Chloe panted as he finished the second mark on the other side of her neck. "Take me, please?"

"Protection?" While the moment had his own desires running high, the ever present concern over children was not something he could easily dismiss. Though his own body ached for relief, he fought it back.

"Protection? Oh. There's an anti-fertility treatment in the ship's water." Chloe moaned as Desmond laid another sucking kiss over her breastbone, right where she would strike it when she went to salute. "You don't have to worry about it, Desmond. It's a universal contraceptive. The military doesn't want folks getting pregnant. The Hegemony requires a parenting license to get the counter-agent, anyway. I'll explain more later!" Chloe groaned, her hips flexing and rolling under him as she tried to get him inside of her. Which was a futile gesture, given their difference in size.

"All right then. One last kiss then, my giant, precious Chloe." Desmond teased, wriggling further up her body to claim her lips. Chloe yipped in excitement as their lips met and tongues dueled for several long seconds while Desmond's hands kneaded her large breasts.

It took him tugging on both her pierced nipples at the same time to break the seal of her lips and that was just because the moan was so loud it sounded like she was lowing like a cow.

"I thought you wanted me inside you?" Desmond laughed gently as he slid backwards to settle into the cradle of her thighs.

"I did. But at the moment, I wanted kisses more," Chloe replied petulantly. Her petulance evaporated with a gasp of desire as Desmond's manhood landed on her sex with a moist slap. "Slowly, Des? Please?" she moaned, spreading her thighs out for him so that he could get into position.

"Slow is required. I can't get good traction down here in 'Lake Chloe'." Desmond teased with a grin. The wet spot had only grown while they kissed, and she recovered.

"Sorry. I'm just that horny right now," Chloe said contritely, both looking embarrassed and slightly proud, with a bit of a smirk.

"Don't worry about it. It's not that bad. Shows that I'm doing something right. Besides, the bedding would be soaked, anyway. Not like we dried off from the shower," Desmond reassured her before reaching down between them and adjusting himself. He tapped her plump lips once with the head of his shaft before slowly pressing into her.

"Oh Suns and Stars..." moaned Chloe as he penetrated her. Desmond bit back his own groan. While Chloe's body had been hot, her insides took it to another level. Her sex closed down on him like a fist, banishing any concerns he'd had about their size earlier.

"Gods, you are tight, Chloe," Desmond groaned, pausing only halfway into her.

"Benefit of being this fit," she groaned. "Why did you stop?"

"Didn't wanna break your hymen too fast." Desmond grunted, taking deep, slow breaths to keep himself under control.

"Hymen? What is that?" Chloe gave him a bewildered look and Desmond started in surprise before laughing.

"Something human women have. It's a, uh, membrane inside the vagina? Not really sure what its purpose was, but its presence was a sign in many cultures of a woman's 'purity' in sex," Desmond explained, slowly rolling his hips as his lover's body relaxed.

"Sounds painful." Chloe murmured, wrapping her arms around him and stroking his back. "That feels good. You can go deeper, Desmond. I don't have a hymen for you to worry about." She looked concerned for a moment before continuing. "Though I do promise, this is my first time being with a man."

"Not something I was worried about, Chloe. Wouldn't change my opinion of you regardless," Desmond reassured her before pushing deeper into her.

Chloe moaned sharply, her legs spreading wider before settling around Desmond's hips, ensnaring and pulling him to go as deep as possible on his next thrust.

"Oh, Stars. That feels so good," Chloe purred. Her eyes grew hooded as she watched Desmond above her.

"Happy...to oblige," Desmond grunted. The process was harder than he was used to, because of their difference in size. But he got a grip on her hips and Chloe's body clamped down tight on him. Desmond knew he had to be careful because it wouldn't take much to drive himself over the peak.

Thrusting slowly, Desmond drove himself in and out of Chloe's orgasming slit. He wished he could reach her lips to kiss her, but the height difference was just too much. So instead, he settled for adding more nips and kisses to the ones he'd already laid over her breasts, since they were within range and jiggling so enticingly.

The erect nipples that capped her swaying mountains begged for his attention, and Desmond was happy to give it to them. Each was as big around as his thumb and stood at attention on her breasts, like two squat peaks on top of a pair of rolling hills. The silver rings piercing them sat like two little handles for him to hold and use to steer her pleasure. Chloe's moans ticked up in volume when he took the first nipple into his mouth and kicked up another notch when he nipped it lightly, threading his tongue against it and using the piercing to tug lightly.

"Don't hold back, please?" she moaned, squeezing him close as her head rolled back and forth, horns whipping through the air above them.

Redoubling his pace, Desmond was surprised when, only

seconds later, Chloe tightened down on him and began to keen loudly in orgasm. Her legs flexed, pulling him hard against her and burying him to the root. Desmond grunted as the sensation of her body clenching tight around him was enough to push him over the edge. His seed pumped out of him and into Chloe's clenching body. The climax continued for what felt like a slice of eternity. Desmond's hips worked back and forth within the tiny space that Chloe allowed him, while her sex continued to pull and milk him as her contractions rolled in like waves.

Their shared climax slowed and finally died away, leaving them both drained, sweaty, and happily satisfied.

"Don't wanna move," Chloe gasped quietly, her chest heaving for breath now that she could finally get her muscles to relax. "Feels too good."

"Agreed. Don't wanna..." Desmond panted back. His member was still buried inside Chloe's sweltering sex and wasn't showing any signs of softening. Turning his head, he nuzzled into the side of her left breast, kissing it lightly. He felt the tingle of his mana settle into the pit of his stomach and chuckled quietly.

"What?" Chloe pushed her sweaty hair out of her face and twisted her head to peer down at where Desmond rested between her breasts. Desmond grinned up at her and, tensing the muscles in his abdomen, made his still unflagging erection jump inside of her, eliciting a gasping moan from the woman under him.

"Again?"

CHAPTER 39

Life in the Hegemony is generally considered to be good. The government works to prevent major issues such as disease, famine, war, and disasters. Though pressures from political rivals always threaten the borders of the Hegemony, the life of the average citizen is fairly idyllic. Mana and technological advancements have eliminated many of the struggles in everyday life.
~A report on the Hegemony, sent back to Terra-Sol-3.

The distant hammering of something on metal drove Desmond out of sleep, and he blinked groggily at what lay in front of him.

A mountain of pale flesh, capped with a peak of dull pink and silver that stood proudly at an angle, hung sideways over him.

Blinking harder, Desmond forced his eyes to focus as the pounding got more insistent.

A single massive breast hung over him and, as Desmond shifted to get his eyes to focus, he felt something soft under his head as well as the shifting of someone beside him. The circular piercing through the nipple over him swayed slightly in time with its owner's slow breathing, glinting in the low light as it moved hypnotically.

The previous night came rushing back to Desmond and he couldn't suppress the grin that spread across his face. He and Chloe had finally slept together. After keeping her up for three more rounds, she had finally run out of energy and pinned him down so she could recover. He'd made good on his idea of using her breasts as a pillow, not that he'd had much choice. Chloe had decided to use him like a body pillow and just wrapped herself around him and promptly fallen asleep.

"Desmond. Cadet-Adept Irongrip is at the door." The jazzy voice that SAUL used broke the muffled quiet of the room, and Chloe groaned petulantly.

"I'd hoped that I was dreaming that," the big woman moaned. As if Monika had heard her through the door, the pounding sound redoubled and got slightly louder.

"I'd better go answer that...she's just going to get more insistent and louder the longer we make her wait." Desmond sighed, glancing around for the time before he remembered he was still wearing his comm-cuff. The metallic cuff was so comfortable on his wrist that he often forgot he had it on until he needed it. "Huh. It's only half an hour earlier than normal. Surprised she waited this long."

Muffling a yawn, Desmond turned to roll out of bed, only to come to a stop when Chloe hooked his waist with one arm and stopped him, scooping him bodily back against her.

"Nope. I'm your guard, Desmond. I'll answer the door," Chloe said, the sleep clearing from her voice as she spoke. "But first, kiss?" The last part was hesitant, as if she didn't quite expect him to be okay with it.

"Yes, kiss. Come here, Precious." Desmond replied with a smile, reaching up to cup her cheeks and draw her into a kiss. It would have been longer, but the thumping of Monika at the door broke them apart with a sigh and Chloe crawled over him, trotting quickly to her room.

A few moments later, Chloe emerged while sealing the magnetic clasps on her pants with one hand. The other had her repeater over her shoulder. She was still bare from the waist up, though, something Desmond made sure to appreciate while she finished dressing.

Chloe made sure the pants were fully secured before crossing to the door. Desmond forced himself to stop staring at her pleasantly jiggling curves at last and slid out of bed to get himself dressed.

"SAUL, confirm who is all at the door?" she called as she crossed the room.

"Cadet-Adept Monika Irongrip and Cadet-Guard Oril'la are outside the door. No others are closer than thirty yards, though there are a few people at their doors," SAUL sang back to her. His cheery voice was cranked up to the normal volume now that he was sure they were awake.

"Open the door for them, SAUL," Chloe called after glancing to make sure Desmond was done getting his pants on.

"Finally! I was worried you two had fallen in and drowned or something!" Monika's voice echoed with the sort of perky enthusiasm that made even morning people cringe while she bounced through the door, with Oril'la following close behind her.

The two of them stopped dead only a few steps into the room when they saw Chloe standing there in just trousers and over a dozen hickies with Desmond still in his room, in the same state of dress. Oril'la's eyes went wide and Monika snorted and began to laugh, a deep rolling belly laugh.

"All right! Was wondering how long you two would pace around each other before you got hot and heavy. Glad to see that Des knows how to treat a lady. Oh he marked you up good, Chloe!" Monika crowed, fighting to laugh, breathe, and talk all at once. Oril'la just rolled her eyes at her companion and turned to trigger the 'close door' pad to give them some privacy.

"Not like it matters with Monika shouting it about like that," the Hyreh woman muttered to herself.

"Oh, I doubt it's a secret to their neighbors. Judging from the marks Chloe's sporting, I'm pretty sure Des had her *singing* last night! Also, you are a freaky girl. Love the jewelry!" Cheered Monika, darting closer to peer at several of the bruises that marked the side of Chloe's breasts.

"Monika..." Chloe began, her face reddening as she

fingered her repeater like she wasn't sure if she should put it away, shoot the Dwerg woman, or just club her with the weapon for being annoying.

"What? I'm happy for you two! Looks like you both had fun, and it was consensual. Glad you got to stake your claim on him early like this, Chloe!" Monika's cheery smile proved to be enough of a 'get out of trouble' pass that Chloe just sighed and gently pushed the shorter woman away from her.

"You honestly think that I'd force myself on someone?" Desmond asked pointedly as he emerged from his room, pulling one of his uniform tops over his head.

"No. While you aren't my particular brand, I know that Chloe's been eying you like a tasty steak for a while. Just glad she got a chance to sample you finally! Had me a bit worried some other woman was gonna swoop in and snatch you up before she got the chance to." Monika's irrepressible cheer was *almost* enough to keep her out of trouble with Desmond. However, he'd had longer to build up a resistance to her 'charm' and instead thumped her in the forehead with a flick of his fingers.

"Ow! What was that for?"

"Interrupting. That's what that was for," Desmond shot back, giving her a slight scowl before turning to Chloe and smiling up at her. "Go finish getting dressed, Chloe, and we'll get breakfast with the pest." Chloe nodded once, smiling down at Desmond and starting to dip towards him before stopping. Seeing her sideways glance at Monika and Oril'la, Desmond guessed what she'd wanted and why she'd stopped. So he reached up to get hold of her left horn again, pulling her down into a kiss that made even Monika blush slightly to see it. Though the Dwerg started giggling a moment later.

"Thank you, Des," Chloe murmured as they parted, her large eyes locked with his again.

"Never feel the need to hesitate to kiss me if you want to, especially in our rooms. Those that matter, don't mind. And those that mind, don't matter to me," he said with a wink before releasing her horn. Chloe stepped back and took a breath to steady herself before turning on her heel and striding into her room to finish dressing.

"Shatter and void it, that was hot!" breathed Monika and Desmond was gratified to see her blushing when he turned back to her.

"What? Do you expect me to change how we act in privacy?" Desmond prodded his friend, not bothering to hide the smirk on his face.

"Oh, Voids, no! Don't you restrain yourself for me." Monika replied with a saucy wink. "Feel free to make out with your sexy hunk of woman whenever you want. I always love free shows."

"Might have to start charging you, then. I will have to ask Chloe," Desmond teased back, before reeling it in to not make Oril'la feel awkward as the Hyreh woman looked like she might pass out if her blush got any deeper. "Anyway, let me grab my stuff and we can get some breakfast. I wanna hear about your run."

<><><>

Breakfast was a relaxed thing. Since Monika had gotten them up earlier than normal, and it looked like a number of cadets were sleeping in as a result of exhaustion from their runs, the mess hall was mostly empty.

They were joined after a short while by Dianne and her guard, Mona, and began swapping stories back and forth. Dianne and Mona had gotten a cave-system, much like Desmond had when he went with the second years, but it was much more relaxed. They both agreed that having the enclosed space made it both more tense, and less at the same time since they could tell where threats might come from, but had fewer avenues to maneuver.

The Rift that Monika and Oril'la had helped suppress had been one of the ones floating in the void. Rather than the pocket leading to a forest or grassland like Desmond's had, it had instead led to what appeared to be the interior of a derelict ship. They went on to describe most of their run in clearing and securing various halls and maintenance tunnels. They had fought off an infestation of creatures that resembled something of a cross between a cockroach and a badger that had a bad habit of tearing through the walls. It'd been easy enough to deal with them, since the creatures would clump up when pissed off.

The others listened raptly when Desmond and Chloe described their run, neither having thought about an 'open space' type of Rift like they'd encountered until that moment.

"Odd that it still basically restricted your path with the trees and undergrowth, but rewarded you going off the path," Mona said at last, looking thoughtful. The slender Yu'Aelfa had been quiet during most of the conversation, only offering the occasional insight while she ate and listened.

"Yeah, I thought that as well. The paths were like game trails, but still broad enough folks could get down. I have to wonder if it's something to do with how the mana is drawn in, since we found stronger creatures at the end of the paths, as well as more concentrations of crystallized mana there too," Desmond replied. He'd eaten quickly to start with and was just nursing a cup of the space coffee right now. It'd taken time, but the odd flavor was growing on him.

"Hard to say, maybe something you three will learn during later years," Mona said with a shrug, turning to look back at Dianne with a small smile. "After all, it's just our job as 'mundies' to keep you safe and let you do the heavy lifting, right?"

"Oh, don't remind me. I am astonished that the veterans didn't just knock that idiot out," Dianne sighed. When everyone gave her questioning looks, she rolled her eyes and explained. "One of the cadet-adepts that was part of the groups sent to our Rift basically tried to co-op the others into letting her lead the entire group and order them around. 'Safety in numbers' and all that, regardless of the fact we couldn't all fit through the tunnels at once." Dianne snorted derisively.

"Heh, that wouldn't have gone over well with our group either..." Desmond snickered as he imagined the reactions from the Sergeant if someone had tried to order her around.

"Oh, that reminds me," Chloe cut in. "Des, did you develop your twist for *Bolt* yesterday? That looked different in the Rift."

Desmond stopped to think about it and nodded. He had only used the *Bolt* spell a few more times during that run, after he'd lost his cool when Chloe had gotten hurt, and each time it had shifted to that double-bit 'barbarian axe', complete with a thundering sound effect.

"I think it was, yeah. I'll have to experiment on the range some," he said after a moment of thought. Which was promptly banished when Monika pestered him to demand he describe what the effects were.

The surrounding crowds grew steadily as they talked and after another half an hour, the group broke up to get on to class.

Chloe fell in as normal on his left, hand on his shoulder. While they were walking through the halls, Chloe's grip on Desmond's shoulder tightened for a moment and she grunted quietly.

"What's wrong, Chloe?" Desmond turned his head to look up at her and the horned woman blushed.

"Sore...little hard to walk straight," she murmured quietly, keeping her eyes forward.

"Can't have that now, can we? I need my guard at full strength, don't I, precious Chloe?" Desmond teased. Chloe trembled slightly and bit her lip before turning a reproachful glare on him. That look morphed into a relieved sigh when Desmond pushed a smaller version of the healing enhancement he'd used on her through their touch.

"Oh...thank you for that, Des. Was worried it would interfere with training." Chloe sighed as the last of the soreness faded from her body.

"Too bad though."

"What's too bad?" Chloe twisted her head to look down at him sharply.

"Your bruises are all faded now," Desmond said with a half-shrug. "Guess I'll have to replace them tonight, then." He added wickedly. Chloe blushed hard again, but a smile crossed her lips and her grip on him tightened slightly before gently massaging his shoulder.

"I'm just glad that Monika didn't comment on them during breakfast. Was bad enough that she saw them in our room and the jokes she made in private..."

"Didn't comment on them *yet*." Desmond reminded her with a smirk.

CHAPTER 40

The fact that the greater universe is ruled by those of the female gender might lead those blinded by bigotry and sexism to believe that the greater universe is a soft, safe place. I assure you, this is not true. Ambassador Steelbender does not bear that name because of her clan or anything silly like that. I challenge any of you to insult her to her face. Just make sure you have your affairs in order beforehand, as there won't be much left of you. I didn't get a warning. I AM the warning, so don't expect to get one yourselves. And she's not even one of these 'adepts'.
~General John Whitton, Terra-Sol-3
military, spoken from his hospital bed.

The first class of the day was back in the Bronze combat range and Throneblood was already waiting when the cadets began to arrive.

Taking their usual lanes for the morning weapons practice, Desmond and Chloe laid their equipment out and got everything ready while the rest of their class slowly filtered in. They'd both agreed over breakfast to practice without armor today, since Chloe's was going to need some repairs given the other damage they'd found the night before and while they weren't sore from wearing it the previous day because of Desmond's healing factor, neither was looking forward to suiting up again right now.

The class gathered steadily over the next half-hour, quietly taking their lanes and setting up for another day of weapons practice. The energy of the class was subdued, as most of them were sluggish after their suppression runs the previous day.

Right before their usual start time, Throneblood broke the aura of silence that her stern presence had cast around them.

"All right, you lot. I've got a few announcements before you all begin practice. Enough of you have gotten to a passing level of accuracy with your weapons that we are rotating focus for the morning classes." There was a mixed murmur of excitement from the class and Throneblood let it go for a short while before continuing.

"While most of you have learned to shoot well enough that you aren't going to hit yourself, your classmates, or your cadet-guards, I cannot say you are *excellent* shots. That sort of thing takes even longer, and I expect you to continue to drill in the evenings. Especially now that you've completed your first Rift and your stipend will be increasing."

That statement got a much louder swell of conversation that snapped off abruptly when the sapphire-haired Uth'ra growled deep in her throat. The sound resonated throughout the room and rattled loose ammunition on the benches.

"Much better. Now, for those that weren't aware. Your stipend will increase by fixed percentages based on your performance in each of the Rift suppressions that you are assigned as part of your assessments. This is an additional measure we are testing this year that the Vice-Admiral thought up. In the past, the bulk of a cadet team's free cash came from the supplies recovered from Rifts. This led to cadets prioritizing collection of supplies over doing their jobs."

Desmond bit back a snicker at that. He had a feeling that Olianna had gotten a talking to after her veterans had reported in.

"So, to help balance that, your stipend will instead be increasing on a sliding scale with the highest performers in efficiency and speed getting an increased weekly pay. Given that, because of the sheer number of cadets, you will only be suppressing two to three Rifts per year, this multiplier can definitely pay dividends for those that try."

One of the cadet-adepts raised their hands with a question and Throneblood nodded to them.

"What if we aren't in the upper end of the pool, Instructor? Is there a negative modifier applied?"

"That is a good question. The answer is, no. There is no negative modifier applied to most of you. It is something that had been considered but was discarded as we do want you all to strive and develop your own style. Only paying out bonuses to the fastest would cause those with specializations that do not encourage speed to fall further behind. Healing specialization, for example, does not lend itself to a headlong charge like the Evocation specialists. Those that do fit the new metric will get a bonus, but those who keep to a steady pace will also gain some benefit on top of their normal pay for recovering important supplies from the Rifts."

"Most of us?" another cadet asked, not bothering to raise her hand. Throneblood didn't chastise her, instead just waving her data-tablet in the woman's direction.

"Most of you. It was decided that, while the ranking system itself will not lower someone below their minimum stipend, losing performance or under-performing can cause you to slide back on the scale. If placing in the top ten percent causes a fifty percent boost in pay for each time you achieve it, then falling out of it will cause a corresponding drop. Maintaining the rank from Rift to Rift will allow for you to stack the bonus on top of past rewards. If you are placed in the top ten, you would get the bonus cumulatively. If you drop out of the top ten, after the Rift you drop out of it on, you will receive a deduction to the rank you fell to, and then will continue to accumulate bonuses at that new rank in the future."

Several of the cadet groups looked confused, but it appeared that Throneblood was done explaining that part of the changes as she moved on.

"The metric being measured, each run will be changing as well. You will only be informed of the metric as you are being launched. It could be anything from individual monsters suppressed, to crystals harvested, to clear speed, to lack of injuries and beyond. So it is important to improve in *every* sector. Do you understand?"

"Yes, Instructor!" came the thundered response, all in unison.

"Good. Now, I have your scores from the last Rift here and I am, frankly, appalled at most of you." Throneblood's tone took a decidedly darker turn as she glared at the students. Most withered, but a few of them remained resolute as her gaze swept over them. Desmond guessed those were the ones that had given it their all and were sure they weren't the reason for the instructor's anger.

"I had been putting off the physical conditioning because the mana enhancements and your gear can make up for a lot of shortfalls. However, it appears that we need to change that. Morning classes from now on will be physical conditioning. You are to meet in the bronze level gym at the usual hour in your standard uniforms. We will be increasing your physical capabilities without the assistance of mana." The grin that twisted Throneblood's lips was made even more intimidating by her fangs. "After all, a solid foundation will let you do more with less. Those of you that have been slacking, now is the time to make it up." A wave of mutters rippled through the assembled cadets.

"Shit," Chloe muttered almost silently behind him, and Desmond glanced up at her. A small, worried expression crossed the horned woman's face before she schooled it to neutrality once more.

"What?"

"If she's going to put us through conditioning like the cadet-guard went through, then it's gonna be rough on you all," Chloe replied before nodding her head for Desmond to put his attention back on the instructor.

"I see that this is displeasing to a good number of you. I'm glad!" Throneblood's voice echoed with malice as she turned her orange-eyed glare on each student in turn that had been grumbling. "It means that you will get something out of this. Did you think your time here was going to be all cushy class time? This is a *military* academy! You earn your rank by blood, sweat, and tears!"

"Not like we had a choice in enrolling," someone near Desmond muttered.

Throneblood, who'd been looking the other direction, whirled in place, eyes locking on the speaker: a regal-looking Va'Aelfa woman who was being hushed by the cadet-guard who was standing next to her, but it was too late.

"Oh, you definitely had a choice, Cadet!" boomed Throneblood, stomping through the class to stand over the top of the lippy cadet. The crowd parted around her like a sea parted before the charge of a battleship. "It might not have been the choice you wanted to accept, but you were given a choice when tested. All adepts serve their time after training. The Hegemony has no need of rogue adepts who refuse to learn and do their part. If you didn't want to do your fair share, then you had the choice of having your dynamo sealed and going back to life as a mundane."

The Va'Aelfa cadet wilted under the instructor's oppressive glare and she nodded once, forcing herself into a shaky attention. Throneblood snorted at her like an enraged bull before turning on heel and stomping back to the front of the class.

"In addition! Afternoons for the next week will be here on the range, but will be a mixture of lectures and practical application of skills. Cadet-Adepts, you will be leaning into a more complex subject that several of you have asked about after the second-years demonstration: Conjuration." That got another swell of murmurs from the class that took a minute to subside despite the instructor's glare.

Once the group had settled down again, Instructor Throneblood continued. "Cadet-Guards, you will have the period to practice with your weapons, as your mornings will no doubt be taken up by getting your cadet-adepts through the physical conditioning. You will have the choice between firearm drills or practicing melee with the instructors. We will divide the range as needed.

"Now, I will be calling each of you to discuss your rankings from the last Rift over this period. The other instructors will be observing if you have questions. Get to it!" Throneblood snarled the last part and there was a scramble from the students to follow directions.

<><><>

Over the next several hours, groups were called up by the instructor to receive the information on their rankings.

Desmond did his best to focus on the range and his practice with the rifle. He'd spent most of the Rift working his enhancements into place, and the majority of the encounters were resolved before he could join in. He knew he could do better. It had him thinking of how to assemble his team for the future while he practiced, though. How to capitalize on the ability to spin enhancements out to his team while maintaining the firepower and pressure they could put forward.

His focus was interrupted eventually by the characteristic bellow of their instructor when it was their turn.

"McLaughlin and Vandenberg, wrap up and come here." Desmond waved a hand over his head to acknowledge without turning, as he still held a loaded weapon in his hand. It was a habit that had been pounded into them over the past several weeks but came easily to him given the amount of attention given to 'firearm safety' that he'd had back on Earth.

Terra, its official designation is Terra-Sol-3 now. He reminded himself as he carefully unloaded the power cell from his rifle and got it plugged into a charging port on the bench in front of him.

Chloe was waiting for him when he set the rifle down and turned. Her repeater was already disarmed, baton shaped energy cell on the charger, before he'd even finished pulling his power cell.

"Show off," he teased gently, getting a playful wink in return from the much larger woman as he went past. Chloe fell into what was rapidly becoming her standard position, just a half step behind him and to his left, her hand settling onto his shoulder naturally.

Surprising how fast this became natural. At first it was just to give her the contact she wanted, but now? Now it feels natural and protective. I know she could jerk me out of the way of just about anything like this, but she's also not getting in the way of my dominant hand either, allowing me to defend myself if need be. Interesting to think about how she started out insisting on being in front of me, but now she lets me walk forward as she watches my back. Desmond thought as they cleared the line of cadets, getting nods of acknowledgment from one of the mundane instructors as they passed. *Whatever, this works for me. If it's a problem, the instructor will say something, otherwise I don't care.*

Throneblood didn't say anything, though one of her bushy, blue eyebrows popped up for a moment as they approached. The eyebrow reset itself as they came to a stop and saluted her. Chloe's hand dropped off his shoulder, but she did not shift from her position on his flank.

"Cadet Adept McLaughlin, and Cadet-Guard Vandenberg reporting, Instructor." Desmond stated as they dropped into attention in front of her.

"At ease, you two," Throneblood snorted. The instructor had commandeered a back corner of the range and had been using it for the reviews. She'd stood in this exact spot for several hours without shifting or moving once, feet planted wide and steady, shoulders back. Desmond couldn't help the idle question floating through his mind.

Doesn't her back hurt standing like that?

"Well. I can't say I am impressed by your performance in the Rift, but neither can I say I am disappointed," Throneblood began, flicking through screens on her data-tablet.

"Instructor?" Desmond inquired. He and Chloe had talked while waiting for the power-cells to charge about what they might expect from the review, but Desmond was entirely unsure of what to make of Throneblood's statement. The Uth'ra had made her ire clear earlier to several pairs of cadets with her bellowing.

"Cadet-Adept McLaughlin, you cleared several challenges without issue. Applied your spells rapidly and without hesitation. Were competent in the directions you gave to your entire team and listened to the advice given by your veterans, though you did hesitate on how to handle the Rift type you encountered. I expect you to study up on the various known types of Rift that exist so you are better prepared in the beginning," Throneblood began, eyes on the data-tablet in front of her like she was reading off a shopping list.

"You spent additional time hunting for resources, though what you recovered was high grade and rare on most fronts for the level of Rift you went into, so the extra time taken is made up in that factor. You even took point on ensuring one of the other teams was safe when they hadn't reported in and went haring off on their own. Sergeant Whist had only positive things to say in her review of your command style. The issue that kept you from the top five percent was that you nearly got yourself killed in a fit of passion."

The instructor's gaze bounced from Desmond to Chloe and back again before turning to Chloe.

"Cadet-Guard Vandenberg, you performed as an exemplar in your grade. You listened to orders and did everything in your power to ensure your adept was safe, even to the point of taking grievous injury to ensure he was safe. I expect nothing less of our cadet-guard, but you have fully embraced a devotion to your duty that bears recognizing. While others of your experience level in their first Rift would have hesitated, the Sergeant reported that you acted without pause. You will be receiving a commendation in your file for your performance. Keep it up, but also, keep your adept on a shorter leash if you can in the future."

Chloe snapped off a sharp salute but did not respond as the instructor's eyes flicked back to Desmond.

"McLaughlin. Your actions endangering yourself are something that, while understandable, is not excusable. Adepts, even cadets, must be protected. That is why you have your guards. Sending you in teams into the Rifts is a calculated risk, but you must also be wary. We can't hold your hand the entire time, after all. And while every one of you will develop your own command style, I expect you to not risk yourself unnecessarily from now on. If this chafes at you, take to heart how it would have felt for your guards if you had been injured after Vandenberg was hurt protecting you." Desmond winced slightly and Throneblood's stern expression softened.

"You understand. Good. The two of you will receive a twenty-five percent bump to your weekly stipend as a reward for your performance. If you can show the same or greater level of competence in the future, *without* receiving injuries or endangering yourselves recklessly, then I expect you to rise higher. You are already investing heavily in your future. Don't think the amount of training you two do goes unnoticed."

Both of the cadets straightened slightly at her words and Throneblood finally let a smile roll across her features.

"The bonus will be applied starting today. You've done well so far, McLaughlin. Better than many in your position would. You two can return to your practice."

Desmond and Chloe saluted the instructor before heading back to their practice lanes. They didn't discuss it until they were back on the range and were loading their weapons again.

"Twenty-five percent pay bump, that's a hell of an increase when you think about how it's going to add up," Desmond muttered out of the side of his mouth.

"Only if we maintain the ranking. Remember, if we drop ranks, it'll penalize us as we 'fall'. You won't see me slacking off, that's for sure. I want that higher pay too," Chloe replied as she carefully went over her repeater, checking all the parts with practiced ease before slotting in her power cell.

"Never thought you would, Chloe. You're not a quitter, proved that to me last night." Desmond grinned at the larger woman, who blushed hotly before setting her lane to produce targets in clusters of three.

Having mercy on her, Desmond changed the subject. "What does the commendation mean?"

"It's a positive mark on my record. If I was still with the regular forces, it'd be a bump towards a promotion. Since you selected me for a guard position, my rank doesn't change since we are outside the normal ranking structure. It does include a onetime bonus, which is good." The last part was said quietly and Desmond almost missed it.

"Oh? Bonuses are always good. Got anything interesting planned for it?" Desmond was curious. Chloe had no known hobbies beyond reading on her tablet in the evenings and the occasional movie that they had watched when too drained to do anything. Knowing more would allow him to surprise her with gifts and he was resolved to not take the horned woman for granted, a mistake that had cost him in the past in relationships.

Chloe was silent at first as she took aim and began sending volleys of laser fire down the range into her targets. Desmond wasn't sure if she'd actually heard his question at first, but she answered quietly a moment later.

"My little brother, actually...the family has some outstanding medical debt that I'm paying down. It's slow but, progress is progress."

Desmond almost kicked himself. He remembered her file stating she had outstanding debts when he'd selected her. He'd assumed it was personal debts, but apparently it was a family debt. They had been so caught up in the training and the new experiences that he'd entirely forgotten about it.

But...if it's for her little brother, wouldn't it be her parents' debt? Unless...

CHAPTER 41

'Prims' or those from primitive worlds. A slur that I got used to hearing so often that it faded into the background. Might have bothered some folks, but to me it was like someone making fun of me for my hair color. Why argue with the truth? Earth is primitive by comparison with these space-wizards. And all the species of the Hegemony started out at this point, even the Aelfa. No, what was disappointing more was the fact that such prejudices and the like are still prevalent in the greater galaxy. I just have to hope my sample just has a disproportionate share of them.
~Desmond McLaughlin, on life aboard the *Valor's Bid*.

Chloe was withdrawn for the rest of the morning class, and Desmond did not press her on it. Instead, he remained quietly supportive of the larger woman and let her work through things in her head. It was clear to him that the medical debt was something that bothered her a lot, and he didn't want to press her on it. If she asked for help or advice, he'd do what he could, but it wasn't his place to pry if she was uncomfortable about it.

The afternoon classes returned to the range as well, this time with Desmond practicing his spells, while Chloe continued to drill with her repeater. During lunch, they'd confirmed with the others that everyone would be moving their schedules to a similar layout, with the day split between physical conditioning and then time at the range. A discussion arose between the cadet-guards about which was more important, improving melee skills or continuing firearm drills, and that had helped break Chloe from her funk.

That evening, Chloe followed Desmond into the shower to clean up without complaint and the two of them had taken it in turns to wash each other before falling into bed once more. Given that they would be doing heavy physical conditioning the next morning, they both agreed that getting up to anything sexual was likely a bad idea. Instead, Desmond fell asleep using Chloe as a pillow, this time with the horned woman on her back and sprawled across Desmond's bed.

<><><>

"Come on Cadet! Is that the best you got?"

"No mana! You pull that again and you'll get another three laps!"

"Move, move, move!"

The four instructors' strident voices intertwined with each other as they chased the unruly herd of cadets around the broad track that circled the outer edges of the massive gym. The oval track was easily wide enough that the entire class only had to go two deep on it if they remained together, and long enough that each lap had to be close to a mile. Desmond hadn't bothered to try to measure it, instead focusing on his breathing and fighting to keep up with Chloe while sweat poured down his body.

The physical conditioning had started with Throneblood telling them to warm up before ordering them onto the track. Apparently, her patience had an extremely short fuse that morning because she'd only given the group of cadets a fifteen second head start before she produced a shock-baton and started chasing them.

The rest of the mundane instructors had joined in along the run, each of them taking a portion of the running cadets to torment as they roared, shouted, threatened, harangued, and in some places, lashed, the cadets into maintaining a steady pace and the adepts into keeping up with their guards.

For their part, the cadet-guards had an easier time of the run with the fact that they had already been doing something similar before being selected. The difference came in that they had to moderate their stride to remain beside their cadet-adept and that was proving a challenge for some. Any who outpaced their cadet-adept or left them behind were quickly called into line at the tender mercies of the instructors.

"Did I tell you to slow down? You are going to wish you were serious about this when you are sprinting for cover!"

Desmond fought the urge to run even a minor enhancement through his body to increase his speed. He was already feeling the lightest tingle throughout his limbs from the bizarre way his body's natural healing worked now, and that was giving him just the barest edge he needed to keep up with Chloe.

"Vandenberg, half stride. You'll run your adept into the ground if you keep that up!" roared Throneblood from the back of their pack. The Uth'ra had been chasing the larger-framed members of the class for most of the run, their longer strides having them leading the class almost exclusively.

Chloe obliged the order, dropping her stride down to a much smaller one that was more of a match for Desmond and put her alongside him rather than two paces in front of him like she had been. Desmond was happy for the reduced stride, but disappointed at the same time. The sight of Chloe's tight bottom bouncing in front of him as he ran had helped keep him distracted from his burning lungs. *All the healing in the world won't help if you can't get the oxygen you need.* He reminded himself and worked to keep his breathing even.

Apparently, Throneblood found someone else to torment as she rounded on another cadet nearby that was huffing and puffing like a diesel engine trying to turn over in the cold.

"You doing okay, Des?" Chloe's breathing was accelerated, but even while her face shone with sweat as she ran.

"Never used to...run much..." Desmond gasped, feeling

like a wrung out rag beside her. "But keeping up. Depends on...how long this keeps going..." he panted heavily. Desmond just hoped that his body's natural healing increase would help him build the lung capacity so he could eventually keep up. His muscles burned with the exertion, but the fire kept fading in and out.

"Don't push too much. It's just going to get worse," Chloe cautioned.

She was proven right only a few minutes later when Throneblood charged through the mass of cadets, scattering them left and right as she went. Once she was at the head of the pack, the instructor began directing them off the track and into a space near the center of the room. The space was enclosed by low walls that blocked vision but had catwalks on them that allowed the instructors to look down on those inside.

"Move! Obstacle course, go! Do not stop. Do not break formation. Stay with your teammates. You can rest when you make it through!" roared the Uth'ra instructor, her orange eyes snapping with inner light. The ragged formation of cadets skidded into a broad turn and angled into the wide mouth of the concealed obstacle course and Desmond learned what Chloe had been talking about.

The obstacle course that they had to move through at a jog would have been easy enough if they had done it first. Most of it was a mixture of balance, ducking, crawling, and dodging obstacles. The cadet-guard were already familiar with it and Desmond relied on Chloe's guidance to suss out the obstacles as they approached each one. His slow regeneration had staved off the cramps from overworking his muscles and the pain from the strain suddenly demanded of them. He'd done his best to maintain the strength that he'd built while working as a welder back home. But it turned out such endurance did not directly translate.

"Watch it!" snarled another cadet-adept, a Hyreh woman whose name escaped him, as they both converged on one of the balance obstacles at the same time. The obstacle was a pit filled with foam 'spikes' at irregular intervals and crossed by a trio of 'logs' that were less than a foot wide. The pit was acting as a bottleneck for the group and no one wanted to wait and see what the instructors had in store for them if they hesitated.

"Go!" Desmond shouted back, dodging to one side as the Hyreh woman pushed past him, dragging her partner behind her, who was also a Hyreh. The two sneered at him and Chloe before staggering out across the beam and off the other side.

"Bitches..." Chloe grumbled before leading the way onto the heavy beam. While it hadn't reacted virtually at all to the two Hyreh women, Chloe's larger size and increased weight made the beam bow and bounce slightly with each step. Moving carefully, Desmond was able to keep his balance as he crossed right behind Chloe.

"Doesn't matter. We just gotta get to the end." Desmond huffed as they dismounted and sprinted up a sharp slope to the edge of another pit. Knotted ropes hung partway out over the pit, simulating hanging vines. Desmond watched as the cadets took it in turn to leap for a rope before tossing it back towards their teammates for them to cross.

"I'll send it back for you," panted Chloe as she got ready to charge across the smaller platform, but Desmond stopped her. Something that he'd noticed while they moved further and further along through the obstacle course was that Chloe's breathing became more labored as her endurance slowly waned. *The changing pace of the run earlier had to have taken a toll on her.* Desmond thought to himself. *That and the well has to have a bottom. Her size works against her at times.*

"No, I'll go first. It's an easier jump for me. Be ready to catch it on the back-swing." Desmond didn't give her time to argue, leaping out into the gap and snatching the rope, letting his momentum swing him forward.

The distant platform was just out of reach and Desmond let himself swing back again before pumping his hips to push himself further out on the second swing, landing on the platform a moment later. Turning back, he nodded to Chloe and sent the rope back to her.

"Idiot prim," growled a voice behind him. Desmond whirled in time to catch an elbow to the chest and the flash of a wicked smile before he tumbled backwards off the lip of the platform and into the pit below.

"Desmond!" Chloe's voice echoed in his head as he fell backwards and time seemed to stretch out as he fell.

Curling up, Desmond did what he could to make sure he didn't land badly. Time abruptly snapped back in on itself when his back slammed into the lightly padded bottom of the pit, some fifteen feet below. The impact drove the air out of his lungs in a rush and Desmond felt his left shoulder give a sickening pop from where he landed on it awkwardly.

Pain washed through his body for a brief second and he bit back a reactive scream. Chloe dropped to the bottom of the pit next to him, her face a mixture of rage and worry.

"Des, are you okay?"

"Shoulder…I think it's dislocated…" he gasped through gritted teeth.

"Vandenberg, can you move him?" The shout came from the catwalks above them. Instructor Gemtooth, the Gaur mundane instructor with gray wings, stood well above them while looking down with a stern expression on her face. Chloe glanced back over at Desmond before nodding up to the instructor. "Extract your adept. He will be seen to when you finish the course."

"Shit…this is going to hurt, Des," Chloe muttered before carefully scooping Desmond up in her arms. The pain from being shifted nearly made Desmond pass out. "I'm sorry, Des…" Chloe's voice was laced with concern and barely restrained rage. Desmond wanted to reassure her, but the tingling from his mana trying to heal the injury was fighting with the pain of the dislocated joint and it was making his head fuzzy.

"Pop it," he gritted through his teeth while Chloe cradled him against her chest as she climbed the steep slope out of the pit on the far side.

"What?" Chloe glanced back down at him, her eyes sharp with worry.

"Back in, pop it back in," Desmond growled, making a punching motion at his left shoulder weakly.

"I'm not a medic, Des. I could hurt you worse," Chloe warned as she charged down the slope on the far side of the swinging obstacle. There was only a hopping balance obstacle left before the end of the course. Desmond fought the urge to scream in pain while his mana struggled to heal, numb the pain, as well as reset his shoulder; all while the injury jostled back and forth as Chloe bounced from obstacle to obstacle.

You'd think the pain would let me pass out...but the damn healing is keeping me awake...

"Vandenberg, what happened?" Throneblood materialized in front of them as if by magic, right as they exited the course.

Maybe it was magic. Fuck if I know, Desmond thought blearily through the pain. He'd dislocated his shoulder before and it hadn't hurt this badly.

"He made it across the rope swing but was knocked off by another cadet, Instructor. Landed badly, left shoulder is dislocated," Chloe reported rapidly, still keeping Desmond cradled to her chest and supporting his arm as best she could. "He told me to pop his shoulder back into place, but I don't have the training."

"Hmm..." Throneblood stared down at Desmond for a moment before snapping her gaze back and forth. There was a ripping sound and Desmond felt something made of cloth stuffed into his mouth. "Bite down on that, McLaughlin."

He was barely given time to comprehend, let alone respond, before a sharp pain seared through his injured shoulder. He choked back a scream, biting hard into the cloth to keep from biting off his tongue. Seconds later, the blessed coolness of his healing sunk in and the pain faded, leaving only a loopy haze from the burn of his adrenaline.

It took a moment for his swimming vision to stabilize, but it did so as his body dragged mana from his cache and fed it into healing him. After less than ten seconds, his shoulder felt good as new.

Coughing weakly, Desmond spit out what appeared to be the wadded sleeve of the instructor's uniform shirt.

"Ow. You can put me down now, Chloe."

Chloe's arm tightened around him protectively for a second, but she slowly relaxed and bent to set him carefully on his feet. Though she did set him down, Chloe did not move from her position, hovering over him protectively, nearly pressed directly to his back. It honestly made Desmond feel a little like a kid again, but in the aftermath of the injury and still dealing with the adrenaline that the injury had dumped into his system, he just leaned back against her. He could feel a hollow sensation in his gut and knew that he'd burned through a good portion of his cache, as his body's automatic drive to heal had consumed the stored mana without his permission.

That...could be bad, Desmond thought. His loopy mind was drifting over the idea of his body just draining away all of his mana to heal an injury in the middle of a fight. If he didn't have control over it and his body burned his cache dry, that would be *very* bad.

The sound of shouting slowly penetrated his adrenaline-fog, and he turned slightly to see Throneblood dressing down a scowling Hyreh. The same Hyreh that had pushed ahead of him on the balance obstacle, he noted idly. While he wasn't hurting anymore, the cocktail of hormones his body had supplied made it hard to understand what Throneblood was saying over the rushing of blood in his ears.

"Des? Are you okay?" Chloe's sweet voice penetrated the fog and Desmond blinked owlishly, turning his head to look up at Chloe. All he really could see was the sweat-soaked underside of her breasts and her horns poking out past them, since he was leaning heavily back into her stomach.

"Yeah...just gonna be a second, Chloe," he panted. "Make... make sure I eat well at lunch. Pretty drained right now."

"Do you need to go to Medical?"

"No. Just let me catch my breath."

"McLaughlin!" Throneblood's stern voice cut through their conversation and Desmond struggled upright, swayed slightly, and then came to full attention.

"Yes, Instructor?" Desmond was silently grateful that he saluted with his right hand and not his left. While his shoulder didn't hurt anymore, he didn't want to test it right away with any sharp movements, either.

"You and Vandenberg are to head to Medical and you are to get checked out."

"I'm fine, Instructor. I can continue," Desmond replied quickly. While he couldn't see the Hyreh woman or her partner in the group watching him right now, the last thing he wanted was to appear weak.

Throneblood gave him a once over with dubious eyes before she responded.

"This isn't some misplaced bravado, is it?"

"No, Instructor. I am confident I can continue. You told us to treat this training like an encounter in a Rift. If I could not continue, I would pull out to preserve my team," Desmond replied stiffly.

"Fine, but no upper body for you. Observe that portion so you can do them on your own. You Terran's are more durable than expected, so I'm trusting your judgment on this. Don't make me a fool."

"Yes, Instructor." Throneblood turned back to the rest of the class and began shouting at them to get them moving out of the exit of the obstacle course as more and more cadets finished it and began walking to cool down.

"What the hell happened, Des? I saw you send the rope

back to me, then you were falling and the Hyreh girl smirking at you." Chloe wrapped her left arm around him now that Throneblood wasn't looming over them, and pulled him tight against her chest. "Throneblood tore that girl a new one for 'interference and sabotage of a fellow cadet'."

"That one that Throneblood was bawling out, she elbowed me off the ledge. I almost landed on my neck." Chloe drew in a sharp breath and squeezed him again, a rumbling growl building deep in her chest.

"I'll kill her…"

"No, you won't, precious Chloe." Desmond had managed to shake off the confusion from the adrenaline finally and gently patted Chloe's forearm with his right hand. "Just keep an eye on her. I bet Throneblood is going to make her life a living hell for pulling that. She said something about 'prims' before she hit me, so I'm sure it's just bigotry."

Chloe growled again, the sound rumbling through her thick chest like a plane engine starting up. It ended up vibrating Desmond's ribs due to their contact. He continued to pat her arm and lean into her until she calmed down enough for them to follow the instructor to the next part of their class.

CHAPTER 42

*You want the answer to existence? You want the answer
to why we are here and what is the 'divine plan'?
It's been lost to time. Whoever wrote it down forgot where
they left it. It's probably under a stack of unpaid bills if we are
lucky and if not, it's got coffee-stains on it and it's illegible.
What is important is the here and now and
finding purpose in every step of our lives.*
~Vice-Admiral Rashona Roaring-Feather, exhorting
a new crop of cadets during a midterm lecture.

The rest of the conditioning class was a mixture of calisthenics and sprints. Desmond followed the instructor's directions and observed while the rest of the class went through the upper body drills. Most of what they did was familiar to him. *After all, there are only so many variations of a push up out there, right?* He mentally promised himself to run through the exercises before bed.

It turned out to be a good thing that he did not push too much during the calisthenics as his much reduced cache levels left him feeling lightheaded. A subtle check of his comm-cuff told him that his internal mana levels were at thirty-four percent and had remained that way throughout the rest of the class.

At lunch, Desmond forced himself to eat more than twice what he normally would, remembering the words of Instructor Tre'shovak from back when the Va'Aelfa had helped get his dynamo moving.

The food helped boost his levels and his dynamo hummed away in his chest, quietly vibrating his breastbone as it processed the ambient mana around him to refill his cache in a snowballing effect as best it could. While he ate, Chloe explained to their friends what had happened, allowing Desmond to focus on eating.

Monika had been, predictably, pissed. The redheaded Dwerg had held a one-person rant about bigots and fools for almost ten minutes, and it took Oril'la actually stuffing some of her food into the Dwerg's mouth to get her to eat so they wouldn't be late to class.

Desmond's effort proved worthwhile, as his cache levels had recovered to roughly sixty percent by the time the afternoon classes came around, and Desmond knew he would need it if they were practicing a new school of magic. He'd been curious about the Conjuration subclass of magic ever since the Vice-Admiral had set up the demonstration with the second years.

<><><>

"Conjuration is one of the more difficult classifications of mana manipulation that you will learn." The class had split, as Throneblood had advised them previously. The cadet-guard were released to practice as they saw fit, while Throneblood lectured the cadet-adepts on the other half of the range. A shimmering force field made up of iridescent purple hexagons divided the room and prevented stray weapons fire from reaching the cadet-adepts as they occupied their half of the range indiscriminately.

Chloe had not been happy to separate from Desmond, especially after what had happened earlier. It'd taken a direct order from Instructor Gemtooth to get the horned woman moving. Even now, Desmond could tell that Chloe was watching him from her place on the firing range. They'd discussed it during lunch, between Monika's rants aimed at getting revenge for Desmond, and she'd elected to drill using his rifle rather than her repeater since it had been a while since she'd used the smaller personal-defense type rifles.

Desmond was fairly certain it was also so she would remain closer to him with something in hand that had range and accuracy, but he hadn't called her out on it. If there was one thing to be said about Chloe, it was that she took protecting him seriously, even in places where he shouldn't need it.

Like earlier, I shouldn't have needed protection, and nearly broke my neck. Desmond pushed the thought aside and focused back on the instructor as she continued her lecture.

"Conjuration takes many forms. From static items used as defenses like a row of sandbags or a temporary *Shield*, to far more complex subjects like you all witnessed the Vice-Admiral produce for the demonstration earlier in the year. What you will practice today is static conjuration. Specifically, a curved-plane *Shield*. If you demonstrate aptitude with this, you'll be moving on to more complex conjurations and maybe even creature type conjurations by the end of the week."

Throneblood demonstrated as she spoke, a slight gesture with one hand called a half-dome shield into place in front of her. It was smooth, unblemished and slightly transparent, but tinged a dark blue like her hair. She dismissed it a moment later before turning back to the class.

"Conjuration can be mana intensive, so pay close attention to what you do. If you can master the basic *Shield* conjuration, then you will be well on your way to protecting yourself and your team in the coming years. With practice, you can narrow it down to manifest for a split-second at a time to catch an attack if necessary."

"What about a specialist? Like the Vice-Admiral?" one of the other cadets asked the question that had been wandering through Desmond's mind. Throneblood glowered at the cadet for interrupting her, but answered anyway.

"That depends. There are as many varieties of Conjuration specialists as there are Evocation specialists.

Twists inevitably branch it further. The Vice-Admiral is a creature specialist that has an easier time summoning multiple copies of the same creature. I've known Conjuration specialists in my time that could conjure weapons that would put anything in the Armory to shame, those that could conjure *Shields* strong enough to be useful in ship-to-ship battles, and those that could summon up creatures of myth and legend to fight for them in a moment of need. It doesn't change the fact that only Transportation tends to be a more costly school to practice in. Even for specialists."

Throneblood glared at the assembled cadets for several more seconds, as if daring another one to interrupt her with a question, before she snorted like an angry bull and gestured for them to get to it.

"Don't forget to carefully formulate your chants and watch your mana levels," the Uth'ra ordered them as they dispersed to have space to practice.

Desmond made his way to the outer edge of the practicing cadets, well away from anyone who had bothered him in the past. This put him closer to the hexagon-pattern shield that divided the range, and a little closer to Chloe, a trade-off he was happy to make. The shriek of laser fire and pop of solid projectiles had become a steady background beat for him weeks ago after long practice at the range. He'd also seen more than a few of the stray shots hit the shield while Throneblood was talking and wasn't concerned, as the shield hadn't even flickered.

Makes sense. They wouldn't put us over here and let them continue shooting if it wasn't solid after all.

Taking a deep breath, Desmond thought for a moment about what sort of mental image or chant he should use on this one. So far, all the magic they'd practiced was just projecting intent into mana while pushing it into the world around them. His *Bolt* spell had taken the shape of the throwing axes he was familiar with for that same reason. It was something he could easily call to mind.

The enhancement spells he'd used were even simpler, especially with the different classifications recorded after the assessment. Focusing on the idea of boosting those individual numbers had allowed him to work the purpose into the mana even easier.

Briefly, he toyed with the idea of using something similar to what Throneblood had shown them, but dismissed it. The shimmering bubble reminded him too much of soap bubbles, which popped all too easily for his liking. Something instinctively told him that the association would weaken the projection. He discarded the idea of something like a tortoise shell either while staring at the hexagons. Striking just right or with enough force would cause that to shatter as well.

Something that I associate with protection...

Movement through the barrier caught his eye, and he watched Chloe set his rifle down on the bench before typing in some commands on her lane. A moment later, a light flashed on the shooting desk and she snapped the rifle up, cycling it and opening fire as targets popped out along her lane.

A smile slid gently onto Desmond's face and he took a deep breath and let it out, allowing the mana to flow as he considered the image. His memory darted back to the fight with the alpha ape-monsters and Chloe's steadfast defense with her shield. Desmond didn't chant or push with the spell, just turned the image over in his head.

"McLaughlin!" The sharp voice nearby made Desmond start in surprise and whirl towards the speaker. He'd been deep in reflection and reacted instinctively, his mana flaring sharply as his heart-rate jumped.

A dark green silhouette burst from his chest to loom over him, slamming down an opaque shield directly in front of him and blocking the speaker from view even as the figure crouched low over him to block him from all directions.

There were a few startled yelps from others nearby and Desmond was so surprised by the appearance of the figure, he couldn't keep his grip on his mana. A moment later the figure faded and dissolved, the mana sliding away from him and revealing the person who'd just startled him.

Instructor Throneblood stood with her hands on her hips, scowling, with one eyebrow cocked questioningly.

"What the hell was that, McLaughlin?" the Uth'ra snapped, eying him up and down speculatively.

"Uh…" he replied smartly, just as startled as she was.

"I asked you a question, Cadet!" Throneblood growled, and the irate tone of her voice produced a natural reaction from Desmond.

Snapping upright into attention, he saluted the instructor and answered.

"*Shield*, Instructor Throneblood."

"How?"

"I was considering what you had shown us as an example and was trying to envision something that would work for me!" he answered quickly, replying automatically as his mind whirled over what happened.

"That was not a static *Shield* you conjured, McLaughlin," drolled the instructor.

"No, Instructor. The demonstration you did felt too… fragile in my mind. It reminded me too much of a soap bubble. Easy to form, but easy to pop as well. I was considering other things that reminded me of solidity and defense and hadn't noticed your approach. When you spoke, I reacted and I am not sure what the result was."

"What the result was, Cadet," Throneblood replied slowly, her eyes never leaving his, "Was that you summoned a copy of your partner in full battle-rattle." She paused for effect. "In less than a second." Another long pause. "Without a chant."

Desmond just blinked up at her, his mind not quite catching up yet.

"Again."

"Instructor?"

"Did I stutter, Cadet? Again!" Throneblood barked the last

word and Desmond shook himself, reaching for that same memory and sensation. He felt his mana reach out and tap it again before flowing out of his chest in a wave and the silhouette flashed into existence around him. Desmond felt his mana continue to spin out at a rapid rate and struggled to hold the *Shield* in place. He could almost see the number spinning down on his comm-cuff.

"Drop it," came the command from the instructor, and Desmond let the mana go, gasping for breath as the loss of mana left him feeling lightheaded again.

"Interesting that your *Shield* took that form...how is your mana doing?" the Uth'ra instructor asked, crossing the distance to him with a thoughtful look on her thick features. Desmond checked his comm-cuff and was shocked to see that the two times he'd cast the spell had sapped away over twenty percent of his mana reserves.

"Uh...lower than I want." He held the cuff up for the instructor to check, not wanting to verbalize his mana levels. "I did what I could to recover after this morning, but was still lower than normal going into class."

Throneblood quickly scanned his comm-cuff, and the frown deepened before she shook it off, turning to eye him speculatively.

"Your healing drained you that much?" she asked, and Desmond nodded in agreement. "Okay, I want you to focus on calling up only a portion of the *Shield*. What you did was a more advanced and omni-directional *Shield*. Not sure how you did it, but you need to focus on a single direction for now to reduce the cost, and start using chants! There is a reason we teach you all to use them. It takes some of the weight off your dynamo and reduces the cost." Throneblood glared around them at the other nearby cadet-adepts, who had been listening in.

Once the eavesdroppers had turned back to what they were doing, she continued.

"The healing your species seems to have is mana

intensive. Which means you need to keep close watch on your cache, so you don't accidentally drain it. It is a weak point and a strength. Don't take your cache below thirty percent today and no practicing after class. Take the evening to recover," she ordered. Desmond nodded again in agreement and the Uth'ra swept off to berate another cadet.

Desmond took a moment to turn over the idea in his head that his healing was a weak point. He'd worried before about it draining his cache dry and that worry rose up again. *I need to get control over it, but it only seems to flare up when I'm hurt or exhausted...*he suppressed a shudder as an unwelcome idea came to mind. Him, taking an injury and his cache draining, then Chloe getting hurt or killed because he couldn't support her.

<><><><>

"Des, what the hell was that?" Chloe hissed as they headed out the door to take their gear back to their suite.

"What was what?" Desmond asked in confusion. While he didn't feel tired, his chest ached slightly from the constant hum of his dynamo as it pulled on the ambient mana. His mana levels had remained stable throughout practice, but hadn't climbed. He'd fought to keep it around the thirty percent mark as warned by the Instructor.

"No, I mean. What the hell did you do?" Chloe whispered in his ear from her position on his left side. Desmond paused to consider what she was saying before he chuckled and answered.

"Instructor told us to conjure a *Shield*. The examples she gave us felt too flimsy, so I used the shield I know best that makes me feel the safest."

"Des, I don't understand. That looked like..." Chloe sounded confused, and he looked over his shoulder to meet her concerned eyes as they shifted down the halls.

"You, Chloe. I was told to conjure a shield and my instincts produced you. A fully manifested and geared version of my guard." Desmond winked up at her, and Chloe blushed furiously. "Doesn't mean I don't need you anymore. Just means that I know I'm safe behind your shield."

Chloe couldn't help the blush as it grew, or the radiant smile that crossed her features at his confirmation that he felt safe with her watching over him. Desmond didn't want to tease her about it at the moment, but she had such a goofy grin going.

CHAPTER 43

You train and you train, hoping to put these skills to use. Then Fate laughs and throws you something you didn't train for and you have to make do with what you know.
~Admiral Lo'Unath, addressing her troops.

Days bled away as the classes continued. Chloe remained vigilant after what had happened on the obstacle course, but there wasn't a second attempt to sabotage or hurt Desmond.

For his part, Desmond was entirely focused on maximizing his conjurations and seeing how his specialty could apply to them. His basic *Shield* took on the shape of the thick metal shield that Chloe carried, but he was able to suppress the conjured body with proper application of willpower and using a chant. He could still summon the whole apparition. But, even with a chant, it ate through his mana at a rapid rate. Something that Throneblood reassured him was normal for Conjuration without a specialty.

Desmond did learn that if he dismissed the constructs, and they were out of contact with his body, the mana that made them up would bleed off into the atmosphere, and he could not recover it. This was a lesson that nearly caused him to pass out when he learned it.

He'd focused on making the ghost-Chloe as resilient as possible in a test case and had stepped away to focus. In seconds, over thirty percent of his mana vanished along with the apparition, and the sudden change of pressure had made him wobble.

After a week of practice, Desmond could replicate the Rift-monsters that he'd fought and Throneblood put him to work practicing with them instead. He moved on to brief conjurations and maneuvering them around, before calling them back to dismiss and reclaim the mana. He found that, if he layered the spells right, he could conjure a weaker version before enhancing the monster's resilience so it wouldn't fall apart immediately.

After a week of practicing Conjuration alone, Throneblood had the class begin working to conjure static defenses and layer their spells together. Only two people showed a specialization for conjuration of creatures, while a full two dozen had for static structures. Desmond was a little jealous of the faux-walls that they had summoned as strong points, but pushed it away while reminding himself that his strength lay in other avenues. This didn't stop the idle dreams of conjuring dragons and other mythical creatures, but they were just that: dreams.

<><><>

"I just don't get it," Desmond griped as he paced back and forth behind the firing line.

The class had let out an hour before and most of the others had already left. Desmond and Chloe had stayed behind and been joined by Monika and Oril'la. Dianne had begged off, saying that she'd drained herself too much in class and needed an early bedtime.

"What I don't get is why you are twisted up like this," Monika huffed as she stood at the ready between Chloe and Oril'la. Chloe was practicing with Desmond's rifle again while Oril'la had an almost mirror match to the rifle in hand. "You are conjuring full creatures weeks ahead of some of us. Hell, there are a few girls in my class that still can't get *Shield* to form."

Sighing, Desmond ordered the construct, a recreation of the ape-monsters from the second Rift, to come loping out from behind cover down the range. The creature dove into a baseball slide as Oril'la opened fire, spraying magnetically accelerated slugs at the creature but missing by a scant margin and having to stop her volley when the creature crossed into Monika's lane.

He and Monika were taking it in turns to conjure a creature for the others to practice on and give each other practice on the different types of monsters that they'd encountered.

Cackling, the Dwerg immediately launched a spell down the range at the creature. Monika had developed her first twist recently, and while the development was unexpected, the spell was not. Her *Bolt* spell shrieked across the distance between her and the enemy and struck it low in the leg. The foot long rivet made of mana yanked its dangling leg down before pinning it to the deck. This prevented it from escaping into cover long enough for Monika to launch a second spell that took the round head off its shoulders and the whole construct collapsed with a puff of green mist. Her twist made it so that the *Bolt* spell acted as an anchor, pinning a target to a surface like it had been riveted in place.

"I'm *twisted up,* as you call it Monika, because I wish I could do more," Desmond muttered halfheartedly. He'd explained it to his friend several times now and the complaint just seemed to sweep over Monika again and the Dwerg didn't really pay it much mind.

"She's right, Des," Chloe said quietly, glancing over her shoulder. "You're ahead of the class with your enhancements and the fact you can reasonably stabilize the conjurations, too."

"Yeah, that was just dandy. As if I needed to be singled out more," Desmond grumbled, aware that he was being hypocritical, since he'd been wanting to be even *further* ahead of the others.

Throneblood had decided to use him as an example to challenge the other cadet-adepts in the class, pointing to the fact that the Hegemony's first Terran could do it on the first day and she expected them to put forth appropriate effort to not let him get too far ahead of them. Nevermind that she also warned him to keep an eye out given the fact someone had actually struck out at him in class. She still used him as a club to beat at and provoke the rest of the class to do better.

It hadn't done him any favors with the other cadet-adepts. The ones that had disliked him now hated him for making them look bad, and the ones that whispered and stared were getting more blatant with their flirting and outright ignoring Chloe's presence at times in an attempt to proposition him in the halls.

"Meh, they can suck void," Monika said with her characteristic lack of caring. "Give it a year and everyone will have covered the basics. From there they turn us loose in independent practice for half the day while the other half is shit like Diplomacy, Tactics, and Piloting." Monika shivered theatrically as she named off the courses the upper tiers took, a reaction which made Oril'la roll her eyes.

"But the Vice-Admiral..." Desmond began a familiar protest as he focused internally and drew out the mental image of the ape-monster again, tossing it out beyond the firing line like he was under-handing a baseball. The rough orb of mana landed and swirled for a moment before the creature solidified. He had to order it to dive to cover immediately, as Monika was already preparing to launch another of her rivet-shaped *Bolt* at it.

"Vice-Admiral Roaring-Feather has been an adept for decades, Desmond," Chloe reminded him in a long-suffering tone, her eyes going forward and rifle coming up as she waited.

Desmond took a moment to check Chloe's cow-tail where it hung from the back of her pants. While he was still learning what the different non-human body signals were, he'd gotten a decent handle on Chloe's. The tail hung steady; the tip swaying back and forth slightly. *Okay, she's not actually irritated, otherwise it'd be switching back and forth.*

Dunno what the tip wiggling means.

At his order, the ape-creature used one of its overly large arms as a catapult to launch it up into an arc over the cover at an angle. Monika snap-fired her *Bolt* too quickly, the sizzling spell arcing below the creature's lower back and slamming into the far wall. The ape-monster never finished the arc as it crossed the line to Chloe's lane, angling towards cover. Before its stubby legs even touched the ground, Chloe had snapped off a long burst on the creature, stitching it from crotch to forehead.

"Bugger, that was even faster than before," Desmond muttered, catching a wink from Chloe and smiling back at her. "Monika, it's your turn. I'm starting to run low on mana."

Monika opened her mouth to say something, but the overhead lights flashed suddenly three times in a row. Moments later, both his and Monika's comm-cuffs chimed sharply three times as well.

"What the? I don't recognize that tone," Desmond mumbled, glancing at his comm-cuff.

"Check it, Des. That's an emergency alert," Chloe called, rapidly removing the power cell from the rifle and hurrying over to him.

Tapping the 'wake up' rune for the comm-cuff, Desmond found a flashing alert on his cuff that he projected onto the small hovering screen to read.

"All hands alert. Report has come in that a Rift in nearby occupied space formed and proved resistant to suppression. Rift went critical less than an hour ago and the detonation has caused extreme damage to a nearby space station." Desmond's eyes grew wide as he read onward. "Station survived the shock-wave due to being on the far side of the system, as well as being in eclipse by the planet it was orbiting?!"

"Oh, no..." The mirth had drained from Monika's voice and Desmond glanced up to see the pale faces of all three women as they circled around him.

"The death toll will be immense..." Oril'la said somberly.

"What does the rest of the alert say, Des?" Chloe urged, sidestepping around him to take up her customary position at his left shoulder, leaning against him and wrapping her right arm over his shoulders and around his front. The fact that she did that rather than put her hand on his shoulder told him that Chloe was as shaken as the other two, but keeping herself in check by focusing on him.

"*Valor's Bid* is diverting to provide emergency assistance in system until relief forces arrive. All cadets are scrambled to be at the ready in their suites in full combat gear. We will receive orders once the academy ship arrives in system in..." he glanced at the time-stamp in the message and then at the ship's clock on his readout, "half an hour? Wow, that happened nearby, didn't it?"

Chloe started to say something when the deck underneath them bounced slightly and, for the first time that Desmond had witnessed, the full alert system sounded throughout the ship.

"All hands, brace. Ship is accelerating to emergency flank speed due to the Rift emergency," the urbane female voice stated coolly and began counting down from thirteen.

Desmond had a moment to ponder why it started at thirteen but was interrupted when Chloe bodily scooped him up with the arm that was already wrapped around him. The horned woman sprinted to the shooting desk, snatching the rifle from the top of it before squatting to brace herself against the desk.

"Chloe, what are—?" Desmond started to protest but stopped when he saw Oril'la doing the exact same thing to Monika, who wasn't fighting her.

"Hold on, Des. The transition is rough," Chloe gritted, pressing herself to the underside of the desk and bracing hard.

"Three, two, one. Secondary Ripple wave forming. Brace," the urbane, mechanical female voice stated. Desmond was posed to ask more questions, but shut up a moment later when the entire ship lurched and jerked underneath him. It felt as if a giant had grabbed the floor underneath their feet and yanked it hard to one side.

A second later the feeling stopped, and he felt a pulsing ripple of mana breeze past them like a shred of windblown fog.

"The hell was that?" Desmond groaned. The sensation had made his stomach flip upside down and, for some reason, his dynamo stuttered as it tried to continue its regular spin while refining mana for him. It felt like a second, irregular heartbeat in his chest and was very disconcerting.

"We need to get suited up. I'll explain on the way. Stay safe, you two." Chloe rose from her position wedged under the shooting bench. Monika and Oril'la dusted themselves off and nodded in return before the group jogged for the exit hall. Chloe set Desmond down once she was sure he was okay and would keep pace. The four of them stayed together for the moment, but their minds were clearly focused on their individual tasks right now.

"So, you know how the Hegemony's ships travel the distances between stars, right?" Chloe asked as they dodged other cadets hurrying down the halls. The group split in half as a wedge of serious faced instructors pounded down the middle of the hallway going the opposite direction like they had a purpose.

"Ripple drive causes an explosion in the subspace foam and the Transport Adept aims it forward like the bow wave of a ship. The Ripple engine hooks onto the distortion in the subspace foam and, through a combination of magic and scientific effects that still escape me, the ripple actually drags us 'below' the subspace foam and out of phase with the visible universe. From there we 'ride' the ripple in the direction we are going," Desmond quoted what he remembered reading in the prior weeks at the Academy. "But I've never felt the ship buck like that before."

"Emergency flank speed outside of combat basically means 'With-All-Due-Haste'," Chloe explained, only to be interrupted by an already panting Monika.

"What she means to say is: Move like the Nebula-hounds are after your ass. They fire the Ripple Drive a second time in phase with the first. It drives us deeper into the subspace foam. It also triples the speed the ship moves at, but there are dangers."

"Like what?" Desmond nimbly dodged to one side around another cadet, a Va'Aelfa, that was hurrying the other direction towards the Armory.

"Creatures live deep in the Astral beneath the subspace foam. You told us about the oceans on your planet and how your species has explored less than ten percent of it, right?" Chloe took back over the description as they separated from Monika and Oril'la upon reaching the hallways to the dormitory area. Desmond nodded that he was following along.

"The Astral beneath the subspace foam isn't explored. It's not hospitable and any attempts to explore usually end with either the exploratory ships vanishing without a trace or returning in tatters. The creatures that inhabit the Astral do not take kindly to intruders. It's fine for quick jaunts, and as long as we stay close to the subspace foam that separates 'real space' from the Astral. But something the size of the *Valor's Bid*? It leaves a wake wherever it goes and this is driving that wake deeper. Things must be dangerous for them to do this, because we are going to drag bits of the Astral back into 'real space' when we come back out."

"And that's bad?" Desmond sent the command ahead of them via his comm-cuff to unlock and open the doors to his suite as they approached.

"Yes. Especially in an area roiling with mana from a Rift detonation. The Astral attracts mana at an even higher rate, and the small bits we will be dragging in our wake are likely going to spawn additional Rifts given time." Chloe looked thoughtful as they slid into their suites and she tossed him the rifle as they separated to go into individual rooms.

"What? I know you had a thought. I recognize that look," Desmond shouted as he rapidly skinned out of his uniform. He briefly wished he had time for a shower, but it would be better to not take the chance.

"They are doing it intentionally. The new Rifts will be more unstable and grow faster, but it'll help stabilize the mana in the region. I'm betting they are either going to leave some teams of second years behind to suppress them when they depart the system or will have contractors come along with the relief forces to do it," Chloe yelled from her room as she did the same.

"Sounds risky, but I think I get it. That prevents another Rift from forming somewhere random and also tones down the levels of mana to something less harmful for non-adepts, right?"

"Got it in one, Des. Clever," Chloe laughed and there was a sharp *clank* as she started pulling on her armor. "Come button me up when you have a second. We've been slacking on getting these repaired."

"I'm not slacking. I was planning on replacing the lot of it when we get paid," Desmond called back as he slid into the armored pants and secured them. The bottom half of his armor felt like a bizarre mixture of hammer-pants and fireman trousers to him as he yanked the heavy suspenders up and tightened the belt over his waistline. A couple of tugs on different straps pulled the armor plates tight on his legs and he tossed the chest armor over the top of it before hurrying to Chloe's assistance.

"Here. Do each other," Chloe said as she saw his armor flapping as he entered the room.

"Don't really have time for that, precious Chloe," Desmond teased, and the horned woman blushed before punching him lightly in the shoulder with a *clank* of metal on metal from her gauntlets, meeting his armor.

"Not what I meant, you horn-dog," she shot back at him before beginning to tug the armor into place and attaching the magnetic straps. Desmond returned the favor silently as he helped force the catches together on hard to reach spots in her armor. Chloe could have done it by herself, but they'd learned in weeks previous that having a hand with it cut the time in half.

"It's funny..." Desmond muttered as he strained with one particular buckle on her left shoulder armor that was still slightly distorted.

"What is?"

"First time you've been back in your room to do something more than grab clothes or your repeater since the Rift, is all. Wanna just move your stuff into my room and turn this one into the gear area?" Desmond didn't look up as he worked, but he felt Chloe's eyes boring into the side of his head.

She had, in fact, shared his bed with him every night for the last week. They'd only made love twice in that time, but had cuddled otherwise, and it was surprisingly easy for Desmond to fall asleep with the large woman in his bed. He'd expected Chloe to retreat to her room for space, but she'd resolutely followed him whenever he'd gone to bed. He could tell from her watchful gaze that she would have gone to her own room if ordered, but she seemed to prefer to share his.

It's not like asking her to move in, anyway. We moved in together when she joined the team. He mentally thumped himself.

"It just feels more practical is all, no reason to..." He continued to ramble.

"Yes, Des. I would love to share your room with you permanently." Chloe silenced him with a quick kiss before bumping the side of his head with her cheek sharply. "You are all secured. Go grab your helmet and the rest of your gear. I can get the rest locked in myself."

"One second." Desmond struggled with one latch at her

hip for a moment before the plate cycled and locked into place, snuggling tight into her side. "There we go. Okay, meet you out in the common space? I don't trust the chairs in full rattle, so couch?"

"Probably for the best," Chloe said, turning back to her rack only to jump in surprise when Desmond smacked her on her armored ass with one hand. The blow didn't even hurt, but it did cause her ass to tense under the armor plates and her to jump.

"See you in a bit, precious Chloe." Desmond winked at her before ducking away laughing.

<><><>

It was roughly twenty minutes after the alert went out that Desmond got an update, but it was via SAUL rather than his comm-cuff.

"Cadet-Adept McLaughlin, you are to report to hangar bay nineteen, pad four, with Cadet-Guard Vandenberg and your combat gear." The jazzy voiced artificial assistant interrupted the quiet conversation the two of them had been having over what they hoped the payout would look like when the Quartermaster's office finally finished refining the materials from their last Rift.

"Thank you, SAUL. Any details on the specifics?" Desmond got to his feet with Chloe beside him.

"Only that you are to report to bay nineteen and pad four and that Armory personnel will meet you there," SAUL replied cheerily. "Best of luck on your mission, Cadet-Adept McLaughlin."

"Desmond, SAUL. Desmond…"

"Right now, sir. I believe it to be better to address you with your full rank and title as you are leaving to do your duty to the Hegemony." Sang the digital assistant. Desmond blinked and then shrugged.

"I guess he has a point."

"I do not have a physical body, Cadet-Adept McLaughlin. It is impossible for me to have any points."

"It was a joke, SAUL." Desmond sighed before taking the stubby carbine rifle from Chloe and shouldering it once he had confirmed the safety was on. "We are on our way."

CHAPTER 44

What happens when a Rift isn't safely collapsed? Chaos reigns and those left behind weep, and that's if they are lucky. If you aren't lucky, you just cease to be and never get to know what it was that snuffed you out. With your atom bombs, you at least get to hear a rumble. When a Rift collapses? It just blots out stars like spilled ink.
~Ambassador Steelbender, speaking to
the United Nations of Terra-Sol-3.

The hangar bay was a study of organized chaos. Streams of cadets flowed at different rates through the several doors to the hangar bays like blood through clogged arteries. The designated clear areas around the shuttles remained entirely untouched, though. Ground crews rapidly worked through their duties and pushed machinery, tools, and other technical pieces through them.

Every pad was occupied with one of the chunky, shark-shaped shuttles, and Desmond noted that there were even ground-crew teams working on the ones that remained in the racks along the walls. Hangar nineteen had space for thirty or more of the shuttles at once and the wall-racks held double that, at least. The shuttles were arranged in three long rows, staggered out of step with each other to maximize space. Every one of the shuttles was oriented nose first towards the exits of the hangar bay.

The large blast-doors that held back the void of space were currently closed. Desmond also felt reassured since he could feel the faint resonance of a mana shield on the inside of the thick metal to reinforce them as well. *My mana sense is getting stronger the longer I practice it.*

"There!" Chloe drew his attention back to the moment as she pointed to their assigned pad in the front row, closest to the massive blast doors and just off of the center of the rows of shuttles. Desmond could see a small crowd of cadets already loitering around the shuttle entrance, nervously checking their weapons as they did so.

He breathed a sigh of relief as they approached. None of the cadets in the group were ones he'd recognized as antagonistic towards him.

"Cadets, over here!" shouted a gruff voice as Desmond and Chloe pushed their way through the crowd. A male Dwerg, the first one he'd seen in the months that he'd been here, hurried over to the landing pad as well, coming from another direction.

The short man had a thick head of black hair that he kept organized in several thick braids that tied into his beard. In his arms was a crate loaded down with boxes of ammunition as well as curious red batons with a series of blue symbols on them that he didn't recognize. What Desmond did recognize was the symbol of the Armory staff on the breast of the man's uniform, barely visible to the side of his neatly braided black beard.

The cadets on the landing pad converged on him first and began collecting ammunition from the box in his arms and slotting it into the different points on their armor.

"Take what you need, emergency supplies from the Academy. Make sure you take plenty of the distress beacons as well. Don't fight over it and don't get greedy!" the Dwerg barked. He set the box down on the deck and tugged out a tablet as he began scanning the cadets and tapping a checklist as they each dove into the box and took what they needed. By the time Desmond and Chloe got there, the box had been heavily picked through. Thankfully, they didn't really need much ammo, given that they always made sure to restock each evening after practice, and Chloe made sure her energy cells were topped up.

"McLaughlin and Vandenberg?" the Armory officer asked as Desmond inspected one of the red and blue tubes.

"That's us, sir," Chloe answered for him.

"Right, you two get what you need from the supply crate. McLaughlin, these are yours. Do *not* lose them." The Armory officer rummaged in a shoulder bag that had been hidden against his side and behind his beard before producing a pair of thick glass vials filled with a shimmering gas. One end of the tubes terminated in a strange sort of mouthpiece with a rubberized section in the shape of a 'U' that looked like the bite guard for a football helmet.

"Sir?" Desmond accepted the vials and inspected them.

"Mana inhalers. Per Instructor Throneblood, you are the designated healer in your group, given..." The Dwerg man squinted at his data-tablet for a moment before shrugging, "given that your racial adaptations allow you to 'bend the rules' as it were. You are to use them *only* in the event of critical mana levels, and you are to reserve any healing assistance to Academy personnel. The distress beacons are for any civilians and will summon teams from Medical to assist them." The Dwerg man looked up from his pad and locked eyes with Desmond, a scowl showing through his thick beard. "Do you understand, Cadet-Adept McLaughlin?"

"Only emergencies, got it." Desmond checked his mana levels, noting that the practice earlier had only drawn him down to roughly fifty percent, thankfully, and it was beginning to tick back up even now. He watched the number flick from fifty-four to fifty-five.

"And you are only to use any sort of healing on the personnel you are dispatched with or others deployed by the *Valor's Bid*." The Dwerg insisted, not looking away.

"Can I ask why, sir?" Desmond felt his gut twisting slightly. Enhancing someone's healing to match his was difficult and costly, but he didn't like the idea of not helping folks that needed it.

And it's costly despite being an enhancement focused adept... he thought bleakly.

"To put it bluntly, you are too precious a resource to risk for a regular citizen. Per Instructor Throneblood's orders," the Dwerg brandished his tablet, "'Anyone in such critical condition that McLaughlin would need to use his powers on them because they won't survive till medical teams arrive, would drain him to the point it would endanger his cache as he isn't certified for healing. This is an emergency measure, McLaughlin. Do your job and let those trained for it do theirs.'" The Dwerg read off to him verbatim.

"Understood, sir." Desmond felt his stomach clench at the thought of leaving someone injured without aid. Like Chloe had been before. His stomach loosened when he felt Chloe's hand land on his shoulder.

"We are combatants, Des. Not healers. It's our job to secure the site and protect the injured. Not treat them," she murmured quietly in his ear. They hadn't donned their helmets yet, so didn't have access to the private channels, but Desmond was sure that the general noise levels of the rest of the hangar would keep folk from overhearing them.

"I just...I don't like the idea of leaving injured behind."

"Stopping to treat one person might cost three more lives. The fact they are issuing ammo and beacons tells me that we are going into a hot zone," Chloe replied before turning her gaze to the Dwerg in front of them. "That is correct, isn't it? The station is damaged and likely there are Rift creatures forming in it?"

"You are correct, Vandenberg," a familiar voice called from behind them.

Turning, Desmond couldn't help the smile of relief that appeared when he saw the familiar quadrupedal shape of Sergeant Whist carefully picking her way over the various hoses and tools of the ground crew while they worked on the shuttle in front of them.

"Sergeant Whist, good to see you. Do you have mission

info?" Desmond asked her before he turned to nod to the Dwerg. "I understand the instructor's orders. Emergencies only." He got a nod in return from the Dwerg, who gestured back to the box of supplies, and Desmond began securing the baton-shaped emergency beacons to his belt.

"Cadets, for those of you who don't know me. I'm Sergeant Hailey Whist, a member of the ship's marine complement. Unlike the Rift exercises, you will instead be under *my* command. So listen when orders come across the tac-net and keep chatter to a minimum." The Sergeant came to a stop in front of the clump of cadets and looked them over with an intent stare, her arms tucked behind her back while the tail on her long, cougar bottom half lashed back and forth.

"The situation is as you have already been informed. A Rift formed locally and was unable to be suppressed in time. Despite advances in technology, Rift stability is something that is unpredictable at best. The resulting detonation sent a shock-wave over local space that has damaged the orbits of four planets in the system we are approaching and obliterated two of the outermost planets in the system." Desmond's eyes went wide, hearing the destruction that had occurred.

"The *Valor's Bid* is operating as a first response unit to stabilize the system. We will be rising back into real-space in less than five minutes and scrambling for emergency response. Your jobs will be similar to Rift suppression. The system was sparsely populated, with most of the population dwelling inside a space-station in geo-synchronous orbit around the second satellite of the star. Reports have come in that the station, while small, still supported a population of just under a million souls before the detonation of the Rift. It is unknown how many survivors there are, but we are to act as first responders and secure the station. Deploy emergency beacons as we find civilians and handle any manifestations of Rift monsters before they can harm the population any further."

"How are there manifestations outside of a Rift?" asked one of the other cadets, a slender Yu'Aelfa that was staring at the much larger sergeant with her wide, yellow eyes.

She must be from one of the other adept classes..., Desmond thought to himself, as he didn't recognize her.

"After a Rift detonation, many things can happen. The entire system is flooded with raw mana at higher than normal levels. While not dangerous for short-term exposure, long term can cause issues and instability that can lead to either mutations in the population or the manifestation of lesser Rift monsters. The basic suits will act to protect you from the mana-radiation, for those non-adepts amongst you. It isn't as concentrated as the ores or crystals you find in a Rift, but it can still be dangerous." Sergeant Whist explained quickly. "Remember, this is a civilian station! Check your lanes of fire and do not shoot any of the civilians. We have no idea if there are Rift monsters manifesting aboard the station, though the likelihood is high given that the station was the largest concentration of mana in the system before the Rift went nova. So it is dragging more and more in by the second."

<><><>

The Sergeant finished the briefing rapidly and chased them all aboard the shuttle without hesitation. Desmond was disappointed to learn that Corporal Ry'taal wouldn't be joining them, but understood given the situation. The Sergeant had been assigned to them purely to lead them as a unit because of their smaller unit sizes. The second year cadets were being turned loose in their own units with specific orders.

Loading onto the shuttle and waiting patiently until they were launched was agonizing. Desmond wished several times that he had some kind of view-screen to observe the system when the *Valor's Bid* arrived outside the orbitals of the planetary bodies for the star and launched its shuttles to actually enter the system. The Sergeant had advised them that the *Valor's Bid* would circle the system perpendicular to the orbit of the planets, launching shuttles as it reached ideal positions to send them to different targets, but would not actually enter the system itself.

Instead, the massive academy ship would use its thick mana wake to try to draw off the dense mana beginning to clump in the system, just as Chloe had theorized earlier.

It's alarming how much mana is like radiation when you think about it. Desmond considered idly as their shuttle arced through space. The jolt when the *Valor's Bid* had surfaced from the subspace foam had sent the entire ship rattling again, but they had all been strapped into the shuttle at the time, so it had been easier to bear. *The more disturbing fact being that I and other adepts are immune to the negative effects of the 'radiation', that is mana. We actually thrive on it.*

Desmond was broken from this line of thinking as the team communication lines crackled for a moment before Sergeant Whist's voice slipped into his helmet. The Sergeant was standing in the middle of the double row of seats, gripping overhead bars tightly to keep herself steady as she spoke to the pilot on a private line up to that point.

"Station is in rough shape. It's venting atmosphere in several places. We are going to be entering near one of those. Our assignment is to sweep and clear, then ensure the damaged section is properly sealed. Medivac is coming in hot behind us, so don't dally girls and boy."

Desmond snorted in amusement. Again, he was the only male aboard the ship and despite living like this for most of the last several months; it was still a strange feeling.

Glancing sidelong at Chloe, who was seated next to him and going over her repeater for the eighth time since the shuttle had launched, he smirked to himself.

Not an unwelcome one, given what's happened, but still.

"Touchdown coming in fifteen seconds. Landing zone

appears secure but take no chances. It appears to have atmosphere but seal suits for environmental hazards."

The order came down from the Sergeant, and the cadets all hit the buttons that caused the seals on their armor to lock magnetically while the small atmospheric scrubbers in their helmets kicked to life automatically.

"Ugh, it smells like feet," Desmond muttered on the private line to Chloe, getting a laugh from the horned woman as the shuttle touched down with a metallic noise.

"Go, go, go! Asses and elbows, ladies! Faster we offload, the faster the shuttle returns with the medical teams!" Sergeant Whist called through the team channel and they hustled to offload into what Desmond would later see as a setting in his nightmares that reminded him of hell.

CHAPTER 45

That day was one of the most horrific of my life. I've seen disasters and the remains of battlefields cluttered with far more bodies in my career. But on that day, I lost innocence. More than that, I mourned the pain of those who survived the disaster, as they have to live on with the memories of what happened and the loved ones lost.
~Desmond McLaughlin, on the
Quinto-2 Rift Nova disaster.

The hangar bay of the station itself had seen better days. Desmond had grown used to the polished metal and neat paint of the *Valor's Bid,* and even its hangars were spotless. The unnamed station they were on was clearly not maintained to the same standard.

Dark stains from retro-thrusters, spilled oil, and metal scarred from heavy items being dragged over it had all left their marks on the tattered decking. But that was only the first thing Desmond noticed as he stepped through the hatch.

Bodies lay strewn across the hangar like scattered leaves. Hunks of shredded metal, dislodged support beams, and tools were scattered about like discarded building blocks amongst the dead. Here and there, flames in several colors shot from damaged fuel lines or dripped from cracked pipes overhead. The walls were marked with stress cracks and tears, as well as several locations that looked like they had been the source of explosions.

It was only the press of bodies exiting the shuttle that kept Desmond from stopping to stare.

"Spread out and move in pairs! Guards, cover your Adepts!

Start checking for life-signs, drop a beacon if you find someone still breathing!" roared the Sergeant as she started across the stained decking. The cadet pairs spread out in a fan from the landing site and the shuttle lifted off again, backing out of the damaged hangar.

Slinging his rifle over his shoulder, Desmond hurried across the deck to the nearest body. She'd been an Aelfa of some kind, that much he could tell from the pointed ear that lay on the deck a few feet from her body, but the rest of her body was a charred mess of burned flesh fused with the metal of the decking.

"Deep breaths…" Desmond muttered as he moved past the dead woman with Chloe close behind. "Deep breaths, focus on those you can help and protect," he reminded himself, fighting the urge to throw up. He wasn't the only one as he heard gagging and a few people retching over the team comms before Sergeant Whist ordered them to 'swallow it and keep moving'.

Working quickly as he dared while keeping to sections of the decking that looked stable, Desmond checked several more groups of bodies. Most were obviously dead. But one woman, a stout Dwerg woman with severe burns on the left side of her body that had scorched her jumpsuit off in several places, was still breathing.

"Got a live one," Desmond called. He yanked one of the emergency beacons off his belt and twisted the bottom half of it to activate it. Chloe had shown him how to use them while they waited to be launched and he followed her directions on auto-pilot.

The red baton flared brightly and the end he had twisted began to blink on and off with a bright red light. Planting the opposite end into the decking, Desmond saw it flash as the other end bonded to the deck beside the downed woman. A moment later, a shimmering field burst out of the baton to encompass her. The gritted expression of pain on her face faded slightly when the anesthetic field settled over her and dulled the worst of the pain.

"Good work, McLaughlin. Keep moving," ordered the Sergeant as Desmond paused over her. His hesitation was broken a moment later as one of the other cadets shouted.

"Contact high!"

Whipping around, Desmond caught sight of something scuttling along the ceiling of the hangar bay a moment before a storm of laser fire tore into the creature and it fell squealing to the decking below with a wet *crunch* on impact and a spray of ichor.

"Eyes up! Confirmed sightings of Rift monsters. Move in teams and continue securing the hangar!" snapped the Sergeant. Her repeater was already deployed and held in her right hand, the stabilizing arm holding it steady as she pointed with her free hand to direct teams.

"Chloe, keep an eye on the sergeant as well. She's the only solo among us," Desmond ordered as they kept moving. Chloe just grunted and began checking over her shoulder on the sergeant every few steps.

Twice more, creatures were sighted and shot down before the hangar space was declared secure. He'd walked close to one when it had been downed and they had a disturbing resemblance to the face hugger from the old *Aliens* movie. He'd avoided it since.

Desmond found a total of three people still moving and set beacons next to each, relying on Chloe to keep watch over him while he checked on people. Each person he left behind made his heart ache, but he knew that the medical teams would be arriving shortly.

Secure the site, that's your job. Do your job and let them do theirs. Desmond reminded himself, but he still felt like the eyes of the dead were watching his back the entire time.

Once the hangar was secure, the Sergeant ordered two of her four two-person teams to secure the other doors while she led the remaining four towards the sector that was venting the atmosphere.

Desmond and Chloe were one of the teams left behind to guard the other exits. While the other pair simply sealed their door closed and stood around, watching the ceiling warily, Desmond and Chloe locked their door open and took positions to either side of the hall, looking down the length of the hall to where it split into a T-Junction.

The station lighting was intermittent, steady in some spots but several panels damaged and flickering all throughout the hangar and into the hallway. Desmond was thankful that there were no bodies in the hallway. The Sergeant had expressly ordered them to stay in the hangar and not proceed deeper by themselves.

"This is really what happens when a Rift goes nova?" Desmond muttered under his breath, forgetting that he had the line open to Chloe until she responded to him.

"Yeah. They are lucky to have been opposite the planet. You heard the Sergeant, the explosion shattered two of the outermost planets, I'm sure that it damaged this one too." Chloe's voice was somber as she kept her focus down the corridor ahead of them. "It's worse if it goes the other way. A Rift collapsing just devours everything within range and it all just…vanishes. At least like this, there are survivors."

Desmond considered her words. He didn't have any real reason to refute what Chloe said. Given the choice between everyone just disappearing and even a handful of folks surviving, he knew which he would prefer. The damage done by the Rift going nova though would also consume numerous resources to recover from.

But it also provides more resources, doesn't it? If what the academy ship is doing causes secondary rifts to form, it means that some of what was lost can be recovered. Not the lives, of course. The thought made Desmond's stomach twist again, and he swallowed bile.

"Movement," Chloe muttered, shifting her grip on her repeater. The Armory had declared her shield unsalvageable and had issued her a new one. Well, a 'new to her' one, at least. It was as battered as her previous shield, but without the dent and stress fractures. She had planted it in the middle of the corridor while she stood watch with her repeater snuggled into the nook of the shield. Desmond's attention snapped forward, and he squinted into the dimly lit corridor.

Straining his eyes, Desmond released the safety on his rifle and stared down the corridor, waiting.

The lighting in the corridor flickered intermittently, and it made it hard to discern movement. Pushing at it, Desmond murmured a brief enhancement to his vision and waited for another bit of movement. The shadows receded as his vision sharpened and he could see a number of additional bloodstains in the hall that he'd been able to ignore before.

A flash of something at the far end of the corridor made him jump. Something low to the ground raced across the T junction some thirty meters down the corridor.

"Saw it again," Chloe said quietly, her hand tightening on the grip of her repeater audibly.

"Same. Be ready." Desmond shifted and keyed the team channel to make a report. "I've got movement in my corridor. Something low to the ground and moving fast."

"Confirm sighting before opening fire, Cadet," Sergeant Whist's voice came back over the line. "We are nearly at the engineering consoles to seal the breach. Once it's locked down, we will be doubling back and we can begin clearing halls."

"Understood, Sergeant," Desmond responded. He spared a glance at the other two left behind as guards. He yelled a warning to them when he spotted movement coming from one vent on the ground and behind them.

The creature that wriggled out of the vent was long and low to the ground, with far too many legs and a sinuous, muscled body. Like someone had grafted a millipede's legs onto a boa constrictor or something. Black scales that reflected the light covered its entire body and each of the legs ended in a needle-sharp looking claw that scored the decking as it crawled free. A wide mouth full of sharp teeth scissored open, and it lunged forward towards the nearest of the other cadets. Unfortunately, they were between him and it, and Desmond didn't feel confident he could make the shot.

Thankfully, his warning came in time. The cadet-guard, a Dwerg woman armed with one of the stubby auto-shotguns, whirled in place and opened fire on it, shredding the creature with a single volley.

"Contact! Watch the vents!" Desmond immediately called into the radio as two more shoved their companions' body out of the way and pushed clear of the vent. At the same time, a furious scratching started from the sealed door behind the two cadets.

"Hold tight, we are sealing and will be doubling back soon," the Sergeant radioed back. As she finished speaking, Desmond heard the distant echo of shots being fired deeper in the station. "Keep the bay secure. Medical is minutes out."

Desmond didn't respond as the two other cadets opened fire on the creatures in rapid order, the auto-shotgun shredding a second one before running out of ammo, the adept handling the other by pinning it to the deck with a *Bolt* spell shaped like a trident made of obsidian.

"Des!" Chloe's voice was sharp, drawing his attention back to their assigned corridor.

Desmond spun in place, rifle coming up to the ready as he searched for whatever it was that gave Chloe's voice that tinge of concern.

"What?" he demanded when he spotted nothing in the hallway.

"Listen, do you hear that?" Chloe hissed at him. Desmond tried to shut out the boom of the other team's weapons as they pushed the creatures back into the vent and clogged it with the corpses of the ones that had tried to make it through. He could hear the scrabbling of claws on metal, though the longer he focused, the more he was sure he could hear it from multiple directions now. One behind him, at the door the other team was covering, and one coming from ahead of them, but echoing oddly.

"Be ready," Desmond murmured, taking a knee to steady his aim while Chloe shifted her head and popped her neck with a dull crackling noise.

The distant sound of scrabbling grew louder, but as the gunfire behind him quieted, he could hear the rhythmic thud of something much larger approaching.

"Steady..." Desmond murmured to Chloe, who didn't respond, still intently focused on the end of the hallway.

A sudden flicker of movement ahead made Desmond twitch and nearly open fire down the hall as something large and misshapen skidded into view. Only a chance flash of light that revealed a determined face streaked with blood stopped him. What appeared to be a resident of the station skidded into view, but there was something wrong with her. She had one arm tucked behind her back while the other held a chunky pistol low at her side.

The rough light made it hard to make out the person or their condition at first, but the enhancement that Desmond had previously worked into his eyes finally let him cut through the gloom. She looked young, maybe only a year younger than him, and was skinny despite her size. She was a dark green in color with a shaggy mane of blue-black striped hair and he made the connection that it was an odd looking Hyreh that was charging towards them with all the speed her sturdy frame could put out.

"Shit!" Chloe barked, shifting to start forward before stopping herself. "She's got kids on her back!" Desmond's gaze snapped to the small shapes that clung to the woman's shoulders and he could make out a trio of small lumps and at least one pair of fearful eyes looking back at him. The arm behind her back was supporting a small group of children while she carried them like a backpack.

"Friendlies! Come this way!" Desmond shouted, slapping the button to broadcast outside his helmet. The woman struggled and finally managed to catch traction after her turn and start forward just before the skittering tide of creatures rounded the corner behind her, spilling like some sort of sick tide that nearly engulfed her in a writhing maelstrom of snapping teeth and sharp legs.

Time seemed to slow for Desmond while the sinuous creatures reared up almost in unison, like a chitinous wave, and the woman struggled to get back up to speed. Desmond's heart pounded once in his ears as he saw the hope go out of her eyes when she realized she wouldn't make it to them.

No.

The word resounded in his mind like a hammer striking an anvil and Desmond felt his mind cast wide, memory racing for something, anything, he could do to help.

Boom. His heart resounded a second time. The creatures lunged, snapping, at the woman's back. He saw one child on her back begin to slip and fall, the little face twisted in fear.

The second stretched out and Desmond felt a surge from deep within his gut. His mana welled up and out of his skin in a shock-wave in response to a particular memory that rose from the depths, the instructor talking about aggressive enhancements used on an enemy and how it was hard to plan for their reactions to it.

Unless you enhance something that they can't plan for. He thought suddenly as his memories crashed into something, eyes focusing on the children on the woman's back.

"May a millstone hang about your neck for threatening these little ones," Desmond called out. He snatched a fistful of mana and scattered it into the air. But the mana was already moving, borne on his intent the second the idea hit him. The words he spoke gave that soundless, sightless wave of intent a grim purpose.

A wash of pressure followed the ripple that lashed out from Desmond with enough force. It sent him reeling backwards even on his knee as something massive and glittering surged down the hallway, a single ringing note rising like the chime of a silver bell.

The surging wave of skittering horrors promptly plowed face first into the ground as the ripple of energy crashed over them. Like a wave striking a wall, the tide of scaled monsters slid to a stop just short of her rear foot, struggling to stand as their bodyweight skyrocketed and slammed them into the decking. Desmond had vastly enhanced the density, and therefore weight, of their thousands of needle-like legs. The pointed claws that their legs ended in punching right through the armored deck, leaving the ones on the bottom trapped, while the ones on top crushed their fellows.

"Move it!" Desmond called down the hallway as the panting woman nearly tripped when the tide didn't get her. Shaking off her surprise, the woman squared her shoulders with a feral snarl that revealed her sharp, Hyreh teeth. One arm went back to steady her burden of young ones just before the last one tumbled out of place.

The expenditure of keeping that many enhancements was draining his cache of mana rapidly, but the effect was wreaking havoc on the serpentine creatures, single-handedly keeping them back as the woman scrambled down the hall and past him. Desmond saw the flicker of something trailing behind her as she ran, but as it wasn't one of the monsters, he disregarded it while he focused.

The second the woman was clear, Chloe opened fire. She blasted in full auto into the struggling wave of enemies. Chloe had spent enough time with Desmond over the last weeks to guess how much it was costing him to maintain effects on that many targets, and she knew she needed to clear them as rapidly as possible.

"Call it off, Des," Chloe barked at him, sparing a glance at the Hyreh woman who had slid to a halt behind them, panting in exhaustion, the trio of children crying in a pile from where they had fallen off her back. *Bloody, but not grievously wounded. And she still has her gun in hand, smart girl.* She noted before turning her attention back to the fight at hand.

"Disengaging," Desmond gritted as he pulled on the threads of mana that spiraled out of him and ripped the enhancement free. His head spun, and he slumped to his knees a moment later. The massed enhancement had sapped most of his remaining mana supply and he didn't need to check his comm-cuff to know that he was running dangerously low at this point.

The monsters reacted immediately as the crushing weight of the spell lifted. Those that had struggled to stand were launched into the air to land back on top of their fellows. Fights broke out as the monsters that had been injured by their fellows lashed back out at them and the squiggling mass devolved into a writhing ball of violence.

"Shatter and void it," Chloe cursed, scooting over slightly to place herself over top of Desmond while he fought to get his head to stop spinning. "Girl, you know how to shoot or are you just waving that thing around as a toy?" Chloe shouted at the young woman where she lay behind them.

"Whazzat?"

"Can you shoot, damn it?!"

Swallowing hard, the Hyreh rolled to her feet with a determined look and shook herself, sending her messy hair flapping before she nodded. Sweat poured down her surprisingly delicate face, and she still panted like a bellows. But it was obvious she wasn't done yet.

"Grab his rifle and start taking shots. He broke their charge, but we have to keep them back." Chloe nudged Desmond's rifle where it had fallen across his chest. A moment later, Desmond's vision was filled by the Hyreh women's fierce face as she bent over him to tug his rifle free.

Desmond was sure that he had to be seeing things, because a pair of erect cat ears looked like they were poking out of the top of her blue and black striped hair. Which wasn't surprising to him as the world continued to spin around him.

"You okay, mister?" she murmured to him, peering intently through his helmet faceplate at him. Desmond gasped again and gave her a shaky thumbs up and a smile. She blushed, surprisingly, before returning the smile with a cute one of her own, despite the dried blood on her face and the sharp teeth of the Hyreh in her mouth. One of the triangular cat-ears on her head flicked as she watched him for a beat longer before she shifted and took a position on Chloe's right with the rifle held steady in her right hand while the left kept her pistol. Despite not being able to steady the carbine properly, she still opened fire with good accuracy alongside the big Taari woman.

The next minute or two, Desmond fought to keep his head from spinning off his neck. His dynamo twirled angrily while it fought to stabilize him some, but the rapid shift in pressure was making it hard to breathe. After he could get his head to slow its whirling, he remembered the two mana-gas inhalers he'd been issued. Fumbling one from his belt, Desmond cracked his faceplate and bit down on the mouthpiece.

As soon as his mouth closed on it, the whole thing fired off and Desmond felt the refined mana gas hit his lungs like the first breath on a snowy morning. The spinning in his head cleared abruptly, and he was able to focus once more. Spitting out the inhaler, he snapped his helmet shut and rolled over onto his stomach, tugging his sidearm out of the holster on his leg to take aim past the side of Chloe's shield.

Between the three of them, they were able to push back the wriggling tide of creatures and disperse them long enough for the sergeant and the others to return. The Sergeant took one look at what was happening and immediately ordered her team of four to split up to assist. The Hyreh woman they had saved eyed everyone warily as the cadets moved around her, but relaxed slightly when Desmond thanked her for backing them up. Behind her, the trio of little ones kept close to her, huddling in a group in her shadow while she stood watch.

The creatures broke just as the shuttle returned with medical teams to evacuate the injured. The Hyreh woman, whom he learned was named Sasha, returned Desmond's rifle once they were sure they were safe. The three small children descended on 'sis-Sasha' as soon as she stepped back from the firing-line, which was how Desmond learned her name.

"Thank you for saving us. I didn't expect to run into an adept..." Sasha's voice trembled slightly as she spoke and her stoic expression cracked for just a moment, but her eyes shone with thankfulness as she fussed over the little ones. A member of the medical team was headed their way, so Desmond just nodded to her with a smile.

"Happy to help. I couldn't let those things get you all. Right, Chloe?" Desmond pushed some of the embarrassment from the thanks onto his partner, who snorted and shook her head.

"Of course you couldn't, Des. I'm glad you and the little ones are safe, miss," Chloe said the last bit directly to Sasha before tilting her head and taking in the woman's clothing at a glance. Sasha was dressed in a rather ragged looking long blouse and pants combo. And Desmond was happy to confirm that he hadn't been seeing things earlier. A pair of blue and black striped cats' ears were nestled in her similarly colored hair.

What is going on? I know that Hyreh don't have that...maybe another crossbreed like Chloe? Maybe a few more generations back?

Rather than stare at her ears, Desmond checked her over for injuries rapidly and was surprised to notice a distinct seam around her right biceps and then a series of lines and traceries that ran down her forearm. Most of her right arm appeared to have been replaced with a prosthetic of some kind that whined quietly as she moved it, but it reacted smoothly with each shift of her body. Pushing that away as well, there were too many oddities about the woman to keep from staring somewhat. He checked the rest of Sasha over for injuries. The woman was *painfully* skinny looking and, between her matted hair and the tattered clothing, had clearly seen better days. The clothes looked like they'd been well maintained recently but had been hard worn.

"Are you going to be okay? Do you have any family on board?" Chloe asked after a moment of looking over the woman.

Sasha's face fell slightly, but she straightened her shoulders and took a deep breath.

"No, no family. I just worked odd jobs around the station and pick up bounty work on occasion nowadays. The little ones are orphans I helped look after on the weekends. We'll get by," she said gamely, her shoulders straight.

Desmond glanced at Chloe questioningly but she didn't return the glance, just looking the girl over again for a long moment before she glanced at Desmond.

"Des, can you give me a minute?"

"Sure, Chloe. I'll go check in with the Sergeant."

Heading over to where Whist stood in the middle of the shuttle bay, Desmond did his best to not think about the dead that surrounded them from the accident. *At least none of the cadets were hurt, right?* He glanced around, but no one appeared injured, though a few of the girls that had gone with Whist had fresh scratches on their armor.

"Damn shame," muttered the Sergeant as he approached.

"About?"

"What happened here," she gestured to the dead surrounding them, "wish that we'd been able to save 'em. But there is nothing we can do. We save those few we can, I suppose." The quadrupedal woman sighed slightly before turning her intent gaze onto Desmond and squinting slightly. "How are you feeling, McLaughlin? You look pale."

"Wrung out, Sergeant. Drew pretty hard to, uh, keep that wave of critters back. Had to use one of the mana-inhalers I was issued for emergencies." The Sergeant's frown deepened.

"Those were supposed to be for emergencies if you needed to enhance regeneration. Like you did for Vandenberg on your last run." The accusation was as thick as the implied question in her tone, and Desmond sighed.

"Overdid it with an enhancement to stem the tide. Pretty sure if I hadn't, they'd have overwhelmed us before you got back. I hadn't used any healing yet. Anyone hurt? The inhaler topped me up enough that I should be safe if it's needed."

"No, we got lucky. The critters never even got close to us other than a few small ambushes. I think most of them were here, trying to get into the hangar or chasing something." The Sergeant's eyes darted to the young woman talking quietly to Chloe on the other side of the hangar. "Or someone. Your friend there, okay? The new one, I mean. I can tell Vandenberg is fine."

"She's bloody, but doesn't look seriously injured. I think she hit her head or something running from those critters." Desmond glanced back at Sasha, meeting her eyes before the woman looked away quickly, blushing.

Uh, what are they talking about? If it was Monika talking to her, I'd be worried, but I doubt Chloe'd do or say anything.

"She did good at evading those creatures for so long, and helping the littles. Given how many creatures there are, I don't have high hopes for many survivors being in the rest of the station, but we'll sweep and clear now that we have the beachhead secured."

"Say the word, Sergeant. Chloe and I are ready to move out when you are." Desmond gave her a quick salute, which she snorted derisively at.

"Knock that shit off in the field, McLaughlin. It's unnecessary for me at least. Help the engineers set up the auto-turrets to cover the doors and any vents you saw the creatures sneaking out of. Once that is set and the medics piss off with the first survivors, we'll march." She gestured to a collection of heavy crates that two regulars were prying open at the moment to reveal oblong metal shapes.

"Sure thing. Why didn't we set these up before you and the others split off?" Desmond asked just before he headed out and got a long-winded sigh from the sergeant.

"Command didn't think they were needed. When we radioed back the contacts, they rushed them to the shuttles to send along with the medics. Someone tried to pinch pennies on this and risked all our lives."

"Sounds like politicians back home." Desmond shot back before turning to help the engineers set them up.

"Politician's everywhere, McLaughlin."

CHAPTER 46

Do you know the feeling? No, of course you don't. You live in a pleasant apartment and have a cushy job where you ask people for info bites to satisfy the talking heads. You wouldn't have an idea of what it's like to be so tired that your teeth hurt and your body feels both burning up and cold at the same time. Your biggest 'sacrifice' to those in need is waiting to photograph the corpses of the fallen until after their faces are covered.
~unknown cadet, to an interviewing reporter for the Star Press, interviewed moments after returning from disaster relief for the Quinto-2 Rift Nova disaster.

Compared to the hectic first few minutes aboard the damaged station, the following nine hours that the cadets spent clearing and securing it while searching for survivors were rather bland. The Rift-monsters had apparently spent the majority of their numbers in that initial push on the landing pad and only occasionally struck from the vents or in attacks of surprise to try to ambush the cadets. With the landing bays secure, Sergeant Whist had them moving in groups of four and going through the station like it was one of the Rifts, marking passages as checked and the like.

They also received further reinforcements as time went by and they met up with other teams that had been inserted through different hangars throughout the damaged station.

The cross-canvassing of the station did turn up far more survivors than expected, with large numbers of people having barricaded themselves in secure rooms as soon as the alerts had gone out. There were still plenty of bodies found, but not as many as Desmond had feared.

Sasha and her three little friends had been evacuated with the other survivors once the injured were stabilized. She'd thanked Desmond and Chloe again. A mixture of sadness and determination showed in her eyes if not on her stoic face. Chloe had given her a brief hug and instructed her to contact them soon. Desmond watched as she loaded aboard the shuttle, urging the little ones ahead of her with the ease of long practice.

"Think she'll be okay?" he asked Chloe as they had formed up to delve deeper into the station.

"Yeah, she's a tough girl. I have faith in her," Chloe replied immediately, with a level of confidence that surprised Desmond.

The end of their rescue efforts came more because of the continued deterioration of the station than completing it. An 'all-call' to return and evacuate went across their systems and the teams retreated rapidly through damaged halls to evacuate.

While on the shuttle out, the Sergeant had advised them that more specialized rescue teams would be going in to fully assess the damage, but what they had done would make things that much easier for the specialists.

"You lot aren't trained for this yet. All they've gone over is combat and magic for you lot. But no one can anticipate these things, and the gods just laugh when they try," Sergeant Whist had explained to the somber team of cadets on the shuttle ride back to the *Valor's Bid*. "You eight have earned your rest. They'll expect a rapid report from me, but I'm dismissing you to your rooms to sleep when we get back to the station."

The exhaustion hadn't hit Desmond until he was seated and the tension was allowed to drain from his body. While he'd had separate spikes of adrenaline throughout the entire process, the extended rescue efforts and intermittent combat had worn on him in a way he wasn't quite ready for. Checking the heads-up display on the helmet he hadn't bothered to remove yet, Desmond sighed gustily.

"What is it, Cadet-Adept McLaughlin?" Apparently, his external speakers were still on.

"Just the time, Sergeant. Morning classes start in three hours." Desmond ended up punching himself in the faceplate of the helmet, though only lightly, as he tried to reach up and rub at his eyes while having already forgotten he was wearing the helmet. Again.

"And?"

"With that little sleep, I personally would rather just stay up. Would just feel like foreplay without the satisfaction." Carefully popping the seals on his helmet, Desmond pulled it off and shook his sweaty hair out.

"Be that as it may, McLaughlin," The Sergeant replied with a wry smirk. "You should learn to take advantage of any sleep you can get. I can only imagine that your instructor will take into account the emergency rescue efforts in your training."

"Yeah. But will they take it easier or make it harder, claiming that 'training while tired is key to the future?'" Desmond groaned.

The Sergeant only chuffed out a laugh.

<><><>

It turned out that mercy was not just for the weak. Throneblood did take into account the fact that every single one of them had been drafted for the emergency response. The *Valor's Bid* had already left the system by the time classes had started, the massive academy ship was unable to linger for long in any system, and the additional instability caused by the massive amount of raw mana flooding the system only shortened that clock.

The instructor had praised them all for their solid work and the lives they'd saved in various positions. Desmond learned that groups of first years had been dispatched to secure surviving installations on the planet, as well as portions of the space station, while the upperclassmen had been sent into more dangerous locations, such as the wreckage of ships in system as well as amongst the debris field of the two shattered planets.

Rather than drill them on the obstacle course or track, Throneblood instead ordered the entire group of still-exhausted cadets to report to the classroom and 'get friendly' with each other to ensure everyone had seats. Desmond hadn't even complained when he ended up on Chloe's lap because of his smaller comparative size to the larger woman. It just felt good to relax against her while Chloe's right hand rubbed at his aching chest.

The pains hadn't struck until Desmond had woken from the brief 'nap' they'd been allowed on returning to the *Valor's Bid*. He'd taken the time to shower but not bothered to do more than chuck his armor at the stand before passing out with Chloe next to him the night before, and his body was complaining about the expenditure of mana to him. While he had only used the mass weight enhancement once, and husbanded his resources afterward, the drain to his cache in one moment had strained his body and his dynamo. As a result, his ribcage ached like he'd just taken several body-shots there from a boxer on par with Chloe in mass and strength.

For the altered morning class, Throneblood instead lectured them again on what happens when Rifts reach critical concentrations and have a breakdown reaction. Desmond noted idly that the instructor looked untouched by the night's exertions, though he had been told by Monika at breakfast that Throneblood had been deployed to the debris field of one of the two shattered planets with a dozen second years, so she had worked just as hard, if not harder, than them.

Throneblood had even shown them a time-lapsed hologram of what was projected to be the events leading up to the Rift collapse and what it had done to the system.

The hologram started out displaying the star system above their heads. The sun was a standard class-G star that reminded Desmond of Sol back home. Orbiting it were seven planets, with three gas giants taking up the middle three of the planets with their customary clouds of satellites, though all three of the gas giants had rings at varying angles from each other.

After a few moments, the hologram scaled outward and the entire system faded above their heads until it was roughly the size of a coin and a dark circle popped into being an enormous distance away.

"The Rift that caused the explosion formed out in the void between stars. We believe that it actually formed on an interstellar visitor, like a comet or a large meteor, that was passing through. The fact that it managed to slip the sensor nets for so long is surprising, but the Hegemony is a vast place." Throneblood zoomed the projection in and they were shown an oblong blur that had a question mark on it. "What we do know is that the sensor net in-system did not catch the specifics. The Rift formed far enough out into the void and off the regular mana-wake lanes that it caught them entirely by surprise."

The shape slowly resolved into a burning dot of light that swelled, then contracted, then swelled again before contracting a second time. This cycle repeated with each swelling, doubling the dot in size until, like a soap bubble getting too much air, it popped. A ripple of light in a rapidly shifting amalgamation of colors spread outward in all directions.

"The system was lucky in that it was over half a light-year away from where the Rift went nova. That distance allowed the shock-wave of mana to settle somewhat as it spread out. That wasn't enough to save the outermost planets, though."

In midair, the image zoomed back over to the system and they watched as the ripple entered the system and struck the outermost satellite in the system. The wave of mana, like an expanding bubble or a supernova on acid, slammed into the planet and engulfed it. The small orb made a brief dent in the shimmering bubble at first before it gave out and scattered like a pumpkin hit with a shotgun blast. While they watched, the second planet fared only slightly better as it was further along its orbital but still on the side of the system, nearer to the blast and scattered as well. The innermost planet was actually knocked off of its orbit and tossed directly into the sun, which swallowed it without a flinch, though a blazing corona of sun-spots flared out the far side of the sun when the mana wave hit it. The second planet, with its accompanying station that Desmond and Chloe had gone to, was partially shielded by the sun itself, but the sun-side of the planet was also licked by that trailing corona of fire. The shock-wave went on to catch the three gas giants and send them wobbling in their orbits, blasting their rings to ribbons.

It took only a handful of seconds for the video to finish playing out. The rippling wave of mana vanished off to the far side of the projection, and then the entire hologram shut off.

Silence reigned in the classroom. While they all understood, at a book level of knowledge, what sort of threats the Rifts posed to populated space, this threw it into far higher relief for them.

"Instructor?" It was one of the cadet-guards who broke the silence finally, a Va'Aelfa woman who was sitting next to her cadet-adept against the wall, the light of the room sparkled off her dusky blue-purple skin and the tiny, mica-like dots that highlighted it. When Throneblood nodded to her, giving permission to continue, the woman did. "Rifts can go both directions. What would have happened if it imploded?"

"A fair question, and the answer is as simple as it is terrifying," Throneblood stated. She adjusted the controls with her data-tablet for a moment before the hologram returned and this time, rather than the dot expanding, it flickered and seemed to invert before everything simply vanished again. "The hologram doesn't do it justice, as there isn't anything visual to track. The explosion took roughly fourteen seconds to cross the distance between the point of origin to the system. Yes, it is capable of moving faster than light. Mana breaks rules all the time after all. It was slow enough for the subspace sensor net to give warning, but comparing it to a supernova is inaccurate. The mana that traveled moved outside the visible spectrum. The coloration in the model was purely to illustrate it. Inversion, or collapse, is actually even faster." Throneblood paused for a moment before shrugging. "If the detonation of the Rift was like burning a piece of paper with a flamethrower; the collapse of a Rift is more like blasting it with a laser cannon. Everything just vanishes."

"What happens to them?" another cadet asked. Desmond couldn't tell who.

Throneblood just shrugged at them, her face neutral.

"No one has ascertained exactly what happens other than the space and all mana concentrated near a Rift that implodes simply ceases to be. It violates scientific laws on several levels, but that is something we are somewhat used to mana doing. And experimenting on Rifts in this manner is illegal as the threat combined with the unpredictability was deemed not worth the risk. Which is why the Hegemony raises up people like all of you. To pacify the Rifts, to protect the rest of the universe. Otherwise, the entire galaxy would be consumed piecemeal as mana slowly siphons away while burning holes in it. Inversions can strip mana away, or consume all matter in the local space."

Desmond was left thinking about what the Instructor had said. The lack of mana in a given area after an implosion and how it could affect the balance of everything.

I wonder, is that why Terra is so barren of mana? How many of these Rift collapses happened that Earth still sails through the void entirely clear of mana and is just now getting back close to an area with any mana at all?

Class continued as a general lecture and Throneblood gave them the afternoon off from range practice, but still exhorted them to get at least an hour of private practice in. She also advised them that they would be getting leave for the next two days to recover after the search and rescue operation, but to not slack off either as they would be diving into their training in the coming months to prepare them for the mid-terms that were coming up.

Chloe and Desmond had gone straight to the range to put in an hour of time as requested, skipping lunch entirely, before they both collapsed into bed and slept until late the next day, taking full advantage of the day off.

CHAPTER 47

She was the best investment I ever made.
~Desmond McLaughlin, regarding his first guard.

"Surprised Monika wasn't pounding on our door again." Desmond muttered as he dressed.

"I would hope that she is learning, but I somehow doubt that." Chloe replied as she dug through the low dresser nearby for clothes as well. She was ignoring the effect she was having on Desmond. Given she wasn't even wearing a towel after the shower and the lights of the room shone off of the bright silver hoops dangling from her pierced nipples. The sparkling of the light off those tiny dangling hoops kept drawing his attention back to the curves of her breasts and from there his eyes would trace over the curve of her hips and her full bottom.

Turning his back on the temptation, they'd already fooled around once on waking up and again in the shower. Desmond cleared his throat.

"I agree, more likely she was just as tired as we were and passed out. Either that or Oril'la has her pinned currently and she can't wiggle free." Desmond smoothed his uniform shirt down and ducked into the bathroom so he could get a look at himself in the mirror. "Huh."

"What is it, Des?" Chloe poked her head through the doorway to the bathroom, working on buttoning her shirt closed over her generous chest. The sleep had done wonders for them both and she looked fit and ready for the day.

"Just occurred to me. I've been here for months and haven't ever really...worn anything besides my uniform or the armor." Desmond glanced back over the mottled black and gray uniform and turned in place.

"Looks good on you regardless, Des." Chloe paused in working her buttons to appreciate how the pants fit him without a single bit of shame.

"Could say the same about you. Just feels odd to me, though. I used to hate wearing uniforms of any kind for work. I was always quick to change out of them after work. Never spent time in the military before either, but this outfit just feels…comfortable." He shrugged before slipping past Chloe, pressing a kiss to the back of her hand as he did so because he didn't want to slow down her dressing.

"Ah! No. Come back here, Des," Chloe protested as he grabbed his sidearm off the hook and belted it on. The horned woman slid up to him as he was adjusting the holster to hang in its spot on his thigh and bent to claim a proper kiss, her hands still working the buttons on the long shirt. "That's better…" she murmured as the kiss completed. "Don't tease me like that."

"Don't tease me like this then, precious Chloe." Desmond smacked her lightly on the rump as he slid past her again. Using his pet name for her made her moan slightly, only to yelp in surprise at the sudden smack that did more to make a noise than actually make her taut bottom jiggle. *Buns of steel.* Desmond thought with a grin. She shot him a mock-glare, but he pointedly ignored it, heading into the main suite of rooms. "SAUL, any new messages?"

"Several notifications from the general system, Desmond. And one from the Quartermasters for both of you," the virtual liaison said in his usual, upbeat voice.

"What are the general notifications? Much as I want to confirm that the message from the Quartermaster is the payout notice for the Rift goods, might as well check them first." Desmond heard a quiet 'thump' and the click of the magnetic catches as Chloe hurried to finish dressing.

"The first is a notification of leave for the next two days.

As you are already aware, no doubt. The second is a notice of payment for 'extra-duty' in relation to the search and rescue mission. You both received four weeks of pay in a bonus as a reward, and have had commendations added to your files for 'Courage in the line of overwhelming odds', as stated in the message."

"Oh, that'll be nice. Two commendations already?" Chloe said as she emerged from their shared room, tucking her shirt into her uniform pants.

"You deserve more, and I'm sure you will earn more." Desmond nudged her gently with his hip as she settled into her familiar place at his side, before he addressed SAUL to learn what he was sure both of them wanted to know.

"Okay, and what did the Quartermasters have to say?"

"The pay for your most recent Rift suppression has been deposited into your accounts. There is an added note that has no signature simply stating 'Don't spend it all in one place.'" Desmond snorted a laugh at that.

"Idioms seem to cross space and time, don't they?" he muttered before turning to look over his shoulder at Chloe. "What do you think, Chloe? Should we go hit the retail zones? Maybe pick up an early lunch there and do some shopping? After sleeping that long, I feel like I need to move some."

"Sure, did you want to go shopping for some casual clothes? You mentioned the issues with your uniform a second ago." Chloe tilted her head to the side inquisitively, her expression soft as she watched him.

"Ehh… I don't want to waste money we could use on gear."

"It's not a waste. Besides, you still don't know how much you have to work with. SAUL, did the Quartermaster give a final total of the goods?" she addressed the second half to the ceiling, a habit she had picked up from Desmond.

"The final total was one hundred and twenty thousand, three hundred and forty Hegemony Interstellar Credits."

Desmond had been in the middle of crossing the room when SAUL announced the number and had tripped over his own feet. Chloe was quick to catch him from her normal position on his flank, righting the smaller man with one hand even as she blinked in surprise at the number.

"Seriously? Split four ways, that's a solid number for sure." Desmond rolled the number around in his head before shrugging slightly and continuing on his path to the door with Chloe right behind him.

"That is the total that was added to Cadet-Guard Vandenberg's account as an equal share of the proceeds."

This time, both of them tripped, and it was only luck and the proximity of the kitchen space that prevented them from ending up on the floor. Chloe caught herself against the counter with one hand while Desmond used one of the stools to prevent a rapid meeting with the floor.

"SAUL…please confirm that what you stated was accurate?" Desmond stuttered in surprise, turning his wide eyed look to Chloe, who looked equally stunned.

"Confirming, you have both received one hundred and twenty thousand, three hundred and forty HICs added to your account. In addition, you both have received a further deposit of four weeks of your pay on top of that."

"Four weeks of pay is a drop in the bucket," Desmond muttered before turning to grin at Chloe. "Definitely have the cash to spare now."

He was surprised to see the look of surprised excitement fade away from Chloe's expression and she turned serious a moment later, biting her lip as she thought intently.

"Chloe?" The one word broke through her serious expression, and she shook herself, turning her gaze back to him.

"Des?"

"Where did you go there? You went distant. Everything okay?" A complex series of emotions crossed Chloe's face one after the other before it finally settled on resignation and she sighed, her eyes falling to the ground.

"Des, you know I have a debt, right?"

"Yeah. It was in your file. We talked about this back when I bid to have you join my team and since then too, Chloe. What is it? Do you need to borrow some money?" Desmond asked gently, turning in place to look up at the larger woman. Chloe's eyes snapped to his, and she stared down at him intently for several moments in stunned surprise before she was able to find her voice.

"What? N...no it's not like that, Desmond. I swear, I'm not...I'd never ask you for..." she stuttered, panic in her voice.

"Deep breaths, Precious," Desmond interrupted the big woman, taking her by the hips and pulling her against him. A brief wish that their sizes were reversed crossed his mind, it was hard to reassuringly cuddle someone so much larger than you, but Desmond pushed it away and did his best with what he could do for now.

Chloe did as he directed, taking a deep breath before letting it out again.

"What is on your mind?" Desmond asked once she had calmed down.

"Des, the debt I have is medical. It's...for my little brother," Chloe explained slowly. Desmond was silent, just waiting and listening to her. "He was hurt in an accident a few years ago. It nearly killed him, but we were able to get him the regeneration therapy to get him back on his feet. The problem is, it basically ruined my family financially."

"And?" Desmond prompted. He wanted to know why this was her problem, but also didn't want to press her. Money troubles were something that had ruined relationships for his friends in the past, so he wanted to only have her say what she wanted to. Apparently, some of it still showed on his face, though.

"I know what you are thinking, Des. 'How is this my problem?' right?" Chloe said quietly, still matching his gaze.

"Actually, I was wondering how you ended up with the debt and not your parents," Desmond replied, squeezing her hips gently where he had hold of her. "Back on my world, it wasn't uncommon to have a load of medical debt, but in a situation like this? It shouldn't land on you unless your parents were…?" He let the question trail off and Chloe shook her head, a small smile on her lips.

"No, my parents are still around. They are taking care of Micah still, but my dad can't really work normally. He and mom were living on their military pension and the medical debt would have destroyed it."

Slowly, Chloe began to relate the whole situation to him. Her brother had been caught up in a mass shooting event in the city that they'd grown up in. His middle school class had been caught in the crossfire of a terrorist attack that had killed several kids and a lot of innocent bystanders while they were on a career-style field trip to the metalworks of the city. Apparently, the terrorists thought that the field trip was the ideal window where security would be lightened, and decided to use it to strike at the foundries. The boy had literally had one of his legs blown off of his body and his right arm was lost at the elbow. Her family had sunk deep into debt to pay for the medical costs of having the limbs regenerated. The family insurance apparently didn't cover acts of terrorism, so they'd been left to shoulder the debt themselves, but no one had bothered to tell the family about it until after Micah's treatment had started. The company that owned the metalworks had sent them part of a onetime settlement they'd received from the government, as an apology for her brother being injured on their premises, but it hadn't really even put a dent in their costs.

"And so, I took out a loan to pay down some of the medical debts for them. I figured that I'd sign up for a minimum term of service with the military and use the option of debt forgiveness they offer to pay the loan off by the time I was out. That would bring the debt down enough that my parents could handle the rest. I ended up having to take it from a somewhat sketchy source, but all the paperwork was through an official bank. It was sort of like a personal loan.

Another reason why I signed up for service to get the debt annulled," Chloe finished with a sigh. They'd moved to the conversation pit at some point during the whole thing, and Desmond was kneading her hand gently while they leaned into each other.

"Okay, that all makes sense. Folk used to do something similar back home, but you had to serve your term first and then the country would pay for a college degree." Desmond had a few friends that had gone into the service for the GI bill after all. "But that was for a regular term, right? What does becoming an adept-guard do to it?"

"Well, it basically cancels the whole debt out. The regular term was ten years of service with a fixed garnishment of wages. Anything left after the ten years is paid off by the Hegemony. Debt-soldiers aren't rare. But for most folks, it's... well, usually their own debts, not someone else's." Chloe sighed, watching as Desmond worked at her left hand. It had become something of an idle habit of his to massage the arm that had been injured before, checking to see if there were any signs of the injury remaining.

"So yeah. Applying and being selected for an adept-guard bumped me off the normal track. I don't get the automatic forgiveness at the end because it's expected that I should be able to pay it off unless it is a truly ridiculous sum. And if I owed that much, it would have excluded me from service to begin with. The issue is that the garnishment isn't just off my regular wages..." Chloe sighed again.

Desmond's jaw clenched, and he took a deep breath to steady himself.

"How much?" Desmond fought to keep his tone even. He hadn't wanted to ask, but he had made a decision and needed to get more information before he made his choice.

"The garnishment? Or the total?"

"Both."

"The garnishment is sixty percent of earnings. Since gear, room, and board is covered at least in basic by the Academy and by the military during deployment, the rest is collected to offset the debt. I either can process the transfer manually, or they do a calculation based on what has come into my account every month and pull that. I was warned to be really careful not to overdraw and make sure to leave enough if I didn't arrange the payments myself. The total for the debt is a little over two hundred thousand credits," Chloe said with a sigh. "Which isn't that bad, honestly. A few more Rift's like the one we did before. I should have it cleared by mid-to-end of next year. It just makes it harder to get my gear up to snuff, is all. But the Academy replaced my shield, so I'm good to go."

Desmond could hear the forced cheer in her voice and it only hardened his resolve. It grated on him that today, which should have been a day of celebration for them given the massive payout, was instead causing heartache for Chloe to this degree. He'd had his own debts for college, but that'd been his own thing. This money had been to help her little brother recover from what should have been a life ending injury.

It doesn't have to be like this. It hamstrings her a bit, but I can still kit her out with my cut, he thought for a moment, considering his options. *But I also know it has to grate on her to have that debt hanging over her head. It's like looking at your first paycheck after the government takes their taxes, just rips at the heart.*

The resolution wasn't even that hard to decide for him. Desmond released Chloe's hand to access his account via the comm-cuff on his hand. A handful of clicks queued up what he wanted. Chloe's murmured excuses trailed off, and she turned to look at him as he dropped his arm back to his side and let out a long breath before picking her left hand up again.

"What did you just do, Des?" Chloe asked quietly, her resigned expression fading away to be replaced by an intense one.

"Made a donation," Desmond said simply. He did not look

up at her as he began digging his thumb into the meat of her palm, eliciting a gentle *pop* from the tendons as he got a knot to release that she hadn't even realized was there.

"What do you..." Chloe's face paled a moment later as she made the connection to what he'd said. "You didn't! Desmond!"

"I did," was all Desmond said in response. "SAUL, dictate the last transaction I made through my shipboard accounts?"

Chloe was silent as the artificial liaison spoke aloud a moment later.

"Your last transaction was a funds transfer to Cadet-Guard Vandenberg totaling one hundred and twenty-five thousand Hegemony Interstellar Credits. The funds transfer is complete and they are available to the recipient. Note attached to transaction: 'What's mine is yours. For your brother.'"

Silence descended on the room that made Desmond feel slightly nervous at first. Chloe didn't speak. Instead, she lifted her arm out of Desmond's reach before she wrapped it tightly around him, pulling him close to her side as she began to cry.

CHAPTER 48

We do our best. There are always people who will try to find a way around the law, thinking that it doesn't apply to them. We catch them when we can, punish them when we catch them. We can only be in so many places at once, though. We do our best, but be careful out there.
~Sergeant Ral'toros, addressing *Valor's Bid* security before a shift.

"I told you, Chloe, we don't have to do this," Desmond protested, not for the first time.

"And I told you before, Des, that I was going to at least spend *some* of my money on getting you something. You literally just crushed my debts and left me with several thousand credits to spend. I want to spend them on you," Chloe shot back airily as they walked through the retail zone.

Once Chloe had gotten her emotions under control, she'd used voice commands to have SAUL request a payoff quote of her debt and eliminate it in total. Which, in turn, also freed her from the garnishments. They'd argued for a bit that it would have been better to spend the money on gear now, but Desmond made an interesting argument that eliminating debts first was better as the weight of the interest on the debts, which was not held back during her time of service, would end up costing them more in the long run. He pointedly did not bring up his own thoughts on the mental strain and how he expected it to have affected her.

Once that had been finished, Chloe had tried to drag him back to the bedroom to give him an even better morning, but Desmond had talked her out of it, stating that he hadn't done it to extort sexual favors from her either, just that it was his duty and pleasure to look after his 'precious Chloe'.

"We are partners, after all. Now we are on even footing. I know you have my back, just like I have yours," he'd said. Which had led to an extended bout of cuddling on the couch while Chloe cried, again, before they finally headed out for the day.

"Yeah. And I told you that I didn't need it. Credits are gonna be tight for a bit and you should save it. Or send some home for the family. You said that your debt was only part of what your parents owed for your brother's treatment?"

"It was enough to get it under control for them. They refused to let me take more out, and it was already at the upper limit of what the lender would give me anyway, without collateral beyond the guaranteed term of service." Chloe quite literally bounced with each step, more so than usual. While she was no less watchful, there was a happy shimmy to her movements that kept a smile on Desmond's face.

"So just to confirm, you are debt free now, precious Chloe?" Desmond bumped sideways with his hip into hers and Chloe smirked down at him.

"Yep," the horned woman said, popping the ending of the word with an even wider grin. "Payment is sent. It's just taking some time for the signal to relay back to the bank on my home-world. Once they confirm the transfer of funds, I'll get the payoff notification, but I triple checked the amount. So it's just waiting for the paperwork to finish."

"That's good. I'm glad for you, Chloe."

"I wouldn't have been able to do it this quickly without your help, Desmond." Chloe bit her lip, glancing around for a moment before towing him out of the flow of traffic. Chloe dragged him into an alcove with a small table in it. "Are you sure that..." She started to question him and Desmond snorted a half-laugh in reply.

Reaching up, he got hold of her left horn and pulled the

much larger woman in for a kiss to shut her up. She didn't resist as soon as his hand was on her horn, moaning into the connection between their lips. Once they separated again, Desmond pressed his cheek to hers, still holding her horn, so he could whisper into her ear.

"Chloe, I wouldn't have done it if I wasn't sure. It's just money."

"It's a lot of money, Des," Chloe countered weakly.

"Easy come, easy go. I never actually *saw* the money, just numbers changing in my digital account." Desmond brushed it off as best he could. It had hit a little harder after the heat of the moment had faded, but he was resolute in it. They'd gotten lucky on the Rift suppression, and the money was going to a good cause. His gear was enough to handle the rest of the year, and it wasn't as if he needed an upgraded weapon. Chloe's repeater and armor could use some improvement, but it had served them well so far.

At least until we start looking into the custom gear that Monika was mentioning the other day. I wonder what sort of bells and whistles can be found out here, or non-standard weapons. Do they have laser-swords? Desmond wondered idly again.

"Still, Des. You shouldered part of the burden for my family, without even asking for anything." Chloe's arms snaked around him and he was treated to another full-body hug from his taurine Taari bodyguard/girlfriend that smushed him face-first into her generous bust.

"Happy to help," Desmond muttered around the face-full of tit-flesh that he was pressed into. A giggle escaped the much larger woman at the sensation, and she released him a moment later.

"You didn't give me all your money, did you?" Chloe asked suspiciously, her eyes narrowing.

"No, I kept back about two thousand credits for myself to cover some minor expenses. I still wanted to take you on a date regardless," Desmond reassured her with a smile.

However, the reassurance fell flat as Chloe's expression turned stern.

"Oh no, we aren't doing this again. I'm taking *you* on a date, Desmond. I know your world has it all backwards, and the male is supposed to be the one doing the courting, but you are out here now, and we do it differently." Chloe smirked, daring him to say otherwise. "Besides, you mentioned something earlier that was bugging you. Why don't we go and look at some more casual clothes? I know we spend most of our time in uniform, but having something comfortable for off days would be nice."

After their conversation earlier about clothes, in between bouts of Chloe crying about his gift and working with SAUL to get the payoff arranged, Desmond had changed back into the only set of casual clothes that he owned, the jeans and a button down he'd brought with him from home. It was the first time he'd changed back into the clothes in the last several months and the cloth felt weird on his skin after the smooth metallics of the uniforms. Even the weight of his sidearm felt odd. He'd used the modular webbing to put it in an underarm carry rather than a thigh carry, as the thigh carry would have made it hard to use his jean pockets.

"Ah, we don't need to do that Chloe," Desmond tried to protest even as his hand rubbed where the rougher cloth of his pants bunched slightly under his belt.

"I want to do something nice for you, Des. And I've got the extra credits rattling around. So we might as well go have a look around and see if anything catches your eye. Besides, I wouldn't mind having some casual clothes either. Some of the girls trashed the few that I brought with me while I was in the barracks, anyway. I'm not saying get us a whole new wardrobe, but an outfit or two might be nice." Chloe gestured to her own outfit. While Desmond was wearing his jeans and button-down, she was still stuck in her uniform.

Chloe's pleading expression eventually convinced Desmond that it would be easier just to go with her. *It would be nice to have something else. Plus, it might be fun to see what kind of styles Chloe likes. I've never seen her in anything besides the uniform or her armor.* Desmond was towed off into the crowd by his grinning partner with his mind full of Chloe in different outfits, a distracted smile on his face.

<><><>

The way that the clothing shops on the station operated was a fair bit different from Desmond was used to.

He was far more used to how things worked back on Earth, with racks in varying sizes and styles and you had to sort through them to find what you liked and if they didn't have your size, you were out of luck.

Instead, in the retail zones for *Valor's Bid*, they had things a bit more archaic. The racks held samples of different kinds of fabric while there were holograms that displayed current styles and outfits that were available and clothes were made to order, at least in the shop that Chloe dragged him into.

"I've never been to a shop like this," Desmond muttered as the larger woman steered him in through the entrance of an upscale looking shop that sported holograms of males of different races in various styles of clothing.

At least the styles are somewhat familiar. Desmond thought to himself as he walked past the displays. He'd quietly been worried that the current trends would be more like something out of a cyberpunk dystopia, based on the variety that he'd seen folk wearing out in the major thoroughfare. *Or something like the Fifth Element.*

"I usually shop secondhand myself, but I've got enough to spare to cover at least one outfit here. You gave me more than I needed, after all. Only fair I spend it back on you," Chloe reassured him, squeezing his shoulder with the hand that rested on it.

Still surprising that I don't feel stifled like this. Desmond thought as they wandered through the racks with Chloe basically glued to his back. *I remember thinking that I would, back when I was traveling with Tre'shovak's group. Figured it'd take a lot longer to get used to that kind of closeness.*

Glancing up at Chloe, he caught her profile as she scanned the racks ahead of them, her horns sweeping back and forth like a tuning fork as her head turned, and he couldn't help the smile. *Pleasant company makes it easier to accept for sure.*

"Good day to you! How can we help you today?" An athletic-figured Va'Aelfa woman slid out from between the racks. She was dressed in what Desmond could only describe as yoga pants in a bright, sky blue and a loose, open-necked white blouse that went from regular fabric directly into ruffles at the bottom of her ribcage and elbows. Her black hair was kept in a neat braid that hung over her right shoulder, contrasting sharply with the white of her blouse. Her sharp brown eyes took in Chloe's outfit before it landed on Desmond and a sensual smile crossed her dark lips. "Oh my, you have such a handsome companion with you, miss."

"Looking for something nice for my partner," Chloe answered before Desmond could speak up. He felt a bit like chocolate on a display rack with the way the shop-helper was staring at him, but brushed it off as his imagination.

"Oh. This will be fun. Any idea of what you might be looking for?" The shop girl eyed Desmond from shoes to eyebrow again, one hand going up to stroke over the single braid of black hair that came around to drape over her shoulder, the light of the shop sparkling off the tiny highlights on her skin.

"Something comfortable but casual, first time shopping somewhere like this," Chloe answered, again before Desmond could speak and he fought to keep his expression pleasant.

Is this what it's like for women back home? Being talked about like I'm not here or just a dressing doll? He thought idly before resolving to talk with Chloe about it later. She wanted to dote on him and this was her culture, so she knew what to expect.

"Let's take some measurements real quick. Come on over

to the fitting station." The shop girl, who still hadn't given her name, gestured for them to follow her, walked backwards between the racks, her eyes still gliding over Desmond and fixating a bit too much on his lower half for his liking.

"Chloe," Desmond murmured to her as they walked between racks.

"It's fine, Desmond. I wanna do this for you," Chloe replied quickly, assuming that he just didn't want her spending the money still. Though that wasn't what he was talking about. He didn't like the way the clerk was eye-fucking him.

They emerged from the racks into an open space in the back corner of the shop. A pedestal that was two feet across and about six inches high stood in the center of the cleared space with a holographic display beside it.

"Hop on up here, cutie. I'll get your measurements real quick and we can find something to polish you up," said the shop girl, and again, it just rubbed Desmond slightly wrong. Swallowing his irritation, he stepped up onto the pedestal. It put him roughly at the same height as the Va'Aelfa shop-girl, though Chloe still towered over them both.

Desmond felt weird while he did his best to stand still while the shop-girl ran a pair of devices over his body. She moved them like one might a regular measuring tape, but they clicked and vibrated as she started with his waist and began to work her way down.

Was just thinking how it was surprising that I didn't feel odd being crowded by Chloe. Now I feel weird that she isn't basically pressed up against me. It did interest him that the girl was using a different setup from what Shelly had used at Shatterstar when measuring him for armor, but he chalked it up to a difference in how armor fit rather than clothes.

His line of thinking was abruptly interrupted as he felt the shop-girl's hand land on his ass, out of Chloe's line of sight, and give it a squeeze. The sudden contact made him jump in surprise, but he forced himself back into position. *There is no way she did that on purpose, was there?*

At his sudden movement, Chloe's attention, which had been more relaxed and wandering, snapped back to him and her expression grew sharp. Desmond shook his head slightly to dismiss it, but Chloe didn't relax as the Va'Aelfa worked her way around the front of Desmond and began measuring his inseam.

Wonder if she's going to try to cop another feel up front or if she's going to behave. The irritated thought ran through Desmond's mind while he resolutely refused to look down and catch an eyeful of the open top of the shop-girl's blouse. *Oop! Well, that answers that question.*

The Va'Aelfa's left hand settled directly over his crotch, only two fingers holding the end of the measuring device in the barest nod towards it being 'taking his measurements' as she groped him, looking up at Desmond with a winsome smile. That winsome smile turned into a surprised yelp when Chloe's hand settled over the top of her head and the much larger woman hauled the handsy assistant away from Desmond by her skull, mussing her perfect braid in the process.

"What the hell?!" screeched the assistant as she was yanked away, grabbing at Desmond to try to steady herself, which just resulted in her squeezing his manhood harder through his pants before she fell back on her ass when Chloe yanked firmly.

"What do you think you are doing, woman?" Chloe barked, her serene expression morphed into one of barely contained rage.

"It's just a handful, damn it. If you are going to buy a fucking escort and trot him around buying gifts, the least you can do is expect people to want to touch!" protested the woman, her previously friendly expression now one of rage. "Besides, he didn't protest, did he? I was just warming the boy up for you!"

"You had no right..." Chloe began, but the shop-assistant shot to her feet, her pretty face twisting into a mask of rage.

"Fuck you, I'm calling security. You could have just let me get a feel. But no, you had to get uppity and put hands on me. Fucking crossbreed whore," she hissed, darting into the racks with a petty smirk on her face.

"Hey!" Chloe shouted and took a step after her before turning to Desmond and covering the feet of distance between them in only two strides, her hands coming up like she wasn't sure if she should just pick him up and run, hug him, or hide her face in her hands. "Des, I'm sorry. I didn't expect her to..."

"It's fine, Chloe. I wasn't expecting it either. Is that normal?" The reassuring feeling of Chloe's close presence helped to calm his racing mind. He'd been offended earlier when the shop-girl had groped him so blatantly, but when Chloe lashed out, his adrenaline had spiked. The building fight between the two women had sent his heart racing, and he'd been working on figuring out how the hell he was going to separate them before Chloe stomped the woman into paste, before the shop girl had darted off to call security.

"Let's just go. I'm sorry, Des. I wanted to do something nice for you and it turned into a mess." Chloe's voice was thick with self-recrimination as she tried to urge him towards the entrance, apparently having settled on the idea of just getting him out of the shop.

"No." Desmond refused to be moved off the pedestal and Chloe, who wasn't about to just pick him up and run, not yet at least, stopped as well.

"No?"

"Chloe, is it normal for someone to just molest a male like this in public?" he asked pointedly.

"No, but I did..." Chloe began, but Desmond interrupted her.

"You protected me. You, my Guard. Protected me, your Adept. You did your duty, and unless molestation is somehow handled differently out here than back home, which I doubt, given the lecture I remember from the instructors, we have nothing to fear," Desmond said gently. He was about to say more when the thunder of running boots entering the shop interrupted them.

"Security, hands in the air!" shouted a voice from on the other side of the rack. Desmond nudged Chloe lightly with an elbow.

"Let me handle this, Chloe." The horned woman looked at him for several long moments before nodding, shifting slightly to take her usual position on his left side as the shop-assistant began to screech tearfully about the 'beast of a half-breed Taari' that had assaulted her while she was working and she was worried they were going to try to rob her.

Moments later, two fully armed and armored security troopers pushed through the hanging cloth racks with their rifles up. Desmond guessed they were both Aelfa based on what he could see through the clear face-plates of their helmets, but enough was blocked from view that he couldn't pick out exactly what sub-breed they were other than confirming they weren't Va'Aelfa due to skin color.

"Hands up!" shouted the one on the left, and Desmond complied. "Step away from the male!"

"The male has a name, Officer," Desmond countered, locking eyes with the speaker.

"The male better shut up if he doesn't want to go down as well," snapped the same officer, refusing to take her eyes off Chloe, though her muzzle tilted towards Desmond.

"Point that rifle at me and I'm going to have Chloe shove it so far up your ass your eyes change color," Desmond replied with a pleasant smile. The words and indifferent tone were enough to startle the security officer into looking directly at him, and her rifle began to drift towards Desmond.

"Are you sure that is a good idea? Pointing a weapon at an adept is a bad idea, let alone one who is a victim in an encounter and being framed? Think very carefully."

That got both of the security officers to stop dead in their tracks, and their eyes went wide.

"Adept? Prove it."

"I'm telling you this as a courtesy, Officer," Desmond said, still smiling at her, though now it was with barely contained rage since their rifles were still aimed up in their direction. Thankfully, neither was directly aimed at him. "I'm going to pull my sleeve down and show you my comm-cuff. Something I was advised is only issued to adepts. If you are still pointing those rifles at my Guard when I do so, then I'll be forced to show you what I am in a more visceral way." The speaking officer opened her mouth to protest, her eyes hard, but he spoke again before she did. "This isn't a threat, Officer. This is a promise. You were lied to, but if you continue to threaten one of mine who was working to protect me, I will act."

Without giving her time to rebut him, Desmond shifted his right hand over and tugged at his left sleeve, pulling the cloth down to reveal the polished bronze of the comm-cuff that hadn't come off since he put it on months previously.

The two guards immediately lowered their rifles, their expressions going from stern to neutral. Desmond and Chloe also lowered their arms, and he could feel Chloe relax from her position at his side.

"Apologies, Adept," the one who had been speaking earlier said. "Can you explain what happened here?"

"To begin with, honesty first. I'm a first year cadet, the name is Desmond McLaughlin. This is my guard, Cadet Chloe Vandenberg. We are on leave rotation after assisting the rescue operation the other day when that unknown Rift went nova. Chloe acted in my defense when she realized the woman who's screeching at your sergeant over there was…" Desmond paused to search for the right words, which was made harder by the tearful falsetto wailing of the shop-girl, "exceeding the bounds of propriety and good conduct. From there, she expressed that Chloe should have 'just let her get a feel' and that she was 'warming me up for her'." As he spoke further, the two women's expressions deepened from neutral back into angry and down into barely suppressed rage.

"So you were molested and when your guard stepped in to do her duty, the offender called security to punish you for speaking out?" the previously silent of the two confirmed. Desmond nodded, pointing at her with one hand.

"Of all the idiotic. Sarge!" The other guard, the one who had been the more vocal of the two, turned to shout the last bit over her shoulder. "You should bring her over here. The 'perps' are cadets, specifically an adept and guard."

"What?!" shrieked the shop-assistant. A moment later, she was dragged through the racks by the third of the security officers, another Aelfa from her features, but a good deal broader than the other two, and with dark mocha skin.

"Explain," barked the sergeant, one gauntleted hand wrapped around the biceps of the blubbering shop-assistant.

The report delivered was quick and precise, and the sergeant glanced between Chloe and Desmond before noting the still-exposed comm-cuff.

"Adept, you are armed, are you not?" the sergeant asked, talking directly over the still protesting shop girl.

"Yes, Sergeant. As I'm on leave, I decided to dress casually. Was actually why we were here, to get some casual clothes to relax in. My sidearm is in a shoulder-holster under my left arm." The sergeant nodded sharply as Desmond explained.

"Please, lift up your shirt to show me. You don't need to draw it, I just want to confirm something," the sergeant asked and Desmond complied. She nodded again before rounding on the shop assistant, still in her grip.

"So you decided it was a good idea to frame two cadets out of the academy because you were so ready to get a handful of dick that you didn't even notice that the boy was packing more than just a stiff rod *and* that he was an adept in training?" The shop-assistant tried to blubber out a rebuttal but was shaken silent by the sergeant. "No! You don't get to change your story now. You accused them of assault and threatening you. I have on record that you were just telling me that the man had said he was going to have his big friend bend you over the counter so he could have you as well. I'd advise you to stop digging before you break through the deck and end up sucking vacuum."

"Sergeant. It's fine," Desmond started, but the sergeant shook her head, her expression stern.

"No it isn't, Cadet. If she'd just stopped at the molestation, then it'd be up to you if you wanted to press charges. She lied on an official record. I have the recording here myself of her accusing you of attempted rape, as well as theft. I can guarantee that there is a security camera or two here that caught the whole thing. It'll be reviewed and, if it confirms that she lied to security and attempted to frame an adept, even a cadet, then there will be hell to pay."

The shop-girl was pale, glancing between the sergeant, Desmond, and back again. Her eyes landed on the comm-cuff and bugged, only to repeat it again after seeing the pistol under Desmond's shoulder.

"All right, Sergeant. Just let us know if you need anything. I just want to get on with my day," Desmond said with a long sigh. Chloe's hand landed on his left shoulder and squeezed reassuringly, drawing his gaze up to hers for a moment.

"You are free to go, Cadet. I have a recording of your statement and will be contacting the owners of the shop to retrieve the security footage. If we need to speak to you again, we will send you a message." The sergeant nodded before gesturing for them to leave.

With a nod and a salute to the security team, Desmond led Chloe out of the shop.

<><><>

"Don't even say it," Desmond said as they emerged from the clothing shop.

"Des, I..."

"Nope, not going to hear you trying to apologize for

something you had no control over Chloe." Desmond towed her away from the shop and into the flow of foot traffic.

"Des! I should have noticed you were uncomfortable sooner. Looking back on it, I should have noticed as soon as she started eying you." Chloe's voice was thick with self-recrimination.

"You had no idea, and neither did I. I sure as hell didn't expect her to try to cop a feel, then try getting us arrested when we protested. Excessive escalation and all that. Not to mention it happened so fast. I mean, damn…She didn't even wait till you weren't looking…"

"Still…"

"Chloe, drop it, please? You had no way of knowing she would have done that, and as soon as you did, you stepped in. It doesn't ruin the gesture you were trying to make with getting me something." Desmond patted her hand on his shoulder, looking up at her so she could see that he didn't blame her. "Though, I have to say, being on this side of the whole groping angle definitely puts some things in perspective." Desmond squeezed her hand on his shoulder again before letting his hands fall to his hips and swayed back and forth in front of her with a faux seductive look on his face. "Though I don't mind if you wanna grab a handful."

"Des!" Chloe protested, blushing hard at his words. It wasn't what he said, but the fact it was in public that made her face heat. That and several speculative looks of passerby, plus one Boghet woman who gave her a broad wink and a thumbs up before disappearing into the crowd.

"What? It's true. Chloe, come on. We gave up modesty a while ago, and it's only going to get more distant as time goes by."

Chloe mulled his words over for a bit as she considered it. They had been living in close proximity for months now and sharing a bed for weeks. And when more people joined the team, it would only get more close. Were they going to change how they acted in front of the rest of their team?

Her blush deepened as she imagined others watching and the nebulous idea of another woman joining them in bed as well.

"Hey, Chloe. Question for you," Desmond's words broke Chloe out of her line of thinking abruptly, and she made a noise deep in her throat and gestured for him to continue. "So, I know that you said before that you aren't allowed to carry a gun when out with me. What about something that isn't a firearm?"

"Like?"

"Like a baton or something. It occurred to me just now that, as a guard, you really are restricted on-board the ship and it makes it hard for you to do your job without a weapon. Not to say you aren't a weapon yourself, but if someone came after us in earnest?"

"It isn't allowed. Only security and the adepts — regular and cadet — are allowed weapons aboard the *Valor's Bid*. The exception being when we are transporting them either to deploy, practice, or taking them to store in our rooms. It's a little more relaxed in the military section of the ship, but even walking a weapon back to our rooms from the shops, it'd be secured in a crate minimum."

"Seems odd that they arbitrarily lift that kind of limitation for adepts."

"I mean, you could cause even more damage with your mana-manipulation after all. Why should they worry about you carrying a gun or a knife?" Chloe said, and Desmond had to concede her point.

"Still, I think we should at least start looking into melee weapons. I know you have that mace thing, but I haven't seen you really practice with it. I wouldn't put it past the instructors to start drilling us with those soon too, us meaning the adepts. They did mention that you could opt to have training with them while I was working on mana manipulation. I know all the veterans and the second years had them. Might as well start looking. At least then we can figure out a budget for it. Same with weapons upgrades."

Chloe was silent for a bit, still beating herself up for putting Desmond in that compromised position, but she nodded after a few more moments. If this was what Desmond wanted to do, she'd do it.

CHAPTER 49

Looking back, I am astonished that I missed the clues back then. In my defense, I'm an idiot male. I didn't think it'd happen given how weird my life already was, being a 'space-wizard'. I'm just glad my girls put up with me being oblivious and have decided to keep me around. Must be my dashing good looks.
~Desmond McLaughlin, moments before being smacked by his laughing guards.

In an effort to shake off the awkward silence that had followed them from the clothing shop, Desmond had insisted on buying some street food from the mobile vendors and eating it while they browsed. Chloe had remained awkward for a bit until Desmond started feeding her bites of his food and stealing bites of hers. The easy familiarity had helped her to relax some while they browsed weapons. Once the blushes calmed down at least.

The shop they were in currently held a selection of different rifles and handguns, and Desmond was browsing through the larger weapons as they talked, considering the options that were present. *The biggest issue we seem to have is stopping power for larger creatures. Chloe can mow enemies down with the repeater right now, but the alpha-apes were an issue and we need to address that. Is there a balance point between the rate of fire and penetration?*

"So, I have been meaning to ask, but what exactly did you pull to slow down the Rift-monsters the other day?" Chloe prodded, interrupting his line of thought.

"Huh? Oh, I enhanced their density, and that increased their body weight. By about six fold. Made them too heavy to really move easily, and they ended up hurting themselves and each other."

"Be careful with that. Was clever, focusing on a neutral or negative aspect of the creatures to enhance, though." The soft smile that crossed Chloe's features brought a grin to Desmond's face as well.

"I remember Throneblood saying something like that. Something to consider, I guess. It sure cost me a lot of mana, but I was also pushing it out fast to try to save Sasha." Desmond sighed in resignation, but explained when Chloe made a questioning noise. "Just wishing that I'd gotten Sasha's contact info. I can only imagine things are going to be rough for her, being a refugee and all. Should see if we can send her some funds as well." He gestured to the racks of weapons all around them. "This is all so far out of our price range that I can't help but think the spare credits I have could be better spent making sure she's getting a future to be proud of instead of just, whatever." The weapons on display *started* around fifty thousand credits and went up from there so rapidly it was ridiculous.

Chloe smiled gently down at Desmond as he rambled, touched by his concern for the young woman, someone they had only met briefly but had risked their lives for. As his rambling wound down, she spoke.

"Don't worry about her, Desmond. I can guarantee she's gonna be just fine. She told me she had a goal in mind already before we separated and the kids that were with her will be taken care of too."

"Oh?" Desmond asked curiously. Chloe chuckled in response to his clueless expression before leaning closer to whisper to Desmond.

"She told me she wants to join up with the army. Something about a heroic adept and his guard saving her and wanting to repay them."

"Wait, what? How?" Chloe laughed again, harder this time at his bemused expression.

"She's signing up like I did: for training with the army corps. If she can make the cut, she is going to apply to be an adept-guard like I am. She's apparently been at loose ends with what to do with her life for a while and the situation gave her a push. She didn't ask outright. I think she was too shy to, but I did tell her I'd put in a good word for her with you. If she's lucky, that'll put her in the running on the next selection bracket after mid-terms. Regardless, she'll also have the third and final one for your first year to earn a spot as well during her training."

"She…what? She joined up specifically to try to be in our unit?"

"Apparently the handsome cadet-adept that saved her life really impressed her. She wanted to pay it forward and prevent others from suffering from Rifts going nova as well. At least that is what she was saying before she loaded up with the kids to evacuate." Chloe's smile turned gentle for a moment before her expression hardened and she met his eyes again. "I didn't promise her anything, though. She needs to impress you first and foremost. I think she's had a rough time of it, but we can't pick her just because she's nice or we want to take care of her."

Desmond started to protest, but Chloe touched his lips to silence him.

"No, Des. I'm not going to budge on this. I know you are kind-hearted, but your life and mine will depend on having a team that we know will function. If Sasha can't make the cut, or doesn't fit the makeup for the team, I don't want you to pick her."

"We could at least tell her what sort of makeup we are going for…" Desmond said around the finger on his lips. It was the only protest he could come up with that made sense in the moment.

"We could, but what if she does take a path that isn't suited for her? She's a Hyreh, which go from mid to heavy, but she's also smaller than normal. And we don't know what her skill set is either. Do you want two heavies on your team if she goes that way? Is that going to work for the style you are building? Do you even *have* a style in mind yet?" Chloe's questions were gentle but pointed and it forced Desmond to think harder.

For the last several months, he'd been more focused on just training his magic and acclimating with Chloe rather than expanding his plans for his team. He'd wanted to do something like Marsden, the second year he'd gone with for his first Rift suppression, had done for her team setup. A balanced team that could adjust to situations as needed. But Marsden hadn't really had a specialty while he did. And Enhancement could make a heavy as quick as an assault despite their far denser armor.

"Think about it, Des. I wasn't sure I wanted to tell you, but figured you deserved to know." Chloe glanced around the room at the different weapons hanging on racks around them and sighed. "Should we just go back to our rooms? It's a little depressing to see these price tags and everything, despite knowing that my debt isn't hanging over my head anymore. Since I'm just thinking about what we could have gotten if that debt hadn't drained you."

"Sure, let's head back for now. I should put more thought into what you said, though, Chloe. About a plan for the future."

<><><>

Desmond and Chloe spent the second day of their leave just relaxing in their rooms. Monika and Dianne, plus their guards, came by to visit and the entire group had spent most of the day chatting. The cadet-adepts discussed different team builds while the guards listened and added in the view from the mundane side of the wall and what they'd seen in their more weapons-oriented training, like different ammunition or squad-tactics that might be adaptable for use with an adept.

Weeks passed into months without anything major happening. Desmond spent most of the time working on refining his spells and coming up with new ways to focus on his enhancements. The mana cost was still ridiculous, but as he practiced, he could build in the efficiencies needed to not bottom himself out, as he enhanced multiple factors. This practice allowed him to build out and stretch his skills and every day he got closer to developing a twist for his Enhancement spells.

The daily physical conditioning continued and Desmond made it a point to stay well away from the antagonistic members of his class that were still watching him. His apparent success and skill showing in the magic classes only seemed to aggravate his detractors more by the day, rather than turn any to his side.

Throneblood had made the announcement that their second mandatory selection for team composition would come up after the midterm exam, to ensure they were all performing up to the expected levels. The order in which they would receive priority for bidding would be determined as a mix of their performance from the previous Rift and their scores for the exam.

Chloe and Desmond continued to share a bed and grow closer as the months passed and Desmond had absolutely no regrets in spending the windfall from looting the Rift on eliminating Chloe's debt. He knew there was still the looming threat of his own student loans back home, but they were worlds away and he highly doubted that there would be problems with dealing with them when he got done with his service to the Hegemony. It was something he pushed off on Future-Desmond to deal with for now and instead focused his attention and time on getting to know Chloe better and improving their training to be ready for future Rifts.

Despite his best attempts, Desmond didn't get the opportunity to take Chloe on what he considered a 'real date', as their few days of leave usually came on the tail end of an exhausting run of training. Chloe didn't seem to mind, but it bothered Desmond.

As they'd both expected, two weeks after their leave time from the Rift explosion, the instructors started training them with melee weapons alongside ranged. The drilling was erratic, to say the least. Most of the cadet-adept's simply opted for a belt knife that they learned the basics of, while the cadet-guards took it more seriously.

Desmond had decided to learn to use a short-handled axe, given the form his *Bolt* spell took. Chloe opted instead for a leaf-bladed sword that in her fist resembled a short-sword, but would have been an arming sword for Desmond. She still carried the collapsible mace on the back of her shield as a backup and practiced with it occasionally as well. Both of them remembered having to hack through the undergrowth to retrieve valuable crystals in their first Rift and wanted to be ready to handle such issues in the future.

Many the cadet-adepts began showing up with custom gear as well, having finally received and spent their bounties from the Rift suppressions. Desmond was surprised to learn that not every team had an equal split between the cadet-adept and their cadet-guard. A little under half of them actually had the cadet-adept taking the lion's share of the Rift harvesting rewards. He did note that those who tended to take a larger share were also largely part of the groups that both looked down on Desmond for being a prim and were either a higher rank in the social power structure or thought of themselves in that way.

They had continued to drill in different setups, with the veteran teams showing up to run obstacle courses with them in simulated combat. The instructors urged them to begin considering how they would train in the next semester, since they would be doing simulated combat with the other cadet teams and would need to at least have an idea of what format they wanted their teams to be. Desmond wanted to invest time on the virtual reality simulators, but the instructors continued to insist that they had to wait until the second term for those.

As the weeks went by, Desmond did his best to put the issue of Sasha and her training out of his head. He'd done a bit of digging and found that, as a disaster relief effort, the academy ship had offered mid-term enlistment to anyone who wished to sign on for active training in the military. It wasn't the best option for those that had lost their homes and livelihoods to the Rift disaster, but it was at least something. Those that did not opt to enlist were dropped off at the next station that the *Valor's Bid* crossed near, with some start-up funds to tide them over while they worked to re-establish themselves. Those that did opt in were put through a crash course bootcamp, to bring them up to speed with the current classes of the regular army being trained on board. For those that made the cut, they could apply to become adept-guards, while those that didn't would have the remainder of the term to try to make it for the second selection in the six months of time that they had left. If they failed to be selected, or opted out of the adept-guard program, they'd be deployed to regular duty posts for the standard five-year term. He'd wanted to send her a message but Chloe had, so far, refused to give him Sasha's contact information, advising him to let her focus on getting through the initial, more difficult, part of training before distracting her.

Despite digging for information, Desmond was unable to discern exactly *how* they were going to be tested when the mid-term exams came up. He couldn't even get information on what the previous year had done for their midterms. So instead, he worked with Chloe to refine all the skills that they had been taught in the first half of the year.

Monika's response to the impending exam was to actually slack off more. This attitude only irritated Oril'la, as the Hyreh woman urged her partner to take things more seriously if only because they needed to place as high as possible to get the best selection for their team.

All too quickly, the months and weeks leading up to the exams ended and the day of the testing arrived. Desmond was surprised to realize that he'd been aboard the *Valor's Bid* for over four months now.

CHAPTER 50

I warned you. Told you someone would get smart. Or in this case, stupid.
~Maya Throneblood, laughing at her fellow instructors after exams.

"As this is an individual test of performance, you will be running the course on your own at first." Instructor Throneblood stood on a podium at the front of the crowd, addressing the entire current class of cadet-adepts and their guards.

"You will be tested on working solo, as well as in tandem with your guards. This year's mid-term exam will be following the format that the adept has somehow been separated from their guard unit and needs to meet back up with them to complete their objectives. Score will be based on time, simulated injuries suffered, and ammunition or mana expended. Don't worry, for those of you with lower yield weapons, there is a separate scoring structure for each style of weapon. So you won't be penalized for using weapons with a higher standard ammo consumption."

"I don't like this," Chloe muttered from her position behind Desmond. The pair of them were towards the back of the group of cadets while listening to Throneblood go over details. It made it harder for Desmond to see, but given Chloe's size, it was more practical for her. Adding in the facts that it kept their backs to a wall and Desmond didn't need to actually *see* the instructor to hear what she was saying, they'd taken to the habit without question.

"Neither do I, but it's the testing format." Desmond shot

back, leaning into her hip with his arms crossed over his chest. The pose had grown more and more natural to him as time went by, to the point where it felt unbelievably odd to not have Chloe touching him in some fashion. He wasn't looking forward to the next semester. Since they'd be selecting a second guard at the beginning, it had already been announced that the cadet-guards could begin rotating assignments during classes to simulate real world work. With one assigned to 'guard' the cadet-adept and the other attending expanded classes if needed to simulate a watch rotation.

Gonna have to get used to that idea. Hopefully, whoever we end up with will be able to keep up with Chloe, Desmond thought to himself. He'd actually tried to check up on Sasha during her training period, but apparently there was an information blackout between the training groups. He would only get access to the list of eligible cadets when the option to bid for another guard position came up. Chloe had messaged her a few times, but the Hyreh had been vague about how she'd been doing and Chloe hadn't wanted to press.

"Still don't like it," Chloe grumbled to herself. Desmond heard the quiet sound of her tail switching back and forth in irritation. He'd gotten better at noting the non-verbal cues of the other cadets. Though there were still several that he was struggling to keep track of, notably the Aelfa, as there were enough variations in species to be confusing.

"We got this, Chloe," Desmond reassured her. He reached up without looking to snag her right horn with his matching hand when it swung down within reach, right behind the Rift-tungsten ring that he had given her. The gesture calmed the much larger woman and she let out a long breath before nodding.

"Yeah. Yeah, we do," she murmured before they had to turn their attention back to Throneblood, who was winding down on her explanations.

"As this is an exam situation, you will not be allowed

to observe those taking the exam until after you have completed it. Once you complete your exam, you are free to use the rest of the day as you see fit. Scores will be sent digitally to you once everyone has completed testing. I expect all of you to finish testing before dinner tonight. Do *not* make me wrong." The Uth'ra instructor paused to glare at the crowd of cadets before gesturing towards the small crowd of other instructors.

From the group, the familiar shape of Instructor Camilla Tre'shovak stepped up onto the podium. Desmond recognized her instantly due to the combination of her unique skin tone and the auburn hair. The Va'Aelfa instructor switched places with Instructor Throneblood and began to speak in a clipped and precise tone.

"Each of the instructors will be in charge of a dual course. We will be running people through the courses in alphabetical order based on the cadet-adept's last name. When you hear the surname of the cadet-adept in your group, head to that instructor. They will direct you from there. Each of the exam courses will have variations, but the goals remain: get through with minimal damage, as efficiently as possible. Cadet-Adepts, you will be measured on mana expended as your heaviest weighed measurement. Cadet-Guards you will be scored on total hit percentages. Adepts, you are not allowed to enhance your guard before they enter the course. We will be watching."

"Damn," Chloe cursed under her breath. While her accuracy with the repeater had improved as she grew more confident, it still wasn't anything compared to what she could do with the conjured enhancements that Desmond could do. She was slightly better when borrowing Desmond's rifle, but the repeater gave a better output overall due to sheer rate of fire.

"Did you catch the important part of that?" Desmond said quietly to her. Chloe cocked her head to look down at him with a question in her eyes. "She said no enhancements 'before going in'. Didn't say anything about before we headed up to the test." Chloe's eyes went wide.

"Des, if you do that...you'll burn through mana too fast."

"My best defense is to get back to my guard as quickly as possible. Lemme think about it," Desmond urged before turning their attention back to Tre'shovak.

"As this is a test of your *skills* and not your wallets, you will be running the course without armor for either of you and with standardized weapons. Upon entering, select one weapon you are most comfortable with, besides the sidearm for the adept. Your time begins when you cross out of the arming room."

"That's gonna suck for some folks." Desmond chuckled when he heard the conditions they'd added. He noted a few of the other students that he knew tended to come from more money than sense were complaining that they wouldn't be able to use the advanced programming of their armor to help with aiming. Chloe remained silent, the hand on his left shoulder sliding around to his right to knead at it slowly while they waited their turn.

<><><>

"McLaughlin, you have thirty seconds to select a weapon. You may take as much ammunition as you feel needed." The instructor that was testing him reeled off the instructions with a bored look on her face while Chloe disappeared through the door that led into the guard arming room. "As soon as your guard exits her arming room, you will be allowed to enter yours. The buzzer will sound at the five second mark, but you can exit your room whenever you are ready. The only other live person inside your course is Cadet-Guard Vandenberg, so be aware of your targets before you fire. Shooting your guard, even a grazing shot, is considered an automatic failure."

"Understood, Instructor," Desmond said, giving the

Hyreh woman a salute before moving to stand directly in front of the sealed door that led to his arming room.

Over the last few hours, the dozen instructors had cycled through the cadets as rapidly as possible. It was a mixed bag, as they worked through the lists by name. A few of the cadets had dragged their heels though, as if that might help them somehow. That was the only time that the instructors really became animated. Clearly, they were looking forward to finishing the testing much more than the cadets were.

After some thought, he had decided to obey the rules and not use any enhancements on Chloe before they were called up. The odds that the instructors might catch it were relatively high, and he didn't want to penalize their score at all.

The door in front of him slid open and Desmond jumped through. He'd caught sight of the room inside while others went through and knew what to expect. Racks of weapons sat on either side, with pre-loaded magazines and energy cells at the ready on their own racks. What was available rotated slightly in variation, as certain weapons tended to be more often selected by the cadets and it took time to bring the weapons back to the beginning of the course.

Thankfully, his preferred choices were available and Desmond jammed a pair of spare magazines for his sidearm into one pocket of his pants and snatched up three power cells and the familiar boxy shape of the standard energy rifle that reminded him of the P90 from back home on Terra. A rapid check of the weapon had it ready to go, and he headed for the door before even half of his arming time was up.

The two of them had discussed it while waiting and decided to maximize their speed as much as possible. They'd noticed that the instructors seemed to vary which order they sent the cadets in, staggering the adept and their guard by anywhere from thirty seconds to a few minutes.

Without knowing what to expect on the far side of the range, they would just have to move quickly and meet up rapidly to cover each other. They'd also decided on a keyword combination to signal each other if needed, trying to come up with something to cover as many eventualities as possible.

The room that Desmond emerged into reminded him of the damaged space station that they had been evacuating people out of when they had found Sasha.

Someone had taken the time to paint the walls with something thick and red that made him think of blood, and he forced the memories down sharply as he started down the corridor at a trot. While he ran, he murmured a small chant to enhance his reflexes while he readied the rifle. While he had practiced extensively with the *Bolt* spell to get used to his first twist some time ago, he still felt more confident with the rifle in hand because of the wind-up speed. He'd seen a few of the cadet-adepts disdain a weapon entirely, simply charging through the arming room and into the course.

You will be judged on mana consumption. Desmond remembered the instructor's words as he spun up the only enhancement he wanted at the moment.

Being ready proved to be a boon, since the pneumatic hiss of the targets emerging was the only warning he got as several cut-out targets of the snake-centipede hybrids emerged from the 'vents' on the ceiling at once. Reacting rapidly, Desmond dropped shots into all of them, sustaining fire on each until it retracted, signaling a kill.

The instructors had swapped up the range time drills only a week earlier, calibrating the targets to different levels of durability to encourage the cadets to ensure that their targets were 'dead' before moving on to the next target. Desmond and Chloe had taken this to heart and upped the range of durability even beyond what the instructors had set it to, working on the same drills in their free time. The goal had been to be ready to move on as soon as a target was confirmed down and to build reflexes around such things.

Picking up speed, Desmond slid to a stop by the door at

the end of the hall, slapping the override button on the wall to open it. Scanning quickly, he checked the room for threats before moving forward. The room in front of him looked like it had been the site of a prolonged battle, with simulated bodies sprawled out at different points in the room.

With his higher reaction speeds, he noticed one body twitched slightly. Since it wasn't one of the bipedal bodies and instead in the quadrupedal shape of a wolf whose mouth ran half the length of its body, he opened fire on the target.

The simulated enemy yelped and struggled to its feet. Attempted ambush foiled, it tried to get to him but Desmond put enough rounds into its head to tag it as killed and shut down the robotic creature.

Another thing they just started drilling us with. Well, drilling the others with. I've been doing something similar with the conjured mobs for the others for a while with Monika during evening free time practice. Desmond thought as he hurried across the room.

Two weeks ago, before they'd started drilling on the durability variants, the instructors had added non-humanoid bots to the shooting ranges. They'd charge along the range and use cover as they moved. They were good, but not the same as the conjured creatures. The programming made the motions less fluid and was far easier to spot.

A booming sound from ahead of him reminded Desmond of gunfire. So he picked up speed, slamming the override to open the gate as he came to the exit on the far side of the room, scanning the hall rapidly before hurrying into it. The pattern of hall, room, then hall again repeated three more times, each room holding a different sort of challenge for him to overcome in the shape of different styles of enemy. One had multiple smaller enemies, one had a single boss-type monster, and the last was littered with line-of-sight obstructions and multiple smaller monsters as well.

He'd gunned down most of the enemies present, only needing to use mana on the boss-type creature, using a trio of *Bolt* spells to hurry it along while firing with his offhand to lay in the damage rapidly.

While they were waiting, he and Chloe had noted that the time between new groups being called up to run the test varied by between ten to fifteen minutes. Desmond had cleared the first four rooms in what he guessed was five minutes, and he could only assume that he should be meeting up with Chloe shortly. The booming sound of gunfire echoed through the hallways every so often and Desmond wasn't sure if it was to help simulate the experience or if he was hearing the sound of Chloe firing on her half of the test range.

Though that doesn't parse, she's not been one for a solid shell weapon, since laser lets her put out more rounds for suppression.

A sudden change in the pitch of the sounds of gunfire answered that question a moment later as Desmond emerged from the last hallway and into a larger, oval room that was divided in half by what appeared to be a pile of girders and rubble.

There were no threats on his half, but the irregular barrier that clogged the center of the room made it hard to see as bits were scattered about. The barrier only took up a small portion of the total size of the room, but he could see Chloe on the other side, taking cover behind a bit of thick girder and firing over the top of it. So he called out his half of their code phrase.

"Nebula!" Chloe's head snapped to the side, her eyes locking on him through the barrier and a grin marked her face.

"Rising!" she shouted back to him over the shriek of weapons' fire, aiming over her barrier and letting loose another blast of fire. "Des, three shooters have me pinned."

The moment crystallized for Desmond as laser fire arced over top of the barrier and slammed into the far wall behind Chloe. The second slowed and stretched as he worked through his options before settling on the one that would work best right now. Chloe needed him, and something was blocking his way.

"Who's gonna stop me?" Desmond murmured under his breath and turned the spinning mana construct in his head loose. He'd been considering different sayings and poems from Earth in ways to work in his enhancements for a while and this one in particular he'd been saving for when he needed to *muscle through* a problem.

The Enhancement spell settled over him like a cloak, and Desmond felt his muscles tense and swell for a moment while his nerves sent out a warning tingle. Everything slowed down further as his reaction speed scaled up.

It'd been only two weeks ago that he'd finally developed his first twist for his Enhancement spells. That twist, which had merged with nearly all of his Enhancement spells, manifested around him in the form of an emerald suit of armor with a high neck guard and a rounded helmet. Whenever he used his enhancements now, on himself or another, portions of the mental image he had conjured to help guide the spell would leak over to the person he was targeting. Once the armor locked into place, he charged the barrier separating them.

Chloe's eyes got wide as she saw the armored figure coalesce around Desmond and she ducked down, covering her head with her arms and turning to put her back to the barrier.

A thunderous crash made the deck underneath him buck when he slammed his way through the barrier, sending metal flying in an arc away from Chloe. Snatching a fallen girder with one magically gauntleted hand, Desmond put his back into it and hefted the set piece off the ground. With a twist of his hips and a heave, he sent the hunk of metal flying down the room to slam into Chloe's attackers.

"Des! What are you doing!?" Desmond could barely hear her over the ringing in his ears from the impact. Shaking himself to try to get his bearings back, Desmond hurried around the damaged barrier to where Chloe was crouched in cover while the rage began to fade from his mind. Ahead of him, he could see the shattered remains of what looked like several of the range dummies and ruined remains of the piece of barrier he'd used as a fastball. It had punched through the wall and into the adjoining room after shredding the dummies.

Taking a deep breath, Desmond reeled in the enhancements, draining the leftover mana he had imbued into himself and returning it to his cache. The glowing armor plates sunk back into his skin and vanished now that he was sure Chloe was safe.

"Stars and suns, Des...that was a bit extreme," Chloe muttered. She peeked over her cover to see the hole quite literally blown through the heavily plated wall ahead of him.

"I would definitely say so," the voice of the instructor who had been administering the test echoed from above them and it sounded familiar. "McLaughlin, you broke the damn exam lane. You were supposed to proceed around the corner to catch the enemy in a cross-fire to free up your guard."

Glancing around, Desmond spotted the oblong shape of a camera hanging on the wall in one corner. Snorting, he rolled his eyes at the camera.

"With all due respect, Instructor, I was given no such direction. I was told I would be graded on mana expended, accuracy, and time. And I was to meet up with my guard with all due haste. No one said I wasn't allowed to damage the surroundings. This was supposed to be to test our skills, and my specialty happens to be Enhancement. Seems dumb to expect me to not use my specialty."

The silence that stretched out from there made Desmond worry that he'd been a bit too flippant with the instructor. Thankfully, a deep chuckle came from the speaker a moment later.

"Fair point, McLaughlin. I remember Throneblood pushing to have more defined testing parameters during the staff meeting when we planned the exams. She said that someone would get clever eventually if we didn't tailor the exam more closely for folks. I remember she got shot down by the others who didn't expect a mid-term first year to be that sneaky. All right, you won't be penalized for damaging the course, but you still need to complete your run. Get moving, you two!"

The last part was snapped out as an order and Chloe was on her feet in an instant, moving forward at a trot. Desmond fell in on her right and slightly behind the larger woman.

"You okay, Chloe?"

"Yeah, it didn't even wing me. They were only firing stunner shots. Did you not notice the color?" Chloe teased him while she shot him a grin over her shoulder and Desmond snorted.

"I thought they were full power shots. Beyond that, I didn't even have time to think. Just saw you taking fire and reacted. You want an enhancement?"

"How's your reserve? I know you can recover some by aborting them early, but that one had *oomph*," Chloe asked as they entered the next room through the shredded breach in the wall. The targets that they would have had to neutralize were already scrap. So they kept moving.

"Down about ten percent, been frugal so far and got back most of what it cost," Desmond replied. He cleared the hall ahead of them with his rifle, taking down the only pneumatic target that he spotted before waving Chloe to take the next door while he covered her.

"Just accuracy for now. Gonna have to make up time for the chat we had with the instructor," Chloe replied, readying herself before bulling through the doorway at a sprint.

The rest of the exam course was fairly straightforward and didn't pose much of a problem for the two of them. The next two rooms were simple shooting galleries, with plenty of cover for them to use. The last room in the now-combined lane was a mixture of the same dummies that had originally had Chloe pinned and the pop-ups that Desmond had dealt with. Between the two of them, they could pick off the enemy targets without a problem. They took turns separating enough to draw the fire of the dummies with the stun-rifles alternately and made sure to never risk each other with their own, more lethal, crossfire.

Emerging from the far end of the range into a larger arming room, the two of them divested themselves of equipment before heading out the other door.

Instructor Gemtooth was waiting on the other side of the door with her tablet out and a stern look on her face. The stern expression was ruined by the amusement dancing in the Gaur woman's eyes.

"McLaughlin and Vandenberg, you have completed the course and scored high enough that you have passed the exam. Actual rankings will be released during morning classes tomorrow. Teammate selection will be tomorrow to give you time to read over the candidate list."

"Understood, Instructor. Does that mean we have access to the candidate list now?" Desmond snapped off a quick salute to the gray-skinned woman.

"Yes. Go get cleaned up. We have to shut this lane down anyway, given that *someone* used excessive force." The instructor smirked slightly before dismissing the two of them.

Chloe elbowed Desmond lightly as they headed out into the main hallways with Chloe slightly behind him.

"If you ask nicely, Des. You can use excessive force when we get back to the suite." Desmond didn't rise to her provocation, instead waiting till she was looking away to check the corridor before he reached up to snag her horn and tug her head to one side lightly. This drew a low moan from the big woman before he released her and raced ahead down the hallway.

Chloe grunted once, then hurried down the hallway after him and back to their suites, her blood still thrumming from the simulated fight of the exam.

SPECIES GLOSSARY

<u>Aelfa</u> - Naturally adapting to varying mana signatures of the universe, Aelfa are diverse in their subspecies. Their ears are their primary means to convey subtle emotions. Height varies between species, some going as short as five feet and others as high as seven. The skin tone varies a great deal depending on subspecies but the majority of them tend towards pale colors with either variance of ear shape, build, or bone structure to delineate which of the subspecies they are part of. Earth lore would call them 'elves'.

<u>Va'Aelfa</u>- Born in zero-gee or on colony ships. They tend to have dark blue-purple skin with tiny iridescent highlights and darker hair colors. Standard 'elven' style ears that sweep back to slight points.

<u>Tu'Aelfa</u> - Born on planets of low gravity and usually high winds. They tend to be small in stature but very sprightly. Pale of skin and fine boned with long limbs and more slender ears.

<u>Se'Aelfa</u> - Born on water worlds or settlements on/in the sea. Their most noticeable feature is larger than average eyes as well as 'finned' ears that come to several points. Harder to notice are the gills in their abdomens. This subspecies has also evolved sharpened predator teeth, but are omnivorous.

<u>Yu'Aelfa</u> - Born to low gravity environments on planetary satellites. pale eyes, pale skin, pale hair. What notes a Yu'Aelfa above others is the fact their iris and sclera are pale yellow to the point that they merge and almost hide amongst the whites of their eyes. The other two can vary, but

their eyes are always that pale color.

Dwerg - Shorter beings, averaging 4-5 feet in height, stocky and strong. While the men tend to cultivate beards, the women instead focus on maintaining their hair as a status symbol and grow it to ridiculous lengths, using elaborate braids to keep it in check. Earth lore would call them 'dwarves'.

Uth'ra - stone-gray skin and large manes of curly hair are common for these creatures, though the colors vary. Nearly all of this species shares the same eye color, a bright orange that glows with an internal light. Predator teeth, primarily consume meat in their diets. On average, Uth'ra stand between six and seven feet tall, with especially large members of their species going as high as eight feet. Closest Earth comparison would be an 'ogre'.

Boghet - Short, green, and with large ears. They appear to be closer in build to the Dwerg than humans or the Hyreh. But while the Dwerg are stocky and strong, the Boghet tend to be more focused on speed and dexterity. Tallest samples of their species top no higher than four feet. Closest Earth comparison would be a 'goblin'.

Gaur - Gray-skinned and hairless, the Gaur are a unique species with their additional appendages of functional wings. Despite having the outward appearance of a predator, they actually have squared off, black teeth and no canines. Their diet consists mostly of hard-shelled fruits and nuts. Their teeth evolved to crack the protective layers of their food. Some posit that they are a side-evolution of the Uth'ra given their similar skin-tones, but this is not true. The Gaur are actually hollow-boned to allow the use of their wings. Closest human equivalent would be 'gargoyles'.

Hyreh - Humanoids with green skin and pronounced lower jaws. Hyreh have lots of sharp teeth in the front half of their mouth. They are not obligate carnivores but definitely lean that way. Possessing very stout bones due to originating on a high-gravity world with a more feudalistic society, despite being on the cutting edge of a great deal of tech movements. Closest human equivalent would be some stories of 'orcs'.

Taari - Taari tend to be an amalgamation between a type of animal and a humanoid of some sort. Taari come in six distinct breeds: Vulpine, Ursine, Canine, Avian, Taurine, or Feline. The six subspecies are stable in their own right and breed true when different sub-breeds cross among the Taari subtypes. It is only when they breed outside of Taari bloodlines that the obvious signs of their Taari heritage begin to fade. A pure blood Taari will have fur, feathers, ears, and tail if their subtype has such. Their facial structure, as well as secondary characteristics (such as horns), will present depending on the subtype.

Latsu - The Latsu are one of the larger species as their bottom half where a human's hips would turn into their thighs actually merges into the shoulders of a larger creature. There are a few variants of the Latsu race, with some that are a mixture of hominid and lizard while others that are a mixture of hominid and cat. There are rumors of a few as well that are mixed with a canine base, but they are even more rare. Latsu tend to not go far from their home systems, being more insular in general. Rumors abound that they are some strange, experimental mix of the Taari, but they vehemently deny this whenever they hear it.

Gan'gari - The Gan'gari are an odd race compared to the others. While only the Taari and the Aelfa have specific subspecies that break their racial molds due to various outside effects, the Gan'gari have a variety of morphic differences to their bodies that can occur at seeming random but certain physiologic traits always remain. Gan'gari are always a mixture reminiscent to a Taari in their composition, of animal and a hominid type. Unlike Taari, they are a distinct and stable mixture of two specific types: Avian and Feline. What subspecies of those two varies from family to family, with mixtures such as a lion and an eagle being slightly more than sixty percent of their population. They still remain bipedal, though all mixtures sport fully functional wings. Gan'gari are relatively insular and prefer to remain in their home systems. Unlike Taari, they still breed true along the normal lines of cross-species relations and unlike the Aelfa, the shifting of their subtypes is not influenced by surroundings. It's theorized that the occasional diversion from familial norms are carry-over genes from a time when mixing between subtypes had not been discouraged as much. Closest human equivalent is 'griffin'.

Yaadi - this species evolved from a symbiotic relationship between a plant and hominid form that eventually fused into its own genotype due to the unique fluctuations of mana flows through their home system. They are capable of existing for a period of weeks on nothing more than water and sunlight if needed, but prefer animal proteins when given the chance. Carbohydrates are unnecessary as they are able to generate their own via photosynthesis. The plant portions of their bodies remain mostly located in the upper torso, with flowers and vines growing amongst their hair to provide the photosynthetic reactions they need, as well as a special makeup to their skin cells that expand that surface further as well as allowing the absorption of nutrients from soil or their environment if necessary. Yaadi rarely develop adept powers, but as a species are slightly sensitive to mana flows as well. There are some who believe Yaadi soothsayers can predict the formation of Rifts with nothing more than their skin and plant growths. As Yaadi age, their skin goes from a softer, leaf-like texture to a rougher, more bark-like texture unless specific treatments are applied. This does not change the color of their skin, which range from a dark mocha brown up to a lush green or a pale silver. Closest human equivalent is 'dryad'.

CHARACTER GLOSSARY

<u>Desmond McLaughlin</u> - **Human** - *Cadet-Adept* - Main character. Desmond is a cadet-adept in training, his specialty lies in Enhancement magic. Brindle-brown hair and green eyes, Desmond is on the shorter side, especially when compared to his girls, at around five and a half feet tall and built stocky.

<u>Chloe Vandenberg</u> - **Taurine Taari/Uth'ra** - *Cadet-Guard* - Standing roughly eight feet tall, Chloe is a mixed breed. Desmond's bodyguard and lover. Blonde hair cut short, bright green eyes, with a power lifters build and generous figure. Chloe sports a pair of curve, black bull's horns that curve out from her temples and are well over a foot long.

<u>Nicholas Kincaid</u> - **Human** - Played against Desmond at the axe-throwing bar.

<u>Agent Carter</u> - **Human** - CIA agent who 'retrieved' Desmond early on. Tazed Desmond.

<u>Agent Tessa Stuart</u> - **Human** - CIA agent, partner to Carter, worked to try and keep Carter in line.

<u>John Whitton</u> - **Human** - General who signed the draft order to recruit Desmond.

<u>Camilla Tre'shovak</u> - **Va'Aelfa** - *Instructor (Adept)* - Red hair and cyan eyes. Instructor aboard the academy ship. Picked Desmond up from Earth.

<u>Ryann Summers</u> - **Tu'Aelfa** - *Adept-Guard (Mundane)* - Part of Camilla's team, pilot of shuttle. Dusky brown skin, black hair. Ryann is one of the few Tu'Aelfa with darker than

normal skin.

Jenneth 'Jen' Sho'tear - **Va'Aelfa** - *Adept-Guard (Mundane)* - Part of Camilla's team. Rough voice, scar on throat, pink eyes and auburn hair.

Ko'an - **Hyreh** - *Adept-Guard (Mundane)* - Part of Camilla's team, gruff voice but well spoken. Dark green skin, only male on Camilla's team.

Olianna Yu'tona - **Se'Aelfa** - *Cadet Adept* - Blonde hair, fin ears, cherry-red eyes. Seems to have something against Desmond.

Monika Irongrip - **Dwerg** - *Cadet Adept* - 'saved' Desmond from Olianna, blunt personality. Red bob haircut, blue eyes, broad figure with thick hips and breasts. Scarred forearms from her work with her family's mechanic business.

Oril'la - **Hyreh** - *Cadet Mundane* - Monika's team, Strong resting-bitch-face but good humored when she speaks. Originally wanted to be a fighter pilot, decided to be adept-guard instead as it paid better with lower fatality.

Dianne Sagejumper - **Uth'ra** - *Cadet Adept* - Friends with Monika. Black hair braided into dreads and kept in a ponytail. 7'6" with a runner's build.

Mona Lu'toru - **Yu'Aelfa** - *Cadet Mundane* - team with Dianne. Willowy build and a bit of a daydreamer attitude.

Iris Marsden - **Vulpine Taari** - *2nd year Adept* - Escorts Desmond during his first rift. Flirty and playful, but serious when things get rough.

Maya Throneblood - **Uth'ra** - *Instructor(Adept)* - Instructor for Desmond. Hardass. 7'4"ft tall, glowing orange eyes, dark-blue mane of hair. Maya would be described as a 'brick-house' with boxer's scars on cheeks and forehead.

Gemtooth - **Gaur** - *Instructor(mundane)* - Assists Throneblood with weapons training after the cadets recruit their first guard. Like most of her kind, she is gray skinned and entirely hairless.

Rashona Roaring-Feather - **Gan'gari (Secretary bird/cheetah)** - *Vice Admiral* - head of the Academy aboard the

Valor's Bid. White wings tipped in black, cheetah-spotted fur on forearms. Very meticulous. Bright gold eyes. More than half leg.

<u>Doctor Astrid</u> - **Uth'ra** - *Doctor* - Point of contact for Desmond, studying the Terran anatomy. Very intense personality and not much of one for small talk, she is very focused on her work.

<u>Connie Leafsong</u> - **Yaadi** - *Cadet Medic* - works under Doctor Astrid. Tends to have to gentle and reassure the patients once Astrid is done with them. Light green hair with leaves scattered through it. Mocha skin.

<u>Shelly</u> - **Boghet** - *Employee at Shatterstar Armory* - helped kit Desmond for armor. robins-egg blue hair was shaved close to her head and inlaid with a zig-zag pattern that was shaved to her skull. Bright red eyes.

<u>Davis</u> - **Taurine Taari** - *Cadet-Guard* - brown fur, short horns. Has a beef with Chloe due to her crossbreed nature.

<u>Hailey Whist</u> - **Latsu** - *Mundane sergeant* - Assigned to Desmond and Chloe for their 2nd rift. Grey eyes, hair shaved to scalp, heavily muscled and quadrupedal cat lower-half. Armed with a smart-gun on the back mounted stabilizer arm.

<u>Gwen Ry'taal</u> - **Tu'Aelfa** - *Mundane corporal* - Helped Whist on the team's second rift. Short, shotgun bearing, keeps her hair back in a ponytail. Excitable and bouncy in personality. Mischief in a uniform.

AUTHOR'S NOTE

Hope that you enjoyed the first step on this long journey with the characters. If you enjoyed this, please leave a review. Reviews are how indie authors get visibility and also what helps spur us on to keep writing. Even if its just a quick message or a comment. Positive feedback is always welcome.

If you want to check out a hub for my works, try my website.
http://www.mtresswrites.com

Other places you can find information on my works and support me:
http://www.patreon.com/user?u=121448296

If you want more Harem content, find people of like minds to talk to, and get the heads up on new content, come join us on Facebook.
Harem Gamelit - https://www.facebook.com/groups/HaremGamelit/

If you want more monster girls (and be honest, you know you do!) come join the rest of us in mischief:
Monster Girl Fiction - https://www.facebook.com/groups/MonsterGirlFiction/

ABOUT THE AUTHOR

M. Tress

I've been a voracious reader for as long as I can remember. According to my parents, that started really young. Apparently, my mother found me in the living room teaching myself to read with the book she'd been reading to me only an hour previous at around the age of four. Apparently, I wasn't done at the same time she was.

Since then, I've been fascinated with the written word. Everything from lore heavy games to literature to tabletop gaming as well. I wrote for the enjoyment of it and spent a fair amount of time in various pennames writing fan fiction, since those stories ended before I was done with them as well.

Now, though, I can appreciate a good ending when the time comes. Especially since, as the author, I'm the one who gets to choose when the story wraps and the curtains close.

It is a good feeling!